Readers love ALBERT NOTHLIT

Life Seed

"Once I started, I couldn't put it down. I put aside a whole day to finish it, because the world-building was so incredibly good, the characters compelling, the story just *chef's kiss.*"

—Lady J's Pawsome Books

Earthshatter

"*Earthshatter* literally shattered my mind, it is an amazing read and for its main genre Sci-Fi it is like absolutely nothing I have read for years."

—On Top Down Under Reviews

Light Shaper

"…fantastic world-building, great characters, and fast-paced plots. It also has elements of a mystery… definitely read this series. Definitely."

—The Novel Approach

By Albert Nothlit

HAVEN PRIME
Earthshatter
Light Shaper

WURL
Life Seed
World Warden

Published by DSP Publications
www.dsppublications.com

world warden

albert nothlit

DSP PUBLICATIONS

Published by
DSP PUBLICATIONS

5032 Capital Circle SW, Suite 2, PMB# 279,
Tallahassee, FL 32305-7886 USA
www.dsppublications.com

This is a work of fiction. Names, characters, places, and incidents either
are the product of author imagination or are used fictitiously, and any
resemblance to actual persons, living or dead, business establishments,
events, or locales is entirely coincidental.

World Warden
© 2022 Albert Nothlit

Cover Art
© 2022 Stef Masciandaro
http://www.stefmasc.com/
Cover content is for illustrative purposes only and any person depicted
on the cover is a model.

All rights reserved. This book is licensed to the original purchaser only.
Duplication or distribution via any means is illegal and a violation of
international copyright law, subject to criminal prosecution and upon
conviction, fines, and/or imprisonment. Any eBook format cannot be le-
gally loaned or given to others. No part of this book may be reproduced
or transmitted in any form or by any means, electronic or mechanical,
including photocopying, recording, or by any information storage and
retrieval system, without the written permission of the Publisher, except
where permitted by law. To request permission and all other inquiries,
contact DSP Publications, 5032 Capital Circle SW, Suite 2, PMB# 279,
Tallahassee, FL 32305-7886, USA, or www.dsppublications.com.

Mass Market Paperback ISBN: 978-1-64108-345-4
Trade Paperback ISBN: 978-1-64108-344-7
Digital ISBN: 978-1-64108-343-0
Mass Market Paperback published October 2022
v. 1.0

Printed in the United States of America

For Luna, Lorena, and Uriel.

chapter 1.
mercy

ELIAS TROST trudged through the mire, followed by his maybe-boyfriend and three wurl with silver scales.

He glanced over his shoulder. Tristan MacLeod walked a few paces behind, panting with effort but tireless as always. Tristan's gaze was fixed on the treacherous ground before him as he picked each step with care. He was slightly taller than Elias, and he had a buzz cut that was beginning to grow out a week after they had left the colony of Portree. Tristan's bushy eyebrows gave his face an appearance of forceful intensity when he furrowed his brow with concentration, as he was doing at the moment. His square jaw was firmly set with evident determination. Tristan was always clean-shaven, even when out in the wild. Elias supposed Tristan was careful about his appearance because of the rigid discipline of the Colony Patrol, but he secretly preferred to see Tristan's cheeks shadowed by dark stubble. In Elias's opinion, it gave Tristan a gruff aura he found hard to resist.

Elias checked his link before he focused on the way ahead once more. The sleek steel contours of the wrist-held computer reflected the diffuse light all around him and showed him a brief reflection of his own face.

Although Elias was the same age as Tristan, nearly seventeen in the long years of the world of New Skye, he looked younger because of his paler skin, his smooth cheeks, and the sharp lines of his trim, angular face.

His features were rather ordinary, with the exception of his eyes.

Elias's eyes were not a hazel shade of brown like Tristan's. His irises were iridescent, mesmerizing, and most definitely not human-looking. Elias had seen himself in a mirror many times since the change, but he did not think he would ever get used to seeing the shifting colors, white and pink and neon green, threading themselves in thousands of different shades every time he contemplated his reflection. He had not been born with such eyes. They were part of the legacy of Sizzra, the Spine wurl queen, with whom Elias had spent many harrowing months. He did not know what the colors meant, but it did remind him of a vow he had made to the weakening queen before she had allowed him to go back to his family.

He had promised to watch over her unborn brood.

It was a vow he meant to keep.

A loud huff to the right made Elias glance in that direction. It was hard to see more than a couple of meters away because of the fog that surrounded them, but as the hulking shadow of a Spine wurl approached, he recognized Narev, one of his three other companions. They were big creatures, standing as tall as Elias on six muscular legs. Narev's body, like Vanor's and Siv's, was covered by metallic-looking scales of flawless silver. They looked like impenetrable armor, but Elias knew that they were not indestructible. He had seen creatures cut through them like an oar slicing through still water—creatures with sizzling talons and huge membranous wings. When he closed his eyes, Elias could still picture the carnage left behind by Dresde's assault a week earlier, and he knew that the images in his memories would haunt him for a very long time.

Narev approached even more until he was walking next to Elias. His many legs sank alarmingly low in the quagmire they were crossing, but he did not appear to be worried about being trapped. In fact his movements were graceful, coordinated, and efficient. Elias's eyes roamed over the dozens of long, wicked spines that covered Narev's back, sides, and shoulders. Like his scales, they were silver. Most of them ended in sharp tips with serrated edges. A few of them were shorter since they were growing back to replace others that had been fired before. Elias had never been on the receiving end of Narev's spines, and he did not want to be. He had seen firsthand how fast and how far an adult Spine wurl was able to fire his spines, and how deadly such an attack could be.

Elias placed his hand on the side of Narev's neck.

"Don't worry," he told him. "We should be out of this swamp in a kilometer or so."

Narev swiveled his spade-shaped head to look at Elias fully, fixing him with a gaze that was alert and attentive as it emanated from all three of his eyes. They were red and glowed softly in the foggy atmosphere, reminding Elias of the electronic lights of the security system he would sometimes see outside the genetics lab back in Portree. However, whereas a year ago Elias would have been terrified of looking into the eye cluster of a wurl, now he was reassured. Through physical contact with Narev, Elias could feel the gist of the wurl's emotions. Narev was as determined as Elias. He was also curious. And a little bit bored.

"I wish there were a quicker way around this awful place," Tristan complained. He had caught up to Elias, and they were walking next to each other. Immediately behind him, the outline of Siv was barely visible at the edges of the fog. Vanor was nowhere to be seen, but Elias could hear him very well. As the largest of the three wurl, it was never difficult to know where Vanor was.

Elias smiled, then grimaced as he felt the furtive brush of something large and many-legged crawling on his neck. He slapped it, shuddering. His hand came back slimy, and he wiped it on his pants.

"I agree," he grumbled. "I never knew there could be so many mosquitoes on this planet."

"Just another of the wonderful consequences of you saving the world," Tristan replied, grinning conspiratorially.

"Right. Yay, me. We should figure out a name for these winged bugs."

"What's wrong with 'mosquitoes'?" Tristan asked.

Elias shrugged. "That's the Terran name, and these insects are not the same. They do suck blood, but they're bigger. And they are *sparkly*." He said that last part while pointing at the smear on his pants leg. The mosquito analogs could have, in fact, been beautiful, if they had not been so infuriating.

"Fine," Tristan conceded. How about 'murder drills with weird screw-shaped stingers'?"

"I... was actually thinking of a scientific name," Elias clarified. "You know, genus and species."

Tristan blinked. "Right. You go right ahead, then. You're the scientist. I'm going to call them mosquitoes, if that's okay."

Elias swatted another one, which was buzzing next to his ear. "Let's keep going. Part of me wishes we hadn't taken this route."

"Me too, but this *is* the quickest way," Tristan said after checking his link for a moment. "If we'd avoided the swamp entirely, we would've had to circle around going north or south. It would've probably added a week to the journey, to say nothing of mountains or hills we'd have to climb."

"I know, I know. And we're almost through."

"Yeah. I wonder if Vanor will let me ride him again," Tristan commented, halting briefly because one of his feet had sunk more than usual in the muck. He tried to yank his leg up, but ended up leaving his shoe behind. "You've got to be—"

Elias chuckled, offering Tristan a hand so he could steady himself while he reached down, cursing. He found his shoe, emptied it as much as he could of its disgusting contents, and put it back on.

"I don't think it's a good idea for us to ride them if we don't have to," Elias told him, gesturing at the wurl around them. "Narev is carrying the pack, and that's heavy enough as is. We don't want any of the wurl to struggle with the terrain more than needed because of our added weight. As soon as we're out of this place and back on more solid ground, I'm sure they'll let us ride them again."

"I hope so. We go much faster that way, and the faster we travel, the faster we get to… her."

Elias nodded, and his expression turned somber. He looked ahead, almost as if he were able to see the distant destination he wanted to reach as fast as possible. He tried to use his eyesight to pierce the ghostly fog that surrounded him on all sides, but to no avail. As far as he could see, the landscape was a dull shade of whitish gray. Sometimes the desiccated trunks of trees would come into view, like sentries watching over the marshy land. They soon disappeared behind Elias and his party, and with few landmarks in the interim to the next one, it felt as though they were making no progress at all. Elias wanted to run, to race to the edge of the continent so he could surge over an entire ocean and get to the volcano where she waited.

Dresde. The Flyer wurl queen. The one who had slain Sizzra by taking advantage of her weakness, attacking in the middle of a storm like a coward.

The one who had taken the priceless white egg in which the next Spine queen slumbered, ready to hatch.

The one who had kidnapped Oscar, his little brother.

Elias closed his eyes briefly.

Oscar, please be okay. I'm coming.

Almost as if sensing that something was wrong, Tristan placed his hand on Elias's shoulder. Elias opened his eyes, surprised. Tristan gave him a warm, reassuring smile. He said nothing, but Elias understood. He took Tristan's hand, squeezed it, and the two of them walked hand in hand for a while.

Despite everything that was happening, there was a bright spark of joy in Elias's chest because he was with Tristan. Elias wasn't sure if he and Tristan were official boyfriends, but he did know that he loved Tristan and always wanted to be by his side. Tristan hadn't reciprocated with the L-word yet, but Elias didn't mind. He knew that Tristan cared about him. Enough, in fact, to leave everything behind and join Elias in a mad dash across an entire continent with no idea of what might lie ahead.

About an hour later, Tristan called for a halt, and Elias agreed. The two of them stopped next to a cluster of fallen dead trees that offered a slight improvement over the moist and muddy terrain they have been traversing.

"I'm so thirsty," Tristan said. He walked over to Narev, who crouched slightly and allowed Tristan to unhook one of the smaller backpacks from his spines. He took out a couple of water bottles and tossed one over to Elias.

"Thanks," Elias said as they both drank. It was hot out, which was to be expected given the fact that it was early summer. However, Elias had never been in a swamp before.

He had also never seen so many bugs before.

They rested for only a couple of minutes before the ceaseless insect assault became too much to bear. The arthropods appeared to be drawn to Tristan and Elias, although they seemed to leave Vanor, Narev, and Siv alone. Some of them were large, like the mosquitoes, but the majority were much smaller. They crawled on the tree trunks, splashed in the mud, and flitted through the air. Elias spotted something that looked like a miniature frog skimming on the surface of the swamp. When it looked as though it was going to bump into the tree trunks, however, it deployed a set of three gossamer wings and took off in a small burst of muddy droplets. Elias followed the creature, marveling at its striped body, and was wholly unprepared for the multi-legged arachnid that jumped out of a crack in the rotted wood of a nearby trunk, snatched the winged frog out of the air with black segmented pincers, and disappeared with its prey into the mud with a faint *plop*.

Elias could not suppress a faint thrill of fascination at discovering so many new species he had never seen or heard of in his life. Months and months ago, he had read the account of Dr. Thomas Wright, where the pioneer colonist described the dazzling biodiversity of New Skye. Elias had found it hard to imagine what that must have been like, but he was finally beginning to understand. Now that the Life Seed had been returned to where it belonged, the planet was teeming with life.

They set off again, and although it took another miserable hour of constant effort, Elias's feet eventually touched solid ground. A few minutes later, he could tell they were out of the swamp for good. Although the fog had not let up, the sun was beginning to go down, and the heat was no longer stifling. A mild breeze blew from the east too, bringing with it a welcome relief from the stench of decaying plant matter that had surrounded them in the swamp.

"We made it," Tristan declared triumphantly. His shoes and pants were caked with dried mud all the way up to the knees.

"Yeah. Now I really want a shower, though."

Tristan nodded enthusiastically. "I'm going to jump straight into the next lake we fi—"

Vanor growled suddenly, loudly enough to drown out the end of Tristan's sentence. The other two wurl stiffened, and both Siv and Narev flared out their spines.

Elias exchanged a worried look with Tristan. All three wurl were looking at the sky.

"Back-to-back," Tristan ordered, his words clipped and efficient. "Weapons out."

He pulled his shock spear, which was slung across his back, in a practiced and fluid motion. The hiss of static electricity as he activated the slender double-tipped weapon was accompanied by a dull flash of blue-white light from either end.

Elias echoed Tristan's motion, but instead of a shock spear, he pulled out a long iridescent spine that was the same color as his eyes. The tip of the spine was stained red, and it was nearly twice as long as any of the spines on the adult wurl who were now backing toward where Elias and Tristan stood, all three facing out and appearing to scan the sky.

Elias felt more confident with his weapon in hand. Sizzra had given it to him, and it had become Elias's constant reminder of his link with her and the world itself. Although the spine was very light and appeared hollow, its edge was sharp enough to cut through most things, and its wicked tip could pierce metal. Elias knew from experience that, with enough force, the spine was able to cut through even the reinforced scales of the Flyer queen. Elias had wounded her with it in their last encounter.

With Tristan's back against his and the Spine wurl all around, Elias studied the sky in earnest. The fog was thick, and even out of the swamp it limited visibility so much that his surroundings were no more than a blur of shifting white and gray, a landscape of muted sounds that carried strangely over the hot, oppressive atmosphere.

These were the perfect conditions for an ambush. Elias recalled the knowledge he had gained from Sizzra's ancestral memories, and he knew that Flyer wurl would often attack when the environment shrouded them from view. They were sneaky, quick, and deadly.

A faint shadow passed directly overhead. Siv growled and fired a single spine upward, but it hit nothing. In the wake of the shadow, a faint current of displaced air brought with it a smell Elias had already learned to associate with Flyers. It was an intense stench that reminded him of burning rock or melting metal.

The smell triggered the recall of much more recent memories in Elias's mind. He remembered a field littered with the dead bodies of Spine wurl. He remembered Sizzra collapsing lifeless as a storm howled around them all. He remembered Dresde most of all, towering above him, majestic, taunting.

Cowardly.

"Stay sharp," Tristan said curtly. "It's coming back around."

"I'm ready," Elias replied. He wasn't afraid. His every muscle was tense, alert, ready to react to the inevitable strike.

The shadow passed again, faster than before. Vanor and Narev fired spines, but the fog swallowed the attacker, and it was gone as fast as it had come.

"Just one, I think," Tristan reported under his breath. "Odd."

Elias nodded, although Tristan couldn't see him directly. Normally Flyers would attack in groups, from many sides at once. They loved to deceive and confuse, to draw their enemy's attention one way while they attacked from behind.

Next to Elias, Narev growled low in his throat.

Something small came sailing through the air and banged against Vanor's metallic scales. A rock, dropped from above. Surprised more than hurt, Vanor was too slow to dodge the second, much bigger rock that plunged from the sky. It hit him on the head.

Elias couldn't help it; he glanced that way.

The Flyer used that opportunity to attack.

It streaked down from the sky like a pouncing falcon, making the air scream in the wake of its mad descent. Elias saw a blur of blue, a flash of large wings, and a sudden collision behind him nearly knocked him off his feet.

"Attack!" Tristan shouted.

Elias whirled about and saw the Flyer take off like a fired arrow after having smashed into Siv. Tristan swiped at empty air with his spear while Narev and Vanor fired spines into nothing. Siv groaned and tried to retaliate, but the buffeting wind from the Flyer made them all stumble. When they recovered, the fog had swallowed the aggressor. Two of Siv's back plates had been punctured by the Flyer's talons, and the holes it had left behind were sizzling.

"Siv!" Elias said. "Are you okay?"

Siv stood up and flared his spines again. It appeared the wounds were not deep.

"Where is it?" Tristan demanded. "Stay vigilant!"

A faint howl from above was his answer. Humans and wurl all looked up in unison and saw the Flyer a split second before it flared out its talons in an unstoppable collision course with Tristan.

Elias's blood ran cold. It was too fast. Tristan would be hit.

Vanor fired two spines.

Thunk, thunk.

The Flyer screamed and smashed into the ground not one meter away from Tristan. Elias had a full glimpse of the Flyer for the first time. It was smaller than the huge cobalt adults he had already seen. This one's scales were a pale shade of sky blue, but its talons and wicked fangs looked every bit as deadly as those of a full-grown Flyer.

Narev pounced on the creature, but even on the ground the Flyer was quick—much quicker than the adults, as Elias realized when he tried to stab the attacking Flyer as it slithered past him. He missed. The Flyer's snakelike coils undulated on the muddy soil and, aided by its legs, allowed the creature to slip away, take off at a run, and leap into the sky.

Siv was ready this time, though. With an angry roar, the much-bulkier Spine wurl launched itself at the Flyer. The two of them collided in midair, and the Flyer screamed again. It slashed with glowing talons, forcing Siv to curl his body into a ball. The Flyer used the distraction to flare out its wings and buffeted them all with wind once again.

Narev and Vanor fired one spine each.

Another scream. The Flyer's wings crumpled underneath him, their membranes pierced by the serrated edges of the silver spines. The attacker fell down in a heap very close to where Elias was standing, and Siv, Vanor, and Narev fired another volley of spines. These impaled the creature's wings and pierced the soil below, pinning the thing to the ground.

Elias was closest to him now. The Flyer squirmed and tried to break free, but his struggling only ripped the delicate membrane on his wings more.

"Elias, now!" Tristan shouted from behind.

Elias raised his own iridescent spine over his head and brought it down in a deadly arc that would strike the creature in the middle of its eye cluster and end its life forever.

"Haaaa!" Elias shouted.

Scared.

The strength of the emotion was so jolting that Elias halted his downward slash less than a handsbreadth away from his victim.

The Flyer was projecting abject terror as he flinched from the killing blow.

Elias blinked, uncomprehending. He was suddenly barraged with the emotions of the creature in front of him. Pain, confusion, and above everything else, fear. The Flyer hadn't wanted to attack them. They were too many. Too strong for him. But she had said to attack them. He couldn't say no. He couldn't. Her voice, her will….

Scared.

Elias looked down at the juvenile Flyer and lifted his weapon away.

A wave of savage glee burst out from the sky-blue juvenile, and he lifted his head, roaring with his throat and his mind. He surged forward as he ripped both his wings, uncaring of the pain, and pounced in a predatory strike that was quicker than thought. All four of his legs were aimed at Elias. His talons sizzled, white-hot with his murderous intent.

Elias realized his mistake, but it was too late.

He was going to die.

"Elias!" Tristan shouted.

The air was knocked out of Elias's lungs by something huge that tackled him to the ground. The impact stunned him. He heard a groan, a growl, and the unmistakable *shwoop* of spines being fired. Then another angry growl, a sound as of meat being shredded.

Finally came a guttural scream cut short, a drawn-out death rattle… and stillness. The fog surrounding Elias was all but smothering him with its heat, and it trapped the smell of blood all around him.

"Elias! Elias, are you okay?"

Tristan was beside him now. Elias focused and tried to take Tristan's hand, but he couldn't get air into his lungs yet. It was a couple of seconds before he managed to stand up, stumbling, and look around.

The Flyer was dead, having been torn to shreds and impaled in five different places by more spines.

Vanor and Siv were standing triumphantly over him, their eyes glowing with rage. They were panting, fangs bared, the bellows of their hot breath loud in Elias's ears. Both of them still scanned the skies, as if daring another creature to come down and challenge them.

Narev was on the ground, unmoving.

"Narev?" Elias said. "Narev!"

Elias rushed to the wurl's side, icy fear stabbing his heart. The fear was replaced with shaky relief when Narev grunted and stood up next to the other two wurl. He looked at the dead Flyer and snarled, radiating anger and defiance.

"You saved me," Elias told him with dawning understanding. "You knocked me away so the Flyer wouldn't get me."

Narev huffed. Then he nosed Elias, gently for a creature that size, as if wanting to make sure Elias was okay. Elias placed his hands on Narev's snout and gasped when he saw the sizzling swipe marks on the side of Narev's head. The Flyer's talons had barely missed Narev's eye cluster, but his scales had been sliced through as if made of paper. Beneath the three parallel gashes, Elias could clearly see charred muscle, and he felt Narev's pain through their shared mental connection.

Elias projected concern with his thoughts, but Narev pushed Elias's hand away and went over to stand next to the other two wurl. He assumed an alert fighting stance and bunched his muscles, flaring out his spines in a threatening display. If anything, the wound on his head made him look more ferocious than ever. He seemed to want Elias to know that he was more than okay. He was ready to fight again.

"Elias, are you okay?" Tristan repeated, placing both his hands on Elias's shoulders and looking into his eyes.

Elias nodded slowly. "Yeah. He… I…. It happened so fast."

Tristan pulled him in for a hug and kissed Elias on the lips. "I'm so glad you're okay," he whispered, choking up slightly.

Elias drew back a little bit and gave Tristan a shaky smile. "Don't worry. I'm fine."

"You could have died," Tristan said. "I tried to help, but I was… I was too far away."

Elias saw real concern on Tristan's face. It touched him deeply, and he put his hands on Tristan's waist. "I'm fine," he said. "Narev saved me. We're all okay." He wanted to be reassuring, but the truth was that the close call had shaken him too. He couldn't erase the image of the snarling Flyer jumping at him, projecting triumphant viciousness at his successful deceit.

Or had it been deceit? The emotions Elias had felt—the fear. It had been real. Elias was sure of it. But then why had the Flyer acted like he had in the end? He had almost seemed possessed.

"I think Narev really cares about you," Tristan commented, bringing Elias out of his reverie.

"Yeah. I think he does."

The five of them left the carcass of the Flyer behind and continued on their way due east. The fog lifted after a while, and the ground sloped gently upward, becoming much rockier and drier. At sunset, the heat of the day finally abated, and the ever-present swarms of flying insects disappeared as well. They were walking over hilly ground now, and a gentle breeze blew from the north. It brought with it the fragrance of blooming flowers and green things growing. Amid the waist-high grass they were traversing, creatures scurried out of the way unseen every few steps. Elias did not know whether the animals were scared of the three wurl stomping a few paces behind or whether they were terrified of two alien creatures walking through the land for maybe the first time ever. Although some people had explored parts of New Skye at the very beginning of colonization, three generations ago, no humans had left Portree in many decades. As far as the vast majority of wildlife on the planet was concerned, Elias and Tristan were incomprehensible visitors from beyond the stars. They posed an unknown threat, and Elias supposed this was the reason why very few individuals of the native wildlife had ventured to come near them in their expedition so far.

Eventually the party ran into an enormous sinkhole, about one hundred meters across, in the middle of the sloping grassy terrain. It appeared to have been filled with rainwater over countless years and resembled a small lake now. Two of the moons had come out by then, and they provided reasonable illumination by which to see the space around it without resorting to the electric flashlights Tristan carried in his backpack. Under the silver moonlight, Elias was once again surprised by the beauty of the world he was exploring. The still surface of the water sparkled, reflecting a few wispy clouds as they raced through the firmament overhead. Bright stars filled the sky, and the air was full of cautious hoots, howls, and chirps coming from sources unknown. A couple of ryddle birds corkscrewed through the air on three wings some distance away, skimming over the surface of the grass and ostensibly looking for prey. A jumping creature with white scales Elias had never seen before appeared briefly over the surface of the grass, evidently startled.

It gave a little squeak of surprise and vaulted away very fast, disappearing over the summit of a nearby hill. It was a peaceful summer's day, relaxing and welcoming.

Part of Elias's mind could faintly detect the web of interconnected spirit-lines that linked every living creature to one another. The vibrant intensity of summertime underscored how the world was healing after having been so long asleep. Despite everything that had happened that day, part of Elias's tension ebbed and was replaced by the balm of balance and unity.

Tristan filled their canteens and water bottles with fresh water from the sinkhole, disinfected it, and then they both proceeded to wash the grime and mud off the clothes they wore.

"That mud was *really* sticky," Tristan grumbled, using a stick as a lever to pry a particularly stubborn patch of mud from the bottom of his pants leg. "And smelly."

"I know," Elias agreed. "We'll avoid swamps from now on. It's too awful."

They were done after half an hour and proceeded to strip down fully to have a swim. Narev, Vanor, and Siv joined them immediately, cannonballing into the water and promptly diving down into the unseen depths of the large sinkhole. They remained there for a very long time, but Elias knew they wouldn't drown. Spine wurl were amphibians, or so he guessed from his observations of their behavior when he had been Sizzra's prisoner months ago. They were also good swimmers and even better hunters underwater.

"Do you think they will catch any big fish?" Elias asked Tristan as the two of them floated in the cool water.

"No idea. But that would only be good news for *you*."

"You could try meat," Elias suggested. "Maybe you won't get sick."

"Oh, no way. It's not worth the risk. My system is incompatible with the meat of this planet, Elias. I don't know why you can eat it, but I think you're the only one."

"Yeah," Elias responded thoughtfully. Three days earlier, Siv had killed a big hairy creature with hooves and a ridge of bony plates along its back that had reminded Elias of a cross between a Dimetrodon-like dinosaur and a cow. It had been big enough for all three wurl, and some meat had been left over for Elias and Tristan to share. He had eaten it, but Tristan hadn't even wanted to try. He was convinced he'd get sick from it like all other humans on New Skye.

Except for Elias.

The two of them did laps in the water for a while longer and then climbed out on the eastern side, where they dried themselves off and put on their clothes again. They then began the now-familiar routine of setting up camp: propping up the tent, building a fire, and taking out the rations they would be having that day. Elias did not speak much as he worked. His mind was elsewhere, recalling the events of a few hours ago. He couldn't stop thinking about what had happened, and a persistent voice in his head insisted that the real reason he hadn't been able to kill the wurl was pure fear.

I was too scared to act. I endangered us all.

"I wonder if it's because of how you've changed," Tristan said as they were heating up water for some tea. He took up their conversation from earlier as if they had been speaking a moment ago. "The reason why you can eat meat."

Elias struggled to understand what Tristan was talking about for a moment. Then he nodded when he remembered.

"I don't know. Maybe."

"It's not only your eyes, either," Tristan continued. He took out a packet of crackers and ripped it open with his teeth, setting half of them on each of two plates they used to have their meals. "It's other things too."

"Like what?" Elias asked, checking to see whether the water was boiling yet.

Tristan shrugged. Behind him, Vanor came out of the water with something in his jaws. The wurl noticed the fire and promptly came over with a mental nudge to Elias to cook the fish for him.

"You have this connection to the world now, right? From the blood rituals with the Life Seed?"

Elias nodded. "It's fainter now, not at all like when I was right there with it. But yeah. It's a little bit like the way Sizzra used to see the world. She could perceive all of the living creatures on this continent."

"That's amazing," Tristan replied. "I see how you communicate with the wurl. It's like you can read their minds."

Elias considered for a moment. "More like their emotions. Sometimes they are very clear. Other times, not so much."

Tristan paused. "Is… is that why you hesitated? Back there?"

He didn't need to be more specific. Elias knew what he referred to, and the memories flashed vividly in his mind again. The wicked glee of the attacking Flyer. The creature's terror and his reluctance to attack them to begin with. The all-consuming fear the blue wurl had felt.

I hesitated because I wanted to save the Flyer's life. Right?

Or was it... cowardice?

"Elias?" Tristan asked.

"I don't want to talk about it," Elias replied, more brusquely than he intended. "Let's eat."

Tristan looked as though he wanted say something else, but instead he simply nodded. "Right. I'm hungry."

As they ate, Siv and then Narev came out of the water with their own catch of the night, two thick, long creatures that resembled overgrown eels of a deep maroon color, with vestigial legs and a surprisingly elongated and tooth-filled mouth. Seeing Narev's raw scar triggered a pang of guilt in Elias's chest, and although Narev appeared to be okay, Elias couldn't help feeling bad. He ate his own food without really tasting it and tried to make amends for his regret by cooking the fish for all three of the wurl. Afterward he helped Tristan pack everything away, and they prepared to settle in for the night.

All three moons had come out by then, and the bright light they reflected from the hidden sun bathed the entire landscape in muted silver with deep black shadows. There were fewer sounds coming from the tall grass around them, as if all of the creatures were also preparing to go to sleep. The heat of the day had fully dissipated, and aside from a few persistent mosquitoes, everything was peaceful. Narev and Siv found resting spots among the grass near the tent while Vanor elected to sleep some distance away, closest to the water. Nevertheless all three of them had chosen positions that formed a rough triangle around the place where Tristan and Elias would be sleeping.

"It's like they're guarding us," Tristan pointed out as he and Elias crawled inside the tent.

Elias zipped it shut behind them, glad to be away from the mosquitoes at last. "They want us to be safe."

"Even Vanor?"

"Yeah," Elias replied as he undressed. It was complicated to take off his clothes in the small space of the tent without bumping into Tristan, but he'd had several days of practice by then. "Vanor is a little bit more independent than the others because he's the strongest. He was Sizzra's mate, and I think that sets him apart somewhat. That doesn't mean he doesn't care."

"But does he only care about saving the egg?" Tristan wanted to know. He peeled off his undershirt to reveal the clearly defined muscles on his torso. There was a scar on his left forearm, jagged and long.

"He wants to save the egg of course. But I think he also cares about us—you especially."

"Me? No way."

Elias shrugged. "The two of you are a lot alike, strong-willed and independent. And he lets you ride him, after all."

"Yeah, he does," Tristan conceded. "Although it's a rather bumpy ride when I do."

He climbed into the large sleeping bag they shared and beckoned for Elias to join him. Elias did so, and he immediately felt safer and more at peace. The tent around them was cozy now that the temperature was beginning to drop with nighttime.

Elias had another mental flash of the Flyer wurl from before. He stiffened in the sleeping bag and turned away from Tristan, resting his head on his biceps.

Tristan hugged him from behind. The contact of his cool skin on Elias's own was reassuring.

"Want to tell me what's on your mind?" Tristan said in a low, deep voice, his mouth close to Elias's ear.

Elias considered saying nothing was wrong, but that would have been a lie. Besides, if he had learned anything from his long months of isolation with the Spine queen, struggling to survive, it was that human company was precious and should be treasured. He'd have given anything back then to have someone who would listen to him, like Tristan now did.

Elias sighed and turned around to face Tristan. He hugged him back and rested his head on Tristan's chest.

"It's my fault Narev got hurt," he admitted in a husky voice. "I hesitated. I had the Flyer right there, and I... I couldn't do it. I couldn't kill him."

Tristan said nothing, but Elias knew he was attentive. Tristan was a good listener.

"I could have died," Elias continued. "Narev could have died. All because of my stupid choice not to kill a creature that wanted to hurt us. But... you know how you mentioned earlier that I can communicate with wurl?"

"Yeah."

"It's not just with Spine wurl. I sense the Flyers too, sometimes. Right as I was about to kill this one, I felt... I don't know. His thoughts, maybe. His emotions. He was terrified, Tristan. He hadn't wanted to attack us, but she'd made him."

"Dresde?"

Elias's brow furrowed at the name. The ancient memories he had received from Sizzra ran deep, and Sizzra had loathed the name of her enemy. He couldn't help but react with animosity whenever he thought about Dresde, her deceit, her violence.

"Yes. She forced him to attack. It made no sense for one single juvenile Flyer wurl to ambush us if you think about it. It was foggy, sure, and that gave him an advantage, but there was one of him and five of us. He couldn't have won."

"But he attacked all the same."

"He did because he was forced to," Elias repeated, and he hoped it was the truth. "And right then, when the Flyer saw that I was about to kill him, he was so scared, Tristan. Terrified, like he had just woken up from a nightmare and found that he was going to die. He hadn't wanted to do any of this. So I... I...."

"You showed him mercy."

Elias shook his head and raised it so he would be looking at Tristan's face. "It was stupid. I think he deceived me, exactly like Dresde would do. As soon as he saw that I was sparing his life, his emotions changed. They became monstrous, twisted. And he attacked me."

"I know. I was so scared," Tristan told him, hugging him tighter for a moment.

Elias looked down. Shame welled up in his heart, and he knew he had to say out loud the thought that had been bothering him for hours now, the pernicious doubt he hadn't been able to get rid of. "What if it wasn't mercy I showed him? What if...? What if it was fear? Tristan, what if I'm just a coward?" Elias closed his eyes. The words hurt coming out.

Tristan was silent for a moment. Then he burst out laughing.

It was so unexpected that Elias drew back from him, opening his eyes again, and propped himself up on one elbow.

"By the generation ship," Tristan said between chuckles, "*that's* what has been bothering you?"

"I, yeah, I think... I mean...," Elias stammered.

Tristan sat up and folded the sleeping bag away. He gave Elias a quick kiss on the lips. "Elias, you're really smart, but that was the stupidest thing you have ever said."

"What? Why?"

Tristan sighed. "Let's do a quick recap, shall we? You defied your entire colony to do the right thing by taking the Life Seed back to where it belonged. Right?"

"Yeah, but—"

"You stood your ground against a gigantic wurl queen who could have killed you with a single bite more than once, right?"

"Yes...."

Tristan raised one of his hands and bent his fingers down with the other as he counted down. "You saved *my* life by challenging Sizzra that one time when she wanted to kill me. You stared her down, remember? You also saved the entire colony of Portree by bringing back seeds that will grow and give us food for the future. You somehow learned to survive out in the wilderness on your own for months. In the wintertime, no less. Oh, and you actually attacked and wounded Dresde herself even though she is *many* times your size."

Elias nodded slowly. All of those things were true, although he hadn't thought about them together like that.

Tristan smiled. "Elias, you're the bravest man I know. You hesitated with that Flyer because you're also the most *compassionate* man I know. You care about life, and you don't kill for fun or because you're angry. When you fight, you do it to protect others. You are selfless and kind, and those are two of the things I like most about you. In fact, you would make a great Colony Patrol soldier if you wanted to be."

"But Narev got hurt," Elias insisted, although a warm feeling suffused his chest at hearing Tristan's words.

"Trust me, it's good that you felt bad about the possibility of killing a living creature, one with emotions. When I think back on the way I gloated about all the wurl I'd killed, like I did back at the Midwinter Feast last year when I showed their spines as trophies, I feel ashamed." Tristan cast his eyes down for a moment, his expression regretful. "And as for Narev, yes, he got hurt, because what we're doing is dangerous. There are no guarantees, and we are going to get hurt sooner or later. Those three wurl outside are ready to fight to the death to save the egg of the new Spine queen, but today you saw that Narev is also willing to die to save *you*. It's a complicated situation, but everyone's fine tonight. That's what's important here. We made it through one more day. I'm thankful for that, and also to be able to spend one more night with you."

"Me too," Elias said softly. He smiled. A great weight was sliding off his shoulders.

"And you are not a coward," Tristan told him with a grin. "You're strong. Resourceful. And very attractive."

Tristan placed his hand on the back of Elias's head and leaned forward to share a long, tender kiss with him. Elias reciprocated, glad to be in Tristan's arms, glad to be safe, and glad to be alive.

Their kiss became more intense and urgent as seconds passed. They made love with the vigor and passion of youth, and afterward it was Elias holding Tristan in the sleeping bag as the two of them panted, hearts still racing, allowing their bodies to relax. Elias caressed Tristan's arm absentmindedly, tracing the outline of the scar.

"Does it still hurt?" Elias asked, remembering how Tristan's forearm had been fractured by the bite of a juvenile Spine wurl last winter.

"No, it healed really well. And I think the scar looks cool."

"It does. Makes you look dangerous."

Tristan grinned. "Nice. Narev will also have a cool scar to show off, you know."

Elias nodded. He was at peace now. "Thank you, Tristan."

"For what?"

"For listening. For saying the things I needed to hear. For being here with me."

"Anytime," Tristan answered in a sleepy voice. "I will always be with you."

"Me too," Elias replied. Then he closed his eyes and, with a yawn, surrendered to sleep. His last fleeting thought was of Oscar, and he hoped his little brother was okay.

chapter 2.
oscar

CRUSHING FORCE. Dizzying motion. Oscar Trost was jostled in so many different directions he stopped being able to tell which way was up and which was down.

He struggled, but it was no use. He tried to bite, he tried to kick. The taloned foot around him merely tightened its grip, threatening to smother him. Panicking, he screamed. He voiced his terror until his throat was hoarse, but no one would help him.

He was thrown violently to the side, together with the creature that held him. The impact was jarring, and Oscar felt one of the sizzling talons dig into his shoulder. Skin burned, muscle tore.

He screamed again. The horrible pain was gone as fast as it had come, but his shoulder did not feel right.

It's broken.

I'm trapped.

Eli!

"Eli!"

Dresde roared, drowning out his desperate cry for help, and he was sure he did not imagine the way he also heard the roar in his mind.

Dresde was angry, bloodthirsty, unpredictable.

However, Oscar also perceived that she was scared. She had been hurt.

Suddenly he was flying. He tried to twist around to see where he was going, but he could not move. He realized he was still clutching something tight against his chest and tried to let go, but he couldn't relax his arms around it.

The egg. I have the egg.

It dug against his abdomen, and he squirmed and twisted until he was able to breathe. He was rising, fast. His legs dangled over nothing, and he saw another big flying reptile from the corner of his eye. This one was blue. There was a girl riding it.

Oscar tried to call for help again, trying to get the girl's attention, but he couldn't even hear himself over the gale. Tears blinded him, and he was forced to close his eyes. His shoulder hurt. He couldn't let go of the egg.

Where is she going? Where are they taking me?

Oscar shouted again, but it was barely audible to him. It was useless to call for help, he realized, and now that he was so high up, he was seized with terror from a new direction.

What if she lets me go?

He froze in a new surge of panic. He would die if Dresde let him go. Or she could crush him at any moment if she wanted to. He could barely breathe as it was, maybe because the grip around him was slowly tightening.

No. Focus.

With an effort of will, Oscar wrenched his attention away from his panicky thoughts and tried to evaluate his situation. He couldn't really think straight. He was trembling, not only from terror but also from the cold. They had reached whatever altitude Dresde had deemed acceptable, but the air at that height was freezing. It sliced cleanly through Oscar's formal clothes and numbed every part of his skin that was exposed to the elements.

Minutes passed. The cold got worse. Oscar realized he was having trouble breathing once more, and he vaguely registered that this time it was because the air seemed thin and insubstantial. Dresde took a dizzying turn at one point, and he was able to see the ground, incredibly far away, a blur of tan and dark green and gray. Another spiral turn a few seconds later made Oscar's stomach heave, and he saw the girl again, flying very close to him on top of that cobalt-scaled wurl.

She has a helmet, like a pilot, he thought to himself, struggling to focus. *So she can breathe in the… In the….*

His consciousness flickered. He came to after what seemed like barely a moment, but the pain in his shoulder had magnified twofold, and he could not open his eyes. He could not feel his face. Panicking yet again, he tried to move, but a white-hot stab of agony in his shoulder forced him to remain stationary.

I can't breathe.

Another jolt. Warmer air. More pain, and it seemed to Oscar as though somebody was holding him by the waist. It was still cold, but he could breathe now. A monumental headache exploded between his temples, and he struggled not to lose consciousness but failed.

He regained awareness choking on some water. It seemed to him that he was not moving anymore. He thought he saw a face in front of his, but it faded.

Consciousness returned, and he trembled in the cold. He was flying again.

Flicker. Freezing rain on his face. *Flicker*. Sleeping in a cave. *Flicker*. Choking down some food. *Flicker*.

Riding on something blue, dozens of kilometers above an endless expanse of a different blue. There was no end to the water below.

Oscar blinked. His mind felt sharper. He took stock of his surroundings and realized he was riding the cobalt wurl, headed for the distant but unmistakable outline of solid ground. And below him….

It's the ocean!

He was jolted to full attention by the realization. He tried to move, but two strong arms restricted his motion. Oscar looked back and saw the girl from before, sitting behind him and holding him by the waist. Her eyes were narrowed to mere slits, and her hair whipped in the wind. Oscar moved his head again and realized he was wearing her helmet, which allowed him to breathe. He wasn't shivering anymore because she had put some sort of tight-fitting jacket around his upper body.

"Who are you?" he tried to ask. His voice was muffled by the helmet. "Where are we going?"

But she made no answer.

It was more than a day before they approached an enormous mountain, nearly conical in shape, rising from the shore of a strange continent. The western flank of the peak looked as if it had been torn away by a titan, exposing dark caves, jagged rocks, and what Oscar could only think of as rivers of flowing lava. It was bizarre. He had never seen anything like it in his life.

Oscar struggled to make sense of the direction they were taking, but it was useless. He was riding on a saddle of some sort, but even so he was in constant danger of sliding off and falling to his death. He used every bit of his strength to keep still when the blue wurl began to descend, heading straight for a cave opening in the side of the mountain, which glowed red in the twilight.

The arms around him tightened their grip until it was painful, and suddenly Dresde flew overhead, terrifying and magnificent as she spread her wings to their full extent and her amethyst scales glittered in the last few rays of the sun.

The descent took much longer than Oscar had expected. They approached the cave in spirals that brought them progressively closer to the ground. Oscar grew dizzy and was forced to close his eyes, using his good arm to hang tight. His left arm was hurting much more now, and the horrible and sudden jostle when the wurl finally hit the ground made Oscar howl in pain.

Someone snatched the helmet off his head. For the first time since his capture, Oscar realized that the wind wasn't screaming in his ears. He felt oddly light-headed, confused by the silence.

"Do not shout again. You understand?" the girl snapped.

Oscar turned back as far as he was able in order to see her face. He was interrupted by her pushing him off the wurl.

"Quickly, male! Doran is taking off!"

Oscar lost his balance and collapsed off the wurl, hitting the ground in a heap. He cried out again, holding his left arm with his hand as he lay on what felt like coarse sand, strangely hot to the touch. A second later the blue wurl took to the air again and blasted them both with wind that reeked of burning rock. The wurl's serpentine body was quickly lost from sight as he appeared to fly off a cliff.

Oscar grunted, trying not to cry from the pain.

"Quiet!" the girl ordered. She stood above him and pulled him to his feet, ignoring his protests.

When he took a step back, Oscar was able to focus on her properly for the first time. She wasn't as old as he had thought at first. She looked to be about the same age as Oscar himself, in fact, but her youthful features contrasted with the severity of her expression. She had beautiful bronze skin, and she wore her long raven-black hair in a tight braid. Her eyes were a shade of emerald green Oscar had never seen in the colony.

"Where am I?" he asked in a shaky voice.

The girl looked at him as though she didn't understand what he was saying.

"Please, you have to help me. Where is my family? What is this place?"

The girl opened her mouth as if to answer, but a shadow blocked out what remained of the sun, and they were almost thrown to the ground by a much more powerful gust of buffeting wind.

Dresde landed nearby with feline grace, folding her massive wings against her body so their back tips would point skyward. She moved on the ground as though stalking prey, her head low, the cluster of three glowing red eyes terrifying in the deepening shadows. There was a slow-flowing river of lava several meters away, and by its reddish light, Oscar saw that in her right front foot, Dresde still carried a large egg of purest white, perfect and unbroken.

The events of the day of the storm flashed by Oscar's mind. His terror was briefly pushed aside and replaced with heart-wrenching concern for his family. He stepped away from the girl and walked toward Dresde, holding his injured arm as he went.

"Where is Eli?" he demanded in as loud a voice as he could muster. From behind him, he clearly heard the girl gasp. "What did you do to him?"

Dresde paused for a moment. Her neck snaked up, and she unfurled her wings halfway.

The little male speaks, she said, and Oscar stumbled, falling onto one knee. Her voice was in his mind, like a shout that blocked out everything else. *How amusing.*

"Whe…," Oscar tried to say, but his tongue felt sluggish. He took a breath, swallowed. Then he tried again. "Where is Eli?"

Oscar's eyes roamed over Dresde's face, and he saw something he had not noticed before: there was a slash mark next to her left nostril. One of her glittering scales had been cut open, and the flesh underneath was still visible.

Dresde lowered her head with shocking speed until her cluster of red eyes was less than an arm's length away from Oscar's face. Under the intensity of her full gaze, Oscar flinched as she stabbed his mind with her overwhelming attention. She forced him to focus on a memory of Elias, seizing it, analyzing it.

You are kin to him, she mused.

Oscar covered one of his ears with his good hand, but it did nothing to block out the voice.

I see. Will he come for you? I wonder….

"Let me go!" Oscar shouted with as much defiance as he could muster.

With a languid flick, Dresde whipped her tail around and slapped Oscar on his injured arm. The pain was beyond imagining. He dropped to the ground, crying.

Dresde smiled with her mind, eyeing Oscar as if enjoying his pain. She brought her tail up again, and Oscar cowered. The mental smile broadened.

Samantha, keep this whelp alive for now. He will come for this one. And when he does….

An emotion shattered Oscar's pain and replaced everything in his mind. It took him an instant to realize that the emotion did not come from him, but from Dresde. It was something like joy, but twisted and bent. Hungry. Evil.

He will pay for daring to attack a goddess, Dresde said, turning her head away slightly so the wound on her snout would not be visible. *I will enjoy breaking him, that little human who wields my sister's spine.*

"Yes, Dresde," the girl called Samantha said. She helped Oscar stand with a rough tug upward.

I will call on you if I need you, Dresde instructed, her mental echo already dismissive. Oscar saw Dresde lift the egg she held and close her foot around it. Her talons glowed in the darkness. She appeared to squeeze, hard, but nothing happened. The egg did not break. *I need to find the solution to a riddle.*

She jumped off the ground without warning, blasting away in the direction of the summit of the volcano. The darkness of the night swallowed her, leaving Oscar alone with Samantha.

Oscar realized he was shaking. His arm felt wrong.

"Please…. Please help me…."

Samantha looked down at the ground briefly, as if conflicted, but when she looked at him again, her eyes were hard.

"This way. Quick, and do not even think of disobeying if you value your life."

"Where are we going?"

"Walk."

Samantha grabbed Oscar's uninjured shoulder and forced him to walk beside her. They went deeper into the cave, and Oscar followed meekly. He was a little bit taller than Samantha, but she projected an aura of such assertive authority that the thought of running away did not once cross his mind. He walked after her instead, stumbling sometimes because he could not see where he was going. There was only ruddy light from the lava river nearby as illumination, throwing harsh black shadows on the rocky walls of the path they had taken, descending the mountain.

The path snaked in and out of caves and narrow passages with so many twists and turns that Oscar was soon completely lost. It was very hot inside the caves and even hotter in the tunnels. Once they exited a particularly narrow shaft and came out into a vast underground gallery with a high vaulted ceiling that looked as though it had been hewn out of the rock by claws. At the bottom of the gallery, hot lava pooled from one of the glowing rivers of molten rock above them. As the lake of lava reached the surface where they were standing, it got progressively cooler until it turned black and solid. The temperature was almost unbearable, and the air was saturated with the stench of sulfur. There was a narrow walkway at the very edge of the cooling lava. Oscar was terrified of falling in and burning alive.

What is this place?

He thought about asking Samantha again, but she was walking fast, and he could scarcely keep up with her. She let go of his arm as they were walking along the edge of the lake of lava, but Oscar still kept as close to her as he could. He was hundreds, maybe thousands of kilometers away from his home, and Samantha was the only one who could help him. Oscar hurried along, holding his injured arm. The shoes he was wearing were terrible for the terrain, since he had put on his one formal pair of glossy black loafers in his bedroom days earlier, so very long ago. The day of the storm.

He sniffled. Samantha turned around, her mouth set in a thin line. "Hurry. It is not good to breathe these fumes for too long."

Oscar nodded with a jerk and obeyed. They entered a low tunnel several minutes later, and Oscar was forced to crouch to walk through it. At the end the path opened up, and he realized that they were still going down. He wondered how long he would have to walk, but after minutes gave way to an hour, he stopped wondering and merely concentrated on not stopping.

Eventually the stifling heat receded. They did not go through tunnels anymore but were going down a much gentler slope. A few minutes later they came out into the open, and Oscar looked up at the sky with relief. It was warm out, but the air was fresh and cool in comparison to what he had endured. The growing claustrophobic sensation he'd had inside the volcano faded slowly.

He followed Samantha downhill until they came to the edge of the place where the mountain appeared as though it had been rent asunder by a titanic beast. There was a drop of several dozen meters straight ahead, where a cliff ended. Far below on a narrow beach, Oscar thought he saw a few winged shapes move about in the darkness, in the midst of large geometric structures that appeared to glitter in mysterious ways. Beyond that he could see the ocean illuminated by the moonlight. To his right the volcano towered like a slumbering predator.

On his left, there was a house.

"Where are we going?" he ventured to ask when they were a few steps away from the building. A single light burned outside a big but crude door made of wood. The structure itself looked more like a barn than a house upon closer inspection.

"*You* are coming this way. Follow me."

Samantha led him to the left, away from the illuminated house and down a path that was treacherous and dark. There were many rocks around, and Oscar kept tripping on the obstacles, which were hard to see with only moonlight to guide his steps. On either side of the path, sometimes close by and sometimes far away, Oscar thought he saw the dark outlines of other buildings or squat houses, but he was not sure. He followed Samantha for nearly ten minutes before they stopped in front of a dark structure, long but not very tall. There were no lights, but Oscar thought he could see two large doors set on either end. They walked to the left one, and Samantha reached forward without hesitation to grab the handle of a door. She pulled, and it creaked as it swung outward.

To the right, a muffled moan answered the creak.

"What's that?" Oscar asked, his tone anxious. It had sounded like an animal.

"In," Samantha ordered, ignoring his question. Oscar glanced in her direction, trying to make out her expression from the shadows that hid most of her face. She carried her helmet under one arm, and her voice was like steel. "Get inside. Now."

"But…."

She stepped forward suddenly until her face was a couple of centimeters away from his, in a threatening gesture so similar to what Dresde had done earlier that Oscar flinched. "I will not say it again, male. In. Now."

Oscar obeyed. He stepped into the darkness, ducking under what could have been a low ceiling. Samantha pushed the door to close it.

"My name is Oscar," he said quickly. "I come from Portree. I know your name is Samantha. Please, help me. I don't know what happened to my family or why I'm here. What's going on? What is this place?"

Samantha paused for an instant, but Oscar could no longer see her face in the darkness.

Then she slammed the door shut. The sound was followed by the clatter of something metallic being placed against it from the outside. When Oscar stepped forward and attempted to push the door open, he realized he could not.

From his left, muffled but still unnervingly close, Oscar heard the moan again.

He waited, frozen and expectant, but there were no other sounds. Samantha did not come back, and Oscar was scared of calling out for her in case Dresde could hear him.

His shoulder hurt. He was hungry and thirsty. His feet hurt from walking for so long, and he could not stop wondering about what might have happened to his family back home.

Eli, where are you? Mom, Dad, I'm sorry....

The sobs came, and he collapsed onto his knees in the darkness. The ground was hard and strangely hot, but Oscar did not care.

He remembered the day of the storm, with the sound of the sirens blaring throughout the colony. He had panicked when he'd heard them from his house. Elias had left to confer with the council earlier that morning, and Oscar had been in the master bedroom talking to his mom.

Then the notification had flashed on all of their links. Sizzra was attacking. Oscar remembered how his mother collapsed on the bed. He remembered shouting for his father, who came in a few seconds later.

And then Oscar hadn't been able to move. He had been so scared. He had seen an adult Spine wurl from the window as his father tried to revive his mother, and he had just… lost it. His father had spoken to him, trying to get him to move so they could go to the shelter in the Main Hall, but Oscar hadn't been able to. He had simply remained there, frozen in the corner, and his father hadn't been able to carry both him and his mother at the same time, so instead they had remained where they were, vulnerable and exposed in their house.

I'm so sorry, Dad. Mom. Eli….

Elias had come back, and Oscar had been so relieved, but the fear had still been too much, and Oscar had not been able to move on his own. Elias had carried him out of the house, and then…. And then….

Oscar covered his eyes with his forearm in the darkness, crying in earnest now.

It was all my fault. I was too scared. I ran away, and Eli had to come back for me. And then Dresde….

It was a blur in his mind. Grabbing the egg. Being taken. But he was certain of one thing—it had been his fault. He had been scared, and this was the result.

A pain stabbed his heart that went much deeper and hurt much more than the sharp ache in his shoulder. Elias had finally come home after months of being away. Oscar's family had been reunited against all odds, and he had ruined everything. What had Dresde done to Elias? Was he okay?

He blinked away tears. An idea had come to him.

My link.

He lifted his injured arm carefully and used his right hand to activate it. Oscar's link blinked to life immediately.

Hope surged in his chest. He opened the messaging application and tried calling home.

He received an error message. He tried again, this time calling his mother directly. Error. He called his dad, Elias, even the director of the colony. Nothing.

I'm too far away. There's no satellite coverage. Unless....

Oscar's fingers flew over the holographic keyboard on his link as he opened the command line editor and created a simple subroutine to scan for faint transmissions. He had interned with his dad all winter, beginning his training as the next telecommunications specialist of Portree. He had worked on many things, but chief among them had been learning about his dad's project to reactivate the satellite that was still in low orbit around the planet, left behind from the days of the *Ionas*.

If Dad managed to activate the satellite, I should be able to pick up a passive transmission, even if I'm on the other side of the planet.

It took him nearly an hour to optimize the gain on his link's tiny onboard computer and its proportionally small antenna. He designed another subroutine that would filter out incoming electromagnetic radiation from any source or wavelength except the one he knew his dad would be using to transmit. Once that was done, he coupled the new program he had created to the messaging app on his link.

He clicked Install.

He waited. Nothing happened. No messages came. As he waited in vain, a thought came to him.

Duh. I won't get anything unless the satellite is passing directly over this hemisphere.

He suppressed a sniffle and tried to swallow his disappointment.

No way. I can't be scared now. I'm on my own. I can't be scared.

It took him a long time, but he was able to stand up again. Cradling his injured arm, he walked until he was able to touch the door, which Samantha had presumably locked from the outside. Then, carefully and methodically, Oscar traced the edge of the door until his foot touched the wall the door was part of. It felt solid, as though made of rock or brick. He followed the wall with slow steps until he reached the corner. It only took him three steps to get there. Then he turned right and shuffled along the new wall. Four steps and he reached another corner. He turned right again. Three steps. Again. Four steps.

It's a prison, he realized. *There are no windows. I'm trapped.*

Something brushed against his leg. Oscar yelped and jumped away. Whatever had touched him had to be crawling on the ground nearby, unseen. Oscar froze and listened. The scurrying halted for a moment, then continued. It halted again, and then the sound changed as whatever was making the noise began to climb the wall immediately to the right of where Oscar was standing. It sounded like many small legs grabbing on to rock, scratching.

With his heart pounding in his chest, Oscar activated the flashlight on his link and pointed it at the wall.

An insect crouched there, nine-legged, as big as his hand. It was pale white and flat, as though it normally crawled through narrow, hidden spaces. Its legs were long and segmented, and its body was nearly triangular in shape, ending in three long, curved fangs that glistened in the light. It had no eyes that Oscar could see, but its legs and body were covered in stiff hairs that looked like spikes standing on end. The creature's mouthparts reminded Oscar of the beak of a Terran octopus, but this beak never stopped moving. It opened and closed, opened and closed, as though already savoring the prey it was about to ambush.

Oscar shifted slightly, his right foot crunching on a rock.

The creature froze instantly. Oscar was almost certain it had not detected the light, but it had definitely heard him. As he watched, horrified, the back end of what must have been the creature's abdomen split open and something long and curved emerged from it. The thing ended in a wicked sharp tip, deep red, and Oscar was certain it was a stinger filled with venom.

The creature scurried along the wall faster than Oscar thought possible. It was closer now, almost near enough to touch. Oscar did not know whether the creature could hear his short, shallow breaths, but he was convinced that the thing was about to attack him.

He froze again in a blind panic, like he had done back home.

Eli.

A thought of his brother came to him, and he seized it for strength. Elias had never been scared. He had been out on his own in the wild, surrounded by wurl, and he had returned a hero. He was brave.

Something clicked in Oscar's brain, and his mind shifted into gear. The fear would always be there, but he could act. If he really tried, he could act in spite of the terror.

Eli. I can be like you too.

I can be—

The creature twitched. Oscar's resolution faltered, as if blown away by a foul wind. He froze, trembling. The creature's stinger pulsated oddly in the light, and the wicked-looking tip was vibrating.

It's going to get me.

I have to move.

But he could not, and he was reduced to staring in fear at the thing until it crawled away along the wall and disappeared underneath a crevice in a corner. Oscar waited, eyes open wide, in case it came back, but it did not reappear.

Relief washed over him, but it quickly turned to bitter shame. He had been terrified *again*.

His shoulders sagged with defeat. He couldn't do it. He couldn't be like Elias, no matter how hard he tried. He would always be a scared boy.

Beep, beep.

Oscar gasped. He activated the link and saw that he had picked up a transmission. He opened the message and realized it was a text file from his father.

"Dad…."

Oscar scanned his prison cell quickly to make sure there were no other creatures nearby and then sat down on the hot ground to read. There was a message from his mother in addition to the one from his father.

When he was done reading, he was crying again, but this time from joy.

They're okay. Mom and Dad are okay. And….

He reread the last paragraph of his father's message. He wanted to make sure that he had understood it correctly.

Eli is coming. He's coming to save me.

Warmth suffused Oscar's chest, and he did not feel alone anymore. Now that he knew his family was safe, his focus changed. He felt stronger, and something like hope kindled a fire in his heart.

I need to know what's going on here. I need to prepare. When Eli comes, I'll be ready.

Oscar touched the top of his forehead with his index and middle fingers, closing his eyes like his father had taught him.

"Thank you," he said out loud.

From the side, as if in response to his words, there was another muffled moan like the one from before. Then there was a scratching at the wall on the left, followed by a gurgling noise. After a pause, there was a sudden crash that made the entire structure shudder and a much louder moan, as though from an animal in agony. An unmistakable note of madness threaded through the horrible sound.

The cell next to me, Oscar realized.

I'm not alone.

chapter 3.
boyfriend

ELIAS WAS the first to wake up the following morning. He thought about Oscar at once and tried to project his thoughts across the distance.

It's going to be okay, Oscar, he thought desperately. *Hold tight. I'm coming.*

The joyful sounds of a world welcoming a new day were all around him, and despite everything, Elias couldn't help but feel a little thrill of satisfaction at perceiving, once again, how the planet was healing after its long slumber. He stepped out of the tent silently, careful not to wake Tristan. He went some distance away to relieve himself and then returned to where Narev was curled up, breathing slow and deep.

"Hey, big guy," Elias whispered, placing his hand on the uninjured side of Narev's head. "How are you doing today?"

Narev stirred and focused his three eyes on Elias. He projected strength and reassurance, and also a need to scratch his face. The scar was itching.

Elias chuckled, relieved to see that Narev was well on his way to recovery. "I can help you with that."

When Tristan woke up, Elias had already prepared a quick breakfast of wheat cakes, tea, and a couple of protein bars. He had also heated up a little bit of the fish that Narev had saved for him and which he had not been in the mood to enjoy the night before.

"Morning," Elias said.

Tristan stretched in the golden rays of the early morning. "Hey. You wake up way too early, you knew that?"

"I suppose I got used to it, living in a cave for months and all. I learned to appreciate the hours of daylight to get work done."

Tristan yawned. "You realize we are *not* in a cave anymore, right?"

Elias smiled. "Come on. Let's have breakfast and get going."

Their routine was efficient. Less than an hour later, everything was clean and they were ready to start the journey again. Elias checked his link briefly as he gazed in the direction of the rising sun. The screen showed him a map of New Skye, with a little dot that approximated his location.

"Nine hundred kilometers left to reach the coast."

"It's not that far," Tristan reassured him. "We're making good time."

They packed everything, distributing their supplies among the backpacks he and Tristan carried. The rest he slung around Narev's back as usual, and he climbed on the wurl with an ease born of practice and settled in a comfortable spot between Narev's spines. He had built a makeshift saddle so he could ride without slipping, and it worked surprisingly well. Tristan approached Vanor, and after a brief moment of almost ritual tension, Vanor lowered his body slightly so Tristan would be able to climb onto his back. Tristan took out his own improvised saddle and adjusted it. When he was seated, Vanor stood up to his full height and grunted. Nearby, Siv was projecting mild annoyance that no one was paying attention to him.

"Let's go," Elias told the three wurl. He broadcast the thought with his mind, but there was no real need. All of them knew where they were headed.

They set off with Vanor in the lead and Siv and Narev flanking him on either side. They moved through the grassy hillsides at a deceptively rapid pace, the undulating movements of each wurl's six legs synchronizing in dizzying efficiency to propel them forward—not quite at a run, but not at a walk either. Elias had once read about Terran wolves and how they could trot tirelessly for hours. The Spine wurl gait reminded him of that. They were able to walk for an entire day with only brief stops for water and food, and with their help he and Tristan were traversing the continent faster than Elias had expected.

"How many days until we reach the coast?" Tristan asked Elias, glancing back from his precarious-looking seat, surrounded by Vanor's sharp and deadly spines.

Elias considered for a moment. "Well, we've been averaging about two hundred and fifty kilometers every day, I would say. Spine wurl travel at about thirty kilometers per hour on flat terrain, but they go more slowly on hilly ground like this. If we run into any big lakes or rivers, or another swamp like yesterday, that's also going to slow us down. So I think we'll get to the ocean in… maybe four days. Five at most."

Tristan looked at his own link and nodded in agreement. "Not bad. It's a good thing the wurl came along with us, or it would have taken us weeks to get this far."

"Yeah," Elias agreed. He reached down and projected gratitude to Narev, whose muscled body moved underneath him, swishing through the overgrown grass. From his vantage point, Elias could look far ahead to the end of the hilly landscape and the beginning of much flatter ground. "We're lucky they came."

They rode in silence for a while, until there was a little *beep, beep* coming from Tristan's link. Elias exchanged a quick look of surprise with him at the unexpected notification. Tristan glanced down and read something on the little screen. A couple of minutes later, he looked up.

"The Colony Patrol tried to send a detachment to help us," Tristan informed Elias. "The morning after we left."

"Was that a message from them?"

"Yeah. Just arrived."

"That means my dad's satellite upgrade worked!" Elias exclaimed, checking his link for any incoming messages.

Beep, beep.

As if on cue, Elias's link flashed with a notification that there was a message from his father and one from his mother waiting in his inbox. "I can't believe it. He really did it!"

"How is he doing this?"

"I'm guessing it has to do with the old satellite the people from the *Ionas* stationed in low orbit around the planet. It helped them with geologic surveys, mapping out the world, and all of those things. We lost contact with it for decades, but my dad's always been obsessed with reactivating it to get in touch with other worlds Out There. This must mean he finally got it to work to broadcast at greater distances than when we used the pad to communicate with Portree from Crescent Valley."

"Wow. Your dad is amazing."

"I know," Elias said, briefly remembering how awful he had been to his father many months ago when he told him that Elias would never want to be the telecommunications specialist of Portree or follow in his footsteps.

"Does this mean we're going to be able to send messages back?" Tristan asked.

"I don't know. Let's find out."

Elias spent some time reading the messages he had received from home, which told him that his mother was doing okay and that both of his parents missed him and hoped he and Oscar were safe, wherever they were. His dad had also sent him two large files. One included a subroutine to improve his link's reception, and the second contained information from the ancient planetary surveyor onboard the *Ionas* on the topography of New Skye. His father hoped it might be helpful having a more detailed map of the world.

After going through everything, Elias tried sending a message back, but he got an error. Tristan was also unsuccessful.

"Too bad," Tristan said.

"It might be because we don't have a big enough transmitter, like they do back at the colony," Elias ventured. "My link might be able to receive messages passively with this upgrade from my father, but we won't be able to transmit stuff back up to the satellite in orbit."

"Well, it's better than nothing. At least we're in touch, kind of."

"Yeah. My mom and dad are doing okay. What about your dad?"

"He's okay too."

"What were you saying before about the Colony Patrol?"

Tristan shifted about on his seat. Vanor appeared to sense that it would be more comfortable for him to walk next to Narev so the two humans could speak, and he slowed his pace to allow Narev to match him. Elias smiled, impressed at how perceptive wurl could be.

"The Colony Patrol tried sending a team after us," Tristan began again, glancing at the screen on his link. "This message is from my dad. He went berserk after he learned that the two of us had gone after Dresde to save Oscar. He demanded a meeting with Commander Rodriguez and convinced her to send a small group with one of the ancient vehicles they have in storage."

"Wait. Vehicles?"

"Don't get too excited—it didn't work. They had an all-terrain four-by-four they tried to start up, but it wouldn't run. They also didn't have any fuel around anymore, and the other vehicles were in even worse shape. They hadn't been used in decades, and it looks as though they won't ever work again."

"So they gave up?" Elias asked.

Tristan shook his head. "My dad set off with Phineas, Rei, and Megan from the Patrol, but they didn't make it far. Flyers attacked them, and they were forced to go back to the colony. After that, the director said that it was too risky to go after us, and now they're working on reinforcing their defenses in case Dresde comes back. Dad says she's talking about building some kind of electrified barrier."

Elias took a moment to digest the information. He hadn't been expecting help from the colony, but knowing that they were officially on their own now made him realize just how vulnerable they were. If something happened to either Tristan or himself, no help would be coming.

"It's up to us, then."

"Yeah. It's a good thing your dad sent us all of this gear with Narev and the others," Tristan added. "I haven't even looked through all of the packs."

"He thought of everything," Elias replied. "Not only the survival stuff, like food or the tent, but also electronics. I think I can build something with them if we ever get some time. Maybe a big transmitter or something."

"Anything for music in there?"

Elias blinked. "What?"

Tristan grinned. "You know. To make the trip more pleasant."

"As a matter of fact, I think I saw something," Elias told him, twisting around so he would be able to reach into one of the larger packs strapped to Narev's back. After rummaging in it for a few seconds, he came up with a cylindrical object about as big as a bottle, bright yellow and rugged-looking. "Found it. Waterproof wireless speaker." He tossed it over to Tristan, who caught it easily.

"Nice. Let me sync it to my link."

A couple of minutes later, the regular beats and snares of an electronic music track blasted out from the speaker. The three wurl froze in place and looked at the source of the noise in alarm.

"It's okay, guys," Elias told them, chuckling. "It's music."

Narev and Siv came over to sniff the speaker curiously. Vanor craned his neck so his eye cluster would be directed at Tristan. After a brief inspection, Vanor grunted and continued walking. The other two wurl took their cue from him and ignored the music from then on.

It was a surreal experience for Elias to ride through the wilderness next to Tristan while listening to music that reminded him of home. He couldn't help but remember how his life had been a year ago, before he had decided to take the Life Seed and return it where it belonged. If he could have somehow gone back in time to tell his younger self where he would be a year from then, there was no way he would have believed it.

"Is it too loud, you think?" Tristan asked after a bit. "Maybe it'll make us easier to find if any Flyers are around."

Elias shook his head. "I don't think the music makes any difference. They can fly. They'll probably be able to see us way before they hear us if they come."

"Right. Do you want to play something from your library?"

"No, I like this. What's it called?"

"This one's a track called 'Remembrance,' by Richard O'Rourke. He was a first-generation passenger on the *Ionas.*"

Elias listened to the music more carefully for the next few minutes. It was pleasant, but there was a hint of sadness interspersed throughout the melody.

"Can you imagine what that must have been like?" he asked Tristan when it ended.

"What do you mean?" Tristan replied, lowering the volume of the music so they could speak without raising their voices.

"I mean, boarding a ship that you'll never leave. The first generation knew they would spend their entire lives traveling through space. It must have been hard."

"Also exciting," Tristan added. "Imagine—traveling where no one has ever gone before."

Elias looked all around him. "That's kind of what we're doing now."

Tristan nodded thoughtfully. "We are. I bet no one from Portree came this far, ever, not even in the good days. We are the first people to see all of this."

"Maybe," Elias said, remembering the fight with Dresde. "Or maybe not."

"You're talking about that girl, right? The one who was riding a Flyer."

"Samantha," Elias said automatically. He still remembered Dresde addressing her by that name. "Where did she come from, Tristan? How is that even possible? Is there another colony that we don't know of?"

"I don't think so," Tristan replied. "There are certain things that are classified, of course, but I doubt the director or Commander Rodriguez would have kept something as big as *that* hidden from everyone. It seems impossible. The *Ionas* was the most advanced ship of its kind when it launched. It was also the first one ever sent to this region of space. We heard that a million times in history class."

"And they would never have sent another ship after the *Ionas* until they heard back from us," Elias added. "That's why my father's work is so important. He's kept trying to get back in touch with other inhabited planets all his life, to tell them we're okay. To tell them we made it, that we are alive. He's never been able to do so, and so the people Out There have no reason to send another ship after us."

"Then where did Samantha come from?" Tristan asked, his tone exasperated. "It makes no sense."

"I don't know," Elias replied quietly. He had fought Samantha the day of the storm, and she had easily defeated him. She was a trained warrior.

The music got tedious after a while, and Tristan switched it off. It was the middle of the day by then, and the tireless pace of the wurl meant they had long since left behind the hilly grasslands. They stopped for a little while to stretch, eat something, and play a bit of shoot-the-bone with the wurl, except they had no bones with them, so it was more of a shoot-the-random-fruit-pit. It was even more difficult with such small targets, but Narev, Vanor, and Siv were all unerring in their aim.

Later, as Elias munched on a tough but tasty plant bulb that Narev had dug up from under a rock, he noticed with some alarm that the sky was beginning to darken with nimbostratus clouds borne on a westward wind. The air itself was fresh and moist, with a hint of approaching precipitation.

It wasn't long after they set out again that the rain began. It was soft but persistent, and both Tristan and Elias took out their waterproof jackets and put them on. Despite the potential threat of another Flyer ambush now that the sky was hidden from view, Elias found himself relaxing with the sound of the rain all around him. The fierce midday summer sun could not break through the cloud cover, and the rain was cool and refreshing. It transformed an uncomfortable and hot summer ride into a pleasant sortie. The landscape they were traversing had changed dramatically too, becoming arid and rocky. According to Elias's link, they were crossing a high plateau that stretched out for dozens of kilometers in every direction. To the north and south, distant mountain peaks hinted at vast expanses of terrain that was completely unexplored. Straight ahead, to the east, the flat and featureless ground was occasionally dotted with short bushes that sported vibrant green and orange leaves, clusters of short, squat trees with light-colored bark, and patches of ground that were covered with countless minuscule dark-green plants that reminded Elias of lichen.

As the hours dragged by, the flat terrain gave way to a dizzying array of elevation shifts. Short broken hills appeared seemingly out of nowhere, leading them down into ravines and ancient riverbeds that cut straight through the hillsides. At some points they had to go single file, with towering walls of rock on either side of them, moist with the drizzle that appeared to be endless, raindrops glistening in the murky light of day. Strange creatures appeared among the rocks and disappeared just as fast, evidently startled. Some of them squeaked, leaving behind trails of cloying flowery scent. Others slithered away like disturbed predators and escaped into the darkness of caves and cracks in the ground. Still others, bolder, stopped for a moment to look at the big wurl and attempted to look intimidating. Elias's favorite was a short lobster-like creature with black-and-white plates. When it saw them approaching, it rose on its hind legs and spread out its remaining three short stubby claws in the air. The pattern on the underside of its body resembled a menacing cluster of three eyes that appeared to belong to an enormous creature, and the illusion was so realistic in the rain that Vanor actually halted for a moment. The unnamed creature hissed and then sprinted away to disappear into a burrow in the ground.

The wurl climbed over steep terrain without a single slip. Kilometer after kilometer went by in what seemed to Elias to be a blur. They came into view of several big lakes at one point. The ground around the bodies of water was completely covered in a carpet of green from the same lichen-like organism Elias had encountered hours earlier. It made for a beautiful landscape, and it was there that the rain finally abated, leaving in its wake the rich smell of petrichor from the wet earth, which spoke of living things being nourished by the water. Off to the south and a couple of kilometers away, ostensibly headed for the largest lake, Elias saw a long line of large ruminant-looking creatures with clusters of three horns on their heads. They were covered in long, thick fur that was bright pink, making them stand out sharply against their surroundings. Elias watched them with interest until they were out of sight. He had stopped counting how many species he had discovered, and he had also stopped trying to name them. Nevertheless, he made a little note on his link, as he had been doing throughout the trip, with a description of the creatures for later reference.

"Always the scientist, huh?" Tristan asked, his voice sounding strangely out of place in the placid calmness of their wild surroundings.

"I guess," Elias answered in a muted tone. There were no creatures around them, but he was strongly inclined to be quiet. He felt like an intruder somehow, and some instinct seemed to warn him that he should be as inconspicuous as possible around the lakes. "It's fascinating."

"You're going to be famous when we get back. You'll be the top biologist of Portree."

Elias smiled. He had entertained that very same fantasy on his own a long time ago. "I'd love to come out here and study how life works on this world. There is so much to discover. So much to learn."

Tristan nodded and fell silent. Elias did too, focusing on the journey instead and the strength of the wurl who carried them. His back ached, and his legs were sore by late afternoon, when Narev, Siv, and Vanor finally stopped for the day at the top of a sharp incline that marked the edge of the plateau they had been traversing. Ahead of them, elevation dropped sharply, and there appeared to be more plants and taller trees in the distance, but they were too far away for Elias to be sure. According to his link's rough approximation, he and Tristan had covered about two hundred and ninety kilometers that day.

Elias got off Narev and made sure to express his gratitude to the wurl for carrying him and the supplies for one more day. After he had unburdened him, Narev immediately bounded away, followed by Vanor and Siv.

"Going hunting?" Tristan asked.

"Yeah," Elias replied, receiving a brief but clear image of the prey Narev had in mind. It was one of the pink, furry creatures they had seen some hours ago. Elias wondered whether there were any of those nearby and how it was that Narev and the other wurl could perceive them if there were. Then he sighed, adding one more question to the mountainous pile of mysteries of the world.

"We made good progress today, but my back is killing me," Tristan reported, stretching. "Want to work out?"

Elias was tired from the trip, but he nodded. "I think we need to. We were sitting for way too many hours."

They set up camp quickly and stripped down to their shorts. The sun was beginning to go down behind them, but there was enough light that they could see well without building a fire just yet. It appeared that the rain had not reached the place where they were, but the temperature was pleasant. The air was invigorating, and Elias was mildly surprised to realize that he was looking forward to his calisthenics session with Tristan.

"What are we doing today?" Elias asked. Tristan was the expert when it came to exercising.

"I'm thinking some interval training and yoga to end. We'll focus on upper body and core for today."

The two of them found a reasonably clear area next to the campsite and got started. Tristan led the way, programming his link to beep at regular intervals to monitor how long they should do each exercise. They did three different kinds of push-up variations for one minute at a time, with five seconds of rest in between. They then switched to crunches, leg lifts, and something Tristan called "manmakers," which were a brutal combination of push-ups, burpees, and explosive jumps. They did three circuits of that, by which point Elias was sweating profusely. His arms were beginning to feel like noodles, and his abdomen was sore from all the crunches.

"Now for the isometrics," Tristan said, panting. "Come on. Stand in front of me."

"Right."

"Now grab my hands," Tristan instructed, and Elias raised his hands above his head and grabbed Tristan's hands, interlinking his fingers with Tristan's.

"Now place your right leg in front. Like that. Your left leg goes back so you're braced forward, as though you want to push against a wall. Great, you got it."

"What now?"

Tristan grinned. "Now? We get to see who's stronger. Push!"

Elias barely had time to prepare himself before Tristan was suddenly pushing against him, using the weight of his body and the strength of his arms. Elias retaliated in kind, stiffening his muscles and resisting Tristan's overpowering strength.

"Try… to make me… take a step back," Tristan grunted, his face already red with effort.

Elias tried. He put everything he had into doing so, all the time struggling not to allow Tristan to do the same to him. He used every bit of power he had.

And realized neither of them was moving.

Sweat beaded on his forehead and dripped over the bridge of his nose, but he didn't budge, and neither did Tristan. As the seconds passed, their arms began to shake with the effort of the sustained contraction, but their strength was evenly matched. If anything, Elias was beginning to feel as though Tristan's resistance was giving way.

Beep.

"Time!" Tristan called, lowering his arms suddenly. Elias was caught off guard, and he collided with Tristan, sending both of them crashing down on the lichen-covered ground. They lay for a couple of seconds like that, chests heaving, with Elias on top. Their faces were less than an inch apart.

"You've gotten… strong," Tristan panted.

"For a moment there… I thought… I was going to win."

"Fat chance," Tristan said to him, playfully pushing Elias away. "I'm still stronger than you."

"Are you sure?"

"Yep. Now come on. Time for yoga."

They did some stretches that Tristan had learned as part of his training for the Colony Patrol. Elias followed easily. Although he had never really exercised at all before the previous winter, he felt in tune with his body and enjoyed the challenge of stretching and holding a single position for a while. By the time they were done, his entire body tingled with energy. He felt great.

"How are you doing that?" Tristan asked him as they were putting their shirts back on.

"Doing what?"

"You move differently," Tristan said, nodding in Elias's direction. "It's like you're more agile or something. Look."

He bent down and picked up a rock. Without warning, he threw it straight at Elias's face.

Elias reacted without thinking. He snatched the rock out of the air with a single effortless motion.

"Like that!" Tristan pointed out excitedly. "Every day we exercise you get better, Elias. I know living in the wilderness toughened you up, but this is something else."

"What do you mean?" Elias asked, looking at the rock in his hand. He wasn't sure how he'd caught it.

"Let me do a little test," Tristan said, walking over to their camp to pick up his shock spear. "Ready?"

"For what?"

Elias's question was answered immediately. Tristan rushed forward and swung the spear in a downward arc, fast enough to make the air whistle in its wake.

Elias reacted as he had done before. He twisted his body out of the way, grabbed the spear as it was coming down, and yanked it out of Tristan's hands. Then he swung it back around, over his head, and stopped the blow right before the spear would have collided with Tristan's shoulder.

"See what I mean?"

"How…?" Elias mumbled. "How…?"

He handed the spear to Tristan.

"It's becoming more noticeable now," Tristan explained. "It's like you're faster in some way. Kind of like them," he added, nodding in the direction of the three muscular shapes that were approaching in the distance. They seemed to be carrying a large carcass between them.

Elias looked at Tristan and then down at his hands.

"Hey," Tristan said, tossing the spear aside and coming in for a hug. "Don't think about it too much. It's a good thing."

"But… I've never trained like you, Tristan. You've spent years strengthening your body. Sharpening your reflexes. I haven't. I shouldn't be able to…."

Tristan shrugged. "We're on a totally different world from what we knew as kids, in case you haven't noticed. You are linked to it now in some way. Maybe this is part of it. Maybe you're getting powers."

"Uh…."

"That would be really cool. My boyfriend, a superhero!"

Tristan appeared to realize what he'd blurted out a split second after the words left his mouth because he froze with an awkward glance in Elias's direction. Then he looked at the ground.

Boyfriend, Elias thought. *It's the first time he's ever called me that.*

Silence stretched between them. Tristan was blushing. Elias wanted to reassure him, but he didn't know what to say. They were saved from the continued awkwardness by the wurl, who had finally made their way to camp and demanded attention with loud grunts. All three of them broadcast pride at their kill and wanted help cooking some of the meat.

"I'll… I'll be…. I'll build a fire," Tristan stammered. He fled back to the tent and busied himself with preparations to cook.

Elias walked over to Narev and placed his hand on the wurl's side. Narev's scales were pliable and polished, like sun-warmed metal.

"I think he's adorable when he gets like that," Elias said to Narev. "What do you think?"

Narev looked at him and cocked his head to the side, at that moment acting very much like a Terran dog. Elias chuckled and helped the wurl drag their prey over to the fireside.

chapter 4.
captive

"OKAY," OSCAR told himself. "Don't panic. Think."

It was the morning after he had arrived at Dresde's volcano. He was pacing in his small cell, which appeared even more oppressive in the faint light of dawn.

"Don't freak out, man. Stay calm."

Oscar mumbled to himself, careful not to make too much noise. He had spent most of the night in fitful bouts of sleep, huddled in a corner of the cell. The ground had been very hard, uncomfortable, and oddly hot, but he had come to appreciate the latter when the warmth of the evening had given way to the coolness of very early morning. Still, the pain in his shoulder had not allowed him to fully relax. He was certain something was wrong with it, and as the hours went by, the pain got worse. As long as he held perfectly still the shoulder did not hurt, but Oscar had never been able to sleep without tossing and turning, and as a result he had barely rested.

He also kept hearing the moans.

Oscar had no idea what kind of animal was in the cell next to him, but at the beginning it had grunted and scratched at the wall separating them whenever Oscar made a noise. It had been unnerving, and Oscar had kept as far away from that wall as he had been able to. He had frequently activated the flashlight on his link to make sure that nothing was coming through that wall, no animal or insect or anything. Whatever was making those noises had to be big. Oscar was terrified of finding out what it was.

Now that morning had come, Oscar was trying to keep himself from panicking. He paced back and forth while holding his injured arm carefully and tried to think of his options.

There weren't many.

"I could try to escape," he whispered to himself, "but then what? I'm halfway across the world. No, I have to wait. Maybe Samantha will help me. Maybe she'll come back. *If* she comes back. What if she leaves me here? With no food, no water? And I need to pee. I hope she comes back soon. I really hope she does."

The temperature slowly rose as the sun climbed up in the sky. The day was not particularly hot, but the odd warmth radiating from the ground made the cell uncomfortable. Oscar began sweating, and after a while he stopped pacing and sat down, grimacing at the pain the change in position jolted through his shoulder.

"Stay calm, man," he told himself. It was starting to become a mantra. "Just stay calm."

He activated his link and tried to send a message to tell his parents and Elias that he was okay, but try as he might he was unable to compensate for the lack of power in the small computer he carried. There was no way for an uplink to the satellite with what he had.

"Stay calm," he whispered, a little bit too loudly.

From nearby, a tired sort of moan came again. Then there was a loud scuffling noise, and after a moment a sudden *THUD* against the wall startled Oscar badly. The scariest part was that, despite the fact that the cells appeared to be made of concrete, the entire structure shook when the creature on the other side hit the wall. Oscar was scared that the prison might simply collapse around him, burying him in rubble.

Stop that, he said to himself. *Focus on the positive. What's good about my position?*

He looked around. There was very little to be thankful for, but he still tried to count his blessings.

I'm still in one piece, sort of. I know my family is okay. And Samantha let me keep her jacket, which I think is keeping my shoulder from dislocating even more.

That last part surprised him, since it was only now he realized that Samantha had not taken her jacket with her. It was tight and form-fitting, and besides keeping him warm during the night, it had also kept his arm from moving too much.

I need to convince Samantha to help me. It's the only way.

Oscar waited patiently, telling himself he didn't really need to pee that badly, and two hours after sunrise he heard footsteps approaching. There was no way to look outside since the only ventilation slots that might have served as windows were set too high up the wall, but Oscar still climbed to his feet, holding his arm, and backed away from the door. He was hopeful and fearful at the same time.

I hope it's her.

There was a sound of keys jangling, and a heavy lock clicked open.

Wait. It's got to be her—I don't think Dresde knows how to use a key.

With a loud crunch, the door swung outward in a flash of blinding morning light. Oscar covered his eyes with his good hand, blinking. The creature in the next cell was strangely quiet.

"Mor-morning," Oscar stammered. He still couldn't see very well. The person who had entered was standing in the doorway, and the light was very bright. "Samantha? Is that you?"

The door opened fully, and the person walked inside. After a few seconds, Oscar realized that it was indeed Samantha. She had a satchel in one hand, and she was wearing completely different clothing from the day before. Instead of a futuristic pilot suit, she now wore sandals, jeans, and a T-shirt that was faded and slightly too big for her. Her hair was still neatly gathered in a braid slung across one of her shoulders. The way she was standing, tense and upright, reminded Oscar of Colony Patrol soldiers on duty. Her demeanor clashed with her casual clothing, and her expression, similar to the day before, was overshadowed by a frown.

"Hi, Samantha," Oscar said as steadily as he could. There was no reply.

"Right," Oscar continued. "I'm so glad you came back. Um, where's the toilet?"

The frown deepened. "If you need to relieve yourself, you are free to go outside."

"O… kay. Sure. Thanks?"

Oscar walked forward until he was a couple of steps away from the door. Samantha stretched out her left arm suddenly, blocking the doorway. "Do not run or think of escaping, male," she said to him. "If you do, you die."

"Wasn't going to, but thanks for the heads-up," Oscar replied. "Be right back, okay? Don't shoot me or stab me or whatever. I promise I won't run."

"Be quick."

Oscar stepped out onto a surprisingly beautiful landscape. He had only seen it at night, and the view that stretched out before him now was simultaneously picturesque and alien.

Under the light of the morning sun, he was able to see across a vast distance. To the right, the volcano rose majestically, its black-and-dark-brown surface an almost perfect cone, neatly outlined against a sky of jewel-like blue. From where he was standing, it was not possible to see the cliffs or the ocean, but the rolling hillsides on which he now stood had a beauty all their own. They were covered in short emerald-colored plants that reminded Oscar of clovers from Earth, and there were odd-looking plants and trees interspersed among them. Many of the trees appeared to grow from three places at once, their thick trunks joining after a few meters and growing skyward only to open again in three different directions, making them look more like sculptures that resembled the skeleton of a pyramid at either end, or perhaps an empty hourglass. In the distance, even more hills were visible, some completely barren, some full of verdure and life.

The buildings he had briefly spotted the night before rose all around his prison, decrepit and dilapidated. They were about a dozen in total, ruins comprised of the charred hulls of what might have once been houses. All that remained of many of them were a couple of thick wooden beams, blackened and splintered. Very few walls still stood, and although the structures appeared to have once been interspersed at regular intervals, nature had claimed most of them, and it gave the landscape a chaotic aspect. Oscar felt as though he was standing in the middle of an abandoned town long after a fire had destroyed every house.

He found a secluded spot and returned to the cell a couple of minutes later, very relieved. Once inside, Samantha approached him.

"My jacket," she told him.

"Oh. Thank you so much, actually. It was great to have it last night and—"

She raised her hand. When she spoke, her tone was clipped, as though annoyed. "Less talk. Give me. My jacket."

"Sure. Let me just try and... ow! Sorry, my shoulder.... Can you help me get it off?"

Samantha stepped behind him and helped Oscar take off the jacket. Oscar was scared that she was going to yank it off and that it would hurt, but she was careful, and the pain was minimal. Now without the jacket, Oscar realized his shoulder was hurting a lot more.

"Sit down," she told him. "Take off your shirt."

"Excuse me?"

She did not answer and instead simply looked at him as though already incredibly annoyed.

"Okay, okay. Hold on a sec." Oscar did his best to remove his shirt with only one hand, but the going was slow. "Sorry about this," he added. "I'm wearing my best shirt, and it has a lot of buttons."

When he was finally able to take it off, he was almost scared of looking at his shoulder, but he could not help doing it.

The skin above his left arm was red and raw, as though burned. He also had many scratches and bruises everywhere from the rough way Dresde had handled him while carrying him. What was most worrisome, though, was the odd way in which his shoulder stuck out to the side. That most definitely was not right.

"Dislocated," Samantha observed. "Hold still."

"Is it bad?" Oscar asked.

"Hold *still*."

Oscar gritted his teeth and shut his eyes. Samantha placed her hands on either side of his shoulder. "Do it. Whatever it is you have to do."

"Three, two, one!" Samantha said and shoved Oscar's shoulder back into place at the last word.

Oscar yelled, but his shout was cut short when he realized the pain was actually fading. "Oh, wow. That feels…. That feels much better, thank you."

Samantha opened her satchel and took out a bottle of water and something that looked like a sandwich. She placed them on the ground, took her things, and stepped out of the cell.

"Wait!" Oscar yelled, standing up, but careful not to approach the doorway. "What's going on? How long are you keeping me here? Who are you, and where did you come from?"

Samantha looked at Oscar for a moment, as though deciding whether to speak. Then she simply shut the door of the cell, locked it, and walked away. Oscar listened to the sound of her fading footsteps until they were no longer audible. He considered shouting after her, but he was scared of disturbing the thing in the cell next to him.

He was also incredibly thirsty and hungry.

He devoured the sandwich-like object and chased it down with the water. His food had not been made of bread, but some kind of tough leaf or tuber he had never tasted before. Inside the sandwich there had been what had tasted like fruits and nuts, and the flavors had also been unfamiliar. It had been delicious, but it was gone all too soon.

At least he had eaten something. Having some food in his stomach cleared Oscar's mind and made the urgency of his situation even more apparent. He was a prisoner, and he did not know what was going to happen to him.

"Keep calm," he repeated to himself. "Eli is coming. Just keep calm."

It was easier said than done. Oscar spent the entire day pacing, thinking of ways to escape and then dismissing them because he had nowhere to go even if he did. The temperature in the cell kept rising as well, and an hour after noon Oscar had to take off his dress shirt and his fancy pants to cool down.

"Mom would kill me if she could see how I've treated my best clothes," Oscar mused, trying his best to keep the panic at bay. The sound of his own voice helped.

"At least that thing in the cell nearby isn't saying anything anymore," he continued. "I wonder what that is."

He bunched up his clothes to make a seat on the ground that would insulate him from the persistent heat coming from beneath his feet and sat down in only his underwear, tapping away at his link and trying to focus on one of the many books that were loaded in the memory of the device. His mind kept drifting away, though, and by late afternoon he had not managed to read a single full page of anything.

He was scared. Not knowing what was going on and being trapped in a cell was triggering his anxiety, and every few minutes he would sit up and listen, hoping he would not hear the sound of large wings flapping.

He dozed off erratically, and when the sun began to set, he actually fell asleep, giving in to the exhaustion of the day.

A sound jolted him awake what seemed like barely a second later.

"Just a minute!" he said, adrenaline pumping through his system and banishing the sleepiness in a moment. He jumped to his feet and tried to put on his pants.

The heavy lock outside his cell clanged open, and the sounds of someone taking it off were joined by the now-familiar sound of keys.

"Give me a sec!" Oscar said loudly, not even minding the fact that the creature in the next cell moaned in answer to his voice.

The door to his cell swung open. Oscar looked in that direction, distracted, standing on one foot and trying to get the other to fit in the correct leg hole of his pants.

He lost his balance and fell to the ground, bumping his left shoulder.

"Ow!"

Samantha pulled on the door and appeared on the threshold. She held something in her hands and looked as though she had been about to come fully into the cell, but hesitated.

Oscar, still in his underwear and with only one leg in his pants, looked up at her awkwardly.

"Uh, hi," he said as casually as he could. "Good afternoon?"

Samantha huffed in what might have been exasperation. "What are you doing?"

"I… I don't know, actually. It was hot in here, you know? I just wasn't expecting any visitors so soon."

"Your food," Samantha responded coldly. She put the satchel she had been carrying on the ground. "Eat."

"Right. Let me get presentable…," Oscar said, struggling into the pants, which he was finally able to do. After zipping them up, he felt much better. "There. Thanks for the breakfast earlier, by the way. Interesting stuff, though I don't think I've ever had any of that in my life. Tasted good, though."

Samantha nodded in the direction of the satchel.

"Oh, you mean eat right *now*?"

"I need to take the containers home. Eat."

"Sure. Can I get a few minutes to, um, heed the call of nature?"

"Yes," she replied. "If you need to wash your hands afterward, there is a stream to the south. Do not go too far if you value your life."

"Right, right, you mentioned something like that this morning. Don't worry, I'll be right back."

Oscar kept his promise and returned a few minutes later. He entered the cell and sat down. Surprisingly, Samantha sat down as well.

"Thanks for keeping me company," Oscar said, opening the satchel. He discovered a bowl full of what looked like dumplings, still hot and steaming. An appetizing smell wafted from them and reminded him of grilled green beans with a hint of garlic. "Ooh, this looks tasty. What's it called?"

Samantha blinked. "Food."

"No, I mean the dish," Oscar said, reaching for one of the dumplings.

"We… we do not name our food."

"For real? That's odd. This nameless dish smells great, though. Let's give it a try."

He put the dumpling in his mouth and bit down. It was delicious—soft and chewy on the outside and full of crunchy vegetables on the inside. The flavor was completely unfamiliar, but the dumpling was savory, well-seasoned, and slightly spicy. "Oh, by the generation ship. This is amazing!"

Samantha's eyes widened. "The generation... ship?"

"It's just an expression," Oscar replied. "Seriously, though, this is very, very good. Did you make this?"

"No. It was made by—"

"By...?"

Her expression hardened. "It is none of your business, male."

"Ouch. You keep calling me that too. It's really demeaning, you know? My name is Oscar."

He received no reply to that. Samantha crossed her arms over her chest and glanced at the satchel.

"Okay, okay. Message received. I'll eat fast."

Oscar finished the rest of his meal in silence, enjoying the exotic flavors. The vegetables were amazing, and he was disappointed when the last dumpling was gone. He had some plain water to go with it, refreshing and cool, with a very slight mineral hint to it. When his meal was over, he sighed with satisfaction. His shoulder was hurting much less, he was full, and the heat of the day was receding now that the sun was going down.

He allowed himself to feel a little bit of hope.

"I have so many questions," he told Samantha. "Where are we, exactly? Who else is here with you? What's the deal with Dresde?"

"Do not say her name!" Samantha snapped.

"Whoops, sorry. We can talk about something else if... uh...."

But Samantha stood up, gathered the satchel, and left the cell without another word. She locked the door from the outside and left Oscar in the growing darkness.

"Weird," Oscar said to himself.

The silence surrounded him. He felt a sudden pang of loneliness but tried to ignore it.

"That was good food," he said to keep the sadness at bay. "I bet Mom would have loved to try it."

But thinking about his mother conjured images of home, of safety, and of everything that wasn't right. Oscar sank down to the ground, and before he knew it he was crying again, holding his knees to his chest. He had tried all day to be strong, but it was exhausting. He was terrified, and he wanted to go home.

He spent a couple of hours composing messages for his mom, his dad, and Elias. He knew they would not reach them, but it was therapeutic for him to write them. They also served as a distraction from his predicament, and when he was done, he saved the messages, turned off his link, and lay down on the hard ground. Sleep claimed him quickly, and when the light woke him up the next day, he knew a brief moment of complete confusion.

Where am I?

For a couple of precious seconds, he thought he was back in his room, waking up to another day of a normal life.

Then he realized he was still in the cell, and reality crushed the brittle calm that the night's sleep had provided him. Full consciousness also made him realize that his arm was hurting again. He whimpered without meaning to.

"Don't cry, man," he told himself. "Stay calm."

Oscar managed not to have a breakdown and instead told himself to look forward to Samantha, who would likely come with more food.

A few hours after sunrise, Oscar's patience was rewarded when he heard her approach. This time he waited for her to open the door of the cell before standing up.

"Good morning," he said, although he realized his voice sounded more tired than the day before.

Samantha did not answer but gestured with her head, indicating he could go outside. He did and came back to have his breakfast. It was the same thing as the day before, something similar to a sandwich with more unfamiliar vegetables and tubers.

Oscar did not attempt to start a conversation. His heart felt heavy, his shoulder hurt, and he barely registered when Samantha left and locked him back in. He spent the day in a haze of dark thoughts, alternating between feeling sorry for himself and fighting against the urge to cry some more. He was ashamed that he was so scared, and the suddenness with which his mood changed from hour to hour was something he had never experienced. When the heat of the day became too much, he took off his clothes and sweated miserably. He put them back on in the afternoon, when he knew Samantha would return.

She did, a little before dusk, and this time brought a bowl with a thick broth of soup that smelled even more enticing than the dumplings had.

"Eat," Samantha said, offering the bowl to him.

"Thank you," Oscar croaked out of habit. He did not know whether there was a time limit for his meal, so he started drinking the soup right away.

He actually gasped after tasting the first mouthful. The soup reminded him of something his mother used to make back when food had been more plentiful in Portree. She had called it minestrone, and it had been one of his favorite things, although mostly it was because whenever she made minestrone it was Italian night, and they'd also had pizza.

Pizza. Soup. A warm home back when his family had been whole.

Oscar tried to choke the sob that welled up in his throat, but it came out anyway.

"Sorry," he said, perfectly aware that Samantha was watching him with her usual inscrutable seriousness. He took another gulp of the soup, but the taste still reminded him of home, and suddenly he was unable to continue eating. He started crying, hiding his face behind his arm, his chest shaking with the sobs he was trying to repress. "Sorry," he said again. "I…."

Samantha stood up. Oscar looked up at her but could not read her expression in the dim twilight. She walked out of the cell and left him alone.

Ashamed but relieved to be on his own, Oscar cried until he felt spent. He wasn't even sure why he had started crying so suddenly, but he was emotionally exhausted, and he didn't care anymore. In the darkness, he leaned back on the wall of his cell and realized that Samantha had left the bowl with him.

Hunger roared in his stomach, and Oscar finished his meal, managing not to cry anymore.

"Keep calm," he told himself at last. The sound of his voice elicited a faint sort of hoarse gurgle from the cell next to his. "Just keep calm."

His voice sounded hollow in his ears. He looked up at the ceiling of his cell and thought of his family until he fell asleep.

chapter 5.
shimmer

NOON THREE days later found Elias and Tristan deep in a tropical forest, hacking their way through the undergrowth with the help of their weapons. They had made good time at first, climbing down from the high plateau and descending onto terrain that was nearly at sea level and had correspondingly higher temperatures. They'd had two full, uneventful days of ground that was easy to traverse, but on the third day they came upon the rain forest, and there was no way around it. According to Tristan's navigation and the maps they had, their path was the shortest one to the coast by far, and some of the old planetary surveys Elias had received from his father indicated that, although the forested region extended for hundreds of kilometers to the north and south, it was a relatively narrow band of vegetation at the point they would cross.

That was little comfort in the thick of it, though. They soon had to dismount from the wurl and continue on foot because the terrain was so choked with vegetation. Elias and Tristan used their spine and spear, respectively, as the entire party wove its way through the treacherous undergrowth threaded with vines and roots. The thick vines appeared to be hosts to a species of parasitic fungus that cascaded down from the thick green ropes and formed delicate but abundant curtains of pale white that blocked their line of sight every few steps. The rain forest contained relatively few trees, but each one of them had a massive trunk, larger than anything Elias had seen up to that point. He estimated the diameter of the trunks at ten meters, and the monumental, moss-covered bark of each tree reached up into the distant forest canopy until it was completely hidden from view by a thick cover of greenery that let only the faintest traces of light reach the ground.

It was hot. And humid. Elias was drenched in sweat within minutes by the tough work of slashing at plants with Sizzra's spine, and the insects in the region must have been drawn to his sweat because they swarmed about him at every opportunity.

"Don't," Tristan grunted, swiping upward with his shock spear, cutting away a particularly stubborn bush-like plant with bulbous red flowers so they would be able to pass. "Forget," he grunted again, swiping down to finish the job. "To drink."

Elias nodded, wiping sweat off his forehead. He was tired and uncomfortable, but they had thankfully stocked up on water before reaching the forest, and they had plenty to drink. "How... much... longer?" he asked, spacing each word between swipes to clear a path big enough for Narev, who was the first one right behind him and Tristan.

Tristan didn't even look at his link. "Maybe two hours. Don't know. Just... keep... going."

Elias slapped his forehead and wished he hadn't. Unidentified goo from whatever bug he had smushed burst between his fingers, and he had to wipe it off on a nearby leaf, which turned out to be covered in very small white hairs. He yanked his hand away, but realized that his palm was now coated in the goo *and* the hairs, which upon closer inspection were moving.

He shuddered and wiped his hand on his clothes, not even caring how dirty they were getting anymore.

"I don't like this place," he said miserably. "I really don't like it!"

Tristan nodded in a distracted fashion. He was busy chasing off something that had looked like a rock buried in the undergrowth at first glance, but which had turned out to be some sort of giant land stomatopod with an exoskeleton that perfectly resembled the dead leaves and random detritus of the forest floor.

"I kind of hate it too," Tristan said, trudging onward. Something had bitten him over his right eyebrow a few minutes earlier, and the skin around it was swollen and red, so much so that it looked as though he had been punched in the face. "Come on."

Elias followed, telling himself it would soon be over. His sense of the living creatures on the world of New Skye seemed to be in overdrive here. There was life literally everywhere. Things slithered and cawed and zoomed and buzzed on the ground, in the air, and on every available surface. The heat and humidity, although not unbearable, made his mind sluggish and unfocused. The mounting exhaustion in his arms from all the hacking and slashing was not helping matters at all.

Glancing over his shoulder, Elias saw that the wurl appeared completely undisturbed by the environment, even if they were slowly getting tired from navigating the tricky terrain. He wondered about that briefly before something that looked like a cross between a dragonfly and a scorpion jumped from a tree trunk nearby and made him yelp in alarm. He decided to leave his scientific musings for later, although he *was* impressed at how well adapted wurl were to the world. He had yet to see an environment in which they struggled. They were truly the apex life form on New Skye.

Movement overhead caught Elias's attention. There was something large in the distant canopy, and he sincerely hoped it wasn't another giant bug. With a shudder, whatever had landed on the tree nearby jumped away.

But not before revealing a brief flash of cobalt scales.

A shiver ran up Elias's spine in spite of the heat. He considered saying something to Tristan, but he decided to hurry instead. The sooner they were out of the trees, the better the situation would be if they were attacked.

Minutes dragged by. Then hours. Tristan's rough estimate had been off, and there appeared to be no end in sight. A particularly nasty episode occurred when Tristan prodded something that had looked like a vine at first, but which turned out to be a large cylindrical reptile with no legs at all. The creature slithered down the trunk where many of its coils had been hidden and attacked Tristan, attempting to bite his face. Only Narev's quick reflexes saved him, since Narev fired a spine that killed the creature before anything worse could happen.

Immediately after the commotion, Elias realized a pursuer was still moving stealthily through the canopy right behind them. This time he saw no flash of cobalt, but the shudders coming from the treetops, along with telltale showers of dead leaves, told him everything he needed to know.

"They're following us," he said to Tristan in a low voice.

"I know. Don't know how many they are, though."

"Do you think they can attack in here?"

Tristan shook his head. "I don't have a lot of experience with Flyers, but it doesn't look like they would have the space. Maybe they're just trailing us, waiting for an opening."

"Waiting for us to tire," Elias said grimly. He was slowly realizing that they were in a trap of their own making; they couldn't stay where they were or the heat, insects, and other animals would make short work of them. But they couldn't leave the forest or the Flyers would attack them.

Tristan appeared to read Elias's mind. "No matter what, we have to get out of here. There's no water around, and we're already running low. We're going to have to take our chances wherever we come out."

"Right. Let's go, then."

They kept up their dogged trudging. Elias experienced tiredness, then exhaustion. After the exhaustion came a kind of exhilaration in which his repetitive motions were a blur. Slash here, step there. Dodge that root. Keep going. Glance up. Yes, the Flyers were still following. Pay them no mind. Hack here, jump there.

A seeming eternity later, although by his link it had only been about six hours, they broke free of the choking vegetation at last. The cool wind that greeted them at the edge of the forest was a welcome shock. Elias had forgotten that there existed something as fresh as the breeze. He could see the sky overhead, bright blue in the afternoon sun. Up ahead the low vegetation was still relatively thick, but the trees were interspersed much farther away from one another, and there were some rocky sections that promised faster going. Among the towering forest trees he saw a different species now. Its bark was rough and flaky, and it was tall but slender. At the top of its stalk, the trunk spread out in three different directions, cupping a roughly triangular section at the very top that had a broad crown of big flat leaves. Nestled immediately underneath the leaves were clusters of long jet-black pods that he estimated were about as big as his arm.

The trees looked like a distorted version of Terran palm trees. According to Elias's link, the party was now less than fifty kilometers away from the coast.

"We're close," he said to Tristan. "The ocean's not far away."

Tristan smiled. "Yeah. It's—" But something caught his attention, and he looked up. Elias followed the direction of his glance.

A phalanx of five adult Flyers swept over the canopy, flying in formation and screeching out a challenge. Vanor burst out of the forest and snarled right back, followed immediately by Siv and Narev. The Flyers did not land, however. They flew past them in the direction of the ocean and were out of sight in a few seconds.

"They want us to know they can attack whenever they want to," Elias said with a frown. "We can't let down our guard."

"Wasn't planning on it," Tristan said, walking over to Vanor. This time Vanor did not challenge Tristan and merely crouched so the young man could easily climb onto his back. "When they come, we'll be ready."

Elias mounted Narev, and the three wurl surged forward through the undergrowth, moving much faster now that there weren't as many obstacles in their way. Elias was on high alert for the next two hours, but nothing happened.

The sun was setting in the west by the time Narev halted on the southern bank of a wide river, panting. Siv and Vanor were nearby, and Elias received a request from Narev for him to dismount.

"Tristan, they want us to get off."

"Sure."

As soon as the two of them were on the ground, the three wurl walked to the edge of the river and drank deeply.

"I'll stand watch," Tristan said.

"Thanks."

Elias filled their water containers, starting the automatic water purifying sequence in their canteens and the larger water packs they carried in a couple of backpacks. He went through their supplies, making sure that everything was in place, and then joined Tristan where he stood scanning the sky.

"I can't see them," Tristan reported.

"They're around," Elias assured him.

"Can you, like, feel them? Like you said you did a couple days ago?"

"No. But now that they've found us, they won't let us go. They're merely waiting for a chance. Flyers don't like to attack headfirst. They like to wait for an opportunity. Maybe as it gets dark. I don't know."

"Should we make camp here?"

"I think we should keep going. Just for a bit."

When the wurl were ready, Tristan and Elias climbed on their respective mounts again, and they continued going east. They followed the river, which grew increasingly wider with the passing kilometers. Elias did not have a record of this river on his link, but he did know that most rivers led to the ocean eventually. Vanor, who was in the lead again, appeared to share Elias's opinion, because he kept close to the riverbank without deviating from it. Occasionally he would stop to glance up at the sky.

They were all on edge, and as twilight came over the land, Elias realized that they had to stop. He was exhausted, and he knew Tristan was too. The wurl might have been in slightly better shape, but if they were attacked at that moment, they would be at a severe disadvantage. They needed to find a place to rest for the night, even if the ocean was so close.

True night had fallen when Elias spotted a cluster of the palm-tree analogs very close to the river's edge. Some of them were growing in the water, and they appeared to take advantage of the fact that the river widened dramatically at that point, forming a wide pool of uncertain depth that stretched north as far as the eye could see. Several large boulders lay haphazardly near the trees, and the ground was cracked and scored in places, as though an ancient cataclysm had befallen the region.

Unbidden, a memory came to Elias of similar devastation he had seen a lifetime ago, on the slopes of the Aberdeen mountains. The ground had also been rent asunder there, but now he realized what he hadn't at that time: these were ancient battlegrounds. The scars on the land were the aftermath of savage battles between wurl queens.

Strangely, though, none of Sizzra's memories recalled this particular place.

Maybe she didn't fight here, or her mothers, Elias thought to himself as they approached. *But if it wasn't a Spine queen, then who did?*

"Flyers!" Tristan shouted, and a screech from the sky echoed his yell.

"Get to the trees!" Elias said, with his voice and with his mind. The wurl obeyed him at once, even Vanor, and they sprinted in the direction of the tree cover.

They were barely in time. As Siv jumped between the tree trunks, one of the Flyer wurl swooped down from the heavens with white-hot glowing talons. Siv curled his body into a ball and fired a spine, but he missed his target.

Elias tumbled off Narev's back and hurriedly relieved the wurl of the packs. Together, the five of them backed farther among the trees. They did not offer much protection, but it was something. One of the boulders was nearby, and Elias gestured to Tristan to stand next to it. Together, their backs to the rock, they unsheathed their weapons and watched the sky.

Two of the moons were out, but their light wasn't enough for them to see more than faint shadows. The sky was clear, and once Elias saw the slender, snakelike outline of a Flyer against the moons, but other than that the night was silent. Too silent. It was as if all of the nearby creatures knew a fight was taking place and were cowering in their burrows, hoping not to be noticed.

"Can't see them," Tristan said under his breath. "Do you think Vanor or Narev can?"

Elias glanced at the wurl, who had spread out around them, spines flared up. He could sense their agitation and anger, but nothing more.

"I don't know," he replied. "Stay alert."

An hour passed. The third moon came out and improved the light conditions, but there was nothing to see.

Standing nearby, Tristan actually stumbled and bumped into Elias.

"Sorry," he said, slurring the word slightly. "Must've dozed off."

"They're doing it on purpose."

"Tiring us out?"

"Exactly," Elias confirmed, pointing in the direction of Narev, who was still standing at attention but was evidently having trouble remaining awake. Siv was lying on the ground, still attentive but radiating exhaustion. Only Vanor refused to show any sign of weakness, but Elias could tell that even he was getting tired. "They'll wait until we go to sleep."

"We can do shifts," Tristan offered. "I can take the first one."

"Maybe. But how long will you be—"

A chorus of screeching in the night jolted them all wide-awake. The phalanx of flying wurl passed overhead, almost touching the treetops, leaving the foul stench of burning rock in their wake. Vanor fired a spine at them, but they were too far away and flew out of sight immediately.

"What can we do?" Elias asked. "Even if we sleep in shifts, I don't know how to tell the wurl to do the same. I don't think they'll go to sleep until they really can't take it anymore, Tristan. The Flyers are waiting for that moment. That's when they'll attack."

The tiredness and multiple frustrations of the day were suddenly too much to bear. Elias knew true desperation.

We're trapped. The Flyers planned it perfectly.

"Here they come!" Tristan shouted, and it was true. The five Flyers came back over the treetops, tucked their wings to their bodies, and attacked.

Narev, Siv, and Vanor fired a volley of spines, and one of the attackers dropped from the sky with a dying scream. The other four were undeterred, though, and they dived at the spot where Vanor was standing. At the last second, Vanor curled into a ball and fired spines to propel himself away, dodging the savage attack but crashing against a tree trunk in the process. Elias rushed forward to help him as he saw Vanor stumble under the exhaustion he had been hiding. On the ground now, four Flyers unfurled their wings and buffeted them with a synchronized blast of air that knocked Elias to the ground. Somewhere to the right, Elias heard Tristan fall down as well.

Elias jumped to his feet, but the Flyers were nowhere to be seen. Siv and Narev roared out their own defiance, looking up. From far off to the north and over the water, Elias heard the howls of the flying wurl, and he felt, clear and ice-cold, the singular overpowering will that was driving their actions. These males would attack until their prey was dead or they themselves died. She wanted it so. She had said to kill them.

"They're coming again!" Elias yelled. "Everybody together!"

Narev and Vanor rushed to where Elias was standing, and Siv flanked Tristan.

The Flyers feinted an attack, forcing Siv to jump up in the air and fire two spines. They flew away, then came in for another attack. Upon landing, Siv stumbled.

There's no way out, Elias thought desperately. The Flyers could keep doing this all night long, until the Spine wurl couldn't react fast enough to dodge an attack.

The Flyers came at them again and landed high on the trunks of four of the nearby trees, dozens of meters above the ground. The bark of the trees sizzled beneath their talons. From their high vantage point, they snarled at the Spine wurl and the humans, their red eyes blazing in the night. They immediately began to weave down the trunks in spiral motions, like snakes, dodging spines as they went. Halfway to the ground, they all vaulted off and took to the air, soaring up with powerful downward thrusts of their wings. They climbed and climbed until they were almost out of sight and then turned, heading north until they were but dark specks against the far shore of the river.

Again, they came.

They're toying with us.

Elias's arms trembled as he held his spine, his muscles threatening to give out. He saw the four winged reptiles skimming the surface of the water as they approached, the silver moonlight outlining their slender scaled bodies, and Elias knew despair.

Suddenly he noticed a shimmer in the water.

Something bubbled in the river and burst out in a spray of warm droplets. Elias flinched, and he saw the Flyers swerve abruptly, almost as if they had hit a wall, and flap away from....

Nothing.

Elias blinked. There were ripples in the water, and the air immediately above it swayed and flickered like a hallucination on a hot day. As he watched, the ripples got bigger. Something was moving in the river, coming closer to shore, but the moonlight showed him—emptiness.

Narev, Siv, and Vanor growled threateningly.

The ripples stopped at the edge of the water. Elias's attention was drawn to that spot. There was something there, but he couldn't see what it was. The Spine wurl could sense it, he was sure.

The Flyers came in for an attack again despite the disturbance. They tucked their wings against their bodies as they had done the first time, eyes blazing, screeching at the top of their lungs.

Pulsating dots of bioluminescent yellow appeared in the river. It was as though a swarm of fireflies had congregated out of nowhere, dancing in the night. The dots outlined something long that broke out of the water entirely and rose meter after meter.

The creature flickered into view instantly when it shed whatever cloaking had made it invisible. Its dripping scales glinted in the moonlight.

It was monstrous and majestic at the same time, a mirage made flesh. Its reptilian body was partially submerged, but Elias descried powerful angular shoulders that ended in what he first thought were forelegs. He soon realized they were instead two moss-green writhing tentacles lined with streaks of yellow bioluminescence, each thick and bulging with muscle as they reached up into the sky. The creature's neck had to be at least a meter long, and it ended in a triangular head that vaguely reminded Elias of the being's Spine and Flyer kin. Its maw was segmented in three different parts, and as it opened, Elias was able to see that the mouth was terrifyingly big, carpeted with wicked teeth like a nightmare version of a Terran deep-sea anglerfish. It had a cluster of three red eyes that shone in the night.

Elias gasped, recognition finally having broken through the shock. He tried to speak, tried to warn Tristan to cover his ears.

He was too late. The creature sang.

It was a sound unlike anything Elias had ever heard. It traveled through the air but also into his mind, a simple but persistent thrum of rhythmical pulses that seized his attention and refused to release it. The beats tugged at his awareness and scrambled his will, and an upward glance revealed that he wasn't the only one affected by it. As if in a dream, he saw the four Flyer wurl halt in midair. Their sudden terror sliced through Elias's addled state, and he was able to focus on them clearly as he tried to block out the song, just in time to see how they attempted to fly away but instead froze again in the air, ensnared by the insidious sound that Elias knew had tunneled through their minds.

The Flyers fell. They hit the water with a splash, and the creature submerged itself in the river with them. Elias caught a fleeting glimpse of blurry yellow bioluminescence, violent ripples and bubbles, and a split second later the thing burst out again with its terrifying fanged maw open wide. It closed its segmented jaws around the exposed neck of one of the Flyers. The victim's mental scream was horrible when six glowing tentacles burst out of the water and enveloped his wings and his body in a crushing, tightening grip. The creature dragged the Flyer underwater, and Elias watched in horror as the Flyer offered no resistance but instead met his own death while still paralyzed by the song.

The echoes of the rhythmical beat stopped when the creature disappeared beneath the river's surface with its prize. Elias looked to the right, but Tristan was still frozen in place, his mouth half-open.

Vanor, Siv, and Narev were shaking their heads as if waking from a dream. On the surface of the water, the remaining three Flyers were doing the same.

Elias recognized the opportunity. "Vanor, Narev, Siv! Get them, now. Aim for their wings—don't kill them!"

The wurl responded to his voice as though jolted fully awake. They focused on the Flyers still helpless in the water and attacked.

Incredibly, Elias realized that the Flyers could swim. They dived in the river and avoided the first volley of spines.

They never resurfaced.

Elias joined the wurl at the edge of the water. He watched until he was certain their attackers wouldn't come back.

Tristan stumbled up to where he was. His voice trembled when he spoke. "What… what was that, Elias? That thing?"

Elias did not answer immediately. Together with the wurl, he scanned the surface of the river in alarm.

Is he still there? Is he hiding? How can I see something that's invisible?

It was only after several minutes had passed that he was sure there was no danger anymore. He allowed his shoulders to relax, and he very nearly collapsed on the ground from exhaustion.

"Elias?" Tristan insisted. "That creature…."

Elias looked into Tristan's eyes, his own mouth set in a grim line. "That was a wurl, Tristan. A Singer. The third kind."

chapter 6.
anger

OSCAR SPENT the next few days of his captivity in a sullen sort of silence, speaking only when absolutely necessary when Samantha came to give him his food. It appeared that his silence suited her perfectly, because she never attempted to start a conversation. In fact Samantha barely looked him in the eyes, and Oscar became convinced that she was only bringing him food because Dresde had told her to keep him alive as bait for his brother.

The hours of those days dragged on with leaden footsteps, punctuated only by random stabs of pain from his shoulder. The confinement started to affect him, and boredom set in. Oscar discovered he couldn't concentrate on anything, and his many attempts to do something useful with his link ended in nothing. He would start reading a document or book and then become distracted with his own thoughts. There was a darkness around him that did not seem to leave, and it was particularly bad at night.

When the shadows lengthened, the creature in the cell next to him would often be more active. Sometimes there would be furtive little scratches on the wall that separated it from Oscar, and he was certain that the thing was looking for a way in. Now that he was silent most of the time, the creature barely moaned during the day, except around mealtimes, strangely. Oscar supposed it was Samantha who opened its cell twice a day, whether to deliver food or for some other unknown purpose.

Something about the darkness appeared to incite the creature to activity. Because of this, Oscar did not rest well at night. He tossed and turned, waking up frequently because of the pain in his shoulder whenever he placed weight on it, and also because he would often startle himself awake and turn on the flashlight in his link, shining in at every corner of his cell to make sure that the pale insect from his first night did not try to crawl back in and sting him as he slept.

There were also other annoyances. At dusk and dawn, winged bugs that resembled the flies he had seen in science textbooks back in Portree would come out. A few of them would flit into the cell and chase him around aggressively. Although they did not seem to drink blood, they appeared to be drawn to something on Oscar's skin, and their high-pitched buzzing was unnerving, as was their size. Even with the wings, they were so small that it was nearly impossible to see them, and yet they made an inordinate amount of noise for beings that tiny. This meant Oscar spent many fruitless minutes swatting away at empty air, trying unsuccessfully to get rid of the creatures.

Finally, he kept having nightmares.

They began on the second night, and after that he had one every single night. Most of the time the bad dream was a variation of the events of the day he had been taken by Dresde. Sometimes he would see Elias killed in front of his eyes by the wurl queen, and he'd be unable to do anything. Other times he would dream that Dresde squeezed him as she carried him in her claws until he couldn't draw breath, or that she would simply let him go as she was flying high overhead and he'd tumble down into the void, screaming. Those visions made Oscar wake up with a jolt, still feeling the desperation of falling. A few times his nightmares involved the conversation he'd had with Dresde at the volcano. He would dream of her shining eye cluster skewering him with her overwhelming attention. Those were the worst nightmares of all because even after he woke up, Oscar was horribly suspicious that Dresde could sense his thoughts somewhat, or that maybe she was stalking him outside the cell. In fact a couple of times he thought he heard large leathery wings flapping in the night, and he could not go back to sleep until the sun rose. When Samantha came with his food every morning, it was simultaneously a relief and a terrifying moment, because Oscar had no idea whether Dresde was coming with her to finish him off.

After a week of barely speaking to anyone and enduring the captivity in silence, however, Oscar realized he couldn't keep it up. He needed to talk to someone— that was the way he'd always been. He suspected that the silence was getting to him much more than the insects or the heat or the fear or the nightmares. Therefore he promised himself that he would attempt to start a conversation with Samantha the next time she came to give him his dinner, that evening.

Punctual as usual, Samantha arrived with the food. Of late she always carried two satchels, although she only ever shared one and left the other outside.

"Hi, good evening," Oscar said as soon as she was in the cell.

Samantha drew breath in sharply, as though surprised he had spoken.

"Yeah, I know," Oscar continued, finding strength in the sound of his own voice. "I'm usually much nicer to be around. Sorry. It's just this awful cell, and being trapped and all."

"Your food," Samantha said, placing a plate with what looked like fruit salad on the floor, although every single ingredient was unknown to Oscar.

"Thanks! Be right back, okay?"

Oscar went outside quickly and washed his hands in the nearby stream when he was done. The sun had set, but there were several cirrus clouds high in the atmosphere that still reflected part of its light in beautiful shades of gold and orange and light pink. For a moment Oscar simply stood there, his hands still dripping wet, and admired the beauty of the world.

Movement in the distance caught his eye. He winced, thinking it was Dresde, and crouched immediately.

He looked for the source of the movement and found it almost immediately. It wasn't Dresde.

It was another person.

Still crouching, Oscar watched in silence for a few moments. It was an old woman with long, braided white hair that reached nearly to her waist. She walked through the hillsides with a basket in the crook of her left arm and stooped every now and then to gather something from the ground. Soon she disappeared behind a cluster of trees, and Oscar stood up again.

"I wonder who that was," he said under his breath.

He returned to the cell and gave a final anxious look at the volcano, making sure that Dresde was nowhere to be seen. Then he went inside his prison with a sigh.

"You took longer than usual," Samantha said, frowning.

"I know, sorry. I saw someone out there actually. An old woman?"

Samantha averted her eyes and did not answer.

"Okay, subject not allowed. I get it."

She stood up as if to leave.

"Wait!" Oscar said, and he was surprised at the note of desperation in his voice. "Don't…. Don't leave yet, okay? I'm going crazy in here. It's so lonely and boring. How about we talk for a bit? Please?"

There was a long pause, at the end of which Samantha actually looked Oscar in the eyes.

Oscar realized she seemed sad.

"Okay," she said. "For a while."

"Awesome," Oscar replied, getting started on his fruit salad. He made an effort to sound cheery. "Where do you get all of this food anyway? Everything's amazing, and I mean it."

"It grows. We collect it."

"Yeah, but do you have, like, a farm somewhere? Back where I'm from, Portree, we had very little food for the longest time. We couldn't grow crops, and the native plants would simply die in the ground. It was a really big deal until Eli…. It was a really big deal. How are you growing these crops here?"

Samantha shook her head. "No farms. The life on the New World does not obey the precepts of human agriculture."

"The New World? You mean New Skye?"

"What is New Skye?" Samantha asked.

Oscar gestured all around him with his left hand, which was a mistake. Such a wide range of motion challenged his shoulder more than he had expected. He grimaced at the pain and tried again with his good arm. "This, everything. The world. You mean you have another name for it?"

"We have always had the same name. This is the New World."

"Okay. I have, like, a million questions, but I want to keep talking about the food. How do you get it, then?"

Samantha shrugged. "I told you. It simply grows."

"But there's no way you can get enough food for an entire village or city just with food growing randomly," Oscar insisted.

"A city? A village?"

Oscar blinked. "Wait. Samantha, how many people live here?"

She glanced down at the ground with an unmistakable expression of anger. "I must leave now. You may keep the dish."

"Wait!"

It was no use. Samantha left, and Oscar mulled over the many questions he still had. He struggled with nightmares that night, but having spoken to someone really helped him. The next morning when Samantha came, he was looking forward to the interaction.

"How about another little talk?" Oscar suggested after finishing his breakfast. "Come on, you can warn me about stuff I'm not supposed to ask you about or whatever. I'm really bored here, and you can't *not* be curious about me. I mean, did you know about us, about Portree?"

"Is that your city?" Samantha asked him.

"Well, city's a bit much. More like a little town. I mean, you were there."

She nodded slowly. "It appeared... big. Many houses. Large buildings."

"Yeah, but the majority of those buildings are empty. It's because of the food shortage, the long winter."

"The long winter?"

"Yeah, because of the Life Seed. Oh, right. You don't know. Let me explain."

Oscar spent the better part of an hour talking, telling Samantha what he knew about the Life Seed, what his brother Elias had done, and how it had been returned to the world. Samantha listened intently and did not interrupt at all until he was done. The last thing he told her was how Elias had returned with modified seeds that would hopefully be the future of humanity on New Skye.

"I understand," Samantha eventually. "This other Flower was taken, all those years ago."

"*Other* Flower?"

"Yes. Exactly like the one here—never mind. But now balance has been restored, correct? Because of your brother, Eli."

Oscar smiled with pride. "Yes. He saved all of us. He was very brave."

"And he is the one I saw. The day of the storm."

"You saw him?"

"The male with iridescent eyes."

"Yeah. That's him. I think his eyes look totally cool, by the way. He says it's because of Sizzra—"

Samantha raised her hand, palm forward, and dropped her voice. "Do not say that name. Sometimes she is listening."

Samantha did not have to clarify who *she* was. Oscar glanced anxiously out the door, looking at the sky and fearing the sight of a winged shape. There was nothing there, however. The cool tropical night was peaceful and welcoming.

"So… let's change the subject," Oscar suggested. "Tell me, why do you have that funny accent?"

"What do you mean? You are the one who has an accent. I find it very odd."

"Oh, no way. You sound like the people in those old-timey shows from the *Ionas*, all fancy and stuff! You kind of don't pronounce your r's, and you have this tone, I guess. Singsongy. Don't get me wrong, I like how it sounds, but it's just so… formal. And you use fancy words all the time. Like you're one second away from heading off to the royal ball at the palace or something."

"Well, *I* think you sound as if you chew on your words," Samantha countered.

Oscar chuckled. "That was funny! You *do* have a sense of humor!"

"I never said I did not."

"I know, but you always act so serious! Like you're a grown-up, even though I'm pretty sure we're the same age. I'm twelve, by the way."

"That has to be a lie. You do not look twelve years old."

"What do you mean?" Oscar asked, perplexed. "I turned twelve a few weeks ago."

"You have to be at least fourteen."

"Uh… no? How old are you?"

"I am fourteen."

"No way. You don't look *that* old."

"But I am fourteen ship years old."

"Ship… oh! I get it. Ship years, *Ionas* years! Like years on Earth. Yeah, in that case I am…." Oscar paused for a second, doing the calculation in his mind. "Uh, fourteen sounds about right. See? We're the same age."

"So you count the passage of time based on the long years in the New World," Samantha observed.

"Of course! This is our home, right? Why do you count years the way you do?"

She shrugged. "Tradition, I suppose."

"Tradition from whom? You guys, your ancestors, also came here aboard the *Ionas*, right? It's the only possibility I can think of. How did you end up here? What happened?"

Samantha shook her head. "I would rather not talk about that, m…."

"Male?" Oscar asked, guessing what she had been about to say.

Samantha averted her eyes. "I think that is enough conversation for one day." She stood up and walked to the door.

"Samantha?"

She paused at the door and looked back. "Yes?"

"What's really going on here? You're angry, I can tell. What happened to this place? Why are all the houses burned like they are? How many people live here? Why do you obey *her*? What's going to happen to me, and what's going to happen to Portree?"

Again, Oscar saw the sadness on Samantha's face. "Rest."

"So that's it?" Oscar asked, the tone of his voice rising with his pent-up frustration. He didn't even care that the creature in the next cell began to moan again in response to the noise. "You're going to let me rot in here because she told you to? This is wrong, Samantha. I know you know it. Are you really leaving me here for however long it takes for Eli to get here just so that Dresde—"

"Do not say her—"

"Just so that *Dresde* gets her way?"

It was odd, but saying her name out loud did have an effect. The unseen prisoner nearby immediately went quiet, and the night seemed somehow more threatening than before. The darkness of the sky outside the cell looked treacherous, as if harboring an unseen predator flying quietly while it approached in the dark.

"Sorry," Oscar said in a small voice. He was scared again, and he hated that he felt that way.

The silence dragged on, loud and oppressive.

"I will speak to her," Samantha said at long last. "Tomorrow, I hope to have an answer to at least one of your questions."

"What do you mean?"

"Rest while you can," Samantha repeated. "You might need your energy tomorrow."

Oscar supposed it was no use arguing anymore, and so he simply nodded. He spent an uneasy night, paranoid that having said Dresde's name out loud would somehow summon her, and she would tear the door to his cell off its hinges, intent on devouring him.

The next morning Samantha was late. Oscar had gotten used to her rigid punctuality, but when an hour passed and then another, he began to get worried.

She said she was going to talk to Dresde, he thought anxiously. *What if something happened to her?*

He grew scared again. He was worried about Samantha, but he was also worried about himself.

If Samantha doesn't come…. If she leaves me here….

The cell felt very small all of a sudden, oppressive and dark. The light of the morning sun scarcely filtered through the tiny ventilation slots at the top, and the air felt thick somehow, choking. Oscar tried not to dwell too much on the fact that if Samantha left him there, he would die of hunger or thirst, and there would be nothing he could do about it.

He began to pace, but the movement only agitated him more. He searched the entirety of the cell for any weakness or any way out, but there was none, and he was scared to bang on the door and draw attention to himself in case something other than Samantha was waiting outside.

He began to breathe faster, pacing.

She's not coming. She's not coming back.

He fiddled with his link, but he couldn't focus. He started pacing the other way, breathing faster still.

She's not coming. What happened to her? What's going to happen to me?

His fingertips started tingling, and Oscar stopped suddenly.

I'm hyperventilating.

"Stay calm," he said to himself aloud, ignoring the odd muffled sound that appeared to echo him from the other cell. "Remember therapy. Stay. Calm."

He closed his eyes and tried to recall what Counselor Kamogawa had said to do when he began to breathe like that.

"He told me to…. He told me to breathe slow. Count to ten and back to one."

He took in a shaky, slow breath. Then he let it out even more slowly.

"One."

Another shaky breath.

"Two."

By the time he got to ten, he was back in control. He sat down, crossed his legs, and counted all the way down to one anyway, reminding himself to stay calm.

His breathing slowed, the tingling sensation in his fingertips stopped, and he opened his eyes again.

Oscar remembered when he had first learned the technique to stop himself from hyperventilating, months and months ago, several weeks after Elias had taken the Life Seed and disappeared. His father had sent him to the counselor, hoping he would be able to help Oscar, and Counselor Kamogawa had been patient. The first time Oscar had gone to see him, Kamogawa had asked a few questions, but Oscar hadn't been in the mood to talk very much. The counselor had merely told Oscar to come back the following week. He hadn't seemed disappointed or angry at the fact that Oscar hadn't wanted to talk about why he was acting out at school. Strangely, Kamogawa's calmness had made Oscar even angrier. He had left that session in a huff, telling himself that he didn't need to talk to anyone.

What could he have said, anyway? That he missed his brother, that he was terrified Elias was dead? That the other students bullied him incessantly, and that the bullying had actually turned physical recently? They called Elias a murderer, a selfish nutcase who had been desperate for some glory and had taken the last hope of the colony with him.

Oscar knew in his heart that Elias would never do anything as horrible as that, but he couldn't understand why his older brother had acted so impulsively that night. Why hadn't he talked to anyone? Why hadn't he talked to Oscar at all?

That was the part that hurt the most. Oscar had always thought Elias and he were close, but ever since Elias had taken to spending his free time at the abandoned lab, it had felt as though his brother was drifting away from his entire family, and there was nothing Oscar could do about it. He had tried reaching out, had tried being there for Elias, but the distance between them had just grown. Oscar had had no idea about the things Elias had discovered in the journal of Thomas Wright, for instance. Hearing them at the Midwinter Feast had been a shock. Oscar found it hard to believe it was true that the colony was doomed to starve. He hadn't paid much attention to the food situation because he was used to the rations, but hearing Elias spell out the certain death of the entire colony in front of everybody had been terrifying.

Oscar had often lain awake at night in bed during that time, his emotions a complicated mess. He missed his brother, and he was scared about his family. He wanted to talk to someone about the possibility of everybody starving to death, but he didn't know whom to talk to. And of course there was the bullying. At first Oscar had simply cried himself to sleep every night, scared. Always scared. His mother had been steadily getting worse back then too, and it seemed to Oscar that his entire family was breaking apart. He didn't know which was worse: going to school and enduring taunts everywhere he went or coming home to an empty house, an empty bed opposite his where Elias had slept, an empty chair at the kitchen table, an empty look in his mother's eyes.

He had tried to be funny, tried to lighten the mood somehow, but it hadn't worked.

After that, Oscar had simply been angry.

He had gotten into his first fight a week before his father had sent him to the counselor, but it wasn't the last one. Many of them Oscar simply did not tell his father about. Punching other kids didn't help, though. At night he still cried. He was still scared. Sometimes he started breathing very fast, feeling that the walls were closing in on him, certain that something awful was going to happen and he couldn't do anything about it.

He tried to focus on doing something useful when that happened, and as a result he started sleeping less and less. When morning would finally come, Oscar would help his father during the hours he worked with him at the telecommunications array, trying to learn as much as he could. Then it was off to school, or off to whatever his duty was for that day. But being around other people meant enduring looks. It meant biting his tongue whenever someone whispered "murderer," just loud enough that Oscar could hear.

Counselor Kamogawa had listened to everything when Oscar had finally opened up to him. He had shown Oscar a way to deal with what was going on, and he had taught Oscar ways to diffuse the oppressive feeling in his chest when he felt as though nothing he did would ever make things right.

With Kamogawa's help, Oscar came to a conclusion after many weeks: being angry did nothing but drag him down. It was like having a big rock strapped to his back that he willingly chose to keep carrying because he couldn't let go of his bitterness and the self-pitying sense of having been wronged. But anger was heavy, and there was no need to drag it around. He could be freer if he simply let it go whenever it came.

Slowly, Oscar had learned to control the anger somewhat. He had returned to being a little bit more like he'd been before Elias left. One of his teachers, Marlene MacLeod, had even said so in his report card for the spring term. She'd written that she was glad Oscar was getting better notes again and that he was back to being the gentle boy she'd always known.

Shortly thereafter Oscar had learned that Elias was alive. The world awoke to true spring like it hadn't done in living memory, and everything in Oscar's life seemed to return to normal—or better than normal. His mother was feeling better, his father smiled more. Oscar became hopeful that Elias would return soon and everything would be like it was.

And now I'm here, Oscar told himself, sitting on the hot floor of his prison. *I'm here and I'm trapped, but Eli is coming. He's coming.*

The thought gave him strength. He told himself that he'd been through worse. He stood up resolutely, and when Samantha finally came, nearly three hours after she normally visited him, Oscar had managed to calm down.

The heavy door opened with its usual loud creaking, and Samantha stepped into the cell. She was sweating and panting.

"I apologize for the delay," she said. "You may… go out," she gestured at the open door. It looked like she was having trouble catching her breath.

"Thanks," Oscar replied. He went outside, relieved himself, and returned.

"I do not have any food today," she told him. "But I do bring news."

"What is it?"

"Come outside with me."

"Um, okay," Oscar replied, wary. "What's going on?"

The two of them stepped onto the soft grass outside the prison building. The air was fragrant with the heavy scent of summertime flowers. Insects buzzed in the air, and the cloudless sky appeared suffused by the light of the sun, radiating energy onto the world.

Samantha crossed her arms in front of her chest. Oscar realized, with a little start, that her left arm was bruised. A long, narrow welt on her smooth chestnut skin was already turning black and blue.

"What happened?" he asked. "Are you okay?"

"What?"

"Your arm. Did someone hit you?"

"I spoke with Dresde," she said instead of answering. "We discussed your... situation."

"And?"

"She has agreed that keeping you in the cell is a waste of potential labor we can use in foraging for food while your brother comes for you. Feeding you while you do nothing is not useful to anyone."

"Okay. What does that mean?"

"As of now, you are free to come and go as you please. You will work to earn your keep of course. I will be responsible for you until such a time as Dresde requires you."

"You're... you're serious? I'm free?" Oscar asked, trying to suppress the note of elation in his voice but being completely unable to.

"Yes," Samantha confirmed. She still frowned, but less deeply than usual. "Dresde was hesitant at first, but I... merely pointed out that it is physically impossible for you to escape. There is an ocean standing in the way of you and your home."

"And you convinced her?" Oscar asked, remembering the crushing power of Dresde's full attention. When she had focused on him, he had felt naked, as if she could read his every thought. He couldn't imagine actually arguing with her. "Wow!"

"It took some time for her to agree," Samantha admitted, touching her bruised arm gingerly, "but in the end she listened."

"Thank you! Samantha, thank you. I mean it!" Oscar beamed. "I'll be glad to work. Just tell me what you want me to do. Anything is better than staying in that tiny, horrible cell."

She nodded stiffly, as if satisfied at his response. "Very good. For now, go wash in the stream. Make sure to be thorough—you stink. I will be there shortly with some soap and spare clothes for you to wear. Make yourself as presentable as possible."

"Presentable? For what?"

"For lunch. I will take you to meet the others."

chapter 7.
doubt

WHEN MORNING came, the overcast summer sky appeared to want to trap the stifling heat of a tropical day close to the surface, adding it to the ever-present humidity that made Elias feel as though he would never be dry again.

He had woken up before everyone else and now stood silent at the edge of the water, watching the river flow past. First he closed his eyes and thought about Oscar, as he did every morning.

Be strong, Oscar, Elias thought, hoping against hope that his little brother would be able to hear him across the distance. *I'm coming.*

He opened his eyes. In the light of day, he could see that the river was massive, much wider than he had first estimated the night before. He could not see the other shore from where he stood, and the water flowed swiftly from left to right. It was impossible to determine the depth of the river from where he was, but based on how the Singer wurl had been able to simply disappear beneath the surface with his prey the previous night, he guessed that the river was very deep. The scale of the torrent was hard to comprehend. He had heard of big rivers and had seen videos of them, but even the mighty Amazon would be dwarfed by what he was seeing here.

It's too big. The world... it's too big.

For the first time since he had set out, his determination faltered. He was beginning to get a true sense of the scale of the planet he was exploring, and he found it overwhelming. There were too many unknowns, and the distances were vast. Unseen dangers lurked everywhere, and each ecosystem they had crossed so far had presented deadly challenges. If it had not been for Narev, Siv, and Vanor, Elias was certain that Tristan and he would have never made it as far as they had.

And now there was another threat in the form of those creatures that could approach unseen and paralyze them all with a beat that was barely a song.

He tried to pierce the surface of the water with his gaze, striving to sense beneath and expand his consciousness into the river, but he could not. Something was different about the watery domain. It felt as if the river were not there.

Elias shook his head.

"Rough night?" a voice nearby said.

"Morning," he replied without turning around. He kept staring at the water.

Tristan walked up to him and hugged him from behind, wrapping his arms around Elias's waist. "You sound worried," Tristan observed. "And you were tossing and turning all night."

Elias sighed. "Yesterday, when it attacked? I didn't know it was there. I didn't *feel* it there."

"You mean the...."

"The Singer wurl. I usually get at least a fleeting sense of the creatures around us. Well, not the Flyers. And I suppose it stands to reason that I wouldn't be able to sense the Singers either. It's just weird, and I can't really explain it very well. Over these last few days, I've gotten used to… sort of used to perceiving the world around me with my mind or whatever. The trees. The insects. The plants. But when I look at this river, I don't see anything. It's like it's part of a different realm."

Tristan allowed a few moments to go by, as if he was digesting the information. "Do you think it'll be back?"

Elias shook his head. "I've been watching since I woke up, and there's nothing in the water. He's gone, probably back to the ocean where he came from."

"Did you know they were like that? So… so alien?"

A few months ago, Elias would have been quick to point out with pedantic insistence that humans were the aliens on New Skye. Now he merely shrugged. "Not really. I have Sizzra's memories, and those are relatively clear. Some of them anyway. Sizzra in turn had the memories of her mothers, but it's hard for me to remember those. They are faint, fuzzy. Hard to understand. And I think that Sizzra herself never fought one of these Singers, although she did see them in the distance from time to time."

"I thought the wurl queens were always at war."

"Yeah. I don't know what's going on. Sizzra must have never had a reason to fight them, or maybe she wasn't interested because she hated Dresde so much. Sizzra's memories do suggest that what we saw last night was only a juvenile, though."

"That… that was a *juvenile*? Elias, you saw what that thing did. He incapacitated everybody. Our wurl couldn't move. I couldn't move. The Flyers dropped down like flies."

"I know," Elias replied. He could not stop going over the events from the night before. In particular, the image of luminescing tentacles erupting from the water had bound itself to his nightmares over the long hours of his attempts at sleep.

"Do you think it's going to come after us now?" Tristan asked, his tone alarmed. "Can that thing walk on land? What if it's invisible again? What's going to happen when we get to the coast? Are there going to be hundreds of those things waiting for us? What are we going to do?"

Nearby, off to the left, Elias caught a glimpse of Narev as he walked up to the river's edge and drank from the water, apparently unworried. Elias received nothing from Narev except mindful awareness of his surroundings. There was no anxiety there. No fear.

He decided to take inspiration from the wurl. They were natives to this planet. They knew where they were going, and they understood the nature of their mission. Despite what Sizzra had thought about males and what she had believed to be their negligible intelligence, Elias was certain that Narev, Vanor, and Siv were smarter than the Spine queen had been willing to admit. If Narev still wanted to keep going despite everything, then Elias decided that so would he.

"I think it's no use asking all of those questions," Elias responded, turning around to embrace Tristan and look into his eyes. "I think all we can do is keep going. Let's stay away from the water if we can, but we should still follow the river. It will lead us to the ocean."

"Right. Do you think Flyers are going to ambush us again today? Maybe I can, I don't know, climb a tree or something? I think there are binoculars in my pack. I could scout, check if I can see any Flyers approaching."

Elias looked up at the gray sky. "I don't think it would be too helpful. You know how Flyers are. They'd simply wait for darkness or a storm or whatever to approach unseen. I think all we can do is remain alert as we go."

"Yeah. You're right. Sorry, it's just…. It's been a lot of close calls lately. I'm trying to process it, is all." Tristan ran his fingers through his hair. His hand trembled slightly. The insect bite on his forehead from the day before was not as swollen, but it still looked painful. His skin was taking on the same weathered tan that Elias's had from being out in the wilderness so much. His clothes were caked with dirt and unidentified muck from their brief expedition through the rain forest, and there was a cut on Tristan's left cheek, which Elias only now noticed.

He realized there was something he needed to say. "Come, Tristan. Let's sit down for a minute."

"Shouldn't we get going?"

"In a bit."

Elias took Tristan's hand and led him a few steps away from the river until he found a good spot next to a tree. They sat down.

"What's going on?" Tristan asked. "Sorry if I sounded freaked out just now. I—"

"Thank you, Tristan," Elias said, placing a hand on Tristan's leg.

"What?"

"I want to say thank you."

"O… kay? For what?"

Elias smiled. "For being here. For coming with me. You didn't have to, but you never even hesitated. We're hundreds of kilometers away from home, surrounded by hostile creatures everywhere we look. Our lives are in danger all the time, and you're still here. I don't have any other choice. I have to save Oscar, and I swore an oath to Sizzra. But you do have a choice. I understand that it's getting to be too much. I was feeling like that a few minutes ago, thinking about how massive this world is. If you want, I can probably convince one of the wurl to take you back to Portree. I can—"

"No," Tristan cut in forcefully. His voice was unusually deep.

"But—"

"Absolutely not. Elias, thank you for saying that. Thanks for offering, but I'm not going anywhere. I told you once already: I'm always going to be by your side."

"But you're hurt," Elias argued, pointing at the cut on Tristan's cheek. "And you have this big bump on your forehead that looks like a...."

Tristan did not say anything, but he raised one eyebrow and looked Elias straight in the eyes. The effect of his skeptical expression with that big welt from the insect bite was incongruously comical, and there was a brittle moment of tense silence between them.

Then both of them broke out laughing.

It started out small, but Elias was soon laughing at Tristan's laughter, which was incredibly contagious. He couldn't stop. They both laughed so hard that Elias was having trouble breathing after a few seconds, and all three wurl came over to see what the commotion was about.

"I... I don't—" Elias tried to say, but Tristan snorted at that moment, and Elias guffawed, rolling around on the ground, trying to get himself to stop.

It was nearly a minute before they were able to reduce their laughter to mere chuckles. Elias was crying from laughter by then, and he wiped a tear from his right eye.

"By the generation ship, I needed that," Elias said.

Tristan nodded enthusiastically. He was also wiping tears from his eyes. "Elias, you have the funniest laugh ever."

Elias adopted a mock serious tone. "Hey, at least I don't snort."

They looked at each other again and tried to contain it, but the laughter came back. This time it didn't last as long, but when it was over, Elias felt relieved.

"You mean that?" he asked. "About wanting to stay?"

"One hundred percent. You mean so much to me, Elias. I—" Tristan hesitated, as if he were about to say something but thought better of it. He stood up and offered his hand to Elias. "I mean, uh, I'm here for you. Okay? Let's get going."

Elias took the proffered hand and stood up as well. He wanted to say so much more about how meaningful it was for Tristan to be there, with him, when their mission was so dangerous and potentially deadly. Instead he simply nodded and walked over to Narev, who was standing close by and radiated concern about the laughter. Elias reassured the wurl with his mind and a brief touch on the creature's forehead.

"All right," he replied. "Let's head out."

They packed up their things and continued going east. After an hour the few remaining trees receded, and the landscape around them changed yet again. They were now walking over moist rocky terrain that stretched out into the distance. No grasses grew among the rocks, but the ground was crisscrossed with cracks left behind from some massive tectonic disturbance in the distant past. Between the cracks lay shallow pools of water, barely a few centimeters deep, and in the pools there grew algae and something that, to Elias, looked suspiciously like coral.

All around them the relatively flat terrain was speared by ancient-looking rocky mounds. They were maybe twice as tall as Elias but were narrow and looked like irregular pillars interspersed at random intervals over the land. Some of them were bulbous in shape, while others were more streamlined. A few were stunted, and others were somewhat thicker than the rest, but they all looked old and weathered. They watched over the land like silent sentries left behind from an ancient era.

The air around Elias smelled different, heavy with the scent of minerals and decomposing plant matter. Out in the open as they were, the heat of the sun was impossible to escape, but every now and then a cool, refreshing breeze would blow from the east. The breeze carried with it a salty scent that Elias had never perceived before but knew to be the smell of the ocean.

There were also fewer insects around, for which Elias was very thankful. He liked the serenity of the place, and its silence. Only the footsteps of the three wurl and the occasional squelch of their large paws on the water broke the peaceful stillness. Once again Elias got the distinct impression that the world was healing, returning to balance. His anxiety from the morning seemed far away now. The muted beauty of the place calmed him.

The river was still to their left, far enough away that they would have time to react to a threat coming from the water, but close enough that Elias knew they were on track to reach the ocean. The sky overhead had cleared, and it was a bright shade of blue, dotted with occasional white clouds.

Elias asked Narev and the other wurl to stop next to one of the mounds with a gentle mental nudge. Dead ahead, Vanor stopped as requested, and Tristan turned around on his makeshift saddle.

"What is it?" Tristan said.

"I wanted a closer look," Elias explained, examining the mound nearby. It appeared to be made of rock, maybe three meters tall, but it was definitely organic in origin. The rock itself looked like fossilized coral.

"What are these?" Tristan asked him.

"I'm almost certain they are stromatolites," Elias replied. "But they're enormous. Wow."

"Stroma… what?"

"Stromatolites. They form over millions and millions of years. They're like fossilized bacterial films. Colonies of bacteria sometimes grow on the surface of rocks in shallow water. They form a living net as they grow, and it traps minerals underneath it. Over time the bacteria die, but the minerals get left behind and harden. New layers of bacterial growth cover *those* minerals, and the process repeats itself over and over. Hundreds of millions of years later you might get this. It was built by microscopic organisms, but it's taller than me. Amazing."

"Are they dangerous?"

Elias chuckled. "No. Just fascinating. There is no record of a stromatolite field like this in any of my biology books. It's incredible, and I wish I had time to study it."

"You will someday," Tristan said, smiling. "Trust me."

Elias echoed the smile. "Yeah. I hope so."

With another mental nudge, Elias asked Siv, Vanor, and Narev to start walking again, which they did immediately.

"You haven't noticed that, have you?" Tristan said after a few seconds.

"What do you mean?"

"I think your connection with the wurl is getting stronger, Elias. You can make them do things now."

"What?"

"Like yesterday. When we were all paralyzed except for you. I heard you order the wurl to attack the Flyers in the water, and they did."

"Yeah, but—"

"And just now," Tristan interrupted. "How did you get all three of them to stop so you could look at the stromatolite, especially Vanor? You didn't even speak this time. Then they all started walking again at the same time when you were done, and I'm pretty sure you asked them to."

Elias considered Tristan's words. He looked to the right, where Siv was bringing up the rear. Siv raised his head and watched Elias for a moment, as if acknowledging him.

"I don't think it's like that," Elias said.

"I don't mean you're ordering them around, like you said Sizzra would do to them. I've been watching, and it's more like you guys can speak without words."

"Sizzra used to think that males were useless and barely intelligent. She never really talked to them. She merely ordered them to do things as if they were slaves."

"Well, I'm not an expert, but I think she was wrong," Tristan offered with a decisive nod.

"I was thinking that same thing earlier," Elias said, grinning. "It's like you can read *my* mind."

"Hey, maybe I can!"

Elias reflected on what Tristan had said for the next few hours. Was it really like that? Was he able to ask Spine wurl to do things now? He was not sure, but he knew that Tristan had a point. His connection to them was getting stronger.

He just hoped the changes he was going through were a good thing.

They arrived at the beach rather suddenly, and it took Elias a moment to take stock of the fact that Narev had stopped moving. Looking around, Elias saw that they had left the stromatolite field behind some time ago, and the three wurl were now standing on a wide, featureless expanse of white sand. Far off to the left, the river they had been following ended in a wide delta. To the right, in the distance, there appeared to be some palm-tree analogs growing very close to the water.

"We're here," he said under his breath.

He dismounted, and so did Tristan. Together they walked forward until they reached the edge of the beach, where gentle waves lapped against their feet.

The smell of the ocean was almost overpowering. It was salty, but it hinted at life. As they stood there, cool ocean spray brushed Elias's face, deposited by the breeze that was blowing from the direction of the water. The sound of the waves crashing against the shore ahead was mesmerizing and rhythmical. It reminded Elias, oddly, of the beats the juvenile Singer had used the day before. This song, however, was not threatening. It was wise.

"It's… it's so big," Tristan said. There was a tone of awe in his voice. "I had seen videos… but I never…."

He didn't finish his sentence, but Elias knew what he meant. The ocean was vast. It was an ever-changing surface of slate blue and white and indigo, broken by approaching waves that kept coming in an unending cycle. It reached as far as he was able to see, limitless. Far away the water appeared to merge with the sky, azure joining cerulean, as if the world itself were nothing but blue immensity everywhere he looked. There was no seeming end to the water, and it made him feel small and insignificant. He had that same sensation of a shift in perspective he'd had when watching the river in the morning, but this time it was not accompanied by a feeling of helplessness. It was more like respect.

"We did it," he said out loud. "We reached the ocean."

Siv walked forward until he stood at the edge of the water. He dipped his front right paw in experimentally. He was followed by Vanor and Narev, all three of whom appeared to be very interested in the new environment.

"Do you think they've never seen it before?" Tristan asked.

"Maybe," Elias replied. "But I think they like it."

As if to confirm his words, Siv and Narev bounded ahead and jumped into the sea, spraying water everywhere. Vanor stayed behind, watching as the other two wurl swam with ease until they were almost out of sight. Then they returned, taking advantage of a large wave. They used the wave's energy to propel themselves forward, and exactly as the wave broke, they launched their bodies out of the water in perfect synchrony, coiling themselves into balls and traveling a surprising amount of distance in the air. Both Siv and Narev uncoiled a split second before hitting the soft sand on the beach a few meters away from where Tristan and Elias were standing. The impact of their arrival sent an even greater shower of sand and spray in every single direction.

Huffing as though annoyed, Vanor retreated a few steps away, shaking the water and sand off his scales. The other two wurl followed him, and Elias got the distinct impression they were inviting him to join them so they all could play.

Elias smiled, glad that despite everything his companions were still able to enjoy themselves.

"Elias?" Tristan asked. His voice sounded worried.

"Yeah?"

"We're here, but… now what?"

Elias looked ahead. The ocean stretched out forever, imposing, unconquerable.

The meaning of Tristan's words sank in slowly, and as it did it was as if something were leeching away the tenuous calm that Elias had managed to cultivate over the course of the day. They had reached the ocean, true. But now the obstacle that Elias had not allowed himself to think about was all around him, and he did not know what they were going to do.

He looked at Tristan, who appeared to have no answer.

There's always a way, Elias told himself, even though doubt was worming into his mind. *There has to be.*

He glanced left. The river offered no help.

He looked at the water again. The peace and awe of a few moments ago were gone, replaced by anxiety in an instant. He was surprised at the suddenness of the change in his emotions. How were they going to cross?

His shoulders sagged. He felt the same wave of helplessness he had experienced in the morning when looking at the river, but multiplied a hundredfold. "I don't know. I don't know how to get to Raasay from here."

A few seconds passed before Tristan spoke up. "Well, if you don't have any ideas, I do have one."

"What is it?"

"We need to cross the ocean, right?"

"Right."

"And there's no way we can ride the wurl all the way across."

Elias activated his link. That, at least, he could answer. "I don't think so. I have no idea how fast they can swim, but Raasay is nearly four thousand kilometers away. There are some small islands between us and the volcano on the other side, and we *did* arrive more or less where we had intended, at the closest point between the two continents, but it's still an entire ocean. It's enormous. I—"

The fragile foundations of Elias's optimism shook, threatening to crumble underneath him.

It's too far away. What was I thinking? How am I my going to get my brother back?

"We can't cross," Elias said, and his voice broke. The mood swing swept over him, and he wasn't able to resist it or understand it. All he knew was that black despair was closing in from every side. "We can't get there. I can't save Oscar, I can't—"

"Hey," Tristan said, stepping closer. "Stop that. It's going to be difficult, but not impossible. I was thinking we build a boat."

"A boat?"

"Yeah. For the two of us. The wurl are amphibians, right? So they can live in the water just fine. They can even help us, towing the boat as they go. It will take some time, but I'm sure we can get to the other side."

"How?"

Tristan nodded off to the right. "I see trees over there. We have two great multipurpose weapons we can use to cut wood and shape it. And we have our links, which have databases of everything. I'm sure there are a couple of articles on how to build a boat. Maybe even some video tutorials from the original *Ionas* database."

Elias took a deep breath, willing himself to calm down. A faint inkling of hope returned as he exhaled. "You think it can work?"

Tristan grinned. "I *know* it will. I used to help my dad build sheds for the greenhouses back home every summer. We used that really tough black wood from the yult trees that grow around Portree too. Really hard to cut and even harder to shape. This'll probably be a little bit more difficult, but not that different. We can do it."

"Yeah," Elias replied slowly. "You're right. We can. We have to."

"It's going to work, you'll see. Come on, Elias. Let's get to those trees and see what we've got."

Elias was filled with a new sense of purpose. They had a plan again. That fact alone gave him focus and allowed him to put things into perspective. Tristan was right. It was going to be difficult, but not impossible. They would reach their destination. They simply had to work together.

The party set out in the direction of the trees, and they arrived about half an hour later. The palms grew thick on that part of the coast, all the way to the ocean. Among them were other tree species that were unfamiliar. Some were short and stubby, with unusually wide trunks of hollow-looking wood. Others towered even above the palms, their slender trunks made from terracotta-colored wood that was very beautiful to look at. The vegetation around the trees was sparse, but there were a few thorny bushes that Elias recognized.

"I can't believe it. Look, Tristan!"

"Are those the bushes that we saw on the mountains?"

Elias nodded, kneeling down next to one of them. He parted the thorns carefully, and sure enough, he was able to see clusters of velvety nuts in between the branches. These nuts were not quite the same, though. They were blue and a little bit larger than the ones he had often eaten at Crescent Valley.

"Check it out over there," Tristan said, pointing farther inland. "There's a cliff."

He was right. About one kilometer away, rising from the ground and partially hidden from view by some trees, a cliff jutted out over the beach. Its ocean-facing surface was rocky, weathered, and devoid of plants. At its base there appeared to be a cave.

"We can use that cave over there as a base while we build," Tristan continued. "I think it's big enough. This place is perfect."

"Yeah," Elias answered quietly.

"Come on, let's see what it's like."

Tristan led the way to the cliff. It was made of white rock that looked like limestone and reminded Elias of a beautiful picture of white seaside buttresses he had once seen in a geography class. The cliff stretched out to the south as it followed the capricious twists and turns of the coastline so that some parts of it were directly exposed to the waves, but some others, like the section with the cave, were more distant from the sea, shielded from the water by the trees that grew nearby.

"Let's hope there's nothing living in it," Tristan said, and he walked straight into the cave.

Elias turned on his link's flashlight and followed suit, signaling for all the wurl to wait outside. He walked after Tristan into a cave that was narrow but very tall.

"It looks like something tried to crack the cliff in two," Tristan observed, shining the light of his own link up above.

"Yeah," Elias agreed. He was able to see the ceiling and disturbed a cluster of small scaly creatures that flew away from the light with high-pitched squeaks. "I don't think this cave is of natural origin."

"There's nothing in here, though. And it's dry."

Elias inspected it. Horizontally the cave was about five meters wide at its entrance, and it narrowed down significantly farther in. It wasn't very deep, but it did encompass a volume that was at least five times larger than the tent in which they had been sleeping. The ground was sandy, with random plant debris here and there, but otherwise clear of rocks, insects, or larger animals. The walls of the cave were polished smooth, and Elias realized that, even if the cave had not been made by a natural process originally, erosion from long years had worked on it, widening it through the action of wind and sand and rain.

"This is amazing," Elias said, his voice echoing in the cave.

"Just what we needed," Tristan replied with a grin. "Told you. We have everything right here."

"It's like... like it was made for us."

Tristan came closer and gave Elias a hug. "Glad you like it. Let's set up camp and get started right away. We can pitch the tent and set it right outside the cave mouth. We're going to have plenty of space to work."

The two of them walked out of the cave, and Elias squinted in the comparatively bright sunlight. The sound of the ocean, which had been muffled inside the stone walls, came roaring back to his ears.

The three wurl came up to them with vague mental questioning. Elias reassured them and tried his best to communicate the fact that they would be staying there for some time. It must have worked, because he felt the wurl relax and immediately turn their attention to exploration of their unfamiliar but interesting environment. Narev and Vanor stood still for a few moments to allow Tristan and Elias to unburden them, and then they left together with Siv in the direction of the trees. As the three silver-scaled wurl disappeared from view,

Elias heard a couple of friendly growls from them, and he was certain they were going to play some more.

"I'll set up the tent," Tristan said, shouldering the largest pack. "Then I'm going to go through my link until I find a tutorial on boats."

"I'll be right there," Elias replied.

He took a few steps away from the cave and gazed at the ocean. The beach in front of him was wide, covered by more white sand, dotted in a few places by large, beautiful shells with a mysterious mother-of-pearl sheen, presumably left behind by mollusks no human had ever seen before. The trees nearby offered perfect cover from the wind, and the tall cliff overhead provided protection from any aerial attacks Flyers might attempt.

Elias walked out past the trees until he reached the edge of the water. The ocean appeared overwhelmingly big, but not impossible to cross anymore. Elias sat down on the sand, contemplative. He had been about to despair earlier, and now it was as if the universe itself were offering him the means to save his brother and the unhatched Spine queen. Everything was there: building materials, safe shelter, support from Tristan and the wurl, food from the plants growing nearby, and even fresh water from the distant river. He was humbled, and although he had never been a particularly spiritual person, part of him wondered at the significance of finding exactly what he needed at the time when he had doubted himself most.

Difficult, but not impossible, he repeated to himself. He noticed that Narev had come over to stand next to him, back from wherever he had been playing, and the wurl bumped Elias's hand with his snout, offering support and friendliness.

We'll cross the entire ocean, Elias thought, resting his hand on Narev's warm scales. *No matter what.*

chapter 8.
family

OSCAR RELISHED being in the water after such a long time in captivity. His body seemed buoyant and light, and the gentle caress of the current felt great on his injured shoulder. It was nice simply being there, his feet barely touching the sandy bottom of the stream he had waded into. The water itself was very pleasant—warm, even. Oscar was not sure whether this was due to the mysterious source of energy that also made the ground hot, but he was not about to complain. It was almost like being in a tub back home, but this was even better. He was out in nature, surrounded by verdure, buzzing insects, and a limitless blue sky.

A couple of small fish corkscrewed through the water around him, and Oscar watched them with curiosity. He was not used to fish at all. Portree was far from any large lakes, and most of the water for the colony was pumped from an underground aquifer. He realized that the fish that lived in this stream were very different indeed from Terran fish he had studied. Their bodies were odd and spiral-shaped, while a couple of disturbances on the streambed, which followed Oscar's own footsteps, betrayed the presence of other fish that lay hidden, their bodies camouflaged almost perfectly with the tan-and-brown sand.

He had no trouble at all looking down to the bottom. The water was completely transparent and presumably pure, although it did have the faintest trace of a mineral odor that reminded Oscar of the bath salts his mother would use every now and then. He wondered where the water came from and where it went. As he floated, he allowed himself to relax, and he cast his thoughts back to his family.

Mom, Dad. I'm okay for now. Don't worry.

With a sigh, Oscar stood up again, just in time to see Samantha arrive at the stream with several things in her arms.

"Hi!" he stammered, trying his best to seem casual in the water while being excruciatingly aware that he was naked and that the stream was crystal clear. "Um, you came back quick."

"Yes," Samantha answered matter-of-factly. "Here are some clothes for you, some soap, and a sponge." She crouched next to the water and offered him the bundle.

"Sure, uh, thanks," Oscar replied, not moving his hands from their strategic position covering his genitals.

"Well, take them," Samantha answered impatiently. "I will be back in thirty minutes, and I expect you to be clean by then."

"Okay," Oscar said, blushing beet red as he half came out of the water to accept the things. "Thank you."

"Thirty minutes," Samantha replied, already turning away. She had not seemed uncomfortable in the least, although Oscar realized she had averted her eyes somewhat when she had given him the stuff.

Alone again, Oscar placed the clothes on a nearby rock so they would remain dry and took the soap and sponge.

"Wow, an actual sponge?" he mused aloud, turning the object over in his hands. He returned to the deep part of the stream and observed it. He was familiar with sponges from his biology lessons, but he had never actually held one. The simple organism was exactly the same as the illustrations he had seen, however. It was a dull hay color, irregular in shape and about as big as his hand. It was also extremely light, riddled with holes both big and small. When he submerged it in water, the sponge absorbed it immediately but retained a somewhat rough texture. When Oscar took it out, he wrung it, and most of the water came out quickly. The sponge retained its shape, none the worse for wear.

Next he analyzed the soap. It had a strange woody smell he could not quite place but that was fresh and pleasant. He dipped it in water and rubbed it on his skin experimentally. It worked like normal soap, apparently, and Oscar scrubbed himself clean diligently over the next few minutes. The sponge came in very handy, and soon he felt renewed. It was odd, but the mere fact of being clean made him feel much better. His shoulder ached a little bit less, and when he came out of the river, he was full of energy.

He allowed the wind and the sun to dry him since there were no towels in sight, although he kept a careful lookout in case Samantha came back. She didn't, though, and soon he was dry enough to try on the clothes she had provided for him. The underwear fit reasonably well, although it was a little bit threadbare. He received a surprise, though, when he saw the rest of the clothes.

"No way," he said to himself as he picked up the shirt. "No *way*!"

He blinked as he studied the shirt, turning it around in his hands. Then he blinked again.

"There is no way," he said again.

Nevertheless, when he looked at the collar and the tag that was still attached to it, he realized the shirt he was holding was authentic.

He held it up at arm's length, admiring it. The colors were much faded, but the light-gray fabric still had the unmistakable logo of the generation ship *Ionas* embroidered in black and gold on the top left. On the right sleeve, near the shoulder, there was an orange V-shaped line, embroidered as well, that indicated this synthetic work shirt would have been worn by a member of the engineering team aboard the spacecraft that had carried his ancestors to the planet.

Oscar put it on reverently, and he marveled at its softness. Other than the somewhat shorter length of the arms, it fit him very well. The pants that came with it were also faded and a bit torn around the knees, but they were original garments of the *Ionas* engineering uniform, black, with the same orange V-shaped indicator tag above the left hip. He put them on and found that they were way too big for him, but he remembered learning in one of his history classes that old clothing such as this often had adjustable belts and drawstrings, so he felt around the waistline until he found a button. He pressed it, and the waist on the pants zipped up automatically until it fit right. He couldn't do much about the rather short length of the legs, but he still felt like someone out of a documentary as he turned around to look at his own reflection on the surface of the stream.

"Wow," he whispered.

He activated his link and took a selfie to make sure he wasn't imagining things. When he looked at the picture he had taken, he smiled.

Oscar sat down, intending to wait, but his link told him that there were still fifteen minutes to go before Samantha came back, and he got restless. He folded his dirty clothes carefully and carried them with him as he set out to try and find his erstwhile captor. He had not gone more than a few steps when he saw her, but she was not headed in his direction.

She was going back to the prison.

Oscar was about to call out to her, but the expression on her face stopped him. She was far away enough that he could have mistaken the somber set of her features for something else, but to Oscar she appeared to be very sad. She was carrying the satchel she often used when she had brought food to him, and Oscar watched, curious, as she arrived at the prison and stopped in front of the other cell.

The one next to where Oscar had stayed. The one with the creature that had moaned and scratched and even hurled itself at the wall separating them.

Oscar stood silently, watching Samantha fiddle with the keys and slide the correct one into the lock. She opened it, put it aside, and took out something from the satchel. It looked like a bowl brimming with food. Samantha stood for a moment outside the cell, and to Oscar it seemed as though she was steeling herself before she entered. Then she opened the door and went inside.

A minute went by. Then another one. Oscar began to worry after five minutes when Samantha still had not reemerged.

What if she's hurt? What if that thing in the cell attacked her? Should I go?

I'm going.

He started walking in the direction of the prison, but Samantha came out a few moments later.

She was crying.

Oscar dropped down to his knees instinctively and watched her from among the tall grass that surrounded him. He noticed she had come out with an empty food bowl, different from the one she had carried in. Samantha locked the cell methodically and then left the way she had come, her eyes cast down, occasionally wiping tears off her cheeks with the back of her hands. She walked resolutely downhill, among the charred ruins of what could have once been houses, until she disappeared from view.

Oscar returned to the stream and sat down on the flattest rock he could find. He had the distinct impression that he had intruded on Samantha's privacy, and he felt bad about it.

At the same time, however, he was intensely curious about the creature in the cell.

What could be there? A wurl?

A few minutes later, Samantha returned.

"Ready?" she asked Oscar.

"Clean and fresh," Oscar replied, smiling and spreading his arms wide. "How do I look?"

Samantha opened her mouth as if to reply, and for an instant, the same sadness swept across her face like a windborne shadow. "The clothes fit. Good."

"Yeah," Oscar said. He considered talking to her about what he had seen, but he still didn't know her very well, and he didn't want to overstep his boundaries. Instead, he opted to try and distract her from whatever was going on. "Where did you get these?" Oscar asked, pointing at the shirt and pants he now wore.

"We had them. I apologize if they are slightly worn out. They are—"

"More than a hundred years old!" Oscar finished for her. He couldn't suppress the excitement in his voice. "People back home would go nuts for original clothing from the *Ionas* in such good condition! My dad says they made things better back then, built to last, but this is insane. I'm wearing actual vintage clothing the colonists wore!"

"Your… dad?" Samantha asked, with an odd catch in her voice.

Oscar nodded enthusiastically. "Yes. Do you want to see him?"

"See him?" Samantha echoed, looking confused. "But he is—"

"I have plenty of photos of my family," Oscar told her, fiddling about with his link until the display showed a picture of his father at his workstation. "This is him. See? His name is Bradford."

Samantha gasped. She looked at the holographic projection in wonder. "Your computer can do that?"

"Well, the lighting's not great, and the projector on my link is a bit old, but yeah. It's my dad. What do you think?"

Samantha looked at him for a long moment. "He looks like a kind man."

Oscar smiled. "He's very patient. I was training under him, since I'm going to be the next telecommunications specialist in Portree. He's taught me all about satellites, remote communication, machine protocols, and so on."

"Interesting."

"I know, right? I think it's fun. Here, let me show you a picture of my entire family," Oscar said, calling up a photo from the Midwinter Feast two years prior. "This is me. This is Elias, but before, you know, everything. This is my dad again, and this is my mom."

"Your family looks happy."

"Yeah, although back then Elias and my dad would fight all the time. And my mom was sick. See how she's so thin? She's doing better now, though."

"I am happy to hear that."

"I think it's because the world is healing," Oscar piped up, feeling relieved at having someone to talk to. "It's weird, but *I* think she was connected to the world in some way. That's why none of the doctors could help her before."

Samantha pointed at the link after Elias shut off the projection of the photos. "Your computer is amazing."

"We call them links. Everyone has one. Don't you?"

"No. I think my grandmother keeps one, but it is broken."

"Your grandmother?"

Samantha nodded. "Yes. Come with me, male. You must be hungry, and lunch should be ready by now. You will meet my family, as I have met yours."

"Sure, let's go!"

Samantha took Oscar back the way he had come when he first arrived. They walked through the husks of buildings long since abandoned and headed in the direction of the cliffs and the only building, aside from the prison, that remained standing.

In the light of day, Oscar saw that his first impression of it resembling a barn had been accurate. The outside looked dilapidated, incongruously rustic next to the high-tech solar panel array that flanked the structure's eastern side. The house was large, and Oscar calculated that it was about three times as big as his own back home. However, most of the windows were boarded up. The walls had no paint to speak of, and creeper vines covered the southern side of the structure completely. He could see only one door, big and imposing and made of what looked like heavy wood. It was outside this door that Samantha and he stopped.

They were close to the ocean now. Oscar realized that it was possible to see a bit of the water from where they were, over the cliff's edge about a hundred meters away. The sea was a deep, dark blue, strangely forbidding. Behind them, due north, the bulk of the volcano loomed overhead. Oscar could not help himself—he looked up at the caldera atop the conical mountain where, he knew, Dresde waited for Elias and her revenge. Oscar shuddered, remembering how she had enjoyed his suffering, how she had hurt him and relished his fear.

The heavy door creaked, startling Oscar out of his reverie.

"Sam?" a voice asked.

"We're here, Oma," Samantha replied.

The door swung out some more, and an elderly woman stepped into the light. She was shorter than Samantha, and her hair was silver-white. She wore a dress, white and immaculate, and her skin was a deep chestnut tone. Her eyes were dark brown, and they were piercing, projecting strength. Despite her evident age and the wrinkles on her face, she moved with undeniable grace. With a start, Oscar realized he had seen this person once before.

The woman looked him up and down carefully, and Oscar had the uncomfortable sensation that he was being judged or assessed in some way.

Then she nodded. "Greetings, male," she said to him. "I am Nadja."

"Nice to meet you," Oscar replied right away. "My name is—"

Nadja held up her hand, which looked oddly stiff. "Your name will not be necessary. Please, this way. Lunch is ready. You may leave your dirty clothes over there."

Oscar obeyed, stashing them nearby. He was the first to step into a dark cavernous space that his eyes had a hard time adjusting to after the bright sunlight outside.

As he crossed the threshold, he glanced back and heard Nadja speaking to Samantha in a soft voice.

"He is very young," Nadja said with a sigh. "What a pity."

Click.

Oscar jumped a bit, startled. Someone had turned on the lights, and he realized he was in the middle of a large kitchen that led into a simple but spacious dining room, with a living room farther down. Despite the fact that it was noon, all the boarded-up windows were covered with what looked like heavy curtains. Nevertheless, the light coming from overhead was bright enough to illuminate the entire space in a warm yellow glow.

There was someone standing by the light switch. It was a woman, older than Samantha but younger than Nadja. She was quite thin, and for an instant she reminded Oscar of his own mother. She was wearing a simple tunic, together with a kitchen apron, and her raven-black hair was braided neatly, with part of the braid falling over her left shoulder like Oscar had seen Samantha wear hers.

"Oh, hi," Oscar said reflexively.

The woman smiled, and Oscar was taken aback at the warmth of the expression. Both Samantha and Nadja had seemed somewhat hard, but this woman actually approached Oscar, beaming. She had a bowl in her hands and held it up to him. The bowl was full of dumplings. She nodded in an evident invitation.

"Thanks!" Oscar replied, realizing he was starving. "I'll go ahead and take one if that's okay."

The woman kept smiling. Oscar reached into the bowl, took one of the dumplings, and popped it into his mouth. It was delicious. He had not tasted anything like this yet. The inside was creamy, and the taste reminded him of mushrooms, but there was a tart, spicy tang that could have been tamarind or chili and complemented the flavor wonderfully. At the very center, there was something crunchy and juicy that tasted similar to a fresh bell pepper.

"Wow, this is amazing!" Oscar observed, chewing still. He covered his mouth and swallowed. "Oops, excuse me. It's really good!"

The woman laughed. Oscar realized that it had been a while now since he had heard anyone laugh, and he found himself grinning from ear to ear.

The door behind him was all but slammed shut, and Oscar glanced back.

"This way, male," Samantha told him, her voice carrying a hint of impatience. "Do not forget to take your shoes off."

"Uh, sure. Thank you so much for the dumpling, um…." He hesitated, looking at the woman.

She kept standing where she was and lifted the bowl, inviting him to take another one with a little nod. Her smile had not wavered, nor had she spoken, and it was at that moment that Oscar realized something was wrong with her.

"That's very nice, dear," Nadja said to the woman, using a tone one would use to talk to a young child. "He really likes your food. Come this way. I'll help you serve."

The woman looked confused for a moment, glancing between Oscar and Nadja. Then she allowed herself to be led away to a nearby kitchen counter where many plates full of enticing-looking food were waiting.

Samantha grabbed Oscar's good shoulder. "Come. We will sit down."

"Okay," Oscar replied.

Samantha led him to the table that occupied the center of the dining space. It was large, easily able to seat twenty people. It appeared to have been built out of the very hard obsidian-black wood of a yult tree.

"This table is incredible," Oscar said, with a last fleeting glance at the middle-aged woman, who was now busying herself with several plates.

"It has been here for a very long time," Samantha replied. She pointed to a seat, which Oscar took. She sat across from him.

"Back home we don't often work with yult wood unless it's something important," Oscar explained. "It's too hard, and you need to be really good at carving it right. Most people have furniture made from artificial polymers. It's light and easy to manufacture."

"Polymers," Samantha echoed. "Large molecules made of identical sections."

"Wow, are you into chemistry?"

"I have received a comprehensive education," she replied. "We keep certain records that provide us with ancient knowledge. I was taught by my grandmother."

"And she is an exceptional student," Nadja commented, setting down a couple of trays of food in front of them. "Very bright. Excellent memory."

"I'd love to help set the table if that's okay," Oscar said, remembering his manners. "Should I bring some plates or pour some water for all of us?"

Nadja looked taken aback for an instant. "No, thank you. You are our guest today. Please make yourself at home."

"Thank you, Mrs., um ...." Oscar hesitated.

Nadja raised an eyebrow. "A marriage title? As if I belonged to a male, and I had taken his family name and forgotten my own? That is not necessary here, young male. Nadja will suffice."

Oscar blushed. "Thank you, Nadja."

The other woman came to the table and placed several plates in front of them while still smiling absentmindedly. She and Nadja set the table quickly and efficiently, pouring water from a rather rough-looking pitcher and distributing silverware, and they then sat down to join Oscar and Samantha. Nadja was at the head of the table to Oscar's right. The middle-aged woman sat next to Samantha. There was an empty seat immediately next to Oscar, and that was all. The rest of the wide, imposing table seemed somehow much larger now that everyone was there.

"Welcome to our home, young male," Nadja said. "I am the head of the household. You already know Samantha, my granddaughter," she added, gesturing with her left hand. It still looked oddly stiff, and Oscar suddenly realized why. It was a prosthetic that did not move. Although it was beautifully carved and each finger had been shaped in a realistic way, the material from which it had been made had a rather dull sheen, and it was a little bit darker than Nadja's natural skin tone.

"Yes," Oscar confirmed, reminding himself not to stare. "Samantha helped me a lot. When Dr—when I was taken and we were flying, she gave me her helmet to help me breathe. I don't think I'd be here if it weren't for her."

Nadja nodded slowly, as if satisfied. "You owe her a debt of gratitude, then. It is good that you realize this. And you have also met my daughter, Ute," she added, gesturing at the smiling woman.

"Nice to meet you," Oscar said to Ute, who nodded in a friendly way.

There were footsteps behind Oscar. He turned his head in time to see a young woman enter. Her hair was blond, and her skin was very pale. She walked confidently, and the faint bulge of her belly contrasting against her slim figure suggested she was pregnant.

"And this is Laurie," Nadja finished. "A dear friend."

Laurie sat down next to Oscar and gave him an odd look but said nothing.

"Um, hello," Oscar replied. "It's nice to meet you."

"Let us eat now," Nadja declared. "Ute, thank you for making this delicious meal for all of us."

Ute appeared to shiver slightly, and she beamed as if thrilled to hear such praise. She then pointed at the array of dishes in front of them.

Samantha took Ute's hand gently and kissed her on the cheek. "Thank you for cooking, Mama."

"It looks delicious," Laurie said, reaching over the table to briefly hold Ute's hand as well.

Ute made a little frown and shook her head, nodding in the direction of Laurie.

"Okay, okay," Laurie replied, almost as if Ute had spoken. "I did help you a little, but you prepared most of the things. I am only your assistant when it comes to the kitchen."

Ute smiled again, appearing satisfied.

The meal began, and the women helped themselves to the many dishes that were arranged on the table. Oscar hesitated at first, but he was hungry, and he reached out experimentally to a plate that was piled high with what looked like steamed greens and some little three-pronged objects that he had never seen before but which resembled peanuts. He scooped some up with a nearby spoon and placed them on his plate. He gave a little start when he realized that the cutlery next to the plate he was about to use, such as the spoon he had just taken, was made of stainless steel and emblazoned with the same official logo from the *Ionas*. He picked up a fork and turned it in the light, feeling as though he had been transported back in time.

Oscar realized Samantha was watching him, and he used his fork to stab some of the greens on his plate and began to eat. His eyes widened as he crunched. Like the dumplings before, this dish was also quite tasty, although it barely had any spices. It was fresh and savory at the same time, and the peanut-like things that went with it were, in particular, crunchy and delicious.

"This is amazing," Oscar said, slightly intimidated at seeing four sets of eyes focus on him as he spoke. He still felt as if he was being examined. "I don't think I've ever had this before."

"You come from far away," Nadja pointed out as she helped herself to something that looked like bright-red bean sprouts and oddly shaped cherry tomatoes. "Most of what we have here should be new to you."

"I'd never left Portree in my entire life," Oscar explained. "I never thought I'd come all the way to Raasay!"

Nadja frowned slightly. "Samantha has told me about Portree, your settlement. What is Raasay?"

"It's… it's here. This continent. That's what we call it anyway."

"I see," Najda replied, sounding thoughtful. "Of course there would be different names for places. Generations of tradition, different knowledge."

"We never knew you guys were here," Oscar told her. "There's no record of a second colony in any of the books. Even Eli, my brother, he had no idea. At least I think he didn't. It's so cool, meeting other people. Back home I know everyone, and they all know me. I think it's the first time I've met someone new!"

He received no reply to that. Samantha and Nadja exchanged a serious look. Ute was eating happily, seemingly oblivious to the conversation going on around her. Laurie, sitting next to him, looked almost angry.

"Uh, so yeah," Oscar continued, trying to break the tension, which was making him uncomfortable. "Back home I never actually went into the wilderness or anything. It was dangerous, so nobody except the Colony Patrol ventured out. Maybe Samantha told you guys about the wurl? They used to be really vicious—"

"No," Samantha cut in.

"Sorry?"

"Do not talk about the scourge at the table."

As soon as she said the word *scourge*, Ute reacted as if she had been shocked with electricity. She let her knife and fork clatter down to the table and looked all around with an alarmed expression on her face. She checked all the windows in succession.

"It is okay, Ute dear," Nadja said quickly, taking Ute's hand. "We are safe. There are no open windows, and they cannot see us. Keep eating. This is delicious, everything you made. Right, Sam? Laurie?"

"It is wonderful," Laurie said, her tone strained. "I have always said that you are the most talented cook among all of us."

"The food is delicious, Mama," Samantha told her, stroking her hair. Slowly, Ute calmed down. After a couple of uncomfortable minutes she resumed eating.

"The young male used a different word to refer to them," Nadja said to Samantha. "Your mother would have not reacted if you had not called them by name."

Samantha nodded. "I know, Oma. I am sorry."

"No need to worry," Nadja said gently. "Perhaps we should use this foreign word to talk about them now. Wurl, you call them? Why?"

"Um...," Oscar began, looking at each of the women in turn. He was starting to sweat. "I think it's because of how they move. You know, how they tumble down hills or slopes? They look like spiked doughnuts, whirling and whirling. I think that's where the name comes.... Oh! Of course, you have never seen them. Well, maybe Samantha has. The ones here fly."

"Fascinating," Nadja interjected. "An entirely new species of... wurl. What are they like?"

"Scary," Oscar answered out of reflex. He remembered the day of the storm and trembled. "They are huge, and they are full of spines as big as my arm. They can shoot them at you, and they are deadly. The scariest one was Sizz—uh, the queen. I saw her once, right before she died. She was enormous."

"And she was also intelligent?" Nadja asked, narrowing her eyes.

"Eli says she was. But she hated us for taking the Life Seed."

"How did your colony survive at all?" Nadja pressed him. "How did you keep her at bay? Do you have a weapon? Something that can kill wurl?"

"Well, the Colony Patrol have shock spears, but they are small. I think we only survived because she, the queen, couldn't leave the place where the Life Seed had been. That's what Eli told us, anyway. When Dr. Wright took the Seed from its resting place, I think the Spine queen nearly died."

Nadja's eyes widened. She exchanged another look with Samantha, one which Oscar could only interpret as conveying excitement. "The Flower at the eyrie," she nearly whispered. "Of course!"

"How many?" Laurie asked suddenly, slamming her right fist down on the table so suddenly that Oscar yelped. When he looked at her, he realized that Laurie looked furious. "How many of you are there?"

"I-I'm not…. Do you mean in Portree? How many people are there in Portree?"

"Laurie…," Nadja warned her.

"I must know, Nadja," Laurie replied. Then she looked back at Oscar with open anger. She had placed both her hands over her belly, as if protecting an unborn child. "Answer, male. How many?"

"I… I think the last census was less than a hundred," Oscar responded. He clicked his link and brought up the file-manager interface. "Let me check the colony records. Hang on a sec…."

Now it was Laurie's turn to gasp. She pointed at Oscar's link. "You have a wrist-held computer?"

"Yes. We all do back home. There are also bigger computers in the labs. Why?"

"No, you do not get to ask that," Laurie said, and Oscar got scared when he saw that her eyes were tearing up in spite of her obvious anger. "*I* get to ask that. Why? Why did none of you ever come, if you had such gadgets? Why did you leave us here?"

"We, uh, we didn't know—"

"You could have saved us," Laurie spat. "Back before he…. Back when we were still…."

"Laurie, that's enough," Nadja said.

"Now it is only us!" Laurie all but shouted. "They could have come before. They have technology. They have dozens of computers, while we have but a single dilapidated terminal!"

Oscar looked at Samantha, alarmed. He expected her to look angry, but she actually looked sad again.

Something clicked in Oscar's brain. He looked around. The large table. The empty spaces. The oppressive sense of fear and loss that he had felt ever since he had set foot inside the building.

"Wait," he said softly. "Is this… is this all of you?"

Nadja nodded somberly. "You could say that, young male. This is all of us."

"But… the buildings outside. And…." He couldn't help it. He glanced at Laurie's belly. If she was pregnant, then there had to have been a father.

Laurie met his eyes with an unblinking defiant glare. Her voice cracked when she next spoke. "Everyone else is dead."

chapter 9.
dream

HEAVY RAIN fell the morning after they reached the beach, and Elias was thankful for the shelter of the cave.

Tristan had set up the tent in such a way that it was partially inside the high ceiling provided by the cleft between the cliff walls. They had spent a comfortable night inside, bothered by far fewer mosquitoes than usual. The sound of the ocean had been hypnotic, like a primal sort of lullaby, and Elias had not slept so deeply or so long since that one wonderful night he had spent back home in Portree after returning from the mountains. The fact that Tristan slept next to him was something that Elias had gotten used to very quickly, and now he could not imagine sleeping on his own again. Tristan made him feel safe, and he loved the way Tristan would sometimes embrace him as they slept. It was as though Tristan were subconsciously trying to protect him.

Elias opened his eyes to the bright-yellow underside of the tent. The patter of the rain was soothing. The temperature was nice, not as hot as the day before, and Elias spent a few moments simply lying on his back, taking in the sensations and savoring the feeling of being well rested.

Tristan yawned. "Morning," he said, rubbing his eyes.

"Morning."

"I dreamed of you."

"Really?" Elias asked. "I hope it was something good."

Tristan turned his head and winked. "It was something sexy."

Elias smiled. "Tell me! Wait—no. Don't tell me."

Tristan chuckled. "It did give me some ideas, for later maybe…."

They kissed, and Elias sat up in the tent. He reached for his shirt and put it on. Tristan did the same and then clapped his hands together once.

"Well, time to begin," he announced.

"Uh, what?"

"With the boat," Tristan explained. "Here, I found a good audio tutorial last night. I'll go ahead and play it on our wireless speaker while we sort breakfast out. It should give us initial instructions so we can begin construction."

Elias stretched and stood up. He left the tent and was pleased to see that Narev, Vanor, and Siv were all curled up next to their shelter like faithful protectors. Narev perked up when Elias walked by, and Elias placed his hand briefly on his scarred scales. From the wurl he received contentment and satisfaction, along with a very fleeting image of an underwater hunt.

"I hope it was a big fish you caught," Elias told him. He looked up at the sky, but it was still pouring out, and he quickly looked down again. "At least *you* don't mind the rain."

By the time he came back from his bathroom sortie, Elias's clothes were soaked. He took off his shirt and pants, opting instead to wear only a pair of shorts that were reasonably water repellent. It was warm enough that he would not be needing a shirt anytime soon.

"That's kind of the way my dream started," Tristan said mischievously, checking Elias out as he sat down next to the fire pit to prepare breakfast. "Then it got steamy."

Elias rolled his eyes, though he also felt warm inside at knowing Tristan considered him attractive.

They had a cold breakfast because it was impossible to start a fire with the rain outside. They were down to about half the rations, in fact, but Elias wasn't worried. The wurl would always be able to hunt something for them, and now that it was high summer, there were always fruits, nuts, and other things for Tristan as well.

As they ate, Elias and Tristan listened to the beginning of the audio tutorial. The sound carried well in the cave despite coming from their small but powerful speaker. As they listened to the correct preparation and the materials and tools they would need, Elias realized that building a boat was rather complicated.

"We don't have half of the tools that woman said we need," he complained after breakfast was over. "Not to say anything about glue, waterproofing agents, and those other things I don't even remember."

"Yeah, but we can improvise," Tristan told him. "Trust me, I've built things before. There's always a workaround."

The rain prevented them from going out for a few hours more, and they used the time to draw up sketches of what they would need and how the inner structure of the boat should look. Tristan appeared to know what he was talking about, and Elias limited himself to offering suggestions and taking notes. From what he was able to understand, they would need to cut down many of the trees nearby and experiment with their wood to find timber that was waterproof and tough but not too dense. They would then need to cut the timber into planks of different widths and sizes, and they would use some of those to build the frame of the boat, which would later be covered by wider planks. The tiny screens on their links were hopeless for detailed technical drawings, but Tristan did not need them. He had no trouble at all understanding things that were essentially incomprehensible to Elias, like the difference between a "ply," a "rib," and "stringers."

Around noon the two of them left the cave with their tools in order to cut down some trees. The wurl were not around, and Elias assumed they were either hunting or exploring. A quick scan of the sky informed him that there were no suspicious Flyers lurking nearby. He felt a brief stab of anxious nervousness when he looked at the ocean, but he supposed that if a Singer came, they would have to face it when it happened. Elias doubted that he would be able to detect them, and he wasn't sure whether the creatures could only turn invisible in the water or also on land.

"Hey," Tristan said, once again seemingly attuned to Elias's thoughts, "The faster we work, the faster we get out of here. It's no use worrying about whether wurl are coming to kill us."

"I know. Let's get some wood."

They selected the most promising trees in the vicinity, and Elias was relieved to see that his spine and the shock spear combined were great tools to cut through bark. The spine was very sharp and was great at making precise cuts. The shock spear, when focused, acted like a laser that burned away wood with great ease, and they soon had felled two palm trees, two of the short and squat stumpy trees, and two of the very tall trees with beautiful terracotta-colored striations.

Elias got Narev and Vanor to help them carry the felled trunks back to the cave when he spotted the wurl basking in the sun nearby. Both of them appeared interested by the project and lifted the heavy ends of the nearest tree with their jaws as if it weighed nothing. With their help, all six trees were soon arranged neatly near the tent.

"Now what?" Elias asked.

"Now we figure how to make decent planks and a frame using only the tools we have."

The rest of the day was spent working. Elias and Tristan spoke very little, but it was a good sort of silence. Tristan took the lead, directing their efforts. As before, he appeared to have a mental image of how the boat should look, and he made a crude estimate on the sand for the length of something he called the center rib. Elias limited himself to being as helpful as he could, improvising from their supplies in order to find the most efficient way to strip away the bark from the trees and cut the wood in the desired shape.

All of their attempts for that day ended in failure, and by the time night came, one of the palm trees had been reduced to splinters and disjointed sections of what might have been the beginning of planks. Unfortunately, Tristan proclaimed that the wood was actually not good for a boat.

"It's not flexible enough," he said when they were having dinner. "It looked good, but I'm not sure. Let's hope we have better luck with some of the other trees."

The next day they began work immediately after breakfast. At lunchtime, Elias's arms ached from all the sawing, but together they had made a plank that Tristan

thought was satisfactory out of the wood of one of the
terracotta trees.

"Let's take it to the ocean, see how it floats,"
Tristan suggested.

They headed in the direction of the sea and got into
the water with their plank. Tristan had also gotten rid of
his shirt the day before, evidently following Elias's lead
and obviously not caring about whether he was wet or
not anymore. They waded in with somewhat awkward
steps until the waves were about waist height. Tristan
then said to place the plank on the surface of the water.
It floated easily.

"Yes!" Tristan exclaimed, beaming. "I think this
will work. We have to wait a few minutes, though. I
want to see if it gets waterlogged or something."

As they waited, Elias could feel the warmth of the
sun on his torso, and the smell of the ocean was all
around him again. He had a brief moment of vertigo,
being so far out in the water. He knew how to swim,
and he had joined the wurl many times in the large
lake on Crescent Valley during his captivity, but this
was something entirely different. It wasn't that he was
afraid of drowning. Rather, he was filled by a sense of
being surrounded by something very big, something
beyond his comprehension.

When the waves came, they moved him gently
along with them. It was disorienting at first, but Elias
soon learned to expect the little bumps and enjoy them.
The sand underneath his feet was cool and very fine,
easily dislodged between his toes. He saw a school of
small fish swimming nearby, and farther out he thought
he saw something dark in the water, which turned out
to be a clump of seaweed. The sky overhead was bril-
liantly blue, as if washed clean by the rain. Aside from

the sound of the waves breaking against the shore, the world was silent.

"It's beautiful out here," he said to Tristan.

"Yeah. And you know what?"

"What's that?"

"We're the first men to *ever* swim in the oceans of New Skye."

"You're right," Elias observed. "I guess we've had so many firsts that it's hard to keep track."

"Yeah, but this one's different. More important."

Elias nodded, looking out over the horizon. Gentle waves came and went. A strange ocean bird, completely black, spiraled through the air overhead and then plummeted down, striking the water. A few moments later it came up again with a bright white fish squirming in its beak. With a graceful burst of speed, the bird took to the air again and was soon lost from sight.

"We should name it," Tristan declared.

"You mean this?" Elias asked, gesturing at the water.

"Yeah. We're the first to see this ocean up close, so we get to name it. That's how it works."

Elias chuckled. "The geography textbooks call this the Eastern Ocean."

Tristan rolled his eyes. "Yeah, and that's boring. Come on. Let's think of a name."

"Um…. Vasty McGee."

Tristan raised an eyebrow. "Where is this funny Elias coming from?"

Elias shrugged. "Okay, you try."

Tristan touched his chin with two fingers as though deep in concentration. Elias experienced another shift in perspective and saw Tristan as if from far away, a human man in an alien ocean, an explorer, a pioneer. It filled Elias with happiness to know that he was sharing all of these discoveries with the man he loved.

"Dyresian Ocean," Tristan said after a few moments.

"That sounds... it sounds nice."

"I think it's Old Terran for division, or something similar. I had a course on dead languages a year ago."

"It's a good name," Elias told him. "This ocean *is* like a divide. It separates us from... her. It also separates the continent of Reena from Raasay. It's kind of at the middle of the world."

"I'm liking it more and more."

"We have to make it official, though. When we return, we should tell Director O'Rourke."

"Okay. For now, though, we have to get back to work. It's been long enough that I know the wood is good for the water. It's flexible, buoyant, and tough. If we could figure out some way to make varnish or something else to seal it up, it would be better, but it's going to have to do."

"What's the next step?" Elias asked.

"Cutting. More cutting. Oh, but first measuring. Remember: measure twice, cut once."

"Sounds fun."

"Are you being sarcastic?"

Elias chuckled. "I'm not sure. If you say that's the way to go, though, then that's the way to go. I'm but your humble assistant."

"Then follow me, *assistant*."

The wurl were invaluable in speeding up their process over the next few days. They helped carry large loads, and their strength came in useful in many other ways. Vanor in particular was an excellent hunter, and he came back every night with ocean fish that were too large for him to finish. He would share his kills with the other two wurl and even with Elias, which was something he had seldom done before. As they spent more time together, Elias got the impression that Vanor was losing his mistrust of humans, along with his attitude of aggressive dominance. He would sometimes even follow Tristan around, as if curious. Whenever that happened Elias would remember what Dr. Wright had written in his journal ages ago regarding the innate curiosity of wurl. However, Elias knew that there was something else behind the apparently simple-minded nosing around. He was almost certain that Vanor had at least a general idea of what they were doing and why it was necessary. Neither he nor Narev nor Siv had made any attempt at crossing the ocean without them, even though they must have been able to do so. To Elias, that was proof that all three of them knew the humans could not cross yet, but they were doing something to be able to get across the water.

More importantly, though, was the fact that Elias knew they all wanted to help. They had a shared purpose: to find Dresde and take back what she had stolen.

On the night eight days after arriving, Elias was lulled back to sleep by the ever-present rhythmic cadence of the waves. When he woke up the next morning he had a faint but persistent impression that he had dreamed of something unusual, something he needed to remember. By the time he was fully awake, however, the remnants of the dream had faded away, and he concentrated on the work of a new day.

Progress was slow at the beginning, but Tristan was patient, and Elias was always there to help. They soon developed a routine: they would gather materials in the morning, work on refining them into usable planks and beams in the afternoon, and use the evening to catalog what they had and plan assembly for the next stage. Over the following month, they grew more efficient at what they were doing. It wasn't long before Tristan declared they had enough material and it was time to put things together.

Whenever they weren't working, Tristan and Elias found interesting ways to pass the time and prepare for their journey at sea. One of the most important problems to solve was how to carry enough freshwater with them to survive the trip. Every few days, either Elias or Tristan would go north on Narev or Vanor to the river, where they would replenish their freshwater supply. Elias spent several hours one day thinking of how to design a larger container for their water, but he settled instead on many smaller containers to help them carry a supply for about a week. As part of their survival gear, Elias's father had also packed them a handheld water condenser, which they could use to get a small amount of drinkable liquid from salt water in the ocean, but Elias knew it would not be enough for two men over a long sea voyage. However, it would supplement their initial supply nicely, enough for them to reach the first island away from the mainland. There they would hopefully be able to resupply and continue their journey. Elias had no idea how long it would take, but he tried to be as prepared as possible and not worry too much about what he could not control.

Elias looked forward to the messages he and Tristan received from Portree every now and then. It was good to know that his parents and Tristan's dad were doing okay, and it was reassuring to hear that no wurl had attacked the colony in his absence. He wished he could answer back, but contented himself with re-reading every letter multiple times. The messages gave him a sense of connection with his home, and they reminded him that there were people who loved him and prayed for his safe return.

Tristan and Elias also spent at least an hour a day practicing with their weapons. Tristan was very good, and he guided Elias and taught him a few moves that he could use in order to defend himself wielding his spine. Every time they practiced, Elias became more fully aware of what Tristan had brought to his attention weeks earlier: somehow Elias's reaction time was decreasing. His reflexes were getting better all the time, and it allowed Elias to dodge attacks with relative ease.

"It's incredible," Tristan said one afternoon, wiping sweat off his brow. "You're really quick, Elias. And you're improving even faster. I can't hit you."

"I think I can sense what you are going to do before you do it. I'm not sure, though."

"Whatever it is, keep it up. The better the two of us can fight, the better it will be when we run into trouble."

"Yeah. Let's go again. This time I'll be the aggressor."

As the work shifted into more technical things and precision work, Elias could offer relatively little assistance. Once all of the individual sections of the boat had been carved out, Elias helped when he could, but Tristan was able to make better progress on his own. Instead of simply getting in the way, Elias decided to use his time wisely and try to create tools that would be useful for later.

His first project was a sonic amplifier. He decided it would be a good way to attempt to boost the signal from their links in order to perhaps send a message back to the orbiting satellite and communicate with Portree. He had plenty of electronics supplies in his pack, so he spent three days tinkering around with the materials.

He disassembled a small solar panel and repurposed it as a power source for a relatively bulky sound array that he created using a second wireless speaker they had been carrying but had used very little up to that point. After some creative retrofitting, he managed to connect together the speaker, power source, and a mechanical amplifier he improvised out of part of the tent's metal rigging. His handiwork was unwieldy, but it could technically be connected to his link via a wireless protocol and would amplify its signal to send out a message using sound waves.

"That thing looks complicated and weird," Tristan observed one night.

Elias poked the fish that Narev had brought him as it cooked over the fire. The creature was bulky and scaly, a nine-finned animal with long whiskers on its snout and a forked tail. It was delicious—Narev had already caught one a few days earlier, and Elias had developed a taste for it.

"You mean my sonic amplifier?" Elias asked.

"If that's what you want to call it. Do you think it'll work?"

"Why don't we find out?"

"Right now?"

Elias nodded. "I finished it today. Let's see if we can use it to send a message back home while the fish cooks. Or we can try sending a message to…."

"To Oscar," Tristan said firmly. "You said he's a telecommunications genius, right? Maybe he found a way to do something similar to this. Maybe we can find out if he's okay, or talk to him even."

Elias avoided Tristan's eyes. That had been his hope all along, but he had kept it hidden, even from himself. If the sonic amplifier worked, he might be able to know whether Oscar was okay.

Or he might be able to learn whether he wasn't. Every link had a built-in vital signs sensor. If Elias was able to establish a connection with Oscar's link, even if there was no answer, he would still be able to see whether Oscar's vital signs were okay. However, Elias was terrified of finding out they were not.

"You know what?" Elias said, suddenly afraid of what he might discover. "Maybe let's leave it for tomorrow."

"Elias, I know you're worried, but we should test it out. Okay?"

"But...."

"Besides, you're always saying how these kinds of communications are better at night because the sun doesn't interfere."

Elias took in a long breath and then sighed. "I just don't think I'm ready."

"You're sure?"

"Yes. No. I mean, the sooner we find out, the better, but...."

"We don't have to do it if you don't want to, but I kind of think you do."

Elias was silent for a moment. "You're right, Tristan. Let's try."

They left the fish cooking over the fire and went outside. It took Elias only a couple of minutes to set up the contraption.

"How does this work, again?" Tristan wanted to know.

"I've essentially built a giant sound system," Elias explained. "Only it's going to transmit ultrasound, so we won't be able to hear it. In theory, if the air around us is not too disturbed by weather, I might be able to get an amplified version of my link's signal all the way to the upper atmosphere. The satellite might pick it up. It's just a theory, though. I actually don't know whether sound waves will travel through the thin upper atmosphere at all, or exactly when the satellite's overhead. I might have been wasting time."

"Only one way to find out."

After some hesitation, Elias nodded again. Then he activated the machine.

The three wurl lying nearby perked up, lifting their heads. Their eyes flashed more brightly for an instant with acknowledgment. Although Elias could hear nothing because the sound was way above the human threshold, he was almost certain that the wurl could hear the sound very well.

"Activating signal," he said aloud, typing some commands on his link. "Sending."

A few minutes passed. Elias received no acknowledgment from the satellite. He tried again, but there was no answer.

"Trying again," he told Tristan.

He tried four times before giving up. The fourth time he almost kicked his creation, but Tristan stopped him.

"Maybe you can try again tomorrow," Tristan suggested gently.

"I don't think it's working. I think I need electromagnetic waves, not sound waves. I have no idea how this telecommunication stuff works, Tristan. I should've had that internship with my dad years ago, instead of turning him down all the time and—"

Elias's voice broke and he sat down on the sand. Tristan sat down next to him and draped his arm over Elias's shoulders.

Tears came out of nowhere, and Elias tried to stifle them but was not successful.

"Hey," Tristan said. "Come here. Let it out."

Elias hugged Tristan hard and let loose the tears that he hadn't allowed himself to shed for days. He wasn't even sure why he was crying, exactly. All he felt was an overwhelming sensation of pressure coming from everywhere, a feeling that something was wrong, but he wasn't sure what.

Crying helped. The fact that Tristan was there helped. Even Narev came over to see what was wrong, and Elias calmed down eventually, flanked on either side by his boyfriend and his best friend. The calm brought clarity and a definite shape to the sense of guilt that was fueling his anxiety.

"I think I've been suppressing a thought," Elias said at last, his voice hoarse. "A specific thought."

Tristan remained silent and listened.

"It was my fault, Tristan. What happened to Oscar."

"That's not true, and you know it."

"Isn't it?" Elias demanded, more loudly than he had intended. The things he had avoided saying for weeks were now bursting out, uncontrollable. "I told him to get the egg. I *told* him to. Why did I do that? When Dresde was attacking, I could've told Oscar to run away. But Oscar listened to me and grabbed the egg. So Dresde took him. It's my fault, Tristan. It's all my fault."

He started crying again. This time he was able to calm down a little bit faster.

"And I'm sick of this, you know?" Elias continued. "The mood swings. I'm okay one time, sad the next. I'm hopeful one day, then full of despair. Like the day when we got here. You had to calm me down, show me the cave and everything. I don't know what's going on.

Sometimes I feel like this, all of this, it's too much. We're so far away from home, and I don't know what's happened to my brother. What if we get all the way to Raasay only to find that Oscar is... that Oscar is... *gone*?"

Tristan nodded. "I've also been thinking about those things."

"You have?"

"Yeah. I'm scared for my dad. I know him, and I know he's going to try something stupid if he doesn't hear back from me. He won't get very far with his leg like it is, and if there are any Flyers around Portree, it's going to be suicide to leave. If the commander doesn't stop him, he's going to try to follow me, and I don't know whether I'll see him again.

"And I'm scared about Oscar, just like you. I worry about him. I'm also tired, sick of the bugs, sick of eating rations all the time, and sick of working all day to build a boat that's way too small for what we need and that I'm not even sure I'm building correctly. But you know what?"

"What's that?"

"I keep going because of you."

"Me?"

"Yes. I told you, I care about you, and I want Oscar to be okay. I want all of this to be okay. This mission we have, it's very important, and not only for you, Oscar, and me. It's for the good of *all* of Portree. If we are somehow able to take down Dresde, we will save everyone back at the colony. What's stopping her from coming back and destroying all of our homes? Nothing, not really. So this thing we're doing, right here, is the most important thing I could be doing."

"I hadn't thought of it like that," Elias admitted.

"I've also felt the way you say. Happy sometimes, irritated at other times. Also sad. But I think it's affecting you more than me. You've always been more sensitive than me, more sensitive than anyone I know, actually. And this new sense you have, this thing where you say you can feel the life around you, maybe it has something to do with it. I see how you smile when you watch Narev playing. I see how you sometimes stop and look out over the ocean, lost in thought for a long time. Yesterday you were sitting outside for nearly an hour, just staring. Meditating or something. There was a really beautiful butterfly fluttering over your head, and at one point you simply reached out your hand and the butterfly landed on it. Like you were speaking to it. I think your connection to the world is part of what's making you have all of these mood swings you talk about. You feel more, you sense more. So things affect you more."

"Maybe."

"And I also think it's normal. This is an awful situation, and adrenaline can only carry you so long. I know all about exhaustion and getting irritable and emotionally imbalanced because of it. When I first said I wanted to join the Colony Patrol, Commander Rodriguez gave me a test. She took me on a patrol mission with Phineas and her, except she didn't tell me I was going to be out in the cold for five days and five nights with only three hours' sleep each night and dreading wurl attacks every minute. It was awful. I got angry, I got sad. Near the end I even swung at Phineas, for goodness' sake."

In spite of himself, Elias perked up. Phineas was a mountain of a man. "You're kidding."

"I wish I was. Phineas smacked me down to the ground, and I kicked him in the face."

"That's…. I can't…. And then what happened?"

"The commander broke up the fight and sent me home. I thought I had flunked the test, that I wouldn't live up to my father's dream of me being a member of the Colony Patrol."

"But…?"

"But a couple of days later the commander showed up at my house and offered me the chance to train with the Patrol. You should've seen my dad. He was so happy."

Elias smiled. "I didn't know. I thought you got handed your spot with the Patrol."

"Not at all. I had to work for it. But that's not important. The point I'm trying to make is that it's okay to sometimes feel out of it. It's okay to cry too. It's your brother's life on the line, and I understand."

Elias glanced at his failed sonic amplifier. "I just wanted to know he was okay. But I was terrified I would find out he wasn't."

"You can try again tomorrow. And the day after that. Whatever happens, remember this, Elias. It's not your fault. Dresde would have come after us sooner or later. She doesn't care about humans at all. There was no way for you to prevent what she did, but there *is* a way for you to make it right. I think that's what's important here."

"Thanks, Tristan. I feel like I say it all the time now, but I mean it. Thanks."

"Don't mention it. Come on, let's have dinner. You can have that fish thing, and I'll make myself some ramen."

That night Elias thought about Oscar before he closed his eyes and tried to remember what Tristan had told him. Tristan's words allowed him to fall asleep without too much trouble.

Elias's dreams were troubled even so. He had the distinct sensation that something was there with him. It was watching, and it was not friendly. The thing was lurking, unseen, mouth agape, wanting to devour him with its hideous maw.

Panting, Elias opened his eyes in the darkness. Tristan slept soundly nearby, and Elias could hear the droning huffs of the wurl outside the tent.

It was a dream, he told himself.

He shifted so he would be lying on his right side. After a few moments, his eyes fluttered shut. He began to dream again, but the presence was still there.

Watching. Waiting to strike.

Elias tried using his sonic amplifier the next day, but it was no use. He gave up on it after a few more tries and instead helped Tristan with the boat. They made good progress, and over the next week, Tristan completed the project. He was very creative, thinking outside the box in order to find a solution to the problem of not having any nails, screws, or adhesive of any kind in order to affix the different parts of the vessel to the sturdy frame he had built earlier.

Elias busied himself in the meantime by preparing supplies for the trip. He gathered as much food as he could from the nearby wilderness and packed it neatly in the backpacks they would be carrying with them. At night he practiced his fighting skills with Tristan and played with the wurl. His rest was peaceful for the most part, except for the persistent nightmares he kept having. Elias decided against saying anything, though. He was certain they were a manifestation of his own anxiety, and he supposed the best way to get rid of them was simply to make progress and leave the beach as soon as they could.

The last step in building the boat was waterproofing it, which Elias helped Tristan do one afternoon with thick sap from a plant they had found at the top of the cliff above them. The plant had a gnarly, twisted trunk, and it oozed sap at regular intervals. The sap itself was a deep red, and many insects were trapped on its surface. Elias was not completely certain, but he thought that the plant was probably carnivorous, and it used the sap as a lure in order to catch insects and then digest them. Whatever the case the material was viscous and sticky enough to serve as a binder and waterproofing agent, according to Tristan. It took them a while, but they collected enough sap to coat the underside of the boat. They carried it down carefully and set to work. It was messy, but the sap was wonderfully fragrant. The only downside was that several bugs were attracted to their work and got stuck on the wood.

When they were done, after about four hours of nonstop activity, Tristan and Elias set the finished boat out on the beach with the help of Siv, who was nearby.

"She's a beauty," Tristan said.

"I can't believe you did it. We have a boat!"

The other wurl came over and sniffed the finished boat with curiosity. It was about as long as one of the big reptiles from end to end. Tristan had built it with two seats in the middle and hollow sections to store their gear and other things at either end. He had also made two sets of oars to help them move and steer.

"There's no sail because I absolutely don't know how to make one from scratch," Tristan informed Elias. "I did, however, make three long ropes we can give to the wurl so they can tow the boat in the water. Together with the oars, it should give us plenty of mobility."

"It's fantastic."

"We should let the coating dry. Maybe a couple days. In the meantime, we can begin packing our gear into the boat."

"That means we're leaving," Elias said, looking back at the cave that had been home for over a month.

"Yes. Time to cross the sea."

Elias spent the better part of the evening packing most of their supplies into the boat. He stashed about half of the rations, the water, and their electronic equipment. He left the other part of the food and most of their outdoor gear near the tent, intending to pack them away the following morning. When he was done, he helped Tristan make dinner.

"I'm breaking out the brownies for this," Tristan announced, taking out a vacuum-sealed package from the second half of their supplies.

"Agreed," Elias said cheerfully. "We deserve them."

They had a feast that night, supplemented with nuts and berries from the nearby plants and bushes, as well as a large yellow fruit with stringy but sweet pulp that Elias had discovered a few days earlier. The wurl appeared to understand something was going on, and they were out hunting for longer than usual. When they returned, they carried a large fish between the three of them, a dark and scaly creature that was almost the size of an adult wurl. It was impossible to cook that much meat, but the wurl didn't seem to mind. They simply settled down nearby and had their own raw fish feast.

It was a good night. After dinner, Elias and Tristan retreated to their tent and cuddled together. As Elias lay there, his left arm wrapped around Tristan in the sleeping bag they shared, he was filled with energy and a sense of purpose. In just a couple of days they would set out into the unknown. They would finally be on the move, closer to saving Oscar and saving the precious white egg.

Elias fell asleep without really noticing. At first his dreams had no shape—they were fleeting sensations and short flashes of disjointed imagery. There was a rhythmical sound in the distance, something like the waves of the ocean but more insistent. Stronger.

Elias's dream changed.

He was outside by the cliff. None of the moons were out, and it was very dark. In spite of this, he knew that the ocean was not far, and he wanted to go there.

He took a step. The sand underneath his feet was cold. He could hear the water and the rhythmical cadence of the surf as it came and went. He knew the water would be warm and inviting. Safe.

Another step. Now he was in the water, knee-deep. It was completely dark… and yet there was light.

Floating around his knees Elias saw flickering, ghostly lights of the most beautiful azure blue. When he moved his right leg, the light flashed more brightly. It was as if someone had dropped glowing paint on the surface of the water, glistening and vivid.

Elias reached down with his hands and dipped his fingers in the welcoming water of the ocean. As soon as they touched the surface, the water around them came alive with the same azure glow. It was mesmerizing. Elias traced a wide arc with one of his hands, and it was like painting on a canvas made of mist. His hand left a trail of neon light that flickered and glowed without producing any heat. Curious, Elias cupped some of the water in his hands. It flashed for a moment, but as soon as he brought it up to his face, it went dark. When he let the water fall, the impact of the droplets triggered more bursts of the light.

He looked back where he had come. He saw something he had not before: when the waves broke against the beach, each crest glowed brightly with that same ethereal light. It was everywhere and nowhere at the same time. The ocean was dark, but anything that disturbed it made the water glow. It was entrancing and relaxing. Elias felt at ease, and he knew it was the ocean embracing him.

Gently, his attention was turned back toward the ocean depths. He should go there. It would be nice there, in the deep.

He took a step. Another one. The water was suddenly up to his neck.

Another step. It was warm there. He liked it. He would—

Whoosh.

Something flew past Elias's left ear. Then the unseen projectile struck something soft.

A bestial scream shattered the night.

The beautiful light surrounding him died away, and everything was swallowed by darkness.

chapter 10.
flying

OSCAR WAS so thankful when the tense meal with Samantha's family was over that he followed her unquestioningly when she led him from the table and up a short flight of stairs. He was glad to get away from Laurie's anger, which had been scary up close. He also did not like the way that Nadja kept looking at him, as if analyzing him. With Samantha, at least, he believed he knew what to expect.

"Up there," Samantha indicated, pointing to a trapdoor in the ceiling and sounding as if she were barking out orders to a soldier. "You will sleep there tonight. You may rest for the remainder of the day, and tomorrow you will accompany me as we go foraging. Make sure to wake up at sunrise."

"Um, how do I get up there?"

Samantha looked around and frowned. "Right. Let me get the ladder. You wait here."

She went back downstairs, and Oscar was left standing on a landing that led into a long hallway that extended to his left and right. There were several doors down its length, but most of them were closed. Only three doors were open, the ones closest to the staircase.

While he was curious, Oscar decided not to move in case Samantha came back quickly. Instead he simply examined the decrepit-looking wooden walls and ceiling and tried to guess how old everything was. At either end of the hallway, there were windows, but they were shuttered, and very little light came through. As a result, the hallway appeared shadowy and slightly sinister. The trapdoor itself, which was directly overhead, was so well camouflaged in the ceiling that Oscar could only distinguish the ring-shaped handle that dangled from it and nothing else.

The house did not smell musty, despite its evident age. In fact Oscar realized that the floors were very clean, and there was art hung on the walls as well.

Click.

Oscar jumped a little bit, startled. Someone had turned on the lights, and the hallway was immediately transformed from its scary dimness into a surprisingly warm and welcoming area. Since Samantha was taking a while returning, and given the light, Oscar was emboldened enough to walk down the hall and explore a bit. He realized that the artwork on the walls had mostly been made by children. His footsteps creaked as he made his way to the shuttered window, and when he reached it, he peered through a small crack in the wood, looking out into the world. He was able to see the green grass that covered the ruins all around this last remaining structure. On the ground below, he noticed a span of carefully tended ground on which the large solar panel array he'd seen before stood. One of the five panels was cracked, but the remaining ones were all clean and correctly angled to receive the maximum amount of sunlight.

More creaking footsteps on the stairs alerted Oscar to the fact that Samantha was returning, and he hurried back to the landing.

"Here is the ladder," she said to him, placing it on the floor. It looked sturdy but old. "You can use it to climb."

She made as if to leave. "Wait!" Oscar said. "What's up there?"

"Your room," she answered. "I prepared it earlier today. It used to… it should be sufficient for you."

"Okay. Thanks."

"I will talk to you tomorrow. Please do not come down if you can help it. Your presence has disturbed my mother enough."

"Sure."

Samantha walked back down, and Oscar dithered for a moment before deciding to set the ladder against the wall and climb up. When he was high enough, he reached for the handle and pulled. The trapdoor slid out easily, revealing wooden steps that, although worn, looked reliable enough to lead him up into what he supposed was the attic.

He climbed and emerged into a room that was bigger than he'd expected. He raised the trapdoor behind him, and the steps he had used folded up smoothly. Now alone in the room, Oscar took a big breath and let it out slowly like he'd learned to do. He realized he was shaking a little bit with a mixture of nervousness and relief. He took a couple of steps back until he stumbled on something that turned out to be a bed. He sat down on it carefully, marveling at its softness. After days and days of sleeping on the hard-packed ground, it was a minor miracle to feel the gentle support of a mattress under his body.

He lay down on the bed and stretched, wincing slightly because of his shoulder. He let tension drain away from his muscles and closed his eyes.

He fell asleep almost immediately. He woke up disoriented and stared with puzzlement into the deep shadows that surrounded him. Then everything fell back into place, and he realized he was still in the attic. Oscar yawned, sitting up on the bed and feeling wonderfully rested. He had not even undressed, but he could not remember having had a better nap in his life. He tapped on his link, curious about the time.

Wow, midnight. I slept the entire afternoon.

He stood up and stretched again. It was dark in the room now, and he had to use the flashlight on his link to locate the light switch. He flicked it, half expecting it not to work. However, a yellow lightbulb overhead blinked to life immediately.

Oscar studied the room for a few minutes. It was a cozy space, kept tidy and clean. There was a closet across from him, a desk with its chair, and a very big window that had been completely boarded up. The floor was adorned with a rug that also came from the *Ionas*, and when Oscar stood up to walk on it with bare feet, he realized it was still very soft, even after more than a century.

Next to the closet stood a guitar, along with a notebook, which Oscar did not touch. All in all, Oscar got the distinct impression that this was a welcoming space, safe. He wondered whether this was Samantha's room, and he was surprised at how nice of her it had been to prepare the room so he would be comfortable. He took a couple more steps in the direction of the boarded-up window, and it was then that he discovered the last items in the room.

Spears. Long and sharpened to wicked points. They appeared to have been made from yult wood, and there were three of them, two as long as Oscar was tall. The last one was broken, and even though the wood was black, Oscar could still tell that one of its points had a thick rust coating that could have been either paint or dried blood. Immediately behind the spears, a conspicuous wooden board covered part of the wall. Oscar gave in to his curiosity and removed it carefully. He did not find a secret compartment or a valuable relic behind it—only the original wall of the attic. But there were three parallel gouge marks on it, coal-black, as if the wood had been burned with a red-hot iron.

Oscar placed the board back where he'd found it and walked to the trapdoor again. He needed to go to the bathroom, but Samantha had said to stay put. He waited for a bit and set an alarm for sunrise the next morning. However, the call of nature won out in the end, and Oscar pushed the trapdoor so the steps would extend down into the hallway. He climbed down and then made his way to ground level, tiptoeing so he wouldn't disturb anyone. Thankfully, the dining room and kitchen were both empty, and he sneaked out of the building until he found the outhouse. He walked back to the front door after washing his hands, and he was about to come inside when he heard voices nearby.

Oscar hesitated, but the voices sounded furtive, almost suspicious, and he walked carefully along the façade of the building until he reached the corner and could peek out from behind it at the space where the solar panels were arranged. Despite the late hour, moonlight enabled him to see the four figures sitting crosslegged in a rough circle as they quietly spoke.

"It is too dangerous," one of the voices said. Oscar realized it was Nadja. "The risk is too high."

"I can do it, Oma," Samantha said. Even though she spoke softly, Oscar could hear the vehemence in her voice. "I can move fast. Doran will be there to take me."

"He will never go against her," Laurie interjected. "You would have to get there on your own."

"I know the way," Samantha countered. "I can get there on foot if need be."

"She would see. She would know," Nadja replied, sounding sad. She placed her hand on the fourth figure, who Oscar guessed was Ute.

"So?" Samantha asked, defiant. "I do not fear death. I would rather die trying to find my freedom than live this way for the rest of my days."

Nadja shook her head slowly. "It is not your death I fear, Sam. It is what might happen if she does not kill you."

There was a choked sound in the night, and it took Oscar a moment to realize that the voice he heard now was Ute's. She had started crying.

"We are upsetting her," Laurie said, also placing her hand on one of Ute's shoulders. "It is best not to remind her of—"

"My father?" Samantha interrupted, raising her voice for the first time. Nearby, Ute sniffled. "He was brave. He tried to defend his family! And Jörgen—"

"No," Laurie cut in, and her voice had the rough, cold edge of an icicle. "You do not get to talk about him."

"He was my *brother*," Samantha retorted, her voice slick with rage.

"And he listened to you, and he will never see his own child," Laurie replied in kind. "Do not *ever* bring up his name in my presence. Do you understand?"

Samantha stood up, hands balled into fists, shoulders held wide and threatening. "He would have wanted us to fight. He would have wanted his child—*my* niece or nephew—to be born free."

"And where is he now, Sam?" Laurie asked, climbing to her feet as well. "Where is he? Do you want to end up like him? Or worse, do you want to end up like your—"

Oscar's foot crunched on a pebble as he shifted his weight, and the two women fell silent at once. Panicking, Oscar rushed into the house, climbed up the stairs to the attic, and shut the trapdoor behind him. He waited, crouched in the darkness, his heart pounding in his chest. He was scared, but he was not sure of what. He only knew that he had definitely heard something he was not supposed to. He had not understood half of the conversation, but the other half was terrifying.

Minutes crawled by, but no one came to reprimand him or drag him back to his cell. Slowly, he relaxed. When his link showed that it was 1:00 a.m., he undressed and slipped back into bed. Oscar thought he would not be able to sleep, but he had underestimated how tired he was. He drifted off quickly once again and was only woken up by the beeping of his alarm at sunrise the next morning.

Almost on cue, the trapdoor to his room creaked. Oscar sat up in bed, rubbing the sleep out of his eyes, and he had just finished putting on his new pair of pants when Samantha came in.

"Are you ready to go?" she asked him.

"Hold on a sec. Let me—"

"I will be outside. You have five minutes."

She did not give him time to answer, and Oscar hurried, getting dressed as fast as he could. He then climbed down to the hallway below his room. Samantha was not there, so he went down to ground level and saw she was standing by the kitchen counter, eating something green and purple from a bowl.

"Eat," she said, gesturing to the container. "It might be a while before we eat again, and you will need your energy."

"Thanks," Oscar replied, approaching slowly. He wondered where the other women were.

"If you are thirsty, there is water over there."

"Right. Um, where we are going, exactly? And for how long?"

"We should be back before sundown," Samantha told him as she ate. "We will be heading east, beyond the Field of Thorns. We should be able to gather some tubers and tari fruit, which is in season."

"Is that far?"

"Walking, yes. About forty kilometers."

"Forty kilometers?" Oscar echoed. "That's going to take forever!"

"It would if we were going to walk there. But we are not," Samantha added cryptically. Oscar considered asking more questions, but he had slept through dinner the day before, and the food looked tantalizing, so he ate instead. After they were both done, Samantha led him outside.

"What now?" Oscar asked as he put on his rather uncomfortable dress shoes.

"You carry this," Samantha said, tossing him a big canvas bag, which he discovered he could wear as a backpack. "And follow me."

She started walking due west toward the cliffs that overlooked the ocean. The golden light of early morning cast long shadows ahead of them that swayed in time to their footsteps as they crunched on loose pebbles. The world was quiet around them. A fresh breeze carried the faint smell of the sea, and Oscar found himself breathing it in and enjoying the walk in spite of everything. This early in the day, it appeared as though Samantha and he were the only ones around, and it was peaceful. Even the volcano, still towering off to the right, appeared less menacing at the beginning of a new day.

"It is rude to eavesdrop, you know," Samantha said out of the blue. She was walking next to him on his left, and she did not look at him as she spoke.

Oscar's face heated with embarrassment. "I'm sorry, really. I, er…." He hesitated, looking for an excuse, but decided against it. "I shouldn't have done that. I apologize."

Samantha nodded slowly. "I accept your apology. I assume you have many questions."

"So many!" Oscar conceded, relief washing over him. "For example, why—"

Samantha raised her hand, indicating he should be quiet. "Accepting your apology does not mean I give you permission to ask me questions. I barely know you, male. For now, be thankful you are not in that cell anymore. Try to be useful during this foraging trip. If you work well, I will think about sharing more information with you."

"Okay, fair. Just, um…. Samantha?"

"Yes?"

"Didn't you say we were going east?"

"That is correct."

"Then why are we going to the edge of those cliffs? That's the opposite of east."

Samantha glanced at him, and for the very first time since he had known her, Oscar saw her face break out in a brief one-sided grin. "I also said we would not be walking."

She stopped a few meters away from the edge of the cliffs, and Oscar followed suit. For a few moments she was silent, almost as if listening for something.

Then she whistled. Loudly. It was a note that went up, then down, and then back up, to the very limits of what Oscar thought a human could make. He jumped at the sound, startled. Up to this point, he'd had the distinct impression that the women avoided being loud at all costs, almost as if they did not want to draw attention to themselves.

"What are you doing?" he asked.

He received no response, and for a few seconds all he did was stand there awkwardly, looking at Samantha, wondering if perhaps she had gone crazy or something.

Then he heard it. The sound of flapping wings.

"Something's coming!" Oscar whispered urgently, chills crawling up his spine. "We have to hide! What if it's her?"

"It is not her."

"But... but...," Oscar stammered, looking everywhere for the source of the sound. The skies were clear, and the sound of flapping seemed to be coming from below them.

Oscar stepped forward until he could see over the edge of the cliff.

He screamed and backed away so fast that he tripped and fell on his bum. Even as he grimaced with the pain of the fall, his eyes widened in shock as two enormous cobalt wings appeared over the edge of the cliff, swiftly followed by the rest of the slender, serpent-like body of a male Flyer wurl.

He scooted away from the edge, but he knew he would never be able to get away in time. His eyes swept over the muscular frame of the creature, from its incredibly long tail to its four legs ending in deadly azure claws. He stared at membranous wings, crisscrossed by indigo veins, that seemed to blot out half the sky, and of course the aerodynamic angular head. The creature's eye cluster gleamed in the morning sun, bloodred and terrifying. All three of his eyes were focused on Oscar. A Flyer had found him.

Oscar's mind flashed back to the day of the storm. The fear from that day came roaring back, and he suddenly found he could not move. His body seized up, and he was left to watch, powerless, as the wurl approached from above.

And went past him.

Mouth agape in disbelief, Oscar followed the wurl with his eyes as he landed gracefully a few meters away and folded his wings into his body with a smooth, almost liquid, motion. His scales looked like sapphires as they reflected the light of the sun, and he wove across the ground with surprising speed, heading straight to where Samantha was standing.

"Look out!" Oscar yelled, jumping to his feet. It was too late, however. The wurl had reached Samantha.

"Do not be afraid," she said to Oscar. She raised her hand and placed it on the side of the head of the male wurl, who held perfectly still and allowed her to touch him.

"Are you *petting* him?" Oscar asked, disbelieving.

As if in response to the question, the wurl's eyes flashed briefly. He was still scary, but the flash was accompanied by something similar to a croon coming from the throat of the large being.

"I missed you too," Samantha whispered. Oscar watched, mouth still agape, as she closed her eyes and rested her forehead on the head of the wurl with no fear whatsoever.

"I... um...." Oscar tried to say something, but he had too many questions at once.

After a couple of seconds Samantha opened her eyes and looked at him. Unnervingly, the wurl did the same thing. He towered above her, but Samantha projected more strength, oddly. It was almost as if she were the hunter and the wurl her hound.

"This is Doran," she said to Oscar. "He is the strongest male in Dresde's brood, and as such he had the privilege to mate with her. He has been my companion for a long time."

Oscar glanced from Samantha to Doran. Then again to Samantha. And again to Doran.

"Nice to... meet you?" he ventured. He had no idea how to introduce himself to a wurl. "I'm Oscar."

Doran lowered his head and approached until he was standing very close. Oscar stood as still as he could while Doran examined him, eyeing him from several directions and even walking a full circle around him once. By the time Doran was done and returned to Samantha, Oscar was drenched in cold sweat.

"What do you think?" Samantha asked Doran.

The male wurl huffed.

"Good enough."

"A-are you for real?" Oscar stammered at last, finally able to break out of his spellbound silence.

"What do you mean?"

"I... okay. Maybe I didn't mention this, but back where I'm from, wurl are scary. The stuff of nightmares. They prowl around in the dark, and they will kill you if you're not careful. Well, not so much after what Eli did, but still. You get the idea. And these ones can *fly*!"

"So?" Samantha asked, raising both eyebrows.

"So? You're telling me you're friends with… with Doran? He doesn't want to kill you? He doesn't want to eat you?"

"No," she answered simply. "He is a friend."

"But," Oscar protested, gesturing at the volcano with his thumb, "you know."

Samantha shrugged. "Wurl, as you call them, have personalities. *She* might be evil, but that does not mean the males in her brood are the same."

"But they attacked my home!" Oscar protested, and his own sudden anger surprised him. "They came in the storm! They descended…."

Doran growled, and a faint smell of burning rock reached Oscar's nostrils.

"I was also there, as you might recall," Samantha said with a scowl. "Did I also attack your home?"

"You… she made you, didn't she? That's why you were there. You didn't have a choice!"

"Exactly," Samantha countered, looking at Doran. "Exactly."

"You mean… oh," Oscar said. "She made him go too."

"They cannot disobey her, not directly. But that does not mean they like what she does."

Oscar took a few seconds to process the information. "Wow, I had never thought about it like that."

"Well, now you have. Now come on, we are wasting valuable daylight. It is time we left on the foraging trip."

"You said we're not walking."

"Correct."

"So that means…," Oscar started to say, looking at Doran and at his wings, which he was beginning to unfurl. "Oh. No. No, no, no. No way."

"Yes. Put these on," Samantha told him, tossing him a small object.

Oscar caught it. "Goggles?"

"Trust me, you do not want an insect hitting you in the eye when we fly. No need to worry. Doran will fly low so a full helmet will not be necessary. Now hurry. You will sit behind me and hold on tight."

"Can't I just walk?" Oscar asked in a small voice.

"No. Today you and I will fly."

Oscar watched as Doran stooped low to allow Samantha to climb onto his back. She jumped up and settled on a saddle strapped ahead of where his wings met his body. The wurl then looked at Oscar and gave him a soft growl.

"Okay," Oscar said, mostly to himself. He put the goggles on and adjusted the strap so they fit snugly. "Okay. I already did this once, though I was sort of dangly that time. I can do this. I can do this."

"Time is ticking."

Oscar clapped his hands, a gesture that appeared to surprise Doran, who raised his head. Oscar nearly lost his nerve at the sudden motion. He simply wasn't used to looking at wurl from so close without needing to fear for his life. Every single instinct in his body told him to run, and it took everything he had to walk forward until he was standing next to Doran.

He reached out gingerly and placed his hand on his scales.

They were warm. Hot, even. Oscar was surprised, and he realized that he had half expected Doran to be cold and slimy, but it was the opposite. The cobalt scales were warm to the touch, hard yet surprisingly yielding, almost like the composite polymer the colony used to make the armor for Patrol officers.

"Just go," Oscar whispered, trying to encourage himself. He grabbed on to Doran and jumped up. "Yaaah!"

He didn't jump far enough, and he bumped his knee against Doran's wing. The motion destabilized him, and he lost his balance. He crashed down to the ground in a puff of dust. Thankfully, the canvas bag on his back cushioned the impact enough that only his pride was wounded. His shoulder did hurt, though.

Samantha looked down on him and tilted her head slightly to the side. "Are all males that clumsy where you come from?"

"Sorry," Oscar grumbled, standing up again while trying to pat the dust away from his clothes. "I'm going to try again, okay? Doran, please don't eat me."

Now slightly more emboldened, since Doran hadn't attacked him, Oscar tried again and managed to jump up behind Samantha's saddle and steady himself.

"Hold on to my waist," she told him.

Oscar hesitated for a second. He hadn't realized how slender Samantha was until then. "Uh…."

The next instant, Oscar felt the muscles of Doran's back ripple, and the wurl launched himself into the sky.

"Aaaah!" Oscar yelled, holding tight to Samantha in a heartbeat. "I'm going to fall!"

"Hold on tight!" Samantha yelled back. "And open your eyes, in case you are closing them. The view is worth it."

Oscar opened his eyes, since he had been indeed clenching them shut, but he immediately closed them again when Doran rose higher into the sky. The motion got Oscar in the pit of his stomach, a sensation that was oddly like falling while never really reaching the ground. With every flap of Doran's powerful wings, Oscar felt himself rising. It brought unpleasant memories of when Dresde had carried him, but the sensations this time were different. He was not in pain. The wind wasn't howling in his face. He could breathe.

Slowly, Oscar opened his eyes one more time.

He gasped.

They were *very* high up. Oscar was assaulted by vertigo at seeing that the cliffs now looked small and Samantha's home was a tiny square almost immediately below them.

"Oh," he said softly. "Oh no."

Samantha moved her right leg ever so slightly, and Doran responded to the motion by turning to face the rising sun. Oscar panicked again and held tight, using his legs as well as his arms to try and anchor himself. The fact that he slid just a bit when Doran turned scared him even more. He had read about the roller coasters of Earth, and he had always wondered what it would have been like to ride one.

Now he knew, and he did not like it one bit.

"Doran, go!" Samantha shouted, and Oscar was slightly taken aback at the almost joyful tone in her voice.

Doran roared in response, opened his wings to their fullest extent, and sped forward like a missile through the wind.

The landscape below blurred by. Oscar decided to avoid looking down because all it did was scare him even more and make him dizzy, and he did not want to throw up if he could help it. Instead he looked straight ahead, past Samantha's whipping braid, and tried to focus on a cloud or something that would not move so fast or so much. It helped, in fact, and after a few minutes he was able to relax more. Doran was flying fast, but his motion was quite steady. Oscar no longer felt like he would slide down to his death at any moment.

"That is the Field of Thorns," Samantha shouted. The wind whipped away her words, but Oscar was able to understand her. "Below us!"

Oscar told himself that he wasn't going to look down, but curiosity got the best of him and he did.

He was pleasantly surprised to find that he did not feel like throwing up anymore. Doran slowed down as well, and Oscar was able to see the place that Samantha called the Field of Thorns. It was a crater-like chasm, enormous, fully overgrown by thick brambles that all ended in glassy thorns that reflected the light of the morning sun like miniature prisms. The brambles themselves were completely black, and the result was a mesmerizing and beautiful interplay of every color in the visible spectrum, swathes of vibrant color splashed onto a black canvas. The place looked almost like a work of art, and Oscar was sorry to leave it behind a few minutes later.

"It was beautiful!" he shouted.

"We can go there later today if we finish early!" Samantha yelled. "We are headed over *there*. Hold on again!"

Oscar did, and not a moment too soon. Although Samantha had not issued a verbal command, Doran appeared to know where Samantha wanted him to land, because he tipped his body forward and began to descend in long, easy spirals. The dizziness came back, and Oscar gritted his teeth and closed his eyes until a gentle *thud* told him they were back on solid ground.

"Here we are," Samantha said, speaking softly in the sudden calm. After the constant noise of the wind, the world seemed almost preternaturally quiet. "Climb down."

Oscar tried his best, but after all that motion, the lack thereof confused him, and he ended up crashing back down to the ground, although less spectacularly than before. He had just gotten back on his feet when Doran jumped into the air with shocking speed, blasted them both with a gust of air, and took off into the sky.

"He's abandoning us here!" Oscar protested as he took off the goggles.

"Not to worry," Samantha told him. "He will be back in the afternoon."

"How do you know? What if he never comes back?"

Samantha actually paused for a moment, as if considering. "I am… not sure. But I know. Doran understands me very well, even without words. Sometimes I even think he understands me better than most people do."

Oscar noticed Samantha appeared to be either embarrassed or annoyed that she had said something so personal, and instead she looked away, gesturing all around them.

"These are the Nightmare Caves," she said. "We can find food here, but be careful. There are things hiding in the dark."

"Okay, that didn't sound creepy at all."

"Most creatures will leave you alone if you do the same," Samantha told him.

Oscar looked around. They were in the midst of a rocky landscape dotted with yawning dark openings into the many tall hillsides. Some of the holes were small, barely big enough for a person to crawl through. In the distance and above him on the sides of imposing hills, Oscar could make out larger cave mouths, all of them black and full of shadows. The air felt cooler too, with the hint of a scent similar to mineral salts and moist earth, which was not altogether unpleasant. The strange quiet continued, however. He could hear no buzzing insects at all, and there was no real wind, so the leaves on the slender, oddly twisted trees that grew at random intervals did not move at all. The bark of the trees was white, but their leaves were black.

The cave closest to them was maybe ten meters away. It was one of the smaller ones. The entrance was ringed with cracked boulders of various sizes, although the rocks all had a peculiar banding on their surface. They almost reminded Oscar of the conduit lines on a motherboard, since they were oddly regular and parallel to each other.

There was the tiniest shuffling noise coming from that cave. Oscar looked more closely. Samantha was busy taking some things out of the pack she carried, and she had not noticed.

The shuffle repeated itself, and something moved in the shadows.

Oscar shivered. "Samantha?"

"Yes?"

"Uh…." Oscar pointed at the cave. The thing peered out of the cave and then stepped slowly into the light, revealing a muscular six-legged body. Although it stood no taller than Oscar's knee, the way it stalked forward was unmistakably threatening. On the front of its body was a fanged, segmented maw, and its eye cluster, white and glassy, seemed almost malevolent. It reminded Oscar of a wolf, but covered by horrible exposed muscle fibers instead of fur. "What's that thing?"

Samantha stood up and stepped back.

There was no time for anything else. The creature snarled and jumped at them with teeth bared and claws outstretched.

chapter 11.
thrum

"ELIAS? ELIAS, wake up!"

Bright sunlight. Elias came to, blinking. He tried to open his eyes, but the sun blinded him.

"What are you doing here?" Tristan demanded.

Elias raised his left arm to block out the sun. He groaned. "What... what time is it?"

"It's past sunrise. And you're lying on the beach."

The fog of sleep blew away in the sharp gust of a half-forgotten memory.

The light in the dark water. The blue light.

Elias sat up, fully awake. Tristan knelt next to him with a worried expression on his face. Narev was also nearby, standing close to him like a guardian. The other two wurl were pacing back and forth by the beach.

"What happened?" Elias asked, realizing his back was sore.

"That's what I'd like you to tell me," Tristan said. "I woke up a few minutes ago and didn't see you. Then I come out and you're here, lying in the middle of the beach, not moving. I thought...." Tristan looked away.

"I'm okay, don't worry," Elias reassured him as he reached for Tristan's hand. He was trying to remember, but the memory fled the more he tried to catch it. "I think I had… a dream."

Narev nuzzled his hand. Siv and Vanor had their spines flared out as if an enemy were approaching.

"How did you get here?"

"I don't know. Maybe I was sleepwalking?"

"You sleepwalk?"

"This would be the first time," Elias admitted. "What's going on? Why are the wurl all worked up?"

"No idea. It's not a Flyer. I don't see any. Might be one of those horrible Singers, but I guess we can't know, can we? With them being invisible and all."

"My dream…." Elias began. "There was light. In the water. Someone screamed, I think. Or something."

"Are you sure it was a dream?" Tristan asked him with a meaningful look.

Elias shook his head slowly. "I don't know. It was weird."

"Come on. Let's get you back to the tent."

"I'm okay, Tristan. Really. Let's prepare breakfast."

"You sure?"

"I'm sure."

Although all five of them were on high alert for the better part of the morning, nothing alarming happened. Eventually, Siv and Vanor stopped pacing, and Narev stopped following Elias around while radiating concern for him. By noon, Siv and Vanor had gone off into the trees, presumably to hunt, but Narev stayed resolutely by the beach, looking out over the water. Every now and then he would growl, sounding menacing and threatening, completely unlike his usual friendly self. He would also glance back at Elias from time to time as if to make sure Elias was still there.

For their part, Elias and Tristan occupied themselves with making the boat ready for the trip. Elias went to the river one last time for a fresh supply of drinkable water. Then they finished packing everything they would need and made a final inventory of all their tools, supplies, gear, and electronics. When everything was accounted for, the two of them carried the boat to the beach, close to the water but away from the reach of the waves.

"What if they're waiting for us in the water?" Tristan asked as he tied the boat to a large boulder. "I've never seen Narev act like that. He just won't relax."

"If they are, we'll need to face them," Elias replied. He had also been thinking about that but had come up with no solution except going. "We're not helpless, and they're not invulnerable."

"I wish we knew more about them. What they can do, how they attack. It's awful, waiting for something but not knowing what it is. At least with the Flyers we know when they're coming."

"I know."

Tristan bent down to reach into the boat and fasten a jug of water to the bottom. When he was done, he stood up with a sigh. "Why are things like this, do you think?" Tristan asked.

"What do you mean?"

Tristan gestured all around, encompassing the world with one hand. "All of this. Why are wurl constantly at each other's throats? They don't prey on each other. They could all live in peace. You're the biologist here. Tell me, does it make sense?"

Elias considered the question. "Each wurl kind seems to be the apex predator of their respective ecosystem. The Spine wurl here, the Flyers on Raasay, and the Singers in the Dyresian Ocean. You're right—they don't really prey on each other. Sometimes in nature large predators of different species will fight with one another over access to resources, like food or territory."

"Yeah, but that's not the case here. You just said it: everybody has their own ecosystem. And I've never seen wurl fight over food. They fight... they kind of fight like humans, you know? They fight to kill."

"Yes. I think it's because of the wurl queens and their conflict. Sizzra was born with the directive imprinted on her to fight and kill the two Others, as she called them. I assume it's the same for Dresde and the Singer queen."

"It doesn't seem right to me, even though I don't know a lot about nature," Tristan argued. "This world is all about balance, right? That's what you kept saying when you took the Life Seed. You wanted to return the world to the equilibrium it once had."

"That's true."

"But if it's all about balance, why are wurl constantly at war? It doesn't make any sense."

Elias took a moment before he answered. Tristan was making some good points, but he was right: his knowledge of biology wasn't as broad as Elias's own. "Some organisms are very intolerant of others, even if they are the same kind. Some social insects are that way, like Terran ants. If a strange ant wanders into a foreign ant colony, the soldiers of the colony will tear it apart. Sometimes entire colonies go to war with one another."

"But wurl aren't ants. They're intelligent."

"Yes, but they are similar to eusocial insects, at least superficially. There is one dominant female at the top of the hierarchy. It's obviously not the same. Most social insects on the planets I know about do have a queen, but the only thing she does is lay eggs. She doesn't really control the other members of the colony and behaves more like a walking reproductive system. With wurl, though, the queens do control all of the males to some extent."

"So wurl are constantly wanting to kill each other because of the queens, like Sizzra," Tristan concluded, sounding dissatisfied.

Elias shrugged. "I suppose. I have no idea. Even though we are learning more about this place all the time, for all intents and purposes it's still an alien world, Tristan. There are many things we don't understand. Maybe that's just the way it is, the way it's always been."

"And the end goal is for one of the queens to kill the others and all of their offspring?" Tristan asked.

"I think so."

"But then why was Dresde unable to break the egg? Remember? You told me how you saw her trying to crush it. She couldn't do it."

Elias hadn't forgotten. "I know, and I can't explain it. I don't think she can either. Dresde got very upset when she realized she couldn't break it."

"Maybe now she's waiting for the egg to break on its own. Do you think she will spare the new Spine queen when she hatches?"

"No," Elias answered with complete certainty. Of that, at least, his mind harbored no doubt. "Dresde will kill the new Spine queen the moment she sees an opportunity to do so. To her, this is war."

"It all feels wrong, somehow," Tristan complained. "All the fighting, the hatred over nothing. But never mind. Let's practice fighting for a little bit ourselves and then do a final check for the trip tomorrow."

"Sounds good."

They went through their training routine, which normally offered Elias a chance to unwind. This time, though, his mind was occupied with the things Tristan had said. He thought about balance and about the age-old conflict between the most powerful creatures on his world.

Even with his mind somewhere else, he was able to dodge most of Tristan's attacks, weaving out of the way and coming in with a retaliatory strike every now and then. Elias realized that his connection to other living things ran deep, and it was sharpening day by day. He could sort of sense Tristan tensing as he prepared to bring his shock spear down in an arc over his head, and he knew he had to sidestep to avoid being hit. When Tristan bent low to jab his spear forward, Elias used Sizzra's spine to block the thrust and pivoted on his left foot in an agile twirl that left him standing to Tristan's right, where he could not retaliate. Elias lifted the spine high in the air and was about to bring it down when Tristan crashed into him with his shoulder, destabilizing him. Instead of falling to the ground, however, Elias allowed the force to sweep through him and did not fight it. Instead he jumped back at the last second in order to allow the momentum of Tristan's shoulder tackle to propel him farther away from harm. His body appeared to move almost before he was able to process what to do through conscious thought. The physical exertion freed his mind and lifted some of the worry off his shoulders.

When they were done, Elias and Tristan were both drenched in sweat.

"I don't even know what to say," Tristan commented, cleaning his shock spear with care. "Soon you'll be able to beat me."

"I like our training," Elias replied, reaching behind him to put the spine in the makeshift scabbard he had made to carry it with ease. "It helps me think. And it's kind of like dancing in a way. You move in, I move out. I attack, you defend."

As he said so, Elias stepped forward until he was very close to Tristan. He placed his hands around Tristan's waist and drew him in close. Elias touched his forehead to Tristan's. He closed his eyes and enjoyed the sensation of Tristan's body so close to his own, feeling the way Tristan's chest rose and fell as he panted, still recovering from the exercise. Tristan's forehead was cool, but his body radiated warmth.

Tristan lifted his hands and placed them over Elias's chest. Elias opened his eyes, looking at Tristan so close to him, and he experienced a brief moment of joy.

I'm so happy. Right now, right this second.

"I'm so lucky to have you," Elias whispered.

Tristan smiled and kissed him gently. "I'm even luckier to have you."

A low growl off to the left jolted Elias back to reality. Glancing in the direction of the beach, he saw that Narev was still standing guard, spines quivering with tension, looking out over the water.

"Let's finish packing up," Tristan suggested.

"Yeah. Let's."

By nightfall everything was ready. They had decided to leave early in the morning the next day, and they had a relatively small dinner. Elias was nervous, and he supposed Tristan was too. Elias wasn't sure whether to feel excited that they were finally going to attempt to cross the ocean or dismayed at how unprepared they were. The scale of what they were attempting to do was not lost on him: in ancient times, people had prepared for voyages at sea for weeks and weeks on end, and they would cross oceans on huge ships that could hold supplies to last for months.

The two of them were going to attempt to cross on a boat that was barely big enough for them to sit side by side, with no real way to cover long distances except for the three tireless wurl that would hopefully not abandon them in the middle of the sea. After the island stop, Elias had no idea how they would get drinking water over the long trek that awaited them, aside from distilling a very small quantity of drinkable liquid at a time using the condenser they would carry with them.

It seemed foolhardy, and Elias was scared that they were trying to do something that was too much for them. Nevertheless, it was the only thing they could do.

We have to try.

As they made preparations to go to sleep in the cave for the last time, Elias walked back out to check on Narev. The wurl had barely moved from his sentry position by the beach. He still growled every now and then, a sound like two metal plates grinding against one another, which in the past would have made Elias's blood run cold.

"Hey, buddy," Elias said, stopping next to Narev. "What's going on?"

Narev looked at Elias briefly but then turned his attention back to the ocean. His unblinking red gaze would have been unnerving if Elias had not known Narev so well.

"Is there something out there?"

Elias accompanied the question with his best attempt at a mental query, but Narev responded only with brief confusion and a vague sense of watchfulness and suppressed aggression aimed at the ocean. Elias shrugged, realizing that his ability to communicate with male wurl had its limits.

Glancing back, Elias saw that Siv and Vanor had already settled down for the night, curling up next to the cave. Tristan's dark outline moved about in the tent. The sound of the surf was rhythmical and somehow comforting. The faint buzzing of insects in the summer night gave the air a quality of vibrant life that Elias thought he would never get used to, having grown up in a world that was slowly dying.

And yet, in spite of all of this, something was wrong with the night. Elias looked out over the dark surface of the ocean.

"It's a Singer, isn't it?" Elias asked Narev in a whisper. In his mind, Elias pictured the tentacled beast they had seen weeks ago. A clammy shudder ran through him in spite of himself.

Narev answered with another low growl. It was as clear a *yes* as any.

"We can't do anything about them, though," Elias continued. "When they come we'll have to be ready. For now, though, we should rest. *You* should rest. Tomorrow is a big day."

Elias received a brief and friendly acknowledgment, but Narev did not move from his position. Resigned, Elias walked back to the cave and went inside the tent.

"Is Narev still out there?" Tristan asked. He had been putting his toothbrush away in a neat package, presumably to take with him in the morning.

"Yes, and he's not moving."

"Maybe it's for the best. That way if one of them comes we'll know."

"I suppose," Elias said, taking off his pants. "I just... I don't know. Something feels wrong. This place, this cave. It felt like home for a while, but now it feels… oppressive."

"Tomorrow we're out of here. We'll finally be making progress. Whatever is wrong here, we'll leave it behind."

"Yeah. I suppose you're right."

"Let's get some rest," Tristan suggested. "Come on, lie down next to me. Tonight you get to be the little spoon. You fall asleep faster that way."

Elias smiled. He finished undressing and settled down next to Tristan. Sleep came quickly, and his dreams were peaceful for most of the night.

Until they weren't.

A shiver woke Elias up. He was dizzy for a moment. He looked around, not really knowing where he was.

Thrum. Thrum.

He sat up, and memories arranged themselves. He was inside the tent. He had been sleeping. And….

Thrum. Thrum.

A sound. Except it was not a sound. It was more like a low-frequency beat, resonant, traveling through the ground and into his mind.

Thrum. Thrum.

"Tristan. Wake up."

"Uh…."

"Wake up. Something's wrong."

Without waiting for Tristan, Elias grabbed his spine and crawled from the tent, blinking in the dim light of early dawn. As soon as he was out, the resonant sound stopped.

Tristan came out of the tent with a grunt of protest. Elias looked all around, trying to see whether anything was missing. Vanor and Siv were still sleeping sound-ly next to the tent. There were no animals nearby, no

Flyers in the air. Narev was still sitting at the edge of the water, watching. He was as still as a statue.

Thrum.

It was like a physical blow. Elias had been about to take a step, but he staggered. Tristan's arms steadied him.

"What's that?" Tristan asked.

The two sleeping wurl uncoiled their bodies and looked around.

Thrum.

Vanor and Siv growled.

"It's getting closer," Elias said. He scanned the ocean and spotted something. "Look, Tristan. Look at the water."

There was a large disturbance on the surface of the water, approaching quickly. Nothing seemed to be making it, however. It was just... there.

Thrum. Thrum.

The disturbance stopped, and the ripples from its passage faded. The low-frequency waves were almost painful now, coming from nowhere and everywhere at the same time.

"What...," Tristan started to say. He did not finish his sentence.

Narev, who had remained motionless up to that point, suddenly jumped up and roared. The other two wurl were close behind, and they all charged, snarling, attacking something invisible.

THRUM.

Vanor and Siv stopped in their tracks. Elias had been about to move after them, but his feet wouldn't obey him. He tried again, but the sound was still in his mind, reverberating, maddening. He couldn't move. The sound wouldn't allow it.

No. Not a sound, Elias realized. *This is a song.*

Elias was reduced to watching as Narev jumped into the water. Of all of them, he alone had not been affected by the sound. There was a big splash as Narev dipped below the waves. He resurfaced a moment later and powered ahead, swimming faster than Elias had ever seen him go.

And he kept swimming. At first Elias thought Narev was heading for whatever invisible attacker was nearby. When moments turned into minutes, though, Narev's outline became a dot in the distance. Then it disappeared entirely.

He's abandoning us, Elias thought desperately. Then he realized Narev would not do that. Someone— something—had made him.

All at once, the spell broke and Elias staggered forward.

"Narev," Elias shouted, running to the edge of the water. "Come back!"

"Elias, be careful!"

Siv and Vanor rushed forward too, stopping barely out of the reach of the waves. They were looking left and right, as if trying to locate the invisible Singer they all knew was there.

"Show yourself!" Elias demanded, slashing at the air with his spine. "Stop being such a coward!"

Something moved in the shallows, much closer than Elias had expected. The water parted as if something were pushing through it.

THRUM.

The thing rose out of the water and decloaked. He was large, as big as Vanor, but his neck was freakishly long, sinuous, and adorned by hanging strands of something that looked like kelp. His triangular head was monstrous, clearly visible now against the light of the rising sun. Three red eyes crowned his forehead, like those of any other wurl, but his jaw was nothing like that of Spine or Flyer. It hung partially open, segmented in three, and its gaping inside surface was riddled with needle-like teeth from which drooled a thick and viscous liquid.

The Singer gave a mighty push and propelled his body forward until it was almost out of the water. The suddenness of his motion created a miniature wave that surged against Elias's legs, but Elias scarcely noticed.

This is not a juvenile, he realized with a sinking heart. *This is a fully grown male.*

The creature he had seen several nights ago had been smaller, much more limber. This new creature was larger, stronger looking, and radiated an aura of confidence and power. His body was covered in scales of different shades of light green and aqua that made it difficult to follow his outline against the water. Protrusions that looked like fins on his back were also covered by the dark-green kelp strands that hung from his neck. His tail was long, almost as long as his entire body, and the wurl flicked it once across the water with shocking speed, almost as if flaunting his strength.

It was the tentacles, though, that drew Elias's terrified gaze.

The creature's body was supported by six tentacles that took the place of his legs. They were hefty and muscular, like his neck and his tail, and they looked deadly. Even in the growing light of the rising sun, spots along the entire length of the tentacles glowed softly with a yellow-green luminescence that made them entrancing to look at. The Singer appeared to stand easily on the beach, using his appendages like legs, and when a particularly large wave receded, exposing the majority of his body, Elias was caught between terror and awe.

There was something about this creature that was different from other wurl. Barnacles encrusted his back, as if granting him armor that had grown over decades. His wicked disjointed maw advertised the fact that this was a being of the depths, a thing that was used to absolute domination of his environment. Even now, almost fully on land, the Singer showed no fear whatsoever.

Standing on either side of Elias, Siv and Vanor had apparently had enough. They roared with an ear-splitting synchronized shriek, and even the Singer wurl hesitated, lowering his neck to look at his land-bound counterparts. As he did, Elias saw something odd. There was a silver spine sticking out from the side of the Singer's neck, near its base. By its length and girth, Elias knew that the spine belonged to Narev.

Elias had a fleeting memory of standing neck-deep in the ocean at night, surrounded by blue biolumines-cence. Something had flown past his ear, striking... striking this Singer, who had been trying to lure him to his death.

In the aftermath of the shriek from the Spine wurl, the Singer pushed back with all six tentacles, spraying them with a mixture of water and stinging sand. The motion propelled his body back to the shelter of the water and made both Vanor and Siv stumble. As the water enveloped him, the Singer opened his triangular maw like a carnivorous plant unfolding its deadly flow-er. Elias expected a roar of defiance.

Instead, there came a song.

It was a deep thrumming that threaded itself through Elias's consciousness, rhythmical, deep, irre-sistible. It spoke of the eternal permanence of the ocean and of the inevitability of waves crashing against the beach. It was simple but undeniable, like the beat of the heart that pumped blood through Elias's body.

Thrum. Thrum.

Its echoes reverberated in the empty chambers of Elias's mind, which had been cleared of any other thought. There was nothing to do but listen to the song. It had always been there, and it would always be there. It was simplicity itself. It was—

Narev. They took Narev.

The thought skewered the cacophony in Elias's mind.

I have to fight this. The Singer is not getting away.

The spine in Elias's hand tingled, and from it Elias registered clarity. It spread through his body like an electric shock, jolting him awake.

"No!" he shouted, raising his weapon in the air. "You won't get awa—"

The creature was gone.

"Watch out!" Tristan shouted next to Elias. "Watch ou—where is it?"

Vanor was partially in the water, looking around as if confused. Siv stood farther back, spines flared, but his anger had no target.

"It's gone," Elias said, his voice heavy with dismay. "It kept us frozen in place and swam away."

"What if it's still here?" Tristan asked, his hands bunched into fists. He hadn't even had time to get his shock spear. "What if it's back to being invisible?"

Elias shook his head. "Even if it's invisible, you can still see its body moving in the water. Tristan, the Singer lured Narev away. We have to go. We need to go now!"

Tristan nodded. "Right. Where?"

"That way," Elias answered with complete certainty. It was faint, but he could still sense Narev's presence. "Let's get in the boat. We won't let them kill him."

There was no need to say anything else. Elias and Tristan packed the last few things they would need into the boat with nearly choreographed efficiency. Both Vanor and Siv appeared to understand that their cooperation would be needed, and they helped push the boat all the way to the edge of the water. Then they allowed Elias and Tristan to tie long, sturdy ropes around their necks.

After the tethers had been secured to both wurl and boat, Elias and Tristan pushed the vessel fully into the water and climbed aboard, managing not to spill any of its precious contents.

Following Elias's mental nudge, both wurl waded into the water. They swam ahead until the ropes connecting them to the boat grew taut, but they experienced a brief moment of confusion. Wurl had never done what they were about to do.

Elias took Tristan's hand. He looked ahead at the horizon, which was burning with shades of pink and red as the sun rose over the water, and he focused his attention on the fading mental echoes of Narev.

Go. Swim, he told the wurl, projecting the urgency of their situation. *Find him!*

chapter 12.
thorns

THE CREATURE sailed through the air, still snarling, in an arc to where Oscar was standing.

"Stand back!" Samantha shouted and snatched something out of her pack. A water bottle.

Oscar shuffled to the side as the creature landed less than two meters away from them and prowled sideways, now focused entirely on Samantha. She, in turn, took a combat stance and held the water bottle like a sword.

Oscar could barely breathe. The creature took a couple of steps, turning its head clockwise in a very odd motion that was accompanied by the threatening gnashing of its bony maw. Samantha did not move but stood at the ready as the creature took another step to the left and then another. The tips of its fangs glistened, and something similar to saliva, but oddly dark red, dripped from its mouth.

The creature attacked with no warning, and Oscar could not even scream. It lunged at Samantha, who appeared to have been expecting the assault. She whipped the water bottle forward and slammed it expertly against the side of the creature's head, hard enough that Oscar heard a *crack*, although whether it had been the bottle or the creature's skull, he could not tell in the midst of the loud yelping that followed.

The creature tumbled to the ground, snarled again, and then turned tail and ran. It disappeared up the side of one of the hills and got lost amid the tree trunks. After it was gone, all that was left was a small pool of its saliva.

"Are you okay?" Oscar asked, concerned.

"Yes," Samantha replied, examining the water bottle. "It was merely a forest hound."

"What if it comes back? What if it has friends?"

Samantha held the bottle up to the sun and sighed, apparently relieved. "Thank goodness. I thought I had cracked it."

"Samantha? What if it comes back?"

She focused on him. "Oh, no need to worry about that. Forest hounds are solitary. This one will not return, I can assure you."

"I thought you said creatures here would leave us alone if we left them alone? What was that all about? Is something going to come out of that cave and try to kill us?"

Samantha shook her head. "It must have been very hungry. I have been here many times, and I have rarely been attacked. I should have brought my spear, though. Just in case."

"Your *spear*?" Oscar asked, disbelieving at first. Then he suddenly remembered the yult-wood spears he had seen in what was now his room.

"I had one the day we attacked Portree," Samantha explained. "It is a good weapon to use when I ride Doran because of its long reach."

"And you casually know all of this cool combat stuff because...."

Samantha shrugged. "I have practiced using weapons since I was young. I was taught from an early age."

"Okay. Wow. At an early age I was taught how to make pictures with glue and macaroni."

Samantha looked as if she were about to crack a smile, but she appeared to contain herself. "In any case, here we are. Follow me. There is work to be done."

Oscar went after Samantha as they trudged up one of the nearby hills, where they approached a particularly large, forbidding, dark cave opening.

Oscar stopped a few steps away from the cave since Samantha appeared to have every intention of going in. "Um, Samantha?"

"Yes?" she asked, turning back. The sun had risen in the sky, and its warm light made Samantha's obsidian-black hair glisten.

"Why are these called the Nightmare Caves?"

She gestured with her head, indicating the cave. "Come in. You'll see."

"I don't like this," Oscar whispered to himself, but as Samantha disappeared inside the cave, he realized that he could either follow or be left out in the open, alone, exposed to whatever other creatures might come. He decided to go in.

The difference in temperature was apparent after just a few steps. It was much cooler inside the cave, although it was quite dark. Oscar clicked his link's flashlight on.

"Turn that off!" Samantha exclaimed.

Click.

"Whoops. Sorry, why do we have to be in the dark?"

"I never use light here," she explained. "I do not know whether anything living here will be bothered by the light."

"Again, not helping to reduce the creepiness factor," Oscar grumbled. "How do you even find your way around, then?"

"Bioluminescent beetles," she said. "Here, take my hand so you do not get lost. It is not far to the first clearing."

"Um...." Oscar hesitated a bit, suddenly nervous about taking Samantha's hand, and she stepped closer and took his left in her right. He realized her hand was smaller than his, although he could tell there was significant strength in her grip.

They began walking, going slowly but in a definite direction. The darkness around them grew, but it never was pitch-black. The air smelled fresh inside the cave, and there was a persistent and gentle breeze blowing past both of them that hadn't been apparent outside.

"Watch your step," Samantha instructed. Her voice echoed in the chamber, which sounded as though it was large. "Use the beetles to guide you."

There were indeed many small beetles with triangular bodies crawling about, giving off a gentle blue glow. Although not very bright, they at least indicated where there was a rock or a solid surface, and Oscar managed not to trip or fall as he stepped after Samantha, reassured by the fact that she was holding his hand.

Before long, Oscar saw literal light at the end of the tunnel, and he realized they were almost out of the cave.

At that moment the howling began.

The gentle breeze that had been blowing past him picked up speed and became a buffeting wind in a couple of seconds. At the same time, an unearthly sound of moaning that sounded like a hungry ghost vibrated through the cave, bounding off the walls and creating echo after echo in such a way that the howling seemed to be all around him, as though Oscar and Samantha were surrounded by specters intent on touching them with their clammy, dead hands.

"Oh man," Oscar said. "That's not an animal, is it?"

"Only the cave," Samantha reassured him.

"How long is it going to last?"

Samantha did not reply, and the two of them waited in silence as the howling multiplied around them. Eventually, though, the wind died down and the creepy sound ended.

"The wind in the caves makes the howling noise," Samantha explained. "My ancestors named these the Nightmare Caves because of the sound, obviously. All of the tunnels and spaces in the limestone rocks of this region are interconnected with one another. Everywhere you go, the wind follows. You can hear the howling here, at the edge of the network of caves, or much deeper in. I have explored the caves very thoroughly. I have even found…."

"Found what?"

"Not important. Now you know why we call them this."

"Right. Can we go, like, to the light? The darkness is creeping me out big-time, and all this ghost stuff is not my thing."

"Of course."

When they finally exited the cave, Oscar was forced to cover his eyes from the glare of the sun after the darkness from before. His eyes teared up as they got used to the light again.

"How come all of these places have names?" he asked, rubbing his face.

"What do you mean?"

"Well, back when I was in prison, I asked you about your food, and you said you guys don't name your food. How come these places *do* have names?"

Samantha paused for a moment, as if thinking of the answer. "I suppose it is because the names here are very old. My ancestors named the Nightmare Caves, the Field of Thorns, and other places too."

Oscar opened his eyes, finally used to the light. "And what happened to them? Your ancestors? Why is it only you guys left here?"

Samantha gave him a quick look that could have been filled with anger, sadness, or something else entirely. "Help me collect food."

"Okay," Oscar said, deciding not to push the subject. "Where?"

"Here. We are surrounded by food."

Oscar looked more closely. He realized they were in a rugged, irregular clearing of sorts amid the network of caves, with a roughly cylindrical skylight above them, spanning the breadth of the clearing. A few plants clung to the edges of the rocky walls that encircled them, and above those Oscar could see the bright-blue morning sky quite clearly. It appeared to him as though the clearing they were in was a huge sinkhole that had opened up in the hillside above, or perhaps someone or something had tunneled straight down until they reached the floor of the clearing in which they stood.

The opening itself, about thirty meters in diameter, was full of life. The rocky ground of the caves was broken and cracked, and from the interstices there grew plants that looked like ferns, but twisted around themselves, reaching up to about waist height. Their trunks were bright blue, almost the same hue as the bioluminescent beetles. Hanging from the trunks were clusters of fruit, trios of plump orbs that were a darker blue than the plants themselves. Near the back of the clearing, an enormous tree grew out of the rock, appearing to essentially have burst out of the wall a couple of meters above them, its trunk extending horizontally for a little bit before the tree had suddenly shifted direction and begun growing skyward again. This tree had many thick branches that turned and twisted at odd ninety-degree angles from which hung larger fruit, oblong yellow objects that looked to be about as big as Oscar's hand.

"Help me," Samantha repeated. "We should collect as much as we can. The grapes are in season, and they are very good."

"These are grapes?" Oscar asked, walking close to one of the blue ferns. He poked one of the round globules of fruit experimentally.

"Not true Terran grapes, obviously. But they resemble them, correct? At least that is what I learned."

"Kind of. I think my aunt experimented with grape DNA at one point."

"Really?"

"Oh yes. Remember I told you about the genetic experiments with the Life Seed? Eli used to spend a lot of time with my aunt before his whole loner, abandoned-lab phase. My aunt did lots of experiments. Very complicated. I never understood anything."

"I find it so hard to believe," Samantha observed, looking up at the sky as if checking for something.

"That I never understood anything?"

"That you have such technology still," she clarified.

"Oh. Ouch."

"That does not mean I think you are incapable of understanding things," she told him. "From what I can see, you appear to be smart."

"Tell *that* to my dad," Oscar said. "He keeps grilling me about Fourier transforms, and I swear I'm never going to get the math through my head."

"I enjoy applied mathematics."

"I know I already sort of asked, but why do you talk like that?" Oscar asked, unable to help himself.

"Like what?"

"You're way too formal. It sounds weird. You talk like my grandma."

Samantha raised her eyebrows. "This is the way I have always spoken."

"Right. So how do I know which grapes are good to pick?"

Samantha showed him how to choose ripe grapes and also good fruit from the big tree, which she called a sweetpod. Together they spent nearly two hours picking fruit, occasionally eating some of it. Both the grapes and the sweetpods were quite tasty, although in different ways. The grapes, unlike their Terran analogs, were somewhat bitter but had an umami undertone that was pleasant and satisfying. The sweetpods, true to their name, were very sweet and fleshy inside. They barely had any seeds, and their oddly spiral-shaped peel was easily opened. To Oscar they seemed almost like improved bananas.

He made sure to stash the fruit he did pick carefully in his pack, and by the end of the second hour he had a sizable load secured.

"This is much faster with two people," Samantha observed, zipping up her pack. "It would have normally taken me around half the day to do this."

"So you come here alone?"

A now-familiar shadow swept across Samantha's features. "Now I do. It is not advisable for Laurie to come this far, not now that she is pregnant, and she has never liked to ride Doran to begin with."

"Oh," Oscar answered gently. He couldn't hold the next words back. "I'm so sorry, Samantha."

She looked at him sharply again, but this time Oscar held her gaze without flinching. He wasn't even completely certain what he was sorry about, but he did know that Samantha had lost her brother, Jörgen, somehow, and he could tell that she was sad. She reminded him a little bit of Elias, back when he had been so preoccupied about hiding his true self from his family and the rest of the world that he had distanced himself from the people he loved.

Samantha opened her mouth as though she was about to say something, but then closed it again. The two of them stood together, sharing an uncomfortable silence while the howling in the caves resumed as another miniature gale began to blow. Oscar realized Samantha looked as though she was trying not to cry.

"There is still time," she said suddenly, her voice brittle. "We should go gather some algae while we can. Follow me."

Oscar did not say anything else for the moment, but as he followed Samantha deeper into the caves, he was thoughtful. He had been so busy being terrified for his own sake that he had not even stopped to consider what life must have been like for Samantha and her family.

They obviously fear Dresde. What did she do? Why is Samantha's house so big when there are only four people living there? Was everyone else killed?

The two of them walked hand in hand for nearly an hour in darkness broken only by the luminescence of the beetles. Oscar had no idea how Samantha knew which way to go. After the first three turns, he was utterly and completely lost. He was fairly certain that his link would be able to retrace his steps and show him the way out, but Samantha did not have a link.

"You explored all of these caves on your own?" Oscar asked eventually, taking advantage of a lull in the howling that had echoed around them a few moments earlier.

"Some, yes. The lake I am leading you to was something I discovered two years ago."

"And you weren't scared? You know, of getting lost down here?"

"I have a good memory," she said to him. She was still holding his hand as she walked forward with confident steps.

"The path we are following, it's going down, isn't it?"

"Yes."

Oscar concentrated on walking and not stumbling, although he realized there were barely any rocks or other tripping hazards around.

"How come there are so few rocks? It almost seems like a path."

"I cleared the path, little by little," Samantha answered. "I find it makes it easier for me when I come."

Oscar took a moment to imagine himself alone, in near darkness and with no link or any form of making light, patiently clearing rocks for days and days at a time.

He shivered.

"Wow" was all he said.

At last they stopped, and Samantha clapped once. The sound echoed, but the reverberations were different. They sounded clearer, perhaps even louder.

"We have arrived," she said. "Look."

With a gentle tug forward, she encouraged Oscar to take a step, and he realized that he could see things in front of him.

No, not in front. Below.

Luminescent fish swam in the darkness. Most of them were quite large, with long dangling fins and spiny-looking whiskers, and they moved slowly, their ethereal white glow filtering up through what must have been water.

"This is the lake?" Oscar asked.

"Yes."

"How big is it?"

"I do not know," Samantha admitted. "There is a rocky wall to the left, and there is debris to the right, which has prevented me from circling the lake. I have not swum very far in it, either. There might be something dangerous in the water."

"Like those fish?" Oscar asked, pointing, although he could barely see his own finger. While the fish were easily visible, their glow was too weak to provide much light to their environment.

"They are harmless. Follow me. We can collect some algae from the shore over here." Samantha led him to a part of the lakeshore that was covered in loose gravel. "Take off your shoes. It will be faster if we wade in."

"In the water?"

"Yes," she confirmed. "You can see the seaweed floating there where the fish are swimming. It looks like black strands against their light. Take as much as you can, but do not go more than knee-deep."

"Sure," Oscar said, although he was anything but. However, Samantha let go of his hand, and soon there was the sound of splashing, so Oscar decided to follow suit. He took off his shoes and socks and waded into the water.

It was warm. He was surprised, as he had been expecting chilly cave water.

"Everything okay?" Samantha asked him.

"Yes. This is very nice, actually."

"Get started. If we finish quickly, we might have time to go to the Field of Thorns."

"I'm on it."

The two of them were done in about an hour and a half, a period of time Oscar enjoyed. He was scared of the fish at first, but they paid him no mind, even when one of them casually swam up against his leg. Pulling up the algae was very easy, and the temperature of the water made it almost feel like he was getting a foot bath. In fact, when Samantha said they were done, Oscar was almost sorry that it was over.

"Here, pack the seaweed in this," she said, giving him an old but serviceable vacuum-sealed bag to store the algae in so he would be able to stash it in his backpack without it leaking over the fruit from earlier.

"All done," Oscar reported after a few minutes.

"Very well. Put on your shoes and we can go."

As they made their way back, Oscar realized he was feeling much less apprehensive. He was getting used to the intermittent howling in the cave system, and he realized he was happy to help. He felt useful for the first time in many days.

"Is it always like this, with the food?" he asked.

"What do you mean?"

"Well, it's right here. We didn't even make a dent in the grapes or the sweetpods. It's still weird to me, seeing so much food, I guess."

"It is summer, so there are many wild plants growing that we can harvest. In the winter, however, it is much more difficult. Sometimes Doran and I have to fly for many days to get to a place where I can harvest something to eat."

"And you've never tried planting things near your home?"

Samantha sighed. "Even if Dresde did not destroy the little farms as soon as she saw them, it would be no good. It is the same here as it was in Portree. You told me about your colony and how you were running out of food because the plants on New Skye do not grow simply because you plant a seed. I think my ancestors tried agriculture at some point, but they also failed. We can only harvest what grows naturally, wherever it wants to grow. It has taken generations for us to find reliable places where we can get food throughout the year. In fact my mother tells me that before I befriended Doran, it was even worse. Since nobody could fly, we were left to walk, and even getting here would have taken days, not minutes. The Field of Thorns is almost impossible to cross on foot."

"I thought life was hard growing up in a little colony surrounded by hostile wurl, but you guys *really* have it hard here. It's amazing how you've been able to survive."

Samantha did not answer. They walked in silence the rest of the way out of the caves until they came to the place where Doran had dropped them off earlier in the day. It was late afternoon, and the midday heat had dissipated. The temperature was quite pleasant, and the smell of growing things, particularly noticeable after the cool mineral atmosphere of the caves, made Oscar smile. Seeing the world full of life as it was would never cease to amaze him.

"There is still time," Samantha said, looking up at the sun. "If you want, I can take you to the Field of Thorns."

"Of course! It looked awesome from the air."

"Appearances can be deceiving. We can go, but stay close in case another creature decides to jump at you from the shadows."

"Uh…," Oscar gulped, looking all about. Then he realized Samantha was very nearly smiling. "Wait. Was that a joke?"

"No. Although unlikely, we might come across another wild creature. I have seen orange hoppers a few times around here."

"Oh no. That was a joke. You *do* have a sense of humor. I knew it!"

Samantha shook her head. "Follow me, male."

The two of them walked for twenty-five minutes, according to Oscar's link, and came to a stop when the grassy landscape on which they had been walking gave way to a sudden break in terrain. On the other side of the divide, the land appeared blackened, as though a great fire had consumed everything and left no single speck of green in sight. There was a noticeable drop in elevation from where Oscar and Samantha were standing to the ground from which the Field of Thorns sprouted.

"What caused this, do you think?" Oscar asked.

"Unclear," Samantha replied. "Did you notice the circular shape of the depression from the air?"

"Yeah. It looked like a crater."

"That is my theory too. Perhaps a meteorite hit this region in the past and left a crater behind, after which the plants you see here began to grow."

"What *are* those plants? They look weird, even by New Skye standards."

"They are called glassthorns. For evident reasons."

"They are beautiful," Oscar said, taking a step forward until he was standing at the very edge of the divide in the landscape. "Wait. They are a bit… I don't know."

He looked more closely. Although the land a few meters below him was blackened and burned, thick vinelike plants grew from the ground and covered nearly every available square centimeter in odd geometric shapes that looked as though someone had taken a normal flexible stalk and decided to see how much it could be bent in on itself without breaking. The midnight-hued plants were very big, and their woody branches were as thick around as a grown man. From the air their size had not been apparent, but now that Oscar was standing next to them, he felt dwarfed by both their girth and their extension. The field they covered appeared to have no end, and from his earlier observations when he had been riding Doran, Oscar knew that the crater, if indeed it was that, was extremely large.

Then there were the thorns. The branches were black, but they were riddled with thick conical growths of a material that appeared to be glass. The combination of the dark wood and the thorns made Oscar think of bramble bushes that had been blown entirely out of proportion. However, these brambles looked sick. Despite the fact that the thorns acted like prisms and covered the black space with every color in the visible spectrum wherever they filtered sunlight, Oscar could not shake the sensation that there was something wrong with the glassthorns, or brambles, or whatever they were.

"They didn't grow right," he said, voicing his inner thoughts.

Samantha drew breath in sharply. "So you feel it too?"

"It's like… they're beautiful, sure. But—"

"But it's like these glassthorns are shrinking away from the sun," Samantha cut in. "Correct?"

Oscar nodded. "Exactly. Like they don't like the light."

"I have always wondered why nothing else grows on the blackened ground underneath the vines. If this is a crater, it must have been here for millions of years, given that an impact to make a crater of this size would have been catastrophic for the region. And yet there are no other plants, only these brambles."

"Have you ever touched one?" Oscar asked. He took a half step and realized he was stepping forward onto thin air. Samantha grabbed his arm and pulled him back.

"Do not get too close," she warned him. Then she whispered, as if afraid to voice her own thought, "At times I feel as though they, or something among them, is hungry. Maybe it is my imagination, but at night, when there is no sunlight to illuminate the thorns, the darkness around this place seems almost to reach out. All animals avoid this region. I wonder if they know something we do not."

Oscar looked in the direction of where he supposed the center of the crater would be. "Something...." His voice trailed off, and he made as if to take another step forward.

Samantha took his hand and led him a few meters away. "We should go back. Doran will be arriving soon."

Let me go! For an instant, Oscar thought about snatching his hand away from her. Then he blinked and looked at Samantha. "Yeah. Let's go wait for him," he said.

He followed her, walking away from the Field of Thorns, and only risked a look back when he was sure he would not be able to see the strange multicolored light amid the blackness of the crater anymore.

chapter 13.
trap

THE SALTWATER spray was blinding at the beginning. Elias had not been prepared for how the water splashed over the sides of the boat, but the waves near the shore made the going unsteady, and the two wurl propelling them forward were swimming so fast that the motion of their makeshift craft reminded Elias of videos he had seen of motorboats speeding through the water, leaving white foam in their wake.

After a few minutes, they were out in open water, and things settled down. There was less stinging spray, and Elias was able to see where they were going more clearly.

"Well, Vanor and Siv can *swim*!" Tristan exclaimed, sitting next to Elias.

Elias nodded but said nothing. He had his eyes fixed on the horizon, urgency pounding in his chest.

Narev. Hold on.

A hand landed on his shoulder. "Don't worry, Elias. We won't let them hurt him."

"Why did the Singer do this?" Elias asked, shielding his face from a random spurt of salty water. "Why not kill us all while we were frozen?"

Tristan shrugged. "Maybe they can't sing and attack at the same time. Who knows? Maybe they thought leading one of the Spine wurl away first would weaken us, make it easy to pick us off one by one."

Elias nodded grimly. "Maybe."

"Let's focus on the positive," Tristan said. "We're on the way. The wurl are swimming so fast that we are going to catch up in no time. And something really important and not to brag, but the boat is holding together."

"You're right," Elias said with a start. He touched the sides of the boat, the seat underneath him. Everything was steady. No water was leaking in. The supplies they had stashed were all in their right spots. "You did it, Tristan."

"*We* did it."

"No, this was you. I and the wurl helped, but only a little. Thank you, Tristan. Thanks to you, now we're at sea."

The sun had fully come out by then, and in the bright light of early morning, Elias looked all around him for the first time and realized something incredible.

"On the open ocean," Elias said, unable to stop the feeling of awe that crept into his heart despite everything else that was happening.

Tristan stood up in the boat. "Open ocean," Tristan echoed. "I can't believe it."

Elias stood up next to him, trying not to move too much so the boat would not be destabilized. Thankfully, Siv and Vanor were swimming in sync with one another as they surged through the water, not even coming up for air. They were, Elias realized, far better than any motor could ever hope to be. Their boat was skimming the water as fast as an arrow fired from a bow.

He looked back. The shore was only faintly visible behind them.

Everywhere else he looked was nothing but the vastness of the ocean.

"It's so beautiful," Tristan said in a hushed voice. "And a little bit scary."

"Yes," Elias agreed. "It's like there's no end to it at all."

Flat. That's the first thing Elias thought as he gazed out onto the water. The horizon was enormous, and there were no trees or mountains to hide it from view. The ocean was so overwhelmingly big that Elias felt insignificant in their little boat. He could not see where the ocean ended. His line of sight was not interrupted, and he experienced odd vertigo mixed with a little bit of agoraphobia. Only water and sky existed. The indigo blue of the ocean faded into the lighter blue of the atmosphere overhead, but the effect was entirely different from what he had experienced back on the beach. Here the sky was an unbroken bowl of vastness above his head, adorned with wispy white clumps of water vapor and, off to the north, a darker section of low-hanging gray clouds. The sun was shining in the middle of all this incomprehensible immensity, and to Elias, who had grown up surrounded by the tall trees of the valley of Portree, the fact that he could see everywhere around him for kilometers on end was dizzying.

He glanced over his shoulder again and noticed that the coast had already disappeared from sight. Another wave of agoraphobia washed over him. Aside from the sun indicating east, there was now no way at all to know where they were or where they were going. It was a humbling sensation of being swallowed by something much greater and larger than anything Elias had ever encountered before. In addition to that, Elias realized that his growing connection to the rest of the world had been completely cut off now that he was out in the water. He could not sense living things in the oceans as he had done on land. He was back to how he had been before he had taken the Life Seed, a lifetime ago.

As soon as he focused on the loss, he felt like he had lost his sense of sight. He was stranded, alone, small. And yet at the same time, he was full of energy and the desperate drive to do what had to be done.

I'm not alone. Tristan is here. Siv and Vanor are swimming as fast as they can. And Narev is somewhere ahead.

Elias glanced at his link and confirmed that they were heading northeast, where Narev had gone. There was nothing but water on the map for hundreds of kilometers now.

"We're on our own," Elias said aloud.

"We've been on our own since we left Portree," Tristan reminded him. "And we're still here."

Elias nodded. "You're right."

Tristan suggested sitting down a little bit later to help the wurl as they towed the boat. Neither Vanor nor Siv had slowed down at all, and Elias knew they would not stop until they reached their destination or their energy gave out. From the fleeting glimpses of emotion he caught from the two large creatures in the water, he knew they were also worried about Narev. The three of them were friends, and they cared about each other.

"I can't believe they haven't come out to breathe since we left," Tristan said eventually. "By my link it's been more than twenty minutes already."

"Remember that they're amphibians," Elias told him. "They are breathing through their gills."

"Right," Tristan replied. Then he scowled, his glance far away and focused on the horizon. "Hey, Elias?"

"Yeah?"

"What do we do if we run into any other wurl? We're really exposed out here. If one of the Singers comes, there's not much we can do about it. I'm not even that good at swimming."

"I know," Elias replied, glancing down at one particular stash of electronic equipment he had been careful to pack the night before. "I think I have a plan if it comes to that."

"What if any Flyers attack?" Tristan insisted. "Out here we're even more vulnerable to attacks from the air."

Elias nodded grimly. "If Flyers come, we try our best to survive."

"You're not scared, are you?" Tristan asked with a faint note of wonder in his voice.

Elias considered. He was anxious. He was worried. But....

"No," he admitted. "I'm not scared. This is the way forward to save Oscar and Sizzra's daughter."

Tristan ran a hand through his hair. "Right. You're right."

They spent the next hour sitting, watchful, their weapons in hand. However, when it became evident that they would not reach Narev anytime soon, wherever he had gone, they relaxed a little. Elias asked Vanor and Siv to slow down and conserve their energy, swimming at a slower pace they would be able to keep up for longer. The wurl obeyed, and the boat sailed more gently on the water.

To the north the distant gray clouds from before had darkened and grown, approaching. They were still far away, but they looked like a solid wall of darkness that advanced a little bit every minute. Elias queried his link to try and see whether it was a storm, but it had insufficient data and was unable to provide an answer.

"I think it's coming closer," Tristan commented after Elias clicked his link off.

"Yeah, same here."

"Not much we can do about that, unfortunately."

"Did you learn a little bit about how to deal with a storm?" Elias asked him.

"Kind of, for bigger boats. For this one we're on, though? There's not really much we can do. If a storm hits, we just pray we don't sink."

Elias sighed. "Right."

"Tell me something, Elias."

"What's that?"

"I know you mentioned this before, but are you sure Sizzra never fought a Singer before? Isn't there anything we can do, any way we can prevent them from paralyzing us?"

Elias paused for a moment, remembering. "Not from Sizzra directly," he admitted. "The closest memory she had was the time she killed a razorback behemoth in the water, but she left before her sister could do anything. She saw a single Singer juvenile once, but no adult males ever."

"And her mothers?" Tristan asked.

"I'm not sure. The memories are fuzzy, and although I can remember many fights between Flyer and Spine wurl, I can't remember fights in the water. Maybe I don't have them."

"Yeah. Maybe," Tristan admitted, although he sounded thoughtful.

A low rumble reached Elias's ears even over the steady splashing of the boat across the water as it moved. He looked left, to where the wall of dark clouds had grown noticeably bigger in a handful of seconds.

"I don't like it," Tristan complained. "We have no idea how bad ocean storms get on this planet."

"To say nothing of the fact that Flyers love to come when there is a storm to hide them from view," Elias added.

"We can steer the boat a little bit, but I never got around to making a sail. If the storm hits and we can't outrun it…."

"We hold on?" Elias ventured.

"As hard as we can."

The low rumbles soon became foreboding thunder. Elias saw no end to the increasingly large wall of anvil-black clouds that were being pushed in their direction by a surprisingly chilly wind that was completely at odds with the tropical heat of the region. Within a few minutes, the clouds surged over them and rain began to fall, consisting of isolated fat droplets that peppered the surface of the ocean with tiny concentric waves after their impact.

At the very beginning, the rain was only sporadic. It was an odd sight—the sky directly above was almost black, but the clouds did not block out the sun to the east, where they were headed, and the interplay of light and shadow made for a bizarre juxtaposition. As the clouds advanced even more, rain began to fall harder. Elias saw a double rainbow forming in the sky behind him, beautiful and ephemeral.

"Better put on our waterproof stuff," Tristan suggested.

"Right."

They did so, and by the time they were finished, the rain was falling in earnest. A bright flash of lightning directly overhead was followed almost immediately by a deafening boom of thunder that was shocking in its violence, out in the open like they were. Elias was certain that the sonic wave had made the entire boat vibrate. Vanor and Siv even came out of the water briefly, looked around, and submerged themselves again, swimming much faster than before.

"Elias?"

"Yeah?"

"I think we better eat something. Like, as much as we can. And drink some water too."

"What's wrong, Tristan?"

Almost as if to answer the question, a sudden gale of chill wind slammed against the side of the boat from the north and made the entire structure shudder.

"I think this is a big storm," Tristan answered, and Elias was surprised to see real fear in his boyfriend's eyes. "I'm not sure…. I'm not sure the boat is going to make it. It might capsize. We might lose the food and the rest of the stuff. I don't know. Maybe we should stash as much as we can in the backpacks, just to be safe, put them on, and—"

Now it was Elias who placed a calming hand on Tristan's shoulder. "Hey. It's okay. Let's pack stuff up, put on the backpacks, and eat something. Let's not freak out quite yet. Maybe the storm will pass us, or maybe we'll skip the worst of it. Vanor and Siv are swimming really fast now. I think they also know about the storm and want to avoid it if they can."

Tristan nodded with a jerk. "Okay. Okay. But…. Elias, I saw some videos of storms, and it gets pretty bad. I have absolutely no idea what to do, and I built the boat, so if something bad happens it's on me."

"Stop that, Tristan. You don't control the weather, understand? Come on. Let's prepare."

Elias spent the next few minutes packing the most vital electronics, food, and some water into one of the backpacks. He made sure to fasten Sizzra's spine to the most secure pocket in the backpack so it wouldn't be washed away. Tristan did some packing of his own, and when they were finished, they shared a large portion of the rations they had not packed away, eating as much as they could and chasing it down with a generous helping of purified water from the river. While they ate, the rain fell even harder. The wind grew colder, and Elias shivered as he put down one of their water containers and placed it carefully underneath the seat behind him. He put on the backpack and secured it around his waist as well as around his shoulders.

Another gust of wind surprised them both and very nearly pushed them over the side of the boat, which now seemed pitifully small.

"I don't… ink we're… ding the sto…," Tristan said.

"What?" Elias yelled. They were sitting next to each other, but the wind was loud.

"I don't think we're avoiding the storm!" Tristan shouted. He reached for Elias's hand, and Elias squeezed it with what he hoped was reassurance.

The truth, however, was that he was also scared now. Really scared.

The storm unleashed its fury without restraint a few minutes later. They were pelted with raindrops that hit them hard enough to hurt and appeared to come in bursts whenever the wind blew nearly horizontally, blinding them. There was suddenly so much water everywhere that Elias lost a sense of ocean and sky and rain in seconds. Everything was the same. Whenever he tried to open his eyes to look at where they were going, he was either blinded by a bolt of lightning or stung by salty water, which forced him to blink and try to clear his sight.

The motion of the ocean was dizzying as well. Elias thought grimly that maybe eating as much as they could had not been a good idea when the entire surface of the world appeared to be shifting up and down. He experienced complete powerlessness and a sense of confused dissociation when large waves pushed the boat up underneath him. Then there was a moment of weightlessness as the vessel hung in midair and the pit of his stomach felt empty and funny, immediately followed by a sinking crash as the boat dropped down into the trough of the wave. He'd seem strangely heavy for an instant, and then the world underneath him would surge upward again, beginning the cycle once more.

It would have been exhilarating if he hadn't also been terrified. The surface of the ocean had transformed itself entirely from the placid flatness he had first experienced to a foamy mess of cresting waves that appeared to race toward them, crashing against the sides of the boat and making the entire thing shudder and creak with ominous violence. He began to fear waves, particularly the big ones that would lift the front of the boat, only to drop it precipitously as they moved away. Those drops were the worst. Elias felt as though he was going to fall headfirst into the ocean, and it was only through Vanor's and Siv's incredible sense of navigation that they avoided simply capsizing after the first big one hit. Nevertheless, the waves kept coming. The horrible swaying, up and down, up and down, never stopped. The wind buffeted them; the rain blinded them. Lightning bolts left ghostly afterimages on Elias's retinas, even when his eyes were shut.

The thunder was the worst of all. It was painfully loud, coming from everywhere at once, and Elias was forced to cover his ears after a particularly booming thunderclap, which only made him unsteady where he was sitting. Before he could reach down and grab the seat as he had been doing, a wave dropped underneath them, and he slid forward, crashing against the wood in front of him with both knees.

It hurt, but the fear was much greater. Elias opened his eyes despite the water and grabbed blindly at something, anything. His hand found the railing of the boat, and he gripped it with all of his strength. It was only after the next wave came that he was able to get his bearings, grab the hand that Tristan was offering while mouthing words that he was almost unable to hear, and sit back next to him.

"We have to… the waves… on!" Tristan shouted next to him.

Elias shook his head. He hadn't been able to hear the entire sentence.

"We have to hit the waves head-on!" Tristan repeated, shouting into his ear. "If they hit us from the side, we'll turn over!"

"What can I do?" Elias yelled back.

"Tell the wurl," Tristan replied. "With your mind!"

Elias nodded and concentrated despite his heaving stomach and aching knees. He tried to project an image of the boat slicing through the waves perpendicularly, and he received a tired sort of acknowledgment from the two wurl who were struggling in the water. The course of their little boat altered just in time to meet a large wave not quite head-on.

They were drenched in a moment. The violence of the water nearly pushed Tristan over the edge of the boat, but Elias grabbed him and used his own legs to steady them both against the barrage of the wave. As the water receded, Elias realized that one of the large packs under the front seat had been washed away. Worse, however, was that one of the wood planks on the bow of the boat had splintered. It looked as though the next big hit would simply tear it away.

The sun disappeared behind the leaden clouds at last, and it was like being plunged headfirst into a nightmare. Elias lost his sense of direction. He stopped caring about the boat, about the food, about his goal. All that mattered was holding on to Tristan with one hand and to the boat with the other. His stomach heaved again and lurched in time with the wild motion of the water as it rose and fell, but he refused to give in to the urge to throw up. He gritted his teeth, closed his eyes tight, and put all of his strength into staying right where he was.

It got progressively harder. Wave after wave crashed against them, and the wind did not let up. It was no better underwater. Elias perceived clearly how Vanor and Siv were doing what they could, but even their vast strength was giving out. They yearned to swim deeper down, all the way to the ocean floor to avoid the storm, following their survival instincts, but they did not do so because they knew it would mean abandoning Elias and Tristan. Nevertheless, every wave took its toll, and they were no longer as nimble as they'd been at the beginning. They were making barely any progress, and dragging the boat behind them was beginning to hurt.

Elias was able to open his eyes for a moment after a lull in the chilly rain, and he witnessed firsthand the initial time Siv's strength gave out momentarily. That meant that it was only Vanor pulling the boat, which made it turn.

Parallel to a crashing wave.

"Look out!" Tristan shouted.

Elias was about to answer, but a wall of water slammed into him with a strength that rivaled Sizzra's and tore him away from Tristan's grasp. He knew a brief moment of utter confusion as he realized he was sailing through the air, and he opened his mouth to scream, but then he crashed against the surface of the water, and the impact stunned him.

He sank.

It took him an instant to realize what had happened.

I'm in the water.

I need to swim!

He tried to move, but the backpack strapped around his body weighed much more than he had anticipated, and it dragged him down. Panicking, he kicked with all his might, and his terror increased tenfold when he realized he did not know which way was up. The water around him roiled and spun him around, and Elias began to feel the burning in his lungs that heralded the moment when he would be forced to breathe in and fill his lungs with water that would drown him.

His vision clouded over. He fumbled with the backpack strap around his waist, but he could not get it loose. In desperation, he made one last-ditch effort to fight against the forces dragging him down, his addled mind realizing that if he fought against that pull, he would be going up. He forced his arms to propel him and kicked as hard as he was able.

He made a little bit of progress. He kept his eyes open in the stinging salty water and saw faint clarity immediately above him. His lungs were on fire by then, and he almost gulped for air, but he clamped down on the reflex with the last erg of strength left to him and, with a mighty heave, broke through the surface of the water at last.

He gulped in a mixture of air and water, but another wave rolled over him and pushed him down.

He tried to swim again, but he did not have the strength. What little air he had been able to inhale merely increased the pain in his chest, and he cast his mind desperately out, trying to call the wurl.

Get Tristan, he told them. *Save him.*

Something large torpedoed through the water and bumped into him, punching the last of the air out of his lungs. Elias grabbed on to the creature, and a split second later, he was able to gulp in blessed air as the two of them broke through the surface and remained there long enough for him to be able to breathe normally again. The storm around him was shockingly violent, but Elias's grip did not loosen. He grabbed Siv's warm body with his legs, not even caring that one of Siv's spines was digging into his thigh.

From Siv he sensed a worried query. Siv did not know what to do next.

Tristan! Elias cast out with his thoughts as soon as his brain cleared slightly. *Find him!*

There was faint mental reassurance from nearby, coming from Vanor. With it there came the wurl's faint sensation of Tristan grabbing on to the underside of his powerful neck.

Elias nearly loosened his grip in sheer relief. He did not do so, though. He knew Siv might not be able to find him and rescue him a second time.

Away from the storm, Elias told both wurl. *Stay together.*

He got tired acknowledgment in response, and Siv swam through the water, spending most of his strength in ensuring that Elias would be able to breathe at reliable intervals, but being forced to dive underneath the waves every few seconds because of the ravaging storm.

Elias nearly passed out twice more, but he forced himself to remain awake. It was only when minutes had gone by and Siv had not submerged himself again that Elias opened his eyes and tried to ascertain where they were.

Something was different. The wind had lessened and no longer howled in his ears. There was still rain, and the waves were big, but the gales were dying off. The booming thunder sounded farther away.

Elias held on until his arms trembled and he feared that his own strength would give out. At long last Siv slowed down, although he still swam in the same north-easterly direction he had been following. Elias was able to clamber onto Siv's back then, avoiding the worst of the spines, and straddled his neck with his legs. Thankfully, Siv's spines had only inflicted superficial wounds on his thigh. He grabbed the scaled neck in front of him with both hands, balancing precariously and wishing he could simply unbuckle the backpack that was incredibly heavy and threatened to destabilize him yet again.

He was almost dizzy with relief when he realized Vanor was swimming not two meters away from them. Sitting on his back, much like Elias, was a bedraggled but conscious Tristan.

They were both too tired to yell, but they shared a glance that spoke volumes. Elias sent a wordless but heartfelt *thank you* to both wurl.

The first ray of sunlight was almost surprising in its brightness more than an hour later. Elias blinked and realized that the black cumulonimbus clouds were behind them now, off to the southwest.

Calm returned to the world as Vanor and Siv still swam. Soon even the last of the clouds overhead had been blown away by the wind, and in their stead was only a vast blue sky where the sun shone and the wind was still. After the violence they had just endured, Elias had trouble understanding the peace of the environment they were traversing. The ocean around them, fathomless, was again flat and restful. The temperature rose until it was as hot as it had been before, and Elias marveled at the fact that he was able to see for endless kilometers in all directions once more.

The ocean is... incomprehensible, he thought to himself.

Siv underneath him acknowledged the thought and offered a fragment of a memory. Elias got a sense of black depths and endless expanse, of swimming near the bottom looking for food, and then—something in the water with him. Something that glowed.

Elias patted Siv. "So you knew the ocean from before, huh? Thank you for saving me back there. I couldn't have made it without you."

Siv did not acknowledge the thought again, but Elias did not mind. Unlike Vanor and Narev, Siv had always been rather distant, much more feral than his two brothers. Nevertheless, the way he had acted during the storm proved that Siv, too, felt kinship toward Elias. He had been willing to endanger his own safety in order to keep the boat afloat and had rushed to find him after the boat had capsized.

Elias waved to Tristan, who was riding on Vanor's back. He received a tired-looking wave in return, and Vanor approached so the two wurl would be swimming side by side.

If it had been possible, Elias would have walked over to Tristan in order to hug him, but he had to make do with a smile.

"Tristan, you're okay. I was scared."

"Me too," Tristan replied. "As soon as Vanor saved me after I fell into the water, I kept screaming at him to find you."

"I did the same thing with Siv."

A couple of seconds passed while they reflected in silence. The only sounds were the paddling of wurl legs through the water.

"We lost the boat," Tristan lamented. "I'm so sorry, Elias."

"That's okay, we're alive."

Tristan shook his head. "I should have made the boat sturdier. Maybe wider, or heavier at the bottom. I didn't know—"

"Tristan, stop that."

"What?"

"That thing where you think you're responsible for our safety. Listen, we're in this together. Out here you're not responsible for me. You are a Colony Patrol officer, but we're not in Portree right now. You don't have to protect me all the time. And besides, like I said before, you don't control the weather. We had no idea a storm was coming."

Tristan nodded.

"I'm just happy we're okay, thanks to Siv and Vanor," Elias continued. "That's all that matters."

"We lost most of our supplies, though," Tristan observed with a worried frown. "All we have left are the backpacks."

"I know."

"We have no idea how we're even going to get where we're going, and we can't ride the wurl all the way across an ocean."

"I know."

"What are we going to do?"

Vanor growled at that moment, interrupting the conversation. Siv echoed the growl a split second later.

Elias looked ahead, and from his vantage point, he was able to see something small and dark on the horizon almost directly east of them.

"What's that?" he asked aloud.

As if in response, Siv growled louder. His spines stiffened, but he relaxed them again in response to Elias's surprised yelp.

Both wurl picked up speed despite their exertion from before. Elias was now fully focused on the black spot, which grew as they approached until it was a diffuse block. At first Elias thought it was an island, but it was too small to be one—it looked more like a floating platform of some kind.

What is that? he asked of the wurl. He received no direct response from either of them, merely a sense of urgency.

That's when he saw that there was a shape on the platform. A large and spiny silver shape.

"Narev!" Elias shouted.

"Is that him?" Tristan asked.

Elias quested forward with his mind. He tried to focus on the prostrate figure that grew larger with every passing second and thought he received a faint mental echo from it. The echo was full of alarm and a desperate call for help.

"It's him," Elias confirmed. "Narev! Come here!"

But Narev did not move, and Elias's anticipation was now tinged with worry.

"What's wrong?" Tristan asked him. "Why's he not moving?"

"I don't know." Elias tried to suppress the faint tingle of fear coursing through his body.

He's okay. He has to be.

They were closer now, close enough to begin making out details. The platform grew as they approached until Elias realized that it was a sort of round surface made out of what looked like thick kelp, dark brown and slimy looking. It was big enough for several adult wurl to stand on, and it appeared to be floating on the water with no discernible means of locomotion, perhaps merely going wherever the wind and the currents took it.

Narev was in the center of it, lying on his side, bound by a multitude of kelp strands.

"Narev!" Elias shouted again, and this time they were close enough that Narev was surely able to hear his voice. The captive wurl struggled, but he was completely entangled in the seaweed and appeared not to be able to move.

"He's trapped somehow," Tristan observed.

"Let's help him. Before something else comes."

Neither Vanor nor Siv needed Elias's mental urging to go faster. Both of them powered through the water, and less than a minute later, they arrived at the edge of the platform. Up close, the surface looked much more unsteady than Elias had assumed. It was a knotted mess of twisted kelp strands nearly as thick as Elias's hand, many of which poked out of the water, where they were many shades of brown and dark green. However, there were pools of water on the platform itself, and it did not look as though it would be able to support the weight of a wurl at all. Underneath the water, Elias could see the strange algae growths extending into the deep, out of sight.

"Vanor, let's go! Up onto it," Tristan said.

Vanor immediately turned, swimming away a little bit and then powering forward through the water, fully intending to land on the platform after leaping out.

"No!" Elias shouted, and incredibly, Vanor halted less than a meter from the platform. The waves in the wake of his motion made the closest brownish kelp sway.

"What's the matter?"

"I think it's a trap," Elias said. "I think the Singer made Narev swim onto this thing until he was entangled by it. Look. He can't move."

As both of them looked at Narev again, it became clear that the wurl must have thrashed with great strength at some point in the past. Wide swaths of the plantlike growth had been torn to shreds, and there were a couple of spines partially submerged in the tangled web of slimy leaves. The place where Narev was now, perhaps twenty meters away and near the center of the floating platform, was the spot where the kelp grew thickest and where its color was darkest.

Narev struggled again, sending out a mental call to all of them with the same insistent alarm Elias had felt earlier.

Elias gasped.

"Elias?"

"He's not calling for help. He's telling us to get away."

"Who? Narev?"

"Yes," Elias confirmed. "He doesn't want us going near him."

"What do we do?"

Tristan was not the only one asking. Both Vanor and Siv sent mental queries to Elias. They wanted to climb onto the platform and help Narev.

No. You're too big, and you'll get tangled in that thing too, Elias told them, hoping they would be able to understand the complexity of his idea. He got confusion in return, so he knew the wurl did not fully grasp his meaning, but they did hold position where they were.

"It's up to us," Elias said.

"You mean the two of us?" Tristan asked him.

"Yes. We climb on and cut Narev loose. We're small enough that we won't sink. I hope."

Tristan looked at the kelp platform, and then back at Elias. A moment later he nodded. "All right. Let's do it."

Bring us close, Elias told Vanor and Siv. *Watch out for danger.*

The wurl complied and swam up to the first leafy strands of the algae that floated, almost lazily, in the balmy tropical water. Carefully, mindful of Siv's spines, Elias climbed down and into the ocean, where he used Siv as support in order to prevent himself from sinking. He almost immediately regretted his decision. He was still carrying the backpack, and it dragged him down like before.

"Leave the backpack!" Tristan shouted from nearby.

"Right," Elias muttered. He unfastened the buckles with much trouble, but managed to do it in the end. He kept Sizzra's spine in his hand, and then he heaved the backpack over the side and onto one of Siv's larger spines, near the base of his neck. The backpack lodged there, and Siv did not seem to mind it.

Now much lighter, Elias swam in the water awkwardly, fully clothed and wearing shoes. He had gotten much better at swimming during his time in Crescent Valley, but this was an entirely new environment, and his clothes did not help him one bit. He kicked hard, though, and used his arms to propel himself forward. He was able to grab the first handful of seaweed, which felt as slimy as it looked, along with quivering gently under his fingers for some reason.

"Gross," Elias said to himself.

Tristan swam nearby, evidently having as much difficulty in the water as Elias.

"Hey," Tristan said, stopping a few meters away. Then he simply swam forward at full speed and, when he reached the algae, grabbed on to them and pushed himself up as if he were climbing out of a swimming pool. The kelp bent under his weight, but it did not break or sink. Tristan swung one leg over and onto it, and then the other. He rolled on the surface of the platform and then knelt up smoothly. "Your turn, Elias."

"Right," Elias responded. He tried to do the same, but his speed did not avail him, and he ended up having to use Tristan's help to clamber onto the platform. He also rolled on the slimy and strangely spongy surface until he was sure it would not give out under him. Only then did he attempt to stand up. Tristan followed suit.

"Well done," Tristan told him.

"I had no idea you were such a good swimmer," Elias observed.

"Let's help Narev."

"Yes," Elias said, distracted. He looked at where Narev was still struggling and felt his acknowledgment but also his alarm. He kept insisting that they go away.

It's okay. We're here now. It's going to be okay.

Elias took one step, and his foot sank amid the seaweed strands, but only partially. Now that he was on top of the platform, the overwhelming stench of rotting and moist plant matter was impossible to ignore. It was everywhere, and as Tristan and he carefully made their way to where Narev was lying, the smell grew even stronger. The surface underneath grew firmer too, and the kelp stiffened the closer they were to the center.

"I had no idea plants could grow like this," Tristan said.

"Neither did I. It looks like seaweed of some kind, but there is no record of anything like this in any of my biology books."

"It's really sturdy here," Tristan pointed out. They were now a handful of meters away from Narev. "Look at the plants. They're a much darker brown here, and my foot doesn't sink anymore. It's almost like this stuff is stiffening now that I'm stepping on it."

"I was thinking the same thing…," Elias said. It was odd. There were no enemies in sight, no Flyers or Singers, and yet Narev's alarm only grew the closer they got to the center. He huffed a couple of times, signaling that they should leave.

Elias stopped a few steps away from Narev. Tristan did so too, with a confused look on his face.

"What's wrong, Elias?"

"I don't know," he said slowly, surveying his surroundings. He motioned for Tristan to be quiet, putting a finger up to his lips.

He listened.

He heard only the faint sound of water washing against the kelp platform, and behind them, the splashes of Vanor and Siv, who were looking at them with concern. There was nothing else, and yet….

Tchk. Tchk.

Both of them heard it at the same time. Narev's alarm reached a crescendo, but Elias did not see anything threatening.

He looked at the algae underneath his feet more carefully. It was exactly like before, thick strands of a leather-like substance, dark brown, almost black.

Wait. This kelp looks too *different.*

He looked closer, taking a careful step nearer to Narev. Near the center of the platform, the seaweed strands were no longer slimy, and they were much sturdier than at the edges. In fact they looked less like kelp and more like taut lines, flexible and strong, reminding Elias of muscle fibers under the microscope.

Tchk. Tchk.

He exchanged a glance with Tristan. The sound was coming from behind Narev. Carefully, both of them edged around the captive wurl until they were able to see what lay past him, having been obscured by Narev's bulk.

"What's that?" Tristan whispered.

There was a dent in the middle of the seaweed platform about a meter away from Narev. It was perfectly round, about two meters in diameter, and completely black. It looked like a hole amid the kelp, and the inside of it was ringed with sharp, stubby spikes.

Tchk. Tchk.

The hole was making that sound. Elias watched, aghast, as the dark opening increased its diameter slightly. The seaweed ropes around Narev tightened and pulled the wurl a few centimeters closer to the yawning opening. Narev struggled, but his bonds tightened in response.

The spikes shuddered again.

Tchk. Tchk.

"Not spikes," Elias said aloud as understanding dawned. His voice rose in volume and urgency as he spoke next. "They are teeth. Tristan, get out of there! These are not kelp strands!"

But his words appeared to disturb the camouflaged organism that had been about to feed, and the surface around them erupted in writhing snakes.

chapter 14.
housework

OSCAR AND Samantha flew back from the Nightmare Caves on Doran. Although it was still scary to hold on for dear life while riding a winged wurl, Oscar was no longer nauseated and actually managed to dismount without falling on his back, which was good given that he was carrying a heavy pack full of food.

"Thank you, Doran," Samantha said after dismounting, placing her hand on his forehead. Doran grunted softly and then bounded away. He jumped with daredevil grace off the cliff from where they had taken off earlier that day. The sun was setting, and Oscar beamed when Doran opened his wings to their full extent midair and began to flap energetically, rising up and away. His scales reflected the light and appeared to blend in with the different colors of the sky.

"Doran is so cool," Oscar said under his breath.

"He is the strongest of the surviving males, and the most agile," Samantha commented, and Oscar could have bet that there was a hint of pride in her voice.

"He's really different from the wurl back home," he added. "So fast and sleek. And he can fly. It's no wonder he beat all the other wurl the day of the storm."

"I would not be so sure," Samantha replied. She sounded thoughtful. "Attacking Portree that day was terrifying. The wurl of your continent may be slower and earthbound, but they have a deadly ranged attack, which neither Doran nor any of the other Flyer males possesses. Dodging those spines was incredibly difficult, and had it not been for the shelter of the storm, I am not sure whether victory would have been ours. You forget, as well, that Doran was the only male from that group to survive."

"Are there any others? Other males?"

"Some remain," Samantha answered. "Although I see fewer every day. Maybe she is still sending them out across the ocean, despite the perils of the journey, to finish what she started. Perhaps she wants them to find your brother. She obsesses about him, you know. She always mentions him when she summons me."

Oscar closed his eyes briefly, trying not to be overwhelmed by fear for himself and for Elias. He tried to find defiance in his heart before he next spoke. "Why doesn't she go herself to find Eli? If she's so obsessed and all."

Samantha sneered. "Because she is a coward. She would see all of her males dead if it meant she could live. Do you remember how she backed away from your brother when he wounded her?"

"Yes. And she sent you and Doran to fight instead, right?"

"Correct. Incidentally, your brother...."

"Yeah?"

Samantha shook her head slightly. "He is brave. None of us have ever hurt her, but he did. I could scarcely believe it when it happened."

"Eli is awesome," Oscar said firmly. "He's coming to save me, I know he is. And he'll help you too. And your family. We can work together, save everyone—"

Samantha held up her hand. "Stop."

"What?"

"Hope is the worst torment of them all. We should go home," she said. She scanned the sky. "It is better not to be out in the open at night."

"Why not?"

For a moment it looked as though Samantha would simply ignore his question as she took a step in the direction of the house. However, she answered as she started walking. "She comes out at dusk to feed."

Oscar shivered and hurried to catch up with Samantha. He watched the sky with apprehension as they went, and he realized that he was developing an almost superstitious fear of Dresde. The fact that he could not even say her name made it worse.

There was a light on above the door of the house, and as they approached, Oscar smelled the enticing aroma of cooking food. His stomach growled with anticipation when the door opened and Nadja came out to greet them.

She hugged Samantha first of all. "Sam. You are safe, thank goodness."

"Yes, Oma. This was a good trip. We collected two packs' worth of food."

Nadja gave Oscar her usual piercing look.

"Um, hi," he said awkwardly. "It, uh, smells good! What are you guys cooking?"

"Was the young male helpful?" Nadja asked Samantha, although still looking directly at him.

"He was. Doran accepted him, and he worked well throughout the day. He did not complain. With his help I was even able to go deep into the caves to gather seaweed."

Nadja nodded slowly. "Good. Come in, both of you. Dinner is ready."

She went on ahead while Samantha and Oscar took off their heavy packs.

"Whew," Oscar said, literally wiping sweat off his brow. "That was intense."

"What do you mean?" Samantha asked as she placed her pack on the ground.

"I think your grandmother doesn't like me. She's super scary."

"She is merely suspicious, like I am, in fact. We have welcomed you into our home, male, but we do not trust you. If you attempt to harm my family in any way, I will—"

"No need to finish that thought," Oscar cut in. "I swear I'm one of the good guys. Tell me what to do and I'll do it, okay? We're on the same side."

"Perhaps."

Samantha led the way into the house, where it was pleasantly warm and the fragrance of mysterious dishes was even stronger. Ute greeted both of them with a smile, hugging Samantha briefly and even waving at Oscar in a friendly way before returning to the kitchen, where she was hard at work watching over several different pots and pans. Oscar put his pack with the day's haul where Samantha told him to, and then he went out again to wash his hands and prepare for dinner. When he returned, all of the women but Ute were seated at the table.

There was an awkward moment of silence. Oscar had no idea whether he was invited to sit down or not. Laurie was watching him with what he could only classify as hostility, and he wasn't particularly sure he wanted to sit next to her again.

"Right," he said, since nobody was speaking up. "Do I, like, go upstairs?"

"You may join us," Nadja replied. "You worked hard today, according to Sam. For that, we thank you."

"No problem," Oscar said. "It was really fun, actually. This place is so different from where I grew up. And Samantha is awesome! I mean, she smacked a forest hound right in the *face*."

"What?" Laurie asked right away. "Sam, there was a forest hound?"

Samantha shot Oscar a dirty look. "A small one, but it left."

"I knew it," Laurie continued. "It is dangerous to go there. Nadja, you should not let Sam go to the Nightmare Caves on her own anymore. She could get hurt!"

"There was no danger," Samantha argued. "The male can vouch for me."

Again, all eyes were on Oscar. Even Ute, who had been busy setting plates, took her place at the table and looked at him intently.

"Samantha... um... was awesome, like I said. Seriously, I don't think she was ever in danger. She saved me, actually. She's really strong."

More silence. It dragged on for a few seemingly eternal seconds before Nadja said, "Sam, please remember to be careful. For your mother's sake."

"I always am, Oma."

There followed a rather uneventful dinner. Oscar was mostly ignored, for which he was thankful. He offered to help do the dishes afterward, but he was again rejected and told to go to his room. He climbed upstairs and sighed with relief when he shut the trap door and could finally relax, alone in the bedroom. He lay down on the bed, closed his eyes, and tried to let the tension ebb away from his body.

His link beeped.

Dad!

It was indeed a message from his family, as Oscar was overjoyed to discover when he tapped the notification. Eager, Oscar opened the text document and started to read. He felt warm inside as he read the words his father had written.

> *Dear Oscar,*
>
> *I write to you tonight hoping you and your brother are well. Your mother and I have hope, each and every day, that both of you will come back to us safe and sound so we can be a family again. I pray nightly, and I know in my heart I will see you again.*
>
> *Elias is resourceful and strong. He said he was going to get you back, and I don't doubt it. However, I know also that you are strong in your own way. Ever since you were little, you have been the heart of this family. You care deeply about others, and you bring a smile with you everywhere you go. Use your strength. Be confident. Wherever you may be, whatever challenge you may be facing, I'm sure you'll find a way to overcome it.*
>
> *Your mother is doing well despite the circumstances, and she says not to worry about her. In fact, her health is better than it has been in many years. She is certain that it's because the world is back to the*

way it should be, and I am starting to think that she's right. There is life everywhere, and for the first time since I can remember, I can see something in the faces of others around me: hope for the future.

We buried Sizzra a few days ago. Some people still think she meant to destroy the colony, but I'm not so sure. I think we owe our lives to her, at least in part, even if she didn't intend to protect us from the other wurl queen.

Some good news: we have started to plant the seeds Elias brought. It's been done very carefully, with each and every seed treated as a precious treasure, which it is. Your aunt hopes that, if everything turns out the way we expect, we can see the first shoots in a few days. We'll send you another message when we know for sure.

By the way, I'm trying to keep the messages as short as I can so the file size is minimal and it can fit into a single data packet, in case the satellite has trouble sending more information to your link.

Take care, Oscar. Remember to be strong, and never give up hope.

Your mother and I love you very, very much.

-Dad

Oscar smiled as he turned the display on his link off. Even though he was so far away from home, and he was scared about pretty much everything around him, knowing that his mom and dad thought about him every day made him feel better. He spent the next half an hour dictating a reply for his dad, although he knew he wouldn't be able to send it. He felt better afterward, almost as if he'd been able to talk with his parents.

He undressed and turned the lights off. He was tired, and he didn't know if he'd have another nightmare that night, but he closed his eyes with a faint smile still on his lips.

The next morning he woke up groggy, and a brief glance at his link told him it was nearly the middle of the day. Surprised, he got dressed as quickly as he could and went downstairs.

Nadja was sitting at the kitchen table, drinking a steaming beverage from a dainty little cup.

"Good morning, Nadja," Oscar said. He still felt weird calling such an elderly person by her first name.

"Good morning."

"Is Samantha around? I'm not sure if I should help her go out for more food today."

"She is not. She was summoned."

Oscar felt a needle of worry. "Why? Is she going to be okay?"

Nadja watched him for a moment before answering. "She will be. Out of all of us, she is the strongest. Why do you ask? Are you worried about her?" Her lips curled up in what could have been a playful or perhaps ironic smile.

"Yeah, of course I'm worried!" Oscar answered immediately. Nadja appeared taken slightly aback at his frankness. "I'm worried about all of you. I know some horrible things have happened here in the past, but I also know that we should try to prevent more awful stuff from happening again. We should, like, draw up a plan or something. When Eli gets here, we should be ready."

"Your brother?"

"Yes. He's coming for me. He's coming to save me, and when he meets you, he'll want to help you too. Just like I do. We can all fight back and get away from here for good."

Nadja looked as if her gaze were lost in the depths of memory. "Fight back." She flicked a strand of white hair away from her forehead. The gesture was only partially successful, given that she had used her prosthetic hand to do so. Oscar tried not to stare.

"Um, yeah. So until Samantha comes back, can I help with something?"

"I assumed you would be tired from yesterday. You worked for many hours."

"I'm fine. I used to help my grandma in the greenhouses all the time when I was younger. I can do some chores, if you want. I learned how to cook when Eli was gone, so I can do that. Or I can clean and stuff."

Nadja's expression softened a tiny bit. "You are a very interesting young male. Very well. Come with me. There is much to do, and I *could* use the help."

At the beginning Oscar still felt awkward working alongside Nadja and following her instructions. He had no idea where Laurie or Ute were, but he didn't see them around the house as he assisted Nadja in fetching water from the river, repairing one of the broken shutters from a ground-floor window, and assisting in the surprisingly complex task of hanging up the seaweed strands he and Samantha had gathered yesterday to dry in the sun.

"This is an excellent source of protein," Nadja explained as she directed him. Her tone was friendlier. Doing the complex work of setting up clotheslines, hanging the dark-green macroalgae exactly right so it would not touch the floor, and securing each with a little pin was obviously hard to do with a prosthetic hand, and Oscar was sure she appreciated his help.

"How long do they last?" Oscar asked, untangling yet another blob of seaweed while being careful not to rip the plant tissues as he did.

"When dry, more than a year. It is good that you and Sam were able to collect so much yesterday. Seaweed is fickle—it may be abundant one day, then disappear entirely for many months. We have yet to understand its life cycle."

They were done with all of the algae around midafternoon, and after a quick snack that consisted of sweetpod slices and some kind of tuber, Oscar and Nadja worked on dusting off the solar array panels.

"Please be very careful with these," Nadja asked. She was showing him how to gently remove the dirt and little grit particles that tended to collect in between the hexagonal arrays. "They provide our energy for cooking, lighting, and heating in the winter. They are irreplaceable."

"Oh, don't worry, I do this all the time," Oscar replied.

"You do?"

"Yeah, back home I'm in charge of cleaning the solar arrays on the roof of our house, and I also help my dad at the telecommunications lab, which has a ton of these. Not as old, though, obviously. Do these come directly from the *Ionas?*"

"They do. We have cared for them diligently for three generations."

"What happened to that one?" Oscar said, pointing at the only broken panel, which he had previously seen from a window upstairs.

Nadja looked in the direction of the volcano.

"Oh," Oscar said. "I get it."

"Thankfully, she appears to think that the panels are merely some kind of amusing toy that keeps us entertained," Nadja explained. "If she knew how important they are to us, I am certain she would destroy them out of spite."

Oscar cast a look of his own at the sky, which was thankfully clear and devoid of any large flying shapes. He was beginning to get tired of having to watch out for Dresde at every moment, and it occurred to him that this was how Samantha and her family had lived all their lives. He couldn't even begin to imagine how awful it must have been.

Oscar focused on dusting the thick reinforced metal casing that anchored the panel he was working on to the ground. He pulled out a weed that was growing nearby and got a very mild zap when he touched the surface of the device with the back of his hand. "Ow! Um, Nadja?"

"Yes?"

"Have you been getting intermittent electricity? Maybe flickering lights in the house? Some machines not working at a hundred percent?"

"We have. In fact our refrigerating unit's performance has decreased dramatically over the last two years. The terminal in the house estimates that the array is operating at sixty-five percent capacity. How do you know?"

Oscar peered closer. "I'd have to look inside the casing, but I think some of the cables here might be short-circuiting. I just got zapped, and that shouldn't happen."

"You can repair the circuitry inside?" she asked, lifting her eyebrows in disbelief.

"Sure, it's no problem. I downloaded all of the schematics for solar panels last year, so I'd need some time to look for the correct model, and also maybe some tools to open the casing. Do you have any?"

"Yes. There is an old toolbox. Are you certain you know how to work on this, young male? If you could repair our energy source, you would be doing us a great service."

"It's really easy," Oscar said, and he found himself smiling. "I can take care of this."

"Very well. But I will supervise you as you work."

Oscar spent the next hour or so familiarizing himself with the appropriate schematics for the solar panels he was working with. They were very similar to the ones back in Portree, with some slight variations because of their age. When he was sure he knew what he should expect, he turned off the entire array and reached for the tools Nadja had brought him in order to open the casing of the panel he had been working on. By this point he was becoming increasingly desensitized to being presented with relic after relic of the generation ship, but he had to gasp slightly as he opened an original shipboard service toolbox from the *Ionas* engineering section. He realized that, together with the clothes he had been given and the circuitry on which he was about to work, he was essentially going to do the same job as an engineer from the actual ship might have done more than a hundred years ago. It gave him a little thrill.

He lay flat on his stomach on the ground and opened the panel casing carefully, using a magnetic screwdriver and a stabilizing cradle to isolate the system. He placed a section of the casing on the cradle after removing it, where it floated in midair, suspended by a magnetic field. He then directed his link's flash-light into the actual circuitry.

"Oh, I see the problem," he said aloud.

"What is it?" Nadja, who was crouching next to him, asked. She was surprisingly nimble for a woman her age.

"I think it's corrosion over time," he explained, poking one of the cables experimentally. "I have to run a diagnostic, but it looks as though salt from the ocean has gradually gotten in, maybe with the breeze, and a little bit of the plastic coating on a few of the cables is gone, so there are short-circuits."

"Can it be fixed?"

"I think so," Oscar said, rummaging through the toolbox. He found a polymer gun almost immediately. "I can use this to patch up the cables that are corroded. First, though, I'm running the diagnostic to see what other places in the network need repairs."

He directed his link to an embossed section of the inner panel, which had a code his computer was able to read, in order to establish a wireless connection be-tween the two systems. He then ran a quick diagnostic that let him know there were four other cable clusters that needed repairs.

Oscar was very careful at every stage, so it took him more than two hours to patch up all the cables that had been damaged as he moved from panel to panel. He felt satisfied and accomplished after he was done, and he re-started the system once everything was back in place.

"Is it done?" Nadja asked.

Oscar showed her his link, where every element in the system was green. "Yep. We can also check the terminal inside, see if it registered the change."

The two of them went back into the house, and Oscar followed Nadja upstairs into a room he had never entered. From the bed and the pictures all around, he assumed it was Nadja's own bedroom.

"One hundred percent!" she exclaimed, pointing at a small console mounted to the wall. "This is incredible!"

In her excitement, she reached to press one of the buttons on the terminal with her left hand, but since it was a prosthetic, she missed and ended up bumping the screen itself instead.

This time there was no pretending Oscar hadn't noticed. He couldn't help himself and looked at the beautifully carved but still artificial hand.

He looked up and met Nadja's eyes.

"Sorry," he said. "Uh…."

Nadja lifted her hand. "Do not be. It is a good hand, a gift from someone who loved me very much."

Oscar knew he shouldn't ask. He told himself it was rude to ask.

He asked anyway.

"What happened?"

Nadja sighed. She sat on her bed and patted the mattress next to her, indicating Oscar could do the same. "When I was young, around Sam's age, I tried to stop the scourge queen from doing something cruel. I stood in her way, and this was my punishment."

Oscar opened his eyes wide. "She bit your *hand* off?"

"She could have done far worse than that," Nadja said, her tone an odd mixture of resignation and anger, "but she wanted me alive. It was a lesson, she said back then. So I would never again defy her will."

Oscar looked at Nadja's hand. He imagined Dresde lunging forward, clamping her jaws shut on young Nadja's wrist, snapping bone and ripping it off.

He shuddered. "I'm so sorry," he said softly. "It must have been horrible."

The two of them exchanged a brief look in which Oscar was almost certain he could see the pain and sadness Nadja had had to live with for so many years.

She stood up. "I should thank you, young male. Repairing our energy source is something none of us would have been able to do. It is an invaluable service, and for that, you have my gratitude."

"You're welcome. I'm happy I was able to help."

"Come. The others should be arriving soon, and it is my turn to cook."

Oscar did his best to help Nadja cook, passing her things and taking over the tasks that required more manual dexterity, such as sautéing greens in a mysterious and unidentified vegetable oil and making sure they didn't burn. Preparing food was soothing. It reminded Oscar of when he'd had to take over as a family cook after Elias had left. His mother had gotten worse around that time, and so Oscar had assumed the responsibility of planning and making meals to help with the house, since his father spent most of his time after work caring for Oscar's mother and taking her frequently to the doctor.

"This is so weird and so fun," he confessed, cutting grapes into tiny slivers so they would look nice when arranged on a plate.

"What is?" Nadja asked.

"Cooking, but with ingredients I have never seen before. The food on this continent is so strange! It's amazing."

"What kind of food did you have where you come from?"

Oscar rinsed his cutting board as he answered. "Mostly genetically modified versions of crops from

Earth. Although we had less and less food each year. Did Samantha tell you?"

"Yes, she explained all about Portree and the food crisis. I still find it hard to believe that scientists were able to use genetic material from the Flower on your continent to force crops to grow."

"It wasn't very successful. We were running out of food fast. If Eli hadn't fixed things with the Life Seed, well... I hope the seeds he brought back are able to grow. My dad told me that they're planting them now."

"You can communicate with your colony?"

"One-way only, sorry. I can only receive messages. The antenna on my link is very small, and I don't have enough power to link to the satellite."

"Oh, I see," Nadja replied, sounding thoughtful. "Would our terminal work?"

"I don't think so. It looks like a simple house management system, but I could try if that's okay."

"You may. I can finish here, in fact, if you would like to attempt it."

"Right now?"

"Of course."

Oscar went upstairs to Nadja's bedroom and connected to the console using his link, but a quick system diagnostic showed that the terminal in the house had no wireless card. It was mostly a hard drive with a variety of different files and some automated programs that managed the house systems, but there was no way to use it to link to the outside world.

Disappointed, Oscar went back down to the kitchen and helped some more. Ute and Laurie arrived a little bit after sunset. They looked exhausted.

"Welcome home," Nadja said to them, giving each of them a hug. "How is...?" She glanced at Oscar and appeared to think better of what she had been about to say. "How was it?"

Ute sighed.

"No change," Laurie replied. "We cleaned everything and replaced the padding on the walls and floor. There were tears and bumps on one of the walls, probably the result of impacts. The toilet was also clogged with the pieces from the wall that had been torn off. Ute and I spent most of the afternoon repairing it, but everything is okay now."

"Thank you so much, Laurie dear," Nadja said to her, flashing a brief sad smile. "You did not have to do any of that."

"You are my family. I owe you all more than I could ever repay. I do this gladly, Nadja."

Ute did not speak, but hugged Laurie gently from behind and rested her head on Laurie's shoulder.

"And Sam?" Laurie asked.

"Still has not returned," Nadja replied. "Come, sit down, both of you. Dinner is ready, and you must be starving."

"We should wait for her," Laurie said, looking worried. "She usually does not keep Sam this long."

"She will be okay," Nadja stated, although her voice wavered slightly on the last syllable. "She always is. She always comes back."

The four of them sat down at the table, but none of them spoke. Ute glanced at a clock on the wall behind her frequently, and Oscar was certain that they all were worried about Samantha. He was worried too, and he couldn't help but imagine how awful it had to be to go up to that volcano to be with Dresde whenever she felt like it. Why had Dresde summoned Samantha this time?

Would she come back?

It was the longest thirty-five minutes of the day, and Oscar breathed out a sigh of relief when he heard footsteps crunch just outside. Ute jumped up with a wide smile and hurried to throw open the door for a bedraggled but otherwise healthy-looking Samantha.

"Sam! Welcome home!" Nadja gushed, the relief evident in her tone.

"Hello, everyone."

"Are you okay?" Laurie asked.

"Yes, although really tired," Samantha replied. She walked over to the table and sank down into her usual chair.

"Why did she summon you?" Nadja asked.

"Catching prey, feeding the Flower, the usual. She cannot get nearly close enough to toss the prey in anymore, so I have to do it. We spent most of the day finding something suitable. The worst part is that the offerings need to be alive now. It is horrible watching them burn."

Oscar did not want to intrude, but he had zero idea what Samantha was talking about, and his curiosity got the better of him. "Feed the Flower? What in the what now?"

Samantha focused on him. "Of course. Live prey are needed regularly to appease its hunger. Is that not the case with the Flower on your continent?"

"Uh… I don't think Eli mentioned anything about that. It sounds messed up."

"We should eat," Nadja interjected. "You three are tired. Young male, help me serve."

"Right away!" Oscar replied. He helped Nadja with the food, bringing smaller plates for everybody, glasses, and pouring fresh water.

"This looks very nice," Samantha commented once they were all seated, looking at the sautéed vegetables and stuffed potato analogs, which Oscar had spent nearly ten minutes arranging so they looked pretty. "Thank you, Oma."

"The young male helped with dinner, along with many other things today," Nadja replied. "He made the work around the house much easier for me."

Samantha met Oscar's eyes. "Thank you," she said.

"No problem!" he said, glad that the awful tension he had always felt at mealtimes was finally fading. "Bon appétit."

They ate in silence for the most part, and Oscar tried to make himself useful both during and after the meal, when he insisted on clearing out the plates and doing the dishes. When he was done, he went straight up to his room, since he sensed the others wanted to talk without him there.

Satisfied and hopeful, he got in bed, tired but certain that things would improve, not only for him but for the four women who had let him into their home. He'd gotten the impression that they hadn't liked him at first, but maybe he had misinterpreted their attitude.

I think they're scared of Dresde, just like me. I want to help them.

I want for all of us to be free.

chapter 15.
maw

"TRISTAN, LOOK out!" Elias exclaimed, jumping away from the grasping tendrils that had burst out of what he had mistaken for a kelp platform.

"What's happening?" Tristan yelled. "What are these things?"

"Behind you!"

Elias tackled Tristan out of the way of three thick velvety strands of the seaweed mimic an instant before they were able to wrap themselves around Tristan's legs. The two of them came crashing down on the hard and muscular surface of what Elias now thought was some sort of predatory organism native to the oceans of the planet. In response to the bump of both men falling on top of it, new tendrils erupted from the surface, seeking, attempting to latch on to something.

Both of them jumped to their feet as fast as they could. Elias dived out of the way of a couple more strands that snaked over the dark-brown surface of the platform like the roots of a plant growing by the second. He stomped on one, but the instant it took him to squash that tendril was enough for another couple of them to wrap themselves around his foot.

He tried yanking it out but could not. The more he pulled, the tighter the binding was, until it was almost painful.

"Elias!" Tristan shouted. A fleeting glance revealed that Tristan was also struggling, standing much closer to Narev.

More ropes erupted from the surface, like bloated black worms looking for nourishment. The stench of rot and decay saturated the air around them, and Elias realized, to his horror, that the circular opening at the center of the creature was now big enough to swallow Narev in one gulp. The sharp conical teeth ringing the dark chasm, which could only be part of the creature's gullet, had come out fully, and Elias was able to see their wicked sharp edges glistening under the noonday sun.

Narev grunted and struggled, even firing one spine that sunk into the creature's muscular flesh underneath him, but it did nothing. Next to him Tristan activated his shock spear, but the fully deployed snaking tendrils from before had already wrapped themselves around his arms, and he was unable to move it effectively. As though from a great distance away, Elias was able to sense Vanor's and Siv's alarm.

No, Elias thought, suddenly angry. *We won't go down like this!*

He brought up his right arm, holding Sizzra's spine in his hand. In a single decisive swipe, he severed the bonds around his foot and stumbled forward, surprised. Although they were incredibly strong, cutting through them had been easier than cutting through soft tofu with a sharp knife.

The effect on the creature was immediate. The entire structure underneath them shuddered, and even more tendrils burst out of its surface.

Tchk. Tchk. Tchk.

The noise the creature made was now more insistent, but Elias spared it no thought. He ran forward, swiping at the strands as he went, and succeeded in cutting the bonds holding Tristan's arms in place. Tristan then used his own weapon and freed his legs. The glowing edges of his shock spear burned through the flesh of the creature.

"Narev," Elias said to Tristan, panting. At the same time, he directed a mental command to the two other wurl still in the water not to come closer.

"I'll cover you," Tristan replied, and in spite of the urgency of the moment, he grinned, and Elias's heart skipped a beat.

The two of them charged, swatting the tendrils away or slicing them cleanly. The creature shuddered even more, and Narev whimpered as the bonds around his body tightened so much that Elias clearly felt Narev's pain and fear. This angered Elias even more, and he hacked at the first thick tendrils around Narev's neck and head, careful not to injure his friend. Then he moved on to his side and freed Narev's legs. Tristan stood behind him swinging his deadly shock spear with expert proficiency, knocking tendrils out of the way, and making sure that Elias could move and focus on Narev.

Elias did not waste a single second. He progressed steadily, cutting and slicing until he had reached the back of Narev's body, where he severed the last remaining bonds around the wurl's tail with a final triumphant swipe. Narev jumped immediately out of the way, now free, and hollered out his defiance with his own metallic, grating roar.

The creature underneath them moved.

Elias did not notice at first since he was busy hacking away at even more snakelike protrusions that quested toward his feet, but a few moments later, all of the tendrils retreated into the black flesh of the creature at the same time, and it was then that he clearly felt the surface on which he was standing tilt to the side.

"It's moving!" Tristan yelled.

Elias looked around and saw how the true extent of the creature's maw was revealed as it began to close its jaws around them, the slimy kelp it had used as camouflage dripping water from the edges as it rose into the air.

Elias was reminded forcefully of a Terran carnivorous plant closing its trap around an insect. They were standing on the inside of the trap, and the teeth-ringed gullet was the center of the creature's mouth, opening even wider to swallow them all.

"We have to go!" Tristan shouted.

No time, Elias thought. The trap was closing around them too quickly. He started to move, intending to run and try anyway, but slipped and fell flat on his face. Stunned for a moment, he pushed himself up and realized that the surface on which he was standing was now slick with some sort of fluid that was being secreted by the creature.

He couldn't stand up—the fluid was too slippery; it reminded him of saliva. Panicking, he did the only thing he could: he grabbed his spine with both hands and stabbed the creature in the mouth with all his strength.

The motion halted. Elias looked back and saw Tristan had also fallen down.

Behind them, Narev had had enough.

He roared again and jumped up into the air, higher than Elias had ever seen him do. Once he was airborne, Narev coiled his entire body into a tight ball and unfurled all of his spines. At the apex of his ascent, he fired three at the same time.

Straight down the throat of the ocean creature.

Narev uncoiled himself and landed with all of his weight right next to the deadly maw that was threatening to swallow him.

A split second later the creature spasmed. The slick fluid on its surface was absorbed back into it in a single heaving motion, and it opened its mouth fully again, flat against the surface of the ocean.

It quivered once more and then lay still.

Elias climbed to his feet and yanked Sizzra's spine out of the creature. It came out covered in viscous goo.

"Are you okay, Elias?" Tristan asked.

"Yeah. Yeah."

"Maybe we should get out of here. Before it tries to eat us again."

Elias shook his head. "I think it's dead. Narev killed it."

In response to hearing his name, Narev bounded over to Elias. He acknowledged Tristan too, bumping into him playfully.

Elias and Tristan were silent for a few moments. Elias was still panting, ready for attack, but it appeared they were safe again.

"Narev's saying thank you," Elias told Tristan. "We saved him."

"And he saved *us*. That was amazing."

Gingerly, Elias approached the fast-closing hole that would have devoured them. In death, the creature's taut and muscular surface was becoming even stiffer, more like hard concrete. Elias listened carefully for a few seconds, even kneeling down to touch the dark flesh under his feet with his fingers, but the creature did not stir again.

"It's dead now for sure," he reported to Tristan and Narev, who were standing nearby.

We're okay, he cast out to Vanor and Siv. The two wurl needed no additional prompting. They jumped out of the water in a burst of bright droplets and landed on the stiff platform made from the creature's body, their heavy footsteps making the entire platform sway a little bit. They rushed to where Narev was standing, and the three wurl touched snouts. All of their eye clusters flashed brightly.

"It's the first time they've done that," Tristan observed.

"They're happy," Elias told him. He had a fleeting flashback to the first time he had seen all three of them, back when they had been fighting for dominance and the right to mate with Sizzra. Back then everything had been snarls, spines, and bites. Vanor had even had one of his chest plates ripped off.

Their behavior could not have been more different now. They were making a low rumbling noise in their throats and circling one another as if they had not seen Narev in ages.

Elias breathed a sigh of relief. His adrenaline high was fading, and his legs felt shaky. He sat down heavily and closed his eyes for a moment.

"The Singer did this," Tristan observed. Elias opened his eyes and realized that Tristan did not appear to be relaxing. He was pacing around, his shock spear still activated. "He lured Narev to this... this thing."

"Ocean maw," Elias said.

"What?"

Elias shrugged. "We might as well keep naming things. We're the first humans to run into all of this."

"Okay. This ocean maw. The Singer probably hoped Narev would be killed by it."

"Yeah."

"But why?" Tristan asked, sounding exasperated. "Why not simply kill Narev directly? Why go through all this trouble?"

"I'm not sure."

"Unless the plan was never…," Tristan began, and his eyes widened. "Never to have the ocean maw kill Narev."

"What do you mean?"

Tristan stopped pacing. "They wanted us here. Maybe they hoped we would kill the creature so we would all be here, easily visible from… the…."

Elias looked up and jumped to his feet, realizing what Tristan had meant. "Sky."

"Flyers," Tristan said in a low voice, also looking at the distant horizon, where a black dot was already visible against the clear blue. "Do we still have binoculars?"

Elias rushed over to Siv and took the backpack off the wurl. He rummaged around but did not find any. "Not here."

Tristan had done the same with Vanor, but he put the backpack down. "Not here either."

The wurl all sensed something was wrong, and a few seconds later, Narev was the first to stiffen his spines and watch the sky.

"Looks like five of them," Tristan reported, shielding his eyes from the glare of the sun. "Maybe more. They're coming in fast."

"We need to prepare," Elias said as he dumped out the contents of the backpack on the ocean maw.

He quickly arranged a bundle of electronics as he took them out of their waterproof container. He armed the device and set it aside.

"It's seven of them, Elias," Tristan told him. "Too many."

Elias stood side by side with Tristan and raised Sizzra's spine. He saw that Tristan was right: seven Flyers were clearly visible now, approaching in perfect formation. They were close enough that Elias was able to see that the three in the front were adults, their cobalt scales dazzling under the sun. The other four were juveniles, and their lighter blue color matched the blue of the sky almost perfectly.

Around them, Narev, Siv, and Vanor took up battle stances, with every spine on their silver bodies erect and ready to fire. They did not feel fear, which reassured Elias.

"We take the big ones out first," Tristan instructed all of them. "They're going to try and swoop in really quick, like they do. Avoid the talons. Remember they burn. Elias, tell Vanor to stand in front. He's going to give us cover from the first attack. If he can bring one of them down, the two of us can stab it and kill it. Siv, Narev. Fire spines. Aim for their wings. If you grab one, shred their wing membranes. That's their weak spot. If they can't fly, they're as good as dead."

"Understood, Tristan." Elias communicated the plan to the wurl as best he was able to. All of them took up positions, and not a moment too soon. The leading Flyer adult screeched as it flew directly overhead, followed by the six others. Siv fired a spine into the air, but they were still out of range.

The phalanx of deadly Flyers turned as one and circled back around. Their grace in the air was

breathtaking, and their red eye clusters blazed malevo-
lently as each tucked his wings into his body and dived
like a bird of prey, straight at their earthbound targets.

There was no time to think. Vanor roared, and it was
echoed by Narev and Siv. The Flyers screamed out their
own challenge and plummeted down from the sky.

The flying attackers raked their talons forward seconds away from impact, but a barrage of spines from
three different sources forced them to halt their dive
and swoop back up. Vanor roared again, but this time
his roar was tinged with frustration. Not a single spine
had found a target. And the Flyers were climbing up
into the sky, coming around for another assault.

"Steady. Stick to the plan," Tristan told all of them,
his voice calm and firm.

Elias watched their attackers reach the zenith of
their ascent, and their slender reptilian shapes were
briefly outlined against the overhead sun. Then all sev-
en of them dived, and Elias knew this time they would
not stop.

"Brace!" Tristan shouted.

The water around them exploded with astonishing
violence. Quicker than thought, shapes burst out of the
waves in a ring around the ocean maw, hulking, writhing, gnashing.

Five, Elias thought, his eyes darting in every direction. His sharpened reflexes allowed him to take in the
entire scene in less than a second. Four of the Singers
were juveniles, with dark-green scales. The fifth one
was a fully grown adult, the same creature he had seen
before and who had a single silver spine sticking out
of the base of his neck. His scales were aqua and light
green, and barnacles covered his back.

All five Singers formed a ring surrounding them. In a synchronized motion, they opened their multijoint-ed, three-sided jaws.

They sang.

But even as the first alien-sounding *THRUM* threatened to echo through the air, the Flyers in the sky and the Spine wurl on the platform appeared to follow a primal instinct unknown even to them and screeched and roared at the top of their lungs, respectively. To-gether, they made a sound Elias had never heard before. The metallic boom coming from Narev, Siv, and Vanor appeared to be amplified by the high-pitched screech-ing of the winged creatures in the sky.

The sound sliced through the air, where it was met by the song of the tentacled monsters in the water.

"Aaaaah!" Elias cried out, falling to his knees. He dimly registered Tristan doing the same thing, but all he could do was bring his hands up to his ears, trying to block out the horrible noise. It seemed to fight in-side his head, insidious paralysis being challenged by something else, something multitonal, dissonant, and powerful. The mind-rending struggle continued for an instant more, and then it simply stopped.

The spell broke. Elias blinked, tears streaming and stinging his eyes. For an instant the scene in front of him remained unchanged, with one big exception. The Singers closed their jaws.

The other wurl canceled the song together!

The balance held for another brittle second that was charged with tension and sizzling animosity.

Then it broke, and it gave way to madness.

Vanor was the first to recover. He jumped up in the air, coiled into a ball, and fired a spine that struck the nearest juvenile Singer in the chest. The creature screamed in response and flickered into nothingness, disappearing from view. A large wave betrayed the fact that it had disappeared underneath the waves, but there were four other Singers surrounding them.

A cobalt missile dropped down, air whistling in his wake, and struck the Singer adult with such force that both of them were catapulted onto the platform, where Siv and Narev barely had time to jump away from the two crashing, struggling shapes. The adult Singer roared in pain, and Elias caught a fleeting glimpse of sizzling Flyer talons digging into the barnacles that protected the Singer's back. The flesh underneath charred and burned, but even as it did, the Singer twisted in the water, brought up its six tentacles, and clamped them down on the Flyer before it could escape. The Flyer screamed and tried to open his wings, but the tentacles tightened around him, and Elias heard bone snapping. Then the Singer dragged his attacker down into the deep, flickering out of view.

"Incoming!" Tristan shouted, roughly pushing Elias out of the way.

Not a moment too soon. A streak of rough, hot wind washed over Elias, and as he fell down hard on the surface of the platform, he caught a glimpse of a streaking shape of light blue smashing into the ocean maw a hand's breadth away.

The juvenile Flyer did not attempt to take flight. He slithered on the ground and used both his powerful wings to buffet Elias, keeping him prostrate. He opened his jaws, exposing his sharp teeth, and his cluster of three red eyes glowed with bloodthirsty anticipation.

He lunged. Elias snatched up his spine from the ground. Swiped. Missed.

Narev slammed into the Flyer from one side with his spines fully extended. The gruesome aftermath of the impact was only revealed when Narev pulled away from the twitching corpse of the attacker, underneath which thick reddish blood began to pool.

Elias sensed the pain and fear of the wounded Flyer, and he registered the exact moment of his death like a wave of cold emptiness.

Elias jumped to his feet and looked around wildly. A few steps ahead, two of the juvenile Singers were threatening to climb onto the platform. Without thinking, Elias charged at the nearest one, slicing at one of his tentacles with Sizzra's spine. He connected, cutting through the flesh and releasing a spurt of warm blood that splattered all over him. The Singer roared and reared up onto four of its tentacles in a macabre parody of a creature with legs.

Two adult Flyers struck the Singer Elias had wounded from either side and sank their talons into his neck. Then they opened their wings and flapped simultaneously, sending Elias stumbling back. In disbelief Elias saw how the two Flyers were able to lift their prey between them as the Singer thrashed helplessly, his moist green scales darkening like charred coal under the glowing grasp of the flying predators. Together the Flyers dragged their victim over the water and then released him, but not before slashing at his neck with their forelegs.

When the Singer died, Elias felt as though his own heart had been struck. The limp body of the tentacled creature sank, and the two murderous Flyers attempted to fly up into the sky once more.

THRUM.

One of them stopped moving and simply dropped into the water, where grasping tentacles enveloped him, but the Flyer squirmed out of their grip and swam away. Elias followed the creature as it propelled itself through the water with its wings, weaving up and down in an attempt to escape the tentacled monster that was less than a second behind him.

The Flyer corkscrewed through the water and dived deeper down.

Unfortunately, the Singer was faster. He surged forward in an unexpected burst of speed and bubbles, seized the Flyer again, and used his many muscular appendages to crush the life out of him.

Again, Elias felt the death of the creature as if amplified.

Stop, he thought to himself. *This is wrong. Stop.*

"Elias! Move!" Tristan screamed.

Elias looked up at the slender shape of a Flyer descending toward him in a blur of speed. Siv was nearby, and Elias ran to him and swung onto his back.

Jump! he told the wurl.

Siv obeyed, and the two of them met the Flyer in the air. Siv absorbed the brunt of the impact, avoiding the deadly talons, but only barely. Elias brought up his spine and stabbed forward as hard as he could, puncturing one of the eyes on the creature's forehead.

He could have pushed in deeper and killed the Flyer, piercing it through the brain, but the Flyer's sudden terror caused his grip to waver.

With a howl of pain, the Flyer pushed away from them, raking the side of Siv's left shoulder with red-hot claws that left glowing marks on the metallic scales. The Flyer attempted to dash away, but Narev was too quick for him. He was suddenly in the air, and he clamped down on one of the attacker's wings, shredding it. The Flyer crashed down to the ground, and his other wing bone broke. Tentacles came out of nowhere and seized him.

More terror. Another death.

Elias scrambled off Siv's back just in time for Siv and Vanor together to launch themselves at the nearest Singer juvenile, firing two spines that struck the creature in its maw right as it was about to sing, preventing the horrible sound from escaping its throat.

There was a huge splash behind Elias. He whipped his head around in time to see another Flyer meet his death, his heart pierced by one of Narev's spines.

Tristan, Elias thought, searching desperately. He saw Tristan at the other edge of the platform, stabbing at one of the Singers with his shock spear. The creature retreated from the weapon, dodging the sizzling edges that would have burned its flesh, and submerged.

Vanor roared, and a great shuddering impact traveled through the platform up Elias's legs and made his teeth chatter. Vanor clamped his teeth on the side of a Flyer's throat and bit down hard, his eyes blazing with victorious fury.

No, Elias thought again. *No.*

He stumbled forward toward the electronic device he'd prepared. A quick glance up told him that there were no more Flyers in the air—they were all dead. That left four surviving Singers, all of which had gone invisible, and the churning and foaming of the water around the platform warned that they had seconds before they were attacked again and paralyzed, killed, or both.

A great hulking shape discarded its invisibility shroud, surging through the surface of the water with such force that the wave he made caused the entire platform to tilt to the side. It was the adult Singer, wounded but still threatening. His tentacles writhed in the light, and his eye cluster surveyed all of them for an instant as he opened his maw to render them all helpless and freeze them in place so the juveniles would be able to tear them apart.

"No!" Elias shouted. His hand closed around the sonic bomb he had made during his long days at the beach. He flicked it on with trembling fingers and tossed it over the side of the platform with as much force as he could.

Three....

Both Spine and Singer wurl watched the slender metallic cylinder sail through the air, uncomprehending.

Two....

It hit the water with a tiny *plop* and immediately sank.

One of the Singer juveniles reached for the ocean maw less than a meter away from Tristan.

One.

The sonic bomb went off in the water, and the most excruciating sound Elias had ever heard blasted both from the transceiver that was even now sinking in the ocean and the wireless loudspeaker that was in one of the backpacks.

As one, the Singers screamed. They flickered in and out of view, seemingly unable to control themselves, and attempted to climb onto the platform.

Spines from Narev, Siv, and Vanor found soft, muscular tentacles, wracking the Singers' bodies with pain from another source. Elias shared the earth-shattering sensory overload of all the Singers as they pushed away from the platform and sank into the waves, where they were met by even more sonic pulses from the sinking bomb that was fast depleting its energy source.

Please work, Elias prayed. *Make them go away.*

He had programmed the sonic bomb to give out one final burst of sound in the frequency range he had theorized would be most painful underwater, and a second later even he was forced to cover his ears a second time as the shrill screeching echoed all around him. The Spine wurl roared in pain, but Elias was able to feel the veritable explosion of agony shared by each of the Singers in their moment of vulnerability. Huge waves betrayed the panicked retreat of four large shapes through the water, swimming away with all of their might.

Then, finally, all was still.

Tristan came running over to him and caught him before Elias's legs gave way.

"They're gone," Elias managed to say. His mind was reeling from the death, the pain, and the noise.

"What did you do? Elias, are you okay?"

Elias took a few shallow breaths, trying very hard not to pass out. Three large shapes approached, blocking out the sun and watching him with concern. Narev in particular came closer. Elias reached out to touch him, and he regained some mental clarity through the contact.

They're gone, he projected to the Spine wurl.

Slowly, he stood up on shaky legs.

"Sit down, Elias. Are you hurt?"

"I'm fine," Elias croaked. "Are you okay?"

"Yes."

"Guys," Elias said again, referring now to the wurl. "Are any of you hurt?"

Only Siv had been wounded on the shoulder, but the wound was not deep. Relieved, Elias closed his eyes and attempted to regain some measure of control. He found he was unable to. His hands were shaking, and he wanted to cry.

"What's wrong, Elias? Talk to me!"

"This is not… this is not the way it's supposed to be," Elias said, choking up. His mind kept reliving the deaths he had witnessed. "This is wrong."

"I… come here, Elias," Tristan said. He stepped forward and enveloped Elias in a bear hug.

The dam broke, and Elias started crying. He wasn't even sure why—they had survived. They were okay. And yet he didn't understand why it felt as though his heart were breaking.

"We're okay," Tristan repeated in a soothing, deep voice. "All of us. You saved us."

"They d—they died," he managed to say between barely suppressed sobs he could not fully control. "So ma-many of them. It's not right. We killed them." The hot tears in his eyes stung as he remembered each of the wurl's pain, fear, and suffering.

"We had to," Tristan reminded him gently, running his hand through Elias's hair. "They attacked us. They would have killed us."

Elias knew Tristan was right. There had been no other choice.

But a small part of him, the part that was connected to the distant Flower on a mountaintop hundreds of kilometers away, warned him that with every senseless death, they got closer and closer to the edge of a horrible cliff at the edge of a bottomless pit.

chapter 16.
bouquet

OSCAR HELPED Samantha many times over the following weeks, and he went out with her on foraging missions where they explored regions of the surrounding area that were both scary and fascinating.

Doran took them to places that Oscar was certain he would never have been able to reach without the help of the strong, surprisingly peaceful wurl. Once Oscar had gotten over his initial fear of Doran, he began to feel more at ease in his company. A few weeks in, Oscar found himself looking forward to the days when he would be flying. The sensation of freedom when both he and Samantha were up in the air was something he had never experienced before, and he started relishing the thrill of landing, the suddenness of jumping off a cliff knowing he would not truly fall, and the calm majesty of flight while soaring on a thermal as he looked down at the world from a vantage point that few creatures ever had.

Samantha and Oscar explored many kinds of environments in their search for food. Some of them were wide plains where edible wildflowers grew in abundant clusters, and where Oscar's chief worry was avoiding beelike insects with three barbed stingers at the end of their abdomens. At other times, Oscar acted as a look-out and support while Samantha daringly rappelled down sheer surfaces in ravines overlooking a foaming river, intent on finding special mushrooms that grew in the moist crevices between oddly striped black rocks.

Once, Doran flew with them for nearly half a day to take them to a small island in the middle of a fresh-water lake, far away from the coast, where Oscar and Samantha spent two days and one night digging in the soil in search of the tubers Oscar had already eaten a few times before and that Samantha said were not only very nutritious but excellent winter food because of how long they kept. That night Doran stayed with them when they made camp, and Oscar was surprised at how safe he felt in the company of the male Flyer. Most creatures gave the wurl a wide berth, and the ever-present heat that Doran seemed to radiate from his entire body kept the faint chill of the night at bay when he curled up to sleep next to Samantha like a giant winged dog. When they returned to the seaside house the next day, Oscar realized he had a kind of fondness for Doran that he would have never expected to feel. He was not a terrifying beast anymore, but a mysterious creature both beautiful and surprisingly intelligent. Oscar began to understand what Elias had meant when he spoke of male wurl the way he had, telling Oscar how he even had made friends with some of them. Oscar doubted that he would be friends with Doran, since the wurl ig-nored him for the most part and appeared to care only for Samantha, but he was happy that Doran tolerated his presence more and more as the days went by.

His interactions with the rest of Samantha's family improved as well. He helped out as much as he could when he stayed home on the days Dresde summoned Samantha, and Nadja expressed her appreciation for the help more than once. Ute did not speak, but she smiled frequently and seemed glad to have him in the house. She reminded Oscar of his mother, always looking out for others and making sure everybody had what they needed. Ute was a great cook, and she was very athletic. For instance, she could climb a tree with ease if it meant she could reach the top branches to collect spicy lichen, which she used for some of the sauces she made in the kitchen. She made house repairs quietly but efficiently, and Oscar was once tasked with helping her replace some of the boards covering the window to his own attic, but from the outside. Ute did not even need a ladder to get to the top level of the house, and she hung by one hand from a windowsill, like a rock climber, while hammering nails into wooden planks with the other—spare nails between her lips.

Laurie was the only one who remained distant and slightly cold. Oscar wondered why that was, but he gave her space and offered to help her only when it was obvious she needed it. As her pregnancy progressed and her belly grew, Laurie's mobility decreased, and she had to rely on others more often. Oscar had no idea how to help when a woman was pregnant, but he did his best to be available in case Laurie needed something brought to her, and he often made little snacks so Laurie would have something to eat if she was hungry in between bouts of morning sickness.

He began to tell them stories at night about three weeks in, mostly because he got bored in his room at night without talking to anyone and he liked the company of other people. He also supposed they would appreciate listening to something new after who knew how many years of talking only to each other, and he was right. Although Nadja, Laurie, and Samantha all rejected his first offer to read them part of *Wild Beginnings*, the serialized novel from his favorite Portree author, Penelope Jones, Ute did not exactly say no, since she never said anything, and Oscar took that as an invitation. He began reading Ute the story, which he had downloaded to his link months earlier, and little by little the others joined.

Soon it became a kind of nightly ritual for all of them to sit in the living room after dinner, drinking some water or tea, while Oscar read for about an hour. He enjoyed seeing their reactions. Nadja and Ute would show rapt attention, while Samantha and Laurie would hang back, almost like they weren't really interested in the story, but every time there was a lot of action, they would sit perfectly still, as if they didn't want to miss a single word. At the cliffhanger at the end of the first book, both of them groaned with frustration, quickly replaced by excitement when Oscar told them he also had the sequel on his link.

Oscar received weekly messages from his family, and he was glad to hear that the colony was doing well. The seeds Elias had brought had all sprouted, and Oscar's aunt Laura was overjoyed, or so Oscar's mom told him in one of her messages. They expected to have the first full harvest in a few months, and they intended to save many of those seeds to build a cache that would be kept in safe storage for future years. According to his mother, the colony would use about ten percent of the first harvest for actual food as a test to see how well it was tolerated, and everyone was excited to find out what the new crops would taste like.

Oscar received no messages from Elias since there was no way for them to communicate, but he was certain that his older brother was still coming to save him, and the thought gave him strength through the days and particularly the nights. He sometimes dreamed that Elias was hurt, and he would wake up in the night and feel like crying. Oscar stayed up and prayed for a bit at those times, and the ritual helped him go back to sleep while still thinking about his brother and hoping he was safe, wherever he was.

Although he was slowly being accepted by Samantha's family, that did not mean the days were easy and carefree. Every person, Oscar included, lived under the constant threat of a winged shadow appearing in the sky. Dresde did not leave her volcano very often, thankfully, but when she did all activity ground to a halt. At those times the five of them would huddle in the house, every window boarded and the door shut tight, and wait for her to fly away and leave. Ute in particular would get a pained look in her face, and Samantha would try to comfort her, but it seemed as though Ute was off in her own world, remembering something that tortured her whenever she so much as caught a glimpse of the wurl queen.

The threat of Dresde's presence was like a worry that never left, an unattended fire that needed to be minded every few minutes, or a faint whisper in the back of the mind that made it impossible to truly relax. Oscar developed the habit of looking up at the sky every now and then when he was outside, much as the others did. During the day the threat was minimized because it was easy to spot Dresde if she decided to fly close to the house. It was much worse during cloudy days or at night because the water vapor and the darkness hid her from view. There were even times, late at night, when Oscar woke up as if from a nightmare. He would sit up in bed, listening. Most of the time there would be nothing but a faint mental nagging, a pale echo of the horrible mental pressure Dresde's attention could inflict.

Other times, however, he would hear furtive noises in the night. Oscar would listen, petrified in his bed, as something scratched the heavy wooden beams of the attic roof overhead. The scratching was slow, almost calculated, and occasionally there would be a faint smell, as if something was burning. The ceiling would creak, small showers of dust raining down from in between the boards, perhaps because of a great weight that shuffled or shifted on the house.

One night in particular, a little over five weeks after Oscar had arrived, he bolted upright in the middle of the night as if somebody had slapped him as he slept. His heart in his throat, Oscar listened intently but heard nothing at first. The air in the room was hot, almost unbearably so, and his wide eyes darted every which way as a sweat rivulet made its way down his forehead and onto the bridge of his nose. The murky blackness of late night made it impossible to see anything.

I'm alone in the room. There's nothing there. It's just shadows.

A loud *snap* startled him badly, followed by an almost gentle wooden creak near the place where the boarded-up window was located.

Oscar could not even scream as the evil red glow of a single unblinking eye bathed his room in crimson radiance the color of blood. The eye moved, ever so slightly, and Oscar had the crushing certainty that it was watching him. *She* was watching him. Her awareness flooded his mind like a raging river, submerging him in a sea of emotions he could never hope to fully understand.

Then the eye was gone. The roof of the house shuddered, and the night was still again. Quiet.

It took Oscar a long time to go back to sleep after that. The next morning, he walked up to the attic window and saw that one of the boards had indeed been ripped out.

He shuddered and went through his morning routine mechanically, hoping that Doran would take them far away from the volcano for their scheduled foraging mission that day.

"Where are we going?" he asked Samantha after he came back from the river, where he had taken a quick bath.

She shook her head. "I've been summoned."

Oscar's heart grew cold. His mind flashed back to the previous night. "No," he said before he could stop himself.

"What did you say?"

Oscar flinched a bit. Samantha still scared him, particularly when she sounded angry. "I meant... um, can you say no? What does she want?"

"I do not know, but I have to go."

"But...." Oscar remembered how Dresde had watched him in his bed, perfectly aware that he was terrified and enjoying every second of it. "Take care, okay?"

"I will. I always have."

Oscar was worried all morning. Nadja appeared to have noticed, and she gave him the afternoon off. She probably meant well, but it was the last thing Oscar needed because now he had nothing to occupy his mind as he waited for Samantha to come back. He dithered around the house, attempting first to compose a message to his family but stopping halfway. Then he tried to concentrate on some schematics he had found to maybe increase the energy efficiency of the water-purifier system, but after an hour he realized he hadn't been able to retain a single word of what he had been studying.

Listless, he left the house near dusk. The temperature was balmy and pleasant, and the smell of the sea reached him clearly. He walked all the way to the edge of the cliffs and looked down, gazing at the beach. It was a beautiful and strange environment in its own right. The sand was black and stretched from the rocks to the edges of the foaming waves that crashed against it ceaselessly. There were large prism-like structures sticking out from the sand at random intervals, their transparent and multifaceted beauty an odd echo of the same kind of contrast Oscar had seen once before at the Field of Thorns. Individually, the structures looked like octahedral crystals, each of them larger than Oscar was tall, or so he estimated, although he had not once been down to the beach. It was a long way down the cliffs, and as far as he could tell, the only way to reach the ocean from where he stood was to fly there. In fact, now that he thought about it, the volcano and its surroundings were like a fortress with natural defenses all around it that made it as difficult as possible to reach from either the sea or the land.

The light of the sinking sun, filtered through the crystals on the beach, resulted in multiple multicolored beams that adorned an otherwise dreary landscape devoid of much life. The few trees close to the cliffs were all dead, their trunks bleached white, their branches stripped bare. They looked almost like bones. Farther out among the waves, more crystals rose from the ocean. Oscar had yet to see a single living creature in the water.

This place is so beautiful. But it feels wrong.

He glanced to the right at the towering bulk of the volcano. Samantha was there somewhere. And so was Dresde.

He turned his back on the cliffs and began walking aimlessly, with the general idea of maybe going to the river again and trying to swim for a bit to relieve the tension. He soon reached the bank but decided against getting in the water. Instead he walked upstream, hands in his pockets, while the sky overhead changed from blue to shades of yellow, orange, and red as the sun went down.

He rounded a bend in the river and saw movement ahead. Surprised, his first instinct was to duck, but then he realized that it was a person. Ute.

Why is she so far away from home?

Oscar approached, curious. Ute was standing in a field of red-and-white wildflowers, a gentle plain that was quite beautiful and peaceful. The river nearby filled the atmosphere with the calming sound of flowing water, and the heady fragrance the waist-high flowers gave off as Oscar moved among them was pleasant and soothing.

Ute still hadn't seen him. She was standing with her back to him, maybe two hundred meters away. Oscar thought of calling out to her, but he did not want to startle her, so he walked closer instead.

Ute knelt down among the wildflowers.

At the same time, the toes on Oscar's right foot bumped against a hard unseen obstacle, and he very nearly fell on his face. He was able to recover, though, and looked down to see what it was.

A weathered rock, almost perfectly rectangular in shape, jutted out from the ground to a height of about ten centimeters. It was clearly artificial. Someone must have cut it to that shape and put it in the ground.

But why?

Oscar knelt down and brushed bits of grass and debris off the rock.

There was a name etched on it.

> *Cmdr. Hugo Wright*
> *3089—3142*
> *FREEDOM ABOVE ALL*

Oscar yanked his hand away and stood up with a sharp intake of breath. He took a few more careful steps, looking down as he searched, and soon stopped in front of a second, larger stone.

> *Lt. Alicia Jones*
> *3119—3142*
> *FREEDOM ABOVE ALL*

As twilight settled over the land, Oscar made his way among more rocks with great care, trying not to step on any of them.

No, not rocks. Tombstones.

One of them, maybe ten paces away, stood out above all the others. It was much more ornate, and it was larger, but the name had been defaced with rough, angry-looking scratches, and a portion of the top of it was missing. Sections of its metal decorations had evidently been torn away in the past.

There were many more tombstones surrounding it. The first twenty or so were regularly spaced, but as he walked forward and closer to where Ute was kneeling, they were spread out more unevenly. The stones themselves were also cut more roughly, and when Oscar reached Ute at last, he saw she was kneeling in front of a simple rock with rough edges on which a single name was written. There was no date.

Jörgen

Ute must have heard him approach by then, but she kept her gaze on the ground. She arranged a flower bouquet so it rested partially on the rock. It was a collection of wildflowers of many different colors, some of which did not grow in the vicinity of the house at all. In particular, Oscar recognized a couple of intricate pink blooms that he was certain grew close to the Nightmare Caves.

She must have walked all the way there, on her own, to get these flowers.

A sniffle betrayed the fact that Ute was crying. Oscar knelt down next to her among the tall grass of the peaceful graveyard as a gentle breeze stirred the petals of the flower bouquet. Oscar remained respectfully silent, wondering what had happened and why there were so many graves in that place.

Ute glanced at him a few minutes later, and she wiped a tear from her cheek. She gave Oscar a sad smile and reached for his hand.

Oscar clasped it in both of his.

"I'm so sorry for your loss," he said softly. He felt like crying too. Although he had never known Jörgen, he could tell how much everyone had loved him. "Was he your son?"

Ute nodded, looking back at the tombstone and touching it lovingly with her fingertips.

"When did he…?" Oscar began to ask, but then decided against it. Ute couldn't answer him, and he didn't want to ask questions that were none of his business.

Ute gave a little shake of her head and pointed instead to another gravestone very close by, next to where Oscar was kneeling. It also bore a beautiful flower bouquet, almost identical to Jörgen's.

Erik

Although the plots dedicated to most of the graves were more or less the same size, Oscar realized that Erik's grave was very small.

Smaller than a kid would have been.

But about the same size as a baby.

Ute reached for that tombstone as well and touched it lightly with the same mixture of sadness and love.

Oscar started crying as understanding dawned.

"I'm sorry" was all he could think of saying.

Ute looked at him for a long moment. She reached for his cheek and wiped off one of his tears with her thumb in a gesture so reminiscent of his mother that Oscar couldn't help himself. He reached forward, arms outstretched, and hugged her.

Ute hugged him back in a warm embrace, and the two of them cried together for a few minutes as the light of day faded around them and the stars began to twinkle overhead.

Eventually Ute let go, and Oscar did the same. They stood up, still looking down at the graves, and Oscar no longer felt awkward standing there. He had shared an important moment with someone who had always been nice to him, and although he didn't understand exactly what had happened, he was glad to have been able to offer at least a little bit of comfort.

Ute swept a lock of hair away from her face and gestured with her head in the direction of the house.

"I agree," Oscar said. "We should go b—"

The words died on his lips the moment he saw a large winged shape soaring through the sky. It was almost directly overhead, flying so high that her violet scales still reflected the light of the setting sun.

I didn't see her coming. She's headed this way.

Oscar's heart sank under the weight of leaden dread. Dresde was coming closer, and it would be seconds before she was able to see them, if she hadn't already. They were exposed. Vulnerable.

"Get down!" Ute yelled, and she tackled Oscar to the ground.

The fall hurt, but Oscar realized that Ute had cradled his head with her hand as they both tumbled down into the grass. She was lying on top of him now, shielding him with her body, her hair obscuring his vision of the sky.

"Be quiet, and do not be scared," Ute whispered. "She will not get you. If she tries, she will have to go through *me*."

Oscar held as still as he could while his mind struggled to process his fear of Dresde and the shock of hearing Ute's voice at the same time.

She can talk. Why hadn't she talked before? What's going on?

It was nearly five minutes before Ute indicated with a gesture that it was okay to stand up again. Oscar said nothing but followed her lead as they made their way to the river. They walked along its course downstream until they were close enough to the house to see the single light burning on the porch. Still silent, the two of them walked to the front door, where Oscar paused before opening it.

"Thank you for protecting me," he said.

Ute gave him a small, distracted nod. She appeared to have reverted back to her usual self, and Oscar was left to wonder exactly what had happened back at the graveyard.

"Mama!" Samantha's voice called out from behind them.

Oscar was relieved to see Samantha safe and sound. She was wearing a bathrobe and had a towel wrapped around her hair. She appeared to also have come from the river, although Oscar did not remember having seen her in the water.

"Hi," he said.

"Where were you?" Samantha demanded. She hugged her mother briefly and gave Oscar an accusatory glance. "Where did you take my mother?"

Oscar raised his hands, palms forward, placating. "I didn't take her anywhere! I found her at the graveyard. We walked back home together."

"At the…," Samantha began. Then her expression softened. "Oh, I see. Are you okay, Mama?"

Ute nodded with a smile.

"Okay," Samantha said. "We should go inside, then, and have something to eat."

All through dinner Oscar kept stealing glances in Ute's direction. He did not understand. From the way everybody else treated her, Oscar had assumed that Ute had some kind of mental disability that limited her speech, or perhaps some of her cognitive abilities. Laurie, Samantha, and Nadja were all quite protective of her, and they were always looking out for her safety, checking that she was comfortable. For the most part, they never left her alone.

Except that this afternoon she was out on her own. And she must leave the house when nobody notices or she wouldn't have been able to get those flowers.

Whatever the case, Oscar smiled at Ute whenever their eyes met. At times she appeared to be off in her own world, but he had seen that she was very much aware of her environment and the threats that surrounded them.

She protected me.

Oscar wondered whether Ute knew who he was, or whether she had merely acted out of instinct. If she could speak but didn't, she had to have a reason. During one of Oscar's therapy sessions back in Portree, Counselor Kamogawa had once mentioned that people reacted to horrible things in different ways. Sometimes, he had said, silence could be a response to mental trauma.

Oscar remembered the two graves, one so much smaller than the other.

What happened here? How did Jörgen and Erik die?

Still thoughtful, Oscar read another chapter from the novel for everybody after dinner. They seemed to enjoy it, although Samantha was a little bit more pensive than usual. Oscar wondered about that, but he was also wary of Samantha's temper, so he chose not to ask her about it and instead went straight up to his room after he finished reading.

There was a knock on the trapdoor a few minutes later.

"Come in!" he said, pushing the contraption down so that the ladder would extend.

Samantha climbed into his room. She had rarely been up there at all since Oscar had moved in. It appeared to disturb her. She took a brief look around before focusing on Oscar, and her eyes lingered on the guitar that still rested on its stand in one of the corners.

The shadow of sadness, so familiar on her features, crossed her face once again.

"If you're going to yell at me about your mom, I swear I didn't take her anywhere," Oscar said preemptively.

"What? Oh, that. Do not worry. My mother can take care of herself. She may not look like it, but she used to be a martial arts specialist. She taught me hand-to-hand combat."

Oscar remembered how easily Ute had tackled him to the ground while simultaneously making sure he wouldn't hurt his head in the fall.

"I definitely believe that," he said. "Um, by the way...."

"Yes?"

Oscar considered telling Samantha about how Ute had spoken, but he chickened out. "Nothing. Did you want something?"

"Correct," she answered with what could have been a hesitant expression. "Rest well if you can today, male."

"Oscar," he corrected automatically.

Samantha ignored him. "I have tried to delay this for as long as I could, but it appears she is either bored or has another motive. I pray it is just the former."

"What are you saying?" Oscar asked, although he could very well guess.

Samantha met his eyes. "Tomorrow you will come with me to the eyrie. Dresde has summoned you."

"Oh. Um, okay."

Oscar's knees went weak. He all but collapsed on the bed when he tried to sit down.

Don't be scared. Stay calm.

"We will leave before sunrise," Samantha continued. "I will take my spear, and I suggest you take one too in case she wants you to participate in the hunt."

"The hunt? Spear?" Oscar's mind was sluggish as he grappled with the fear. He glanced to his right, at the place where one of the boards that used to cover his window had been ripped out the previous night.

She did that. She was watching me. She likes to see me scared.

"I believe there are spears here," Samantha replied, walking farther into the room until she reached the spot where the extra yult weapons still lay. Oscar hadn't touched them at all. "Take one of these tomorrow, just in case. She has lately asked me to capture bigger and bigger prey to feed the Flower, and the hunts can be dangerous."

"Hunting. Right."

Samantha picked up the spears, chose one, and gave it to Oscar. He accepted it without really registering what he was doing.

"Any questions?" she asked him. She made her way to the trapdoor and began to descend.

"One," Oscar said quietly.

"What is it?"

He swallowed. The spear in his hands felt very heavy. "Will I come back?"

He hated that his voice sounded so fearful, but he couldn't do anything about it.

Samantha gave him a sympathetic look that scared Oscar even more. For her to look at him like that must mean she felt sorry for him.

Her voice was regretful when she answered. "I do not know."

chapter 17.
water

AFTER THE carnage of the battle between Flyer, Singer, and Spine wurl, the placid calmness of the ocean waters was almost mocking.

Elias sat on his backpack, hugging his knees to his chest, and witnessed the sun going down over the western horizon. It was a beautiful spectacle—something he had never seen in fact. He watched as the sky went from blue to golden, orange, and red. The disk of the sun diminished in brightness as it appeared to touch the edge of the water, where a brilliant stripe of red-gold light was reflected on the flat and featureless expanse that was the ocean all around him. Faster than he would have liked, the sun sank into the fathomless abyss and disappeared from view as the entire world turned away from its star for one more day. The sun left a lingering brightness on the horizon, light pink and fast fading. Overhead countless twinkling stars had appeared, and two of the moons were out, their irregular surfaces reflecting sunlight only partially, looking like two silver-white sickles on a field of deep azure littered with sparkling diamonds.

Elias tried to admire all of this beauty, but he felt only emptiness. Loss.

His left hand twitched as he flinched, involuntarily, from the memory of what it had been like to die impaled by spines.

That wasn't me.

He called his attention back to the present, but another memory flashed in his mind. He remembered how it had been to fall down from the sky, terrified and paralyzed, only to be grabbed by horrid muscular tentacles that had snapped his bones and crushed the life out of him.

No. That was not me.

Unbidden, his mind flashed even further back, to the dull burning agony that Sizzra had endured during the last months of her life as the raging, burning wound from the Life Seed had slowly eaten away at the flesh on her snout.

A choked sound escaped Elias, almost a whimper. Heavy footsteps behind him heralded the approach of Narev, who came closer until his face was level with Elias's head.

Elias placed his hand on Narev's head and closed his eyes. Narev knew something was wrong, but he did not understand what it was.

That makes two of us, Elias thought miserably.

The stifling warmth of late afternoon gave way slowly to gentler, balmier weather. Eventually the light of the sun died away completely, leaving only starlight and moonlight to illuminate the incomprehensible vastness of the sea. The air smelled like salt and kelp, and also like blood. There was no wind, and the world was mostly silent. Only gentle splashes every now and then indicated that they were all still in motion, being carried away by unseen oceanic currents in whichever random direction they pleased, atop the dead carcass of a carnivorous ocean maw.

"Are you hungry?" Tristan asked softly, coming to sit next to Elias. Narev wandered off to where Siv and Vanor were resting and lay down, making the entire platform tremble under his weight.

"Not really," Elias replied. He felt cold, but that made no sense, not in the tropics like he was.

"You should eat something even so. Here, I had been saving these. I call them flanties."

He offered something roughly circular to Elias, an object that was about the size of a large pear and vaguely the same shape, except for the fact that its skin was almost completely white, ridged, and rough.

"It's a fruit I found back at the beach," Tristan explained. "Well, Siv found one first. He shared a bit of it with me, and it's really good. Then I went out looking for more, but I only found these two. I put them in my backpack for later, and I remembered just now. They're very sweet. You should give one a try, skin and all."

Elias did not feel at all like eating, but he realized Tristan was worried about him and was trying to help, so he obliged, biting into the fruit despite his misgivings. He had expected the flesh inside to be tough, but it was the complete opposite: soft, moist, and wonderfully juicy. The fruit was sweet, but not overpoweringly so. It was also fresh, completely unlike most of the things Elias had eaten growing up, which had always been pickled or made into marmalade or otherwise preserved. As Elias ate, part of the soul of the world awoke inside him once more. It was as if New Skye were sharing its energy with him. Its life force.

"This is amazing," Elias said, and he meant it.

Tristan nodded, mouth full. He had bitten into his own fruit, and juice was running down his chin.

Elias ate some more. "What do you call these again?"

"Flanties. What do you think of the name?"

"I think we're going to run out of names for stuff one day, since we keep discovering new things all the time, so this one's great."

Elias finished his fruit and realized he had been thirsty and hungry. He placed his hand on Tristan's leg and smiled. "Thanks for looking out for me, Tristan."

Tristan nodded, but his brow was furrowed. The faint silver light of the moons steeped part of his face in deep, dark shadows. "What's wrong, Elias? What happened to you after the battle?"

The battle, Elias thought. *Fitting name. This feels like war.*

"I'm not sure. Do you remember that time I wasn't able to kill the Flyer, weeks and weeks ago?"

"Yeah."

"It was like that again, only more. I could feel them dying around me, Tristan. I could feel their pain, their fear."

"Is this because of your connection to the Life Seed?"

Elias shrugged. "I don't know anymore. All I know is it's wrong. It's like you said, wurl don't prey on one another. They don't even compete for the same ecological niche. Them fighting like this—it's not right. It just isn't. I don't understand it. I mean, the Flyers I get, kind of. Dresde is making them do this. But the Singers? Why did they attack us the moment they saw us? What did we ever do to them?"

A few silent moments passed. From nearby the heavy, reassuring bellows of three wurl sleeping reached Elias's ears.

"I have been thinking about that, you know," Tristan told him. "It's odd. The way Singers have acted so far is weird."

"Yeah. They lured Narev to his death here on this horrible ocean maw. Then they attacked us. They set a trap, like you said."

"Maybe," Tristan conceded, but he sounded thoughtful.

"What do you mean?"

"I don't know yet. It doesn't make sense. I just hope they don't come back."

Elias looked out over the ocean. The water reflected the sky faintly, and for a moment it seemed as though he were floating in the middle of a vast dark marble, surrounded by stars everywhere he looked.

"I don't think they will come back, not for a while," Elias said. He still remembered how painful the sonic bomb had been.

"Can you scare them away again if they do?" Tristan asked. "With that awful sound you played?"

Elias shook his head. "The electronics are fried. I overloaded the circuitry on purpose for that one time, and all we have left are our links and a wireless speaker that doesn't work anymore. If they come back, we won't have any way to get rid of them."

"Except fighting them."

"I hope it doesn't come to that."

"It looks like tonight, at least, we're safe," Tristan pointed out. "And I think we need to rest. Come on, Elias. We can sleep with the wurl."

"Right," Elias answered, and a wave of exhaustion swept over his body, surprising him. "Sleeping is a good idea."

Tristan took Elias's hand and led him to where their three companions were already resting. Vanor awoke only briefly, his red eyes glowing in the dark as he acknowledged them for an instant and then fell promptly back asleep.

Elias lay down on the rough, leathery surface of the ocean maw and used his backpack as a pillow. Tristan settled down behind him. Elias grabbed Tristan's hands over his own stomach and closed his eyes, grateful for the feeling of safety he experienced when surrounded by friends and the man he loved.

His eyes fluttered shut. He fell asleep almost immediately.

He had nightmares and woke once or twice in the night. He tried to remain quiet nevertheless. He did not want to disturb Tristan, who slept soundly next to him. The hours went by slowly, though, and the next morning he had already been awake for some time before the first rays of the sun caressed the eastern horizon.

He stood up and examined his unfamiliar surroundings. The sky was as cloudless as the day before. The temperature was mild, but he knew that the rising sun would soon change that. The air smelled cleaner that morning, or maybe it was simply the fact that he had gotten used to the odor of kelp drying in the sun. None of the Spine wurl were on the platform, but Elias was not worried. He suspected they were underwater, hunting. They would come back up in time.

"Morning, Tristan," he said when Tristan finally woke up.

"Hey. Where are the wurl?"

"In the water, I think. Don't worry. They'll be back."

"Oh yeah. I always forget that they can breathe underwater."

"They're amazing creatures."

The sun had fully risen in the sky by the time Tristan and Elias sat down together near the center of the platform, flanking a small pile of objects, food, and water containers.

"All right. We need to make a plan," Tristan said, adopting the authoritative tone that reminded Elias of Tristan wearing his Colony Patrol uniform, bossing people around.

Elias smiled. In a crisis, he definitely wanted Tristan on his team. "I'm all ears."

Tristan patted the surface underneath him. "First, this thing. The ocean maw."

"What about it?"

"Is it going to sink, do you think?"

"I don't know," Elias admitted. "But I don't think so. I think this is an organism that evolved to resemble a bunch of floating kelp, camouflaging itself so it's able to trap anything that climbs onto it. Maybe it normally feeds on ocean birds or something like that."

"But now it's dead."

"Yeah, but I don't think that makes any difference. This is a plant, not an animal. At least I'm ninety percent sure."

"Okay?" Tristan said, indicating he did not follow.

"That means that its structural integrity will probably remain unchanged for a while. Even if it has died, like this one. I'm not totally convinced of this, but considering the fact that we spent all night on it, with the weight of two guys and three wurl, I don't think it's going to sink right away. If it is a kind of plant, the creature probably does not have any means of locomotion, or a way to swim on its own through the water. My theory is that it simply floats wherever the currents take it, and the shape of its body is optimized for that." He brought up his link. He had long since lost the GPS signal that connected him to Portree, but the link was still able to track distance covered in approximate numbers. "According to my link, we have traveled about fifty kilometers since last night. The creature did not move on its own, which means that we are being carried by the current, floating along."

"Okay. Good. That takes care of one problem, then."

"Yeah. At least we don't have to ride the wurl—yet."

"Which leads me to the second problem," Tristan said. "Navigation."

"The platform is too big," Elias told Tristan. "I don't think the wurl will be able to tow it the way they did with our boat. Besides, we don't even have the ropes anymore. They would have to push it somehow, and I'm concerned that if they do, they might simply crush sections of the maw, and *then* we will sink."

Tristan nodded. "Yeah. I was thinking more or less the same thing."

Elias pointed at their worryingly small pile of supplies. "This means that this, right here, is most of what we have. The wurl will probably share some of what they kill with us, but you can't eat it."

"I can try," Tristan said.

"Yeah, but we need to be prepared. If you can't digest it, that means you should eat most of the food here, which isn't much."

It was not an understatement. Most of their supplies had been lost with the boat. They had some dried food in their sealed metallic envelopes, about two liters of water, a change of clothes, and some fire-starting equipment that had been soaked and was therefore useless. Critically, however, they did have one other item—the water condenser.

"I'm not concerned about the food, not that much," Tristan said, nodding at the condenser.

"Water," Elias said, agreeing with him. "I know."

"We need to look at it like it is, Elias. Okay?"

Elias looked into Tristan's eyes and nodded. "Okay."

"Here's the situation. We're stranded. In the middle of the ocean. We have no real way of knowing where we are aside from the maps on our links, but they can't track our position anymore, so where we are is anybody's guess. We have a little bit of food, even less water. With what we have now, we won't make it. Not even if we each ride a wurl and leave everything else behind."

Elias gulped. Hearing it said out loud made the situation scarier.

"We have to make a choice: go back or continue. If we go back, there's no guarantee we will make it, even if we keep going west until we reach land. I'm not even sure the wurl would be able to carry us that far, or whether they would even want to. After all, they are trying to save their future queen, just like we are trying to save Oscar... but if we keep going forward, it's almost certain we won't survive."

"I know," Elias said quietly. Images flashed through his mind. Oscar screaming as Dresde took him away. Sizzra's reminder that his promise would bind him forever. "But I have to try."

Tristan crossed his arms over his chest. Then he smiled. "I thought you'd say that. In that case, let's see what we can do."

They spent the better part of that morning organizing their supplies and setting up the condenser right away. The wurl came back a couple of hours later, and

Elias saw that Narev held a spike-covered sphere in his jaws when he surfaced. The wurl heaved himself onto the platform, making it wobble, and trotted over to Elias, radiating contentment. Vanor and Siv had not brought anything to share, but they were also projecting the satisfaction that usually followed a successful hunt. The two of them settled on the opposite edge of the platform and relaxed, sunning themselves.

"What's this, Narev?" Elias asked. The spiky ball Narev had dropped at his feet was unlike anything he had ever seen. He was not even sure whether it was a fish or something else.

Still dripping water everywhere, Narev poked the sphere with his front foreleg, hard.

The sphere uncurled.

"Oh. Gross!" Elias said, taking a step back involuntarily.

Narev projected confusion, but Elias did not think he could approach the thing the wurl had hunted. It had to be an overgrown crustacean of some kind, like a gigantic shrimp with dozens upon dozens of short articulated legs that hung limp in the light of the noonday sun. The center of the creature had been cleanly speared by a silver spine, and only when he made certain that the thing was really dead did Elias approach again, gingerly.

"What in the generation ship is that?" Tristan asked from nearby. He sounded as disgusted as Elias felt.

"Some kind of copepod analog," Elias answered, still unwilling to touch the animal.

"Some kind of what?"

"A crustacean, like a Terran lobster. But I didn't know it was possible for crustaceans this big to exist."

Again, Narev projected contentment. Elias received a faint mental image of Narev scouring the bottom of the sea, looking for the tasty creatures that he had only tasted once before in his life.

"So this is a treat, huh?" Elias asked the large wurl, placing his hand on Narev's forehead. Through the contact, as usual, his perceptions of Narev's experiences sharpened, and he was able to see clearly how the wurl had killed and eaten one of the crustaceans underwater, spending some time afterward trying to find another one to bring back up. It had been difficult, but he had managed, even shooing Siv away from his kill.

"A treat?" Tristan echoed.

"I think wurl love eating this animal. Narev got one for us to share."

"Uh… okay. Thanks?"

The seemingly dead creature twitched, and both Elias and Tristan flinched. Narev grunted, confused.

"Thank you, Narev," Elias told him. "I'm going to try to cook this somehow."

"Good luck with that," Tristan told him. "I can't eat animals, and I'm not going to start with this thing. I'll stick to the rations if that's okay with you."

"Yeah. Of course. I'll eat whatever Narev brings me. You eat the other food we carry."

Tristan proceeded to sit down and enjoy a package of dried food that he claimed was lentil curry, while Elias was left with the alien-looking giant shrimp.

"I'm not even going to give it a name," he grumbled, reaching for a knife.

He spent the next hour essentially dissecting the animal, trying to find which parts he could eat. It was not pleasant work, but at the end of it, he had managed to pry open the surprisingly tough exoskeleton of the creature to expose white, glistening meat that appeared to be moist and supple.

Narev was still standing next to him, mentally urging him to take a bite.

"Okay," Elias mumbled. "Here goes nothing."

He carved out a piece of the meat, closed his eyes, and put it in his mouth.

It was tart, tough, and a little bit slimy, but not as bad as he had expected. It had ample moisture, and the savory juice filled his mouth as he chewed. The flavor reminded him of breaded shrimp sticks he'd had back home, when there had still been some, but mixed in the seafood tang there was a hint of spice to it, which was not altogether unpleasant.

"How is it?" Tristan wanted to know.

Elias swallowed. He shrugged. "I think I could get used to it."

"Good. I'm going to eat over there if you don't mind. Far away from this, uh, thing."

After eating as much as he could, Elias set aside a few more pieces of meat for dinner and gave the rest of the creature to Narev, who happily devoured it in three bites.

"I think we should check out the ocean maw from beneath," Tristan suggested after they were done. "You know, to make sure it's dead."

"Yeah. Good idea."

The two of them stripped down to their underwear and jumped into the ocean. The water was warm, and Elias was reassured when Vanor decided to jump in with them and hang out nearby.

"Do we dive down?" Elias asked.

"Yeah. Let's see what we can see."

Elias took a big breath and then plunged his head into the water. He used both hands and feet to go farther down and then opened his eyes, fighting against the sting of the salt. As quickly as he could, he took stock of what he could see.

He had imagined the ocean maw to be a large organism, but it appeared to be quite flat, even from beneath. Kicking hard with his legs, Elias swam beneath the platform as far as he was able to go and saw only kelp strands, or something that looked quite similar to it, hanging from the underside of the dead maw. There were no roots extending down into the water, no main stalk. The maw was like a giant lily pad, wide but not very thick, with the exception of three strange dark growths near the center of the platform which appeared to be big enough to each contain two wurl side by side.

Elias's lungs demanded oxygen, and he swam away until he was able to come up to the surface for air. Sputtering, he waited for Tristan to come up.

"Anything?" Tristan asked him.

"It's dead," Elias reported.

"Did you see the things near the center?"

"Yeah. I'm guessing that would be the stomach."

"Is it a threat, do you think?"

"No," Elias said confidently. "The plant won't be trying to eat any of us anymore."

"Okay. Good."

Elias followed Tristan back onto the platform. Together, they checked the progress of their condenser, which had captured enough moisture out of the air to fill about a fifth of a drinking glass of water.

"Not much," Tristan observed.

"I know."

The rest of the day went by uneventfully, although Elias had a mild sunburn after being all day out in the open. He slept as fitfully that night as the night before, and he was tired the next morning.

There followed several days that blurred together in their monotony. Elias tried to do as Tristan instructed, sticking to a routine to help while away the minutes, but it was hard. There was almost nothing to do other than read the occasional message from Portree. In the mornings he would eat whatever fish or strange creature Narev brought for him, and that was the high point of the day. Afterward, as the merciless sun climbed ever higher in the sky, he and Tristan would sometimes simply lie next to one of the wurl, sheltering from the heat in the shade they provided, using their own clothing or the empty backpacks to cover their faces or their heads and trying to escape the ever-present danger of heat stroke.

In the early afternoon they would swim for a bit, but as their food reserves dwindled, it became clear that spending energy in frivolous activities was out of the question. Elias was very worried about what they would do once the dried food ran out. He knew he would not starve—Narev would not allow it. However, Elias had no idea how they would get food for Tristan if they were unable to find a vegetable source of nourishment.

Far more urgent than the food was the water, a constant reminder of their perilous situation. They had rationed it, but on the fourth day of their aimless drifting at sea, it ran out. They were left with the condenser only, but it produced less than two full glasses per day, and it was simply not enough for two men.

Elias favored Tristan once again, arguing that he could get some moisture from the flesh of the animals that Narev brought to him, which was true. Tristan had

resisted at the beginning, but on the fifth day he finally gave in and drank most of the water himself. Elias
was parched, but he did not say anything. He knew that
their resources were stretched to the limit now, and they
would need to find a way to keep going if they wanted
to live.

Elias began dreading the sunrise, because with
it came heat and thirst. It was maddening to be surrounded by water that he could not drink, and during
the hottest hours of the day, both Tristan and he would
lie quietly, scarcely talking, each second dragging on
like an hour. Elias took to looking at his link every few
minutes, staring at the estimate of the distance they had
crossed. It was pitiful. Whatever ocean current was
dragging them along only took them about forty kilometers per day, due east. They needed to cross thousands of kilometers to get to Raasay.

Irritability began to thread its insidious tendrils
into everyday interactions. At first it was little things,
like deciding whose turn it was to check on the condenser and make sure it hadn't turned over. As the days
went by, though, Elias found that many more things
made his temper flare. It could be the heat, or finding
that Tristan had sat down on his spot in the shade next
to the wurl. It was also watching him eat the last few
remnants of their dried food while Elias was reduced
to eating raw fish that he had long since stopped being
disgusted by, but which was by no means enjoyable.

At night Elias began to wake up with every little
noise. If Tristan got up in the night to pee overboard,
Elias woke up and resented him for it. If one of the wurl
tossed in his sleep, Elias would grit his teeth and try to
find release in his own dreams, often unsuccessfully.
When he did fall asleep, the nightmares from the battle

reared their ugly heads as if they had been waiting for him to let his guard down.

The mornings brought no relief. On the seventh day, near noon, he realized his entire body ached. He was tired, thirsty, and bored out of his mind.

He took out his link and made the same calculation he had already made several dozen times over.

"At the rate we're going," he said weakly, lying next to Tristan in the shade of Siv's body, "It's going to take seventy days to reach the coast. That's seventy full days. Two months."

"Hmmm," Tristan grunted noncommittally.

"And that's if the currents don't change."

"Hmmm."

"And if we don't run into any other storms. There's no way the water will last us that long, or the food. To say nothing of more Singers or Flyers. If they attack us, we have no defense."

"Hmmm."

"Also, assuming we don't—"

"Stop that, Elias," Tristan snapped, his voice sharper than Elias had ever heard it.

"What?" Elias retorted, hurt.

"Listing every single way we're completely screwed. I know we are, okay? I don't need to hear it every single day."

"Sorry for being informative," Elias spat back.

"That's not being informative. That's being negative."

"Oh, so it's negative to be realistic about our situation?"

"Yes."

"I don't have to deal with this," Elias huffed. He sat up quickly, and his head spun for a minute from the motion, compounded by his exhaustion. When he recovered, he walked over to Narev and sat next to him to sulk.

"That's right, run away from a proper discussion or admitting you were wrong," Tristan called.

"Leave me alone, Tristan."

"Fine," Tristan replied sarcastically.

"Fine."

The remainder of the day crawled miserably by in an uncomfortable silence. When his thirst got too bad that afternoon, Elias went for a quick dip in the ocean water, but it was torture. He climbed back onto the platform, wondering if he should attempt to eat the kelp that still clung to the ocean maw or if that would be suicide. He had no idea whether the tissues of the kelp would be saturated with salt or not.

He sat with his feet over the edge of the platform and wondered where the wurl were. They had dived into the ocean around noon and had yet to return. He had eaten part of a fish Narev had brought him in the morning, but the meat had been tough and difficult to swallow. In fact, now that he thought about it, he wondered whether eating it had been a mistake. If he remembered correctly from his physiology textbook, digestion used up a lot of water.

An electronic beep jolted him into full alertness. He turned to face the center of the platform, where the condenser was notifying them that it had finished producing five hundred milliliters of water.

The water was there. Right there, in its transparent little container. Elias looked at it, and then at Tristan, who had stood up and was walking to the container to retrieve the precious liquid.

The two of them locked eyes for a moment. They hadn't spoken at all since the fight in the morning.

Elias looked away and tried to think of something that was not water. He was scared, lonely, and really thirsty. He began to think that it had been a mistake to embark on a quest halfway across the world he did not know, completely unprepared, trusting blind luck.

I'm sorry, Oscar, he thought to himself. *I don't know if I'm going to make it.*

He heard Tristan approach behind him. Elias stiffened and did not look at Tristan as he sat down next to him with a sigh. A torturous *slosh* of liquid in a bottle was all-too easily audible in the quiet of late afternoon.

"Here," Tristan said.

Elias considered ignoring him. They had never fought before, and although he was angry, he realized he was also scared and sad.

He glanced at Tristan, who was smiling, holding the bottle out for him. It was still full. He hadn't drunk a single drop.

"I know you're thirsty," Tristan said. His own lips were cracked, parched from lack of moisture. "You should have this."

Something melted in Elias's heart, and his anger vanished. He reached for the water container and carefully set it aside. Then he fell into Tristan's arms, hugging him tightly.

"I'm so sorry, Tristan."

"I'm sorry too," he replied, hugging him back. "I shouldn't have spoken to you like that. I apologize. I—"

"You were thirsty. Tired," Elias finished for him. "I am too. I understand. I shouldn't have snapped at you."

"I *am* thirsty," Tristan conceded, "but you being angry at me, that was so much worse."

Elias smiled. "I love you."

Tristan opened his mouth, hesitated, and instead said, "Come on. You should drink."

Elias's brief burst of hope was squashed as quickly as it had appeared.

He can't say it. He doesn't love me.

I can't make him love me.

"Are you okay?" Tristan asked gently.

Elias closed his eyes for a moment. *It's okay. I can't change the way I feel about him, and he can't change the way he feels.*

"I'm okay," Elias replied. He even managed a weak grin.

"Let's share the water, then. It will do us both good."

That night, as Elias held Tristan in his arms, he took a moment to give silent thanks for having Tristan with him. Again Elias reminded himself that Tristan could have chosen not to come on this desperate quest at all, but he had done so freely. He'd had many opportunities to go back, but he had never done so. He had been true.

Even if he doesn't love me, he's always been there for me, Elias reminded himself. *He's never given up on me.*

He remembered how Tristan had found him at Crescent Valley all those months ago, and how Tristan had told him that he had never given up hope that Elias was still alive. He remembered the now countless times Tristan had saved his life, and he realized that he was not sad that Tristan could not reciprocate his feelings for him.

Instead Elias was scared.

He looked up at the star-filled sky and tried not to cry.

I led him here.

The recrimination rang true in his mind, and it would not stop bouncing in the close confines of his guilt-stricken skull. If they were in this situation, it was because this was the plan Elias had come up with. If they were now adrift and lost, it was Elias's responsibility to fix it. And he could not.

Elias hugged the sleeping Tristan more tightly in the darkness, a couple of tears running silently down his cheeks. His heart burned with guilt, worry, and desperation. He was not scared for himself, but he was terrified for Tristan.

I led him here, he told himself again, every word hurting like a lash. *If he dies… it's on me.*

chapter 18.
eyrie

OSCAR SLEPT very little that night, terrified about going to see Dresde the following morning. He had nightmares that were similar to the ones he'd had while he had been in the prison. He relived the anguish he had experienced while Dresde had carried him, and he also remembered the brief conversation with her when he had first arrived at the volcano. He recalled the way she had slapped his injured arm with her tail, knowing full well how much it would hurt. He kept having flashbacks of how quickly Dresde had approached him until she was standing close enough to end his life with a single bite.

The night brought him little rest, and he was almost glad when his link beeped, telling him it was time to wake up.

He got ready quickly and efficiently, grabbed the spear, and went downstairs. He barely tasted his breakfast.

"We are leaving now, Oma," Samantha told Nadja as Oscar was putting on his shoes by the door.

"Be safe, both of you," she replied.

Oscar looked up from tying his shoelaces, surprised. *Did she include me?*

"We will," Samantha said firmly.

Outside the air was fresh and invigorating, which helped Oscar focus, given that he was equal parts nervous and sleepy. The sun was about to rise, and the now-familiar landscape around the house was illuminated by the gentle light of dawn. It was very quiet, and only the far-off sound of waves breaking reached Oscar's ears.

He tried to tell himself it was going to be okay, but he wasn't sure he believed it.

He shouldered the backpack Samantha had assigned to him, which contained provisions and some water. It wasn't very heavy, for which he was grateful. He had no idea how long he would have to carry it.

"Follow me," Samantha said, heading uphill with her own spear in hand. "Doran has been sent elsewhere, so we will have to get to the eyrie on foot, and it is about three hours to the Flower chamber."

"Three hours. Right," Oscar replied, gulping. "Lead the way."

Samantha walked a couple of paces ahead of him, apparently unafraid, but Oscar couldn't help but remember the last time he'd taken this route with her.

It had been weeks ago, and he had tried his best to forget, but as they left the cliffside behind and headed for a distant cave on the upper slopes of the volcano, Oscar recalled vividly how awful it had been the night he'd first gotten there. His shoulder had hurt a lot. He had been confused, with no idea of where he was or what was going to happen to him.

My shoulder is better now.

He rotated his arms experimentally and felt no pain.

I'm also stronger than I was back then. I know where I am. And I think I'm not alone.

With three quick steps, he caught up to Samantha.

"What do you think she wants with me?" he asked, trying his best to sound casual.

Samantha shook her head briefly. "I do not know. As I said yesterday, sometimes she is simply bored. There have been times when she summons me only to talk."

"Talk? Like, as if she was your friend?"

Samantha's tightened her lips into a line. "No, nothing like that."

"Then what do you do?"

"Mostly, I listen. I think human speech amuses her. She can convey meaning without words—it has happened a few times—but I think she enjoys talking to me and forming sentences in her mind. I do not know how to explain. I intuit this. She is very intelligent, and sometimes I think she likes bouncing ideas off of another intelligent creature."

"And what do you guys talk about?"

"Sometimes inconsequential things," Samantha replied. The sun had come out fully, and the first golden rays of the morning appeared to caress her skin and made her inquisitive emerald eyes take on the color of amber.

Oscar realized he had been staring and turned his attention back to the increasingly steep path full of dark-gray gravel and some rocks of larger size that made the going tricky now they were actually climbing. He tried to use his spear as a walking stick, and it helped give him some stability.

"Sometimes?" he said to keep the conversation going.

Samantha sighed. "I would rather not go into detail about what she chooses to discuss. You should know this, however. She is a cruel creature. If you show her weakness, she will pounce on it. If she sees that her words hurt, she will keep talking and talking, hoping to break you. Show her nothing. Let her words wash over you, but never let them sink in."

"It sounds hard to do," Oscar said quietly.

Samantha gave him a rueful grin. "I have had many years to practice."

"How long have you, you know, been Dresde's, uh...."

"You can say it, male. Say it openly. I am her slave, as all in my family are, and now you. I may be her favorite plaything, but I am not free, and I never forget that. When she orders me to come, I come. When she orders me to fight, I fight. I never wanted to fly halfway across the world to duel with your brother and invade your home, but I had no choice."

"Why you, though?" Oscar asked, unable to suppress the question, even if it made Samantha mad. "You're the youngest. It's not fair."

Samantha appeared to think for a long while. Eventually they reached the entrance to the cave that led into the side of the volcano, and she went in without hesitation. Oscar followed close by, wincing at the sulfur-laden smell that reminded him even more strongly of the last time he had been there. When Samantha spoke next, her voice echoed faintly off the rocky walls around them.

"Why me? I suppose it is because I have stood up to her the most. Perhaps. My grandmother and Laurie interact with her as little as possible, and they never talk back."

"That's weird," Oscar commented. "Your grandma and Laurie are scary. Like, it wouldn't be easy to intimidate them."

"Oh, they are not intimidated. It is simply that they have too much to lose."

"What do you mean?" Oscar asked, although he was certain he wouldn't like the answer.

"They could lose me, male," Samantha said matter-of-factly. "Dresde threatens us with the only thing of value we have, which is our family. Therefore, out of love for me, they never challenge her. They know what would happen if they do. My mother…." There was a long pause Oscar dared not interrupt. "She paid the price for defying her, and she is now broken."

Oscar teared up at the catch in Samantha's voice.

"She's not broken. She can still talk," he almost whispered.

Samantha stopped so suddenly that Oscar bumped into her in the shadowy confines of the tunnel they had reached.

"What?"

"She can," Oscar insisted. "Yesterday we were at the graveyard together, before you came home. We saw D—we saw her, flying overhead. Ute tackled me to the ground and told me to be quiet. She told me she would protect me."

Samantha turned to face him, still standing very close. Oscar perceived clearly the faint citrus fragrance of her hair.

"You are certain of this?"

Oscar nodded vigorously. "I'm not making it up, I swear. I was really surprised."

Samantha ran a hand through her hair. "I always suspected she still… but why with you?"

"To be honest, I don't think she knew it was me. I mean, I think maybe she mistook me for someone else. It was weird. At that moment she looked so different. Strong, determined, fierce, awesome. Kind of, uh, like you."

Oscar realized he must be blushing, and he was thankful for the dim light that hid it from view.

Samantha resumed walking.

"Thank you for telling me this," she said. "It gives me hope, cruel though it may turn out to be."

Climbing the volcano was hard, and Oscar soon had no breath to spare for conversation. Although they had begun by taking a path that was similar to the one he had descended weeks ago, Oscar realized they might be going higher this time. Samantha led him ever upward, through tunnels of rock, caves, and breathtakingly beautiful but really scary sections out in the open on the exposed flank of the volcano.

After about an hour and a half of climbing nonstop, they finally had a brief break on an exposed ledge that looked south, where they had come from.

The view was spectacular. The sharp slope of the volcano was clearly outlined below them, and Oscar was able to follow the contours of the rolling landscape until, very far away, a hint of green showed him where the house should be. He was too high up to see anything in great detail, however, and other than a very thin and sparkling line that he supposed was the river, he could not distinguish any landmarks.

To the right the ocean spread out in all its immensity. Low-hanging clouds looked close enough to touch, and despite the fact that it was summertime and the sun was shining, Oscar shivered a little bit with the bite of the relentless wind that blew past him. The rock on which he was sitting was hot, though, and it counteracted the chill with a strong and pervasive warmth, which made Oscar wonder, not for the first time, why it was that the rock all around the volcano, as well as the water in the river, was always so warm. He wasn't an expert in geology, but he didn't think it was normal.

They had some food and drank most of the water in Oscar's pack while they rested. Oscar used the time to massage his legs, which were shaky after the relent-less hike. He was careful not to let his spear roll away, because if it fell off the side, he would never be able to retrieve it.

"How much farther till we reach the top?" he asked. He had to raise his voice a little bit to be heard over the wind.

Samantha looked up at the sun. "About an hour and a half more, I estimate. But we are not going all the way to the top."

"We aren't?"

"No. The caldera is a mysterious place where only Dresde goes. Our destination is the eyrie, which is below."

"Was that the place where we first arrived, after I was brought here?"

"No, that was but one of the many caves that face the ocean. The males often use them to rest at night, or at least they did before. I rarely see any males anymore other than Doran. The eyrie is above that, and it is a much larger chamber. You will see it very soon."

"Yay, sounds like fun," Oscar grumbled.

"We should go or we will be late. Dresde does not like to be kept waiting."

"Right," Oscar complained as he stood up, leaning on the spear. "Let's not make Her Majesty wait."

"You say it as a joke, but she really thinks of herself as the queen of the world," Samantha pointed out. The two of them made their way back into a nearby tunnel that led up. "She thinks every other creature on the planet is beneath her, and that includes her sisters."

"And what do you think?"

"I think she could be a great queen if she tried, but I also think she lost control of herself long ago."

"What does that mean?"

Oscar received no answer to that, and soon he was out of breath again. The climb was even more arduous than before, with the added complication of the temperature. It was tolerable at first, but the more they climbed the hotter it got. When they reached the vast underground chamber lit by a lake of molten rock that oozed slowly from a crack on the volcano's massive wall, it was all Oscar could do to remain focused and put one foot in front of the other. The air was stifling, and it was also noxious. Oscar hurried behind Samantha to leave the chamber behind as soon as possible, and he took in great gulps of fresh air as they reached a cave that he recognized. It was where he'd first arrived what seemed like ages ago. There was another magnificent view of the ocean at the mouth of the large chamber, but he had little time to appreciate it because Samantha kept going.

They took a rough path that was treacherous because of all the loose rocks. It was also narrow, barely big enough for one person at a time to use, and Oscar realized that the climb had only then begun in earnest. He was soon on all fours, panting, his only focus to keep going, telling himself to ignore the fierce headache that throbbed between his temples. He managed, but it cost him.

The next minutes were a blur of exhaustion. The temperature fluctuated between uncomfortably hot and chilly, and every rock held the potential for injury if Oscar trusted it too much and it ended up moving under his weight to potentially send him tumbling down the way he had come as he broke every bone in his body. Oscar got scared that he wouldn't be able to reach the top or, worse, that Samantha would leave him behind to fend for himself with no idea how to get back down at all.

He was obsessing over this last worry when he bumped into Samantha once more as she finally stopped.

"Our last break," she said, very nearly whispering. "We are close."

She offered him water from her pack, which Oscar gulped gratefully once he stopped panting. As he handed the half-empty bottle over, he realized that Samantha had made it so they had drunk the water in his pack earlier, as well as eaten the food he had carried, so his backpack would be lighter for the hard part of the climb.

She climbed all this way with a backpack full of water and rations.

"I can't believe you do this all the time. You don't even look tired!"

Samantha shrugged. "I have come here many times. I am used to it."

"Still, wow. How close are we?"

"Close enough for you to keep your voice down. Remember, do as she says. Do not contradict her. With luck, she will get bored of you and we can be back home before sundown."

Oscar tried not to be too obvious about the fact that he was terrified and gave what he thought should look like a brave nod. Samantha packed the water bottle, picked up her spear, and resumed climbing, with Oscar close behind.

They broke into the eyrie with very little warning, climbing up from the path they had been following and through a hole in what had looked like the rocky ceiling of a tunnel.

Oscar followed Samantha up through the opening. He struggled to heave himself up but could not. Samantha lent him a hand, reaching down through the hole, and he was able to push with his legs and finally come out and stumble onto the floor of the largest rock chamber he had ever seen. His spear fell to the floor, and he scarcely noticed, distracted by what he saw.

"We are here," Samantha said. "The eyrie."

"It's… enormous," Oscar whispered.

He could barely see the walls on the far end of a vast cave that sprawled overhead, its domed ceiling so high up that even the stalactites that hung from it looked like tiny twigs. One side of the dome, which looked out over the ocean, had either collapsed or been sliced clear off the side of the volcano, and it offered the most dramatic view of the distant blue vastness of the sky Oscar had yet seen during his climb. He took a couple of tentative steps in that direction, marveling at the magnificence displayed before him. He had climbed so high that even the clouds were beneath him from where he stood. The wind howled in the cave, as if to say that he had reached the end of the world. He felt as though he were standing on the observation deck of the tallest skyscraper ever built, but on a scale that was not meant for humans. What would have been a window was instead an opening so large that his entire house would have easily been able to fit through it with room to spare.

He took another step toward the edge. He felt as though he needed to see, to peer over and look down. It was a mixture of morbid curiosity and sheer amazement.

Crack.

A hand on his shoulder stopped him. Oscar looked down at the source of the noise, where Samantha was pointing.

A bone?

Oscar examined the long white object he had snapped in two under his foot. The thing appeared to indeed be a bone, but it was different from all others

Oscar had ever seen. It was hollow inside and spiral-shaped. It was also long enough to have belonged to an adult person.

He took a few more steps, more carefully this time.

Crack.

Samantha brought her index finger up to her lips, telling him to be silent. Oscar stopped moving and instead let his eyes roam over the ground of the gigantic cave. He realized now that there were many piles of white things strewn carelessly around as far as his eye could see. Hundreds upon hundreds, maybe thousands.

All of them were bones.

There were skulls, wings, claws, and disembodied vertebral columns. Many were crushed to near powder, and he saw bones of every size. They made the cave look like the trash heap of a slaughterhouse, but with the conspicuous absence of anything other than ossified debris. There was no fur, there were no feathers, there were no scales, and there was no blood. Every bone had been picked clean of the last remnant of flesh that might have stuck to it, and the result was eerie. There was no smell of death or decay. In fact, everything appeared too clean, too aseptic, almost as if intentionally robbed of every trace of life. The only hint to the fact that there had ever been activity in the space besides the bones were countless black gashes in the rock that looked as though they had been made with a red-hot poker dragged over the ground.

Oscar met Samantha's eyes, more scared by the second. She gestured with her head and, taking his hand, led him away from the sheer drop and certain death at the edge of the cave and closer to its center.

Dresde was nowhere to be seen, for which Oscar was very thankful. It took the two of them nearly a minute to reach what Oscar guessed was the center of the space.

It was hot there, almost unbearably so. Samantha stopped rather suddenly and prevented Oscar from moving forward with her hand.

Something red and glowing dripped from above.

Plop.

Hiss….

The rock a few steps away from Oscar's feet sizzled as the reddish substance touched it. The drop of liquid bubbled immediately, like liquid nitrogen boiling away at room temperature, and a few seconds later there was no trace of it left.

Plop.

"Do not look up," Samantha whispered.

Oscar glanced at her just as another viscous drop flashed by his peripheral vision.

He couldn't help his reflex. He glanced up.

And immediately wished he hadn't.

He opened his mouth to scream, but Samantha clamped her hand over it with irresistible strength. Oscar managed to cut short the shout that had been fighting to break free from his throat, and as Samantha let go of him, he merely stared, his terrified eyes wide, at the thing that hung from the ceiling of the cave and constantly dripped thick red liquid that was so hot it was glowing.

It might have been a plant at one point, but all Oscar saw now was a grotesque parody of a living thing. Thick vines snaked through the ceiling of the cave, coming from all sides and looking like the pulsating veins in the living tissue of a creature larger than comprehension. The vines all met at a single point at the very center of the cave, and there the three largest ones threaded themselves into a tight braid that reached down halfway to the floor.

At the point where they all met, suspended maybe five meters above the rocky ground, was the Flower.

It was bigger than Oscar had imagined it to be, but not so big that he wouldn't be able to carry it. Hanging from the vines like a corrupted growth, its three fleshy petals drooped under the pull of gravity. There were hints of crimson on the petals, and glowing ooze dripped incessantly from their tips, hissing when it touched the rock below.

However, the vibrant red of the Flower appeared to be all but gone, nearly overtaken by unmistakable black corruption.

The vines on the ceiling were dark, so similar to the twisted brambles of the Field of Thorns and the black sand on the beach by the cliffs that Oscar was not surprised to see the same spiny, glasslike growths on the vines overhead as well. The thorns were perfectly transparent, like miniature prisms, but instead of looking beautiful, they were almost obscene in the twisted way in which they refracted light. It was like they offered a glimpse into a reality of twisted colors that had no place in the world of sanity.

The black that complemented the prismatic display was not limited only to the vines. The Flower itself had been all but engulfed by the darkness as well. The intricate capillary array on the surface of its petals glistened also with miniature versions of the same crystalline growths, making it look like rotting fruit overgrown with glassy fungus. The Flower's center was completely dark as well, and to Oscar it was like a gaping void into which he looked, unable to tear his gaze away from the corruption, the decay, the abomination.

A pull.

Oscar yelped, and he was halfway through taking a step forward so he could get closer to the Flower before Samantha stopped him.

"No closer," she snapped. "It can draw you in. Be careful."

"It's dead," Oscar whispered, full of equal parts revulsion and sadness. "The Flower is *dead*."

"No. It is much worse than that. It is—"

Hungry.

It was not a word. It was the most exquisitely distilled essence of a maddening sensation that blasted past all of Oscar's thoughts and banished them, leaving only itself in their place. He had never felt such hunger. He was going to starve. He needed to eat, to consume, to devour.

"Get back!" Samantha said, pulling him away. Her voice sounded distant despite its urgency. There was only the hunger, loud in its deafening silence. "I should not have brought you this close to it."

Oscar resisted her. He planted his feet and admired the thick, velvety blackness over the petals of the Flower.

It wasn't as repulsive anymore, now that he thought about it. The contrast between black and crystalline prismatic reflections was actually quite beautiful and entrancing. The black appeared to drink in the light, that hateful light that was like a plague on all of existence. It was safe here, inside this cave with no sun. There was very little brilliance except for the light the Flower itself generated from its red-hot, sizzling petals, and even that was finally dying out. As the light dimmed, the darkness grew.

But the darkness was hungry. It needed to be fed. Something, anything.

Oscar glanced at Samantha. Should he give her to the darkness?

No, too strong. But I can offer myself.

He took another step. Someone was restraining him, and he struggled with every erg of strength he could muster.

"Leave me alone!" he shouted, trying to push Samantha away. His shout echoed throughout the cave. He needed to get closer to the Flower. It hung high above him, yes, but he could try jumping. Climbing.

"Stop!" Samantha yelled.

Then she punched him.

Her fist hit him on the cheek, and the sudden pain snapped Oscar out of the trance even as he stumbled to the ground, narrowly avoiding falling on a brittle collection of bones. He looked up at Samantha, one hand on his cheek and one hand still on the ground, and registered her worried expression at last.

His vision cleared. She offered him her hand, and he took it. He lurched back to his feet, cradling his cheek.

"I am used to it, so it does not affect me as much," Samantha said. "But it is your first time. I should have known. We should not have come so close to the Flower. We should—"

What an amusing show this is, a silken voice said. Its echoing tenor dripped with contempt and amusement. *Does the tiny human male wish to offer himself to feed the hunger?*

Her claws appeared first, glowing as they gripped the ceiling of the cave at its far end, where the enormous opening exposed the chamber to the wind and the elements. Her head followed immediately afterward, and her sinuous body slithered into the cave even as she kept crawling on its ceiling like a spider, her talons gouging red-hot marks into the rock. Her wings were folded close to her body, but even then they were so large that they seemed to blot out the faint traces of sunlight that struggled to illuminate the eyrie.

"Dresde," Oscar whispered.

The glowing eye cluster on the queen's forehead zeroed in on him, and her attention overwhelmed Oscar's mind. Her awareness was different from the seething madness of the black Flower. Her mind was precise, sharp, like a scalpel used with expert precision to slice through mental barriers with irresistible cruelty.

Dresde dropped down from the ceiling, crushing bones under her claws. She half opened her wings as she approached, and Oscar was compelled to admire her. She was beautiful. The amethyst and violet of her scales appeared to sparkle, even in the dim light, and the way in which she moved, so confident and agile, spoke of power beyond his ability to grasp.

Welcome, she said, smiling with her mind. *I think we will have fun together, you and I.... I wonder. How loud can you scream?*

chapter 19.
light

ANOTHER SUNRISE greeted Elias and Tristan with the same monotonous promise of quiet suffering. It was day ten at sea by Elias's count, and there was nothing to look forward to.

That morning the dried food ran out. When Narev brought half of a dead spiral fish that was three times the size of its lake-dwelling brethren, Elias skinned it with now-practiced efficiency, using Sizzra's spine. He then carved out two large fillets and carried them over to Tristan.

"Do you... want to try?" Elias asked, holding one of them out.

Tristan looked at the pinkish, chewy-looking fillet and then at Elias.

"What if I can't, you know, digest it?"

"That would be really bad," Elias conceded. "If you get sick now, or get diarrhea, you're going to dehydrate even faster."

"Yeah. That's what I thought. But... I'm really hungry, Elias."

His voice cracked as he said that last word. Elias's heart felt as if it had cracked too.

"I don't know what to say," he told Tristan. "I think the decision should be yours."

"I never communed with the Life Seed like you did. I don't think I have the same connection you do. I never feel that thing you sometimes say when eating fruit."

"Like I'm sharing the soul of the world?"

"Exactly. To me it's simply food. And this… the colonists tried, right? When they first arrived on New Skye?"

"Yeah. They couldn't digest the animals here. Nobody has been able to, not in all this time. People back at Portree have tried many different things, but nothing has worked."

"But maybe things are different now. You said it yourself—the Life Seed has changed."

"The Flower is different now, yes. It was forced to adapt and evolve."

Tristan was silent for a long moment. "Okay. I suppose it's worth a shot. Let's… let's have breakfast."

Tristan took one of the fish fillets. He brought it up to his mouth, hesitated, and then took a bite.

"How is it?" Elias asked, taking a bite out of his own meal. This particular fish was relatively tasty, even raw. The meat was flaky and quite moist, which was a very welcome sensation in Elias's parched mouth.

Tristan chewed and swallowed. "Not bad." He took another bite, bigger this time, and he even grinned. "Not bad at all."

"That's incredible," Elias said, releasing a pent-up breath that had been full of anxiety. "This means you can eat meat too! We won't run out of food, then, as long as Narev keeps hunting."

"Oh," Tristan said, blinking quickly. "Oh."

"Tristan? What's the matter?"

Tristan shut his lips tight and appeared to want to hold in a burp. "Nothing. It felt weird, is all. Maybe I—"

But he did not finish his sentence. Tristan barely had time to scramble over to the side of the platform before he vomited. Elias rushed over to him, not knowing what to do. Tristan kept retching even after the contents of his stomach had been emptied into the sea. He clenched his midsection with both arms, as if in great pain.

"Tristan! Tristan, talk to me!"

Elias placed a hand on Tristan's back and felt him tremble.

"Wait a second. I'll get some water," Elias said.

He rushed over to the condenser and yanked its receptacle out. There was only a little liquid inside, but he hoped it would help. He hurried back to where Tristan was still on hands and knees, leaning over the side of the platform, eyes closed.

"Here," Elias told him, holding the bottle up to his lips. "Drink some water."

Tristan reached for it with trembling fingers and drank a couple of sips. Then he began to cough, sputtering. He retched again. He eventually sat back on the platform, breathing quickly through his nose. His forehead glistened with sweat, and when Elias wiped it off, it felt cold.

"Can't…," Tristan said, but he was sick again before he could get another word out.

Elias got out of the way and then helped Tristan sit back down.

"Don't speak," Elias told him. "Easy now. I'm here."

Elias held him for a long time. Tristan kept trembling, and he was only able to keep water down in very small sips. It was full noon by the time his shivering stopped. The water had run out, and Elias let go of

Tristan for a few moments while he set up the condenser once again. Then he went back to where Tristan was sitting and held him in his arms.

"It was awful," Tristan whispered after a while. "It was like poison."

"You're okay now," Elias said in what he hoped was a reassuring tone. The truth was he had no idea whether it was true. "You got it out. You only had a couple bites."

"It still hurts," Tristan replied, leaning into Elias a little bit more. "I've never felt like this before."

"Rest. It's going to be okay."

"I'm sleepy."

"You should take a nap. I'll be here."

Tristan dozed off alarmingly fast, and Elias spent the next few hours holding Tristan's hand, making sure he was still breathing. The guilt from before came roaring back with a vengeance.

I shouldn't have let him eat that. I shouldn't have offered him the stupid fish.

He'd had no idea that the reaction would be so violent. Nothing he had read in Dr. Wright's diaries had prepared him for this. However, now that he thought about it, he had never once heard a person in Portree suggesting they eat meat from any of the animals around the colony, despite the increasing shortages of food they had endured for decades. None of the genetic experiments to procure more food had ever involved anything other than plants and fungi, and Elias's aunt had never suggested using animal tissue to create lab-grown meat.

They probably knew this would be the reaction if they tried, he reasoned. *I hope the worst part is over.*

In the afternoon, the three wurl returned from their underwater hunt and immediately noticed that something was wrong. Vanor in particular approached closer than usual, even nudging Tristan once or twice to try and get a reaction. Elias tried his best to reassure him, as well as Siv and Narev, but he was scared. He had no idea whether there would be any other permanent consequences. He feared Tristan would have an allergic reaction that would close up his airways, and he was terrified that the meat would turn out to be literal poison.

By sunset Elias was at his wits' end. Tristan hadn't yet woken up, and Elias didn't know whether it was because Tristan was tired or because of something more serious.

"Tristan?" he asked at last, unable to bear it anymore. He shook him gently. "Tristan, wake up."

For a few torturous seconds nothing happened. Then Tristan's eyes fluttered open.

"Eli," he said softly.

"Hey. I'm here."

"What... what happened?"

"You ate something bad," Elias replied. "How are you feeling?"

"My tummy hurts."

A cold shiver crawled down the back of Elias's neck. *What if the meat damaged his digestive system?*

"It's okay, Tristan. Just rest, all right? I'm going to bring you some water."

Elias himself had not drunk a single drop that day, but the thought did not even cross his mind. He brought what little water the device had been able to condense and offered it to Tristan, making sure to pace the sips. It took quite a long time, but Tristan managed to drink all of the water and keep it down.

"I'm tired," Tristan said. The lack of energy in his voice was alarming. "I'm going to...."

He drifted off before finishing his sentence, and Elias teetered on the edge of panic. He had no idea what to do. He was thousands of kilometers away from the nearest doctor. He had no water, no food. He could not help Tristan. He could not help *himself*. He was trapped. He was trapped, and the cage was the ocean, with no way out. They were both trapped, and they wouldn't get out at all, and it hurt and it was unbearable.

A choked sound escaped his lips, but he did not allow himself to scream.

I'm having a panic attack, he told himself. *That's all. I'm having a panic attack.*

He would have made a noise, but he was scared of waking Tristan up.

I'm trapped here. I'm trapped!

Three large creatures approached and looked at him with clusters of unblinking red eyes. All of them, even Siv, appeared to sense that he was in great distress, and they were projecting a single, surprisingly clear message.

Reassurance.

Elias looked at all of them in turn, then down at Tristan in his arms.

Is he going to be okay? he asked the wurl.

They did not understand the question fully, but they did settle down around the two of them, still projecting reassurance in waves. Night fell, but the wurl did not move from where they were. Elias realized they were acting like guards again, protecting both of them from the night.

No, more than that, he corrected himself. *They are acting like friends.*

Elias tried to stay awake, but exhaustion got the best of him. He was so tired that not even his nightmares were able to wake him up. He only blinked his eyes awake after bright daylight disturbed him the next morning.

Tristan.

He panicked when he realized Tristan was not lying next to him. He sat upright, heart hammering, and looked around the platform.

"Good morning," Tristan said. It looked like he had been petting Vanor.

Words failed Elias for a moment. "Tristan? Tristan!"

Elias jumped to his feet, ignoring the wave of dizziness, and all but ran toward Tristan. He stopped short of crashing into him, still concerned.

"Come here," Tristan said to him, opening his arms wide.

The two men embraced, and Elias was relieved to see that Tristan was no longer trembling. "How are you doing? How are you feeling? Does your stomach hurt? Have you been ill again?"

Tristan chuckled. "Slow down, slow down. I'm okay, I think. Nothing hurts anymore, although I'm really thirsty. And hungry. That's nothing new, though, right?"

"Are you sure? How about your throat? Do you have a fever, or do you feel funny in any way?"

"No, Eli. I'm fine."

Eli. It's the second time he's called me that, Elias realized. Only his family had ever used that nickname for him.

Elias closed his eyes and gave a silent prayer of thanks. "I'm so happy, Tristan. I thought... I thought the worst yesterday."

"So did I, to be honest," Tristan admitted. "I'm not doing great, mind you, but I don't think I'm going to die because I tried to eat something that I wasn't supposed to."

"I'm so sorry I offered you the fish. I thought—"

"Don't do that to yourself. I decided to eat it. We had to know, right? And now we do: only you can eat meat. I suppose the rest of us normal humans on New Skye will have to remain vegetarian. Can't say I'm sad about it either. That fish was slimy and gross."

Elias laughed nervously, releasing part of the tension that had kept him on high alert ever since the previous morning. "It *is* kind of slimy."

"And *you* should be really thirsty," Tristan told him. "I don't remember much from yesterday, but I do remember you giving me water. You didn't drink anything, did you?"

Even the mention of water was painful. Elias shook his head.

"I suspected as much. Come on, let's check the condenser. Whatever's in there, that's for you."

"You were sick," Elias argued. "You probably lost a lot of fluids, and dehydration is a big danger. You should have it."

Tristan sighed theatrically. "Fine. Fifty-fifty."

They each drank some water while the wurl milled about, projecting happiness at Tristan's recovery. It was such a pure emotion that Elias could not help but smile, thankful that his family was safe.

My family.

The thought was surprising as he first put it into words, but it rang true. He had a deep connection to each of the four beings that had decided to accompany him on his desperate journey. Every one unique in their own way, he felt connected to them all, even if three of them could not speak.

The happiness and relief faded as the hours bled into one another, a haze of thirst under the searing overhead light of the sun. The reflections on the surface of the water were blinding, and when Narev offered part of his catch of that day to Elias, he realized he was far too thirsty to care about food anymore.

He and Tristan sat together, sheltering in the shade of the wurl and fashioning improvised hats out of their shirts, which they put over their heads to protect themselves from the heat. They held hands, but Elias could tell that Tristan was very weak. Tristan napped intermittently as the unbearable hours of midday went by and only woke up fully when the sun was already close to the horizon in the west.

When Elias realized Tristan was awake, he opened his mouth to ask him how he was, but his own lips were so parched that he could not get words out. He contented himself with a faint smile, squeezing Tristan's hand. He received a weak squeeze in return.

The three wurl, but in particular Narev and Vanor, began to radiate concern again. It was hard for Elias to explain to them why they had not eaten any of the fish Narev had caught, or why they were so thirsty when the wurl themselves did not have that problem. A tired part of Elias's mind attempted to consider the interesting scientific question of discovering how the wurl were able to remain hydrated in the salty environment of the ocean, but his thoughts were disordered. He found he was having a hard time concentrating.

Dusk brought some relief, but neither Tristan nor he moved from where they sat. They shared what little water the condenser had been able to procure, but having a few mouthfuls of precious liquid was somehow worse than enduring the thirst in quiet resignation.

The two of them sat down again, their backs against each other providing mutual support. Elias clearly felt Tristan's warmth on his own back and perceived also the steady rise and fall of his boyfriend's breath. They did not speak. Elias watched the interminable slate of the ocean water stretching out forever, featureless, dark. He wrestled with resignation, with more guilt.

This was a mistake, he thought miserably. There was not enough water. Simply not enough. The ocean— the world itself—was too big, too dangerous.

He would have cried if he had been able to, but all he did was shut his eyes tight, utterly defeated. The reality of their situation crushed him with its overwhelming weight.

We are going to die out here. We are going to die, and I can't do anything about it.

He realized he felt disappointment most of all. He had been so certain he could save his brother and Sizzra's daughter. He had been so confident in his own strength. Now that his luck had finally run out, he realized his bravado had been foolish, perhaps from the very beginning.

A choked sound escaped him, halfway between a grunt and a scream.

"Don't beat yourself up too much," Tristan said, his voice barely above a whisper, responding to Elias's thoughts in that uncanny way of his, almost as if he had been able to read them. "We tried."

"I should have planned better. I should have considered so many things."

"We did what we could," Tristan responded calmly. "We got far."

Not far enough, Elias thought, but something about the tone in Tristan's words stopped his self-destructive train of thought. He fell silent for a while, thinking about what Tristan had said. Eventually he experienced a shift in perspective and realized Tristan was right. This was out of their control. They had tried.

"Yeah," Elias said at last, his tone both rueful and accepting. "We got far."

The absence of the sun submerged them in the familiar inky blackness of the ocean at night, and the welcome coolness made the thirst less of an insistent scream and more of a background drone. For a while, Elias and Tristan watched the night.

The wurl suddenly jumped onto their feet, their eye clusters flashing in the dark. Almost as if they had rehearsed it, all three jumped into the water simultaneously, with a big splash that made the entire ocean maw wobble. Elias had expected to hear the familiar bubbling sound of them diving to the bottom to hunt, but instead he clearly heard all of them swimming away from the platform, due north, so fast that it was less than a minute before he was not able to hear their splashes anymore.

It had been unexpected, and it somehow hurt. Elias had the distinct impression that the wurl were abandoning them at last.

"Where are they going, do you think?" Tristan asked quietly.

Elias shrugged. Even that motion tired him out. "Maybe they're going to try on their own now. Maybe they understand that this last part of the journey is for us alone."

"Good for them," Tristan replied, with no hint of resentment. "They protected us as much as they could."

"Yeah. I do hope they'll try to save Oscar, as well as the new Spine queen."

"Do you think they'll have a chance? The three of them, on their own?"

"They're strong. Intelligent. I think they learned a lot during this journey with us, so yeah. They have a shot."

"Good."

More silence. None of the moons were out, so the blackness was particularly dense. The stars overhead were the only things that gave Elias any sense of direction, of where they were.

"We never did name any constellations," he said eventually. "A few of these are not visible from Portree."

"Any ideas?"

"I'm not sure. You see that red star over there?"

Tristan shifted, very slowly, so he would be able to see in the direction Elias was pointing. "Yeah."

"There are two other stars nearby, fainter, but also kind of reddish. The three of them make a kind of triangle."

"I see them."

"What do they remind you of?"

"Maybe…," Tristan began but then fell silent for a few seconds. "It's like their eyes. Like the eyes of a wurl."

"That's what I was thinking. And look, I think there's a nebula surrounding the stars. Kind of looks like a crown around the eyes, doesn't it?"

"Kind of."

"It reminds me of her."

"Sizzra?" Tristan asked.

"Yes. Maybe we can name the constellation after her. We can call it the Spine Queen."

"That's a great idea, Elias. You should add that to the stellar cartography charts when we…."

Elias reached for Tristan's hand. "That's okay. The two of us will know."

The stars were a seemingly endless canopy that appeared to shelter them. Some of them were reflected on the water itself, faint lights in the distance that shimmered and swayed in ghostly shades of purple and pink. As the ocean currents carried them onward, the lights on the surface of the water got brighter, blinking lazily, almost beckoning.

Wait. Those aren't stars.

Elias sat up straighter and looked again, squinting. He was not imagining it. In the distance, there were faint blinking pinpoints that phosphoresced very close to the water.

"Tristan, look."

The two of them sat side by side so they would be able to observe the strange phenomenon together.

"What are those?"

"No idea," Elias replied.

A few minutes later, they reached the first of the lights. Elias watched, entranced, as he realized that the glow was produced by bioluminescence from some kind of slender and immobile organism that poked out of the surface of the water, almost like the stalk of a tall reed growing in a river. A thin tube or stem rose about three meters into the air, where it ended in a starfish-like cap with many glowing and swaying tendrils that produced the same ethereal light, pink and purple and light blue. The tendrils floated gently in the air like leaves in the breeze. Under the water, the stalks of the plants were visible for quite a distance, bioluminescent as well. The entire structure pulsated slowly, going from full brightness to dim nothingness, and then back to its wondrous shine.

It was also not the only one. There were dozens upon dozens of the structures all around them now, and the currents took them through a veritable maze of the strange trees that would briefly burst with even brighter light if touched accidentally by their floating platform. As Elias and Tristan went deeper into the bioluminescent forest, the soothing light appeared to suffuse the atmosphere around them with a pleasant floral scent of growing things blooming.

"This is amazing," said Tristan with unmistakable awe.

"It's so beautiful," Elias agreed, noticing small fluttering specks of light among the trees. One of these specks floated closer, swaying in the air, and landed on Elias's knee. It was a small insect of some kind, with three V-shaped wings that gave off a magenta glow. Elias smiled, marveling at the beauty of the tiny creature as it took off into the night after a few moments. More creatures like it darted in and out of sight, like Terran fireflies or fallen stars from the sky above come to illuminate their way.

The forest appeared to be never-ending. Within it Elias saw other creatures in the water, darting in and out of the roots of the ocean trees. Some of those beings glowed in other shades—yellow and lime and violet. Many did not, but their shapes were clearly visible in the water nevertheless. Elias knew a brief moment of vertigo as he realized he was floating above an endless expanse of water, an entire world within a world with secrets he could never hope to understand. He had thought the things he had seen so far had given him an idea of the vastness of the planet he called home, but he now understood that there was no possible way to comprehend everything that surrounded him. Oddly, the idea gave him peace. It was okay to be a small individual human. Somehow, the majesty of nature reassured him.

Elias's link blinked once and then beeped with a very specific ringtone, the electronic sound completely at odds with the natural wonders around them. Elias silenced the link with a tap and smiled.

"What was that?" Tristan asked.

"A reminder of something important."

"Something important?"

"It's past midnight now," Elias explained. "And today is July the fifth."

"Today is…."

"Happy birthday, Tristan." Elias leaned forward and kissed Tristan on the lips. "Today you turn seventeen. You're officially an adult."

Tristan appeared not to know what to say. The bioluminescence around them allowed Elias to see Tristan's face as it broke into a bittersweet smile. "Thank you, Eli."

"I didn't get you anything," Elias apologized.

"You're here. That's the best coming-of-age present I could ask for."

Elias thought for a moment. "On the plus side, you are one of only two humans to ever see the Forest of Light."

"Nice name," Tristan commented. "You're right. This *is* a very nice present. And Eli?"

"Yeah?"

"I love you."

Elias gasped.

"Tristan, you—"

"I mean it," Tristan interrupted. He touched Elias's cheek gently with his fingertips. "You're my soulmate. I was scared to admit it before. I'm not sure why. But these past few weeks with you have been amazing and scary and wonderful, and I'm not afraid anymore. Life's too short to keep hiding how I really feel. If this is it for us, I just wanted you to know how much I love you. I want to be with you always, if that's okay."

Tristan gave him a shy smile.

Elias's heart overflowed with love.

He kissed Tristan and held him in his arms as he experienced pure joy.

"I love you too," Elias whispered into Tristan's ear. "With all my heart."

They shared another kiss and then admired the trees that were slowly thinning as they appeared to be exiting the forest. Elias's happiness went deeper than the exhaustion and thirst. He felt at peace.

"How old would I be in *Ionas* years?" Tristan asked after a bit. "You know, like on Earth."

Elias did some quick math. "You'd be about twenty years and, uh, four months old."

"Gotcha. We should have a party when we get back. Celebrate your birthday and mine. Yours is in November, right? The seventeenth."

"You remember?"

"Of course. You used to invite me over to your house for your birthday parties when we were little. You know, before your antisocial, sarcastic loner phase."

Elias chuckled softly. "I deserve that. And you're right. We should have a big party when we get back."

They fell silent again as they left the Forest of Light behind. The night was completely quiet, so it was easy for Elias to notice the sound.

"What's that?" he asked. It sounded like splashing in the distance.

"Don't know."

The two of them remained alert while the splashing got louder. Very soon, glowing eye clusters intermittently visible in the dark revealed the fact that wurl were approaching.

"Are those Singers?" Tristan asked.

A faint mental message reached Elias. It was full of urgency.

"No," he replied. "It's the guys. But they're in a hurry. In a *big* hurry."

The three approaching wurl raised a ruckus with their splashing and reached the platform in a few minutes. Siv remained in the water while Vanor and Narev jumped up and rushed to where Elias and Tristan sat.

Elias received the urgent emotion much more clearly now, from all three of them.

Vanor and Narev lowered their bodies.

"They want us to ride them," he told Tristan. "And we have to hurry."

"Why? What is so—"

At that moment, the night stillness was rent by a sound. It was a huge noise of rushing air and bubbling water, but on a scale that Elias had never heard before. The entire ocean appeared to tremble, and a wave reached them, coming from the north.

Hurry, the wurl echoed, almost shaping thought into words. *Hurry.*

"We have to get on," Elias told Tristan. "Now."

"But—the equipment. The condenser."

Another sound, alarmingly close this time. Something was moving over the surface of the water, distant, indistinct in the darkness.

Something big enough to block out a large portion of the stars in the sky.

Hurry.

Elias stashed the condenser in his pocket.

"We need to go!" he said.

There was another wave, and the sound of rushing air repeated itself, much more clearly.

It sounds like breathing, Elias thought as he used the last of his remaining energy to climb onto Narev's back, securing his position as best as he was able to. The only thing he took with him was Sizzra's spine.

"I'm ready!" Tristan called from nearby. He was already atop Vanor with his shock spear in hand.

"Go," Elias told the wurl.

They jumped into the ocean and torpedoed through the water. Elias struggled, simply holding on, completely blinded by the droplets spraying in his face. In brief bursts of clarity, he saw that the gargantuan shape that moved through the sea was getting closer. It was much, much larger than he had initially thought.

"Narev, it's getting closer!" Elias yelled, urging the wurl to swim in a different direction to avoid whatever thing was almost on top of them. "Swim away!"

But Narev ignored him, powering ahead as fast as he could swim.

Straight for a moving island.

chapter 20.
bait

THE VERY air around Dresde shimmered with the heat her enormous body radiated.

Oscar stood motionless, scared beyond his wits, and watched her slink forward like a stalking feline about to pounce. Her size shocked Oscar anew. He had gotten used to seeing Doran, who was big, but Dresde was an order of magnitude larger than any of the male wurl, and everything about her spoke of danger, strength, and speed.

Dresde flicked her tail through the air, making it crack like a whip.

Oscar squealed.

Marvelous, she said, doing it again. Oscar flinched. *You are so much more skittish than Samantha, little male. Are you afraid?*

Oscar tried to speak but found he could not. He knew Samantha was nearby, but such was the force of Dresde's full focus that he felt cut off from the entire world. He was alone and isolated. He was powerless to do anything but tremble while the wurl queen decided his fate.

I see you were admiring my Flower, Dresde continued, prowling in a wide circle around Oscar. *Is it not beautiful? Such exquisite darkness. And its transformation is almost complete. What do you think of it? Answer me.*

Dresde's mental pressure on Oscar's mind ceased so suddenly that he actually lurched forward as if he had been fighting against physical pressure. He realized he had control over his body once again, but Dresde's will was still there, directing his attention to the Flower behind him.

He didn't want to look, but he had no choice.

He was farther away from it now, and yet the Flower still yawned like a punctured hole of nothingness in the fabric of reality. It drew his attention, calling to him. Still hungry. Still a foul abomination of unspeakable ugliness.

"Your Flower is beautiful, Dresde," Oscar said, lying through his teeth. "It's magnificent."

Such a bad liar, Dresde said, yanking his attention back to her. *If you think it is so beautiful, why do you not go touch it?*

Oscar's blood ran cold at the words. If Dresde made him touch the Flower, he would not be able to resist. He also intuited that he would die in a horrible way. What had Samantha said? Weren't they now feeding the Flower with live prey?

Go, human male, Dresde coaxed him. *Touch it!*

"Please…," Oscar begged, but all he received in return was a mental prod. He was forced to take a step back and approach the black thing behind him.

He resisted, but it was no use; his feet dragged over the ground as if of their own accord, and he took another step back. He did not look behind him, but he heard something that sounded like a wet squelching noise, like something opening hungrily, dripping with thick saliva.

"No, please," Oscar whimpered.

Touch it, Dresde replied, gleeful. *Jump. See if you can reach it.*

Another step back. Something sizzled on the ground immediately behind Oscar.

"Dresde, if I may," Samantha cut in, yanking Oscar roughly away from the Flower, "I think this male might be more useful to us alive."

Dresde shifted the full power of her attention to Samantha. Relief washed over Oscar when the mental pressure on his mind eased. He glanced at Samantha, expecting her to be paralyzed under the force of Dresde's will, just as he had been. Maybe she would be terrified as well, trembling.

She was none of those things. Her eyes were defiant, her jaw firmly set. Even when Dresde took a step forward, Samantha did not back down.

Useful? Dresde asked. *How can he be useful, Samantha?*

"He is bait for his brother to come, like you said weeks ago. As long as he is alive, Elias will come to you, and you will enact your revenge for the… injuries you sustained."

Oscar blinked, and it was as though Samantha's words had shattered a glamour that had been placed over his vision to prevent him from noticing anything but perfection when he looked at Dresde. All of a sudden, he was able to see imperfections. Wounds. Scars.

The delicate membranes on Dresde's wings showed uneven tissue in several places, small circular patches that were slightly redder than the rest of the wing, with each about as wide across as a spine from a wurl.

Around the top of her neck were big jagged breaks in her beautiful amethyst scales, places where new scales had grown, but which were a noticeably lighter color than the others. The breaks were all aligned in a semi-circle. It looked almost as if someone had attempted to take a bite out of her neck.

The last wound was also the most noticeable. On Dresde's snout, a large violet scale had barely begun to heal. Oscar's mind flashed back to the day of the storm. That was when Elias had wounded her.

Dresde flared her wings out, and Oscar cowered away.

Injuries? she asked Samantha, her tone angry and disbelieving. *I was not injured by those lowly earthbound worms. I was the victor! For the first time in the age-old battle between sisters, I destroyed my rival without being killed in return! Sizzra is dead, and I live!*

"Still," Samantha insisted, "the male might prove useful if we keep him alive."

Is that so? Dresde asked, her mental tone half-disdain, half-sarcasm. She slinked to the side, still tracing a wide circle around Oscar and Samantha. The cave in which they stood was so large that she had ample room to do this, even when she fluttered her wings over her head. *Yes, you may be right. He is my bait, is he not?*

"Exactly," Samantha confirmed.

Dresde paused, one clawed foot still in the air, looking almost thoughtful. Then she cocked her head to the side in open mockery. *Or perhaps you are merely trying to save his life. Maybe you have grown attached to him in so short a time?*

"What? No, I—"

I know all, Samantha. I know this puny male has no way to communicate with his kin. If I were to kill him now, the older male with my sister's eyes would still come to me, oblivious to the fact that his quest is in vain. There is nothing stopping me from having fun with this one here. In fact, it may even be sweeter to end his life and then look into his brother's eyes when he realizes there is nothing he can do anymore.

A choked sort of groan escaped Oscar's throat. It was born out of despair, because Dresde's words were infused with her will, and through them Oscar knew that she was not making empty threats. She was truly considering killing him, right then, with no remorse whatsoever. He was nothing to her. He was going to die, and he had no way to defend himself. He had even discarded his spear earlier, and his hands were empty. Only Samantha still had her weapon, but it looked like a toothpick compared to Dresde.

The wurl queen shifted her attention back to Oscar, still circling around them. It was unnerving watching her slender body move with such grace, her muscles rippling underneath her scales and the way glowing gouge marks were left on the floor whenever she lifted her talons. With her proximity, the temperature in the eyrie was quickly becoming unbearable. She was terrifying beyond belief.

You never answered my question, she said to him. *How loud can you scream?*

She pounced on him, snarling.

Samantha yanked him with unbelievable strength and pulled him away from the place where Dresde's jaws snapped shut a split second later. He careened uncontrollably for a moment before tumbling down to the ground less than a meter away from the Flower.

Dresde whipped her head around and pierced Samantha with a flashing glare.

How dare you?

She whipped her tail again and struck Samantha in the face.

"Samantha!" Oscar shouted, breaking free of the spell keeping him silent.

She fell backward under the force of the impact and landed a couple paces away from him. When she moved her hand away from her face, Oscar saw that there was a red welt on her cheek and the corner of her mouth was bleeding.

"Leave her alone!" he exclaimed without thinking. He jumped to his feet.

Oh? Is this defiance I hear?

Oscar walked forward so he could stand between Samantha and Dresde. He knew the gesture was futile, but he also knew he couldn't stand by while Samantha was hurt because of him. He spread his arms wide in a protective gesture and faced down the queen.

Let us test it, shall we?

Dresde snarled again and crouched as if she were going to leap. Her talons began to glow even brighter, and the rock underneath them started to smoke.

Die, human!

Dresde swiped forward with one of her front claws.

Oscar screamed and ran away.

Laughing in her mind, Dresde slithered over the floor of the eyrie and cut off his escape. Oscar tried running to the side, but she cut him off again. He was forced to run back to where Samantha was still sitting on the floor, dangerously close to the Flower.

Dresde looked as if she wanted to pursue him further, but she stopped suddenly with a very brief but crystal-clear moment of fear in her mind. She backed away from Oscar and Samantha and resumed pacing in a wide circle around them.

Oscar looked up at the Flower. He glanced at Dresde and then at Samantha. Why had Samantha brought him so close to the Flower in the first place? Could it be that it was the only place that was safe?

You are very amusing, little male, Dresde said in a tone that was anything but amused. *I have decided not to kill you for now. Come closer. There is something I wish to show you, since you have climbed all this way to visit me.*

Oscar exchanged a panicked look with Samantha. He was not going to be able to resist the direct order from Dresde, not if she focused her entire attention on him.

Samantha, however, merely stood up and grabbed her spear. She looked away from Oscar and directed her gaze up to the Flower.

Come.

Powerless again, Oscar was compelled to walk to where Dresde was standing.

This way, she said, leading him to the far end of the dome.

Oscar walked. He was not sure where Dresde was taking him, and he could not even glance back to look at Samantha because Dresde's will saturated his consciousness and left no room for anything but obedience. He followed her like an automaton until they stood at the darkest section of the eyrie, a place that was even hotter than the rest of the cave. Oscar started to sweat profusely, and he felt as though he couldn't breathe.

What do you see?

He glanced ahead and choked out an answer. "I see an uneven wall, Dresde. Like a cave-in. Many big rocks, piled high."

Appearances can be deceiving, she told him and used her powerful front feet to move two enormous boulders that stood directly in front of them. The motion destabilized the entire pile of rocks and debris, which collapsed in on itself and kicked up an enormous cloud of choking grainy dust.

Oscar coughed, blinded, but Dresde flapped her wings forward once, and such was the force of the beat that the dust cloud vanished instantaneously. The view forward was clear, and Oscar gasped in awe.

An opening yawned in front of them now, offering a magnificent view of what looked like a lake in the distance.

Go forward.

Oscar did as he was told, walking carefully over small rocks and making his way to the edge of the opening. A sudden gust of cool wind made him stumble backward, but he recovered quickly and gazed out over the largest volcanic crater he had ever seen. From where he was standing to the opposite wall could have easily been a kilometer. Not even in videos had he ever looked at such a wide inverted bowl, filled nearly to the brim with pastel-blue water that smoked and bubbled as it hinted at the unquenchable fire of the magma beneath it. The crater walls were nearly black, and such was its extent that some of the bubbling water condensed into wispy clouds within the caldera itself, like a miniature weather system.

There were cracks in the walls of the crater, and some of them glowed red.

Behold, Dresde gloated. *My triumph.*

She forced his gaze immediately below them. Perhaps a hundred meters down, lava bubbled up from unseen cracks in the volcano. Some of it had long cooled into thick undulating curves of solid rock that bore the

memory of flowing magma, and sand had collected on
it over eons. Parts of it were still liquid, and they radiated stifling heat, even at a distance.

Partly submerged in the lava pool he saw a twinkling reflection given off by an egg of purest white.

Oscar recognized it.

You know this egg.

"I do, Dresde."

*Sadly, it will not break, or crack, or melt. It is a
puzzle, but all puzzles have solutions. Interesting, however. I thought only my own brood would be able to
withstand such heat.*

She gestured with her mind, and again it was as
though reality itself shimmered, or as if a veneer had
been lifted from Oscar's mind and he was able to see
what lay beyond the white egg. It was an enormous pile
of much smaller oval-shaped eggs, dozens upon dozens
of them, each of them a beautiful shade of sky blue.

"These are—" Oscar began.

Unimportant, Dresde answered dismissively.

Oscar's gaze roamed over the huge pile of what he
was sure were Dresde's eggs. They lay all over the place,
haphazardly, and a few of them had been evidently
crushed just moments earlier when Dresde had carelessly moved the boulders out of the way and some smaller
rocks must have tumbled down the slope. Some of the
eggs were dangerously close to the steaming water of the
crater, and a few were half buried in the sand.

At the very edge of the pile, lying as if forgotten
and floating in the red-hot lava, Oscar saw another egg,
much bigger than the others. It was a glittering vibrant
crimson.

"And that is...." His voice trailed off since he did
not dare to express what was so evident.

Only the present matters! Dresde proclaimed, yanking Oscar's attention back to her. She walked away from her crater nest, pushing one of the boulders back to where it had been, but she used too much force and the boulder sailed through the air and crashed right into the pile of vulnerable blue eggs below. Oscar cringed as he heard *crack* after *crack*.

Witness me, little male. What does the future matter when I exist?

Dresde compelled him to admire her, and he did. She flared out her wings and demanded to be praised.

"You are beautiful beyond compare," Oscar said, his voice hollow. He gazed in tired awe at the creature before him. "Your scales eclipse the majesty of the setting sun."

Indeed. You speak the—

Dresde's attention shifted away from him, and Oscar stumbled forward once again, freed from the awful pressure.

Oh, Samantha. What a devious little creature you are.

Oscar glanced to his left, following Dresde's lead, and saw that Samantha had been standing with her spear cocked back like a javelin, one of her legs flexed, frozen in the moment right before she had been about to hurl her spear straight at the black Flower.

Dresde bounded toward her, and the floor of the eyrie trembled in her wake.

Let your weapon go!

Samantha appeared to struggle and managed to throw it, but there was no strength behind her motion, and the spear missed its mark. It clattered to the ground a moment later. Dresde remained entirely focused on her, and Oscar approached the two of them with care. He did not know what had happened, but it looked as though Samantha had been about to try to hit the Flower that Dresde protected.

Using the young male as bait to distract me? Dresde asked, this time sounding genuinely amused. *I underestimated how underhanded and cowardly you aliens can be. I think this warrants a punishment. Would you not agree?*

Samantha looked ferocious as she glared at Dresde. Her body remained tense, and Oscar realized that Dresde was keeping her in that position against her will.

Answer me!

"Yes, Dresde," Samantha said between gritted teeth.

She suddenly stumbled forward in the same way Oscar had done, and Oscar hurried to where she was. He reached her a couple of seconds later and offered a hand to help her up.

How touching, Dresde commented. *I shall think of a fitting punishment for you, Samantha, but not yet. I will have fun devising something special. For now, leave, both of you. Now.*

Samantha took Oscar's hand and led him away. They moved quickly, and it was only after Oscar had jumped down the hole that led onto the path that would take them away from the eyrie that the punishing mental pressure of Dresde's attention faded enough for him to actually be able to speak.

"What happened there? What were you doing?"

"Walk," Samantha replied curtly.

"But she—"

"Walk!" she snarled. "She might change her mind. We have to get away from here. Fast."

Oscar obeyed.

They descended quickly. Samantha kept looking over her shoulder as they did. After half an hour had gone by, however, she appeared to finally relax a little bit.

"It appears she really is letting us go," she said. The two of them were making their way along a narrow rock face that overlooked a sheer drop to the distant ocean below.

"Well, she said she would, right?" Oscar asked. He was trying hard not to look down and instead focused on Samantha.

She studied the sky before answering, as if verifying that Dresde wasn't flying above them. "Sometimes she lies to give others false hope. She might have found it amusing to let us believe we were going to get away, only to swoop down at the last second and kill us."

Oscar shivered, and it had nothing to do with the wind blowing past him.

After Samantha's words he only felt truly safe hours later, when they were past the lake of lava and trudging through the narrow rock tunnel that led to the oceanside cliffs at the foot of the volcano. The tunnel was not big enough for Dresde to fit inside, and Oscar finally let out the pent-up tension he had been holding. As he did so, though, the survival adrenaline left his system, leaving him with nothing but exhaustion.

And shame.

He stopped walking. After a few steps, Samantha must have realized he was not following because she stopped and looked back.

"Is something wrong?" she asked.

Oscar shook his head, although he was unsure whether Samantha could see him clearly in the tunnel gloom.

"In that case, keep going. I do not want to be in this place longer than I have to."

Oscar started walking again, keeping his eyes on the ground. His sense of guilt and shame only increased when Samantha was nice to him, such as when she shared the last bit of water from her pack right before exiting the tunnel mouth. She had even taken his hand once or twice during the descent in dangerous places to make sure he wouldn't hurt himself.

And I was a coward. Again.

Coming out into the open air and the fresh breeze wafting from the ocean was like waking up from a long nightmare. The sun was still relatively high in the sky, and Oscar was surprised when his link told him that it was barely a couple of hours after noon. His legs were shaky with exhaustion, and his knees threatened to buckle under his own weight after every step he took. The straps of the backpack he carried chafed, and he was certain he had never sweated so much in his entire life. He was dusty, and he ached all over. He felt like he had gone through a grueling marathon of a workout.

His mind flashed back to Dresde pouncing on him. He stopped walking again.

"Is anything the matter?" Samantha asked impatiently, stopping as well.

She turned around, and Oscar was able to see, quite clearly, the awful red welt on her cheek where Dresde had struck her. He realized he had already seen her hurt like this once before, and it made him mad at the same time it filled the pit of his stomach with even more caustic shame.

Oscar hung his head low. "I'm sorry, Samantha."

She took a moment to reply, almost as if surprised. "Sorry? What for?"

"I…," Oscar began. "I ran away."

He shut his eyes tight as if to block the memory that clawed at the back of his mind. He saw himself running away like a coward and leaving Samantha to face Dresde's attack on her own. He recalled his own panic, the way he had screamed. He had tried to be brave, and it had all been for nothing.

Again.

Samantha stepped closer and placed her hand on Oscar's shoulder. After a few moments, Oscar looked up into her eyes.

"There is nothing to be sorry about," she said, and her voice lost the hard edge it usually had.

"I was a coward," Oscar confessed, and the words burned as they came out. "I left you there when she attacked. I'm so sorry."

Samantha let go of his shoulder and looked up at the sky, appearing pensive. "Not many people would have done what you did."

"I didn't do anything."

"Are you certain? I know how terrible her mind can be. I am used to it, and even I find it hard to resist it sometimes. This was only the second time you spoke to her, and you tried to stand your ground."

"But—"

"Running away from her is not cowardice," Samantha interrupted. "It is common sense. What could you have done? No creature on this planet can match her power. Even her sister perished under her talons. Besides, I believe it is *I* who should be apologizing to *you*."

Oscar furrowed his brow, confused. "I'm sorry?"

Samantha sighed, turning around. She walked downhill, and Oscar followed, keeping pace with her.

"I used you as bait, young male," she said to him, not meeting his eyes.

"You mean what Dresde said?"

"Yes. I knew she would be interested in you. I knew she would probably fixate on you, trying to terrorize you or getting you to admire her, vain as she is. Things went better than expected, in fact. She even showed you her clutch, and for that time, crucially, she was distracted."

"You used me to distract her?"

"I did, and I am sorry. I deliberately put your life at risk, but it was the only way."

Oscar remembered how Samantha had been about to throw her spear at the Flower, an instant before Dresde had frozen her in her tracks.

"You wanted to destroy the Flower." Oscar said, voicing his realization.

Samantha nodded. "I tried. I had thrown my spear at it several times already before she noticed me, but to no avail. It simply bounced off the black petals each time. I'd also tried to reach it with my hands, but it dangles too high up. When she discovered me, I was trying to impale the vines above it instead."

"That was really dangerous."

"Yes, but I had to try. I had often wondered whether harming the Flower was worth it, but I only knew for sure that it is her one weakness after what you told me. Sizzra was incapacitated when her Flower was ripped from its resting place, was she not?"

"Yeah. That's what Eli told me. It took her decades to be able to move again, I think."

"Exactly. So if I could but rip that Flower from the vines that hold it, she would be powerless. We would be *free*."

"That's why she freaked out," Oscar said. "She knew that's what you were trying to do."

"Oh yes. Make no mistake, young male. She may have let us go, but she does not forget. Even now she must be plotting the punishment she will give me. I can almost feel her amusement and anger through the link we share. I doubt she will ever let me go back to the eyrie after what happened today. I had one chance to save my family, and I-I failed."

Her shoulders sagged, and Oscar felt sorry for the enormous weight Samantha evidently carried. She seemed utterly dejected.

"You could have told me," he said. "About the plan, I mean. I would've helped. I can be really annoying and distracting when I want to, and I would've kept her busy even longer."

Samantha met his eyes and gave him a tired-looking smile as she nodded. It was the first sincere friendly expression Oscar had ever seen from her.

"I see that now. I misjudged you. I thought you were not to be trusted, that you would betray us the moment you could benefit from it so that you could save yourself. I have been told this is how strangers often are, and you are the first stranger I have come to know in my entire life. You are not like that, however. If only I had trusted you, things would have been different. I will not make that mistake again."

Oscar felt like he should say something, but he couldn't think of anything smart or witty, so instead he simply nodded in a jerky way and smiled.

They walked the rest of the way home in silence, but it was a companionable sort of quiet. Oscar was almost sorry when they finally reached the house.

"I will go in and let them know we are safe," Samantha said. "You can go ahead to the river if you want to take a bath."

"Do I," Oscar replied. "I don't think I've ever been this dirty in my life."

"I will catch up shortly and bring you some clean clothes."

"Okay, sounds good," he said, taking the hint that maybe Samantha wanted some alone time with her family.

He dropped his backpack on the porch and went straight to the river. When he sat down by the bank to peel off his shoes and socks, he groaned with more aches than he could count.

"I hope I never have to climb that volcano again," he grumbled to himself.

He took off all his clothes and arranged them as neatly as he could on a nearby rock. He then slipped into the water, which was bubbly and warm.

It was blissful. He sighed with contentment and swam forward for a bit. He took a big breath and then allowed himself to sink underwater until his feet touched the soft sandy bottom of the riverbed. He stayed down as long as he could and then kicked back up to the surface. For a few minutes afterward, he simply floated, enjoying the sensation of the warm current caressing his skin and easing away the aches and pains of the day. In particular the water did wonders to wash away the soreness on his shoulders and back. He massaged his legs and feet for a while, and although he had not brought any soap with him, he still scrubbed his hair and rubbed his skin until he was sure that he had gotten rid of all the grit and dust from the volcano. When he was done, he relaxed in the water, anchoring himself to the bank with one hand.

A faint swish of steps on tall grass alerted him to the fact that Samantha was coming mere moments before she arrived.

"I brought you clothes," she said.

Oscar flip-flopped awkwardly for a moment and hurriedly made sure his lower body would be relatively invisible underwater. Once again, he was painfully aware of the fact that he was completely naked with Samantha right in front of him.

"Um, thanks," he said, trying not to blush. He knew he was failing.

"How is the water?" she asked, placing the pile of clothes she had brought on another rock.

"It's amazing," Oscar replied, wondering how he was going to get out of the water this time.

"Good. Here, soap." Samantha tossed him a bar, which he caught with one hand. The other remained strategically fixed in position.

Samantha kicked off her shoes and started unbuttoning her shirt.

"Samantha?"

"Yes?"

"What are you doing?"

"Getting into the water," she said matter-of-factly. "What else would I be doing?"

Oscar gulped and looked away when he realized Samantha was about to take off her shirt. He did his best to focus intensely on the bar of soap in his hand and used it to clean himself as fast as he could.

Splash.

"The water *is* amazing," Samantha sighed from very close by.

Oscar gulped again.

"Could you pass me the soap, please?"

He shut his eyes tight and stretched out his arm behind him until Samantha took it.

"Thank you," she said. "Is something wrong?"

"Um, uh… I'm done," he replied. "Thanks for bringing me new clothes."

"I hope they fit."

"I'm sure they will!" Oscar said, trying not to sound shrill as he climbed out of the river. He toweled himself dry faster than he ever had in his entire life. Only when he had put on his new pants did he relax. He still dared not look at the river, though, and he put on his shirt in a hurry. He grabbed his dirty clothes as he set out. "See you back at the house!" he called.

"Okay," Samantha said, sounding confused.

Oscar escaped and hid in the solar panel array for a while rather than go into the house. He was flustered and a little bit confused. A few minutes later, when he saw Samantha walking up the path, he experienced a weird fluttery sensation that he firmly told himself was indigestion.

He only walked up to the house after he was certain Samantha had already entered. He was nervous about going inside for some reason, but he also knew he couldn't stay out by the array forever. He pushed the heavy door open and walked in.

"Here you are," Samantha said. "I was wondering whether you had gotten lost."

"I'm here," he announced. Laurie, Ute, and Nadja were all in the kitchen. "Thank you for the clean clothes, by the way."

Ute smiled at him and approached, holding her arms out. At first Oscar thought she was going to hug him, but she merely reached for the pile of dirty clothes he carried.

"Oh, sure," he said awkwardly. "Thanks."

"Sit down, both of you," Nadja told them. "Tell us what happened over dinner."

Oscar obeyed, taking his usual place at the table next to Laurie, who gave him an odd look.

"Hi," Oscar said to her. "How's the baby?"

If he could have kicked himself, he would have.

What kind of a question is that?

Surprisingly, though, Laurie merely nodded. "I am well, thank you. Or rather, we are well." She glanced at her belly.

"That's great," Oscar replied. He had no idea what to say after that.

Fortunately, Nadja and Ute saved him from the situation by placing several plates of delicious-looking dishes in front of them. Samantha took a seat opposite Oscar and immediately reached for a seaweed wrap.

"Go ahead, eat," Nadja said to him. "Laurie, you too. Ute and I will be with you in a minute."

It was a bit early for dinner, but Oscar was so hungry that he didn't care. He spent the next half an hour helping himself to anything within reach. His favorite was a savory soup made of the odd mushrooms that Samantha had risked so much to pick a couple of weeks back. The soup was thick and spicy, with a hint of something sweet that was unlike anything Oscar had tried up to that point.

"This is amazing," he said when he was pouring himself another bowl. "Ute, you're the best chef I know."

Ute smiled at him.

Samantha did too.

Oscar was taken aback at the gesture and actually stopped what he was doing, his spoon in midair for a couple of seconds before he remembered he could move.

"I think it is time to tell you what happened," Samantha said to the rest of them. "As we supposed, she was curious about the young male. She was even fully distracted for a few seconds."

Laurie leaned forward, looking eager. "Then you were able to…." She gave Oscar a quick look, as if she didn't trust herself to finish the sentence with him in earshot.

Samantha shook her head. "I was not able to take the Flower or hit it with my spear, no," she replied.

Laurie scowled. "Sam, the male is right here."

"Yes, and he should hear this," she said firmly, looking also at Nadja and Ute. "We decided not to tell him about the plan, and it backfired. He could have entertained her for longer. Instead she realized what I was doing and stopped me before I could be successful. I failed, and I do not believe I will ever get another opportunity like this again."

Laurie looked disappointed. Nadja appeared sad and reached across the table so she could hold one of Samantha's hands in her own.

"It's okay, Sam," Nadja said to her.

"Dresde was very angry," Samantha said quietly. Ute bunched her hands into fists when she heard the name spoken aloud. "I am sorry, Mama. However, I have started to think that all of this secrecy, all of this hiding, is what is keeping us trapped here. We should not be afraid to say her name. We should not be afraid to try and trust others."

Laurie frowned. "We do not know whether this male here is trustworthy. He could—"

"Try to save my life?" Samantha cut in.

There was silence after her words.

"Yes," Samantha continued. "Dresde was very angry, and she was going to hurt me. I know her better than any of you, and I know how impulsive she can be. She kills for fun in the heat of the moment and experiences no regret.

"The young male stood between her and me today. He tried to protect me and distracted her long enough for me to even attempt my attack on the Flower."

Ute, Nadja, and Laurie all looked at Oscar at the same time.

"Is this true? Did you stand up to the wurl queen?" Nadja asked him.

"Uh, I mean, I tried, but then she attacked me and I ran away. It wasn't my best moment, to be honest. I'm not sure I even did anything."

"You did enough," Samantha replied.

Both Nadja and Laurie fixed Oscar with long silent looks. It might have been Oscar's imagination, but he thought he saw their expressions soften, particularly Laurie's.

"I failed, but I still obtained valuable information," Samantha informed everyone. "I confirmed what we have long suspected: Dresde cannot approach the Flower."

Oscar remembered the very brief but clear flash of fear he had felt when Dresde had tried to pursue him close to the Flower. "You mean, that's why we always stood near the center of the eyrie?"

"Yes. I assumed we would be safest there, even if the Flower itself is dangerous."

"This is important," Nadja said. "What else did you learn?"

"Threatening her eggs, as Laurie had proposed, will be ineffective," Samantha replied. "The young male here can attest to this."

"How so?" Laurie asked Oscar.

Once again, he felt as though he had been put on the spot. "Well, she doesn't seem to care about them," he said, remembering how Dresde had acted. "I actually think she crushed some of the eggs with a big rock when she was showing me her nest and everything. And she didn't even care about the red egg."

"The next queen," Nadja said.

"Right," Oscar agreed. "It was the same size as Sizzra's egg, but red. It was just lying there, like she couldn't be bothered to think about it."

"Interesting," Laurie commented. "So it appears our only option is the Flower."

"Correct," Samantha confirmed. "It is her only weakness."

"But she will not allow you near it again," Nadja pointed out.

"Perhaps," Samantha said. "However, there may be a way, something we have not thought about. We should think."

"We should also be careful," Laurie told her. She looked worried. "This time you came back. Next time you may not be so lucky."

"Another chance will come. I am sure of it," Samantha proclaimed fiercely. She looked at each member of the table in turn. "And when it does, I will be ready. I will set us free—or die trying."

chapter 21.
reprieve

ELIAS DID everything he could not to fall off Narev's back as the wurl swam with an incredible burst of speed, remaining on the surface of the water so Elias would be able to breathe. He was weak, dizzy, and it was only a few seconds before his arms started to tremble.

Can't hold on much longer, he told the wurl.

Elias was not sure whether Narev even acknowledged his thought. There was another loud sound in the night, the same enormous spraying of water and a rush of air that was like a giant breathing out. Elias, utterly confused by the speed and the darkness and his own lightheadedness, began to slip out of consciousness. His grip on Narev's neck slackened.

The sense of urgency Narev was projecting reached a crescendo. Elias was not sure whether Narev was worried about him or about the thing they were approaching, but he could not focus on the thought properly. His strength was leaving him quickly.

Keep breathing. Stay awake.

The world went black for a moment. Elias came to, realizing he had been about to slip backward onto one of Narev's dangerous spines. The fear and adrenaline allowed him to reposition his body, but he was exhausted and out of breath after he did so.

He was entirely unprepared for the sudden disturbance in the water.

A wave came out of nowhere and slammed into the two of them. From somewhere in the distance, Elias heard Tristan cry out. Narev shuddered with the force of the impact and dived straight down. Into the water.

Elias had had no warning, and the water was suddenly all around him, pushing, shoving, choking. He panicked, having no idea what was happening anymore. He couldn't even hold his breath.

This is it. I'm sorry, Oscar.

Narev shot out of the water at that moment, and Elias breathed in air instead of the water that would have filled his lungs and spelled his doom. He registered momentary weightlessness, and then a hard impact as Narev landed on something solid. The crash shook Elias to the core, and he lost his grip. His consciousness flickered, and this time there was no holding on anymore.

He was falling. Then… nothing.

THE HEAT of day finally made Elias come to. With a groan, he opened his eyes and immediately closed them. The sun was straight overhead, roasting the entire world with its incessant waves of light.

Elias realized Narev was nearby, and he clearly received a mental image from him. Water.

Water? Elias asked, confused. Narev was quite distressed, and he pushed Elias with his snout, as if attempting to help Elias stand up.

It took a few minutes before Elias had gathered himself enough to attempt to stand. The first time he tried, he simply fell back down on the grass. Slowly, a centimeter at a time, he attempted to stand once more. He leaned heavily on Narev and managed to balance on his feet with unsteady legs. His mind was foggy, sluggish.

Narev urged him again and sent the image of water. The ravaging thirst roared awake, and Elias knew a moment of exquisite torment. He did not know why Narev was taunting him with ideas of water like this.

He was being pushed gently, and he dragged his foot forward. Then he did it again. He stumbled, blinking in the light, entirely focused on not falling and taking small, halting steps. When he tired after four, Narev growled and urged him to continue moving. Elias had a moment of anger at being pushed around like that, but it was quickly superseded by overwhelming exhaustion.

I need to lie down.

Narev growled again, glancing back to stare at Elias with his eye cluster. Then he whimpered and kept urging Elias to move, projecting the image of water.

Why are you doing this, Narev? Why, except….

Elias heard the water before he saw it. There was a faint gurgling noise ahead of him, and he struggled to focus on its source. Narev led him through places with alternating light and shadow, and Elias thought he saw trees above him but realized he was probably hallucinating. Still, he kept walking, since Narev would not let him stop. An eternity later, when Elias was certain he could not take another step, Narev projected another emotion suddenly, loud and clear.

Happiness. Satisfaction.

Elias blinked in the sun. There was water ahead. Not the ocean. There was…

Water!

In his haste, he felt to his knees and crawled, stumbling, the remaining distance to the shore of a sizable body of water. As soon as his hands touched the blessed liquid coolness, he plunged his head into it and drank.

His position was awkward, however, and he had gulped too much water to begin with, so he choked on it briefly. When he recovered, he knelt in front of what looked like a lake and used his hands to cup water to drink. As soon as the liquid touched his lips, he felt like life was flowing back into him. The sparkling coolness flooded his parched mouth, and when he swallowed, he was so happy it was as though nothing in the world would ever be wrong again. He drank slowly, pacing himself, part of his mind reminding him that it was not good to drink too much at once after so many hours of being dehydrated.

It was only after he had quenched the thirst that had tortured him for days and days on end that he paused to think what kind of water he was drinking. It did not taste salty.

How can this be?

He looked around. He was surrounded by the palm-tree analogs that he had seen growing by the beach. Short grass covered the ground and—

Tristan.

Every other thought was pushed out of Elias's mind. Haltingly, leaning on Narev, he stood up again and tried not to lose his balance as a wave of dizziness made his legs wobble. His heart was hammering unsteadily in his chest.

Take me to Tristan, please, he told Narev.

With a grunt, Narev indicated he understood. The two of them began walking again and made their way through the undergrowth of what looked like a tropical forest. Elias concentrated on not falling, and it was but a few minutes later that they arrived at a clearing beyond which the ocean was visible. Lying on the beach, still unconscious and being nudged by both Vanor and Siv, was Tristan.

Elias rushed over to him, finding strength born of desperation.

"Tristan? Tristan!"

Elias cradled Tristan's head in his lap and tried to shake him awake very gently.

"Tristan, wake up."

Tristan did not react, and Elias grew even more alarmed. "Guys, help me. We have to take him to the lake."

The wurl acknowledged Elias's request. Vanor in particular was worried, as Elias could tell by the mental waves of anxiety that he sent out, and he was the first to stand perfectly still and allow Elias to pull Tristan up and onto Vanor's back. It was difficult since Elias was so weak, but Siv helped, and together they managed to place Tristan safely amid the spines of the larger wurl.

"Let's go," Elias told them. "Hurry."

Siv and Vanor went ahead, walking fast. Elias followed with Narev immediately behind, and was there to help bring Tristan down to the shore of the lake. Elias's strength failed him then, however, and Tristan ended up falling partway, centimeters from the water.

"Wh-what's happening?" Tristan mumbled as Elias struggled to manage the weight of his body and bring Tristan to a sitting position.

Elias was so relieved to hear Tristan speak that he started crying. His relief was mirrored by the three wurl, who had been standing around them anxiously.

"Tristan," Elias said. "Tristan, we have water."

"Water?"

Elias cupped his hands again and poured a little bit of moisture into Tristan's lips. The effect was immediate—Tristan opened his eyes fully.

"Water!" Tristan exclaimed, his voice weak and hoarse.

"Here, drink. Slowly, slowly."

Elias helped Tristan drink a few sips and then forced Tristan to wait for a few minutes before giving him more water. He repeated the process two more times and was relieved to see that Tristan was slowly becoming more alert. After about an hour, Tristan was able to dip his hands in the lake and drink his fill on his own.

"Can't believe it," Tristan said between sips. "I can't believe it."

Elias smiled and looked at their three silver-scaled companions. "It was the wurl. They saved us."

It took the better part of a day for both Elias and Tristan to feel well enough to stand without the help of either Vanor or Narev. Elias had insisted that they still drink a little bit at a time, and despite some rather painful stomach cramps during the night, Elias felt more like himself than he had in a long time when the next morning dawned. Tristan was also doing much better, although he had been more severely dehydrated and was still rather weak.

Neither of them had left the lakeside at all, and the wurl had remained by their side. In fact the three of them had stayed awake all night to guard them, as far as Elias had been able to tell.

"We're better now," he told the wurl as the sun climbed in the sky. "You should go hunt. You must be hungry."

They hesitated.

"Go, guys," Tristan said as well. He was sitting with his back to a large rock, and his voice sounded much more energetic. "We'll be okay."

Siv and Narev looked at Vanor, who made a gesture with his head that looked almost like a nod. Then Vanor turned around and bounded away into the forest, followed by the other two. There were soon three loud splashes in the distance.

"I'm hungry too, you know," Tristan told Elias. He grinned as he said it, however.

Elias's stomach appeared to agree. "I know. You stay here, okay? I'll go see if I can find anything."

"Oh, don't worry, Eli. I don't think I could move too much, even if I wanted to."

Despite the fact that their situation was still urgent, hope surged in Elias as he stood up and began his search for something edible. He had never realized it, not once in his life, but the absence of thirst was the best sensation in the world. His mind was sharper than it had been in days, and he shuffled around the lake with careful but surefooted steps.

A few minutes later, he noticed the fruit.

"I don't believe it," he said to himself. He walked away from the lake and into the jungle, batting a large feathery insect out of the way. Growing in a clearing were a group of three white trees with bark that was veined in maroon. Their trunks were thick and squat, but their branches reached up quite high into the air. Oddly, the trees appeared to have no leaves whatsoever. Instead the uppermost branches looked as though they were covered in fur, deep ochre, and they reflected the morning sunlight.

Elias paid little attention to the details of the trees themselves. All he cared about was the food.

The lowermost branches of each tree were heavy with pearlike fruits that Elias recognized. They were flanties, like the one Tristan had shared with Elias at the beginning of their journey on the ocean maw. Elias staggered forward, overjoyed, and plucked as many of the plump veined fruits as he could. He made his way back to where Tristan was sitting with more than a dozen flanties in his arms.

"Hey, Tristan?" he said, coming up behind him. He knelt down next to Tristan and showed him his bounty. "Check this out."

"No way. Flanties? Wow!"

"What are you waiting for? Dig in!"

They ate. Elias had been so hungry that the first taste of the sweet, juicy pulp inside the fruits made him moan with contentment. He limited himself to just one, knowing that he could always eat whatever fish Narev caught, but Tristan did not have as many sources of nourishment.

"Eat another one," Tristan told him.

"Not a chance. This food is for you."

"Were these the only ones?"

Elias smiled. "Oh no. There are probably hundreds more."

"Then eat, Eli! They're delicious."

Elias's considered for a brief instant and then nodded. Later, he returned to pick fruit three more times, more than enough for both Tristan and himself to eat as much as they wanted. There was still plenty of food left, and Elias had glimpsed a couple more of the maroon-veined trees in the forest, as well as some promising bushes and other fruit-bearing plants growing on the opposite shore of the lake.

It was a feast, and after it was over, Elias knew unabashed happiness.

"That was amazing," Tristan commented.

"The best meal I've ever had in my life."

"I know. And now that we've eaten, I have a great idea."

"What's that?"

Tristan yawned. "Let's take a nap."

Elias wiped sweet juice off his chin and nodded, smiling. He found a comfortable spot on a sun-warmed rock, sat down with his back to it, and opened his arms, beckoning Tristan to join him. Tristan came and leaned back with his head resting on Elias's chest. Elias held Tristan close, enjoying his warmth. Neither of them had shirts anymore, having lost them in the desperate rush from earlier. However, the day was neither hot nor cold, and Elias was as comfortable as he had ever been.

"I'm so happy you're okay," he told Tristan, caressing his face with the backs of his fingers. Tristan's cheeks were covered with a patchy dark-brown beard that had grown, unkempt, over their time at sea. His skin was deeply tanned, and his hair was stiff, bleached slightly from all the sun and the salt. "You look really hot, by the way."

Tristan's face broke into a smile. "That was random."

Elias placed his hand on Tristan's muscular chest, his fingers tracing gentle circles over the patch of dark hair that grew between Tristan's pectoral muscles. "It's the truth."

"You also look great," Tristan said in a deeper voice than before. "Less like a wood elf now, and more like a wild fisherman with iridescent eyes. And great abs."

The two of them kissed, and Elias allowed relief to wash over him in silent contentment. He leaned back and closed his eyes, enjoying the moment for what it was.

"Where are we, do you think?" Tristan asked him. "This can't be an island. There are no landmasses in this part of the ocean."

"I think we'll find out soon enough," Elias speculated. He remembered the sound of rushing air he had heard two nights ago, as Narev had made his desperate dash toward something in the night while carrying Elias on his back. "For now, though, let's just sleep."

Elias did not dream for the first part of the night. He rested deeply, and only woke up once to go relieve himself. After he settled down next to Tristan again and closed his eyes, however, he had a dream of a vague yearning within him, something that was drawing him in. It was unsettling and enormous, but Elias did not know what it was or what to do. When morning came and he woke up, he had a faint déjà vu of having dreamed something similar in the past.

He did not cling too hard to the recollection, and it was soon forgotten as daylight showed him another beautiful morning, free of clouds. He felt much better, far stronger than the day before, and for the first time in more than a week, he did not fear the rising sun and the heat it would bring.

He went to the lake and belatedly realized he had not even thought about purifying the water before drinking it, as Tristan and he had been doing throughout their journey. He was thankful neither of them had gotten sick. The lake, however, was incredibly clear, and its water resembled that of a mountain spring. It was possible to see the bottom all the way out the twenty or so meters it spanned. The bottom of the lake was not rocky, but rather smooth and dark, almost black. No debris of any kind had collected there, which was odd.

There were also no fish or anything else in the water. It looked pristine, but unnaturally so.

"Morning, Eli."

"Hi, Tristan," Elias replied, glancing back. Tristan hugged him briefly and gave him a kiss on the cheek.

"What are you looking at?"

"The lake. It's odd—I have never seen one this clean. There's no sand at the bottom, no fish, nothing."

"Sounds like we need to investigate."

"Yeah."

"Before we do, though… breakfast?" Tristan proposed, scratching his beard.

"You read my mind. Let's see what we can find."

They walked halfway around the lake until they came to the bushes Elias had seen earlier. Small light-pink berries grew in clusters of three among their leafy branches, and Elias plucked one to try it.

"Oh. Gross," he said, spitting it out immediately.

"Bad?"

"Very bitter, probably not a good sign. Best not try our luck with those."

"How about these?" Tristan asked, pointing at a new tree whose trunk was a near-perfect spiral. The wood of its convoluted yet beautiful trunk was a pale tan color. At several points among the twists and turns of the spiral, spiked branches poked out, from which hung long, cylindrical fruit that ended in the same odd pattern as the main trunk. The skin of the fruit alternated between green, red, and orange, and it grew six at a time, each one a slightly different shade.

Elias walked over to the tree and gently tugged at one of the green fruits. It came off easily. "They look like weird bananas."

"Yeah," Tristan agreed, taking a red one. "Let me try them first."

"Sure."

"Uh…," Tristan mumbled, puzzling over the fruit, "how do I peel this?"

He ended up breaking the fruit in half, revealing pulp that was a completely unexpected indigo hue and dotted with tiny black seeds.

"Wow, blue," Elias said.

Tristan shrugged. "Here goes nothing."

He bit into the fruit and made a face. Then he sort of smiled. Then he grimaced. "It's… aw, man, the peel is bitter. But the flesh is really good. Don't eat the peel."

Elias tore off the peel as best as he could, but the inside of his fruit was white instead of blue. He bit into it and immediately realized it was not ripe. "Ugh. This is awful."

"Maybe the green ones aren't good yet," Tristan suggested.

Elias tried a red one instead and peeled it carefully. He bit into the soft, silky flesh and was pleasantly surprised. The taste was creamy, with a hint of nuttiness and a very satisfying umami aftertaste.

"It's like an almond and a tomato had a baby," Elias said in between bites.

"Yeah. Not bad. Weird, but not bad."

"What do we call them?"

"Um, blue almonds?" Tristan suggested. "No, wait. That name sucks."

"How about…. Blue bananas. Blunanas. Or weird bananas. Wananas."

Tristan chuckled. "Wananas it is."

"We need to get better at naming stuff," Elias said.

"Hey, I came up with flanties, which is great."

"If you say so," Elias responded in a playful tone.

They each ate about four of the fruits in total. Elias realized that he already felt quite satisfied.

"Those fill you up really fast," he commented.

"They taste nutritious," Tristan said. "I hope they are."

"Yeah, me too."

"So, you want to go explore? Figure out where we are and how the wurl were able to get us to this island when the maps show no islands anywhere near this region?"

"Are you feeling okay?" Elias asked, concerned. "Wouldn't you rather just rest?"

"I'm all right, Eli. Really. Not at my best, but I can definitely walk for a bit. Besides, I'm really curious."

"Okay. Let's go."

They walked to the opposite shore of the lake. The vegetation around them reminded Elias of a jungle, but there was an odd quality to it he could not quite place. It was not as chaotic or stifling as the other tropical forest he had already crossed with Tristan before arriving at the beach weeks ago. The plants here grew farther apart from one another, and the canopy did not completely cover every inch of available sunlight in a desperate fight for light between different plants. There were also barely any animals around, with only a few insects here and there.

"The lake," Tristan said, pointing. "Look. It's perfectly round."

Elias checked and realized Tristan was correct. From farther away it was clear that the lake was indeed a perfect circle.

"That's weird," Elias said, beginning to feel unsettled. "Lakes don't usually look like that."

"It's also odd how black the bottom is. Kind of looks like obsidian."

"Let's go to the beach where I found you," Elias proposed. "We need more information, and that's a good place to start exploring. Maybe the wurl are around."

"Sure," Tristan replied with a last suspicious look at the lake. "Lead the way."

Elias and Tristan circled all the way around the lake and stepped into the forest proper. Elias hoped he remembered correctly where Narev had led him to the beach two days earlier and did his best to pick his way around the trampled vegetation that indicated one or more wurl had gone through in the recent past. Once inside the forest, Elias realized there was very little noise. There was no incessant bird chatter in the upper branches of the trees, for instance. A few insects buzzed in the air, but aside from them, and the gentle swaying of the plants in the breeze, nothing moved.

Elias hurried his pace somewhat and was glad to come out of the forest after a few minutes. He stepped out onto a sharply sloping beach of oddly regular, striated rocks that led down into the ocean. There were no wurl in sight.

"Here's where I found you," Elias said, walking out onto the beach. The rocks underfoot were slick with water, and instead of being haphazardly strewn about, Elias realized they were perfectly aligned with one another in interlocking patterns. They reminded him of the tissue of the ocean maw, in fact, and that was not a pleasant association. Now that he was out of the forest, Elias also realized that the gentle breeze he felt did not stop. It blew constantly in a single direction.

"Look at the water," Tristan said, joining Elias at the edge of the beach. "It's all frothy."

"You're right. Those aren't normal waves. It looks more like...," Elias began, understanding dawning in his mind. "Like...."

Instead of finishing his sentence, Elias activated his link and brought up the approximation of distance traveled in the last day. His eyes widened in shock.

"What's wrong?" Tristan asked.

"Tristan, open the distance tracker on your link. What does it say?"

"Hang on a sec," Tristan replied, tapping his left wrist to call up the data. "Distance for yesterday is... what?"

"I have 405 kilometers," Elias told him. "It says we traveled 405 kilometers in a single day."

"I... I have more or less the same thing. How?"

At that moment the entire island shuddered. Then there came a loud noise of air rushing out, huge, seeming to come from everywhere at once. The gentle breeze changed into a violent gale in an instant, and Elias was forcefully reminded of being in the wind tunnel of Portree's atmospheric dynamics lab when he was fourteen. The wind pushed against him now, as it had then, and he clamped his palms over his ears as he tried his best not to fall. The sound was overwhelming. It was like a hurricane or a huge factory exhaust. It got louder, almost to the point of being unbearable, and then suddenly stopped.

The wind stopped too, at the same time as the sound. Elias stumbled forward into Tristan, who had also been covering his ears. They shared a confused look, and Elias opened his mouth to say something.

Before he could, another sound replaced the first, completely different. It was almost like a sucking in, like air around them was being absorbed. The wind changed direction, but it was not as loud or as violent as before. After a few seconds the sound and the wind stopped once again.

"Eli?" Tristan said after enough time had passed that they were reasonably sure the sound would not repeat itself.

"Yeah?"

"You said that two nights ago the wurl were approaching something, right? Something that moved?"

"Yeah."

"These rocks here," Tristan continued, pointing down at the beach. "What if they're not rocks?"

A memory came to Elias. Sizzra, fighting a creature in the water that was many times her size. A being so ancient that its life-spark was hidden even from the Life Seed. What had she called it?

"A razorback behemoth," he said out loud.

"That's it, isn't it? This island isn't an island. It's alive."

Almost as if to punctuate Tristan's words, the same deafening sound of rushing air came back, receded, and was replaced by the other sound, as if a mountain were breathing in and out.

When the noise had died away, Elias pointed ahead. "There's an easy way to find out. Let's see if this island has a head."

Both of them walked along the edge of the beach, their footsteps quick. Glancing at the ocean, Elias now understood why the water looked the way it did. They were traveling, moving through the water at a constant but significant speed. It was faster than any boat, and the motion never stopped.

Islands don't swim, he told himself.

About fifteen minutes later, the beach ran out. Elias and Tristan walked back into the forest and hiked through the same lively but sparse vegetation as before. A couple of minutes later, they emerged at a wide, flat clearing.

"By the generation ship," Elias whispered.

"It's enormous," Tristan said. "It's…."

Words failed him, and Elias could not blame him. He could do nothing but look on, mouth agape in astonishment.

They were standing on the back of a creature that was larger than anything Elias had ever seen, a living organism whose size defied comprehension. From where they stood, he saw clearly how the creature's back sloped down in a sharp, cliff-like drop all the way to the ocean dozens of meters below. Halfway under the waterline, though, there was a massive, leathery head. This head moved very slowly, partially submerged beneath the waves, its rugged surface encrusted with barnacles. It was vaguely triangular in shape, grayish-brown, and at the top of it there were three large eyes that looked directly skyward. The eyes were milky white orbs, each larger than Elias himself. Just below them, the head sloped back up into what looked like a wicked beak of pure jade green, but it was difficult to tell given the distance and the refraction of the water. Only the top of the section of the beak that must correspond to the lower jaw of the creature poked out of the water, razor-sharp and tall, like the prow of a ship cutting through the ocean.

From where Elias stood, he was able to see a large part of the back of the creature he had mistaken for an island, and he realized that this was not the same being Sizzra had once fought in the deep. It did not have the same spikes on its back, and it was larger than anything even Sizzra had seen. On impulse, Elias knelt down and placed his hands on the being's shell where it was exposed, uncovered by soil or plants. He closed his eyes and concentrated.

He simply felt life. There was no complexity to it, no real thought. It was a blindingly bright spark of energy, a life force completely different to anything he had ever experienced. Elias was not sure he even comprehended what he was sensing—this being was too old, too big for him to understand. He was like a single bacterium trying to understand an entire human body. It was simply not possible for him to comprehend.

"Is it dangerous?" Tristan asked after Elias stood up.

"No," Elias responded with complete certainty. "I don't think it even knows we're here. I think it's swimming wherever it goes, and we're hitching a ride."

"It's going fast," Tristan pointed out.

"For its size, I actually think it's swimming really slowly," Elias pointed out. "Maybe, when you're this big, you don't need to hurry to do anything."

"Good point. Hey, Vanor and the others knew!" Tristan exclaimed.

Elias nodded. "That's why they swam away that night. That's why they came back, making us hurry. They wanted to catch up to this... this being. This Island Behemoth."

"The Island Behemoth," Tristan echoed quietly. "That wind we felt earlier. It was breathing, right?"

"I think so."

"Wow. Just... wow."

They watched the creature in silence for a long time, but it took no notice of them whatsoever. Eventually, when it was clear that they were safe, they headed back to the lake.

Along the way they ran into Narev, who projected happiness at seeing them.

"It's great seeing you too," Elias told him, placing his hand briefly on his friend's scaly neck. "Where are the others?"

Elias received images of wurl hunting, but not in the water this time.

"So," he told the wurl and Tristan. "You guys are out hunting on the island. Don't let me keep you, then."

Narev bounded away happily.

"All of them are here? On the Behemoth?" Tristan asked him.

"Yeah. They seem to like it here. Narev was very pleased with himself at seeing us doing better."

"It's amazing, the way they saved us," Tristan said. "They knew we were dying."

"It's like I've always said. Wurl are more intelligent than anyone gives them credit for."

"You're right. Do you think, maybe, it's because Sizzra isn't here anymore?"

Elias thought for a moment, considering Tristan's question. "I don't know. I don't think so. She didn't think much of the males, but for the most part she let them be. I think it has more to do with the fact that the Life Seed is where it should be. One of the three Flowers of this world has returned to its rightful place, and the Spine wurl are reacting to that. Or at least that's what I guess is happening. I really don't know."

"Well, whatever it is, their quick thinking saved us. If they hadn't carried us here, we would've died of thirst on that horrible maw. Instead, now we have plenty of food, shelter, and we're hidden from view in case any attackers come."

"Right," Elias replied, realizing he had barely thought about Flyers or Singers at all for the last few days. "I wonder why they've left us alone."

"Well, the Flyers Dresde sent after us are probably all dead, or most of them anyway. I can't imagine it's easy to fly over an entire ocean without stopping, so maybe it's going to be a while before reinforcements come."

"And the Singers? Why didn't they finish us off?" Elias wondered. "We were such easy prey, all of us, a couple days ago."

"I think they…," Tristan began, then appeared to catch himself. "Actually, I don't know. I'm just glad they aren't around."

Elias shuddered, remembering the carnage of the last fight once again and how awful it had been. "I hope they don't come back at all."

Tristan yawned. "Hey, mind if I take a nap?"

"No, of course not. Let's go back to the lake so you can rest and recover."

"Except it's not a lake," Tristan pointed out. "What do you think it is, speaking as a biologist?"

"Maybe it's, I don't know, something like a pore on the Behemoth's body," Elias ventured. "You know, the place where it gets rid of excess moisture after having filtered the salt out in some way. Similar to our own sweat glands, although the parallel is not perfect."

"So you're saying we're drinking Behemoth sweat?" Tristan asked, lifting an eyebrow.

"Kind of, yeah. Except it's purified water. Well, we're drinking the purified sweat of a massive ocean-going creature with an island growing on its back."

Tristan sighed. "You know what's messed up? That's not even the weirdest thing I've heard you say since we started this journey."

Elias laughed, enjoying the luxury of being able to do so. Tristan and he returned to the edge of the water, and while Tristan rested, Elias went over the practice moves Tristan had taught him, fighting an invisible opponent with Sizzra's spine in his hand. It felt good to exercise, and to have energy to do so. It felt even better to be safe, at least for the time being.

For the next three days, Elias simply enjoyed Tristan's company. Narev, Vanor, and Siv came by every now and then to play or rest next to them, and as they explored the island more, they discovered a wide variety of vegetable-based foods that were a welcome addition to the flanties and wananas that made the backbone of their daily meals. They did not have any of their survival gear with them anymore, but Elias realized that he did not miss it or need it very much. Compared to his first time surviving on his own, when he had shivered every night in the unforgiving winter, sheltering in a narrow cave on the side of a mountain and constantly fearing for his life should Sizzra ever decide that he was no longer necessary, this new hiatus felt almost like a vacation. Food was plentiful, and the temperature was nice. There were no mosquitoes at all, which Elias was incredibly thankful for after having endured them for weeks in the earlier part of the trip.

Building a fire was not a priority, and even though Elias had essentially been reduced to wearing a pair of pants and nothing else, he did not feel exposed or vulnerable. Neither the lack of light at night nor the lack of protection for his body seemed wrong. Quite the opposite, in fact. He felt in touch with nature, and even though he had lost his ability to sense other living things around him ever since he had taken to the ocean, he still had a sense of connection that made him glad to share in the beautiful summer of a world that had too long been dormant.

The only interruption to the blissful respite that the island provided came at night. On their second night on the Behemoth, Elias sensed clearly that there was something tugging at his consciousness. It was still faint, but its entrancing urge was impossible to ignore. At first it was merely annoying. His dreams reminded him vaguely of being thirsty a few days ago and made him keenly aware of how awful it had been to wait for hours and hours on end for the condenser to fill a glass so he would have a mere mouthful of water. The glass was never filled in what soon became nightmares. He was forced to wait, hearing the torturous *drip, drip* of water he would never drink.

On the third morning, Elias woke up somewhat disquieted. There was something scratching at Elias's mind, something that demanded his attention and would not be denied. It was intruding into normal dreams and twisting them, dowsing them in unpleasant urgency that felt like an emptiness, like a void demanding to be filled. It was cold. It was unending.

The urgency of the sensation faded away as he woke up fully. He tried to focus his mind on other things, like exploring the island with Tristan. However, a few hours later, when Elias was sitting on his own at the edge of the Behemoth's back and looking out over the water, he began to fancy that he could feel the sensation again, even during the daytime. He said nothing to Tristan when they had dinner and tried to ignore it as best he could.

That night, the dream took on the tint of a nightmare much more quickly. He could not move. He lay on the leathery surface of the ocean maw again, completely exposed to the blistering noonday sun, and he could not escape it.

Drip. Drip.

Elias wanted to turn his head, to look at the condenser and see whether the glass was ready, whether he would be able to drink and assuage the burning thirst in his throat. He struggled in vain.

Drip.

The dream blurred at the edges, and he was suddenly thirteen years old, hungry at night. Director O'Rourke had recently made ration cuts for all the families in Portree, and Elias hadn't had enough to eat for dinner. He was hungry, even though his father had given both him and Oscar half of his own ration.

He walked to the fridge, stealthily, in the middle of the night. He could not wake his parents. He felt bad that he was stealing food, but he was so hungry. He really needed to eat something.

He reached for the handle of the fridge, and it crumbled under his fingers.

No.

He reached for the door of the fridge itself and, triumphant, yanked it open—but the inside was empty. There was nothing to eat.

No!

He looked over his shoulder, and he was back on the ocean maw again. Weak. Elias fell to his knees, utterly confused. The wurl had left them days ago, and Tristan…. Tristan had not made it. Elias was too weak to cry, too weak to move. He could not hunt for himself, and his stomach threatened to devour him from within.

All he could do was watch the condenser, drop by drop by drop.

Drip.

He knew he would never drink the water. He would never have food again. It was all he desired, all his own voice screamed in his mind, but he could not move. He could not even crawl to the condenser to save his own life, and the sun was coming up again. That merciless, horrid star full of hateful brilliance and incessant radiant light. The sun would sear the skin off his flesh. The sun was coming, and there was no stopping it.

Elias woke up with a scream.

"Eli? Eli, what's wrong?"

Elias realized he was grabbing fistfuls of soil and grass he had yanked from the ground somehow. For an instant he glanced up at the sky, terrified of seeing the sun again.

It's nighttime. It's nighttime. I'm safe.

He took a couple of shaky breaths and relaxed his hands.

"Eli?"

"It's okay. I am—I'm okay," he lied, regretting the fact that he had woken Tristan in the middle of the night.

"It's not okay. Come here," Tristan told him, and drew him into a strong embrace. The two of them were lying on the bed they had improvised of soft grass, underneath one of the taller palm trees by the lake. The night was quiet, almost eerily so, and particularly after Elias's loud scream. "What were you dreaming about?"

"I was thirsty," Elias responded automatically. He tried to remember the specifics of his dream, but it was hard. "I was so thirsty, like before. And you weren't there. You'd di—I was alone. It was horrible."

"It's okay," Tristan said gently. "It was only a dream."

"Sorry I woke you up."

Tristan kissed Elias's forehead and wiped the sweat off his brow. "Never mind that. You want to tell me what's going on?"

"What do you mean?"

"Your dreams. You're having nightmares every night."

"You noticed?" Elias asked. He could see Tristan's face in the moonlight as Tristan nodded.

"I was waiting for you to say something, but I didn't want to intrude. What is it?"

"It's like… it's like those dreams I'd been having back at the beach. When the Singer male was trying to lure me to the edge of the water."

"What?" Tristan said, stiffening. "Eli, you should've told me. What if they're out there? Trying to lure you to your death?"

"I don't know. I'm not sure. It doesn't feel exactly like that, just similar. When it was a Singer, I could sort of hear a voice. This is different, Tristan. It's like…." Elias paused for a moment, collecting his thoughts. He could still feel the sensation in the back of his mind, like a whisper he could barely hear. It never stopped, and it demanded to be heard, thought about. It would not, could not, be denied. "It's like a… hunger," he finished in a small voice, and as he said the word he knew it was true. "It's like a hunger in my mind."

Elias expected Tristan to tell him he was imagining things or was going crazy, but Tristan merely frowned and said, "Is it bad?"

"I'm not sure. I can't ignore it. I think…. I think I've begun to hear it in the daytime too."

Tristan was silent for a few seconds. "I don't like this. The Singers know we are here. They have to. They haven't attacked, so maybe they're trying to separate us again. Like when they made Narev swim away."

"You think?" Elias asked him.

"Maybe. There's something odd about the way Singers have behaved. They could have killed us so many times over already, and they haven't. That leaves only two logical explanations. Either they can't or they won't. If they can't, we need to figure out why. If they won't, we need to understand why as well. Maybe they want something from us. Something from you specifically."

"Like what?"

"I have no idea," Tristan admitted. "I keep thinking about it a lot, though. Why lure Narev out into the ocean so he would be trapped by the ocean maw? Why didn't they attack us while we were nearly dead from thirst? Why didn't they pick us off in the middle of the storm, when our boat capsized?"

Elias sat up in the dark, and Tristan followed suit.

"I don't know if it has anything to do with that, but that sensation, that... thing in my dreams. It's getting louder," Elias told Tristan. "I think we're going to wherever it's coming from. And there's something else."

"What is it?"

Elias tapped his link, and the screen blinked awake, painfully bright in the starlit night. After a few moments, Elias was able to look at it without squinting. He brought up the map of the world.

"According to the estimates from the computer here, we've traveled around 1200 kilometers since we started."

"Right."

"For the most part, we've been traveling northeast, although the Behemoth hasn't followed a straight path. I've been plotting its course, approximating where we were when the wurl led us here. Look." Elias tapped a virtual key, and the map zoomed in to show clearly the outlines of both continents, Reena in the west and Raasay in the east. Separating them was the ocean. "We set out on the boat around here," Elias said, tapping a spot on the wavering and uneven outline of Reena's eastern coast. A small glowing dot indicated the place.

"Right. Then we traveled on the boat with the wurl until the storm hit. We were going northeast."

"And we found Narev more or less here," Elias continued, tapping another point not very far from the coast. "That's where we had to fight, and from there we rode the ocean maw, but we didn't travel a long way. That plantlike organism evolved to drift with the currents, not to swim. I estimate that we were riding an easterly current that took us all the way up to here, where we found the Forest of Light." With a tap, another indicator shone. It was still not too distant from the mainland, and the vastness of the ocean sprawled ahead.

"That's where the wurl took us to this Behemoth," Tristan added.

"Yes. It's only been four days since then, but I've been watching the sun and the stars to try and figure out which way we are going. If I'm right, we've traveled in *this* direction, and we should be around *here*." Elias scrolled through the map and zoomed out, tapping again and making a new dot appear. This indicator was dramatically farther away from the others. "I estimate we've traveled nearly halfway across the ocean."

"We're in the middle of nowhere."

Elias paused. "Not... not quite."

"What do you mean? There are no landmasses in this region of the ocean—it's just water. The few islands that we wanted to visit are very far south. There's nothing here."

"It may not show on your link, but...." Elias zoomed in with his map. Then he zoomed in again. "I have extrapolated where our current course will take us. I cross-referenced it with the planetary surveyor data my dad sent us when we still had a connection to Portree. I hadn't had a chance to do it, but I integrated the data these past couple of days, while you rested. The new information allowed me to refine the map, particularly for this area here, in the ocean. And I found... this."

He zoomed in one more time, to the limits of the map's resolution. There was a tiny black blob there.

"What's that supposed to be?" Tristan asked him.

"I'm not sure. It might be an island, but it's really small. Or maybe its several tiny islands."

"In the middle of the ocean?"

"It's not as weird as you think. It looks like this entire region of the ocean floor is quite shallow, if the gravity fluctuation readings are to be trusted. Some kind of continental shelf extension is responsible for it. If so, what we're seeing here, making this island or whatever it is, might not be more than a few meters tall. It could be a coral reef poking out of the water, for instance."

"And we're going in that general direction?"

Elias turned off his link. In the absence of the light, the night appeared dark and threatening. "We're headed *straight* there. It's not a coincidence. That's... that's where the thing is coming from. That horrible sensation, that hunger."

"So the Island Behemoth is taking us there."

"Yeah."

"Then whatever this thing is, affecting your dreams...," Tristan began.

"Is powerful enough to control a creature as large as the Behemoth."

chapter 22.
ledge

THE FOLLOWING weeks were tense. Oscar kept
waiting for Dresde to show up one day and punish Samantha, as she had said she would, and he kept an eye
on the sky every single day as he went about his chores.
The constant mental unrest and vague anxiety were insidious, but he did his best to concentrate on the good
things and make the best of his current situation.

He was able to sleep better at night, for one. Samantha and he had replaced the missing board over his
window a few days after the volcano ascent, and Dresde had not come back to torment him at night. This was
a big improvement, and Oscar had fewer nightmares as
a result, even if he still woke up in a cold sweat every
now and then when he dreamed that Dresde had somehow found Elias and was about to hurt him. However,
despite the ever-present faint threat of Dresde showing
up, the fact that he could rest meant he was more alert
during the day. He had more energy, and he could help
more around the house.

He often accompanied Samantha on her foraging
trips, and together they explored new places and revis-
ited others. They went to the Nightmare Caves often,

in particular, since abundant food grew in many of the isolated galleries and spaces in that confusing and seemingly endless labyrinth of rock and water. Oscar began to feel comfortable navigating the tunnels and caves, even in near-total darkness with only the faint bioluminescent bugs to serve as markers. He helped Samantha gather all kinds of things, from seeds to tubers to water plants that grew in total darkness and whose thick and fleshy white stalks were delicious when fried in vegetable oil. He was also able to increase the amount of food they could gather, not only through his manual labor but also by using his link. Its many functions proved invaluable more than once, such as when he created maps of the surrounding region along with detailed data entries on what kind of food source was located at each place.

Once, he also used the microphones on the link to track a particular kind of burrowing feathered animal that often made its tunnels very close to a species of pungent underground fungus that Samantha liked to collect. The fungus reproduced via mushrooms that were delicious but very difficult to find. With his link, though, Oscar was able to track the sound signature of the bird-like creature, and he actually located a portion of overturned earth in one of the dark caves that, upon closer analysis, led them to a large cluster of the networked fungus. Afterward they spent several hours collecting pieces of it and bringing their haul back to the house.

Oscar was carrying his last bag of pale-yellow mushrooms back to the main entrance on his own when he heard something strange.

Rrrr.

It was halfway between a purr and a growl, and it sounded vaguely threatening. He stopped.

"Hello? Samantha?"

He received no answer. Samantha was still gathering food deeper in the cave complex.

Rrrr.

Oscar heard little clinks in the darkness to his right. They sounded as though someone was walking on hard rock using tiny stilts made of metal.

"Hello?" he said again.

A skylit opening a few paces ahead of him led onto one of the many breaks in the cave tunnels. He walked in that direction, although it would take him away from his planned route.

Rrrr.

He started walking faster. The clinking of metal on rock increased its tempo.

It was coming after him.

"Aaaaah!" Oscar yelled. He dropped his bag in a panic and ran the rest of the way into the light. In his mad rush he almost didn't see a root protruding from the undergrowth. He leaped over it and avoided tripping, but a moment later he smacked his shoulder against the thick trunk of a reedlike plant.

He lost his balance and fell forward in the moist earth, disturbing a cloud of mosquitoes.

Rrrr.

Oscar whirled about on the ground so he was on his back and sat up, panting.

The arthropod came out of the darkness of the cave slowly, its six large appendages clinking over rock as it went. It was horrendous, nearly as big as Oscar himself, although most of its heft was due to its legs. They were thorny, ebony black, and they ended in wicked points that stabbed the cave wall as it crawled. Waves of motion ran along them in perfect synchrony, like the strings of a piano being struck one after the other in consecutive octaves, again and again.

Its body was neon orange, shockingly bright, and segmented in three like a nightmarish version of a cricket whose mandibles resembled scythes. Three freakishly long antennae swept ceaselessly over the space in front of the being as if palpating to detect prey.

And it hopped. Its hind legs were massive, and they made a sharp *skree* every time the creature jumped. Stubby wings on the arthropod's exoskeleton fluttered when it was airborne and increased its range of motion.

Oscar moved slightly, and the creature's antennae froze. A moment later it rotated its body, and Oscar realized that the top of its chitinous head had a horrible cluster of countless little black eyes, shiny globules with no lids that appeared to focus on him.

Rrrr.

Oscar tried to stand up, and the creature jumped at him.

Doran fell from the sky so fast that Oscar didn't even have time to scream. The wurl came down in a blast of hot air and shredded the bug to pieces with glowing talons. He then jumped out of the way before its still twitching mandibles could touch him.

For a couple of seconds, the only sound in the clearing was Oscar's scared panting. Some of the creature's legs were jerking on the ground, even detached from the thing's crushed carapace.

"Th-thank you," Oscar stammered.

Doran walked over to him, almost as if he wanted to check whether Oscar was okay.

"I'm all right."

Doran projected a faint idea that was part acknowledgment and part warning, overlaid on the image of the creature he had just killed.

"Those hopper things are dangerous. Got it. Thank you, Doran. Really."

Doran glanced at him briefly and then unfurled his wings. He jumped and flapped hard, rising in the air until he was out of sight.

Relieved and thoroughly creeped out, Oscar went back into the cave, picked up his bag of fungi, and made sure to triple check there were no more dreadful bugs desiring to get him on the way out.

AT THE house, Oscar assisted with repairs and did his best to optimize whatever electronic system he could help with. Samantha was sometimes away on Doran without him, and Nadja usually left a couple of times every day with food, headed for the prison where Oscar had been kept after his arrival. At those times Oscar helped Laurie and Ute around the house. They even let him cook from time to time, and it was stressful, but he managed to produce dishes that were actually tasty.

Laurie was not very talkative with him, but ever since the day when he and Samantha had visited the eyrie, Oscar had noticed a change in Laurie's attitude toward him. She was no longer as hostile or angry.

One morning shortly after dawn, Oscar was helping her overturn the compost pile they had dug up some distance away from the house when he stepped on a sharp rock.

"Ow!"

"Is something the matter?" Laurie asked, leaning on the shovel she had been using. Despite her noticeable belly, she was still active, and physical activity seemed to energize her rather than tire her out. She often mentioned that it would be good for the baby.

"A rock, I think," Oscar complained, hopping on one foot. "Ow. Let me take off my shoe."

The problem was evident as soon as he did. The sole was worn through underneath the place where the ball of his foot should be, and it provided no protection anymore.

"How long have you been walking with those shoes?" Laurie asked him.

"Since I came here? These were my dress shoes. I'm kind of surprised they lasted this long, actually, especially after I climbed that volcano."

"This will not do. You might get injured."

Oscar shrugged. "I don't know how to repair shoes, and you guys all have small feet. I don't think any of your shoes will fit me."

Laurie placed her shovel against a nearby tree. "Not *our* shoes, true. Follow me."

Intrigued, Oscar followed her back to the house as he tried not to step on any more sharp rocks. Ute was reading in the living room, and neither Samantha nor Nadja were around.

"This way," Laurie indicated, heading upstairs.

Oscar followed her to her room, where he had never actually been. He stopped at the threshold, unsure whether he should go in.

"Come in," she said. "I think it should be around here somewhere."

Oscar stepped inside carefully while Laurie rummaged around in a closet. He looked around, curious, and realized Laurie was much the same as Samantha when it came to her room. She was very organized and clean. Everything was in its place, and the only striking thing about her personal space was the large mural that had been painted on the wooden wall directly opposite the door. It was a riot of color, with many swirls and symbols in orange, blue, purple, and yellow. In the center of the mural were two right handprints, one slightly larger than the other, with names underneath them.

Lauren. Jörgen.

"Here, finally," Laurie exclaimed, stepping back from the closet while holding a midsized rectangular box in her hands.

"What's that?" Oscar asked.

Laurie sat down on her bed slowly, one hand holding the box and the other resting on her belly. Oscar would have offered to hold the box for her, but he knew Laurie well enough already to know that she did not like to be offered help.

"Shoes," she said simply. She offered the box to him. "They should be about your size."

"For me?"

"Yes, take it."

Oscar took the box and set it on the floor with care. He knelt next to it and opened it.

"Sweet!" he exclaimed. Inside was a pair of hiking boots, rugged and well-worn. He took one of them out of the box and admired it. The shoe had the *Ionas* logo stamped near the heel, and it appeared to be made of synthetic leather or a similar material. The sole was made of thick rubber that promised to offer a solid grip on many kinds of surfaces, and the shoelaces were a vibrant shade of orange that contrasted with the black of the rest of the shoe. Oscar would have bet his link that these were shoes meant for the engineering crew of the generation ship.

"Try them on," Laurie said.

"Okay!"

He made sure to dust off his socks and then slipped his right foot in. The shoe was a little big, but he tied the laces tightly to compensate. He did the same with the other shoe and then stood up.

"How do they feel?" Laurie asked him.

Oscar took a couple of experimental steps. "Wow. This is amazing!"

"Do they fit?"

"Yeah! Laurie, thank you! These are actual shoes from the generation ship. I know you guys have all sorts of relics around, but these… oh man. My friends back home would be so jealous of me right now. How did you even get these?"

Laurie did not answer immediately but instead looked to the side, at the mural with the two handprints.

Oscar glanced at her gravely. "Oh. They were his?"

Laurie gave the tiniest of nods.

"I can't accept them," Oscar said quickly, making as if to take them off. "I—"

"Please do. They do no one any good sitting in a box like that. You have helped us greatly, young male. You have proven yourself." Laurie glanced back at Oscar, flicking her blond locks out of her face. "At the beginning, I was opposed to you being in the house. If Samantha had not insisted so much, we would have kept you in the prison cell where we could have been certain you would not do anything to harm us. We did not know you, and I did not know whether you could be trusted. You could also have unwittingly attracted *her* attention to us, encouraging the wurl queen to watch us even more than she already does.

"And in a way, you did," she continued. "I heard her coming to torment you in the attic weeks ago, late at night. She must have found it amusing to terrorize you. I expected you to complain, but you never did."

"You knew?"

She sighed. "I have years of practice listening anxiously for noises coming from the attic. I know how horrible it can be, and I have experienced her twisted kind of mental torture firsthand. But you did not cave in, and you kept helping us. You even protected Sam at your own peril. You stood up to the queen, something few of us have been able to do. I see now that my suspicions were unfounded. It is like Sam says: we made a mistake by not trusting you at the beginning. This is my way of apologizing. Take his shoes and use them well. He would have wanted for someone to—"

She choked up, and Oscar had absolutely no idea how to react. He felt like he should go and comfort her, but he also intuited that she would not like it. Instead he stood there, in the middle of her room, anxiously waiting until she regained her composure.

"Sam should be ready soon," Laurie said eventually. "She mentioned she would like for you to go out with her today. You should get ready."

"Right. I'm going, then," he replied, backing out of the room. He stopped at the threshold, though. "Laurie?"

"Yes?"

"Thank you so much," he said with a gentle smile. "I know how much this means to you, and I really appreciate it."

She gave him another nod and turned her gaze to the mural. Oscar left, feeling happy and sad at the same time. He was happy that Laurie trusted him. He was sad at the darkness Dresde had brought to her life, and he wished he could do something to help.

Samantha and Nadja returned to the house together about an hour later, which surprised Oscar because he thought they had been in their bedrooms, still asleep. They carried empty food containers and some cleaning supplies. Samantha's eyes were red, as if she had been crying, and Ute gave her a long hug as soon as Samantha came in.

Oscar tried to stay out of the way and sat down at the far end of the living room. He reviewed the chapter of *Wild Beginnings* he was going to read them that night while the women talked. They all went upstairs at one point, and a few minutes later Oscar's link beeped.

Excited, Oscar opened the message that had arrived, this time from his mother.

> *Dear Oscar,*
>
> *I hope you are well. I had a dream last night, and you and your brother were in it. In my dream you came home, but you were little children. I was so happy. I ran forward and hugged you both, and I never wanted to let you go. Through this dream, I know both of you are out there, somewhere, and my faith will keep me going until you return. I have to be strong until you do.*
>
> *Counselor Kamogawa says your father is depressed. I can understand why. He's had to be strong for too long while I was sick, caring not only for me but also for you while Eli was missing. Now that both of you are gone, I think the strain of the uncertainty might be finally getting to him, but don't worry. I'm feeling much better now, and I'm here to keep your father*

focused and prevent him from spending too long at work. I have started going to the gym, in fact, since my strength has fully returned. I take your father with me often, and I think the physical activity energizes him. Your grandmother visits us frequently too, and her presence helps.

On a lighter note, I have big news. A few of the plants that grew from the seeds Eli brought were finally harvested and proclaimed safe! Your aunt has made genetic analyses, and the seeds are edible. In fact, she was the first person in Portree to try a soup made from the grains, which resemble rice, and the legumes, which are similar to beans or lentils. After a couple of weeks of health screenings, no adverse effects were observed in her or any of the other tester volunteers. We can eat these crops! They are nutritious and, as far as I have heard, quite delicious.

The yield of these plants is unfortunately low, completely different from domesticated crops such as our ancestors brought with them on the generation ship, but Laura assures me that even if the low yield means our colony on this planet can never grow too large, it will certainly prevent us from ever fearing starvation again. Our future is truly secured for the first time since we made planetfall.

I cannot tell you how happy everyone is. Director O'Rourke is considering creating a holiday and naming it after Eli! She

*says she wants to honor him for what he
did for us and make sure future generations
don't forget. They sent out a colony-wide
survey today, in fact, asking for suggestions to name the holiday. I think I'm going
to submit the name "Hope Day." I feel like
Eli gave us all hope.*

    *Please be safe, Oscar dear. I keep
praying for your safe return, and I know
my dream will come true. I know you and
your brother won't come back to me as
little children, but instead you'll come back
as men. I can't wait to hold both of you in
my arms again.*

    Love,
    Mom.

Oscar smiled and made sure to save the message in his special folder. It made him happy to know that his parents were okay, even if his dad was having a hard time. He really wished he could tell them that he was doing well, but he contented himself with dictating a detailed letter of his experiences thus far, like he had been doing for a while. He hoped his entire family would be able to read them one day.

Eli, I know you're out there. I know you're still coming to save me. Be safe.

Oscar closed his eyes for a bit and thought about his brother. Despite his bad dreams, he was sure Elias was alive and getting closer to him all the time. It had been months, but Oscar knew Elias would reach him no matter what. It was a comforting thought, and Oscar was smiling when Samantha came downstairs and waved at him.

"Good morning," she said.

"Morning. Everything okay?"

She paused for a moment as if considering. Then she merely shook her head. "Yes. We are going to a place with fjords today. This time of year the tidal pools dry out considerably, and there are plants we can harvest."

Oscar stood up. He realized he was still wearing his boots in the house, so he hurriedly took them off. "Fjords? Sounds exciting!"

"We should pack some food and go. Doran is probably waiting for us already."

Oscar helped Samantha with the usual routine of stashing food in backpacks, filling the water bottles, and making sure they had all their gear. He then stepped out into the early morning and put on his shoes again. He relished the smooth way in which the laces tightened as he tied the knots to secure the shoes to his feet.

"I have new shoes!" he told Samantha brightly "Look! Laurie gave them to me."

She gave him a little smile that was tinged with sadness. "I am glad. Your other shoes were worn through."

"I know. It's so cool to have good shoes again." As they started walking, Oscar purposefully walked on top of rocks he would have avoided the day before. The shoes were not only sturdy, but very comfortable. He barely noticed the fact that they were a bit too big.

They walked to the cliffside where Doran was waiting for them, as they often did.

"Hey, bud," Oscar called out. He was no longer scared of the wurl.

Doran walked forward, half opening his wings, and went straight to Samantha, nuzzling her outstretched hand.

"Right, ignore me," Oscar grumbled. "I brought you a treat, you know."

After a moment, Doran turned his large head and looked at Oscar, radiating expectation. Oscar rummaged around in his backpack until he found what Samantha and the others called a greenhead, a large and fibrous plant that was similar to a lettuce but with thick leaves on the outside and a juicy interior.

Doran gave a playful growl.

"Catch!" Oscar shouted, running straight at the cliff's edge. He tossed the greenhead down with all his strength, and the treat plummeted under the relentless pull of gravity.

Doran slithered over the ground and launched himself after it with lightning speed, wings tucked tight to his body, and fell like a missile for nearly two seconds in pursuit of his prize. He snatched it out of the air with his jaws and then threw open his wings, coming to a graceful stop on the black sand far below, from where the sound of his contented crunching reached them.

"I think he likes you," Samantha said.

"Yeah, because I *bribe* him," Oscar complained. He cupped his hands over his mouth to yell. "Right, big boy?"

Doran glanced up, still chewing, and bounded up the cliffside with a graceful leap. He appeared to defy gravity as he began running on the vertical surface at the same time he flapped his wings, scaling with evident ease.

"That is *so* cool," Oscar whispered.

Doran reached them a few seconds later and crouched so they could climb on his back. When they were secure, he took off, and they were airborne.

"This is seriously the best!" Oscar shouted, holding on to Samantha's waist where he sat behind her.

"I thought you were scared of this?" she called back.

"Nope, not anymore. I. Love. Flying!"

Almost as in response to his comment, Doran flapped harder and rose significantly higher than he usually went. From their vantage point, Oscar had a breathtaking view of the landscape stretching out before him. They were going north this time, following the coast, and he was easily able to see the frothing ocean far below him as it crashed continuously against the intricate curves of the beaches and cliffs. A few seconds later, just when the air was getting too thin to breathe comfortably, Doran tilted his center of gravity forward and the three of them sped down in a controlled dive that was exhilarating and a little bit terrifying.

"Aaaaaah!" Oscar shouted, gripping Doran's back with his legs, using all his strength. "This is awesome!"

"Yes!" Samantha shouted as well, a rare note of joy in her voice. "Doran, go faster! Show us what you can do!"

Doran grunted and projected agreement, anticipation, and a hint of mischief.

"Uh-oh," Oscar said. "Samantha, he's taking it as a challenge!"

"Go!" Samantha yelled happily.

Doran obeyed. If Oscar had previously thought he had seen how fast a male wurl could fly, he had been sorely mistaken. Doran's wings began to flap faster than he had ever seen them move, and a quick glance back revealed that he was also doing something with his tail, using it as a sort of rudder to guide him as he propelled both himself and the two humans riding him through the air so fast that the wind in his face took Oscar's breath away while he tried his very best to hang on in the slipstream.

The dizzying blur of motion was more exciting than any flight he had experienced thus far, and it seemed to go by in an instant, although it lasted about ten minutes, according to his link. His heart was still going a mile a minute when Doran finally slowed down and glided in a slow-moving spiral toward their destination on the ground, a large fjord with tall rocky ledges leading inland along a narrow channel that was partially flooded by what looked like a combination of seawater and the current of a snowmelt river that flowed from the east.

After landing, Oscar and Samantha spent most of the day wading through tidal pools nestled among the sharp rocks at the bottom of the fjord. It was difficult work, and it was necessary to be on the lookout at all times so as to not have a nasty fall, but it was also fun and fascinating.

"What do you call this one?" Oscar asked at one point around noon, gesturing at a strange creature that looked like a fist-sized ball with nine very long spikes radiating out from its body. Oscar watched, mesmerized, as the creature moved slowly but steadily over the shallow water of a large tidal pool with emerald-green water. It appeared to use its spikes as legs, and it had no eyes or mouth that Oscar could see.

"I do not think it has a name," Samantha replied. "I believe you are the second person to ever see these, after me."

"Ooh, let's name it."

"Very well. Any suggestions?"

"Spike face. No, wait. Prickly ball. Uh... pokey-dokey?"

Samantha smiled. "I like the last one."

"Are pokey-dokeys dangerous?" Oscar asked, wading through the ankle-deep water gingerly. He had taken off his new shoes, which he now wore around his neck with the shoelaces tied together, and he was stepping barefoot on a soft carpet of purple-and-pink moss that grew on the rocks. It was slippery at times, so he moved forward really slowly. "You know, venomous or something?"

"I have never touched one, so I would not know. The rays on its body look sharp, however. I would advise you to be careful."

"Right. Doran, what do you think?"

The wurl crouched on a large jutting rock a few meters above them. The sun was almost directly overhead, and Doran appeared to enjoy opening his wings to catch as much sunlight as possible. The thin membranes on each appendage looked almost electric blue from below with light shining through them. Oscar could see the intricate network of capillary vessels in the wings from where he stood, and he marveled at the complexity and beauty of an apex predator of the world.

"Doran?" Oscar repeated, since the wurl had given no indication that he had heard.

In response, Doran jumped down from his perch and landed at the far end of the tidal pool with a big splash. He approached with care until he had reached the spiny creature, then lowered his snout to sniff it. At that moment, the pokey-dokey rolled forward and one of its rays poked Doran in the nose.

Doran did a sort of half growl, half whimper and projected pain and surprise with his mind. He jumped straight up, flapped hard with his wings, and returned to his rock, all the while glaring at the innocent pokey-dokey, which continued moving slowly, apparently oblivious to anything that had happened.

"Ouch," Oscar commiserated. "Sorry, bud. Lesson learned: don't touch those."

"Poor Doran," Samantha said. "Sometimes he is too curious for his own good."

"So I'm giving the pokey-dokey a wide berth."

"Good idea. You should be looking for the star plants."

"Right. You said they're at the bottom of the pools, right? Growing on the rocks?"

"Yes," Samantha confirmed, crouching down a few paces away. She reached down into the water and pulled. An instant later she brought up a flat dark-red organism that looked like a star with only three points, about as big as her hand. "They look like this."

"They look slimy," Oscar complained. "You sure they're good?"

"My mother steams them, and they are chewy but tasty."

"They kind of look like starfish."

"These are not animals. We cannot eat the animals of this world."

"I always wondered about that, you know. Why?"

"They are not compatible with our digestive system," Samantha said matter-of-factly.

"I know that, but why can Eli eat them?"

"Your brother can eat them?"

"Yeah, after his mystical bond with the Life Seed or whatever. Not sure."

Samantha shrugged. "Good for him, but I would rather not try. Oma says you can get really sick if you do."

"Right. Vegan life it is. So, let's find more of these star plants and... what were the others?"

"Redbulbs. And whitepetals."

Oscar lifted an eyebrow. "Very descriptive names. Creative."

"Are you being sarcastic? I came up with them," Samantha replied, storing the star plant in her pack and then placing her fists on her hips.

"No, no," Oscar said in a playfully sarcastic tone. "It's just, maybe you could've come up with less literal names?"

"Says the male who came out with *pokey-dokey*."

"Hey, no fair! You said you liked the name."

"I was being polite."

They glared at each other in silence for a heartbeat, in mock seriousness. Then they both grinned.

Several hours later both their backpacks were heavy, full of a variety of different marine plants that could only be found in the brackish waters of the tidal pools. It was late afternoon, and Oscar was tired but happy.

"All done," he proclaimed, zipping up his pack after making sure the plastic containers inside weren't leaking. "Although we could keep going if you want."

"I think we have enough," Samantha told him. "It is surprising to know that you still have energy, however."

"Why is it surprising?"

Samantha looked up at the sky and then back down at him. "Well, when you first came here, you were... shall I say... weak."

"Weak?"

"Yes. Pale, stringy. As if you had never known physical labor in all your life."

"Thank you?"

Samantha shook her head. "It is different now. You have adapted well, and you help me quite a lot. You also *look* stronger."

Oscar's heart fluttered at the praise. He pretended he was fiddling with something from his pack to surreptitiously check out his reflection in the water and realized Samantha's words made him feel all warm inside.

Maybe she thinks I'm shredded and hot!

He examined himself. It was true that he was stronger now than he had been when he first arrived. He could feel it. For instance, working all day in the sun did not bother him anymore. His body had changed and adapted. He was still lean, but now it wasn't due to the chronic food shortages in Portree. He was eating well, much better than at home, in fact, and Oscar thought he had put on at least a little bit of muscle. He wondered whether he had a tan, and he supposed he did, but the changes had been so gradual that he could not tell the difference when he looked at himself in the mirror, or at his own reflection in the water like he was doing. Only his hair was longer than he usually wore it, but he thought the wavy jet-black locks falling partially over his forehead made him look mysterious.

"Ready to go?" Samantha asked, startling him.

"Sure! We heading back home?"

Samantha whistled loudly, calling for Doran, who was out of sight somewhere. "Not yet. I would like to show you something."

"What is it?"

"I think you will like it."

Doran came less than a minute later, and they climbed onto his back. Samantha leaned forward right as he was taking off and whispered something to the wurl. Intrigued, Oscar held on like he usually did and wondered what she had said, and also how deep the bond between Samantha and Doran really was. He had no idea whether Doran could understand human speech, but sometimes it certainly seemed like it.

"Uh, Samantha?"

"Yes?"

"Doran is taking us the wrong way. We're still going north."

"I know."

With that cryptic remark, Oscar was left to wonder where they were going. Doran flew low to the ground, going north for what Oscar estimated to be around ten kilometers while still following the coastline. As they went, fjords gave way to cliffs that grew taller and taller until they rivaled those near the house. These cliffs, however, were almost preternaturally smooth and made of beautiful white stone that looked like chalk from a distance. The cliffs were crowned with greenery, a collection of small plants that covered every available surface as the land spread out to the east.

Doran flew out over the ocean and then returned to the rock wall, going relatively fast. It seemed like he was on a collision course with a particularly tall cliff that rose above them, but a few seconds later Oscar realized there was a ledge about a third of the way from the top, a highly irregular platform jutting out from the otherwise perfectly uniform cliff face.

"Samantha?" Oscar yelled against the wind in his face.

"Yes?" she called back.

"I think we're going to crash!"

The cliff was much closer now, and Doran still hadn't slowed down.

"Hold on!" Oscar shouted, shutting his eyes tight.

Instead they came to a rough but even stop with much flapping, and that was followed by silence punctuated only by the distant sound of breaking waves.

Oscar opened his eyes cautiously.

"Here we are," Samantha announced, jumping off Doran.

Oscar followed, being particularly careful because Doran had landed on the platform he had seen earlier, a long and narrow outcrop of white rock a little bit over the size of the body of a male Flyer wurl. In fact, now that Oscar looked at the cliff more closely, it was evident that the back of the platform had been hewn out of the rock by powerful claws that had scraped the rock away to create an alcove in the cliff itself.

"What is this place?" Oscar asked, setting down his pack with care near the back of the space. Tall cliff walls rose up on either side of him, creating a rather cozy, cavelike feeling. Ahead of him, the outcrop extended into a ledge that looked like a diving board into nothing.

Samantha put her pack down next to his and then stepped forward, fearless, to the very edge of the ledge. She ran her hands through her hair and breathed deeply once, sighing with what appeared to be contentment.

"This is my special place. My shelter."

Behind them, Doran settled down on the back portion of the ledge. He folded his wings to his body and curled up in the space, which was perfectly sized for him.

Oscar took a few very slow steps toward Samantha while telling himself not to look down. The ledge was wide enough for maybe four people to stand side by side, but there was no railing, and he was keenly aware of the fact that if he fell he would be screaming for a long time.

He fought against his lingering fear until it was squashed enough for him to feel wonder.

"It's… it's amazing," Oscar said.

He meant it. From where they stood, it felt as if they were at the edge of the world. The ocean spread out, immense, and appeared to fill the entire bottom half of Oscar's field of vision. The sun was setting across the water, creating red and golden reflections on the waves. The indigo sky overhead appeared to be screened off by a latticework of long clouds, intertwined in a pattern tinged in orange and vermilion. The sound of the surf far below was like a gentle backdrop to the entire scene, and the cool breeze brought with it a mineral scent that was oddly refreshing. A flock of marine birds flew close to the water, their white plumage reflecting the light of the sun as they corkscrewed through the air.

Samantha sat down with her legs dangling over the lip of the ledge. Oscar hesitated, then copied her. It was exhilarating to be sitting like that, and it felt like the three of them were the only living creatures in the entire world.

"I come here when I want to be alone," Samantha said quietly. Oscar admired the beautiful color of her eyes in the light of dusk, like emeralds with a burning core of flame, which he always found breathtaking. "Here, not even Dresde can hear me, and I can speak freely."

"How did you find his place?" Oscar replied, speaking just as quietly. It seemed unnecessary to raise his voice above a gentle murmur.

"Doran showed me," she replied, glancing back briefly with a fond smile that was answered by a brief huff from Doran's powerful lungs. "I must have been around nine years old then, and he and I had only just begun to truly bond. I was sad often at the time, and I suppose Doran felt it. He brought me here. I was scared, but he stayed with me, and I cried for a long time that first day, holding on to him. We even spent the night here, and I was not cold because Doran is always so warm. The next day I felt so much better. Ever since then we have come here to escape from the world."

"Did Doran carve this?" Oscar asked, pointing at the claw marks still visible on parts of the rock.

"Yes, over time. I believe this was his own refuge, a place where he could come to be away from Dresde and the other males."

Oscar nodded. He could easily imagine Doran feeling concern for Samantha as a little girl, and bringing her to the place he thought was safest.

"How did you two meet?" Oscar asked her. "I mean, no one else in your family seems to be friends with him."

"By accident. I was out foraging one day, but I was a silly child. I disturbed a nest of ghost scorpions near the house while looking for wildflowers."

"Ghost scorpions?"

"Yes. You are lucky you have never seen one. They are about as big as your hand, very pale, which is why they have their name. They are blind but are very sensitive to vibrations. They also have a long stinger that comes out of their abdomen, and they like to hunt at night. It is said that even a scratch from that stinger is enough to kill a grown woman."

Oscar shuddered a little bit, remembering his very first night in the prison and the horrible creature that had come into his cell. He was almost certain he had already seen one.

"Anyway," Samantha continued, "it was dark that day, and when I saw dozens of ghost scorpions crawl out of the ground, I panicked and screamed. Doran came down from the sky and snatched me up. I thought he was going to kill me, but he set me down gently near the graveyard, and I felt… I do not know. Something from him. I had grown up hearing that all the scourge— the wurl—were bloodthirsty monsters, but I saw something different then."

"I know," Oscar replied. "It was the same with me."

"From then on Doran began to follow me around. At first Oma was terrified. She attacked Doran once to shoo him away, even knowing full well that Dresde would be furious, but the following weeks he still came to visit me when no one was watching, and over time they all came to accept him when they saw he was not a threat. He became my friend."

"He's very nice," Oscar said. "I think he didn't like me at first, but now he sort of tolerates me. Maybe it's because I bribe him with treats all the time."

"You have proven yourself, and he is fond of you now," Samantha told him. There was a little pause. "As am I, Oscar."

Oscar gasped. "Did you just…?"

Samantha glanced down, allowing some of her hair to obscure her features. She was silent for a few seconds. Then she looked at Oscar, moving her hair out of her face and fixing him with a defiant frown.

"We do not do that awful dehumanizing thing of referring to boys and men as 'males' because we want to. She makes us do it."

"Dresde?"

"Yes," Samantha hissed. Her scowl deepened. "To her, only females are worthy of being considered sentient creatures. Of her own brood, only Doran still has a name, and that is because he remembers it from when she named him a long time ago, when Dresde hatched. As time has gone by, she has forgotten the names of all other males except him. She considers them little more than slaves and does not care for them at all. Surely you have seen how there are no other males left around the eyrie."

"I wondered about that, yeah," Oscar said.

"I believe she sent them all on suicide missions to try and find your brother. She does not care about the fact that flying for thousands of kilometers over water is a brutal endeavor or about how it weakens them. She also does not care about the fact that there are things in the oceans, creatures that shine in the night. I have seen them only a couple of times, but I fear them. Those creatures have voices."

"That doesn't seem so bad."

"They ensnare you with their song. If you do not fly far away as fast as you can, you will simply plummet to the ocean, never to be seen again. I have witnessed it before. Doran is strong, so he has not been taken. But every time Dresde sends out males in pursuit of your brother, many die in this way. I know because they never come back. Now I am all but certain that only Doran remains."

"Wow. Why is she like that, do you think?"

"I do not know, and I do not *care*!" Samantha shouted. She pounded the rock with her fists.

Oscar flinched at the sudden outburst. "Hey, it's okay," Oscar said, terrified of the fact that he could see the beginnings of tears in Samantha's eyes. He was not used to seeing her so vulnerable.

"It is *not* okay, Oscar. It is not okay," she said, her voice thick with suppressed emotion. When she next spoke, she whispered. "You do not know. You have not seen the horrors. You have not met…. I was born into slavery, as was my mother and her mother before her. Dresde keeps us alive, the females, the only ones she deems worthy of existing. She terrorizes us. She fills our days with dread, and now I am her soldier against my will.

"To her, we are toys," she went on, her volume rising with every word. "She allows us to eke out our meager existence because we amuse her. She gives us just enough freedom to think we can maybe build happiness for ourselves, and then she snatches it away! It brings her a twisted kind of joy to see our pain. She is a horrible creature. I have wanted to end her life from the moment I could hold a spear, and one day I *will*."

Oscar shrunk away slightly at the ferocity in Samantha's voice. She had always appeared so stoic, so unfazed by events around her, that Oscar had not once suspected the depths of her rage. He realized he was in the presence of true hatred for another creature.

He was also reminded of his own anger. After Elias had left, Oscar had been angry at the entire world. He had been hurt by heartless bullies so much that he had begun to lose himself in his own boiling wrath. Wounded, he had tried to hurt others in turn. He had begun to change into a violent person, and had it not been for therapy, he was scared to think of what he might have turned into.

"Anger is heavy," he heard himself whisper.

"What did you say?" Samantha snapped.

Oscar met her blazing eyes with his own sad expression. The sun had set by then, and the wind had a slight chill to it.

"You should try to let go of the hate, if you can."

She drew away from him. "How *dare* you! You have no idea what you are talking about. You have no idea what I have been through, what my family has been through!"

"I have been angry too. I have gone through some tough times."

"Oh, tough times," she mocked him. "What tough times could you have faced, Oscar? You were born in a city of peace. You never had to fear for your life each single day of your existence. You never had to huddle in the dark every time *she* flew by, you never had to see your—your—"

She started crying. Oscar edged closer to her but did not dare touch her.

"I can never understand what you've gone through," he said gently. "Of course not. And yeah, compared to you I've been a pampered kid all my life. You fight for your survival every day out here. All I had to worry about was school.

"But," he continued, "I do know about anger, and I know how it feels. My counselor told me once that anger is like an addiction. You hate how it makes you feel, but you keep going back to it again and again. It feeds on you to keep going, like a fire that doesn't go out. It's best to let go, if you can."

"I cannot," Samantha declared, wiping tears from her cheeks. "I will never forget, and I will *never* forgive. Dresde will die one day, and it will be by my hand."

Oscar nodded slowly. He was sad, but the ironclad determination in Samantha's eyes was unmistakable. "I don't understand, but I'm with you, every step of the way," he told her. This time he did reach for her hand, and she took his. "I only hope you won't have to do it."

Samantha looked out over the ocean, where the twin moons were like pearls reflected on the waves. She let go of his hand after a moment and stood up.

"It is time, I think," she told him. "Maybe this will help you understand."

"Time? For what?"

"For you to meet my father."

chapter 23.
atoll

ELIAS SPENT the entirety of the morning after talking about his nightmares with Tristan in a state of alert, stopping frequently to listen for something he couldn't quite hear. He knew they would arrive at whatever place the Behemoth was taking them sooner rather than later, and he wanted to be prepared.

Around noon Elias walked all the way to the front end of the gigantic creature and sat down at the edge of its leathery shell. He could not quite get used to the size of the being he was now riding, and he spent more than a couple of hours watching the Behemoth swim, looking at the way it would lift its massive head above the surface of the water every now and then to breathe. Elias wondered whether the creature had any sense that he was carrying intelligent beings on his back or whether the creature simply moved because of something similar to instinct.

Guided by whatever is controlling him, he thought grimly.

The more time passed, the more pernicious the vague sensation of disquiet and hunger became. Elias imagined they would arrive at their destination very soon, and he tried to understand what was happening based on what he had observed. Why were they being transported to the middle of the ocean?

Tristan was right. The Singers had had plentiful opportunities to get rid of them but had not done so.

What do they want from us? Why are they taking us here?

Elias wrestled with the feeling of not being in control of where he was going or why he was being taken there. He knew that both Tristan and he would be dead already if they hadn't found the Behemoth, but that did not make his current situation any more agreeable. He felt as though powerful forces in the largely alien world around him had seized control of his destiny without him realizing it had happened. All he wanted was to save his brother and keep his promise to Sizzra. He had no quarrel with the denizens of the ocean and hoped that, whatever happened next, he would be able to find a way to reach Dresde's lair.

"Brought you lunch," Tristan said, coming to sit nearby. He handed Elias a large leaf on which he had arranged a selection of the fruits, tubers, and nut analogs they had discovered were good for eating.

"Thank you," Elias told him, realizing that the hunger was not only in his mind, but in his stomach. He had not eaten much since he had woken up, preoccupied as he had been.

"Is it getting worse? That feeling you said you got during the night?"

Elias popped a crunchy nut with a bright green shell in his mouth. "Yeah. It's more distinct."

"What do you think it is?"

Elias shrugged. "I think we will find out soon enough. According to my link, we will be at the island, or whatever it is, very soon."

Loud rustling and stomping behind them betrayed the fact that large creatures were approaching, and a few seconds later Narev, Vanor, and Siv appeared and sat down next to them.

"Even they know something's going on," Tristan observed.

Elias listened with his mind and perceived, very clearly, the state of heightened alertness of all three wurl. "Yes, they do. I wonder if they know what it is."

Tristan and Elias ate lunch in silence, and Elias kept his gaze focused on the horizon. In late afternoon, after hours of traversing featureless oceanic terrain, he finally spotted something dark ahead.

"Is that…?" Tristan began.

Elias stood up, squinting. The dark speck was growing larger. "Yes," he confirmed, his heart speeding up with anticipation and dread in equal amounts. "I think we've arrived."

It took the Behemoth another hour to reach the first small island, a stretch of land no bigger than a hundred meters long, completely flat. Elias and Tristan watched, expecting the creature to stop, but it did not. Instead, it swam farther north until it reached another island, much bigger and rocky, one of its sides jutting out from the ocean like a miniature mountain. There the mighty being finally slowed down and stopped.

"This is it," Elias announced, clutching Sizzra's spine tightly. "Let's go."

"Or we could just stay here," Tristan proposed. He held his shock spear in both hands. "We don't have to get off just because someone or something wants us to."

"I have a feeling that we will be attacked if we don't do what the Singers want."

"Right," Tristan said. "Then down we go."

They made their way off the Behemoth's shell, followed by the wurl. Elias jumped onto the soft sand at the edge of the rocky island easily. He knew a brief moment of disorientation at feeling himself on actual solid ground instead of on a floating platform of some kind, but he recovered quickly and helped Tristan jump. The wurl joined them on the island with no trace of hesitation.

Elias took a moment to breathe. The air was hot but not stifling. The bulk of the island, though relatively small, rose sharply above sea level not far from where they were. Its surface was bare except for a few short, spiny-looking bushes at regular intervals. There were no large trees in sight, and he felt terribly exposed after having spent a few days under the cover of the trees that grew on the back of the living island.

"Let's explore," Elias said at last, "and find out why we're here."

"Why don't we climb that hill?" Tristan suggested, pointing at the nearby summit of the island. "We'll get a better view from there."

"Good idea."

Elias followed Tristan as they walked along sandy ground, which quickly turned into sun-warmed rock as they left the narrow beach. Their bare feet hardly made any sound as they walked, and even the wurl behind them were stealthy, almost as if it would be best not to make too much noise. All five of them climbed to the top of the island in less than ten minutes. From it, Elias examined the magnificent scenery.

"We are…," Tristan began. "This is like a collection of little specks of land."

"Yeah. It's incredible."

From their high vantage point, Elias realized they were standing on one of the islands that made up an archipelago of at least seven landmasses of varying sizes. The island on which they stood was the largest one, but each of them was visible, even if they rose kilometers away from the next.

"Weird," Tristan pointed out. "The islands, they make—"

"A circle," Elias finished for him. "A really big circle."

Elias had noticed it too. The archipelago of islands stretched out over a large distance, but from the top of the rocky outcrop it was clear that they were all arranged around the perimeter of an enormous circle. Even the most distant island, a mere speck of green Elias was barely able to spot across the azure water, was placed in such a way that it was diametrically opposite the island where Elias and Tristan were standing.

Looking back, Elias got his first good view of the Island Behemoth from a distance.

"Tristan, look," he said.

He watched the creature that had served as their transport, and from afar its size was even more impressive. Its shell was essentially a forest, twice as large as the place where they were standing now. The creature had lifted its head out of the water to take a loud, long breath, and although whatever means of locomotion it used was hidden beneath the waves, looking at its face from the side and realizing its beak was big enough to eat a wurl in a single gulp drove home the point of how massive the Behemoth really was.

"It's not swimming away," Tristan observed.

"I don't think it will," Elias said. "It brought us here for a reason. It won't let us leave."

"Not that we could. We have no boat, no equipment, nothing. These islands are too small for much of anything to grow."

"Maybe we should—" Elias began, but a sharp mental jab stopped him midsentence.

"Eli?"

Elias turned his head to the left, gazing out over the water at the center of the circle. The sensation in his mind came again, sharper. It was so clear that he actually clutched his stomach involuntarily.

Hungry. I'm— It's hungry.

"Eli? What's going on?"

"There's something there," Elias answered in a small voice, pointing at the deceptively placid expanse of ocean in the middle of the archipelago.

"I don't... I don't see anything. Are you sure?"

Elias wrenched his attention away and looked at Tristan. The horrible mental echoes subsided at once.

"Not sure. I... I don't know."

"Come here. It's almost sunset. I suggest we go back to the Behemoth, sleep there, and figure out what needs to be done tomorrow. Okay?"

Elias nodded. "Okay."

They walked back to the beach, but they were still several meters away from the Behemoth when the gigantic creature growled.

"What the...!" Tristan exclaimed.

It felt like an earthquake. Elias stopped, trying to regain his balance, and he saw how the Behemoth pushed away from the edge of the island with a mighty heave that created tall waves in its wake. Much faster than Elias would have ever thought possible, the Behemoth retreated, swimming away in a burst of speed that appeared to be completely at odds with a creature that size.

In a few seconds, the Behemoth was entirely out of reach. After a couple of minutes, it was out of sight.

"We're on our own," Elias said, mostly to himself. A small wave of fear washed over him. "We have no food, no water. We're literally in the middle of nowhere. And our ride just left us."

"We're together," Tristan reminded him. "Let's not freak out until we have to. One thing at a time. Night is coming. We should find a place to rest."

"You're right. You're right," he told Tristan, giving him a brief hug. "Let's find a place to spend the night."

"I think I saw a nook in the rocks back that way. We can check it out."

After searching for some time, Elias sat down next to Tristan in a natural alcove in the western flank of the island. They were protected from the gentle breeze that was blowing, and they watched the sun go down together. Narev curled up nearby, as he often did, while Siv and Vanor found comfortable spots on the beach itself.

"Try to rest," Tristan told Elias. "I know those nightmares have been keeping you up at night."

Elias shuddered involuntarily. "I suspect I'm going to have another one tonight."

"Well, I'll be here if you do. Come on, Eli. Close your eyes and rest."

Elias tried to do so, and he attempted to ignore the dozens of unanswered questions in his mind. He had no idea why they were there, or what they would do, or even how they would survive. He had never felt so exposed or adrift.

As darkness fell, Elias's accumulated tiredness from the last few nights made itself felt. He yawned and rested his head on Tristan's shoulder.

"Go to sleep, Eli. I'll stay awake for a bit to wake you up if you have another nightmare."

"You don't have to do that."

"That's okay. Try to get some rest."

Elias was going to argue, but another yawn interrupted him. "Okay. Thanks, Tristan."

"Don't mention it. Now go to sleep."

Elias was already drifting off. He slipped into a dream so smoothly that at first he did not realize anything had changed, and as the dream took hold, Elias's mind began to wander.

He dreamed of Sizzra this time. His own memories were mixed with hers, and he was suddenly trapped at the bottom of a mountain, snow piling on his once-muscular scaled body. He struggled to move, but he could not.

The Flower. Those aliens took my Flower.

The aftermath of that horrible wrenching sensation had not left him. Elias, as Sizzra, stewed in his own anger and tried to find enough strength to stand up again.

Time passed, and the hunger came. He was ravenous, but he could do nothing. Summer followed winter, but the world did not wake as it should. The Flower was missing, the center of all life, and without it Sizzra's domain was doomed.

Elias-as-Sizzra was humiliated when Spine males brought him food for the first time. He was hungry, however, so he ate. Like an invalid, he was nursed back to a semblance of his former self over the slow grind of years. Gradually, he tried to find in himself enough strength to stand up. It was a long time before he was able to do so, and an entire mountain still loomed above him, unconquerable and imposing, where before the strength of his beautiful body covered in spines would have been able to climb any peak with barely an effort.

One day he finally overcame the weakness and began to climb, but his progress was excruciatingly slow. The hunger did not leave him but instead grew stronger. He seethed with rage at the creatures come from another world who had hurt him so and vowed to destroy them all. Soon they would witness his strength. He was the queen of the land, and he would teach them how dearly they would pay for their abominable transgression against the world.

The climb was arduous, painful, and full of peril. His body did not respond correctly. More than once he feared he would fall back down, to die the most ignominious death any of his mothers had ever had before him. The mere thought of it kept him going, even after his strength had long since given out, and so he made his way to the Flower chamber one morning at long, long last.

He rested there and regained his strength over several months. The place itself was unbearable. Where before the Flower had radiated its life energy across the entire continent through the mighty vines that connected it to every living thing, there was now... nothing. The place where the Flower had grown was empty, and that emptiness was hungry.

Elias-as-Sizzra grew strong enough one day to stand up again. He knew where the aliens were, and the time had come for his revenge. He walked away from the Flower chamber with murder in his mind, determined to slay every single one of those creatures and find a way to return the Flower to where it needed to be. He would not be stopped. He would impale them on glittering, iridescent spines and tear the invaders apart with his claws and his teeth. He would—

He did not understand, not at first. Elias-as-Sizzra had been about to leave the Flower chamber, but he could not. Confused, he rested for a while and attempted it again the next day.

He could not. At first he thought it was his own weak body giving out again, but this was something different.

The third time he tried to leave, he realized that something was holding him back. And pulling him in.

Elias-as-Sizzra looked back and focused his eye cluster on the thing he had avoided looking at directly out of rejection, out of anger, and out of a tiny shred of fear.

The center of the chamber yawned, empty. Three vines came together and joined into nothing. Where the Flower should have been, there was nothing now.

No, not nothing. Or perhaps precisely that. There was a void there. An empty, grasping, pulling void.

The ravenous void wanted to swallow the entire world. And it was pulling him in.

Elias woke up from the dream and managed not to scream this time. He blinked in the starlit night and was not surprised to find his forehead and chest covered in clammy sweat. It took a moment for his mind to readjust to the shift in perspective.

That was a memory. I'm not Sizzra.

Carefully, mindful of not waking Tristan, Elias stood up from where the two of them had been sleeping and walked to the beach. Vanor took notice of him, lifting his head and focusing his glowing eye cluster on Elias as he walked to the edge of the water. Elias tried to reassure him with a brief mental pat, and Vanor curled back up after a few moments. Alone, Elias sat down on the sand. Two of the moons were setting in the distance, and the night was perfectly quiet.

I can still feel it, Elias realized. *That thing. That hunger.*

Elias had almost forgotten, but the dream-memory had forced him to remember. Sizzra had also felt this awful sensation. It was the reason she had been unable to leave the mountaintop for so long. She had been trapped, trying not to get pulled into that emptiness, that ravenous yearning that Elias was experiencing yet again, but coming from a completely different direction.

Almost as if acknowledging the fact that Elias was thinking about it, the insidious sensation in his mind sharpened, sizzling like an electric shock.

Elias stood up and walked resolutely away from the beach.

I need to know. I need to see.

The part of the island where he was faced west, out to open ocean, so Elias walked around it until he had reached the eastern shore that faced the archipelago and the circle around which all of the islands were arranged.

There was very little light, but Elias did not need it to see the thing at the center of the circle, the second nexus of the world, the thing that should be protected above all else.

It's revealed with the tide, Elias realized. *It was underwater before. But now....*

He could not see it with his eyes, but he could feel it as it reached for him with unseen spirit-lines of an entirely different kind to what he had already experienced on a mountaintop. These spirit-lines went deep. They held in them the cold touch of water that flows quietly in the darkness of unknowable depths.

Elias took a step forward, his foot dipping into that water that connected everything. As he did, the sensation sharpened. The call grew louder.

It's like the other one, Elias thought. *Big, all-encompassing. A network of energy and life and.... Something else.*

He took another step, standing ankle-deep in the water. He could feel the call, and also more insidious and sinister undertones that appeared to want to draw him in and engulf him. The sensation was so similar to what Sizzra had experienced that Elias shared her same aversion, her same fear.

What's wrong with it?

He took another step into the water.

"Eli?" a voice called, but it sounded far away. "Eli!"

Another step. The water was welcoming, warm.

The loud, painful sound of metallic claws scraping against rock made Elias hesitate. It was followed by rumbling steps, a loud splash, and Narev was suddenly in front of him, blocking the way forward.

"Narev?" Elias asked, confused. "What are you doing here?"

"Eli!" Tristan yelled.

This time Elias turned around and noticed Tristan coming as fast as he could.

"Tristan?"

"Narev, get him out of there!" Tristan shouted.

Narev approached Elias and pushed him back gently. Elias resisted.

Growling, Narev shoved him back with far more strength and sent him stumbling back to fall on his bottom with a jarring impact.

"Ow! It's... wow, it's okay, Narev," Elias said, coming fully back to his senses with the pain of the fall. "Thank you for stopping me."

Narev nuzzled him, radiating concern still.

Elias got back on his feet with Narev's help and returned to the beach to sit on a rock. Tristan was with him a moment later.

"Eli, are you okay?"

"Look, Tristan," Elias replied, pointing out over the water. "The second Flower."

Tristan looked in the direction Elias indicated. "I don't see anything. It's too dark."

"It's there," Elias said quietly. "I can feel it. It's calling to me."

"Is that—is that why we were brought here?"

Elias shrugged. "I don't know. But I think I have to go there, Tristan."

"Okay, but we're *all* going. And not in the middle of the night. We wait for morning, okay?"

Elias wrenched his gaze away from the Flower with an effort. "You're right. You're right. I almost.... It's weird. It reminds me of what Sizzra felt...."

"Sizzra?" Tristan echoed. "What does she have to do with this?"

"Nothing, I think. I'm not sure. I feel weird."

"Come here. Whatever it is, we'll do it together in the light of day."

"Okay. All right. Could you... hold me?" Elias asked.

"Of course."

Neither of them slept for the remainder of the night. It was hard for Elias to ignore the insistent call to come closer, and every time he was about to doze off, it seemed to him that the call came louder and attempted to take over his thoughts and his volition. Tristan helped as best he could. He talked to Elias, held him, and helped him stay put and wait for the sun.

When morning finally came, Elias was tired. The constant back-and-forth in his mind had been exhausting, but as the light grew, part of the pressure in his thoughts appeared to abate.

"I see the place now," Tristan said after the sun had risen fully. "It's right in the middle of the circle."

Elias stood up. "That's where we have to go."

The Flower was not visible from so far out, but a structure had appeared with the low tide, rising over the waves. It looked like an atoll, roughly triangular in shape, its sandy edges almost white in the morning sun. It was very narrow, a thin sliver of land with a band of green in between the white.

Tristan lifted his shock spear out of the sand. "If you say that's where we go, then we go. Together, all right?"

"Yes. Let's find out what brought us here." Elias looked at Siv, Narev, and Vanor. "You guys don't have to come," he told them. "We don't know what's out there."

None of the wurl walked away. If anything, they projected firm determination more clearly than before, as well as a desire to accompany them. Narev approached Elias, and Vanor walked over to Tristan's side. Siv waded into the water and looked back in a clear invitation.

"Looks like they want to come with us," Tristan observed.

"Okay. As a team."

Elias climbed onto Narev's back, and Tristan did the same on Vanor. Gripping Sizzra's spine tightly in his right hand, Elias directed his thoughts at the wurl.

Let's go.

Vanor and Narev walked into the water. They began to swim after Siv.

Elias was nervous, and he tried to be on high alert. He looked everywhere around him as they swam but saw nothing threatening. Their destination was barely a couple of kilometers away, according to his link, and he expected to be there in a few minutes. As they quickly approached, Elias kept scanning the water.

It was a rather beautiful place they were crossing. The Spine wurl were swimming over the continental shelf that Elias had identified with help from his link, and as a result of the low depth to the seafloor, the water was a sparkling medley of aqua, emerald, and light blue. It looked like the waterfront of an expensive beach resort on one of the settled worlds, a magnificent seascape fit to be immortalized in a painting, a destination worth crossing half the world to reach.

A few meters below, Elias could see a veritable forest of coral covering the shallows, the sessile organisms sporting a breathtaking array of different shapes. The sections of seafloor not covered by coral had white sand instead, which reflected the morning light in a striking way. The water was so clear that Elias had no trouble looking all the way down, and it felt to him as though he were in a huge outdoor aquarium or a natural swimming pool of sorts that should have been teeming with life. Some of the coral even grew out of the water, making incredible sculptures of natural origin that had been carved by erosion over millennia. A few of the coral columns spread out at the top, looking like irregular rocky tables balancing precariously on flimsy foundations, their sun-facing surfaces green and lush. Many sported capricious geometric shapes that were odd yet entrancing, and the entire place looked like the epitome of what an ocean paradise should be.

Except for the fact that something was missing.

That's odd, Elias thought as Narev sped through the water with a graceful paddling motion aided by his muscular tail. *There are no fish.*

The submerged coral reef was devoid of anything that moved. There were no small crustaceans scuttling about, no fish darting in and out of cover. It was odd and slightly disquieting. Even out over the open ocean Elias had frequently seen fish swimming about, and the Spine wurl had never had trouble finding something to eat. Here, however, there was nothing. Even the coral looked odd. Although beautifully shaped, Elias realized now that most of it, both above and below the water, was white, bleached.

Dead.

Almost as if sensing his stress, Vanor and Siv approached so all three wurl would be swimming very close to one another in a tight formation.

"What's wrong, Eli?" Tristan asked. The place was so quiet that his voice carried easily.

"There's nothing here," Elias answered, pointing all around him. "No life."

"Maybe this is how it's supposed to look."

Elias shook his head. "No. Something's wrong. This is the place where the second Flower rests. It should be the epicenter of life in the ocean. Instead, it's… it looks abandoned. Like a disease took hold and killed everything."

"Okay. Stay alert, whatever happens."

The atoll was fast approaching. The closer they got, the more nervous Elias felt. He avoided looking directly at their final destination, in fact, and only realized they had arrived when Narev grunted and climbed onto solid ground.

"By the generation ship," Tristan said under his breath. He pointed with his shock spear. "Eli, that's…."

Unable to avoid looking anymore, Elias took in the entire scene in a single glance.

They were standing on a very narrow strip of land that was almost perfectly triangular. It appeared to have been made out of the coral reef, and it was about ten paces wide although very long, each one of its three sides spanning a considerable distance of at least half a kilometer from end to end. Sparse vegetation grew on it, but it looked brittle, and it crumbled underfoot when the three wurl walked closer to the other edge.

The other side overlooked a chasm.

The change in the color of the water was shocking. Behind them, the water was a gentle shade of blue-green. In front of them, however, the water inside the triangular atoll was the shade of the sky at dusk, a deep indigo that darkened with shocking suddenness. In places it was almost black, and the contrast was not only stark but also mildly threatening.

"Why is it like that?" Tristan asked quietly. "Why is the water so dark?"

"There must be a huge abyssal pit underneath," Elias explained, trying to remain rational despite the fact that he was shaken for a reason he could not quite place. "Behind us the water is not very deep. Five or so meters at most. And here? It could be thousands of meters. This chasm could lead all the way down to the blackest depths of the ocean floor. There's no knowing how far this goes."

"And…," Tristan began, and his voice, usually so steady, shook slightly. "At the center, there…."

Elias lifted his gaze and met the object at the center of the world, unblinking. "That's the Flower of the
Deep."

The wurl made a sound very close to a whimper.
All three of them stood stock-still, looking ahead. Elias
remained motionless next to Tristan, finding himself
unable to do anything except gaze at the second nexus
of life on New Skye.

The Flower that rose from the ocean had the exact
same shape as the Flower that grew on a windswept
mountaintop, and yet it was completely different in
almost every way. Where the Flower that Sizzra had
once guarded had sported iridescent petals of white
and green and light pink, shifting endlessly in the light,
this Flower had petals that mirrored the ever-changing
shades of the gold-plated radiance of the sun. The Flower glistened, its petals dripping moisture as if covered
by water, although they were rising out of the waves.
Immediately below it, three thick vines were partially
visible before they disappeared into the depths below, a
perfect mirror of the vines that had connected the other
Flower to the rest of the world.

Elias could feel its energy. It was not like before,
when he had been entirely cut off from the world as an
alien and had been able to hold the Life Seed in his hands.
He was now part of the world, and he felt the power coming from the Flower. He understood perfectly why the
Spine wurl did not want to approach any farther.

No creature should ever touch the Flowers, none of
them. Not even their guardians.

"It's calling me," Elias said, his voice barely above
a whisper. "It wants…."

Narev, still carrying Elias on his back, took a step
forward. Then another one. He did not want to, and

Elias was not sure whether he wanted to be there, but the call was urgent, impossible to ignore. Vanor moved as well, as did Siv.

Together, the three wurl crossed the narrow atoll and jumped into the dark waters that surrounded the Flower.

At the same instant, one adult and two juvenile Singers discarded their camouflage and flickered into view, revealing the fact that they had been lurking beneath the water's surface. They screamed and launched themselves at the intruders with grasping tentacles writhing.

"Incoming!" Tristan shouted, an instant before madness broke out.

The three Singers were like living bullets that shot straight for the Spine wurl. Elias had only a moment to register their attack before Narev used all of his strength to propel himself to the right, barely avoiding one of the juveniles that came, jaws gnashing, within centimeters of Elias's leg.

Watch out! Elias thought, urging Narev to swing forward just as the second of the juveniles came upon them. One of his tentacles reached out to grab Elias, but Narev was able to avoid him by coiling his body and submerging himself as he powered down through the water with his tail.

Elias gasped as he was completely submerged along with his ride. The water felt different, as if saturated with something foul. It pressed all around him and appeared to want to take something important away.

He opened his eyes underwater and caught a glimpse of something that luminesced faintly in the deep dark, an afterimage of light blue in the blackness all around, but Narev twisted in the water at that moment, and Elias was forced to shut his eyes tight and hang on to Narev's scales with all of his strength.

The two of them burst out of the water, and Elias looked around wildly, taking stock of the situation. He could not see Vanor or Tristan, and Siv was trying to keep one of the juveniles at bay.

Ahead of them, the adult Singer appeared out of his shroud of invisibility and roared.

Elias recognized him by the silver spine still embedded in his neck. He was a terrifying vision, a powerful creature of the ocean who radiated strength and deadly agility.

Narev stopped his forward motion with an effort, attempting to swim to the side, but the Singer reached forward with its two front tentacles, aiming for Elias. He was too fast. There was no time to move away.

Narev's entire body stiffened underneath Elias as Narev fired two spines that whistled through the air and met their mark an instant later, piercing the flesh at the tip of each of the two tentacles that had been about to grab Elias.

The Singer howled, and the sound paralyzed Elias momentarily. He fought against it with everything he had until he was able to move again.

The atoll! he told Narev. *We have the upper hand if we fight them on land!*

Narev understood and swam away at once, aiming for the nearest sliver of land, but he was cut off by a juvenile. He swerved, avoiding another tentacle from an unseen source, and swam as fast as he could across the depths of the atoll and toward the shore at the far end.

The Singers pursued. Elias could only hold on, and he glimpsed both Vanor and Tristan chasing, trying to help, but they were too far away to do anything.

Narev scrambled onto the atoll and whirled about, roaring out his own grating defiance. Elias jumped off him and whipped out Sizzra's spine, assuming a fighting stance.

"We don't have to do this!" he shouted out over the water, hoping against hope that the mad creatures about to come upon them would understand. "We don't have to fight!"

Three Singers went invisible and dived under. Behind them, Vanor and Siv were in hot pursuit.

"Where…?" Elias began.

This question was answered immediately when big splashes to his left and right indicated that at least two of the Singers had surfaced again and were climbing onto the atoll on either side, still invisible, but betrayed by the dents their heavy bodies made on the brittle grass and the narrow sand-covered platform.

Thwock!

Narev fired a spine at the nearest Singer. It struck the creature, who howled in pain and shuddered into view.

"Eli!" Tristan shouted, close enough to be heard. Elias glanced in his direction in time to see the adult Singer appear suddenly, fully visible, and slap the water with his tentacles as he blocked the way, preventing Vanor, with Tristan on his back, from approaching.

To his right, Elias heard something slither very close.

He slashed at the air with his spine. It caught on something, and an instant later the second juvenile became visible with a brief spurt of hot red blood. It had been about to grab Elias with a tentacle, but the creature backed away from the spine in his hand.

"Stop this!" Elias shouted, swiping with his weapon to make the creature back away further. "We aren't your enemies!"

A roar behind him yanked his attention in that direction. Narev jumped out of the way of the Singer on the other side, coiling his body into a ball. He fired two more spines, but the Singer leaped into the water and avoided them. Narev landed on the ground, hard, and roared again at the juvenile still on land, who Elias was trying to fend off.

There was commotion in the water, but Elias could not look. The Singer in front of him was not going away. He approached again, his tentacles dodging Elias's swipes, reaching, intending to grab.

There were too many tentacles. Elias sidestepped one, punched another one away, but the third one slithered under his weapon and coiled around his waist.

Vanor came out of nowhere. He fired a spine that struck the creature in the shoulder, and it screamed.

No, Elias thought, flinching as though he had been hit. *This isn't right.*

"Eli!" Tristan yelled, jumping off Vanor's back and running at him. Siv launched himself out of the water an instant later and landed next to Vanor. Together, the three Spine wurl retreated until they were standing back to back, surrounding Elias and Tristan in a protective triangle of dozens of upright, quivering spines ready to fire and kill.

The adult Singer opened its segmented maw and screamed again. It was not a song, but he was still terrifying as he propelled himself out of the waves created by his own motion and landed with a tectonic tremor on the atoll before Vanor, his barnacle-encrusted body a wall of muscle and scales. The two other juveniles retreated to the water but remained close, blocking every avenue of escape.

Elias clearly felt the burning determination in Narev, Siv, and Vanor as they prepared for a fight to the death. There was no fear, only defiance and a fierce challenge from which there was no backing off.

They are going to die protecting us, he realized.

The fully grown Singer opened his segmented maw again, exposing his rows upon rows of needle teeth.

"This is wrong," Elias said under his breath.

The Singer moved forward immediately in front of Vanor, almost as if he sensed that Vanor was the strongest of the Spine wurl.

"You're right," Tristan said suddenly. "We have to stop this."

The two male wurl in their prime looked at each other for an eternal, fragile second. Then they attacked.

"No!" Tristan shouted at the top of his lungs, and with a last look at Elias, he ran forward, faster even than Vanor, and stood immediately in front of the adult Singer wurl with shock spear in hand.

"Tristan!" Elias screamed.

Tristan lifted his shock spear, its deadly ends sizzling with electricity. The creature in front of him appeared to recognize he was holding a weapon and reared its entire front body on four of its tentacles, using the other two to slash at the air.

"Tristan, duck!"

Instead, Tristan tossed his only weapon aside.

Elias watched, horrified, as the shock spear sailed through the air and fell to the ground, inert. Tristan stood defenseless against a creature as large as Vanor with no means of defense. The Singer fell forward onto all six of his tentacles and rushed the last few meters to where Tristan stood.

Tristan did not move away.

Elias watched, shocked, as the Singer stopped and did not attack.

"We're here," Tristan said in a loud, clear voice. "I don't know if you can understand me, but we are here. Whatever the reason you brought us to this place, we can help."

"Tristan!" Elias yelled again, and jumped over Narev's tail to run to where Tristan was standing.

"It's okay, Elias," Tristan told him without breaking eye contact with the Singer adult. "I finally understand. These wurl never attacked us. All they wanted was to bring us here."

Elias's eyes flicked between Tristan and the Singer, who remained where he was, his massive scaly chest heaving, his eye cluster fixed on Tristan almost as if he were able to understand. "What?"

"The first time we saw one. A Singer. Remember?"

"At the river," Elias answered, sparing a nervous glance backward. The three Spine wurl were standing at attention, ready to fight, but the Singer juveniles behind them were also standing still. It was surreal, almost as if somebody had paused a scene in the middle of a video or frozen time.

"Right," Tristan confirmed. "A juvenile. He didn't attack us. He attacked the Flyers."

Elias remembered the event well. "We were paralyzed by the song."

"Yes, but the Singer did not attack us. He scared the Flyers away and killed one."

"But at the beach...."

"They were trying to lure you to them. He, specifically," Tristan said, lifting his finger to point at the adult Singer in front of them. The creature made a low sort of gurgle with its throat in response to the gesture. "That's why you were having the dreams. But Narev intervened."

Elias looked at the spine still embedded on the side of the creature's neck. "That night, in the darkness, I thought Narev had saved me."

"I think that's why they lured Narev away later," Tristan continued. "To separate him from you so they would be able to get you."

"But there was a battle. On the ocean maw," Elias countered. "So many died."

"And yet Singers did not attack *us* directly, only the Flyers. Think back. They were protecting us, Eli."

"Protecting us? But...." He remembered the carnage. The chaos. And yet, not once during that entire interaction had a Singer attacked him directly. In fact, now that he thought about it, the Singers had killed all of the Flyers and then left after the sonic bomb had gone off.

"Finally, they did not attack us when we were on the ocean maw, even though we were very vulnerable," Tristan explained. "It made no sense to me. Why avoid us when we were so weak we could barely stand? And just now. They could have paralyzed all of us with a song, but they haven't done so. Why?"

Elias took a step forward. "Why?"

Elias did not let go of Sizzra's spine, but he raised his other hand, palm outstretched, and stepped forward again.

Why? he asked with his mind, attempting to reach the creature in front of him.

Another step forward.

Why?

The adult Singer did not move away. Elias heard Narev growling out a warning, but Elias realized Tristan was right. The creatures wanted him here for some reason.

Tell me, he said to the Singer. The creature remained still.

He allowed Elias to touch him.

A mental wave exploded in Elias's mind with the force of a tsunami. He staggered backward into Tristan's arms.

"Eli!"

The three Singers made a sound that reverberated with absolute fear and vanished from sight. They fled away from the atoll, and only when they were in the clear waters beyond did they discard their camouflage and become visible again. Even so they continued swimming away, eventually disappearing under the surface of the water.

"What's happening, Eli?"

Narev, Vanor, and Siv whimpered at the same time. They crouched low to the ground and flattened the spines on their bodies in submission.

Elias looked at Tristan again and realized he was trembling.

"Eli, speak to me."

The mental wave came again, brutal. Elias stumbled, and Tristan had to steady him once more.

"Something…," Elias tried to say. It was hard to concentrate.

"Something what?"

Elias looked forward at the vast pool of midnight-blue water that reached down and down to the untold depths of the ocean, down where there was perpetual darkness and absolute cold.

He tried to point but could not.

"Something…," he tried again.

There was a tremor. The still water at the center of the atoll bloomed up, small concentric ripples radiating from the middle.

"Eli, you're scaring me," Tristan said urgently.

Another tremor, and this time there were actual waves in the water, waves coming from nowhere.

No, not nowhere, Elias corrected himself. *They're coming from below.*

Enormous bubbles floated up through the dark water and burst, followed by bigger waves.

"Tristan, run," Elias managed to whisper at last.

"Run?"

In the depths, lights began to appear. They were visible even in the brightness of the morning sun, fleeting glimpses of ghostly blue and ethereal white, flashing for only a moment before being swallowed by the murk.

Elias forced himself to speak. "There's something in the water!"

"In the—"

But the mental wave came again, and this time even Tristan appeared to feel it. His eyes lost their focus. A moment later, Elias's own mind was assailed by a force unlike anything he had ever experienced. It could not be denied. It could only be obeyed.

Elias stood up, with Tristan by his side. As if sleepwalking, the two of them waded into the water and began to swim until they were several meters away from the atoll.

What's happening?

Elias struggled to regain control. His grip tightened on the weapon he still held.

The overwhelming pressure of the mental wave receded, and his vision cleared. He realized he was in the ocean now.

"Tristan?"

"Eli?" Tristan asked, appearing to blink back into consciousness again. He looked down and appeared to be shocked to see he was in the water. "What the…?"

From below Elias felt a current. Gasping, he looked down into the indigo depths but saw nothing.

"We have to get out," Tristan said. "Didn't you say there was something in the water?"

"Yes, let's—ahhh!"

The mental wave crashed against Elias, so loud it was painful, and Elias covered his ears with his hands in a useless gesture to try and block out the sound that was not a sound. He thought he heard Tristan's voice for a moment, but he could not swim and began to sink, still clutching the sides of his head, down into the bottomless pit.

A second later Elias blinked and realized he was underwater. He was confused for a second and had an awful déjà vu of sinking and being tossed around by a storm with no idea how to reach the surface.

Which way is up?

He looked straight ahead. Dark.

Above me!

The surface was close. Glancing to the side, Elias realized Tristan was also underwater, pressing his palms against his ears. Elias swam over to him and grabbed his hand, intending to pull him up as well. His lungs were already beginning to demand oxygen, and he kicked once, fighting against gravity.

He felt the current again, close by. And then he saw the lights.

He froze in place, still holding Tristan's hand, helpless in the face of such beauty. The water around him was alive with lights, like blinking stars against the night sky and myriad pinpoints of white-and-blue brilliance that pulsated gently in a dazzling display of hypnotic beauty.

I'm surrounded by light, Elias thought, enraptured.

The lights shifted to the left, moving as one, almost as if they were connected in some way. Elias wanted to keep watching, but he could not hold his breath any longer. He gathered his strength and swam to the surface, yanking Tristan with him.

The two of them broke out of the water, coughing and sputtering.

"What was that thing?" Tristan said, his eyes wide with fear. "That thing in my head, that force?"

"Not a—not a thing."

But a large disturbance in the darkness below them robbed Elias of the ability to talk. The water became distorted, bulging outward as something big swam up from the deep. Bioluminescence was everywhere now, that mesmerizing light show of flickering points of brilliance that was so entrancing and so dangerously beautiful.

The surface tension of the sea held for an instant and then broke at the same time as something massive burst out of it in the midst of a breaking wave and a blinding spray of droplets. Elias and Tristan were pushed away, but not far away enough. They were reduced to looking up at the creature that had finally appeared in the midst of rivulets of dripping water, an imposing and slender outline against the merciless blue sky.

"It's her," Elias said in a choked voice.

A voice larger than life itself proclaimed her name in his mind.

Lyrana.

chapter 24.
papa

IT WAS already dark as they flew back to the house on Doran's back, but all three moons were out, and under their combined light Oscar was able to see the vague outlines of the landscape from where he sat.

He was anxious and a little bit confused.

I'm going to meet Samantha's father. How am I going to meet him?

He could think of only two possibilities. Either Samantha was taking him to the graveyard, perhaps to show him where her father's remains lay, or she was taking him to the prison.

He remembered the first few days after he had arrived. There had been something in the cell next to him, a thing that had sounded like an animal and that had thrown itself at the wall many times. It had reacted whenever it heard Oscar's voice, but there had been no words in the creature's utterances. Nothing to suggest it had been human.

But they go to the prison every day. They bring food to whatever—whomever—is in there.

He recalled how sad Samantha had been the first time he'd seen her after she returned from the prison.

Many more times afterward, either Samantha or one of the others would return from that place with deep sadness on her face.

Is he in there? In that cell? And if he is, why don't they let him out?

Doran flew swiftly, and they arrived home a little over an hour later. Oscar and Samantha thanked him, and he left by jumping off the cliff and flying out to whatever resting place he preferred.

"Samantha?" Oscar asked once they were alone.

"Yes?"

"What do you mean we are going to see your dad?"

"Follow me."

Together they walked down the now-familiar path that led to the house, where they stopped briefly to leave their haul of the day and most of their things. Samantha stepped inside for a few minutes, presumably to let everyone know they had returned safely. She came out holding a satchel that, judging from its smell and the way it steamed, contained food.

"Where are we going?" Oscar asked.

"Not far."

He followed Samantha as they made their way in the very same direction they had gone that first night when Oscar had arrived. Like then, the yawning outlines of the blackened ruins of what must have been houses at one time rose up from the ground in sharp contrasts of silver and black under the light of the moons. Although the night was warm still, there was a faint hint of fall in the air. Fewer unseen insects made noise in the grass around them, and the atmosphere was quieter, almost expectant.

Oscar was not surprised when they stopped in front of the prison building. He had avoided coming near it in the intervening months, and he was surprised at how vividly it brought back memories of his time as a prisoner. The heavy padlocked door to what had been his cell was closed, and next to it was another door, identical in every way.

"He might be surprised to see someone new, and particularly a young man," Samantha told Oscar, passing him the satchel with food. She then rummaged around in her pockets until she found a key ring from which many different keys dangled. "Stay back at the beginning while I introduce you. Try not to make any sudden movements, and speak softly if you can. My father is not dangerous, not to others, but he might react unpredictably."

"Um, okay," Oscar replied. He had about a million questions, but he didn't know how to ask them.

"One more thing," Samantha indicated as she picked one of the keys and approached the padlock that secured the door. "No matter what, do *not* mention the wurl."

"All right. Yes."

Samantha opened the padlock, which clicked loudly.

From inside the prison cell, something like a moan reached their ears, but muffled as if from far away.

Oscar took breath in sharply, and Samantha glanced at him. "No need to be afraid."

He nodded. He *was* scared but also curious, and he guessed that for Samantha to be willing to allow him to meet her father was a very big deal.

"I'm fine," he told her, trying to smile but failing. "Let's go."

"Very well."

Samantha grabbed the heavy door handle and pulled.

Oscar expected a deranged lunatic to jump out at them the second the door was wide enough to allow for a person to go through it, but nothing of the sort happened. When the door was open, there was only silence.

Samantha stepped inside and gestured for Oscar to follow her. After a very brief moment of hesitation, he did.

It was dark inside. It was also soft. When Samantha closed the door behind them, which shut with a rather disturbing *clunk*, he could not see anything at all.

"Hello, Papa," Samantha called out in the gloom. "I have brought you some dinner."

A sound as of something shuffling reached Oscar's ears, like fabric rustling against a hard surface, but it seemed to be coming from below them. Oscar was getting majorly creeped out, and he nearly jumped when Samantha touched his shoulder.

"Take off your shoes," she said to him in a very quiet voice. "The dimmer takes a moment to activate. Sudden changes in brightness disturb him."

Oscar tried not to stumble or drop the satchel while he untied his shoelaces and placed his shoes against what he assumed was the door. When he stood on the oddly soft floor barefoot, he could feel little bumps and ridges on the surface. It was also a little bit bouncy, similar to walking on a mattress.

The air smelled odd. It was not a bad smell; rather he could perceive a mildly chemical, antiseptic note that mixed with the much more welcoming smells of wood and sap.

Click.

"That is the dimmer," Samantha said. "The lights will be coming on now."

In response to her voice, the rustling sounds underneath them increased in volume. There was also a faint but deep grunt. Oscar backed away from the sounds until he bumped into a wall, which was also soft, and stood there with the satchel of food in both hands.

Slowly the light level grew enough for him to be able to make out details. The increase in brightness was very gradual, so much so that he was surprised to realize he could finally see.

He was standing in a rectangular room that was perhaps twice the size of what his cell had been. There were no windows except for a large skylight directly above them. Aside from that the room was mostly bare. As the light grew it revealed that the walls and floor were partially covered in the mattress-like material, although it was irregular and patchy, as though it had been put together from fragments of other things. When the lights reached full brightness, Oscar realized there were dents and bumps in the wall, as well as scratch marks in many different places. In particular, the padding separating this cell from the contiguous one, where he had been a prisoner once, had been mostly torn away.

In the center of the room a square hole led down to another level, dark. From where he stood, the only thing Oscar was able to see was the lip of a wooden ladder that appeared to descend into whatever was beneath them.

"He will come out when he is ready," Samantha said, answering Oscar's unspoken question. "Sometimes it takes him longer than others. He might also not want to come out at all, but I am confident he will."

"Okay," Oscar replied.

The effect of his voice was immediate. Something threw itself against the ladder, making it shudder with a loud *bam* that made Oscar yelp.

"Papa, move softly, remember?" Samantha called, approaching the hole and sounding perfectly unconcerned. "Soft steps."

A groan answered her words, exactly the sound that Oscar had heard in his confinement, but several times more disturbing now that he knew a human being was making it. Oscar glanced at Samantha with alarm, but she wore a bland smile as she looked down at whatever the darkness below hid from view.

This is crazy. What if her dad comes out and attacks me?

The ladder creaked.

"Very good, Papa. Soft steps."

She took a step back and, a couple of seconds later, Oscar saw Samantha's father for the first time.

He appeared to be around the same age as Oscar's own dad, a man in his forties with a small bald spot on the top of his head. His buzzed hair was jet black, like Samantha's, and his skin was the same bronze tone as hers. He had a full beard, which was surprisingly kempt, and as he climbed out onto the padded floor, Oscar saw he was a big man, with wide shoulders, and taller than Oscar by several centimeters. He was wearing sweatpants and a turtleneck, both white and spotless.

For a couple of seconds, as Samantha's dad smiled and reached for his daughter to embrace her, it seemed to Oscar as though he was a perfectly normal man.

Then her father caught sight of him.

The calm in his eyes shattered and was replaced with shards of evident raw anxiety in a split second. He let go of Samantha carefully and then backed away as fast as he could, half tripping over the ladder, and slammed his back against the farthest wall in the cell. The entire structure vibrated with the impact, and the man whimpered, crouching down to the floor and hugging himself.

"This is Oscar," Samantha said, again without the slightest trace of alarm. Her tone and demeanor were so mild they could have easily been sitting in a living room somewhere, sipping tea. "He is a friend. I wanted you to meet him. Oscar, this is my father. His name is Johann."

"Nice to meet you," Oscar said tentatively.

Johann started breathing quickly through his nose, exhaling forcefully.

"Big breaths," Samantha said. She approached him slowly and sat down next to him. She rested her hand on one of Johann's knees. "Like this: in... out." She showed him how to take deep breaths while Johann's frantic eyes flicked between her and Oscar. He was still breathing fast, and the more he kept going, the more Oscar became concerned he was going to hyperventilate and pass out.

Maybe I should go.

Oscar had come into the cell feeling scared that Samantha's father was going to attack him, but now that he saw the trembling man cowering on the floor a few steps away, he actually felt sorry for him.

He's scared. Of me.

Oscar smiled, trying to appear as nonthreatening as possible.

"In... out," Samantha continued, breathing deeply.

It took a while, but Johann's breathing slowed eventually, hinting at the fact that Samantha was being successful at helping him relax. Oscar decided to sit down on the floor as well so he wouldn't be the only one standing up, and he did so very slowly. When he first started moving Johann gasped audibly, but Oscar kept smiling until he was sitting cross-legged at the same level as Johann and Samantha.

The change in position appeared to soothe Johann, because a couple of minutes later he had relaxed enough that Samantha stopped telling him to breathe deeply and glanced at Oscar instead.

"Oscar has brought you dinner today, Papa," she said. "Would you like to have some?"

Johann hesitated. Again his gaze shifted quickly between Samantha and Oscar. Finally it settled on the satchel of food.

He gave a nearly imperceptible nod. "Yes," he croaked.

"Very well!" Samantha said with a happy note in her voice that sounded brittle. "Oscar, would you like to share dinner with my father?"

"Yeah, yes. Of course."

She gestured for him to come closer. "We can all have some. Right, Papa?"

Carefully, moving as slowly as he could, Oscar made his way around the hole in the center of the room and approached Samantha and her father. He kept smiling the entire time, and he was rewarded when Johann did not attempt to escape after Oscar sat down a meter away from Samantha and him.

He offered the satchel to Samantha, but she shook her head and indicated that he should give it to Johann directly.

Wordless, Oscar did so. Johann drew back slightly at the beginning, but either curiosity or hunger appeared to get the better of him in the end because he reached forward cautiously until he was able to touch the satchel. He took it from Oscar with another small nod and what could have been a fleeting smile.

"What do we have for dinner tonight?" Samantha asked. Although her tone was not condescending, Oscar could tell from her eyes that it was hard for her to speak to her father as if he were a child. "Can we see?"

Johann opened the satchel carefully and took out a bowl of triangular mushroom buns that Oscar had already had on a few occasions. Ute usually made them, and they were both savory and very tasty.

"That looks delicious!" Samantha said.

Johann nodded. "Delicious. Thank you, Sam."

He reached for one of the buns and offered it to Samantha, who accepted. He then took a second bun out of the bowl and offered it to Oscar.

Oscar exchanged a quick look with Samantha, who gestured affirmatively.

"Thank you, Johann," Oscar said, accepting the food.

Johann did not meet his eyes fully, but he did nod again. Then he took a third bun and bit into it with gusto.

They spent the majority of the meal in silence, and although Oscar had been hungry earlier, he lost his appetite at seeing the state Johann was in. He seemed healthy, physically at least, but the slightest noise or movement startled him. When an insect flitted by overhead, briefly outlined against a moon through the skylight, he dropped his food and had to be calmed down again over several minutes. He spoke very little, and although he did not meet Oscar's eyes at all while he ate, Johann would often steal quick glances at Oscar, almost as if afraid that his visitor was going to hurt him.

After the food was gone, Johann and Samantha descended into the lower level, what Oscar supposed was the basement or bedroom of the prison structure. They spent a few minutes down there, and Oscar did not follow, although he did hear how Samantha kept her voice deliberately upbeat and soothing as she spoke. Eventually she came back up, looking as though she wanted to cry.

Oscar had an impulse to reach out to Samantha and maybe try to comfort her, but he stifled it. Instead he picked up the satchel before he followed her out of the cell and into the freshness of the night, which Oscar had almost forgotten inside that claustrophobic space. Only when the door was locked and secured did Samantha look at him under the moonlight.

"That is my father," she said, almost sounding apologetic.

"He's nice. He looks strong."

"He is," she agreed. "When you were in the other cell, I was concerned that he was going to break the wall separating you two. He became very distressed those first days. We often had to stay with him for long stretches of time."

"Does he hurt himself?" Oscar asked, remembering the padded floor and walls.

"Not anymore, but in the past he did," Samantha answered, beginning to walk toward the house. Oscar followed. The night around them appeared even quieter somehow now that he knew that there was another person living in the area, someone who spent his days as a prisoner. "We only allowed him access to the underground bunker after we were sure he wouldn't be in any danger going up and down that ladder."

Oscar wanted to ask why, but he didn't know how. Instead he said, "So you guys care for him. That's why I see either you or Nadja or Laurie come here so often."

"Yes. My mother comes too. It is harder for her than for the rest of us, but she does it anyway."

More silence followed her words, and they kept walking with only their footsteps disturbing the quiet of the night. Oscar could see that Samantha was hurting, and he felt powerless and desperate. He did not know what to do or what to say to make her feel better. The sensation in his chest grew in intensity with every step until Oscar couldn't take it anymore.

He stopped walking. "Why? What happened to your parents, Samantha? Why doesn't your mother speak? Why is your dad in that prison? What *happened* here?"

She stopped walking as well, but she did not turn around to face him. "Did you notice the sweater he was wearing?"

"The turtleneck? Yeah."

"My mother made it for him, from clothes our ancestors brought to this world. He has a couple of them, and he seems to like them. They hide the scars."

Oscar shivered, although the night was far from cold. "The… scars?"

Samantha's voice was thick with emotion. "Burns, mostly. He has them over most of his body. Some are… some are…."

She started crying in earnest all of a sudden, and the sound pierced Oscar's heart. He couldn't hold back the need to comfort her anymore.

He walked over to Samantha and hugged her.

She stiffened in his arms at first, but her resistance dissolved almost immediately, and she turned around to allow Oscar to hold her in his arms. Her hands were pressed against his chest while she allowed the tears to flow. Oscar had no idea what to say, so he simply stood there while sobs racked Samantha's body. Tears started rolling down his cheeks too, out of empathy for a person who, he realized now, had been forced to grow tough and strong to face a world that had hurt her and her family more deeply than Oscar could ever understand. He wished he could help, feverishly so. He wished he could tell her that it was okay, but he knew it wasn't okay. They were all in a horrible situation against their will, and the one responsible for all of it was Dresde.

Samantha pushed Oscar gently away after a few minutes and wiped tears off her cheeks with her sleeve.

"I apologize for that," she said.

"Don't."

"He used to be a great man, you know," Samantha told him. "He built the attic by himself, and he also dug up the underground bunker over which the prison is now built. Our ancestors made that bunker, but it had been lost to us until my father found it again. He did many other things besides. Oma says he was an amazing engineer."

"I'm sure of it," Oscar said. "He has sharp, intelligent eyes, like yours."

Samantha looked up at the sky briefly, as all of them often did, but there was no flying shape obscuring the stars. She then glanced back at Oscar with determination on her face, and she bunched her hands into fists.

"We must do something. This is all her *fault*."

"I'm with you. You already know that."

"I do. Come with me, Oscar."

"She can hear you here! Just call me 'male.'"

"I have stopped caring about what she can and cannot hear, and even she has limits. She cannot hear individual words from so far away—it is physically impossible. Her name she can probably sense because it is so closely linked to her, but I do not think she can hear anything else unless she is nearby. This superstitious fear of speaking freely needs to end."

"Are you sure?"

"Yes. I make my stand now. And for that, I need your help."

"What are you talking about?"

Her reply was to walk in the direction of the house. Together they reached the building a few minutes later, and as soon as Oscar took off his shoes and walked through the door, he sensed the tension in the atmosphere. He glanced to the right and saw that everyone was sitting in the living room, apparently waiting for them. Even Ute was there, looking far more alert than usual.

"Are you okay, Sam?" Laurie asked.

"I am."

"And your father?" Nadja joined in.

"He is well. He was surprised at the beginning, but we ate together, and he even gave Oscar—" Everybody gasped. "—*Oscar* some of his food. Oma, Laurie, Mama, it is time."

"Are you sure about this?" Nadja asked.

Samantha made her way to the living room and sat down. Oscar took a seat next to her.

"I am," Samantha told everyone else. "Our attempt on the Flower failed, so our only other option is to go away."

"If we do this and we fail, she will kill us all… or worse," Laurie pointed out. She did not sound scared.

"I know," Samantha agreed, "so before we proceed, I want to ask you. I will not do this unless we are unanimous. Should we try to reactivate the shuttle?"

"Yes," Laurie said almost immediately.

"Oma?"

"Yes."

"Mama?"

Samantha's mother did not speak, but she did nod.

"Good. And you, Oscar?"

He glanced quickly around the room. "I'm… going to need a little bit of an explanation. This is going too fast. Shuttle? What are we talking about here?"

Samantha looked at Nadja.

"Young male," Nadja began, "Sam says she now trusts you fully, and therefore we all trust you. There are things you do not know, but tonight we will share them with you, and to understand you must know our past. Tonight you met Sam's father, my son-in-law. He used to be a lively and resourceful man in years gone by. Ute and he were happy, for a time."

"What happened?" Oscar asked timidly.

"My grandson, Jörgen, was born," Nadja answered.

Ute made a small choked sound in her throat, and Samantha and Laurie each took one of her hands in both of theirs.

"Jörgen was Samantha's brother, right?" Oscar said.

"That is correct," Nadja replied. "He was their firstborn son, but instead of being happy when he came into the world, we were all terrified. You see, young man, the wurl queen does not tolerate males. She allows the women and the girls to live, but she kills most of the boys when they are born. Over three generations our population has dwindled because *she* has only allowed a very small number of males to live. The queen told me once that my son-in-law was to be the last male to live in her domain because she had gotten bored of humans. We are like vermin to her, or like trapped animals that should be culled. Now that our novelty has worn off, she wants to see us die out completely.

"When we saw that the baby was a boy, we quickly devised a plan to trick her. We hid him away, and Ute told the queen that the baby had been stillborn. Sam's father built the attic in the interim, and it was there that Jörgen lived, hidden."

Nadja glanced at Laurie, whose expression was stormy as she spoke up. "I grew up knowing of him, but we were not allowed to interact," she recalled. "I would often listen for noises in the attic when I was in my room, and I would know it was Jörgen, but we barely saw each other at all while we were children. It was all done to prevent the scourge queen from knowing he lived. Over time we developed a way to communicate without speaking. He would rap on the floor of the attic, and I would answer by tapping my bedroom ceiling. We became very good at sending messages that way, one letter at a time."

"Laurie's parents died soon after my grandson was born," Nadja added, "in an incident by the cliffs. To this day, we do not know whether it truly was an accident or not. With them gone our numbers dwindled even more.

"The more years went by, the more difficult it became to hide Jörgen from the queen. He was growing, and he was restless. He wanted to be let out of the attic, but we could not risk it. Johann found the underground bunker around this time, and he built what is now the prison, imagining that he would be able to hide his son there instead, where he would be safer.

"Shortly after the prison was completed, Ute became pregnant again. We were happy but also scared. Then Sam was born, and we were greatly relieved because she was a girl. We knew a couple of peaceful years… but then Ute and Johann had another child. A son they named Erik."

Oscar glanced at Ute, who was crying silently. He felt tears burning in his eyes, threatening to spill out, because he knew what was coming now. He had seen the tombstone in the graveyard.

"This time there was no tricking the wurl queen," Nadja said bitterly. "She came flying in the night one week after the child was born and demanded to see him. We were all with the baby that night, all but Jörgen, who was in the bunker. Ute attempted to lie again, saying the baby had been stillborn, but this time the lie did not work.

"The queen demanded to be given the baby so she could kill him. Johann refused, shouting that she would have to go through him first, and attacked her. He was no match for such a powerful creature, of course. She knocked him unconscious, and she… she…."

Nadja paused, evidently unable to speak. A lonely tear rolled down her cheek. Then her expression hardened.

"After she murdered Erik, she kept us there until Johann came to. Ute was screaming. Laurie was terrified out of her wits, and I was trying simultaneously to hold on to her, protect Sam, who was a toddler, and prevent my daughter from attacking the queen and dying. It was chaos.

"As soon as Johann was conscious again, the queen announced his punishment. You see, Oscar, our ancestors originally called her the scourge because of her cruelty. She enjoys suffering. She seems to feed on it. To her, the very worst punishment she can give you is not death, but life. She said that she would give Johann a long life, the longest one possible, and that every second of it he would beg for death but would never have it. She said… she said she would torture him forever."

Everyone but Samantha and Nadja was crying by then. Oscar had guessed some of what Nadja was telling him, but the depths of the horror shocked him. He could not even begin to imagine what Laurie must have gone through, witnessing all of that as a young child. Merely thinking about what Ute and Johann must have felt that night after Erik's murder gave him chills. He had known Dresde was violent and cruel, but he'd had no idea. This was a million times worse than anything he could have dared think.

"The wurl queen allowed me to leave with Laurie and Sam," Nadja said in a flat, apparently emotionless tone that simmered underneath with what could only be rage. "I took the girls home, and I waited. Many hours later, as dawn was breaking, Ute came back. She was filthy and covered in dirt, and Johann was not with her. She did not answer my questions and has rarely spoken since. I did not know what to do. I needed to go out and see whether Johann was still alive, but I could not leave the house with two little girls and my own daughter, who appeared to be catatonic. I also had Jörgen to think of, alone in the bunker. It took me most of the day to get Ute to react enough so that she would be able to mind Laurie and Sam while I went outside to check on Jörgen and then go look for Johann.

"I will not describe how I found my son-in-law, but suffice it to say that he bears the scars to this day. The queen had been true to her word: despite the gruesome injuries, he was still alive. She demanded for him to be cared for and placed in the erstwhile prison, and for a big skylight to be installed so she would be able to torment him whenever she wished. I acquiesced out of desperation, because I knew she would kill us all if I refused. I thought I had known her cruelty before, when she bit off my hand after I begged for my own father's life to be spared, but now I understood that she was mad. There is no reasoning with a being as corrupted by evil as she is."

"My brother grew up hating her," Samantha joined in. She was looking straight ahead, but her gaze was far away. "He was forced to hide all his life. After my father was put in the prison, Jörgen went back to the attic, and he stayed there for *years*. He had to be quiet, always. Every single time he went outside, it was in the middle of the night, and we were always afraid that she or one of her males would see him. We were lucky, and he survived... or so we thought."

There was a pause, heavy with what could only be memory. Eventually, Laurie spoke up.

"After I became pregnant, Jörgen grew afraid for the baby. He also began to say that he could hear voices in the night, and that something was outside the attic, watching him."

The clammy hand of recollection squeezed the back of Oscar's neck. He knew what that was like.

"A month before you came here," Laurie continued, "Jörgen went to the river to bathe. He had not gone in weeks, and he was desperate to be outside for a little while. I did not want to let him, but he insisted. He almost did not sound like himself that night."

"I was there," Samantha added. "I offered to go with him, to defend him, but he said no."

"He never returned," Laurie said dully. "He is dead."

"The queen told me that she always knew," Samantha told Oscar between gritted teeth. "From the day Jörgen was born, she knew about him. She let all of us believe that we had deceived her. She let us go through the awful pantomime of hiding my brother away from her all his life, simply because it amused her. When she grew bored, she killed him with no compassion, no mercy, nothing. She is *evil*."

The silence that followed stretched on for what seemed like a very long time. Oscar was reeling from everything he had heard. He looked at each of the women in turn and realized that they were living in a perpetual nightmare. Something from which there was no escape.

Unless....

"I am very, very sorry," Oscar said to them, his voice unsteady with emotion. "I can never understand what you went through, but if I can help you, I will. You guys mentioned a shuttle."

"Yes," Samantha confirmed.

"Is this a shuttle from the *Ionas*?"

"Indeed," Nadja answered. "It is the vehicle our ancestors used when they arrived on this planet."

"Where is it?" Oscar asked.

"Hidden," Laurie replied. "Only Sam knows its precise location."

Oscar frowned. "Why haven't you used it before? If the shuttle still works, you guys could fly to Portree. Escape from this place."

"It will not open for me," Samantha explained. "I have tried for years, but the ancient mechanisms that keep it sealed prevent me from accessing it."

"We believe a computer interface is needed," Nadja added. "Like the one you carry."

Oscar lifted his left forearm. "My link?"

"Yes," Nadja confirmed. "We tried to repair the links of our ancestors years ago, but we lack the necessary technological expertise, and none of them are operational anymore. We believe a working interface may allow us entry to the shuttle. We are not certain, of course. It may be that the software is incompatible, but it is worth a try. It is our only option now."

"I will take you to the shuttle, if you agree," Samantha said to Oscar.

"Of course. When should we go? Maybe we should give Dres—I mean, we should give the queen some time to cool off before we try anything."

Samantha shook her head. "That will not happen. She is now aware of the fact that we all know her Flower is her weakness. She may decide to kill us tonight, for all we know, or she may allow us to stew in our own fear before punishing us all for what I tried to do."

"So…," Oscar began.

"So we leave tomorrow," Samantha indicated. "I would leave tonight, but Doran and I do not usually go on a foraging trip after dusk. If I summon him and she notices, she will stop us. Tomorrow, before dawn, we will leave as if we were going to gather fruit from the Nightmare Caves. If all goes well, we should be able to make the shuttle operational and return with it to pick everyone else up. If we fail or we need more time, we can always return on subsequent trips."

"Wait," Oscar said, looking at everyone else in turn. "If we're able to pilot the shuttle, we're leaving? Tomorrow?"

"Yes," Nadja answered, her tone firm.

"But this is so sudden," Oscar argued. "We're not prepared to leave, are we? We need to pack food, and Eli and Tristan are coming for me. They're coming this way. We can't just leave."

"Food is not a problem," Laurie replied. "If the shuttle works, it should be fast enough to get us across the ocean in a few hours."

"And we have not forgotten about your brother or his companion," Samantha joined in. "We should be able to track them down with the shuttle and pick them up. We would all go together back to your colony from there."

"But… but…," Oscar stammered. "She will follow us, even if we escape. We would be leading her straight to Portree!"

"An inevitable conflict," Nadja answered. "You will use the communications array on the shuttle to contact Portree and warn them of the danger, something for which they should already have prepared as well as they can. They have had months to ready any weaponry they have for the inevitable return of the queen."

"The shuttle should be fast enough to give us a grace period of several hours to days before she arrives at the colony after we get there," Laurie commented. "We will stand and fight with your people, but it is a fight that must be fought. They should be aware of it too. If they have not prepared well enough, then we will all perish."

Oscar ran a hand through his hair, hard. "It's… this is so sudden. I don't even…."

"It is the only way," Samantha said to him, placing her hand on his shoulder. "She may be powerful, but if we catch her by surprise and fight together, we have a chance. Are you with us, Oscar?"

He tried to steady the fluttering in the pit of his stomach. He was scared, yes. But he was also tired of being scared. "Yeah. Let's do this."

chapter 25.
lyrana

IN THE wake of her name, all semblance of conscious thought vanished. Elias could only gaze in enraptured awe as the third wurl queen revealed herself at last.

She towered over them both, a gigantic sea serpent come to life. Her incomprehensibly long form rose above the surface in a cascade of water droplets that ran down segment after segment of shieldlike scales, tightly packed and angular. The armored plating on her body was a magnificent shade of glittering gold that warned of one thing only: danger.

She appeared to be massive, larger than either of her sisters could ever hope to be. Six disturbingly long tentacles erupted from breaks in the segments that made up her torso and writhed incessantly beneath the surface. When she cloaked again, her body blended into the sea itself, and it was distinguishable only by the beautiful bioluminescence that she gave off. The water became alive with the blinking lights of a thousand stars.

Lyrana dived down, and another large wave was the only thing to betray her motion in the wake of her descent. Invisible, she swam underneath them, and Elias was mesmerized by the bioluminescence from her body.

It was impossible to ignore, the myriad points of light mysterious and alluring at the same time. He did not even attempt to flee when Lyrana surfaced again on the other side of where he and Tristan still floated. She became visible again and dipped her head closer to them, allowing him to look into her eyes for the first time.

Her head was as large as Sizzra's had been, but it was adorned with finlike protrusions that looked almost like kelp strands, each of them a deep azure against the glistening cosmic shimmer of her golden scales. Her eye cluster, unblinking, sat amid an angular forehead that ended in the same monstrously segmented jaw male Singers had. Six long and sinuous whiskers dangled from it, and even out of the water they shone with complex sequences of light in shifting shades of white and yellow and blue. The brilliance appeared to run down each of the whiskers in a nonstop sequence, like the lights along a landing strip on a runway. Whenever she moved her head even slightly, the eye was distracted away from her dangerous maw and focused instead on the entrancing interplay of color underneath it.

Lyrana's neck and most of her body were covered by other dangerous-looking and yet delicate rays that reminded Elias of the fins of a Terran lionfish, but he suddenly realized that, although she had appeared massive at first glance, her heft was mostly an illusion. Her neck, thin and scale-covered, looked almost fragile. Her body underneath the water was quite slender as well. The bioluminescence and the interplay of the kelp-analog as it swayed made her appear enormous, but she was in fact a creature of delicate beauty, the intricate protrusions that covered her a filigree of fascinating and misleading complexity. Even her tentacles were slim, several times longer than those of an adult

Singer male but looking as if they had been made not for power, but for dexterity. Her rudder-shaped tail underneath the surface was the only part of her body that appeared to be muscular and strong, but it was partially hidden by the kelp that enshrouded her like a veil, and Elias was not able to get a complete picture of the queen. She was a living mystery, a being that lived in a medium Elias would never comprehend.

"We…," Elias tried to say, but the words were silenced by her glare.

Lyrana opened her enormous jaw and began to sing.

Elias lost control of his body. He and Tristan sank again beneath the waves, and as they did Lyrana descended with them. As soon as they were fully underwater, her song was audible in all its multitonal beauty, and Elias was enraptured. It was a voice unlike any he had ever heard, a song that was true music, unlike the primitive and simple repetitive beats Singer males used to paralyze their enemies. Lyrana's melody was everywhere, in the water and inside Elias's mind, and as she dragged them down into the depths without ever touching them, Elias knew only wonder and awe.

Underwater he was able to admire Lyrana's true beauty. Her delicate body, veiled in kelp, glowed in the darkness and appeared to sway without moving, like algae moving with the tide, like the arms of an anemone in an ocean current.

Something was burning in Elias's hand. He was devoid of volition, surrounded by salty ocean water, and yet something was burning him.

The song got louder, and Lyrana approached, her tentacles fanning out around her like those of a monstrous jellyfish. Her whiskers swayed and spread out, commanding his attention. There was only light and motion in the water, only music, only wonder. As if in a dream, he faintly remembered he needed to breathe. There was pain in his chest, but it seemed unimportant. All he wanted to do was listen to that haunting melody that threaded itself through his consciousness and built a hypnotic tapestry that coiled itself around him, smothering him. It was a refreshing and constricting embrace he did not ever want to end.

The burning in his hand increased until it became searing pain that jolted his consciousness awake in a burst of clarity.

Stop. Stop singing.

The song reached a crescendo, and his mind went blank again. It was dark everywhere now. The magnificent bioluminescence was gone. Lyrana faded from view as if swallowed by the darkness. Elias was alone, sinking still, and he felt abandoned and forlorn. Where had she gone? Where was the music and the light? Why was there so much pain in his chest? Why was there so much darkness?

His hand throbbed with heat again, and he came to, shocked.

I'm—we're drowning! Narev!

Something torpedoed through the murk and grabbed Elias around the chest, a rough and metal-tipped claw that surged up with him in tow. The contact cleared Elias's mind even more. He realized Narev was saving him.

Get Tristan!

Narev did not slow down. He brought Elias up to the surface of the water and kept him there. An instant later Vanor and Siv appeared with Tristan.

"Tristan, are you okay?" Elias asked.

Tristan coughed up some water. "I think… so."

Lyrana came up at that moment, silent now, and looked at them with another paralyzing glare. She sent out a massive mental wave, and Narev stiffened next to Elias. The Spine wurl sank into the water, helpless, along with Vanor and Siv.

With an almost languid motion, the Singer queen approached once again and raised two of her tentacles above the surface of the water, where she held them, motionless, above Elias and Tristan.

She did not speak, but Elias sensed something close to curiosity, mixed with anger and something else, an emotion that was muddled and hard to recognize.

Lyrana brought one of her tentacles down as if she were about to grab Tristan and crush the life out of him.

Stop! Elias shouted in his mind, and he held aloft the thing that had been burning his hand, even in the water, the iridescent spine he had not let go of and that had allowed him to break the spell of the song and call for help even as he had been about to drown.

The effect was immediate. Lyrana hesitated and lowered her head to look more closely at Elias's only weapon.

"That's right!" Elias shouted, treading water awkwardly while holding the spine up in the air. "This belonged to Sizzra. Your sister."

He received wordless acknowledgment, and her curiosity intensified.

"We mean you no harm. Please, let us go."

Lyrana's eyes glowed more brightly for an instant. There was a question in her look. With a start, Elias realized that he could understand, even though she did not use words.

"You don't know what we are," he said aloud. "We're... we're from another world. We came here. From the stars."

Every bioluminescent point on Lyrana's body flashed bright white at the mention of the word *stars*. She bared her teeth, radiating hostility.

"No! Stop!" Elias shouted. "We want to live in peace. We're not here to hurt you. We're just passing through."

Curiosity again. Slowly Lyrana closed her fearsome jaw.

Elias exchanged a quick glance with Tristan, who appeared to be at a complete loss for words. Then he looked back at Lyrana.

"Just let us go, okay? We don't know why the Singer males brought us here. We'll go and never come back. Okay?"

Lyrana turned to look behind her, and Elias realized that all the Singer males were standing on the atoll, watching the scene unfold. Upon seeing them, Lyrana projected acknowledgment, even fondness. The males, hesitant, waded into the water.

"We'll go," Elias repeated. He reached out with his mind and was able to locate Narev and Vanor underwater. Siv appeared to be close by. "We'll swim away. We won't go near your Flower at all—"

Lyrana screamed, a mind-rending noise that was the diametrical opposite to the beautiful song from before. It was a sound born out of desperation and pain and loathing. It paralyzed Elias completely, and even after it was gone he realized he could still hear it, or part of it, echoing in his thoughts.

Lyrana's bioluminescence shifted horribly, and dread clawed at Elias's heart as he realized that the beautiful blue-and-white pinpoints of light on her scales were now glowing blood-soaked red.

Aghast, he watched the Singer queen as her body stiffened in response to the terrible color. Her eye cluster glazed over, and her tentacles, so graceful and slender, became crooked parodies of themselves, bending inward like the legs of a dead spider.

Hunger.

The thought was like a grenade blast in Elias's mind. It was louder than anything he had ever heard, louder than the song, louder than life itself. And it did not come from Lyrana.

Horrified, Elias turned his head slowly until he was able to look behind him.

It was the Flower, its beautiful petals gone dark like the void, reaching forward as though with invisible vines that wanted to pull Elias in to choke him, to devour him and everything else in the world.

Lyrana jerked forward in the water and snatched both Elias and Tristan out from the surface with terrifying strength. She held them aloft and began to squeeze.

Stop! Elias shouted in his mind, because the air had been forced out of his lungs. His right arm was pinned against his body, and he could not use Sizzra's spine. *Stop! Please!*

The hunger pulsated again, and Lyrana echoed its ravenous demand for nourishment. She stiffened as though gathering her strength.

Lyrana! Don't do this!

She ignored him. Lyrana coiled her tentacles tighter, drew both Elias and Tristan back, and then threw them forward at the ravenous Flower.

Elias sailed through the air and barely had time to brace himself for the impact as he crashed into the water and sank. This time he was free to move, however, and he quickly resurfaced again.

"Tristan!" Elias shouted, and the two of them swam until they were next to each other. Elias reached for Tristan's hand and held it firmly.

"The water," Tristan said, teeth chattering.

It was ice-cold. Elias felt again that awful sensation, as if there was something in the water that was draining him of everything. The cold reached into his body and beyond, leeching his energy, his will, and his mind.

"We need to m-move," Tristan stuttered. "We c-can...."

But the hunger towered behind them, and they were forced to look back. They had landed less than a meter away from one of the huge vines that protruded from the surface of the water and met at the nexus of the ocean, crowned by the Flower of the Deep.

Elias let go of Tristan's hand. He was compelled to swim until he was at the vine, and he grabbed it, pulling himself out of the water while slipping occasionally on its slick surface. Tristan was close behind him. Together they climbed it and reached the place where the vines had coiled into themselves and made a large spiral-shaped platform above the water on which the Flower rested. Elias jumped onto this platform, feeling the leathery toughness of the vines underfoot as he landed. They thrummed with energy, with life.

With hunger.

The two of them now stood in front of the Flower and looked at its petals, which were a velvety black still, each projecting a yearning and reaching and grasping. Although it could not move, Elias still felt as though the Flower was pulling him in with irresistible force. He was close enough now that he could also sense the heat coming from it, a searing sort of energy that would destroy him if he dared approach it, as it had destroyed Sizzra, who had touched the Flower of the Earth. The proximity hurt. Elias was so deeply attuned to the life of New Skye that he realized he could never touch any of the Flowers again, not without being destroyed.

But this one tugged at his will. It forced him to take another step forward, closer to the veritable furnace. It needed him, it yearned to consume him and everything else in existence. It was an emptiness that would never be satisfied until it devoured the entire world, full of the same relentless pull that had kept Sizzra trapped in a mountaintop cave for decades, but here it was much stronger. The Flower Elias was commanded to look at was diseased, wrong, warped. The horrible black petals looked as if they had died.

Another step forward. Elias began to sweat, trying to avert his face from the infernal blast that was the energy coming from the Flower. It was unbearable. As soon as he touched it, he feared his entire body would go up in flames, enduring in an instant what that horrible smoldering wound had done to the flesh on Sizzra's snout over agonizing weeks and months.

He took another step. The next one would be fatal.

He lifted his leg, and the air was rent by a song.

It was not the complex melody of Lyrana. It was a simple *thrum* that paralyzed Elias just as he was about to meet his doom. He could not move.

Thrum.

The voice of a Singer male, louder. Elias heard frantic splashing nearby.

Thrum.

Now the voice was joined by three others, juveniles, and together they prevented Elias and Tristan from moving forward to their destruction.

Thrum.

The hunger radiating from the Flower intensified, but at the same time the song that kept Elias motionless shifted, commanding him to move away.

He tried, and there was an agonizing moment of teetering conflict between the two forces wrestling over control of him. Elias began to sweat and tremble, the muscles in his body contracting forcefully as though he were attempting to move an enormous boulder out of the way.

Thrum.

With a snap, the ravenous will of the Flower was overwhelmed by the song, and Elias stumbled back, falling down hard on the rough surface of the platform.

The pain of the fall helped. Blinking, Elias struggled to get up and slipped on several large, jewel-like golden scales that were strewn about on the platform itself.

He had barely managed to stand up fully and glance over at Tristan when the hunger surged again, clawing at his will, demanding to be fed.

"Run!" Elias managed to shout to Tristan, but then he lost the ability to talk and took a step forward, closer to the Flower. Then another one. Everything was happening again, and this time he was too close to it. Its will could not be denied.

From the water, two large shapes surged out with a large splash and climbed the vines up to the platform in a shocking display of agility, Singer juveniles slithering over the ground on their many tentacles. They were still singing, but their voices had no effect anymore. Eyes blazing, without even stopping their forward momentum, each rushed at Elias and Tristan and whipped out one of their tentacles.

Elias would have flinched if he had still been in control of his body, but instead he simply stood as the tentacles slammed into him and Tristan and sent them both flying backward.

Away from the Flower.

The combination of the impact and the distance from the Flower itself allowed Elias to regain control of his actions in time to see the juveniles stumble. The brave Singer males had managed to push both Tristan and Elias away, but in doing so they had gotten too close to the Flower of the Deep.

The hunger pulsated in Elias's mind.

"No!" Elias shouted, but even as he did, he knew it was too late. The Singers' bodies jerked, almost as if being pulled by the same invisible vines Elias had felt wrapping themselves around his mind, and the creatures fell into the open petals of the dark Flower.

Elias was not sure if it was him screaming or the juveniles, but all he knew for a moment was pain. Elias reached out his hand in a futile gesture to help the creatures that had saved them, but could do nothing before they touched the Flower and sealed their fate. The instant the contact happened, the Singers burned alive.

The horrid heat obliterated scales, flesh, and sinew with horrifying speed. A couple of seconds later, all that was left of the creatures was hollowed-out white skeletons that clattered to the ground.

The hunger subsided ever so slightly. It had been fed, and Elias had the fleeting impression that the sustenance had been channeled to the dark unknown, where something large grew as it took shape.

"No, no!" Elias yelled, realizing he was crying.

"They saved us," Tristan said quietly. "They... they brought us here, and—"

But a loud scream interrupted Tristan's words, and the two of them whirled about as Lyrana swam forward, straight at them, her body still luminescing with that red glow, her tentacles contorted by the will of the hunger. Her eyes were dull and unseeing. As she closed the distance between them, Elias had the absolute certainty that she would push them into the Flower to feed its insatiable urge for nourishment.

Seconds before she reached them, the surviving Singer juvenile and the adult male breached the surface of the water and stood in the way of their own queen.

They slammed into Lyrana and wrapped their tentacles around her, restricting her motion. The queen, enraged, thrashed and began to sing once more.

Yet again, Elias was ensnared by the song, only for it to be interrupted immediately by a complementary cacophony coming from the males, a dissonant chord that shattered the spell before it could dominate them.

Lyrana struggled against the two males, infuriated beyond rational thought, and brought two of her slender tentacles up above her head. She then wrapped them around the juvenile, immobilizing him, and used all of her strength to throw him into the Flower.

"Stop! Lyrana, this isn't you," Elias shouted. "Fight. Fight the hunger!"

The young Singer was also consumed. Now only one adult male stood against Lyrana.

"She's coming to kill us," Tristan said quickly. "The males, they brought us here to help them. To help *her*."

"But what do we do?" Elias answered desperately. "It's the Flower, Tristan. You felt it, right? The hunger. It's driven Lyrana insane."

"Yes," Tristan said, backing away from the edge of the platform. "I felt it. I feel it."

"Something's wrong with the Flower. Something is terribly wrong, and I can't touch it. It burns. It's unbearable! No creature from New Skye can, and now I'm like them!"

Tristan took another step back. At the same time, Lyrana struck the male who was attempting to hold her in place with her muscular tail. The impact was so powerful that Elias clearly felt how the adult Singer stiffened with pain and then immediately lost consciousness. Helpless, he began to sink.

"What are you doing?" Elias asked.

"No creature from New Skye," Tristan echoed, "but I can."

"Tristan, no!"

Lyrana rushed forward through the water, a nightmare vision of terrifying agility. In a heartbeat, she had raised herself up to the platform by grabbing it with her front tentacles.

Tristan ran until he was standing next to the Flower. Elias tried to go after him, but Lyrana snatched him out of the air with an iron grip.

"Tristan!" Elias yelled, struggling in vain against the constricting tentacle of the crazed queen.

"Let him go!" Tristan demanded. He reached forward until his fingers were mere centimeters away from the Flower. "Let him go," he repeated in a menacing tone. "Or I destroy this."

Lyrana screamed again and brought a tentacle down like a whip, aiming directly for Tristan.

Tristan rolled out of the way and snatched something up from the ground.

Lyrana tried again, slashing at the air with her tentacle, and this time Tristan blocked the blow with something that shimmered, a shield that appeared to shift between deep gold and complete invisibility.

Fuming, Lyrana began to squeeze Elias more tightly, radiating madness and threat.

Tristan lowered the scale he had been holding and approached the Flower again.

"I'll tear the Flower out if you don't let him go," Tristan said in a voice that carried. "We did it once before, and Sizzra is now dead. You're next if you don't let. Him. Go."

Lyrana whipped her head between Elias and Tristan, teeth bared, growling with frustration.

"Do it," Elias managed to say. "Do it, T-Tristan."

The grip around him constricted even more. Elias was certain one of his bones would snap at any moment.

"Let him go!" Tristan demanded.

Lyrana slammed another tentacle onto Tristan, who was forced to deflect the blow with the scale he still held.

"Do it!" Elias urged him. "Do it now!"

Tristan hesitated for a moment, but then his look hardened. "Okay."

He dropped the scale and reached forward even as Lyrana let go of Elias and threw herself at Tristan, teeth gnashing.

Tristan grabbed the Flower with both hands and tore it out of the world with a single massive pull.

Elias hit the ground but did not register the impact. He thought he heard the sound of a large creature falling into water, but all he knew was pain.

He screamed in his mind and was reminded of the way Sizzra had suffered once before, falling down from a mountain when her Flower had been ripped out of the networked consciousness of the planet. It was happening again now, and it was torturous.

Time stopped having any meaning. All Elias knew was that something terrible had happened, something that should never have been, and every single living creature in the oceans shared the sense of overwhelming loss with their own ravaged consciousness. For a moment Elias's mind brushed against Lyrana's, and both of them were lost in agonizing confusion, blind to the world, struggling to understand how it was that the spirit-lines that had anchored the delicate balance of the world were suddenly unmoored, mindless, torn to shreds.

And yet this time the pain faded much more quickly. Elias came back to himself and blinked, opening his eyes to the real world and struggling to focus. He felt as though he were coming back into his body from a distant place or had traveled a vast distance to return to himself. In the midst of the confusion, he realized Tristan was offering a hand. It took a moment, but Elias remembered how to move his own body. He reached forward and took the proffered hand.

"Eli! Are you okay?" Tristan asked, his face full of concern.

"I... I...." Elias struggled to make a sentence and realized that Tristan was carrying the Flower under one arm. Slowly, his thoughts ordered themselves. The pain faded. "You took it."

"There's something wrong. Can you stand?"

"I... I think," Elias answered, and he was surprised to feel strength returning to his muscles. He wasn't paralyzed and helpless, as Sizzra had been.

"Quick, before she recovers."

A glance at the water showed Elias that Lyrana floated on the surface, motionless, her tentacles crumpled underneath her. She appeared to still be para-lyzed from the pain of losing her Flower.

"Okay. What's wrong?" Elias asked.

Tristan held his hand and led him back to the nexus of vines where the Flower had been. His voice dripped with disgust as he spoke. "*That*."

Elias gasped. It was only now, after Tristan had ripped the Flower away from its resting place, that the truth was revealed.

Underneath the place where the Flower of the Deep had rested, there was a thing.

Elias shuddered. He was filled with revulsion as he beheld a dark, semiliquid blackness pooled around the vines that linked all life together. In its midst, faint flashes coming from minute and strange crystals blinked in and out of existence with fleeting reflections of refracted multicolored light.

"That… thing," Elias said between gritted teeth. "That thing is not right."

Tristan nodded. From his face, Elias realized he was also feeling the same instinctual aversion to seeing something that was truly *wrong*.

"We have to kill it," Tristan said. "It was feeding on the Flower. Look."

Elias flinched, backing away from the Flower and its still-deadly heat, but Tristan was unharmed by it as he held it up so Elias would be able to see underneath it.

"By the generation ship," Elias said under his breath.

The Flower's roots had been corroded, eaten away by something evil over an untold amount of time. Now that it had been ripped out, the Flower was wilting, dying, and yet it radiated no hunger whatsoever. The only sensation Elias got from the Flower was unity. Connection.

"*That* thing is the hunger," Tristan said, pointing at the dark oozing pool among the vines with a deep frown. "That's the thing that was driving Lyrana insane."

"Yes," Elias agreed, completely certain that Tristan was right. "And we have to kill it."

He took a step forward, together with Tristan, and was revolted at the way the liquid darkness appeared to congeal and then, impossibly, shrink away from the two men as they approached it. The thing quivered, attempting to ooze upward into a Flower that was no longer there. It hid beneath the vines, but it sent a projection of itself upward, like the malformed proboscis of a mutated bug. It met air as it stretched.

And sunlight.

The darkness screeched, a mental note of vileness suffused with terror, and Elias remembered the insidious fear he had felt when the hunger had first attached itself to his mind. He recalled fearing the sun, hating the source of all light and warmth with the same vehemence this thing did.

"It's the sunlight," Elias said, tightening his grip around Sizzra's spine.

"It hates it," Tristan confirmed. "I can feel it."

"I think I know what to do."

Elias stepped forward with the spine, moving as fast as his newfound agility allowed him to, and even though the darkness coiled around itself and attempted to avoid the weapon, Elias was still able to impale it in a single lightning-quick stab.

Touching the thing through the spine numbed his arm with a cold that was deeper than any chill found on a living planet. It was the cold of the void, an absolute emptiness that had frozen solid in the forgotten abyss at the edges of the universe. It shot up Elias's arm and attempted to latch on to his body, but Elias yanked the vile darkness straight up into the air with every erg of strength he was able to muster and ripped it out of its hiding spot, sending it flying overhead.

It sailed up into the bright, warm midday sun of a summer sky.

The thing shattered. It sent out a last piercing cry of dissonant corruption that appeared to want to reach across the distance to another part of the world, and then it was suddenly cut off, obliterated by the thing it hated the most.

After the light of the sun destroyed it, every trace of the darkness vanished. It left behind nothing, not even smoke, to betray where it had been.

And in the wake of its destruction, the hunger abated and disappeared.

Elias fell to his knees, his right hand still gripping the spine tightly. The horrible chill in his body was slowly replaced by tingling warmth, and Sizzra's spine appeared more beautiful than ever before in the light, iridescing in beautiful patterns.

"Elias!" Tristan cried out, dumping the Flower on the ground and kneeling down next to him.

"I'm okay. It's gone."

"What was that thing?"

Elias trembled, and he fancied that a little bit of that ravaging, piercing cold still lingered on his fingertips. He recalled how Lyrana had reacted earlier, when he had said the word *stars*.

"I don't know," he answered, "but it's dead. Whatever it was, if it ever was alive even, it's gone."

"It was destroying the Flower," Tristan said, picking up the bud with care. Elias backed away again from its blistering energy. "It wanted to consume... everything."

"But we stopped it," Elias replied. Then he smiled and realized that a horrible weight had been lifted off his shoulders, a weight he had felt ever since he had taken to the ocean, where the hunger had always pulsed in the back of his mind, even if he had not understood what it was at first. Now, in its place, there was only peace.

"What now?" Tristan asked him.

"Now we set things right."

They walked to the place where the Flower had rested, although Elias kept his distance. In the water, Lyrana stirred.

"Do I put it where it was?" Tristan asked Elias.

"Yes. Return it to the world."

The vines at the center of the platform appeared to want to reach up and meet the Flower at the same time Tristan brought it back, placing it gently on the place it belonged.

The instant the Flower made contact with the vines, it linked itself to them, and its petals discarded the horrible empty black for the last time. Instead, they now became perfect mirrors of Lyrana's scales, a beautiful display of deep gold that shifted hypnotically into invisibility and back into metallic yellow, making it seem as though the Flower was sometimes there and sometimes not at all.

"Thank you, Tristan," Elias breathed, sinking to his knees with an overwhelming sensation of relief. The radiant life force in the Flower was no longer full of mindless hunger, but instead projected balance. "You've saved the ocean."

A slender serpentine neck raised above them and approached, dripping water that pattered around both Elias and Tristan. Lyrana lowered her head until it was level with them and watched them both in silence for an eternal second.

She was still deadly, still incomprehensible, and yet her beauty had returned. Her scales appeared to shine, brilliant under the sun. The mesmerizing biolumines-cence of her body was once again a delicate shade of blue interspersed with purest white, and her entire body mimicked the shifting patterns of the Flower, phasing in and out of sight in a mysterious yet entrancing way.

Elias stood up, facing her, Sizzra's spine still in his hand. Tristan walked up to where he was, and the two of them waited, motionless. Elias realized that the sky overhead appeared more vibrant, and the ocean that surrounded them beckoned with mystery instead of si-lent threat. The air itself appeared to be buzzing with energy and something very akin to joy.

Lyrana reached out a delicate tentacle, but this time Elias sensed no intent to kill. The appendage stopped centimeters away from them, bioluminescing gently, and the invitation was clear.

Elias reached out his hand. He was keenly aware of the fact that Lyrana could end his life in a moment with a single bite of her terrifying maw, but he felt no fear.

"You too, Tristan," he said. "I think she wants to talk to you too."

"Okay," Tristan said, his voice wavering slightly. "We just… touch her?"

"Yes. We do."

Elias lowered his hand and, with no hesitation, touched Lyrana.

The world around him vanished. He was in a men-tal space that was similar to Sizzra's and yet different in too many ways to count. Where Elias had been able to sense Sizzra's thoughts as though they were his own, this time he was aware of the fact that he was still himself: tiny, transient, small.

But there was a presence with him, towering over everything in his mind space.

Lyrana, Elias said without speaking. *Hello.*

He caught a vague sort of acknowledgment, but the presence surrounding him was too big, too vast to limit itself to words. Instead of speaking, she showed him.

chapter 26.
archaeus

OSCAR BARELY slept the night following the revelation that a shuttle from the *Ionas* remained on the planet of New Skye. He woke up frequently, his bedsheets tangled around his legs, and tried to calm down by breathing like his counselor had taught him, but found it nearly impossible to do. He kept repeating his mantra to stay calm, but to no avail.

It wasn't merely fear. It was also nervousness and the tiniest thread of anticipation. For the first time since his arrival, there was something concrete he could do, something *they* could do to take control of their own fate. He had gotten used to the constant threat of Dresde maybe showing up one day to torment him or do something worse, but now he had hope that wasn't tied to Elias coming to save him.

Of course the mere thought of facing Dresde if she somehow found out about the plan made his stomach churn, and he had absolutely no idea what they would do if she discovered them. He was worried, expectant, tense. He was relieved when his alarm went off and, bleary-eyed but determined, left his room and met Samantha downstairs in the kitchen.

They packed like they usually would for a foraging trip, but this time they did so in silence. Everyone was awake, and the way they hugged Samantha and waved goodbye as they left gave Oscar the distinct impression that each and every member of her family, with the possible exception of her oblivious father, was ready to sacrifice everything and abandon their home at a moment's notice if it meant they could have a shot at freedom. He felt a strange finality as they waited for Doran to arrive, and Oscar's gaze lingered for a while on the house he had come to call home as he soared above it on Doran's back.

Samantha spoke very little, and Oscar had no idea whether he was even allowed to talk about the plan while Doran was in earshot, so he stayed quiet while they flew over the now-familiar landscape leading to the Nightmare Caves. As they went over the Field of Thorns, Oscar's lip curled up in disgust. Those horrible black brambles with their prismatic sharp spikes looked too much like the growth that had infected Dresde's Flower for it to be a coincidence.

Doran landed gently a few minutes later in the same clearing he always used when bringing them to the Nightmare Caves. Oscar hopped down and walked a few steps away from the large wurl before noticing that Samantha wasn't coming with him.

"What's wrong?" he asked her. She was still straddling Doran's back.

"I… I need a moment," she all but whispered. She placed a hand on the side of Doran's neck in a loving gesture. "Just in case this is goodbye."

Oscar gave her some space. He made his way to the nearest cave and sat down at the entrance, watching Samantha and Doran from a distance. It looked as though Samantha was talking, although she was too far away to make out her words. Eventually she dismounted and walked until she was standing next to Doran's head. She leaned forward and touched her forehead to his for a long moment. Then she turned around, wiping her cheeks with the back of her hands, and joined Oscar with a resolute expression on her face.

"Are you okay?" Oscar asked.

"Yes," she answered, although she sounded a little hoarse. "I needed to tell him thanks."

"Don't you think he would help us?" Oscar wondered as the two of them entered the cave, where the familiar coolness of the rocky environment enveloped them. After a few steps they were in near-total darkness. "I mean, if you told him the plan."

Samantha was silent for a bit. The two of them held hands as usual and followed the invisible path deeper into the cave complex, which by then was no longer an insurmountable challenge for Oscar. The faint bioluminescence from the beetles on the floor or on rocks around them were enough of a marker to guide them as they walked.

"I think he would try to help," Samantha replied eventually. "However, I do not believe Doran could ever disobey her directly. If she told him to kill us, he would do so without hesitation. Perhaps."

"Oh. That's awful."

"This is why we should keep up appearances as much as we can. If we are unsuccessful today, we will keep coming back until we are able to reactivate the shuttle. Doran will be none the wiser, and neither will she."

"Do you think the shuttle will work after a hundred years?"

"Perhaps. It depends on its power source. If it has an engine that relies on a fission reactor, it should still be operational. The worst possibility is if it relies on fuel of some kind, as most of it will likely have evaporated or congealed. If it relies on a hybrid system, we might be able to repair it."

The wind started blowing at that moment, and Oscar had to wait for the creepy howling to subside before asking his next question.

"Where is the shuttle, exactly?"

"Deep in the caves here. I found it by accident. I got lost during one of the first expeditions I made here on my own. I walked farther into the network of caves than I ever had, and I came out into a very small sinkhole, similar to the one where we gather sweetpods and grapes. It was narrow but very deep. It was also almost completely overgrown with plants and young trees, so much so in fact that at first I did not notice the shuttle at all."

"Wait, is the shuttle visible from the sky?"

"No. I have flown over the area on Doran a couple of times, and not only is the sinkhole small and unremarkable, but the greenery hides everything."

"And you tried to open the shuttle?"

"Many times," Samantha admitted. "I had to be careful whenever I tried, since I did not want to draw attention to what I was doing in case there were prying eyes in the sky. Remember that in the past, this area was full of male wurl, who would fly around looking for prey. It took me a long time to fully explore the shuttle from the outside in an inconspicuous manner. The craft is fully sealed, and I believe nothing short of breaking it open with a power tool would work—unless we had an interface."

"I understand. How long till we get there?"

"About two hours, I estimate."

"Whoa!" Oscar exclaimed, loud enough for the echo of his question to bounce back to his ears in the dark confines they were traversing. "Sorry. That's quite a bit."

"Yes. Now be silent so I can remember the way."

Oscar did his best to hush and followed Samantha through the dark labyrinth. They passed through caves both familiar and new, and occasionally came out into the sunlight in the form of a sinkhole. Some open-air spaces were overgrown with vegetation, while others were treacherous and partially flooded, with snakelike animals with triangular fins swimming in the murk. The deeper into the cave system they went, the more isolated Oscar felt. He saw strange fauna observing him intently from tree perches in the sinkholes, and he heard odd noises in the dark sections of the caves. The howling and moaning effect from the wind blowing through the rocks became more eerie, and the temperature descended as they came closer to what Oscar supposed was the heart of the cave network.

Nearly two hours later they stumbled into yet another sinkhole, narrower than most but still spacious enough to hold a small house within it. The sky overhead was invisible due to the thick plant cover that appeared to choke every square meter of space, from ground level to the unseen rim of the eroded depression in the walls of the caves. The air was moist and cool, and it was dim out in the open despite the fact that noon was approaching.

"This way," Samantha said, walking purposefully to the center of the space.

Oscar followed in her footsteps, batting away wide leaves with oddly moist surfaces and velvety undersides and trying not to get tangled in a kind of milk-white creeper that snaked up from the ground and hung in loose coils from some of the trees that grew higher up, their trunks perpendicular to the walls of the cave. Oscar's and Samantha's movements disturbed a cluster of small insects with shiny wings of beautiful silver, similar to butterflies, that exploded out of a bell-shaped flower nearby.

In the aftermath of the rush of movement, Samantha stopped in front of what looked to be a big mound overgrown with moss and fungi.

"This is it," she announced. "The shuttle."

Oscar approached carefully. Greenery rose to well above his own height dead ahead, with plants of all kinds growing over one another and covering a sizable portion of the space inside the sinkhole. A few thick fallen tree trunks had been all but engulfed by the raucous flora all around, and had he not been expecting to find a large vehicle of some kind, Oscar would have simply supposed the raised structure in front of him was natural in origin.

"Where's the door? Or hatch? I'm not even sure what you call it," Oscar said.

"To the side," Samantha indicated. She walked in a counterclockwise direction for a few steps, her hand making loose contact with the edge of the towering mound. She ducked under a particularly thick vine and stopped, facing the fronds of a plant with beautiful orange-and-yellow leaves. "I have not been here in months, but it should be around here. Help me uncover it."

She leaned forward and grabbed a fistful of the plants, yanking hard. The greenery did not give way, so Samantha reached into her backpack and pulled out a knife. With its help, she began hacking at the undergrowth.

Oscar assisted her with the knife from his back-pack, but even with two people working on it, getting rid of enough of the plant cover to see what was underneath took them nearly thirty minutes. Oscar was all but drenched in sweat by the time Samantha's knife struck something solid that gave off a metallic clang.

"Found it," she said triumphantly.

"Finally," Oscar complained. "Mosquitoes have been stinging me nonstop."

"Pull here," she indicated, pointing at a leaf-covered lattice of what looked like the roots of a tree immediately in front of them. "I will pull from the side. Ready?"

Oscar stood on tiptoe and grabbed two handfuls of the roots, trying not to get any dirt into his mouth. "Ready."

"Pull on three. One. Two. Three!"

Oscar yanked the roots down and met resistance. He put his entire body weight into it, and a gradual rip vibrated under his palms until there came a sudden *snap*. He stumbled backward with Samantha, but they dragged along with them a section of the mixture of roots, moss, leaves, and other components of the carpet of growing things that had been hiding the side of the shuttle from view.

Oscar let go of the roots and wiped his hands on his pants. They had uncovered only a small fraction of the entire structure, but it was enough.

"This is the hatch," Samantha said.

Oscar took a careful step forward and then another, until he was close enough to rest his hand on the metal surface they had revealed.

"I can't believe it," he whispered.

He had been expecting it, but seeing proof in front of him and being able to touch it was something else entirely. He was looking at the reinforced metal exterior of the shuttle that had belonged to the generation ship itself. The metal was neither rusty nor corroded, and it was solid under his palm. The hatch was taller than him by several centimeters and looked imposing, even though he was seeing only a small fragment of it.

On the side, in faded yellow, there were letters.

EUS

"What's that?" Oscar asked.

"The name of the shuttle."

He reached to his left and pulled additional roots and plants out of the way until he was able to dislodge another section of the living blanket that had decked the craft. As soon as he ripped it off, he was able to see the full name etched on the metal in capital letters.

ARCHAEUS

"Wow," Oscar said. "This is so cool! Weird name, though."

"Were you not familiar with it?"

He shook his head. "We didn't learn about this in history class. I didn't even know the *Ionas* had a shuttle!"

"That is odd," Samantha replied. "I wonder why it was not mentioned."

"No clue. Hey, that looks like an access panel," Oscar pointed out. Below the name *Archaeus* was a cracked plastic surface immediately to the right of a deep seam in the fuselage.

"This? I thought it was decoration of some sort."

"Looks like a panel to me. Let me tap it." He did, but nothing happened. "Okay, that didn't work."

"I have tried many things over the years. I have banged on the doors. I even tried breaking the cockpit windows on the upper level once, but nothing has worked. It remains sealed tight."

"Time for plan B, then. Let's see if I can establish a connection with my link."

Samantha approached and looked on while Oscar activated his link's short-range wireless network scanner.

"What are you doing?" Samantha asked.

"Well, if this thing still has any energy at all, there should be a wireless network of some kind here. If that's the case, I can—"

Beep.

"What was that, Oscar?"

Beep, beep.

"My link. On the display, look."

>Scanning....

>Wireless network found: ARCHAEUS-LR01

>Performing handshake....

>Access failure.

>INVALID FIRMWARE VERSION

>Manual update required.

"What does that mean?" Samantha asked.

"I'm not sure. Let me try downloading older firmware versions. Hold on."

"How are you going to do that?"

"I have a compatibility optimizer subroutine here I worked on with my dad for the satellite back home. Let me tweak it a little bit."

It took Oscar about an hour of multiple tries and numerous edits to the code on his link to finally compile an executable file that would be able to interact with the shuttle and download its software version. He then had to install it and debug it, which took the better part of another hour. All the while Samantha paced back and forth, keeping mosquitoes and other bugs away from him but otherwise remaining quiet so he could concentrate.

"I got it!" Oscar exclaimed at last.

"You can open the shuttle?"

"No, I installed the firmware. Now I restart my link," he said as he did so, "and this is the part where we cross our fingers. If everything's right, I should have the old version of the CLI installed now, running on this virtual machine in the link partition I created. That should let me talk to the shuttle. Ready?"

"Do it."

Oscar brought up the new interface.

>Starting....

> Start-up complete.

>Scanning....

> Wireless network found: ARCHAEUS-LR01

> Performing handshake....

> Access failure.

>Parsing error 31A1B0C

"Crap," Oscar swore. "Wait, I forgot to delete the local libraries. It's probably messing with the older versions of the code. Just a sec.... There."

> Performing handshake....

> Connection established.

> ARCHAEUS-LR01:

"Yes!" Oscar exclaimed. "Not to be dramatic, but I'm in."

"You can interact with the shuttle now?"

"Yes. My link should be able to translate any commands I give into the proper code for the onboard computer."

"So we can go inside?"

"I don't know, but let's try it out. Ahem. *Archaeus,* open the main hatch."

CLUNK.

"By the generation ship," Oscar whispered, taking a step back.

"Oscar, the hatch."

"Yeah. It's opening."

"At last," Samantha said.

A hiss of pressurized air was accompanied by the movement of a section of the fuselage that appeared to sink into itself. It then moved to the left with smooth efficiency, exposing a dark opening into the craft large enough for two people to enter side by side.

Samantha walked in without hesitation, brushing a stray vine out of the way as she did. Oscar paused for a moment and then followed her.

The first thing he registered was the smell. He had expected the space to be musty and foul, with an atmosphere that suggested something long abandoned, but instead the air smelled clean and crisp. There was a faint hint of plastic and another odor he could not quite place but which reminded him strongly of his counselor's office.

The door behind them slid shut and snapped into place with a definite clicking that suggested an interlocking mechanism. They were now in complete darkness. Although the air was clean and relatively fresh, there was now a pressure in his ears that was mildly uncomfortable. He wondered whether the atmosphere inside the shuttle was fully isolated from the outside in some way.

Might make sense, given that this thing once flew through space.

"Can you turn on the lights?" Samantha asked nearby. Her voice echoed slightly in the enclosed space.

Oscar edged to the side. His left boot bumped into something with a dull *clang*. The surface underneath his feet felt metallic but hollow, as if he was walking on a grate.

"You can also give commands with the name of the shuttle."

"*Archaeus*, turn on the lights," Samantha ordered.

There was a buzz and then a pause when nothing happened. His link beeped and then flashed with a text message.

> *Main start-up sequence failure.*

> *ERROR D10C: main solar battery depleted.*

> *Engage emergency backup systems?*

"I got an error," Oscar told Samantha. "Let me see. *Archaeus,* engage the emergency systems."

> *Engaging....*

> *Success.*

> *Analyzing user ID....*

> *Invalid user ID. Name: OSCAR TROST not found in database.*

> *Analyzing user link time signature....*

> *Time signature analyzed. Running warning protocol.*

> *Please stand by.*

"What was all that?" Samantha asked him in the dark.

Oscar held his link up to where he guessed she was so she would be able to read. "I have no idea. I'm assuming there's some kind of emergency system thing? Not sure what it meant by warning protocol, though."

The lights came on when he finished speaking, flickering at first and then steadying as they bathed the space in a cool white glow.

Samantha ran her hand along her braid. "This is—"

"Amazing," Oscar finished for her.

They were in a sprawling oval space that was twice as large as the living room back at the house. The floor was a solid-looking metal grate, and the far wall to the left supported a semicircular row of seats with harnesses, all of them empty. Two other concentric rows of seats followed the first, and the nearest seat was the one Oscar had bumped with his boot earlier. There appeared to be seating for forty in total, covering most of the space from the middle to the left.

On the right a sturdy-looking metal partition ran the entire length of the shuttle and blocked access to whatever lay behind it. A sign above it read Storage.

"Is this it?" Oscar asked.

"There," Samantha said, pointing at the far end of the last row of seats. "A ladder leading up to what has to be the second level."

They made their way toward it carefully. Other than the faint whirr of an unidentified mechanical system, the space was eerily quiet, and Oscar tried his best not to be creeped out. They reached the ladder in a few steps, and Samantha ascended first. Oscar followed, unwilling to be left behind in the cavernous space below. All those empty seats were disturbing. He felt as if the space were filled with ghosts.

"Oscar, look at this," Samantha said from above.

He hurried and climbed out onto the second level of the shuttle.

"A window!" was the first thing he said.

"This is the cockpit, surely. Look at the instruments."

Oscar scanned the room. It was much smaller than the space below, barely big enough for three or four people standing. Two large seats rested immediately in front of the largest and most complicated control panel Oscar had ever seen. The seats featured straps and buckles, along with helmets and what looked like oxygen masks for what had to have been the pilots. Ahead of the seats and above the controls, an enormous curved window dominated the view. The inside lights shone through it and illuminated a complex tapestry of dirt, roots, and small wriggling arthropods on the outside that had evidently been disturbed by the sudden brightness in their dark domain.

"Oh, gross," Oscar said, pointing at a particularly large pale worm with what looked like dozens of breathing tubes or legs protruding out of its body and retreating back in as it writhed on the smooth surface of the window. "So many bugs."

"None inside, however," Samantha observed. "The shuttle was hermetically sealed."

"Everything's so well-preserved. I bet the view from this window is amazing without all the dirt. Can you imagine? Someone flew through space and down to New Skye in this."

"Not just one person. Many. My ancestors." She made her way through the room and sat in the left-hand seat with care, placing her hands gently on the armrests. "How do we activate the systems?"

Welcome, a disembodied mechanical voice called from unseen speakers all around the cockpit.

"What in the—jeez!" Oscar exclaimed, startled.

Please identify yourselves, the voice indicated.

"I am Samantha."

Acknowledged. Second user, please identify yourself.

"Um, I'm Oscar Trost."

Thank you. Access granted: Samantha and Oscar Trost.

"Good," Samantha said. "*Archaeus*, can you fly?"

Flight capabilities are contingent on the warning protocol.

"What is the warning protocol?" she asked the shuttle.

Stand by. Accessing video log.

Oscar used the brief lull to take a seat to Saman-tha's right. A metal buckle poked him in the back, and he was fiddling with the seatbelts when one of the mon-itors set in the control panel flickered to life. The still image on the screen showed a woman in her twenties, sitting in what had to be the very same cockpit where they now were. She wore a tight-fitting pilot suit that reminded Oscar of the first time he had seen Samantha. The woman had freckles adorning a youthful-looking face, and brown shoulder-length hair framed delicate features. Both her grin and the wild green eyes that stared into the camera from beneath slender eyebrows hinted at energy about her.

The shuttle voice spoke and a video started.

PLAYING VIDEO log one.

"This is the video log of Lieutenant Alicia Jones, pilot of—"

Jones appeared to have been interrupted by some-thing that sounded like wild cheering in the distance.

"Sounds like a party down there," a male voice said, although the speaker remained hidden.

"Can't blame them, Commander," Jones answered. "We did it! Freedom above all!"

Her words had an immediate effect. The sound of many voices, muffled with distance, reached them a split second later, chanting, "Freedom above all!"

"Hell yeah!" Jones exclaimed, pumping her fist. "We're free, people!"

"Lieutenant," the unseen commander observed, "you were about to begin the video log. I will mind the navigation systems while you record. Bear in mind: this is a historic day. It is important to document the events for posterity."

"Right. Yes, sir." Jones centered herself more fully in the frame and appeared to want to put on a serious face, but her smile resisted the attempt. "This is the video log of Lieutenant Alicia Jones, pilot of the shuttle *Archaeus*. It is April the third, 3142. Today, under the leadership of Commander Hugo Wright, and following the vision of Illuminate Zendaya, we have finally gained our freedom. We have left behind the oppression we endured on board the generation ship *Ionas* and have set out to carve our own path in this bountiful new world.

"Our secession was achieved without bloodshed. Captain MacLeod and the other senior crewmembers knew nothing of the plan until the day of its execution. While the senior crew was occupied performing planetary surveys after reaching a stable orbit around our new home world, a total of forty-seven people worked together under their noses and prepped, stocked, and boarded the ship's only shuttle at 0300 hours today. By the time MacLeod found out, our engines were already running, and he was forced to either open the cargo bay and let us go or risk having the shuttle crash through it anyway, permanently damaging the *Ionas* so it wouldn't be able to make planetfall. He gave in, needless to say. It was *awesome!*"

"Lieutenant," Wright interrupted.

"Sorry, Commander. It's just—wow! Your plan went by without a hitch. We're free! We can settle wherever we want, make our own future and *vote* on it, not simply obey whatever the captain says. Who gave him all that authority? Did you know he wants to name the planet New Skye and the first settlement Portree? I don't care if his ancestors were Scottish, he didn't even put the name up for a referendum! He decided to name everything on his own, and don't even get me *started* on the site he chose. Why build a new home in a land-locked mountainous region when you have literally an entire planet to choose from? I mean, the coast is by far the best option, like *we* decided. It gives us potential for growth, communication, access to ocean resources, so many things!"

"Jones, you're rambling."

"I am? Sorry."

Wright chuckled. "It's okay. I am excited too, but maybe we should leave the video log for another time."

"Right. Of course, Commander. Should I have a look at navigation?"

"Please do. We need to bring this home, quite literally."

"Not a problem. That's why I'm here," Jones answered, and suddenly she was all business as she clicked numerous buttons and appeared to type, judging from the sound. "Approach vector is stable. Three hours until we begin our descent. All systems nominal, heat shield prepared. The *Ionas* has not pursued or changed its own trajectory, although they have deployed a satellite, presumably to track us."

"Let them," Wright replied. "Our settlements will be on opposite sides of the world. MacLeod should have realized by now that the planet is big enough for all of us, wherever we decide to live."

"Yeah!" Jones exclaimed. "I wonder how it's going to be down there. I mean, it's one thing to have data from the probes, but Commander, we're heading to a new world!"

"A new beginning," Wright declared. "A better beginning."

There was a brief pause, during which Jones appeared pensive.

"Commander?"

"Yes, Lieutenant?"

"She was right. Illuminate Zendaya was right."

"Indeed, her prophecy has come true."

Jones leaned closer to the still unseen Wright and spared a brief glance backward, where the faint sounds of excited voices were still discernible. "I did not believe at first," she said in a tone that sounded like a confession. "I had no real faith."

"Understandable."

"I mean," Jones pressed on, "a woman who can see the future? I thought it was, well, I don't want to say stupid, but I thought it was stupid. Then Leanne roped me into one of the gatherings and I saw you were there!"

"I remember. I was very surprised to see you enter."

"I bet! Seeing you there, Commander, well, it made the entire thing believable, even with all the chanting and hocus pocus and the rituals. And then she came out. She had something about her. It's like...."

"An aura," Wright finished for her.

Jones nodded enthusiastically. "Yes. An aura. And when she started talking about our new home, about leaving the pseudomilitary bureaucracy of the generation ship behind, I found myself listening."

"The Illuminate is wise," Wright replied. "She shows us the way."

"She shows us the way," Jones echoed with ritual intonation. "And it came true! She said we would break free. She said we would live far away from judgmental glances and the ridicule of others, and here we are! You know my family held an intervention for me?"

"Really?"

"Yeah. A week ago. Everyone was there, all the way up to my insufferable aunt Ileana, who left her lofty post in Engineering for an entire hour to lecture me on how I was part of a cult. Ugh."

"They don't understand. Remember, the Illuminate teaches us forgiveness for those who do not see the way."

"I know, I know."

There was another pause, during which Jones appeared to be checking instruments and typing on the console.

"Commander, do you think the rest of the prophecy will come true?"

"I do," Wright answered immediately.

Jones smiled. "It's going to be so cool. Our own home in *paradise*. Practically the same gravity as Earth, nearly identical atmospheric composition, tons of water, and it's right there! What do you think she'll call the planet?"

END OF video log one, the disembodied ship voice announced.

"What was that about?" Oscar asked.

"The hero, Alicia Jones," Samantha whispered, half reaching for the monitor. "I cannot believe it."

"You recognize her?"

"Yes, in a way. My ancestors spoke of how she saved them, all of them, once. *Archaeus*, are there any more video logs?"

Yes. They are part of the warning protocol.

"Play the next one."

Acknowledged.

The monitor flickered to life again. This time half of the image showed a wider view of the cockpit from above, as if it was the feed from a security camera. The second half of the image was divided in two. One of the parts showed what was evidently the room below, with all of the chairs, and every single one was occupied. The last quarter of the image showed blue-and-white sky.

PLAYING VIDEO log two.

When the video started playing, the images shook. The harsh blaring of an alarm filled the craft.

"That was a direct hit!" Jones shouted over the alarm. "Approach vector compromised. Compensating!"

"What was that?" Wright demanded.

"I don't know! As soon as we entered the lower atmosphere we were hit by—"

BANG.

The entire shuttle shuddered. There were screams from the passengers strapped to their chairs. The impact slammed Jones back into her seat, and a second alarm was activated, adding its whine to the din.

Wright punched some controls until the alarms stopped.

"Lieutenant, report!" he demanded.

"I don't know, Commander!" Jones replied while she frantically typed and checked multiple consoles. "Something is hitting us from outside!"

"How are the engines?"

"Still operational, but we are burning fuel to stabilize! We won't be able to get to the projected landing site."

"Can we make it to solid land?"

"I'm trying."

"Jones, we can't land in the ocean. This shuttle doesn't float. Everyone will drown."

"I know, I know! If only I knew what the hell keeps—"

BANG.

More screams. The third image on the monitor still showed the blue of the sky, but there was a brief blur of something else. A flash of cobalt in the wake of the impact.

"Again!" Wright shouted. "Something's attacking us!"

"Not possible," Jones shouted back, her hands flying over the nearest console. "The *Ionas* doesn't have any weapons!"

"Not the generation ship. Something from the planet."

BANG.

Jones grunted in the aftermath of the hit. People still screamed in their seats on the lower level. "I don't care *what* it is. I'm going to land this thing."

"Illuminate, what are you doing?" Wright asked suddenly, speaking into what looked like a communications mic.

There was no verbal response, but the image showed a single person standing up belowdecks, unstrapping herself from her seat. She turned to face the people and lifted her arms. The screaming ceased immediately.

"Illuminate, please sit down," Wright urged. "We might be hit again!"

"We will not," Illuminate Zendaya replied in a calm, deep voice. "We will be safe, and we will land. Lieutenant Jones, I foresee your success."

There was silence for a beat. Then Jones spoke up.

"I have visual!" she announced. "There's the coastline... and land! Adjusting vector. Deploying fins."

"Our new home," Zendaya said with evident confidence. "I see fire."

"Well, it's a volcano, so there's your fire," Jones muttered, sweat beading on her forehead. Her concentration was palpable. "I'm going to try not to kill us all. Everyone, hold *on*!"

PLAYING VIDEO log three.

This time there was only a single image coming from a camera that was evidently in motion. To Oscar it looked as though the footage had been captured with a bodycam.

"So much for our glorious planetfall," Jones grumbled. Her voice sounded very close by, and she was presumably the person wearing the camera.

"But we are alive," Wright answered, and he was fully visible for the first time when Jones stopped moving and faced him. He appeared to be a man in his fifties, with buzzed salt-and-pepper hair, a trim mustache, and a forceful chin. "You saved us all, Alicia."

"What attacked us?" she asked, walking again. The camera panned to the right and showed the side of the shuttle. There were deep scores on the fuselage. Whatever had struck the ship had partially melted the plated metal. "I can't think of anything that can do this kind of damage."

"We will face whatever it was together, and we will persevere," Zendaya interjected. Jones turned to face her and revealed that she was a middle-aged woman with waist-long black hair and heavy-lidded eyes. She was wearing a lot of makeup. "This is the beginning of the future I have foreseen."

"Yes, Illuminate," Jones replied, although her tone was dubious.

"We are all unhurt, thanks to you, my child," Zendaya continued with a motherly smile. "Today we celebrate your heroism, and I confer upon you the honor to name our new home. Tomorrow we start building and begin walking the wondrous path I have foreseen."

"Me? Name the… the *planet*? Illuminate, I am not worthy."

"You are."

PLAYING VIDEO log four.

"I'm recording now, Commander," said Jones. She was presumably wearing her bodycam again, and the image showed a landscape that was familiar to Oscar. It looked like she was near the Nightmare Caves.

"Good," Wright replied. "We should keep a record of this. Step forward to the edge so the camera can capture the crater better."

"Will do."

Jones moved, and the camera now showed a vast blackened depression in the ground, covered with black brambles with glassy thorns Oscar knew only too well.

"What *are* those things?" Jones wondered.

"They are not radioactive, if the shuttle's sensors are to be trusted. I don't like them, though. The energy readings they give out are very strange."

"Me neither. Good thing we're building close to the cliffs and away from these nightmarish caves. I *hate* the howling. I don't care if it's the wind; it sounds like a ghost with a hangover."

"Yes. Construction is going faster than expected. I hope we will have at least six complete houses finished using the supplies we brought from the generation ship. If all goes well, we should be in very good shape to face the coming winte—"

"Commander, look!"

The camera wavered wildly. Oscar caught a glimpse of the sky and deep-blue wings.

"Is that a bird?" Wright asked quickly.

"Not possible. Or maybe. It's very high up. It looks more like a… like a dragon."

"Nonsense. Try to track it."

"No dice," Jones informed him. "It's already out of range and flying away *real* fast. Commander, do you think that was the thing that attacked us? Some kind of predator?"

"Maybe, but if so why doesn't it attack now? We are vulnerable here."

"Maybe it's doing recon."

"Surely not. Besides, the Illuminate would have foreseen it."

Jones let out a derisive sigh.

"Lieutenant?"

"Sorry, Commander. I know she's supposed to be wise and everything, but I've begun to kind of think she's winging it. A lot of her prophecies didn't come true, and now she's changing them as we go. Like how she said we would find paradise and instead we're stuck near a volcano and all we can eat is plants. You know, Schäfer grilled a fish from the river a week ago and ate it? She *still* has diarrhea. What's wrong with this planet?"

"We need unity, Jones, now more than ever. If the Illuminate can provide leadership, we stand a much better chance at survival with her than without her… *despite* our personal misgivings. Is that understood?"

Another sigh. "Understood, sir."

"Very good."

"But," Jones insisted, "why did the Illuminate make me hide the shuttle in the Nightmare Caves? Shouldn't we keep it nearby, just in case? It's banged up, but it can still fly."

"It might be a temptation," Wright explained. "Some might try to use it to join the other settlers across the ocean."

"So we're pretending we never had a shuttle? What if there's an emergency?"

"There won't be."

Jones grunted, sounding unconvinced.

"Lieutenant, remember: unity. If it makes the Illuminate happy to sever our last connection with the other colonists and our past, it is a small price to pay for the chance to build a future together here."

"If you say so, Commander."

"Let's return to the colony. There is much to do."

PLAYING VIDEO log five.

"Commander Wright is gone," Jones began abruptly. She was sitting facing a camera in what appeared to be a plain well-lit room, and she looked exhausted and sunburned. She ran a hand over her face. "Nobody knows where he is, and I've spent two days looking for him."

Jones looked surreptitiously around her before continuing. "Zendaya is pretending this is another one of her idiotic prophecies, but I'm sick of it. She doesn't know what's going on any more than we do. We've been on this planet for five whole months, and we're barely scraping by. Sure, we have houses and a solar array and even a shiny underground bunker for emergencies, but almost no food! She told us this'd be paradise. We didn't bring any big tech from the *Ionas* because this was supposed to be a world of plenty, but we're reduced to foraging for plants and fruits, discovering which of those are edible through trial and error. If it weren't for those banana things I found at the Nightmare Caves, I'm sure fights would have already broken out over food."

She sighed and took a sip from a water bottle.

"Then there's the virus. Nearly everyone got sick. I only had fever and headache for two days, but most others are still suffering from it. The thing isn't deadly, but they say it's like having a cold every single day, and it doesn't go away. Productivity is going down, and winter is approaching. If we don't build stores of food, I have no idea how we're going to make it. Zendaya doesn't know this, but I have tried sending messages to the *Ionas* via the shuttle, asking for help, but I'm not getting an answer. I *know* they're listening. Why won't they come get us? Is MacLeod really that petty?"

There was a knock at the door. "Alicia honey?" a female voice called.

"Yeah, Leanne! Coming!"

PLAYING VIDEO log six.

"I saw the predator again today," Jones said into the camera. Both her clothes and the background were the same, but her hair was tied up in a ponytail this time. "It's been two weeks now, and no amount of prophecy can hide the fact that Wright is dead. Zendaya keeps saying maybe he wandered off on his own, but that's the stupidest thing she has said yet. Wright orchestrated this entire thing. He would never abandon us! I'm sure the predator took him. I've been watching the sky, and I've seen it a couple times. It flies really high up, but

I used the shuttle's sensors to track it. The thing looks like a dragon, with blue scales and three creepy eyes on its forehead. Why does everything on this planet have three of everything?

"I'm sure the predator killed Wright. I've suggested that we all sleep in the shuttle just to be safe in case it comes back, but Zendaya said no. She denies the fact that the predator exists, although I literally have telemetry that proves it's out there. There's also video, although it's blurry. Why don't people listen to me? Only Leanne seems to care."

PLAY VIDEO log seven.

Jones appeared again, this time slumping into her pilot's chair inside the cockpit of the shuttle. She looked bedraggled, and a scratch above her left eyebrow was bleeding. She was also panting, and when she brought up a hand to brush her hair away from her face, it was shaking. Her other hand appeared to be frantically pressing buttons.

"Come on, come on! Now!" she shouted, losing all trace of composure. "All systems nominal. Start *up!*"

The shuttle hummed.

"Yes!" she exclaimed, patting the control panel in front of her. "Hurry up, girl. We can still save them. Warm up the engines and go!"

Ninety seconds to takeoff, the shuttle's voice said.

Jones looked around and swallowed. Then she looked straight at the camera. "This is… this is…." She panted and appeared to be unable to finish her sentence. She took a few moments to steady her breath, closing her eyes. When she opened them again, they were bright with unshed tears. "This is Lieutenant Alicia Jones of the generation ship *Ionas.* I'm making this recording to warn others if they ever come across this transmission. Portree settlers, if you're listening, stay away. The promise of paradise on this planet was a *lie*.

"Zendaya is dead. Leanne… Leanne is dead. Others too, not sure how many. I escaped from the colony with Schäfer and Hino, but they died keeping the aliens away from me. I thought there was just one predator, but there are *scores* of them. Blue. Glowing red eyes. Enormous wings. They came flying in the night, and they attacked us, rounding us up like cattle. I made it out in the confusion after the fuel tank in Zendaya's house exploded. I intend to fly back on the *Archaeus* and pick up as many people as I can, and from there we're headed to Portree. It's the only safe place now."

Sixty seconds to takeoff.

"Maybe I can take some of the predators out with the shuttle, even though it has no weapons. They aren't that big, and I should be able to ram them or outfly them."

She spent the next few seconds typing, muttering to herself about data backups and protocols, and she connected her link to what looked like the shuttle's main computer.

"All set. In case I don't make it, I've uploaded all relevant information to the shuttle into a warning protocol. I'm now ready for takeoff. I hope the babies are safe. I'm going to…."

Her eyes lost their focus suddenly, and her entire body appeared to relax.

Ten seconds to takeoff.

Jones did not react.

Please confirm takeoff.

Jones sat in her chair, looking at nothing.

Takeoff sequence aborted. Please restart manually.

Moving strangely, almost like an automaton, Jones undid the buckles in her seat belt and stood up. She walked away from the camera, toward the ladder that would take her down to the lower level of the shuttle.

The camera caught a last glimpse of her as she descended. She stiffened suddenly, as if someone had struck her, and then she spoke a response to a command none but her could hear.

"Yes, Dresde."

She disappeared from view and the recording ended.

chapter 27.
balance

THE ECHOES of Lyrana's name resounded deep in Elias's mind, and with them came memories.

She was already ancient when the world was young.

Lyrana lived in the fathomless depths, a queen of unrivaled power and unmatched wisdom. Her domain spanned the entire planet through enormous oceans that dwarfed even the continents in their immensity. She was the ruler of the still and silent waters that slumbered underneath the ice at the poles of the world, vast expanses perpetually covered by glaciers that had not melted since time beyond memory. In these places there lived creatures both minuscule and enormous, and the cold currents thrummed with the promise of life.

She ruled over the warm, sun-drenched waters of the tropics, full of color and competition and the flamboyant beauty of untamed wildness. Tropical fish of every visible hue acknowledged her presence and darted out of the way whenever she approached. She watched over them, but she could also end their lives with the first note of a single song.

She was at home in the scalding waters surrounding undersea fissures that reached down into the crust of the planet, places from which glowing magma erupted onto the surface and made water bubble as it slowly added new mineral-rich nutrients to the bottom of the ocean floor. In these places there was very little life, but still Lyrana enjoyed them. She knew the names of the tiny creatures that existed without any form of nourishment other than the inorganic molecules that welled up from the planet itself. She knew the names of the colonies of sightless, colorless crustaceans that clustered around the vents and formed enormous communities in absolute safety, protected from everyone but her by the blistering temperatures of their underwater environment.

And she also knew of hidden places, vast chasms where the sun's light would never reach, areas that were bigger than continents where the crushing pressure and perpetual darkness created forms of life both magnificent and strange.

It was there that she felt most at home, because her beauty was most stunning in total darkness.

If she chose to, she could dazzle all around her with her bioluminescent glory, bringing the majesty of the night sky to the deepest recesses of the abyss. Where she swam, wonder and beauty followed. The underwater inhabitants of the deep respected and feared her, but they also loved her. She had existed for so long that she had known every creature in the ocean from the moment it was born. Her mind, linked to the Flower of the Deep, allowed her to sense every speck of life in her domain, even those that might appear to be hidden to others.

Lyrana knew of the Behemoths that lived in the oceans of the world, creatures that were old and yet still younger than her. Some of them were predators, with armored backs covered in razor-sharp blades and long fanged snouts that snatched unsuspecting prey in the darkness of the deep. Others were peaceful herbivores, and they spent centuries floating idly on the surface, feeding on sunlight, becoming larger than islands over countless seasons. Every now and then she would sing for these creatures, and they would in turn stop and admire her, expressing their awe, their wonder, their devotion.

And yet, out of all the creatures in the oceans, it was her brood-siblings she loved the most.

They were also old, hundreds while she was one, and they populated the waters of her domain in a fiercely territorial fashion that she found both endearing and amusing. The strongest among them had claimed the deepest trenches in the ocean floor and had grown powerful over untold eons, fighting for supremacy in the hopes of one day gaining the right to mate with her. Others remained as juveniles, limber and agile, exploring the limits of the sea with never-ending curiosity. Some even ventured out of the water every now and then in order to spend time with their brothers of the land and their brothers of the sky.

For time beyond memory she had ruled in peace. Together with her sisters, Lyrana had watched over the world, eldest among them.

But one day something happened.

It had been sudden, unexpected, incomprehensible. A foreign thing had arrived in her domain in a fireball from the sky. It was something she did not know, and that in itself was not possible. Lyrana knew everything. Nevertheless, that... *intrusion*, it appeared one day where before there had been nothing. As it came into the world, Lyrana realized that the thing had fractured, becoming not one, but three.

It was a dangerous force. That, at least, Lyrana knew.

On that day, she had swum halfway across the world in a burst of strength that no other creature could have matched. Instinct told her that she needed to get to her Flower. She needed to protect it from that nameless thing.

Lyrana had surged through the waves quicker than a tsunami. Her body had sliced through the water as if it had been air, and she had used the currents themselves to propel her forward. She had been fast, but not fast enough. She first felt the thing latching on to the Flower of the Sky, because that is where the fireball had crashed into the world. Lyrana shuddered even as she swam with frantic intensity, and she clearly felt how her winged sister screamed and plummeted down from the heavens in the wake of the violation.

The next Flower to be attacked was her own. Lyrana did not arrive in time to protect it, and she was still an entire continent away when the darkness found her Flower, drilled into the precious petals, and stabbed the roots that linked it to the vines at the nexus of the world.

For an instant there was absolute confusion. Lyrana had never experienced anything like it—the Flowers were the only thing more ancient than her. They were everything. Nothing in the world could touch them; nothing could ever hope to change them.

Nevertheless, this thing, this… hunger. It tried.

Eventually Lyrana reached her Flower, but by then the corruption had taken hold. She witnessed how the beautiful petals began to glow with an abhorrent prismatic luminescence that was almost a mockery of her own beauty. Some of her brood-siblings gathered around her, having sensed the danger, and they attacked the darkness, that hungry thing that was devouring the sacred Flower from within.

They all died. None could approach the Flower, and they all perished in horrible agony.

Lyrana tried as well, but she could not get close. The Flower was too bright, too full of energy to ever be touched without Lyrana herself being destroyed by the contact. She raged and struggled, but it was in vain. And so, confused, she retreated.

For a while nothing else happened. Lyrana began to forget that the thing had ever come, and as years turned into decades and then centuries, she regained a measure of the balance that had been stolen from her on that horrible day. She resumed watching over her domain, taking care of the world that had been entrusted to her. She spent entire years in total darkness, patrolling the vast depths of the ocean. Much later, when the trauma and the memory had faded with time, she resurfaced and spent some years in the shallow waters, accompanying the peaceful Behemoths that made their slow, ponderous rounds close to the shores.

It was during one of those days that she first saw her sisters fight.

She knew their names then, and they knew hers. Venaya, Earth queen, and Jalei, Sky queen. They had been Lyrana's companions for as long as she had existed. Each of the three had her domain, and together they protected the world and everything in it. They were each powerful in their own way, but that power had never been tested because it had never been challenged.

Until that day.

Lyrana watched, horrified, as Jalei attacked Venaya, diving like a missile from the heavens themselves. Venaya had not expected the traitorous attack, and it was only because of her crown of spines that she survived, but barely. The left side of her neck had been clawed open by the red-hot talons of her sister, and blood began to pool underneath her like a disturbingly hot waterfall.

Lyrana experienced a wrenching sensation she had never felt, and she realized that Venaya was going to die.

Lyrana tried to help, but it was too late. Venaya screamed out an earth-shattering cry of vengeance and fired a single spine into the air with her last remaining strength. Jalei, drunk on her murderous glee, did not see it coming until the projectile skewered the scales on her chest and pierced her heart scale. She died a moment later, and her body crashed down to merciless rocks, where it broke, never to move again.

Venaya died shortly thereafter in a pool of her own blood.

And from then on, the war never ceased.

At first Lyrana attempted to stop them, but the rage of vengeance in each of her sisters' daughters did not abate, and she paid the price for her attempts at peaceful intervention dearly. Her beloved brood-siblings died, one after the other, as Lyrana sent them on hopeless missions to try and stop the mad conflict that had taken hold of the world. Not even Song could stop the violence.

Generations upon generations of Earth and Sky queens were born with undying hatred of the other, and every generation ended in the same bloody display of senseless violence that appeared to hunger for something that could never be satisfied.

Eventually Lyrana stopped helping. The oceans, her home, were empty of Song, where before her brood-siblings had filled the water with their voices. The sorrow she felt could only be matched by the pain of the mad cycle of sister killing sister. When only five of her ancient brood-siblings remained, Lyrana retreated to the depths and took them with her, far away into the darkest part of the ocean where they could never be reached. There, under the crushing weight of the water, Lyrana used every ounce of her willpower to resist the urge. The call.

The hunger.

Slowly, she understood why her sisters now hated one another. The thing, the darkness in the Flowers, had never gone away. It fed on death and destruction, and all it thought about was consuming.

The hunger was strongest in the Sky Flower, because that is where it had first appeared.

It was weakest in the Earth Flower, although Lyrana did not understand why.

And in her own Flower…? It kept calling to her. Tempting her. Torturing her mind.

Decades passed. Then centuries. Lyrana lived in the abyss and never left. She could feel the insidious darkness urging her to kill. It commanded her to leave her domain and, with a single one of her Songs, destroy both of her other sisters and kill their daughters so only she would remain in the world, uncontested and triumphant, sated. Lyrana fought successfully against the incessant cacophony of violent urges, but it slowly chipped away at her will, weakening a mind that had been tempered through ages. The hunger filled every part of her waking consciousness, slowly, insidiously, and one day she realized she would not be able to fight it much longer. When aliens came to the world from the distant stars, she had no strength left to challenge them.

At the edge of madness, despair overwhelming her completely, she had been about to give in to a destiny of mindless hunger when the miracle happened.

There was pain in the world, horrible, rending pain as one of the Flowers had been torn away from its roots. The aliens had done it. Even though it had been the Earth

Flower, Lyrana screamed in the sunless depths at the top of her voice, and she knew only horror laced with agony.

A Flower was missing. It was *missing*.

And yet....

Over decades that were a mere moment in the life of one so ancient, Lyrana realized that the abominable event had briefly snapped the mental vines that the hunger had ensnared her with. She was able to recover a fraction of her own will, and when the Earth Flower was returned at last, albeit changed, she was able to gather enough strength to think of something, a solution. It was a last-ditch effort that hinged on the alien creatures that had committed the abominable act in the first place.

She sent her brood-siblings then, the four who still remained—one adult male and three juveniles—to go in search of the creatures. She told them to find them and bring them to the Flower of the Deep.

She hoped they would be able to arrive before she succumbed to the madness and killed everything in the world. She did not know how much longer she would be able to resist, but she knew that her strength was at its limit. And if she were to sing a Song of Death, the terrible aftermath would defy comprehension.

ELIAS REALIZED he was standing still as a statue, his hand in the air. Before him Lyrana had gently withdrawn her tentacles and was now watching Tristan and him with intent, intelligent eyes.

Elias reached his right hand to take Tristan's. Together they waited for the queen to decide their fate.

Lyrana sank into the waves and, an instant later, appeared on the other side of the platform formed by the vines. She gazed at the Flower, keeping her distance from its energy and yet radiating a sense of completion, of satisfaction. She examined every inch of its golden petals with care, almost as if making sure it was okay, and then returned to where Tristan and Elias still stood.

In silence, she beheld them. The energy she projected was completely different from what Elias had perceived when he first met her. The creature before him was still incomprehensible but also peaceful. Lyrana was wise, completely different from her sisters. Now that Elias had shared her mind for a moment, he realized the true extent of Lyrana's power, and he knew that it was only because of her great strength that the world had not collapsed into death and chaos.

"We will make it right," Elias heard himself say. "I will protect the Earth queen, Sizzra's daughter. That's why we were traveling. We have to go to where Dresde awaits."

Lyrana did not give any outward indication that she understood, and yet Elias was certain she did. She acknowledged the mental image of Dresde taking Sizzra's egg away, and sent an idea of her own in return. It was not an image, not a word. It was a sensation, a feeling of completion, of...

"Balance," Tristan said aloud. "Lyrana wants balance."

At the sound of his voice, Lyrana lowered her head so it would be level with Tristan's own.

"What's happening?" he asked.

"It's okay," Elias reassured him. "She won't hurt you."

Slowly, as though everything she did held the patience of a century of centuries, Lyrana gazed at Tristan and appeared to appraise him. After a pause, she reached forward with one of her tentacles and grabbed something lying at Tristan's feet. A scale. She picked it up with surprising dexterity, lifted it to the sun briefly, and then struck it with another tentacle. The scale vibrated instantly and gave off a pure musical note that suffused the air around them with calm, peaceful energy for a moment. Elias relaxed, almost as if the sound were inviting him to rest.

After the note died away, Lyrana offered the scale to Tristan.

"F-for me?" Tristan stammered.

Lyrana did not move. She held her gift out to him, a beautiful angular jewel that was the fierce gold of the noonday sun.

"You can take it," Elias told him. "She's giving it to you."

Tristan reached forward reverently and grasped the scale with both hands. Lyrana let go and projected approval with her mind. In Tristan's hands the enormous scale looked almost like a shield, and when Tristan held it against his body it shimmered and became invisible, partially hiding him from view.

"Thank you," Tristan said, his voice a little shaky. "I am honored, Lyrana."

The Singer queen turned her attention to Elias next, and the two of them regarded each other earnestly for a timeless second. Then Lyrana beckoned Elias forward and lowered her head. With another wordless message, she asked Elias to touch her forehead.

With a nod, he stepped forward and made contact with Lyrana.

The sea around him opened itself up to his perception.

Elias cried out in a mixture of surprise and wonder. Lyrana helped him link to the Flower of the Deep, the same way he and Sizzra had done it what seemed like a lifetime ago. In his mind's eye, he saw the oceans of the world stretching out in all directions. He could feel the life-spark of enormous Behemoths in the distance. He could clearly sense Lyrana's last remaining brood-sibling,

Alinor, as he regained consciousness and began to swim up to the surface a moment later. In the depths he also perceived Narev, Siv, and Vanor, and he was able to link with them and call them up with a thought. Farther out, Elias marveled at everything he could see. There was life everywhere in the ocean. He could sense predators and prey, creatures both enormous and microscopic.

Lyrana lifted her head, and as the contact between them was broken, Elias was filled with gratitude.

"Thank you," he told her. Around them, figures appeared on the surface of the water. Narev, Vanor, and Siv kept their distance, still wary of the queen, but Alinor swam straight up to Lyrana and touched her with one of his tentacles, projecting his unbridled joy at her freedom.

"What happened?" Tristan asked.

Elias smiled. "I can see now. She has shared her vision with me."

"And what… what do you see?"

Elias closed his eyes. He could sense the Flower of the Deep next to him as a blinding source of energy. Far away, the Flower of the Earth also shone brightly, its light different now that it was linked to human beings as well.

And beyond—far away, at the limits of his perception—Elias sensed the last Flower. The one Lyrana had called the Flower of the Sky.

It was dark. It was hungry, and its energy had been driven mad.

"I see where we have to go," he answered quietly. "We need to go save Sizzra's daughter and Oscar. But we also need to save Dresde."

"What?"

"That thing. The darkness—it's driven her mad, Tristan, like it almost did with Lyrana. We need to save her from herself."

Tristan looked at Lyrana and then back at Elias. He gripped the shimmering scale more tightly in his hands. "Okay. Let's do this."

"We could use your help," Elias told Lyrana. "Come with us."

But Lyrana projected the mental equivalent of a negative response. She beckoned Alinor closer to her, and together they began to sink beneath the waves.

"She's not coming?" Tristan asked.

"No," Elias answered. "And I can't blame her. She needs time to heal, and this isn't really her fight. It's ours."

Lyrana sent out acknowledgment, and before disappearing underwater, she sang.

It was a melody more beautiful than anything Elias had ever heard. She sang about life, about perseverance, about strength, and about light itself. Threaded through the notes there was also a call. Elias did not fully understand it, but he was still moved to tears by the beauty of the song he heard. Lyrana kept singing even as she submerged herself completely, and the echoes of her voice lingered in the air after she had gone, followed by her last brood-sibling, to live in peace in the darkness of the ocean depths.

"She's gone," Elias said when the last of the song had faded. "I wonder if we'll ever see her again."

"We're on our own, then," Tristan said.

The three Spine wurl jumped onto the platform, giving the Flower a wide berth, and they greeted Elias and Tristan with happy little grunts. Even Siv joined in.

"We do have a problem, though," Tristan pointed out. "We're in the middle of the ocean, and we don't have a ship."

"Don't worry about that," Elias told Tristan, grinning. "Right before she left, Lyrana called us a ride."

"A ride?"

"Wait," Elias said, closing his eyes briefly. "I can sense it approaching."

Something appeared on the horizon. It was small at first, but it rapidly grew into the familiar outline of the Island Behemoth.

"It came back!" Tristan exclaimed. "Is it going to take us all the way to Raasay?"

"I think so. Lyrana asked it to. Come on, let's meet it at the edge of the atoll."

Tristan climbed onto Vanor, and Elias did the same on Narev. Siv followed, and the five of them jumped into the water surrounding the Flower of the Deep. The ocean felt wonderfully friendly, open, and warm. Being partially submerged sharpened Elias's perception of the creatures in the ocean, and he was clearly able to sense the life-spark of every living thing around him. He enjoyed the short trip to the edge of the atoll, where they made a brief pause so Tristan could retrieve his spear.

They met the Island Behemoth shortly thereafter, and the enormous creature waited patiently until they were safely on top of its massive jungle-covered back. Elias and Tristan made their way to the top of the Behemoth's shell, to the clearing overlooking its gigantic head.

Elias knelt down and placed his hand on the Behemoth. "Take us there. Please."

The creature acknowledged him for the first time and began to swim in the direction of that distant volcano that even now beckoned, threatening, enshrouded by the hungry darkness that consumed it.

"We're on our way, Oscar," Elias said as he stood up. Tristan wrapped an arm gently around Elias's waist, and together they sailed. "We're almost there."

chapter 28.
fire

WARNING PROTOCOL complete, the shuttle announced.

Oscar and Samantha exchanged a long look.

"I see," Samantha said quietly. "I always wondered why the shuttle was hidden here."

"That was awful!" Oscar exclaimed. "All those people.... Dres—the queen killed them?"

"Not all of them, no. She kept some, my ancestors, as slaves."

"But she waited so long to attack. What did Jones say? Five months?"

"Maybe longer," Samantha guessed.

"Why, though? She knew they had arrived, right? One of the males even attacked the shuttle as it was trying to land!"

Samantha appeared to consider the question. "She is crafty, ruthless, but most of all cautious. She was probably observing them and taking her time to attack. Then again, perhaps she was merely toying with them. Giving people hope and taking it away is one of her favorite pastimes, as you may recall."

"Hey, Samantha?"

"Yes?"

"Jones said *her* name at the end. The queen's name."

"Yes. She was probably forced to leave the shuttle."

"But then… if she found Jones… doesn't that mean the queen knows about the *Archaeus*?"

"Perhaps not," Samantha said, although her voice wavered slightly. "It is possible Jones followed the mental command from a distance. The wurl queen might not have known where Jones was."

"But she saw the shuttle land. Eli said that a wurl queen can see everything the males see. And you just said that she was probably monitoring your ancestors all the time. Wouldn't she have seen them fly the shuttle to this sinkhole in the first place, when Zendaya told Jones to hide it here?"

"What if she did?" Samantha cut in, nearly shouting all of a sudden. "I apologize. Oscar, this is our only chance. We must try."

"Right, I get it. I was wondering, is all. Sorry."

"This has to work. It *has* to. *Archaeus*, begin liftoff sequence. Show me how to fly this craft."

Do you wish to engage the autopilot?

"Yes," Samantha replied. "How do I give you a destination?"

Exact coordinates are best transmitted via link interface.

"Oscar, can you do that?"

"Yep."

"Send the coordinates to the house, and then the coordinates of Portree."

"Already on it," Oscar replied, transferring the data wirelessly from his link.

"*Archaeus*, how long to liftoff?"

System checks underway. Rerouting emergency power to engines. Estimated time for diagnostic and navigation system restart, seven hours.

"Okay. Let me know as soon as you're ready to fly."

Understood, Pilot Samantha.

"Oh wow," Oscar said. "This is really happening. We're going to fly."

"That remains to be seen."

"We have a lot of time. Is it okay if I contact Portree and my brother? This shuttle should have a powerful enough antenna to transmit information to the satellite when it passes overhead, which should be in about… four hours or so."

"Yes, please do. In the meantime I will go below and see if anything useful remains on board."

"Okay."

Oscar spent the next couple of hours figuring out the intricacies of a computer interface that was over a hundred years old. Surprisingly, not much had changed in terms of operating systems, and he was eventually able to access the telecommunications array connected to the shuttle's mainframe.

"Dad, you would be *so* jealous," he muttered to himself as he typed. As the telecommunications specialist in Portree, Oscar's father had taught him many things about transmitting and receiving information through electromagnetic waves during Oscar's internship several months earlier. Oscar was sure his father would have been thrilled to have the chance to work on an original colonist system like the one in the *Archaeus*.

Once Oscar had a stable connection established, he uploaded all the letters he had composed to his family over the months to the shuttle and compressed them in a small text file, ready to send. He then spent around thirty minutes composing a message to the Portree council, explaining everything that had happened and telling them of the possibility that Dresde might follow after the shuttle when they returned. He tried to be succinct so the file would be as small as possible, in case he had bandwidth trouble when connecting to the satellite.

The next thing he did was write a message to Elias and Tristan. He was not certain whether either of them would be able to receive the transmission, but as long as their links worked, it was likely, given their wireless reception antennas and short-range link-to-link communications capabilities. He made sure to tell them about the shuttle and about the plan to pick both of them up on their way to Portree. Once the messages were ready, he checked his link and saw that the satellite should be in range overhead, so he tried to establish a connection with it.

It took him nearly an hour to do so. Although both the satellite and the shuttle had once been part of the same system on board the *Ionas*, it was tricky to get them to communicate, and the handshakes kept failing because the satellite had been modified to expect only signals being transmitted from the telecom array in Portree. It was only through some clever programming that Oscar was able to establish a reliable connection by tricking the satellite into thinking that the shuttle's signal came from Portree's location, using his link's geopositioning history as a data source for the dummy origin point.

"Yes!" Oscar said after he finally received an acknowledgment from both systems.

"Did you succeed?" Samantha asked him. She was sitting in the other chair, reading what appeared to be a flight manual that was displayed on one of the monitors.

"Yeah. Now for the moment of truth: I'm going to transmit the data."

"Good luck."

"Thanks. Here we go."

Oscar sent the warning letter to Portree first of all. Despite its small file size, the data took nearly a minute to transmit and then another minute for the reception verification stamp to be sent back. Next he sent the message to Elias and Tristan, which was also transmitted correctly. The last thing he transmitted was the much larger file with all of his letters to his parents. It took most of the remaining transmission window for it to go through, and Oscar was unable to receive an acknowledgment, but he hoped it would be received.

"Done," he said, collapsing back in his chair. He was mentally exhausted.

"All messages were sent?"

"Yeah. Portree will get the warning when the satellite comes back around to their hemisphere in a few hours."

"And your brother?"

"I don't know. I told him to look out for a shuttle. I've loaded his link's MAC address to the navigation system so we can find it as we fly, but the shuttle has limited range. Depending on where he is, we might simply miss him."

"We will not," Samantha reassured him. "No one gets left behind. I will make sure of it."

"Thanks. It means a lot."

"I would have never been able to access the shuttle without you, Oscar. I should thank *you*. And we will get through this, all of us. We will survive."

Oscar smiled. When Samantha said it was going to be all right, he really believed her.

"You're awesome, you know?" he blurted.

"What?"

Oscar's face warmed, and he knew he was blushing, but he had already started, and the words poured out of his lips like a torrent. "You're strong. You've taken care of your family all this time, and now we're maybe about to save them. Your life hasn't been easy, but you've kept going, and you're even nice to other people, like me. And you're brave. I wish I had a tiny bit of that bravery."

Oscar was sure Samantha was going to tell him to shut up, but instead she said, "You are also brave, Oscar."

"No, I'm not. I always run away from things. I'm always crying. It's my fault I got captured in the first place all those months ago."

Samantha swiveled her seat and leaned forward, closer to him. "You are not to blame for what happened to you. You were abducted against your will, and you have made the best of this situation. You have helped my family, and you have helped me. I am glad to have met you."

Oscar faced her as well. When he next spoke, his voice was a bit deeper. "Me too. I'm so glad I met you. Really."

They looked into each other's eyes, and the tension held for another heartbeat.

Oscar leaned forward and pursed his lips at the same time Samantha leaned back. She stood up, and Oscar was left looking up at her in total embarrassment.

"We should eat," she said. "We still have a few hours before takeoff, but we should be ready."

"Oh, right. Eat. Yeah."

She went downstairs first. Oscar stayed behind and tried to tell himself he hadn't just experienced the most cringeworthy moment of his life.

"Nice moves," he muttered, punching his own thigh.

He followed Samantha down to the lower level to eat, and then the two of them spent some time exploring what had been the cargo bay of the shuttle but was now completely empty, aside from a single metal crate that had nothing in it. Afterward they went back up to the cockpit, where they had to kill some more time. Oscar didn't know what to say to Samantha in the aftermath of his failed attempt at a kiss, and she seemed absorbed in her reading of the flight manual anyway, so he spent the time trying to figure out what all the little buttons on the console did. It was boring, however, so he ended up dozing off.

System check successful, the shuttle's voice announced out of nowhere. Oscar jumped up in his seat, fully awake in an instant. *Navigation and flight systems ready. Awaiting instructions.*

"Take off and head to the first location, my house," Samantha instructed without missing a beat. "Once there, wait for further instructions."

Acknowledged, Pilot Samantha. Initiating engine sequence.

"Whoa, do you feel that?" Oscar asked, rubbing the sleep out of his eyes. "My seat's vibrating."

"Not the seat. The shuttle."

Samantha was right. The cockpit began to shake noticeably as a low hum reached Oscar's ears.

Obstruction detected in engine three. Compensating.

The hum intensified and was followed by a loud *snap* that made the entire shuttle rattle.

Obstruction in engine three removed. Ninety seconds to takeoff.

"Thank you, *Archaeus*," Samantha said. She placed her hand on a tactile interface on the console in front of her with confidence and called up a complicated-looking menu from which she selected an option that in turn displayed what looked like a three-dimensional rendering of the area they were in.

"Can you fly this thing?" Oscar asked, trying to suppress the note of anxiety in his voice.

"Of course not. The autopilot will do most of it, but I did learn how to make minor trajectory adjustments from the manual."

"Great. Um, Samantha?"

"What is it?"

"We're still completely covered in dirt and plants and stuff."

Samantha grinned. "Not for long."

The vibrations intensified.

Sixty seconds to takeoff.

"Look, Samantha! The windshield!"

The amalgamation of dirt and roots that covered the wide curved glass began to shift and move as if under the influence of a great wind. As the seconds ticked, the movement became more noticeable, until a large chunk of the debris covering the outside of the cockpit appeared to be torn away by an outside force.

Thirty seconds to takeoff.

"Buckle up," Samantha indicated.

"Oh. Right," Oscar replied, fumbling about with the straps for a while until he was able to secure himself to the seat.

Ten seconds to takeoff. Please confirm.

"Confirmed," Samantha said firmly.

Takeoff.

Oscar cried out when the shuttle began to rise. The movement was smooth for a fraction of a second, and then it stopped. There was resistance.

CRACK.

The sounds of things snapping and crumbling surrounded them. Light lanced through gaps in the plant cover as it broke away, and as the shuttle rose and freed itself from the shroud that had hidden it from view for generations, its movement became smoother, faster. When the last fragment of debris tumbled away, the windshield offered a spectacular view of the miniature hurricane the shuttle's engines had kicked up inside the sinkhole as their rotors spun. Powerful floodlights illuminated a space where dirt and torn-up plants spun violently at the mercy of the downdrafts.

The mechanical hum reached a higher pitch, and the craft rose still more. One meter. Two meters. Five. Oscar felt the motion in his gut.

"We're flying," Oscar said, scarcely able to believe. "Samantha, we're flying!"

"Yes," she replied, setting her features in a determined frown. "*Archaeus*, go. Let's save my family."

Acknowledged.

The shuttle ripped vines out of the ground and splintered tree trunks like matchsticks in its inexorable rise to the sky. It collided briefly with the rocky wall of the sinkhole, throwing Oscar and Samantha to the side, but their seat buckles held fast, and the craft recovered quickly. The sound of its engines suggested a shift in gear a few seconds later and was accompanied by a burst of speed. The upward acceleration and dizzying shift in inertia reminded Oscar of how it felt to cling to Doran's back when he rose in the air, but this was an order of magnitude more intense. Rocks and plants were a blur through the windshield, and then they disappeared from view.

The shuttle halted its rise so suddenly that Oscar floated briefly in a split second of zero gravity.

"Oscar, look!"

"By the generation ship," Oscar said. "It's beautiful."

They had cleared the sinkhole and were hovering over the entire network of intricate depressions and greenery-choked mounds that made up the surface of the Nightmare Caves. Ahead of them, the sky stretched out in all its immensity. It was late afternoon, and the rays of the sun suffused the entire scene with golden light. There were no clouds overhead, but two of the moons shone silver and appeared to watch over the entire landscape with their quiet, gentle glow.

It was surreal to see all of it from a perfectly stable vantage point. When riding Doran, the goggles restricted Oscar's view, and there was always motion of some kind. The wind was in his face, and there was often a small fear that he might fall off. Oscar experienced none of that while sitting in the cockpit of a mechanical craft. He had never even been inside a vehicle of any kind because Portree was so small. It was exhilarating, but also slightly terrifying. His life and Samantha's life were in the hands of a hundred-year-old autopilot program.

Scanning. Satellite link established.

"It's *that* way," Samantha said with evident impatience. She jabbed the navigation panel in front of her with her finger, indicating the direction. "Hurry up!"

Calculating route. Please wait.

"It won't be long," Oscar reassured her. "We're almost—"

"We have no time!" she interrupted with unexpected intensity. "You don't understand. Doran will have heard the shuttle taking off. He will either fly here and attack us or go warn Dresde. Every second counts!"

Route established. Engaging.

A heavy *clunk* on either side of the shuttle was accompanied by movement. Oscar looked to the right and watched as one of the engines on the outside rotated a full ninety degrees. For a fraction of a second, it felt as though the shuttle would simply drop out of the sky. Then they surged forward.

Oscar was pressed back into his seat. They were going *fast*.

"Whoa!" he exclaimed.

"Down there!" Samantha said, pointing.

"No way."

A slender cobalt shape rose in the sky ahead of them, flapping frantically, and immediately pursued. It opened its mouth and appeared to roar, lunging forward to attack, but the shuttle was too quick. They left Doran behind in seconds and sped over the landscape. The Nightmare Caves were gone in the blink of an eye. The Field of Thorns was little more than a blur.

"When we arrive," Samantha instructed, her gaze fixed straight ahead, "you go into the house and get everyone. I'll go to the prison and free my father. Understood?"

"Yes, got it."

"We must get everyone in here and be airborne again as fast as possible. Doran has seen us, so by your brother's logic, Dresde has too."

"You can count on me," Oscar said firmly. His heart was beating like mad in his chest, but he was determined.

Samantha gave him a brief nod. "I know I can."

Approaching destination.

"Land by the house and hover," Samantha told the shuttle as she unbuckled herself from the seat. "Open the lower hatch. Take off again as soon as six people are on board."

Acknowledged, Pilot Samantha.

"We're close," Oscar informed her, unbuckling himself as well. He could see the ocean and the cliffs already, and an odd column of what appeared to be smoke in the distance. A few seconds later they flew over the river. "Is something burning over there?"

"Follow me down to the hatch," Samantha ordered, ignoring the question and standing up. "We should be by the hatch door the moment we…."

The color drained from her face and she froze, looking through the windshield.

Oscar followed her gaze, and the icy hand of despair constricted his throat when he registered the scene in front of his eyes. It was suddenly hard to breathe.

"*No*," he gasped.

Fire. Even as the shuttle slowed down in its final approach, all he could see was fire.

The building that had once been the prison was engulfed in flames, hungry pillars that flickered and danced on the blackened walls as they devoured them. The inferno mushroomed into a quickly growing cloud of black smoke that choked the light out of the sky and contorted into more horrible shapes the higher it rose.

In the fire itself, coiled like a constrictor around its prey, was a shape larger than the collapsing building. Glittering violet scales reflected the light from the blaze as the shape moved, unfurling gigantic membranous wings.

Welcome home, little humans, Dresde sang, her voice loud in Oscar's head. Each word dripped with venom-laced notes of cruel amusement. *Are you surprised?*

She flapped her wings once, and so powerful was the blast of air that the shuttle itself wobbled even as it came down, mindlessly obedient, and hovered above the ground. The fire was extinguished instantaneously, and the lull revealed Dresde in all her malevolent glory. Her glowing talons sank into the floor of the prison as she moved, and the wooden frame of the structure burst into flame again wherever they touched it.

Oscar looked for the metal ladder that led down to Johann's bunker. It was a blackened mess, and the metal had warped and partially melted with the heat.

No one hiding underground could have possibly survived.

"No!" Samantha screamed. "*Papa!*"

Yes, Dresde crooned, smiling with her mind. Her eye cluster blazed, and she sprang forward with terrifying agility, landing on the shuttle and seeming to envelop it with her wings. The craft crashed to the ground under her weight and stopped moving. Dresde lowered her head so she could look right at Samantha through the transparent barrier that separated them. *He is dead! Now come out, Samantha!*

Dresde grabbed the windshield with her two front claws. Her talons sank into the glass as if it were butter, and then she pulled, hard. She ripped the windshield off its hinges in a shower of broken shards and tossed it to the side as if it weighed nothing. Choking-hot air full of noxious smoke and Dresde's brimstone stench rushed into the cabin, stinging Oscar's eyes and clogging his throat.

"Papa!" Samantha screamed again, and she barely avoided a swipe from Dresde's claw by falling backward. The wurl queen's talons raked the control panel instead and destroyed the delicate electronics therein.

"Samantha! This way!" Oscar shouted, running to the back of the cockpit. He grabbed Samantha's hand and all but shoved her down the ladder leading to the cargo bay. He jumped in after her with not a moment to spare. The metal fuselage of the shuttle groaned and then snapped. Dresde's red-hot talons pierced the reinforced plates where some of the passenger chairs had been and then retreated.

Hiding, Samantha? Dresde asked calmly at the same time she rent the side of the shuttle asunder with horrifying ease. *I expected more from you.*

Oscar dragged Samantha along with him, and they half ran, half stumbled forward until they reached the still-open outer hatch.

"Jump out!" Oscar urged, bracing himself against one of the seats while the shuttle shuddered yet again. "Now!"

Samantha hesitated, eyes wide, seeming unable to focus. Oscar thought she might be in shock, so he grabbed her by the waist and jumped out with her.

They crashed to the ground in a heap, but Oscar had no time to think about the pain. He scrambled upright and helped Samantha move out of the way.

Dresde jumped on top of the shuttle and looked down at them from her perch.

What an interesting machine this is, she observed, stalking forward until she reached one of the *Archaeus*'s engines. *It has been a long time since I last saw it fly.*

With an almost languid motion, she grabbed the engine with her claws and twisted. The entire propeller came off, and its moving parts splintered into a thousand pieces. Dresde discarded it slowly and moved to the next engine. She tore it off as well and then jumped down to the ground with unhurried grace.

Oscar looked all around, desperate for a way out. The house was too far away. The shuttle blocked the way to the cliffs. To the right, the smoldering ruins of the prison boxed them in. Fire had started again, and the heat coming from the place made the air around it waver and shift like a mirage. Billowing smoke collected and spread low to the ground, as if drawn to the presence of the wurl queen.

Samantha was panting, almost as if she had been running. Then her eyes settled on the prison, and she yelled.

"Papa!" She ran forward. To the fire.

"Samantha, no!" Oscar yelled.

She ignored him, so he sprinted and tackled her to the ground.

They fell together in a tumble of elbows and knees, and a sharp rock jabbed Oscar in the back.

"Get off me!" Samantha shouted and kicked Oscar in the chest.

He was knocked off-balance and was powerless to stop her as she climbed to her feet, a manic look of desperation in her eyes.

How very amusing, Dresde said and slammed her tail in Samantha's path, forcing her to stop. *I so enjoy watching humans fight.*

"Out of the way!"

No, Samantha. I will not allow you to die looking for a dead male human. You will be the last *to die.*

"Papa…," Samantha sobbed.

This is your punishment! Dresde crowed triumphantly. She radiated twisted enjoyment. *I told you that you would be punished. I told you, did I not? And you chose the best possible retribution yourself! I often wondered how long it would take you to try to use this flying machine to attempt an escape. So secretive you were, thinking that you could hide your great discovery from me. I see all. What was it that decided you to finally do so? Tell me!*

Samantha glanced at Oscar as if someone were forcing her to turn her head. He stood up slowly, edging closer to her.

Oh, I see. The little male brought something with him. An object to activate the machine. Around his forearm?

"Where is the rest of my family?" Samantha demanded.

Dresde snaked her head above them, appearing to look at something that approached. She gave them another mental smile.

See for yourself.

"Sam!" A loud yell reached them. Nadja's voice.

"Sam!" Laurie shouted.

Oscar turned around in time to see three figures burst through the thick smoke screen that had hidden them from view.

"Mama!"

Ute ran with Nadja and Laurie close behind. The three of them carried spears, and they looked ferocious in the combined light of the setting sun and the flames, like raging warriors charging to destroy an enemy army.

The scariest one by far was Ute. "Get away from my daughter, you monster!" she shouted as she skidded to a stop in front of Samantha, shielding her from Dresde with her body. She raised her weapon and assumed a fighting stance.

Oh? Dresde said. *You speak again, Ute? I suppose it is fitting now, at the end.*

Dresde lunged forward, but Ute was quick. She vaulted out of the way of skewering teeth like a gymnast, and Dresde's fanged jaws snapped shut around empty air. The instant she landed, Ute swung the yult spear with a guttural grunt and smacked the side of

Dresde's mouth so hard Oscar heard the sharp *crack* of one of her scales.

Insolent little insect! Dresde bellowed, but instead of attacking she drew her head back.

"Always a coward," Ute spat. Her voice shook with rage. She took a step forward, her knuckles white around the polished black shaft of her weapon. "You murdered my sons. You murdered my husband. But you will *not* kill my daughter as long as I live."

Nadja and Laurie arrived and flanked her on either side with their own spears at the ready.

And what can you do? Dresde asked, the timbre of her mental voice ringing with laughter. *What can weaklings do against a goddess?*

"We can fight," Nadja replied.

"We will not be slaves anymore," Laurie declared. "My child will be born free."

Samantha walked up to stand next to her mother. She assumed a fighting stance, and the two of them exchanged a brief smile.

Oscar stepped forward as well. There was no possibility of hiding, no way to escape Dresde, and the certainty of the inescapable threat gave him a strange clarity. He was terrified, but he was done running away from things. He joined the women and raised his fists.

"You cannot stop us all at once," Samantha said with a sneer. "Come and *fight*."

The air appeared to crackle with tension for two long seconds while Dresde regarded them in simmering silence, jaws slightly agape. Flames licked at her feet, and the malevolence in her eye cluster was the visual projection of the hate she radiated incessantly.

The tense silence was shattered by the roar of a wurl in the sky. Oscar looked up and saw Doran rocketing through the air.

Excellent, Dresde said, stepping farther back. *Doran, come here now!*

Doran spiraled through the air once and then plummeted to the ground. He unfurled his wings at the last second and landed hard amid a cloud of dust and smoke. When the air cleared, Oscar took a step back in fear, and he wasn't the only one.

He had gotten used to seeing Doran the way he normally was, friendly and helpful. What he saw now before him was something else entirely, a terrifying creature with blazing eyes, wicked fangs, and sharp talons. Like a beloved pet gone rabid, Doran was a nightmarish betrayal and somehow even scarier than the much larger wurl queen behind him.

Kill them! Dresde ordered, her voice manic. *Kill them all but the male and Samantha! Leave those to me.*

Doran stalked forward slowly, head hung low, growling. His wings were folded against his body, and crimson reflections from the fire danced on his scales as he circled them.

"Doran, do not do this," Samantha pleaded. "You do not want to attack us. I know you."

Doran hesitated, one of his forelegs lifted in the air.

I said kill them! Dresde screamed, and Doran's entire body shook. His eyes appeared to dim, and he snarled.

He leaped forward with liquid grace and swiped at Nadja, who was closest. The air whistled. Nadja parried the blow, but Doran's glowing claws sliced clean through the spear, breaking it in two and sending her tumbling backward into Ute.

"Oma!" Samantha screamed.

Doran crouched as if preparing to attack again.

There is no escape! Dresde gloated. *Doran is the strongest, and the last! He will tear you limb from limb. He will—*

Both she and Doran froze. In unison, their heads lifted and turned toward the volcano.

You tricked me, Dresde hissed. *You tricked me!*

Oscar glanced at Samantha, who looked as confused as he was.

At that instant Oscar's link buzzed. In disbelief, Oscar realized he was getting a short-range call.

"Oscar?" Elias's voice asked, barely distinguishable through the static. Oscar listened in utter shock. "O… car? Are y… there? Os…?"

Dresde unfurled her wings, buffeting them with a gust of wind that sent blinding dust everywhere. *You distracted me to give those males a chance! You will regret this. Now I will* not *kill you, any of you! You will curse the day you were born, treacherous little aliens!*

She appeared to gather strength for an instant and then launched herself into the air like an arrow fired from a bow, splintering the ground where she kicked off. She flew faster than Oscar had ever thought possible, and it was only a faint echo of her mind-voice that reached them.

Doran! Bring Samantha and the male to the eyrie. Alive.

chapter 29.
climb

THE BLACK beach was majestic and desolate at once.

Elias and Tristan stood hand in hand in the shallows and watched the Behemoth as it retreated to deeper water. It remained there like a sentry, waiting.

"Can't it help us?" Tristan asked.

Elias shook his head. "I don't think it can leave the water."

"Yeah, I kind of guessed," Tristan said. "So. We're here. Raasay."

Elias analyzed his surroundings with a mixture of excitement and apprehension. Water swirled around his ankles, and the sound of the sea was the only thing that could be heard. It sounded forlorn to him somehow. Jagged gray rocks rose halfway above the water all around, and some of them had been shaped into spectacular forms by erosion over untold decades or centuries. Waves crashed regularly against the tallest formations and exploded into foam that infused the air with the salty fragrance of the ocean.

Elias turned away and glanced toward land. Tristan and he walked forward, out of the water, followed by the three hulking Spine wurl. The sand underfoot was soft and toasty with the warmth of the afternoon sun, but a shiver ran up Elias's spine as he left the ocean behind. It was more than the sudden loss of his mental perception now that he was finally on solid ground.

"What's the matter?" Tristan asked, evidently having noticed Elias's discomfort.

"Something's wrong with this place," Elias answered. "It feels empty."

He had already experienced how it felt to be cut off from the spirit-lines that linked him to the world when he had first entered Lyrana's domain, and he knew that it would happen again now that he was on the continent where only Dresde ruled. However, the void he perceived whenever his toes sank into the black sand underneath was entirely different from his past experience. He could feel something that was almost an echo of a wail, an ancient moan of something having been irrevocably lost. The desolation around him added to that impression, and each step farther inland reinforced the idea that something horrible had happened in the distant past.

He came to the first crystal cluster after six steps. He had avoided the ones in the water, but this one was directly in front of him, and he approached it unwillingly.

"Neat," Tristan commented. "What are these, do you think? Giant diamonds?"

"No," Elias replied with absolute certainty. He felt nothing but revulsion as he studied the multifaceted gems that protruded from the ground. The biggest one was as tall as he, a nearly perfect three-dimensional rhomboid that filtered the fading light from the sun like a prism. The black sand behind it was colored by vibrant light in all the wavelengths of the rainbow, but instead of looking beautiful, the display seemed to Elias like a warped mockery of light itself.

There were many such crystal formations of different sizes scattered throughout the beach, piercing the ground like parasitic arthropods that fed on the life of the world and grew fat with their stolen sustenance. Although they evidently did not move, Elias found himself keeping an eye on the glassy protrusions. He was unsettled by the way they spread out and reached all the way to the towering cliffs that made an abrupt end to the beach.

The cliffs were huge walls that rose a few meters ahead, forbidding and somehow threatening. Elias craned his neck up and could barely see where they ended. To the left and to the right, the rock stretched, seemingly without end, a natural barrier that only those who could fly might easily overcome.

"That's going to be a problem," Tristan observed, pointing straight ahead. "We don't have climbing gear at all."

"There has to be a way. The volcano is very close. We're almost there."

Although hidden at the moment because the cliffs were in the way, Elias had watched the volcano grow larger and larger on the horizon throughout their two-week trip on the Island Behemoth. He had watched its odd western slope with interest, wondering why it looked as though titanic forces had sliced it to expose a cross-section of the mountain to the elements.

Vanor walked up to Tristan with heavy footsteps, but the wurl gave the nearest crystals as wide a berth as possible. He nosed Lyrana's scale with interest instead.

"I think he likes it," Tristan commented, raising the beautiful golden object.

"It's a precious gift," Elias replied.

"Yeah, although it's really awkward to carry," Tristan continued. "I have to use both hands or hold it under one arm, and I can't use it and my shock spear at the same time. Maybe I could drill a couple of holes into it or use some adhesive to attach a strap. Then it could be a shield. I'll do it first thing when we return."

Elias looked at Tristan in silence for a moment. "When we return," he repeated.

"Yes," Tristan said vehemently. "We'll go back, Eli. *All* of us."

He brought the scale down hard, presumably to sink it into the sand and emphasize his point, but Tristan hit a half-buried rock instead.

Clang.

Elias relaxed the instant he heard the musical note. Just like when Lyrana had made it, the sound coming from the scale made him feel peaceful and at ease. The tension he had been holding left his shoulders, and he was caressed by relief.

Tristan relaxed visibly too, and he was not the only one.

"Tristan, look," Elias said, pointing at the wurl.

"Oh wow."

Narev, Vanor, and Siv had all lain down on the sand. They looked almost paralyzed, and they only moved again when Tristan picked up the scale and stopped its vibration.

"That was amazing," Elias said.

"Yeah. And maybe it can come in handy."

Elias looked up at the sky, and his apprehension came back. "We should be ready. Dresde could send Flyers to attack us at any second."

"Maybe. Although we haven't seen any since the atoll."

"That's true," Elias conceded. "I wonder if maybe there aren't any more left."

Beep, beep.

Elias and Tristan glanced down at their links at the same time. Their notification indicator was blinking.

"A message," Tristan said. "Maybe it's from our parents."

"Yeah," Elias said, opening the file.

His eyes widened in shock. He looked at Tristan, who looked dumbstruck.

"Eli," Tristan whispered. "This is from Oscar!"

Heart hammering in his chest, Elias looked at his link again and read.

> *Dear Eli and Tristan,*
> *I hope you're okay. I'm sending this message with the help of the* Archaeus, *a shuttle from the generation ship that Samantha and I are trying to get to fly again. If this works, we'll pick up Samantha's family and then look for you guys before heading to Portree. Dresde is probably going to chase us, so we don't have much time. Please set your links to broadcast your position starting now, even if it drains the battery. Look for a shuttle in the sky.*
> *Oscar.*

"He's alive," Elias said under his breath. Then he raised his voice. "He's alive!"

He could scarcely believe it. Tears of happiness welled up in his eyes.

"I knew it!" Tristan added, smiling. He hugged Elias and gave him a quick kiss on the lips. "Your brother is tough."

"Thank you, thank you," Elias whispered, touching his forehead reverently. "I had been so worried, Tristan. I was scared that he… that he…."

"I know. He's okay, though! That's the important part. And what's this about a shuttle?"

"Not sure. I wonder why the message was so short."

"In any case, let's activate the position broadcast."

"Right," Elias replied, tapping his link while barely able to contain his excitement.

"This is amazing. And this person, Samantha? Is that the girl from the day of the storm?"

"I think so, yeah," Elias said, remembering that Dresde had called the girl by that name. "Looks like she's with Oscar now."

"We need to get up there, over those cliffs. If Oscar's nearby we might even be able to call him without the interference from the rocks. He can't be far. We'll find him, Eli! We need to get to him as soon as we can."

Elias grinned and took a happy step forward, but a moment later he stopped. His shoulders slumped.

"No." His voice was ashen.

Tristan blinked. "What?"

Elias walked up to Narev. The wurl crouched down obediently and allowed him to mount. Vanor and Siv grunted, sensing his inner turmoil. Narev himself projected concern.

"We can't go to him, Tristan."

"Why the hell not?" he asked, looking flabbergasted.

Elias closed his eyes briefly. "This is a chance."

"A chance for what, exactly?"

"Oscar sent this message just now. He said that Dresde was likely going to pursue him, and that means she's going to be distracted. She won't be guarding her Flower. She'll fly out to intercept Oscar and Samantha, wherever they may be."

"Oh. So we can use this time to climb the volcano."

"Yes. If we get to the Flower of the Sky and tear it out, she'll be incapacitated. We'll be able to find Sizzra's egg, which is almost certainly going to be in the vicinity. Then we can go get Oscar. Once we have everyone together, you'll return the Flower to its rightful place and we'll move out."

"But Oscar is going to be in danger," Tristan protested. "What if Dresde reaches him before we get to the Flower?"

Elias's lower lip quivered, but he set his features in iron determination. "This is our best chance. It's the best strategy. You're a soldier—I'm sure you agree."

Tristan scowled. After a couple of seconds, though, he sighed and gave a reluctant nod. "Without Sizzra we don't stand a chance against Dresde, not even with the help of Vanor, Narev, and Siv. She's too powerful."

"Exactly," Elias confirmed.

"Are you sure about this plan?"

"Yes. Oscar's giving us this chance, and we can't waste it. Remember, even if we save Oscar and Sizzra's daughter, we'll never make it back to Portree without Dresde catching us first. We need to incapacitate her, and then…." He trailed off, unwilling to say what he knew had to be done to eliminate the threat of the wurl queen permanently.

"We'll think about that when the time comes, okay?" Tristan told him, placing his hand on Elias's leg. He picked up his scale from the sand and walked up to

Vanor. A moment later he vaulted over the wurl's spiked back. "Like I said at the beginning of this, Eli, I'm with you. If this is what you want to do, I'll support you."

Elias smiled. "Thank you, Tristan. Really."

"Now we need to figure out how in the world we're going to get up there."

"I think I know how. Give me a moment. Guys, come here."

As he spoke, he projected the request, and the three wurl walked closer together until they were standing in a rough triangle, snouts touching.

We're here, Elias thought, projecting his ideas with as much clarity as he could. He could sense Narev's consciousness most clearly, but Vanor and Siv were also listening. *We've traveled far to get here, to save Sizzra's daughter. Help me find her.*

He focused on his memory of the brief brush of awareness he had experienced the day of the storm, when Dresde had taken the egg. He tried to recall every detail of the beautiful white luster of the shell that encased the future Spine queen. As he did so, he quested out with his mind across the distance. Although he could get no real sense of the life around him because it belonged to another's domain, he was still connected to Sizzra's daughter, and he looked for her life-spark in the darkness.

The wurl helped. They understood what Elias was trying to do and added their strength to his. Narev and Siv were focused out of the devotion they'd held for Sizzra, but Vanor's impetus to find the egg was far stronger and more urgent. This was *his* daughter. His mind burned with a desire to find her and save her.

A flicker of light. Elias sensed it as if from a great distance, but it was difficult to know where it was in the swirling shadows of the mind space. A moment later the light was gone; he had lost it, as if the emptiness itself had swallowed it.

Help me, guys.

Elias tried again, pouring more strength into the attempt. At first he sensed only shadows, and he grew scared, thinking he had lost the contact for good, but a sudden twinkle at the edge of his perception drew his attention, and he focused on it with everything he had. His mind reached out and was rewarded by recognition. He sensed a mind that still slumbered, a consciousness that resembled Sizzra and yet was different from her.

From the contact, Elias expanded his perception so distance and position would be clearer. He sensed great height and a specific direction.

There.

His eyes snapped open. "I found her."

Tristan grinned. "Great! Let's go!"

Vanor, Narev, and Siv roared at the same time, and their eyes flashed with the intensity of their emotions. They needed no encouragement. Under Elias's direction they turned to the northeast and bounded forward, knocking a crystal out of the way in the wake of their stampede. They ran straight at the cliff wall and showed no intention of stopping.

"Eli?" Tristan said, sounding anxious. "What's happening?"

"They know what to do. Hold on!"

He leaned forward and grabbed two of Narev's spines not a moment too soon. With but a few meters left before he would have collided with the rocks, Narev launched himself at the sheer vertical surface with a mighty leap that sent him and Elias flying through the air. A moment later Elias's teeth rattled with the impact against the rocks, and he braced himself for a fall that never came.

Cautiously, Elias opened his eyes.

"We're on the wall," Tristan exclaimed to Elias's left. "We're *on* the *wall*!"

Elias gripped the sides of Narev's back with his legs and held tight to the spines.

Let's go up.

Narev's sharp metallic-sheened claws had sunk into the rock as if it had been nothing but paper. Under Elias's direction he lifted his front right foot, reached above him, and pierced the rock again as he secured a new hold. He did the same with his left, and then his other four feet. The cliff wall gave way as though it posed no challenge at all.

Then Narev climbed.

Elias had never considered whether Spine wurl could scale vertical surfaces, but now he had his answer. Despite their heft, all three male wurl clawed their way up the cliff with ponderous but unhesitating proficiency. The more they rose, the smoother their climb became, almost as if they were finding it easier by the second. Elias concentrated on not moving, and he kept his gaze resolutely fixed on the back of Narev's head, but after nearly half an hour had gone by, he could no longer resist the urge to look down, and he peeked for a moment.

He wished he hadn't. They were already dizzyingly high up, and if he let go of the spines, there would be nothing stopping him from a fatal fall where his body would break against the black sand and the horrible crystals that looked like grains of rice from his vantage point. The wind had picked up, and it tousled his hair, bringing with it the musty scent of rotting algae and also something else, a vague hint that suggested something burning.

Claw followed claw, and Narev, tireless, scaled with precise strikes into the rock. Elias's arms began to tremble, but he did not risk looking straight up to see how much farther they had to go out of fear of destabilizing both Narev and himself and making them fall.

It was therefore an abrupt surprise when Narev crested the cliff and heaved his body over the lip with a loud grunt.

"You did it," Elias praised him, letting go of the spines. "Good boy."

He patted Narev's silver scales and dismounted to give him a chance to breathe.

"Took you long enough," Tristan said playfully. He and Vanor were already there. Tristan was panting, but Vanor radiated energy and purpose.

Siv reached them a few seconds later. Once they were all together, Elias gazed around him in wonder.

"This place is beautiful," he said, and he meant it.

The rolling slopes on which he stood were covered by greenery, an emerald carpet that spread out far into the distance. The sky overhead was a cloudless blue that reminded Elias of the water in the atoll, and the air was warm but had a faint crispness that suggested the first stirrings of autumn. He could see the thin outline of a river to the southeast, and there were strange trees dotting the landscape farther south.

The volcano towered above it all, majestic and forbidding at once. It drew the eye unerringly.

Narev grunted again. Vanor and Siv did the same after a moment.

"It's there," Elias said with complete certainty. He pointed up at the cone of the smoking mountain. "That's where we need to go."

"Hey, Eli, what's that down there?"

Elias glanced back. "Where?"

"Over there, on the lower slopes. Those dark things. They don't look like trees."

"Maybe they're rocks. We're too far away to tell."

"Maybe," Tristan conceded, "but they're odd. The big one in particular. Kind of looks like a house."

Elias squinted. It was possible Tristan was right.

"Whatever it is, we have no time," Elias said. "We need to get going."

"Okay."

They mounted again, and the wurl ran forward. It was rough going, but speed was everything, and they could not afford to lose a single minute. Before long they reached steeper slopes with loose rocks and boulders, and Narev was forced to slow down to make his way across the treacherous terrain.

They saw a cave in the side of the mountain and tried it, but it soon narrowed down into a tunnel where no adult wurl could fit, and so they came back out into the open.

"We're going to have to climb on the outside again," Elias said, eyeing the western side of the volcano. The rocks were similar to the cliffs they had scaled, and he guessed they would be able to do the same thing: scale them with nothing but raw strength.

"Looks like it," Tristan agreed. "This isn't going to be fun."

"On the positive side, the walls here aren't vertical," Elias pointed out. "They are steep, but nothing like the cliff. We can do this."

"Yes. We can. Right, Vanor?"

A decided huff was Vanor's prompt reply.

Elias guided the wurl up to the point where he guessed it would be easiest to begin climbing, but after that he left the ascent to the wurl themselves and their instincts. They never hesitated. Vanor in the lead, they used their claws and tails to help themselves along as they climbed the volcano. It was a brutal, strenuous effort, and one where a single mistake meant the difference between life and death.

When they reached a part of the rocky wall that jutted out at a steep angle overhead, far exceeding verticality, Elias thought they would have to go around it and waste more time.

Instead, Vanor and Narev fired four spines in total. They sunk into the rock at regular intervals and provided anchor points that the wurl used to grab on to as they scrambled up the surface like rock climbers, at one point hanging nearly horizontal directly over the chasm below. Elias was beyond relieved when they left that obstacle behind.

Progress was nerve-racking but steady. The sun descended, ever closer to the horizon, and minutes became an hour.

They paused briefly at a ledge with about a third of the way to go and resumed after they had all steadied their breath. Neither Elias nor Tristan spoke anymore. It took all of Elias's concentration simply to hold on, and he was sure that it was even harder for Tristan because he had to balance himself on Vanor while simultaneously making sure he didn't drop Lyrana's scale.

Siv stumbled once and nearly killed them all. He had been climbing ahead of the other two but then trusted his entire weight to a boulder that became dislodged under the stress. With a panicked mental cry, Siv let go of the rock and jumped to the side, only avoiding a fall because Narev fired a spine underneath him that Siv used to stabilize his lower body. Vanor was forced to flatten his body against the volcano to avoid the boulder, which tumbled and fell for so long that Elias never heard it hit the ground.

The hour turned to two. The wurl were slowing down, even their prodigious strength being tested by the horrendous ascent. The wind blew mercilessly at the altitude they had reached, and the air was not only chilly but also thin. Elias got a mild headache, and he was nauseated from the constant swaying and tilting and the anxiety of falling down. To calm himself, he closed his eyes and focused on the pinpoint of light, which was growing brighter by the second. He could sense Sizzra's daughter much more clearly now, but his perception registered something else in her vicinity as well.

Elias shivered once more, and it had nothing to do with the cold gale that whipped his hair and caressed his exposed back and shoulders with icy fingers. The thing he sensed was unmistakable. It was the same hunger that had tormented Lyrana for ages, but it was different. More focused. The more they climbed, the colder Elias felt. Rather than ascending a volcano, it felt as though he were sliding down a bottomless pit where light could never reach. The sensation eventually became so strong that Elias lost track of the egg he wished to save. When Narev came to a stop, still holding on to the rocks on a steep slope very near the summit, he did not register the change at first.

"Eli, look."

Elias did not respond. He was having a hard time focusing as the hunger needled itself through his consciousness. It was more tangible here. It was less a nebulous threat, such as he had perceived at the atoll, and more of a... presence.

"Eli!"

Elias heard Tristan's voice fully and wrenched his attention away from the darkness with an effort. "Tristan?"

"What's wrong?"

"I'm not sure."

"Look over there," Tristan told him, nodding with his head. "Down there by the cliffs we left earlier."

Unsteadying though it was, Elias craned his neck to the side and looked down the southern slope.

"Do you see it?" Tristan asked.

It took a moment, but then Elias registered something rising in the air, very far away. It looked like a tiny black and cloudy pillar.

"What's that?" Elias asked.

"It started a few minutes ago. I think it's smoke."

"Smoke?" he repeated, and he realized Tristan was right. "Something's burning down there."

Oscar.

"Hurry, guys," Elias urged the wurl, with renewed energy fueled entirely by adrenaline. "We have to reach the Flower."

All three acknowledged the words, and they used their remaining strength in a final push that took them all the way to an enormous cleft in the rock that looked like a cave carved in the side of the volcano itself. Narev scrambled over the edge and all but collapsed on level ground, panting. His entire body was trembling with exhaustion. Vanor and Siv were no better off.

"Thank you, Narev," Elias said, and he dismounted as fast as he could.

He activated his link and searched for nearby user signatures. There was Tristan's, of course….

And another one.

"Tristan, I see him. His link!"

"Oscar?"

"Yes! He's in range of the scanner."

Elias typed as he spoke and all but smashed his thumb on the button to place a call.

"Come on, come on," he said urgently.

Ring. Ring.

With a mixture of disbelief and hope, Elias glanced at Tristan. The call had been established.

"Go on," Tristan said. "Talk to him."

"Oscar?" Elias asked, holding his link close to his mouth. "Are you there? Oscar!"

The call was terminated. The message on the display reported too much static and an unstable connection.

"No!" Elias yelled. "Oscar!"

He tried again, but it was no use. Tristan tried as well, but the connection failed.

"I'm sorry, Eli."

"That's okay," Elias replied, trying to suppress his frustration. "We're here. That's what matters. We need to find—"

Something bubbled not far off. It was a mental sensation, not really a sound. Elias lost his train of thought.

"We're here," he repeated, whispering.

He took a full look at the space where he stood for the first time. The golden light of sunset bathed the space in warmth, but all Elias perceived as he eyed the cavernous gallery that yawned around him was cold.

The cave was gigantic. He took a careful step away from the edge and then another to see it better. It had been made by Dresde, of that there was no doubt. It looked like a place where Flyer wurl would come to roost, but instead of being a safe haven where a nest could be found, there was only death. Piles upon piles of bones littered the space and made it look like an open graveyard. Elias crouched down next to a skull with three openings for what could have been eyes. He picked it up, and it felt brittle under his fingers.

"Are these her kills, do you think?" Tristan asked, stopping next to Elias.

"Not her kills. Something else happened to this animal." He applied the faintest amount of pressure, and the skull crumbled in his hand. "Something drained it of life."

They walked deeper into the space, trying not to step on any bones. Although he knew Dresde was not there, Elias still felt the need to be stealthy. He passed the place where an unexpected object lay on the ground but did not touch it. It looked like a spear made of black wood, oddly incongruous to its surroundings.

The hunger grew the more he walked. He started feeling something akin to a magnetic pull that wanted to draw him in and consume him. It was uncomfortably hot and chilling at once.

"Eli, it's over there. Hanging from the ceiling."

"Yes, I see it." Elias swallowed and took Tristan's hand to steady himself. He came to a stop once again, not far from the center of the chamber. "The Flower of the Sky."

It was even more hideous than he could have imagined. Lyrana's Flower had been black, but the corruption had been mostly superficial, limited to the Flower itself. Here, the taint of the dark unknown was everywhere. It had radiated out from the Flower and forced itself into the vines that were the basis of the spirit-lines that held the tapestry of the world together. The corruption was nearly tangible, and the plant stems themselves looked diseased, bloated with ichor that threatened to burst out of them at the slightest touch.

The greatest horror by far, however, was the thing that dangled from the nexus of vines, its majesty having been utterly destroyed.

Traces of its former red petals were faintly visible, but they were the dying gasp of a critically injured life form. The hunger had overtaken it so thoroughly that its horrific crystals had pierced the Flower itself, growing like deformed mushrooms colonizing necrotic flesh. The crystals appeared to drink in the light of the sun, and they transformed it into the now-familiar prismatic shades that were nothing more than an aberration of light, a facsimile of color on a backdrop of purest black. Each crystal, transparent though it was, appeared to Elias like a puncture in the fabric of reality, an object that should not exist.

The hunger in the Flower registered his presence and focused on him. His will crumbled under its command.

Elias reached out his hand. The hunger drew him in, compounding the furnace-like heat of the Flower's energy. He knew he would be destroyed if he touched it, but there was no denying the call. He would willingly give himself to satiate the darkness, if only for an instant. He had to do it. He *wanted* to do it.

"Eli, snap out of it!" Tristan yelled. He tugged on Elias's hand.

Elias pushed Tristan away.

"Oh no," Tristan said. "We're not doing this again."

Tristan dropped Lyrana's scale and grabbed Elias around the waist. Elias struggled in his grip, but Tristan was relentless. He forcefully dragged Elias several meters away and dumped him next to a bone pile. Then he went back for his scale.

Elias's mind cleared. He backed farther away from the Flower of his own volition and took out Sizzra's spine. The contact of his fingers around its smooth surface helped, and he was able to recover fully.

"It's horrible," he said when Tristan came back. "The Flower's nearly dead."

"That black thing is everywhere. It's much worse than back at the atoll."

"Yes. It wants to devour us."

"We won't let it. Hold this," Tristan told him, handing Lyrana's scale and his shock spear to Elias.

"Tristan, wait!"

Unheeding, Tristan sprinted forward until he was almost below the Flower and then jumped. He reached above his head at the apex of his path, but he hadn't even come close. His fingers were at least three meters below the nearest black petal.

Tristan landed hard. He backed up to get a running start and tried again twice more, but he failed to grab the Flower each time.

"It's too high up," Tristan complained. "I can't reach it on my own."

"Maybe if you climb on my shoulders," Elias suggested.

"No way. You'd have to get close to that thing, and I'm not risking it. Hand me my spear. Maybe I can knock it off the vines."

Elias gave Tristan the spear, which still worked, although it was dented and tarnished after their long journey.

"Don't damage the Flower," Elias warned him. "We need to restore it later."

"Don't worry. Stand back."

Tristan crouched slightly and adopted a running stance with the spear in one hand. The clearly defined muscles in his legs contracted in the split second before he powered forward.

He froze.

You will stop, little human males, a voice echoed in Elias's head. *Sneaky, treacherous creatures.*

Tristan made a choked sound in his throat and appeared to struggle against unseen restraints, but it was no use. He spun around, away from the Flower, and stood up straight with a jerk. A vein on his forehead became visible under the strain he was enduring.

Elias rushed over to him. He had just reached Tristan when the bloodred light of dusk was eclipsed by an enormous shadow that rose at the far end of the chamber, obstructing the view of the sky.

Elias's heart constricted with despair as Dresde stepped through the entrance to the cave. Her great body blocked the light as she flapped, seeming to drown the entire space in darkness. For an instant her shape appeared as if wreathed in shadow, and only her three glowing red eyes blazed with hostility and sly intelligence.

To think your plan nearly succeeded, she hissed, her sinuous body flowing into the space. Every beat of her membranous wings was accompanied by a burst of hot air that reeked of burning rock. *I should have known you were working together with Samantha. Insects! But now you* die.

She landed hard enough to make the ground tremble. She approached Elias and Tristan carefully, and her gaze never wavered from Tristan, who was still frozen under her spell.

With a blur of silver, serrated missiles flew through the air.

Vanor roared out a booming challenge that made the stalactites on the ceiling reverberate; at the same time, he fired three long metallic-plated spines that glinted in the light. Narev and Siv added their voices to the sound a moment later, and the three male wurl, last survivors of Sizzra's brood, attacked the one who had slain their queen. They fired spines as they charged and, snarling, pounced from three sides at once.

Dresde reacted instantly. She jumped with such speed that most spines missed their mark and buried themselves in the rock instead. The few that struck her simply clattered off her impervious violet scales.

In response to the attack, she answered with a roar of her own as she came down and tucked her wings close to her body. An instant before Vanor reached her, she coiled into a ball and then stretched out with shocking agility, her tail cracking through the air like a whip.

"Look out!" Elias shouted, but it was too late.

Dresde's tail found its mark and struck Vanor on the side. Silver scales cracked and splintered. Vanor projected a single thought drowned in bewilderment and pain before he was catapulted through the air by the force of the impact and sailed out the entrance to the cave, his body limp. An instant later he fell out of sight to tumble down the mountain.

"No!" Tristan yelled. "Vanor!"

Narev and Siv did not waste the chance Dresde's brief distraction gave them. They seized her and dug their claws into her flesh.

Dresde screamed in pain and threw herself to the ground, rolling to knock them off. Narev and Siv held on firmly at first, firing spines intermittently, but when

Dresde unfurled her wings and blasted the space around her with a gust of air, they very nearly lost their grip. Each was barely holding on to one of her back legs.

Die, die! Dresde yelled.

Narev bit her leg, hard. Siv fired two spines that punctured the membrane on her left wing. Dresde projected waves of panic with her mind and kicked off from the ground, flapping so vigorously that the piles of bones on the ground flew in every direction in the hurricane of her downdraft.

Twisting in the air, she launched herself out of the cave.

"Narev, let go!" Elias urged. "Siv!"

He and Tristan watched in earthbound powerlessness as Dresde hovered in the air outside and, arching her flexible back, clamped her jaws down on Siv.

Siv fired every spine left on his body and forced Dresde to snatch her head away, but it came at a cost. He lost his grip and fell.

Dresde roared and dived back into the cave, angling the fall so her back leg would hit the ground first. Narev stood no chance. He bore the brunt of the impact, twitched once, and then lay still. Triumphant, Dresde smacked his body with her tail and sent him careening over the edge like his brothers.

"Narev!" Elias shouted. His vision clouded over with rage and he charged, weapon in hand, straight at the wurl queen.

Tristan roared out a wordless battle cry, running at her at the same time.

Dresde whipped her head to face them and bared her fangs as they approached. She crouched on the ground and lifted her front foot in a single fluid motion.

That's enough! she proclaimed.

Her talons began to glow. A second later she swiped her claw across the ground in a violent arc that forced Elias and Tristan to stop before they were torn in half. Dresde had carved a deep swath in the ground itself, and its molten edges were glowing. She had sliced solid rock as if it had been butter.

The two men looked up at Dresde in defiant silence. The ground in front of them sizzled as its glow faded away. Fuming, the queen radiated heat from her entire body, and her wings quivered with the rage she projected with her mind.

I have waited for this moment for some time, she said. She was looking at Elias now. Her voice appeared strangely calm, a stark contrast to the glow that surrounded her feet and illuminated her from beneath, making her appear tenebrous. *There is no more help, human with my sister's eyes. You will pay for daring to attack a goddess.*

"You'll have to go through me!" Tristan shouted in response, activating his shock spear. The endpoints of the weapon crackled and came alive with electricity.

"Tristan, no!"

How touching, Dresde said in open sarcasm. She directed her speech at Elias. *I wonder, is this your mate? What would it do to you to see him suffer? To see him die?*

"Leave Tristan alone!" Elias yelled. "Your fight is with me."

He jumped over the cooling swath of torn-up ground and held his spine aloft, ready to attack and simultaneously shielding Tristan with his body. Silently he prayed Tristan would understand. He was going to try to distract Dresde as long as he could, even if it cost him his life, so Tristan would have another chance to grab the Flower.

Almost as if she had read his mind, Dresde slithered on the ground and positioned herself so she would be standing between them and her only weakness.

You think you are so clever, all of you, Dresde said, *but I see all! You will never touch the Flower of the Sky as long as I am its guardian. You will know despair itself instead!*

The sound of another pair of flapping wings reached Elias. It was coming from the cave opening.

Just in time, Dresde commented, sounding pleased. *Doran, this way. Bring the hostages over.*

Elias glanced back. The sun had already set, but the twilight was enough for him to notice a magnificent cobalt-scaled male wurl.

On his back were two people. One of them was the girl he had once fought, Samantha.

Elias's heart almost skipped a beat. The other one was his little brother.

"Eli!" Oscar yelled at the top of his lungs, "Eli!"

"Oscar!"

Elias made as if to go to them, but Doran soared overhead with surprising agility and brought his riders to Dresde instead.

A family reunion! Dresde mocked them. *Doran, throw them on the ground!*

The male wurl complied immediately. He landed and bucked at the same time, sending both Oscar and Samantha sailing through the air. They hit the ground and cried out in pain at Dresde's feet.

"No!" Elias shouted.

Dresde lifted one of her glowing claws immediately above Oscar's head. The wicked talons quivered with anticipation, and her eyes flashed.

Witness my revenge.

chapter 30.
crystalline

OSCAR ROLLED over on the ground so he was facing the stalactite-thorned ceiling and tried to get his breath back. He had fallen hard, but the pain of the impact and the struggle to fill his lungs with air were nothing compared to the horrifying vision of Dresde towering over him and Samantha, her jaws bathed in the white-hot glow of her talons.

"Eli!" Oscar screamed in desperation. He was going to be torn apart.

He kicked off the ground, trying to get up, but Dresde focused her gleeful gaze on him and his muscles seized and stopped obeying him.

Enough struggle, she said.

She swiped at him.

A spine rocketed through the air and knocked her claw out of the way, destabilizing Dresde's attack enough that the nearest talon sank into the ground not a meter away from Oscar's head, close enough that it felt like he had opened the door to an oven and stuck his head inside. The sudden impact broke the mental spell, and the bonds holding Oscar in place snapped.

He wasted no time. He scrabbled away and jumped to his feet alongside Samantha.

Another spine whistled by, quicker than vision, and embedded itself in the vulnerable connective tissue between Dresde's talons.

She raised her voice in an earsplitting scream and jumped back, narrowly avoiding two more spines.

Why won't you die*?*

From the shadows at the entrance to the cave, a veritable mountain of muscle approached. Oscar gasped when the largest male wurl he had ever seen came into full view. His shoulders and back bristled with long serrated spines, and his eye cluster gleamed in the twilit haze that outlined his massive heft. He was limping, but the ferocious aura he projected made his wounds inconsequential. He was dangerous in a primal way that left no room for any other sensation but fear.

The wurl came ever closer slowly, rotating his head from side to side, his jaws half-open in a deep-voiced snarl. Oscar realized that many of the silver scales on his side had shattered, and his middle right foot was bent at an unnatural angle. It looked broken.

"Vanor!" Tristan yelled.

The wurl ignored Tristan's voice. Oscar backed away out of instinct, reaching for Samantha's hand and leading her out of the path of the enraged Spine male.

"He's enormous," Samantha whispered.

Vanor fired another spine, but now Dresde was ready for him. She swatted it out of the air with apparent ease.

Brave little male, Dresde said with open sarcasm. *You may be the strongest of your brood, but not even your mate could kill me!*

That was evidently the wrong thing to say. Vanor growled even deeper in his throat and projected a simple but clear idea with perfect clarity.

He was summoning his brothers.

Two roars answered him, and Oscar watched in astonishment as two other hulking outlines staggered into the cave, hurt as well but radiating hostility and determination. Even the wurl with no spines left on his body looked ferocious.

"Narev!" Elias said, his face a mixture of surprise and relief. "Siv!"

Fearless, Doran jumped in front of the path of any more spines and unfurled his wings to their full extent, appearing three times as big for a moment. He roared in defiance, his guttural cry completely different from the metallic grating of the Spine wurl.

"Doran, no," Samantha whispered. She clutched Oscar's hand more tightly. "They are too many."

Doran crouched, ready to pounce. His three enemies fanned out, heads low, and prepared to strike.

There will be no need for that, Dresde said, her every word drenched in dismissive overconfidence. *Doran. Move out of the way.*

Doran hesitated. To Oscar, his emotions were clear. He wanted to protect Dresde.

I said move! Dresde boomed, and she smacked Doran with the side of her tail. Doran cried out in surprise and reeled from the unexpected betrayal.

"Doran!" Samantha yelled.

Dresde ignored everyone but her three scaled opponents. She yanked Vanor's spine out of her foot with her teeth.

This has gone on for too long. I decree your end, last males of my sister's brood. Even as she spoke, something started moving in the ceiling of the cave. *You should have fallen to your deaths instead of defying me again, but now your fate shall be worse than death. You will give your essence to the hunger!*

Dresde plunged her front feet into the ground, and something appeared to flow into the rock, detaching itself from Dresde's body. It looked like a shadow that was gone in an instant.

The ceiling rumbled. Some stalactites fell in the vicinity of the three Spine wurl, cracking on impact.

Oscar looked up, and he wasn't the only one.

"Narev!" Elias shouted. "Look out!"

It was too late. The vines that spread across the ceiling in a latticework of green and black came to life and, writhing, shot down like harpoons.

The Spine wurl tried to jump out of the way, but the vines were too quick. They snatched the three of them out of the ground like the malformed fingers of a grasping hand and coiled themselves around their bodies. The wurl struggled, but more vines burst forth and ensnared them more tightly.

"No!" Tristan yelled. He ran toward Vanor, brandishing his shock spear, but the vines retreated and hoisted their entangled prey out of reach.

Yes, Dresde replied, evidently enjoying herself. *Now watch, humans. The prodigious life energy of these three will provide nourishment to that which still slumbers. With this offering, it may even awaken!*

The vines tightened. There was a sickening *crunch*, as of metal being warped. The captive wurl projected defiance at first, and Narev even fired one of his spines into the nearest plant.

Then the darkness came. It sped through the vines like a voracious infection, black overtaking green, and it attached itself to the wurl. Their scales went dark. There was a single spike of horror coming from their three minds before their bodies went limp. Their heads sagged into their bonds, and the red luminescence in their eyes dimmed to barely a spark.

Thorns began to grow out of the dark constricting vines, glassy and curved, sprouting all along their lengths.

"Narev?" Elias asked, his voice shaking. "Narev?" He turned to Dresde. "What did you do to them?"

I did nothing, Dresde said innocently. *And they are not yet dead. The hunger takes time digesting its prey. Is that not so, Samantha?*

"Stop this," she said, gritting her teeth. She let go of Oscar's hand and raised her fists. "You have killed enough people. This ends here."

Dresde laughed. *And what will you do? You may be the queen of your human brood, but you are nothing compared to me, nothing!*

"I will stop you," she declared.

Despite having known her for months, Oscar took a step back from Samantha. She looked like an assassin about to strike her target down.

Do try, Dresde prodded her, *but I promised you a fitting punishment, did I not? You have seen the first part of it already. Now for the finale. Doran!*

Like a trained soldier, Doran jumped forward. He held one of his wings against his body where Dresde had struck him earlier, but there was no hint of pain in the thoughts he projected. There was only obedience.

Dresde's malevolent face towered over Doran, making her appear like a puppet master about to pull on the strings.

Do you think I did not know about your pitiful attempts to befriend Doran, Samantha? I know of every interaction you ever had with him. I know of how he saved you when you were still but a whelp. I know of your so-called secret place, where you would go to cry so no one could see you. But I could! You thought you were smart, but I was always there! Doran was never your friend. He followed my orders and deceived you from the start.

Doran stalked forward and bared his fangs at Samantha. He looked nothing like himself.

"No." Samantha said in a low voice. "You lie."

How does this last betrayal feel? Tell me!

"Doran," Samantha pleaded, ignoring Dresde. Tears glistened in her eyes. "I am here. Do not do this."

He will. He has no choice.

Samantha kept her gaze on the wurl who had been her companion for years. "There is always a choice. You are free to make your own."

You attempt to reason with a male*? They are little more than animals!*

"No!" Samantha snapped. She lifted her head to look at Dresde. "That is your greatest mistake. We are all living creatures. You may be stronger, but that does not give you the right to treat others like slaves. A true queen rules with compassion, not cruelty."

Let me show you how much your compassion is worth, Dresde sneered. *Doran. Kill her.*

Doran howled and attacked.

He pounced on Samantha, but she somersaulted backward and avoided his gnashing teeth.

"You can fight her!" Samantha urged. "You can defy her!"

Doran appeared not to hear her. He charged and swiped at her midsection, but Samantha jumped out of the way and grabbed a bone from the nearest pile. She hurled it at Doran, who was forced to stop briefly to avoid the projectile.

Samantha used the pause well. She sprinted across the floor of the eyrie nearly all the way to the edge as if looking for something and threw herself to the ground at the last second, avoiding Doran's tail by a millimeter. She snatched the object of her search even as she fell, rolled on the ground, and jumped upright in a graceful flow.

"Stay back!" she warned, holding a sharpened yult spear with both hands. She crouched into a fighting stance, one hand in front of the other, the point of her weapon aimed at Doran's face. "I do not want to hurt you."

Doran's onslaught halted momentarily as he considered the new threat. He growled, and his talons began to glow. They were even more terrifying than usual in the growing murk as twilight faded fast from the world.

Samantha and Doran circled one another in a deadly dance that appeared to be perfectly balanced.

Oscar's link buzzed.

"I know your weak points," Samantha threatened Doran. "I have seen you fight many times. You have seen how deadly I am with this weapon. Stand. *Down*."

She bluffs, Dresde countered, slithering closer to the fight. *She is merely a human with a stick. Cut her down, Doran. Uphold your honor as my mate!*

"She does not care about you," Samantha said, keeping her voice even. "All she cares about is herself. You have seen how she treats the vulnerable eggs of the next generation, *your* children!"

Doran paused at the words.

"She crushed many under an avalanche of rock last time we were here and barely noticed," Samantha continued. "To her they are worthless when they should be precious. And you defend her?"

Finish her! Do it now!

"She is mad, Doran. She fights for the hunger that has corrupted her heart."

Obey me!

"I fight for life. And I trust you."

Samantha's shoulders relaxed and she breathed out, letting go of her spear. Even as it fell, Doran launched himself at her, glowing talons outstretched, deadly fangs lit from beneath.

Samantha smiled.

Doran's eyes blazed in the darkness. He unfurled his wings, flapped once, and twisted in the air, abruptly changing his trajectory away from Samantha. He landed in a pile of bones that sizzled under his feet and jumped upright, still terrifying but looking like himself at last. He radiated a pure emotion, unmistakable in its simplicity.

Love.

Samantha walked up to him and reached out her hand. Doran touched it briefly with his snout.

"I love you too," she said to him.

That was a mistake.

Dresde opened her wings wide. The light of her talons dwarfed Doran's, and when she took a step the entire cave ceiling appeared to tremble. More stalactites fell all around them, and Oscar was forced to jump out of the way when one crashed dangerously close to him.

Betrayer, Dresde accused Doran.

In response, he positioned himself so he would stand between Dresde and Samantha. He roared out his defiance and projected no fear whatsoever.

Very well. Die.

Dresde attacked so fast that her talons were a blur of light streaks in the darkness. Doran jumped out of the way and struck Dresde's shoulder with his back feet, leaving glowing parallel marks on her scales. When she swiped at him next, Doran dived underneath her and slithered on the ground, twisting so he would be able to rake her belly with all four of his feet.

Dresde reared up on her hind legs and cried out in pain.

"Yes!" Oscar said. For an instant he allowed himself to hope that Doran would be strong enough to do the impossible.

Then Doran froze. He was still lying on the ground, his wings under his body, and he wasn't moving. Oscar felt the razor-sharp intensity of Dresde's will only in passing, but he knew that the object of her silent command would find it impossible to resist.

Dresde said nothing as she dropped back down on all fours and covered the distance separating them in an instant. Doran made a choked sort of sound, as if struggling to break free, but his body remained paralyzed.

Dresde brought up her left front claw and stabbed Doran in the chest.

"No!" Samantha screamed. "Doran!"

Oscar felt the moment when he died, a ripping away of something incredibly delicate, like the last hint of a beautiful dream vanishing after being jolted awake in the darkness of deepest night.

Goodbye, traitor, Dresde said, but her mind-voice trembled for the first time. She looked at her bloodied claw, and the color of her scales appeared to waver for an instant, shifting away from violet and into a red that reminded Oscar of the petals of the Flower.

"Murderer!" Samantha yelled.

Oscar's link buzzed again. This time he looked down, wrenching his attention away from the scene, and realized it was a text message from Elias.

Tristan hoists you up. Get Flower. RUN.

Oscar glanced behind him, heart hammering in his chest. Tristan had stealthily positioned himself underneath the Flower while Dresde was distracted.

In a flash, Oscar understood.

He ran to him with every last bit of strength he had.

Behind him he heard Samantha yelling, but he tuned it out. Dresde stomped, but he ignored it. He was close. He glanced at Elias, whose eyes were full of silent intensity. Tristan was nodding, urging Oscar along. Tristan linked his hands, palms up, and crouched as he held them forward in front of his hips.

Oscar was a second away.

What is that little human male—no!

Oscar jumped onto Tristan's hands. He braced himself, and Tristan catapulted him up into the air with a powerful burst of strength. Oscar compensated for the dizzying acceleration and stretched out his arms as he sailed toward the ceiling, reaching for the Flower.

Stop!

Dresde's iron will wrapped itself around Oscar, and his fingers froze. An instant later he heard Samantha yell and then a loud *crack.* Something broke Dresde's spell for a single moment.

It was enough. He grabbed the Flower of the Sky with both arms and tore it out of its mooring using his entire weight as gravity pulled him down.

Dresde screamed. Elias screamed. Oscar realized he was about to have a bad fall a second before he hit the ground, but Tristan caught him. The two of them crashed down on some bones with loud grunts.

Tristan was first on his knees. "Oscar, are you okay?"

"Yeah," Oscar panted. The object in his arms felt cold. "I—whoa!"

He threw the Flower as far away as he could. It was moving, convulsing like a dying creature.

Tristan helped him to his feet.

"Eli?" Oscar asked. It was much harder to see now in the darkness of early night. "Eli!"

"Eli!" Tristan echoed, and together the two of them rushed over to where Elias was lying prostrate on the ground.

"I'm okay," Elias muttered. "I'm okay. Just the shock."

Oscar's eyes brimmed with tears, and he hugged Elias with all of his strength. Sniffling, he helped his older brother up.

"Eli," Oscar whispered. "You're here! You came for me. You came!"

"I'm here," Elias replied, fiercely returning the hug once he was on his feet. "You're safe. I was so scared."

"I knew you'd save me," Oscar said. "I knew it."

Elias placed his hands on Oscar's shoulders. "I think you saved *us*."

Oscar looked at Tristan, who was standing to the side. "Thank you, Tristan. You also came to save me. You didn't have to, but you came."

Tristan grinned. "Least I could do."

A faint tremor ran through the ground. Anxiety surged through Oscar's body once again. "Where's Dresde?"

"Here," Samantha answered in the distance. Her voice was dull. "She's over here."

"Let's go," Elias said, picking up Sizzra's spine.

Tristan gathered his shock spear and something that looked to Oscar like a shield.

The three of them activated the flashlights on their links and rushed deeper into the lugubrious space of the eyrie. Oscar spared one last glance at the quivering thing that was Dresde's Flower and then looked away in disgust. Their three beams of light pierced the darkness as they walked. The vines on the ceiling were moving ever so slightly, and the thorns along their lengths appeared to drink in the light of Oscar's link when he aimed it overhead.

He did not look at the place where the Flower had been attached to the three thickest vines. Something was making a noise there, and he was afraid to see what it was. Instead he jumped over a pile of bones and ran the rest of the way to where Samantha was standing, black spear in hand.

Lying before her, seemingly paralyzed, was Dresde.

"Samantha!" Oscar yelled, skidding to a stop next to her. "Are you okay?"

"I am. Thank you, Oscar. You succeeded where I failed, and now this monster is helpless before us."

Oscar glanced at Dresde. She was lying on her side, one of her wings crumpled underneath her body. Her eye cluster still shone, but she did not move, and she no longer projected her terrifying aura of mental pressure and stifling heat. It was almost surreal to contemplate her while standing barely a couple of steps away from the deadly curved talons that could melt solid rock but which were now utterly devoid of their glow. In the light of his link, Dresde's scales appeared an even deeper purple, but instead of looking beautiful, they now reminded Oscar of rotting fruit.

Elias and Tristan joined them, but they remained silent. Samantha stepped forward and placed her right foot on Dresde's chest.

"Murderer," Samantha hissed, sounding nothing like herself. Her voice held a venomous note of hatred. "You killed my brothers. You killed Doran. You killed my *father*."

She set her foot back on the ground and pointed her spear at Dresde. With barely a pause, she placed the tip of her weapon on the edge of a specific scale on the wurl queen's chest, a particularly large violet plate that was thicker than the rest, as though it protected something important.

Samantha braced herself and pushed until she penetrated the space between the scales. Then she shifted her stance. She heaved the shaft to the side using her entire body weight. The spear became a lever, and the scale began to move.

"What are you doing?" Oscar asked her.

Samantha grunted and threw herself at the spear again. The scale ripped out of its mooring with a sickening tearing sound, and she pushed it out of the way with a wordless cry.

As though dampened with great distance, Oscar felt an echo of Dresde's pain. Her chest scale clattered to the ground.

"I know wurl very well," Samantha said in a sinister tone. "I have seen many males die over the years. When they fought for dominance for the right to be Dresde's mate, Doran ripped this same scale out of the chest of his fiercest rival before killing him. It is the heart scale."

Oscar shined his flashlight on the exposed flesh Samantha had uncovered. It was raw and red, and it twitched ever so slightly in a rhythm that could only have corresponded to the beating of a massive heart.

Samantha lifted her spear above her head, gripping it with both hands. Her lip was curled in a sneer, and her eyes appeared to blaze with anger.

"Wurl may have three eyes," Samantha whispered, "but they have only one heart."

She brought her spear down.

"Samantha, no!" Oscar shouted and jumped in the way of the weapon.

She was forced to stop. "What are you doing?"

"Don't," Oscar pleaded. "This isn't you."

"How dare you?" she hissed. "Stand aside!"

"No!" Oscar shouted, swallowing his fear. "If you kill her, you'll also be a murderer. You will be no better than her."

"She killed my father!" Samantha yelled. A tear rolled down her cheek. "She killed Jörgen. She killed Erik. She made my family and me her slaves!"

"There has to be another way," Oscar insisted. In desperation he looked at Elias and Tristan, but they shook their heads with evident sadness. He met her eyes again. "Don't do this, Samantha. Please. Anger is heavy, remember?"

Her expression wavered for an instant. Hatred was replaced with sorrow, loss, pain.

Her shoulders sagged.

"I am sorry, Oscar," Samantha said quietly. "There is no other way."

She kicked Oscar in the chest so fast that he was sailing through the air before he fully registered what had happened. He crashed into Elias and was horrified to see Samantha lift her weapon again, roaring out her hatred. A second later Samantha thrust her spear down and stabbed the wurl queen in the chest.

Vines shot down from the ceiling like striking snakes aiming their fangs at Samantha. One of them snapped her spear in two before she could sink it fully into her target.

"Samantha!" Oscar yelled.

She jumped out of the way and narrowly avoided being grabbed by another vine. One of its glassy thorns scratched her cheek.

"Watch out!" Tristan shouted.

More vines came, but they were not after the humans. They were after Dresde.

Dozens wrapped themselves around the queen as though shielding her from harm. They enveloped her, forming a cocoon of darkness that bristled with glassy thorns that consumed the light from the links and projected the same horrid palette of every color in the rainbow, like miniature distorted prisms.

Despite her heft, the vines lifted Dresde in her entirety, out of the reach of any of them. She now hung like the three Spine wurl, motionless and unreachable.

"No!" Samantha cursed and threw the half of the spear she still held at Dresde. It struck its mark and sank into one of the protective vines, which burst with the impact and spurted out a black liquid that stank of death. Dresde herself was unharmed.

"We need to move," Elias said. "Oscar, Tristan, get the Flower. Go."

"Yes," Tristan said immediately. "Oscar, come on."

The vines overhead were moving. Oscar did not want to, but he left Samantha behind for a moment and ran back to the place where he had dropped the Flower.

It was still there, lying on its side much like Dresde had been. It was no longer twitching.

"What the—" Oscar said.

The Flower was now showing hints of a beautiful crimson sheen. The petals held noticeable traces of the color in large splotches, and it looked as though the black was slowly draining out of it. The small crystals that had grown on its flesh were gone.

"You grab it," Tristan said to him. "I'll cover you if any vines try to attack us."

Oscar scooped the Flower out of some bones and held it against his chest, although it remained as clammy as when he had first torn it out. His flashlight showed him a pool of black liquid on the ground where the Flower had lain. It looked like infected blood that had poured out of a wound. There were also glassy shards strewn about, floating on the foul substance.

"This way!" Elias commanded. "We have to find the egg!"

"Vanor," Tristan whispered, shining his light above them. The three Spine wurl still hung motionless, their eye clusters barely shining. "We'll be back for you guys."

"Hurry!" Elias said.

Oscar and Tristan ran back to where Elias and Samantha were standing.

"Samantha, you can't reach her," Elias was saying. "We need to get out of here. Tell me, where is Sizzra's egg?"

Samantha appeared not to hear. She was still staring at the ceiling. "I failed again," she said.

"No, you didn't," Oscar told her. He put the Flower in the crook of his left elbow and reached for

Samantha's hand. "Let's go. Eli, Tristan, I know where the white egg is. Follow me."

Samantha allowed herself to be led away. Oscar held her hand firmly and led the party to the far end of the cave. He stopped at the place where boulders blocked the way.

"Here," he indicated. "We can move that rock there. It'll lead us out of here, where the eggs are."

"Got it," Elias answered. "Everyone, let's do it. Oscar, you hold on to the Flower."

Although reluctant at first, Samantha helped Tristan and Elias to move the nearest boulder. Oscar stood to the side, anxiously looking over his shoulder in case Dresde came back or freed herself somehow, but he saw nothing of the sort.

"Tristan, put your shock spear here," Elias said. "Samantha, help me push it down."

"I think the boulder is stuck," Tristan said. "Hold on a second. I'm going to try something."

Oscar stepped back involuntarily when Tristan activated his shock spear. Both ends of the weapon crackled with electricity, blindingly bright in the darkness.

Samantha pointed. "What is that?"

"Patrol weapon," Tristan explained. "Let me see if I can carve a little bit out of this rock here so we can move it."

He applied one of the glowing tips of the spear to the boulder, but it sizzled out. He did the same with the other and was also unsuccessful. The rock they were trying to move was taller than all of them and wouldn't budge. Oscar remembered how easily Dresde had pushed it when he had last been there, and the recollection made him realize how strong the wurl queen was.

"Okay, whatever," Tristan said. "It's going to break, but I think it's the only way. Samantha, Eli, I'm going to brace this against the rock, and you guys jump on it when I say so."

"Did you say jump?" Samantha asked.

"Yes. Ready?"

Elias and Samantha nodded.

"Great. On three. One, two, now!"

They jumped at the same time as Tristan used his own body weight to push. There was a loud *snap* and then a much deeper *crack*, accompanied by a groaning of rock shifting.

"Out of the way!" Tristan yelled.

They moved aside a few moments before the boulder tilted forward, first slowly and then much faster. It hit the ground with a crunching noise and kicked up a cloud of dirt.

"Nice," Elias said, coughing. "Too bad about your spear, though."

"Had to happen," Tristan replied, kicking away the broken halves of his weapon. "Oscar, Samantha? You guys okay?"

"I'm fine," Oscar said. "Samantha?"

"I am here."

"Okay," Oscar continued. "Follow me, everyone. Watch out. There's a drop ahead."

He went first, followed by Samantha. Tristan and Elias brought up the rear. Oscar picked his way carefully among the rocks, shining his light everywhere so he would know whether it was safe. It was treacherous going for the first minute, but he suddenly found himself outside, at the upper edge of the caldera at the heart of the volcano.

He had been there once before, during the day. At night, the landscape around him was simultaneously terrifying and spectacular.

Although the darkness hid the far crater walls from sight, the water that formed a lake perhaps one hundred meters below him was visible as a nearly perfect mirror of the sky overhead. All three of the moons shone down upon them, bathing the scenery in a quiet silver glow, and a chill wind coursed through the enormous space. The water wasn't bubbling or smoking as it had previously been, but Oscar found the apparent calm somehow more ominous. He did not think the volcano was going to erupt, but there was something about the place that he found deeply disturbing. It was more than the fact that he felt as though he was gazing down at a hostile alien environment. It had to do with something his mind couldn't quite place.

The lava added to the otherworldliness of their surroundings. It glowed red, spewing forth slowly but steadily out of many cracks along the edge of the crater wall. Immediately below them, the largest crack of all had enabled lava to pool on the ground in a hollow depression that was close to the water. The heat coming from the lava reached Oscar very quickly, and he started to sweat in spite of the wind. There was a sulfurous smell in the air, and he was keenly aware of the fact that one false step would send him tumbling down to molten rock and a horrible death.

In the glowing pool were several objects. Two in particular were clearly visible. They appeared dark due to the light, but Oscar knew better. He knew one of them was the pure white of newly fallen snow, and the other was a deep crimson, not unlike lava itself.

"Down there," he said to the rest. "That's Sizzra's egg, and Dresde's egg too."

"I see them," Tristan said.

"I can sense them," Elias added. "They sleep, both of them."

"We need to climb down," Oscar explained. "Careful, though. I haven't done this before."

Still in the lead, he picked his way down the crater slope with as much care as he could muster, balancing the Flower first in one arm, then in both. Boulders gave way to rocks as he descended, which in turn gave way to gravel. He tried to go down at an angle so he would skirt the lava, and although it was nerve-racking, Oscar managed to make it down to flat ground in one piece. He now walked over soft sand the same deep black as the oceanside cliffs. The mineral stench was stronger where he stood, and he could hear the water in the crater lake as it lapped oddly against the shores. Looking up, Oscar felt as though the crater itself wanted to swallow him. He had never felt so confined and yet so exposed at once.

Elias approached the lava pool first. Oscar and the others followed.

"I'm here, Sizzra," Elias whispered, stopping at the edge of the glowing viscous liquid. "I've kept my vow."

The pool was large but narrow, and Elias used his iridescent spine to reach out over the lava. When he made contact with the white egg, he gasped.

"Eli?" Oscar asked.

"I'm okay," Elias responded. "She's in there. She's alive."

It took a few minutes, but Elias was able to poke and prod the egg until it came within reach. He pushed it out of the lava with a final effort, and Oscar approached, illuminating the egg with his link.

"It's really beautiful," he observed. He had forgotten how it looked, but he remembered what it had felt like to hold on to it on the day Dresde had kidnapped him.

"Don't touch it yet," Tristan said. "Let it cool down."

"The other egg," Samantha mentioned, speaking up. "We should also collect it."

"That Flyer queen is innocent," Elias warned her. "Whatever Dresde did, her daughter is not to blame."

"I know," she replied with a sigh. She sounded spent. "I want to keep it safe. I don't think it's supposed to float in the lava like that."

"Okay," Elias said, although he looked doubtful. "I'll try to fish it out."

A few minutes later, Elias had managed to take the egg out of its liquid cradle, and he gently pushed it so it would be lying next to Sizzra's egg.

"It's like they're jewels," Oscar said, admiring the two eggs.

Samantha knelt next to the crimson egg. She scooped it into her arms.

"Whoa!" Tristan exclaimed. "Drop it, you'll get burned!"

"Samantha!" Oscar yelled.

"No need for concern," she said, too calmly to be in agonizing pain. "The egg is not hot. Dresde and her brood are impervious to high temperatures. The other eggs will be the same," she added, pointing at the far end of the lava pool. A veritable mound of sky-blue eggs lay partially in the lava. Some had been smashed, but many were still intact.

"Do you feel it?" Elias asked Samantha, pointing at the egg she carried. "The life within?"

Samantha closed her eyes for a moment. "I do. A little bit."

"All right, as soon the white egg is cool enough to carry, we should get going," Tristan told them. "We'll climb back up and try to free Vanor, Narev, and Siv. If they're okay, they'll be able to get us down the mountain."

"If not, I know of a way down through the volcano," Samantha offered. "Oscar has taken the route as well."

"Good," Tristan said, nodding. "The sooner we're out of here, the better."

"And what about Dresde?" Oscar asked. "Do we just leave her there?"

Yes, a sarcastic voice said from above. *What about me?*

They all gasped. Oscar looked up at the opening in the crater wall they had used to descend and was dismayed to see a slender head appear with an unhurried motion, her eye cluster glinting in the darkness.

You should have killed me when you had the chance, Samantha, Dresde said, bursting through the rock with a mighty heave. Boulders gave way under her onslaught, and her entire body broke through an instant later. She jumped down, flapping once before she landed.

She hit the ground too hard, however, and she stumbled. Oscar noticed her right wing hadn't opened fully.

I will admit, I underestimated humans. And particularly males. You are so very deceitful.

As she spoke she stalked over the black sand, whipping her tail in the air. The glow from the lava made her appear even more dangerous than before. When she opened her jaws, sharp teeth glistened in the ruddy light.

"Stay back," Elias warned her. "We have your Flower. Samantha has your egg."

Are you trying to blackmail me, human with my sister's eyes?

"I'm warning you," Elias replied, holding his spine in front of him like a sword. "Leave us alone or we destroy your Flower, your only daughter, and your entire legacy."

Dresde laughed. *Such threats! I can see your thoughts, human.* You *are bound to the world, as I am. You will never harm the Flower willingly. To destroy it would be to destroy all life in a third of the planet. You cannot even touch it!*

"Maybe he can't, but I can," Oscar said, surprising himself.

Dresde pierced him with her laser focus. Oscar staggered under the mental onslaught, but he didn't give way.

I think I will kill you last, smallest male. I see why Samantha has made you her personal slave.

"Oscar is not my slave, and he never was," Samantha said loudly. She started walking forward, straight to where Dresde was. In her arms she carried the egg that reflected light like a ruby. "He is my friend. Like Doran was my friend."

Dresde flinched visibly at the mention of the name.

"Indeed," Samantha continued, relentless. "Your *mate*. The one you murdered in cold blood."

He defied me, Dresde growled. *A mere male defied me, the goddess of the world! He valued your life more than my will, and the punishment for that is death.*

"He did not value only my life. He valued *all* life." Samantha gestured with one arm all around her. "These are his children. This is his daughter. You are supposed to be their guardian, and instead you have betrayed them!"

I....

For the first time, Dresde appeared to be at a loss for words.

Behind her, black vines slithered out of the cave opening.

"If you want to kill me, go ahead," Samantha challenged her, "but if you attack, I will smash this egg and kill your daughter. *You* might not have been able to break your sister's egg, but I guarantee you I can break yours. I am not of this world, remember? I am an alien, an invader. Your laws do not apply to me. Whatever protects the queen eggs is powerless against me."

Dresde's talons began to glow. She attempted to unfurl her wings, but evident pain halted the motion.

Despicable vermin! she raged. Oscar noticed that she stood in such a way that her missing heart scale would not be fully exposed. *You will pay for this, Samantha. I will enjoy destroying everything you hold dear!*

"So you keep saying. Try it and your line dies, along with the life in all of your domain. If Oscar's brother will not harm the Flower, I will, and they will not be able to stop me. It is your choice, Dresde. Do you want revenge, or do you want life?"

Samantha stopped dangerously close to the wurl queen. If Dresde wished, she had but to pounce forward to strike and kill her.

However, Samantha held the egg in a precarious way and looked ready to smash it against the ground. Oscar trembled. He wasn't sure whether Samantha was bluffing, but he had a feeling that she wasn't. She would try to break the egg, and maybe she'd be able to.

Give me that egg, Dresde ordered. *Obey me!*

"No," Samantha said simply. "You will command me no longer. I can resist your will long enough to do what must be done, and you know it. Go ahead, try to control Oscar or one of the others to get the egg from me. In the time it will take you to do so, I drop it and she dies."

The vines oozed over the crater wall. They reached the edge of the lava and stopped there, tips held aloft, almost as if they were listening.

The sand underneath Dresde's feet started to melt. Oscar could barely stand her buffeting rage, and it took all of his concentration to focus on clutching the Flower tightly. He did not know how Samantha could face her like that.

"Decide. Now," Samantha ordered. "My life or your daughter's."

Dresde reared up. *You do not threaten me, human queen! I am the sovereign of the sky!*

She fell back down on her front legs, and the earth shook. She bared her fangs in a snarl, but Samantha did not budge.

Seconds stretched between them, crackling with tension. The two females glared at each other unblinkingly in a silent contest.

Dresde's eye cluster focused on the egg. Her rage was fleetingly replaced with something else, and Oscar's eyes widened when he realized what it was Dresde was feeling.

Concern. Desperation. The urge to protect.

Her talons stopped glowing. She folded her wings against her body.

My daughter must live, she conceded, her mind-voice almost quiet.

The vines behind Dresde erupted at her words.

They were everywhere at once. The ground itself seemed to come alive when some broke through the rocks underfoot in a shower of sharp fragments, and they no longer resembled snakes but bloated worms intent on feeding. The nearest ones shot forward directly over the lava. A couple of them burned under the heat, but many of them didn't.

They were all converging on a single spot—the place where Dresde and Samantha were standing.

"Watch out!" Oscar yelled, but he was too far away to do anything.

He watched in horror as more than a dozen thick vines attacked.

Samantha jumped out of the way of the first one and very nearly dropped the egg. The vine slammed on the ground where she had been, kicking up a cloud of black sand. Samantha recovered by rolling on the ground, and then she jumped to her feet. She ran away from two other vines that were chasing her, weaving as she went, and only barely dodged another bulbous whip that shot by her head.

Dresde roared in defiance and slashed at the nearest vine with her talons, cleaving it as though it were putty. The ground shuddered in response, and black liquid burst out of the stump like a disturbing parody of a geyser. Drops flew through the air, and one of them landed on Oscar's arm.

He yelped and wiped it off. It was cold as ice, and it burned.

More vines came at Dresde from all sides in a horridly concerted effort. Snarling, Dresde hacked and slashed in a deadly dance so quick that all Oscar could see were the light-trails of her talons through the air. She cut more vines down, and the black liquid pooled on the ground. The detached sections of each writhed and strained, still jerking forward and attempting to reach her.

Elias cried out. Oscar jerked his head back to see his brother fall on one knee.

"Eli!" Oscar yelled, rushing over to him.

"Eli, what's wrong?" Tristan asked urgently.

Elias was panting. He ignored the questions and crawled on the ground until he was able to pick up Sizzra's egg. He then closed his eyes, and the contact seemed to calm him down. A moment later, he opened them and looked at Oscar. The iridescence in his irises was almost luminous for an instant.

"The spirit-lines," he told them. "Something's really wrong."

An earsplitting roar yanked their attention back to the fight. Samantha had run all the way to the edge of the lake, but her advance had been cut off by three particularly large and thorny vines. They swayed in the air and struck the ground whenever she attempted to escape the rough triangle in which they had penned her.

"We have to help!" Oscar yelled.

He held the Flower tightly and ran to Samantha.

The vines whipped forward at the same time, zeroing in on the egg. Oscar wouldn't reach her in time. Samantha was cornered with no way out.

"No!" Oscar shouted.

Dresde was a blur of speed and heat. She jumped in front of Samantha and buffeted the nearest black tentacle with her wings. The blast of wind was as powerful as ever, and even Oscar was sent stumbling back.

Dresde radiated pain, and her right wing now hung limp, but she remained indomitable. She struck a vine that had been about to impale Samantha and the egg, severing its tip with her tail. Samantha dodged the last one, and a moment later Dresde clamped her jaws on its thick, pulsating stem. It burst like the rest and twitched on the ground.

"Dresde, behind you!" Samantha warned.

The wurl queen reacted, but not fast enough. A fat vine burst out of the sand and coiled itself around her chest and back. Glassy thorns dug into her flesh, and blood began to flow from the cuts. Dresde struggled and snapped, but her bond constricted. It appeared to grow around her, pinning her left wing to her side.

Crack.

Dresde howled in pain. Her other wing bone had snapped, but the vine was not done. Its tip wriggled, first one way and then the other, as though palpating. Looking for something.

It stopped just above the left side of her chest, where the heart scale had been removed.

"No!" Elias yelled. "She'll be born of her death!"

Oscar had no idea what he meant, but he was horrified as he watched the powerful queen struggle. Her chest heaved, and she slashed at the air, but her talons kept missing their mark. Slowly she was being pinned lower and lower to the ground. The fragments of vines that had been cut were converging on her like hungry leeches preparing to feast.

I am the sovereign of the sky, Dresde said. Her mind-voice sounded exhausted, but there was something different about its tone.

The thorny vine struck down, intending to impale her exposed heart.

I am not your slave!

Dresde's eye cluster flashed with terrifying brightness, and her scales changed. The deep shade of rotting violet was overwhelmed by a new color that shimmered with its own faint light, unmistakable in the darkness of night.

Oscar yelped. The Flower in his arms grew very hot, and something intangible flowed out of it, suffusing the air with warmth and a sense of connection. Its petals began to glow in a mirror of the change overtaking Dresde.

Her scales turned crimson. They were exactly the same ruby tone as the petals of the Flower.

Dresde braced her body against the ground and pushed. The vine held taut for a moment and then snapped. It retreated back into the ground, showering them all with freezing black liquid amid an overpowering smell of burnt plant matter. The other vines followed suit, and they were all soon gone, as though absorbed back into the depths from whence they had come.

Panting, Dresde lifted her head and roared a proclamation of her victory. The sound rebounded off the walls of the crater, amplified and somehow beautiful. As the sound faded, the Flower appeared to answer her. Oscar sensed a kind of questing contact reaching out from it.

Dresde focused her piercing gaze on Oscar, who was still holding the Flower. Then she slowly looked all around. She projected curiosity, almost as if she was seeing everything for the first time.

So, Dresde said quietly. She glanced at her own body, lifting her front right claw as if to examine it. *This is what I had been robbed of. This is the freedom denied my mothers for an age.*

She focused on Samantha and the ruby egg.

Give it to me.

"No," Samantha replied.

You have protected my daughter. Give me the egg and I will spare you. Refuse and you die.

Samantha opened her mouth to answer, but the ground rumbled and drowned the sound of her voice.

Dresde crouched as if readying herself for an attack.

"What's happening?" Oscar said.

Elias couldn't quite suppress a horrified moan. He carefully placed Sizzra's egg on the ground. "Oscar, watch this egg, but don't let the Flower touch it, okay?"

"Why? What's going on?" Oscar asked.

A deep tremor shook the surface, almost like an earthquake.

"It's too late," Elias replied, his face ashen.

"Too late for what?" Tristan asked with open confusion.

Elias did not answer. He walked to where Dresde and Samantha were standing.

Tristan hesitated for a second. "Stay here, Oscar, okay?" He then caught up to Elias.

Samantha, give my daughter's egg to the young male, Dresde ordered.

"Why?" she asked suspiciously.

The water in the crater began to bubble.

Do it! Dresde shouted, and Oscar was taken aback at the unmistakable note of panicky fear in her voice. *Do it now.*

For once, Samantha obeyed. She ran to Oscar and placed the egg she carried next to Sizzra's. "Watch over them," she said. Then she ran back.

"Samantha, wait!"

A tremor came again, but this time it didn't end. It had to be an earthquake, but Oscar didn't know of any earthquakes that lasted entire minutes.

Dresde faced the crater lake, where the once-placid mirror of water that had reflected the moonlight was now smoking. Bubbles burst on its surface, and more were coming as the seconds ticked by. With them there came a smell, something that reminded Oscar of the damp and dark places of the world, but the miasma that soon grew thick and choking held a quality that inspired nothing but revulsion. Oscar had no name for the fetor he was perceiving. It was a stench that challenged his conception of what should be allowed to exist in a normal, ordered reality.

The water roiled now like a boiling cauldron. The earth kept shaking. The very center of the lake turned convex, as if something were pushing the water from below.

"What is that?" Samantha demanded.

"It's too late," Elias repeated. "She has fed enough."

Indeed, Dresde agreed. She sounded dismayed, but her tone held an edge of fierce determination. *She has stolen enough life from the world, and now… she is being born.*

"What?" Tristan asked. "Eli, what's coming?"

An answer was not necessary.

They all witnessed the birth.

The tremors stopped. The bubbles ended. Tiny shimmering lights glittered in the depths of the lake, yellow and blue and red and green and violet and orange. It would have been beautiful had the spectacle not been accompanied by an inescapable sense of dread that was reinforced by the appearance of the crystals.

They rose out of the water, rhomboids and tetrahedrons and irregular shards, perfectly transparent and multifaceted like diamonds. They were like the thorns on the vines and the objects growing on the cliffside beach, but these were larger than any of them by far. They grew at an impossible speed, cresting the surface of the lake at random intervals, each of them appearing to feast on the light of the moons overhead and replace it with darkness. Soon they rimmed the entire circumference of the crater lake, like a horrible inverted crown of vile decadence.

The lights in the water died out. For a couple of fear-choked seconds, not a single sound could be heard.

Then there came a blast of mental energy so strong and so sudden that Oscar screamed. He collapsed on the ground, nearly dropping the Flower. It radiated from the lake in waves, and Oscar had never felt anything like it before. It was not like the iron manacles of Dresde's will at all. This was cold in a way that appeared to rob him of breath itself. It was emptiness, ravenous. Its echoes held the absolute silence that reigns in the absence of life.

Something burst out of the water, enormous. Oscar struggled onto his knees and, from there, looked up in horrified awe.

The water around the shape boiled away. It started out slowly, but the lake was soon a frothing mass of bubbles and vapor that obscured its occupant from view.

"She is here," Elias whispered.

"Impossible," Samantha protested. "It cannot be. Is this the queen of the oceans?"

Dresde bared her fangs at the towering apparition. *This is not my sister. It is something much more ancient. One of my mothers named her, once. The day she came down from the stars.*

"What is it?" Samantha asked. "Who is it?"

Dresde couldn't quite suppress the slight waver in her mind-voice.

It is She Who Hungers.

The thing in the lake moved, and the vapor that enshrouded her was blasted away. Oscar gasped, climbing to his feet. There was no water left in the lake anymore.

A gigantic chrysalis of thorny vines bloomed in the darkness, opening like a corrupted flower. The vines withered as they fell away and shriveled into nothing.

All that was left was her.

She was beautiful beyond comprehension and terrifying beyond belief. She Who Hungers stood in the center of the crater, a vision of darkness and light.

She was as large as Dresde, but her body was much stockier, reminiscent of Sizzra's heft. Her neck was disturbingly long, like that of a snake, and it ended in a spade-shaped head in which three eyes glowed—but instead of the red of a wurl, her eyes blazed in every color of the visible spectrum, like prisms filtering the light of the sun. It was mesmerizing and horrifying at once. It appeared as though each one of her eyes was a bottomless orb from which no escape was possible.

Her scales were black. They were so dark that looking at her body was like watching a jagged tear in the fabric of space-time itself.

She would have been all but invisible in the darkness but for the crystalline spines.

They grew all over her body, long and serrated, like a parody of Sizzra herself. Each spine was a sculpture of glass, shimmering faintly from within in ever-shifting colors of the rainbow. They grew on her back, down her shoulders, and on her tail, bristling and quivering. Her head was crowned with spines as well, and they wreathed her face in terrible beauty. Every centimeter of her spoke of danger.

The creature moved, and Oscar realized she had no legs.

Tentacles sprouted from her body instead, six of them, muscular and covered in spines. They slithered on the ground, and faint luminescence twinkled in their scales. They were nothing like the vines that had come out of the ground. These appendages looked powerful, and they moved with exquisite precision. They lifted the creature's massive body with ease, and their overpowering strength was evident as they crushed rocks that were in her way. Their tips were made of crystal, exactly like her spines, and each skewered the ground like a stinger sinking into tender flesh.

When she opened her wings, Oscar very nearly cried. It was too much horror. The cyclopean membranous appendages were exactly like Dresde's, but instead of crimson they were black, the veins in them shimmering conduits of the same prismatic luminescence that coursed through her entire body. The mesmerizing glow ran up her neck and appeared to concentrate around the edge of her maw, a monstrous thing that was held half-open. It was segmented in three parts, each of them needled with long, wicked-looking teeth.

Oscar backed away. She was dazzling and tenebrous at once. She was a vision of brilliant darkness.

You go no further, Dresde said. Her thought boomed with command. *You will besmirch my domain no longer.*

The creature paused.

She Who Hungers focused fully on Dresde and rotated her head to the left ever so slightly, as if appraising her enemy. She did not speak, nor did she project intent or conscious thought with her mind.

Instead she fired a spine at Dresde's heart.

chapter 31.
her

ELIAS SENSED the deadly projectile an instant before it was shot, but even with his heightened reflexes, he was shocked at the sudden brutality with which She Who Hungers attacked.

For a moment, a large spine on her shoulder glittered with prismatic otherworldliness. Every wavelength in the rainbow coursed briefly along its shaft.

Then she launched it. The air cracked in a sonic boom. Elias jerked his head to the side, expecting to see Dresde impaled on the glass needle.

Impostor! Dresde accused, vaulting through the air with exquisite precision. She dodged the spine by a hair's breadth as it sailed past her chest, and she landed a moment later in a burst of sparks when her glowing talons struck the ground. Dresde sneered with her mind. *You are an abomination, born of stolen life!*

She Who Hungers crouched and smashed the crystalline tips of her tentacles into the ground.

A fractal latticework of glowing polychromatic fissures splintered the rock and spread out from the six puncture wounds in the earth. The world groaned.

Elias's breath caught in his throat. He almost let go of Sizzra's spine when his mind registered what the creature was doing.

"Eli!" Tristan said. "What's wrong?"

Sweat beaded on his forehead, and it took him a moment to be able to answer in a strained gasp, "Everything."

The spirit-lines of the world were being drained. He could feel the horrible rending as She Who Hungers drew sustenance from the network of life around her and used it to bolster her strength. Life forms in the far-off continent of Reena were dying, falling to the ground, and the oceans shuddered as living things seized up in their last moments and then sank to the depths as corpses. It was as though every victim dropped into nameless darkness to disappear forever. The Flowers could no longer find them in death. They had been ripped from the world itself.

Through the contact Elias caught a glimpse of the mind of She Who Hungers, and he teetered on the brink of despair. There was nothing there. The enormous reptilian monster before him, the amalgamation of stolen life energy from the three guardians of the world, was a mindless hungry void.

You dared make a thrall of me, Dresde hissed. Her eye cluster blazed, and she radiated the heat of the midday sun. She slunk forward without a hint of hesitation, approaching her rival.

The spines along the monster's entire length shone brighter with the rapturous beauty of shimmering multicolored light. A moment later she jumped up, dizzyingly high, and flapped with wings that were at once blacker than night and brighter than the moons.

You should have never dared take physical form, Dresde threatened. *A body can be killed!*

She jumped with a wild roar. She Who Hungers flapped harder, as if wanting to rise out of reach, but Dresde was too fast. She collided with the intruder in a burst of sparks and raked the creature's black scales with all four of her glowing talons.

You try to fly away from the queen of the sky? Dresde demanded with arrogant ferocity. *Your stolen wings are nothing in the face of my power!*

Dresde twisted out of the way of spine after spine and slithered to the back of the resplendent abomination. She snapped her jaws shut at the spot where a dark wing sprouted from a nest of aberrant crystals and crunched bone into splinters. She braced herself for a heartbeat, gathering strength, and then ripped the wing from muscle with a sickening tearing sound.

She Who Hungers dropped to the ground.

Dresde vaulted away and landed gracefully on her feet, tossing the bleeding wing to the bottom of the crater a moment later. She Who Hungers crashed down in a spray of black sand that forced Elias to cover his face. When he was able to open his eyes again, he saw the creature already up on her thick wriggling tentacles, her remaining right wing a mangled mess that had been torn to shreds by her own spines in the fall.

Incompetent newborn! Dresde crowed, facing her squarely. *You are nothing but a facsimile of true life. You can barely wield the strength you hold!*

She Who Hungers gave no outward indication of pain or fear. Instead she lifted her serpentine neck, and the twinkling light along its length began to pulse, faster and faster.

Time to end your life, Dresde declared with supreme confidence. She pounced.

She Who Hungers opened threefold-segmented jaws that resembled the petals of a carnivorous flower, and she screamed.

Her voice was the sound of countless creatures dying. It was a painfully strident chorus of death that sliced a path through the air and appeared to rend the very molecules asunder.

Dresde's body was paralyzed. Her jump was cut short, and now it was she who crashed down in the sand, helpless, mere centimeters away from the lava and the clutch of sky-blue eggs.

She wasn't the only one. Elias couldn't even cry out as the creature's ragged shout ravaged his brain. The stridulating notes were so loud that he was sure his ears were bleeding, but he couldn't lift his hands to cover them. He was awash in pain, but that was only part of the reason that his mind was blanketed in stifling horror. This howling scream could not exist in a world with life. It was the deafening sound of the emptiness between the stars, an echo of the titanic convulsions of a dying sun. All who heard it had to die.

There was no escape. She Who Hungers approached Dresde with insolent calm, and the Flyer queen was powerless in her dissonant grasp.

A new song pierced the rattling chaos like an arrow sailing through thick fog. The ravenous cacophony was disturbed by a pure and gentle sound, a single musical note that vibrated through the air and then grew, joined by harmonic layers that built upon one another until the song became a multifaceted arrangement of melody of ever-increasing complexity.

She Who Hungers hesitated and screeched again, more loudly. Pain sliced through Elias's mind, but an instant later the song in the distance reached a crescendo, and it shattered the dissonance into irretrievable fragments.

Fathomless silence followed.

Dresde struggled to get up but failed. Elias barely avoided losing his balance when he regained control of his body. He and Tristan exchanged a quick look as the last echoes of the harmonious song faded away. Both of them knew who had sung.

Samantha and Oscar screamed when she flickered into view, discarding her mantle of invisibility.

Lyrana came through the rubble at the mouth of the eyrie, tossing boulders out of the way as if they were pebbles. Her head and blazing eye cluster were visible first, but she smashed rocks into fragments and burst out into the open a moment later. Her terrifying jaw was still open, its three segments displaying its fearsome teeth, but it was not that which made Elias shrink away from her out of sheer animal instinct.

Lyrana was walking.

Her slender golden tentacles stabbed the ground with every step she took. They no longer appeared graceful and dexterous. They were bent at right angles and moved with the disturbing synchronicity of the legs of a spider. They lifted Lyrana's diaphanous form off the ground as she went, making her look like a gigantic arthropod from whose body there hung still-dripping kelp like the tattered remnants of a veil.

Lyrana jumped down to where She Who Hungers stood motionless, as if in utter shock. With unmistakable wordless clarity, the queen of the ocean proclaimed immense anger, defiance, and condemnation.

Her mind-voice was like a balm that washed over the raw wounds left behind by the monster before her. Elias found himself reaching out with his own mind, supporting her, but Lyrana paid him no heed. She was entirely focused on her enemy.

"Beautiful," Samantha whispered nearby.

Lyrana was a mirage of ethereal splendor. Even out of the water, the countless pinpoints of white-and-azure bioluminescence on her scales were magnificent. They outlined not only her tentacles and streamlined body, but also decorated the length of her serpentine neck and twinkled around her head and the long whiskers under her jaw. It was like seeing the night sky itself, a spectacle that eclipsed even the beauty of the setting sun. Elias was filled with hope at seeing the eldest of all creatures in the world come to fight at long last. He knew from Lyrana's own memories that her power was vast.

She Who Hungers slithered back on her bloated tentacles as if attempting to flee, and Lyrana sang again.

The air appeared to stand still, and then it boomed with a missile of pure sound that blasted away a wide swathe of sand along its cylindrical path. It was a sonic onslaught impossible to avoid. Elias was thrown back by the wave, but instead of hope he trembled with icy foreboding. The sound was not directed at him, and yet he recognized it, although he had never heard the doom-ridden notes before. It was the weapon that Lyrana had resisted using through the long decades and centuries of her confinement as she had clung to the tattered remnants of her sanity, the thing she had never dared unleash out of fear for the destiny of the world. Her ultimate attack.

The Song of Death.

Elias had never heard such a heartrending harmony. The very earth under his feet appeared to resonate with energy from the spirit-lines themselves, intent on doing one thing only. Destroying.

She Who Hungers was thrown back by the blast and then appeared to convulse. Her tentacles flailed in the air under the onslaught, but Lyrana did not stop. She rushed forward, still singing, her jaws dripping saliva, and positioned herself for the killing blow.

Lyrana struck. Her maw closed on the vulnerable throat of her enemy with the viciousness of a starving predator, and she tore out an entire chunk of black flesh from which dangled long cords of vibrating tissue. Lyrana consumed it and reared up as she sang again, skewering She Who Hungers with a second assault of the song.

In apparent panic, She Who Hungers jumped back with such force that she sailed high enough to grab on to several boulders protruding from the curved sides of the far crater wall. She hung there like a cornered beast, bleeding, and screamed out her defiance.

Except she was unable to make a sound.

Lyrana's voice wavered. Elias sensed her confusion clearly—She Who Hungers should not be able to move. She should have been killed instantly. Lyrana resumed the song, but a horrible clawing dissonance struck at each and every note and latched on to it, draining it of power, destroying the critical melody. Black ooze pooled in Lyrana's mouth, and part of the luminescence along her neck was snuffed out.

A second before it happened, Elias understood.

"It's inside her," he whispered in naked terror.

Crystals burst through Lyrana's neck with a gut-wrenching scrape of sharp glass rupturing flesh. They sliced through her scales in a fountain of blood, and her song was silenced forever.

Lyrana stumbled. Elias's heart seemed to skip a beat when the crushing realization hit him as Lyrana herself understood. The Song of Death was useless against She Who Hungers.

It's impossible to kill something that isn't alive.

With an almost triumphant flash of her eyes, She Who Hungers vaulted off the crater wall. She blazed with kaleidoscopic brilliance along her path like a meteor burning in the atmosphere of its victim planet, and then she fired.

Every spine on her body glittered and then shot through the air in a dazzling chromatic explosion that had but a single target.

Lyrana.

It was too sudden. Too fast. Lyrana's body was impaled by hundreds of wicked crystals that struck her with unbridled brutality. For a single moment she was able to project a last emotion, something akin to the sadness of ages.

Then her life-spark was destroyed.

"No! Lyrana!" Elias shouted, bursting into tears.

Her body collapsed to never move again. Her luminescence faded. The multitude of spines that had killed her lost their polychrome intensity and became transparent, seemingly drinking from the void itself.

She Who Hungers landed in a cloud of dust. Half obscured by it, she opened her multijointed jaw as if to proclaim her triumph, but no sound came out. She tried again, and there was nothing. She whipped her head from side to side with apparent animalistic confusion.

None hear her final Song and go unscathed, Dresde said, climbing onto her feet with evident difficulty. *My elder sister tore off your vocal cords. Your misbegotten voice is gone.*

She Who Hungers focused on Dresde again. Her body was now devoid of spines, and without them, she was almost entirely black. Only her eye cluster still glimmered with its shifting prismatic radiance.

She crouched when Dresde stood up fully, but this time She Who Hungers did not back away. Still mindless and now voiceless, she thrust the tips of her tentacles into the ground once more, and the rock underneath her glowed along the radiating cracks she inflicted on the world.

Elias cried out in pain. She was stealing more life, feeding her never-ending hunger, and creatures were dying. However, now the essence she leeched coursed through her body with an additional horrifying effect.

"No," Samantha whispered. "It can't be."

The spines on the body of She Who Hungers were regenerating. Like crystals growing at a speed that defied nature, glassy multicolored stubs pierced through the black scales on her shoulders and back, along her neck, down her tentacles, and along the length of her tail.

So many tricks you have, Dresde said, attempting to project sarcasm. Elias wasn't fooled. Dresde was scared.

It wasn't only the spines that were reforming themselves. Tissue was growing on the stump of her left wing where it had been torn off. Membrane knit itself together. Bone reconstituted and lengthened. The gash in her throat was closing.

"Impossible," Tristan cried out in dismay. "No, no!"

Interesting, Dresde said, *but too slow!*

She snarled and pounced on She Who Hungers. The creature took barely a moment to disentangle herself from the world she was ravaging, but it was enough. Dresde struck her side and slashed with her back feet, severing one of the tentacles cleanly. Before the beast could recover, Dresde tackled her to the ground.

She Who Hungers writhed and flailed. She managed to push Dresde off, but the wurl queen wasn't done. She reared back on her hind legs and swiped at the abomination's face. Her talons found their mark, and she shredded all three prismatic eyes to bloody ribbons.

Even that which does not die can be destroyed!

Dresde seized the creature's neck with her front claws in triumphant bloodlust, hacking at her flesh. She Who Hungers struggled ferociously but to no avail. She could not break free, and after a *snap* of what could only be the bones in her spinal column, she went still. Elias dared to hope for a moment.

Then She Who Hungers engulfed Dresde in an embrace.

She raised her heft on her two thickest tentacles and spread the remaining three as wide as their length would allow. The appendages bent at right angles along invisible joints with horrible loud crunches, turning into crooked lances tipped with crystalline blades. She Who Hungers fell into Dresde, pulling her close, and stabbed the Flyer queen in the back.

"No," Elias whispered. His legs felt as though they would give way.

He felt the sharp spike of Dresde's pain and then a horrible emptiness as her consciousness faded. The three tentacles had sunk into her flesh, impaling her completely with a mortal wound.

She Who Hungers did not allow Dresde to drop to the ground. She held her tight instead and started to feed, drinking from Dresde's essence to fuel her own corrupted healing. One of her eyes reformed. Several long spines on her shoulders grew to full size.

"This is the end," Samantha said in audible despair. "That thing will destroy the world."

The creature's tentacles shimmered with their stolen energy. But in their midst, a spark began to glow.

It started on Dresde's back. The edges of a single scale started to shine, as though there were an irresistible source of golden radiance below it.

Dresde twitched.

The light spread across her back. Yellow brilliance became orange and then vermillion. Her scales themselves were progressively infused with bright energy that turned them into crimson plates, like red-hot slabs of metal in the depths of a furnace. A moment later heat radiated from Dresde again, ferocious and undeniable. Elias gasped when the first wave reached him. It felt as though he had been thrust into the stifling confines of an iron oven and the door was about to shut behind him, trapping him to roast to death.

Shatterer of worlds, Dresde panted with a tattered voice, *your corruption ends here.*

The heat became even stronger. Dresde clamped all four of her legs around the body of She Who Hungers, and the glow in her glittering ruby scales resembled magma itself.

Be destroyed!

Dresde's scales begin to melt. They fused together for a moment and then began to flow around her body like lava given life.

Flesh sizzled, but it was not Dresde's.

She Who Hungers flailed her neck from side to side in a silent, soul-rending scream as her tentacles burned. The half-formed crystals of many new spines exploded. Her black scales smoked under the onslaught of the inescapable heat and light as she attempted to break free but could not, and every time she struggled, her body was further consumed by the inferno.

Dresde glanced back, and her face was blinding. It was like looking at the molten core of the planet itself.

She gazed at Samantha for a timeless moment with an expression of unreadable complexity.

Dresde raised her left foot and tore off one of her talons with her jaws. She threw it in Samantha's direction, where it glowed on the ground for a moment before its light went out.

Dresde's last look was for the crimson egg.

Remember, daughter.

She roared with her ultimate strength, and the light from within consumed her form. Her body shone as she immolated herself in order to destroy the ravenous creature in her grasp. For an instant, her sinuous length appeared to be entirely made of molten bronze, and she was a blazing vision of liquid grace incarnate.

She Who Hungers squirmed in her grasp like a worm and brought her two remaining tentacles to bear. She stabbed Dresde through the heart and spasmed as both her appendages were destroyed.

Dresde's body collapsed and tumbled down to the bottom of what had once been a beautiful lake at the top of her domain, a place where land met water and sky. She never moved again.

Elias clutched at his chest the moment he felt the rending loss of Dresde's death. Before him, She Who Hungers was a mangled mess of twitching and smoking flesh. All of her tentacles were gone, and her neck had been half obliterated by the heat. Her tail was a charred stump.

But she was still moving.

Elias gritted his teeth and slashed at the air with his spine.

"We're not done."

"I'm here," Tristan said at once.

"As am I," Samantha joined in. She rushed to the place where Dresde's talon lay and picked it up. In her hands it looked like a scimitar with a bloody handle made of crimson scales.

She Who Hungers bucked and flipped onto her back. Her tentacles were already regenerating.

"We end this. Now!" Elias declared.

The three of them charged. They ran over glassy sand and fragments of dead vines. They ran past Lyrana's body and avoided pools of black ichor.

She Who Hungers appeared to sense them coming. She opened her jaws and tried to lift her neck to attack them but failed.

Elias was first to reach her. He jumped onto her hideous belly and kept running. He slipped several times, but he made it to the very center of her exposed chest. There he grasped his spine with both hands and plunged it down.

The scales were too thick. The spine sank only halfway.

A drop of icy drool fell on Elias's shoulder.

Elias realized what was happening an instant too late. She Who Hungers twisted her body, and her neck crunched as it regained its full range of motion. She unhinged her maw and bit down on him savagely like a striking snake.

There was no time to get away. All Elias's reflexes enabled him to do was realize the certainty of his own death.

"Eli!" Tristan shouted.

He jumped in front of Elias with Lyrana's scale in both hands.

Clang.

Needle jaws collided against the shield and broke off. She Who Hungers was paralyzed for a moment with the clear note that resounded through the air, vibrating with the unmistakable echo of the voice of the Singer queen.

"Tristan!" Elias cried out.

The impact pushed Tristan over the side and to the ground. The scale tumbled out of his hands.

She Who Hungers bent her horrendous neck in his direction.

Something glinted in the darkness with kaleidoscopic light.

"No!" Elias shouted at the same moment the creature fired one of her fully formed spines. There was a horrible metallic groan when the projectile hit.

Elias almost jumped off in desperation, but Samantha grabbed his wrist with a grip of steel.

"Elias, no!"

He struggled briefly against her, but She Who Hungers reared her head over them again, forcing him to hold on to his spine to avoid being thrown off.

Clang.

Impossibly, Lyrana's scale rang again. The abomination froze for an instant.

"Heart scale," Samantha whispered.

Dresde's talon began to glow in her hands, and Samantha stabbed She Who Hungers with the wicked edge of the blazing weapon. Its hooked tip cleaved black armored plates with terrifying ease, and Samantha roared out a wordless cry as she ripped the chest of the creature open.

Black scales parted, exposing the heart.

Elias yanked his spine out and gasped. The monster's nexus was a perfect octahedral crystal, pulsating with otherworldly light in every color he could perceive and in others he could not, but which nevertheless reached into his consciousness with their terrifying energy. Cold enshrouded it as it floated in a pool of utter blackness. There were no veins, no muscles. She Who Hungers was an empty husk.

"Not alive," Elias said.

"Now!" Samantha urged.

She Who Hungers fired a serrated projectile at him, but Elias knocked it out of the air. He lifted Sizzra's spine above his head and plunged it down with all of his strength, roaring with unrestrained ferocity.

He pierced the perfect surface of the bloodless heart and cleaved it to the core.

The crystal shattered. She Who Hungers convulsed once, and then the light animating her body vanished from sight, as if fleeing to the void of night itself. The prismatic radiance was snuffed out in a single instant, and her body collapsed.

"Get off her!" Elias yelled. He took Samantha's hand, and they jumped.

They landed and rolled. When Elias leaped to his feet, he saw that the corpse of the thing that had once moved was now boiling and bubbling, melting into a pool of black decay.

"Tristan!" Elias shouted, tossing his weapon away as he broke into a run. He skirted around the diminishing pile of vile flesh and skidded to a stop on the other side.

Three metal-clad wurl were huddled together. The glassy spine She Who Hungers had fired lay on the ground as a pile of harmless shards, along with a torn silver scale.

"Guys?" Elias asked, disbelieving.

Narev, Vanor, and Siv gave him flashes of acknowledgment and parted to reveal Tristan crouching in their midst.

Safe.

"Tristan!" Elias exclaimed.

Tristan grinned and stood up fully. He opened his arms wide, and Elias gave him the fiercest hug of his life. He kissed Tristan on the lips, hard, shedding tears of joy and relief.

"I thought…," Elias sobbed. "I thought—"

"I'm here, Eli. I'll always be with you."

"I love you so much," Elias said, still crying.

"I love you too," Tristan said with a smile, gently wiping Elias's tears away. "More than life itself, and I think I proved it just then!"

Elias chuckled at the unexpected humor, the dam of anxiety and fear and stress breaking all at once with Tristan's words. "That was stupid," he reprimanded Tristan.

"And that's why you love me."

"Eli!" Oscar shouted, rushing over to them. "Tristan!"

"Oscar!" Elias replied.

He hugged his little brother, and they cried together for a few blissful seconds. It was as though the world around Elias disappeared and the only thing he focused on was an inexhaustible surge of gratitude. His family was safe. Tristan and Oscar and the wurl were with him, and it made every sacrifice worth it. For the first time in months, his heart was light, and the last remnants of shadowy worry were dispelled by true happiness.

Elias gently pulled away from the hug and looked at Oscar, smiling.

"I'm so sorry for everything," Oscar sobbed. "It was my fault, Eli. The day of the storm, I was so scared. It's my fault you and Tristan had to c-cross the world to find me."

"It wasn't your fault," Elias contradicted. "You were taken. And you survived."

"But if only I h-had been different. Stronger."

"You *are* different now," Elias told him. "You've grown strong. You've grown brave."

Oscar's eyes pooled with more tears even as he smiled, as though the praise were reaching his very heart. "I always wanted—" He hiccupped. "I always wanted to be brave like you. To stop being scared."

Elias shook his head. "I think I should be more like *you*, Oscar. Gentle. Kind. Caring. You were the only one to show Dresde compassion, and you were right. You've always been right."

"I think we're all amazing," Tristan interjected, clapping Oscar on the shoulder.

They looked at him for an instant and then laughed. Elias let the adrenaline-fueled tension evaporate as it was replaced with joyful relief.

As though on cue, Narev bumped against Elias, demanding attention. Vanor and Siv were slightly more dignified, but they also came close. Vanor was limping, but they were all safe.

"Narev!" Elias exclaimed. "I'm so glad you're okay. Siv, you look weird without your spines."

"'Sup," Tristan said to Vanor. He received a grunt in response.

Elias gave another silent, heartfelt thanks. His heart brimmed with happiness.

"Let's sit for a bit," he proposed, "and then we go home."

chapter 32.
free

THEY SAT together in the sand for what felt like a long time, resting.

Oscar held Elias's hand for a while. The contact reassured him. He was having a hard time comprehending that his older brother was there, next to him. He hadn't abandoned him, and he hadn't come alone.

Oscar wasn't freaked out by the three large silver wurl a few steps away. He might have been in the past, but he knew these were friends. He admired the way their scales reflected the moonlight, and the length of their beautiful spines. He watched them as minutes passed and became an hour. The moons moved across the sky. Behind them, the horrible mass of black goo had shrunk to barely a puddle, and its noxious odor was dissipating at long last, leaving in its place the icy freshness of the mountaintop wind.

Samantha was sitting by herself, closer to the warmth of the lava. She hugged her knees close to her chest, and her eyes were on the pile of sky-blue eggs, but her gaze appeared to be lost in the distance.

Oscar squeezed Elias's hand once and stood up. He walked over to Samantha and took a seat, not saying a word. They spent several minutes in companionable silence.

"It has ended," Samantha said eventually.

"Yeah," Oscar replied. "It's over."

"My father…." Samantha shut her eyes, and a tear rolled down her cheek.

Oscar reached for her hand. "I'm so sorry."

She nodded and did not pull her hand away. It took her a while to be able to speak again.

"Doran fought by my side at the end," she all but whispered. She looked at Oscar with a bittersweet smile.

"I know," Oscar replied, smiling too. "He loved you."

"I loved him too. He was my only friend before you came."

"He was amazing. And he let me ride him so many times! Remember how I screamed the first time I flew with you guys?"

Samantha chuckled as though in spite of herself. "I remember. He liked you from the start."

"Are you sure?" Oscar asked. "I always thought he didn't."

"He was just being protective of me. But when he came to know you, he trusted you, like I do."

They fell silent again, but a small part of the pressure of sorrowful loss had lifted. Oscar looked to the right, where the crimson Flower lay in the sand, no trace of darkness on it whatsoever. Some distance away, two large and beautiful eggs rested side by side.

Of the creature there was no trace anymore. The severed sections of black vines had shriveled and crumbled like ash in the wind. Crystals large and small had seemingly vanished. The foul tissue of her body had bubbled into nothing.

Samantha touched a faint dark scratch on her cheek. "My family is free," she said in a low voice. Then she spoke louder. "*I* am free."

She looked at Oscar, and her eyes widened, as though she truly realized what her words meant.

He grinned. "That's right. You can do what you want. You don't have to live here anymore. I mean, if you don't want to."

Samantha took a long breath in and let it out slowly. "This place is full of sorrow. I would be glad to leave it, but where would my family and I go?"

Oscar raised an eyebrow. "Duh? You guys are coming with us. Back home. That was the plan, right? With the shuttle and all."

"I suppose, but I have been thinking. Will your people accept us?"

"Are you kidding? Everyone's going to freak!" Oscar exclaimed. "In a good way, I mean. There's so few of us, you guys are going to be like celebrities. If you want, you can live in one of the empty houses next to mine. We can be neighbors!"

Samantha nodded slowly. "That would be nice."

Elias and Tristan had stood up. Oscar followed suit and offered his hand to Samantha. "Let's go."

She sighed with a last glance at the edge of the erstwhile lake, where Dresde's remains rested. "Yes."

After helping Samantha stand, Oscar walked over to the Flower and picked it up. It was no longer blazing hot, but it radiated wonderful warmth nevertheless.

"Is the Flower all right?" Elias asked, although he kept his distance from it.

"I think so," Oscar replied. "It's so beautiful now."

"We must return it," Elias said. "But first…."

He approached the eggs and knelt beside them. He placed a hand on each, his right on the porcelain-white one, his left on the ruby shell. Elias then closed his eyes and appeared to commune with the unborn queens.

"This is a new beginning," Elias said under his breath. "The bloodshed can end."

Oscar felt something. It was coming from the Flower in his arms, a faint sensation, almost like the brush of a dormant mind.

Elias stood up with Sizzra's egg in his hands. He looked at Samantha.

"Will you take the other one?" he asked her. "It should be placed at the top of the clutch, above the males."

Samantha looked down at the fragile object not two steps away from her. For a moment Oscar grew afraid when he saw something like rage flash across her face. However, the emotion faded from view as quickly as it had come, and Samantha said instead, "I will."

With unusual care, Samantha scooped the egg up and held it in the crook of her left elbow. She then walked a few steps away and picked up Dresde's talon. It looked dull in the moonlight, but Oscar felt the faintest hint of heat coming from it as Samantha fastened it through her belt.

"Over here," Elias said.

Samantha followed him. Oscar hung back, careful to keep the Flower away from any of the eggs.

"Place her there," Elias instructed, pointing at a spot where the pile of blue shells was tallest. They were lit from below by the lava, each one a perfect jewel.

Samantha hesitated. "Will she be my enemy?"

"No," Elias assured her. "She will remember."

"I do not understand."

"She will know what her mother knew. She will know what you did."

"Very well," Samantha said. She laid the ruby egg down on its rightful place.

"When will it hatch?" Tristan asked, standing behind them.

Elias shrugged. "I don't know. Maybe soon, maybe not for a long time. All I remember from Sizzra is that she was born around the same time as Dresde."

"And…," Tristan said again. He looked at Lyrana's body, beautiful even in death. "Her daughter?"

Elias closed his eyes. "I'm not sure. Maybe I'll know when we're in the water again."

"She was Dresde's sister, right?" Oscar asked.

"And Sizzra's," Elias confirmed. "Lyrana was the oldest creature in the world."

"She was beautiful," Oscar said. "And scary."

"You should see her mate," Tristan commented. "Alinor is terrifying."

"We ought to leave," Samantha reminded them. "I need to see if my family is well."

"Let's go," Elias said. "Oscar, you're up. It's time to make things right."

They climbed over boulders and pebbles and reached the entrance to the eyrie with little trouble. Oscar focused on not dropping the Flower, but once he was about to enter the cave, he couldn't suppress a slight shudder.

"What if those horrible vines are still there?" he asked Elias. "What if they attack us?"

"They won't," Elias said with audible certainty. "The darkness is gone."

"Okay," Oscar replied.

The eyrie was empty and forlorn. Their footsteps appeared to echo off the cave walls, and evidence of the fight was visible in many places under the beams of the link flashlights. The ground was covered with broken stalactites, and there were deep scores in the ground.

There was also a body. Samantha and Oscar walked over to it in solemn silence.

"Thank you, Doran," Samantha said softly. She placed her hand on his scales. "I will always remember you."

Oscar gave Samantha some privacy and picked his way carefully through the chamber until he came to its very center. Tristan was with him, but Elias and the three wurl remained several paces away.

"I don't think we can get any closer," Elias said. He wiped sweat off his brow, holding the white egg under his other arm. "Something's happening to the Flower."

"It's getting hotter," Oscar observed. It wasn't painful yet, but the crimson petals were giving off a faint radiance that was accompanied by palpable waves of heat.

"In its natural state, this Flower is as hot as molten rock," Elias explained. "Maybe She Who Hungers had nearly extinguished its energy, but I think it's coming back. You guys better hurry."

"Right," Tristan replied. "Oscar, come over here. Climb onto my shoulders."

"Okay," Oscar said.

It was tricky but manageable. Tristan crouched so Oscar would be able to place his feet on either side of Tristan's head, but keeping balance while simultaneously holding the increasingly hot Flower was hard, and they had to try several times. Oscar nearly fell on the fourth attempt, but Tristan grabbed his ankles and stabilized them.

"Ready?" Tristan asked.

"Yes."

Tristan stood up fully underneath the place where three long vines drooped, almost as if questing for the thing that was missing from the world. Even with the added height, however, there was still nearly a meter of distance between Oscar's outstretched arms and the vines.

The Flower was getting so hot it was painful to hold.

"I'm going to jump," Oscar announced. "Tristan, this might hurt."

"Do it," Tristan said. "I'll catch you."

Oscar craned his neck up, gauged the distance, and then jumped as high as he could.

At the same time as he sailed through the air, the vines extended. They did not move much, but it was enough. Oscar smashed the Flower against them, and he felt the slight pull when they made contact. In that instant he perceived a faint inkling of something vast and peaceful, like an enormous networked consciousness spanning the entire world.

Then he fell. Tristan caught him, and they once again tumbled to the ground in a heap. Oscar banged his hip against the ground, and Tristan's shoulder hit an old bone that snapped.

"Ouch," Tristan complained.

Oscar grunted as well. He suspected he was going to get a big bruise, but he was okay. "Thanks, Tristan."

"Don't mention it."

Oscar rolled onto his back and shone the beam of his flashlight at the ceiling.

"Tristan?" he said.

"Yeah?"

"Get out of the way!"

The two of them scrambled to their feet and were barely in time to avoid a single drop of bright red liquid that hissed and smoked when it hit the ground.

"That was close," Tristan commented.

"Oh wow," Oscar said. "Look."

The Flower was transforming. Its petals no longer hung limp but instead opened fully in an intricately beautiful array. Each of them blazed with inner light that grew brighter by the second. Their edges and sides resembled liquid bronze.

"They look like her," he whispered. "At the end."

A warm hand touched his shoulder. Elias was standing next to him, smiling.

"Thank you, Oscar. Tristan." He closed his eyes for a moment and breathed in as though inhaling pure bliss. "The world is whole again."

They watched the Flower for nearly a minute and witnessed how its inner light spread through the vines themselves, slowly and steadily. Each plant conduit began to glow softly in the same crimson hue, and the radiant splendor of them all soon covered the entire ceiling of the eyrie. The cavern was fully lit from above, and the effect was wondrous in the darkness of night.

"This is how it should have looked," Elias told them. "It's the true majesty of the Flower of the Sky."

Samantha joined them where they stood. Oscar glanced at her, and she nodded. It looked like she had been crying, but she managed a tenuous smile.

"I never saw it like this," she observed. "I do not think any of my ancestors every did."

"There was darkness in here for centuries. An age," Elias said. "But it's been banished at last."

"Good," Samantha replied. Then she turned around. "I will show you the way down. Follow me."

She led them to the opening to the tunnel that would take them down to the volcano. She jumped down, but a problem became apparent.

"Um, tiny logistics issue," Oscar pointed out. "The wurl won't fit through there."

"They can descend the way they came," Samantha said. "Even the injured one should manage."

"Right," Oscar agreed. "Eli? Let's go down."

Elias looked at the wurl. "Guys, we'll be going down this way, is that okay? We'll meet down below."

Vanor huffed and touched the white egg with his snout. Then he positioned himself between Elias and the tunnel, blocking the way.

"He's having none of that," Tristan said. "I don't think these guys are going to let that egg out of their sight."

Elias sighed. "Fine. I'll go down with you three. Narev, you'll carry me, but be careful, okay? Oscar, Tristan, you go down with Samantha."

"Sure," Oscar said, although he felt uneasy about leaving his brother. "You'll be there, right?"

Elias grinned. "Of course I will."

They said goodbye, and Oscar and Tristan followed Samantha down the tunnel.

They spoke little at first. It was difficult going in the dark despite the light of two links, and Oscar was very tired. He could tell Samantha and Tristan weren't any better off, but they didn't complain.

Eventually, however, the silence was too much for Oscar.

"Hey, Tristan?" he asked.

"Yeah?"

"Thanks again," Oscar told him, skirting an unsteady-looking boulder in his path. "You came all this way for me although this wasn't your fight."

"Yes, it was," Tristan said right away. "I protect people. It's my job as an officer of the Colony Patrol."

"We're kind of far away from the colony, though."

Tristan glanced in Oscar's direction briefly. He smiled. "And I also did it for Elias."

Oscar grinned. "You love him, right?"

"With all my heart."

Oscar hugged him. Tristan appeared surprised, but he stopped walking momentarily and returned the hug.

"That makes me really happy," Oscar said. "You guys are such a great couple."

The arduous descent soon demanded their full attention again. It was almost two hours later that they finally reached the gentler section of the path near the narrow tunnel that would lead them out of the volcano. Oscar's legs were trembling by then, and his throat was parched.

"We should've brought water," he complained.

"Almost there," Samantha answered. There was an edge to her voice. "We are almost out of here."

"They're all right," Oscar reassured her. "I know they are."

"I hope so," she said.

When they finally came out into the open, it was an enormous relief.

"Took you long enough!" Elias called out. He was sitting on Narev, safe and sound, Sizzra's egg in his arms. Siv and Vanor stood on either side of him like bodyguards.

"Eli!" Oscar yelled. He half ran, half stumbled over to him.

"You guys okay?" Elias asked.

Oscar nodded several times. "We are. And you?"

"Well, Vanor here had some issues going down because of his leg and *wouldn't* ask for help, but other than that we're fine."

Vanor grunted. Oscar got the distinct impression that if the wurl could have rolled his eyes, he would have.

"This way," Samantha said, walking past without stopping.

Oscar patted Elias's leg briefly. "Eli, I'll go ahead with Samantha. Is that okay?"

"Sure. We'll be right behind you."

"Thanks."

Oscar hurried until he caught up with her. She was walking fast, her hands bunched into fists.

It was very dark when they came to the house. The moons had all set, and daybreak was still hours away.

It was also silent. Deathly so.

"Mama?" Samantha called as they approached the main door. "Oma? Laurie?"

There was fraught silence for a couple of seconds. Oscar feared the worst.

Then the door burst open.

"Sam!" Nadja exclaimed. "Oh goodness, Sam!"

Ute and Laurie were immediately behind her.

They rushed into each other's arms, hugging and crying. Samantha kissed her mother's cheeks, held Laurie's hand, and stroked Nadja's hair. Oscar stood a few steps away, smiling. He was very happy to see they were all okay.

"I thought I would never see you again," Nadja sniffled. "I thought Dresde would...."

"I am here," Samantha reassured her. "I am safe. We all are."

"And her?" Laurie asked. "Is she—"

"Dead," Samantha interrupted. "Dresde is dead and gone forever."

Laurie teared up. "At long, long last."

Ute beamed. "I am so proud of you, Sam."

"Mama!"

"Your father would have been proud as well," Ute continued. Her voice was hoarse but firm.

Samantha looked down with evident sorrow. "Did he suffer?"

Ute shook her head. "He fought until the end. He still held a knife in his hand when I found him."

"Papa," Samantha sobbed.

Nadja walked over to Oscar and took his right hand in both of hers. "You have brought my granddaughter safely to us once again, Oscar. You have my undying thanks."

"Uh, actually Samantha sort of brought *me* back safely. She did most of the saving. And my brother and Tristan."

"Your brother is here?" Nadja asked.

"Yes. Look!"

The women backed away in evident horror when they saw Elias and Tristan approach, and Oscar had to admit that their wurl companions looked terrifying. Their eye clusters gleamed red, and their loud breathing betrayed their size and heft.

"It's okay!" Oscar said. "They're friendly."

"What are they?" Laurie asked.

"Wurl," Samantha answered. "From across the ocean."

"I see a rider," Nadja said. She then stepped forward unhesitatingly. "Greetings."

Elias dismounted and approached, together with Tristan. "Greetings," he replied in a formal tone. "I am Elias Trost."

"I am Tristan MacLeod."

"My name is Nadja. Welcome."

"It's very nice to meet you," Elias said. "Thank you for keeping my brother safe."

Nadja nodded solemnly. "You are welcome. We are thankful to him too. For many things."

After all the introductions were made, Elias spoke up. He addressed Nadja as the head of the household. "We would like to offer you to come back with us, to Portree."

"Is there a home for us there?" Nadja asked. "Oscar spoke of it, but we know little about your colony. Will we be treated with dignity and equality?"

"Yes," Elias replied.

"But you are not part of the governing body, the council, as Oscar has told us," Nadja argued. "How can you assure us that we will not be treated unfairly, relegated to the outskirts of your city, or exiled outright? My ancestors fled persecution. It is why they came here."

"Um…," Elias stammered.

"I can vouch for that," Tristan added. "I am a member of the Colony Patrol. I know my commander will see things the way we do."

"Plus everyone will vote or something, right?" Oscar asked. "You can be made citizens, and then you'll be free to choose whatever profession you want, do whatever you wish to do."

"Free," Nadja whispered. Then she looked at her family. "What shall we do?"

"We go," Laurie said immediately.

Ute nodded. "We go."

"Sam?" Nadja asked.

Samantha looked determined. "This was our home," she said, "but not anymore. There is too much death, too much sorrow here. I would like to go with Oscar."

Nadja walked up to the house and placed her hand on the weathered wall. "When I was a child here, I spent many a night awake, dreaming the impossible dream of freedom. I would often imagine a life away from the scourge of Dresde's shadow." She sighed. "My parents would be happy to know my dream came true, all these years later. I still find it hard to believe."

"The nightmare is over," Samantha assured her. "She can never hurt us again."

Nadja looked at Tristan and Elias. "We will go with you, Elias Trost and Tristan MacLeod. But we will hold you to your word and your promise of equality."

"If it weren't for you, Oscar wouldn't be here," Elias replied. "On my gratitude to you, I swear you'll find a new life in Portree. A better life."

Nadja smiled. "I can hardly wait."

Oscar's stomach chose that moment to growl loudly. "Sorry," he said. Everyone was looking at him. "Can we have something to eat?"

With formalities over, they all went into the house and shared a simple but large meal at the dining table while the wurl waited outside. It was surreal to Oscar to see his brother and Tristan sitting with him. It was almost like a dream that wouldn't end.

Afterward Nadja offered her new guests one of the empty bedrooms to rest, but Elias declined.

"We have spent many months sleeping in the open with the wurl," he explained. "We are used to it. And besides, they want to be close to the egg."

He stepped outside with Tristan after thanking his hosts for the meal.

"Before we rest as well," Nadja said, "there is one more thing to do."

"I will dig the grave," Samantha announced.

"As will I," Ute joined in.

"I will help if I can," Laurie added.

They made as if to go out, but Oscar hung back, unsure what to do.

Samantha looked at him. "Are you not coming?"

"I, um, yeah. I just didn't know if I... if this was a family thing."

"You should come," Nadja said gently. "We would be glad to have you there."

Oscar nodded and followed them.

They had the funeral as the sun was coming up, as if it wanted to remind them that warmth existed. Oscar seemed to float in a state of consciousness that went beyond exhaustion and into true connection with the people around him. He couldn't help crying at the eulogies that each of them gave. He had barely known Johann, but seeing his gravestone next to Jörgen's and Erik's really drove home everything Samantha and her family had endured for decades. They bore wounds that would take a very long time to heal, if they ever did. There was irreplaceable loss and fathomless grief.

Ute was the last person to say goodbye. She knelt on the ground and whispered something inaudible, tears running down her cheeks. Then she glanced at the two other graves and placed her hands over her heart.

Samantha helped her up, and they all left the graveyard behind for the last time. Morning was returning to the world, and Oscar felt lighter with every step he took. He looked up once at the sky and scanned for a threatening winged shape out of habit but then realized there was no need to do so anymore.

"She is gone," Samantha said, coming up beside him. She reached for his hand, and he took hers. "Forever."

"Are you all right?" he asked.

She appeared to consider. "I will be. In time."

chapter 33.
bach

THEY LEFT the next afternoon. Elias would have liked to have stayed longer and explored the fascinating wilderness of the new continent, but he also wanted to take Oscar home. They lingered only long enough to stock up on supplies and prepare for the journey.

Nadja was a gracious hostess. She gave both Tristan and Elias clean new clothing that was in surprisingly good shape for garments that had once been worn on the generation ship itself. Oscar took them up to the attic of the house the next afternoon so they could change into them.

Elias put on a matching set of tough-looking shirt and pants that had once belonged to an engineer on the ship. They were a bit small, particularly the former, but to Elias it was an inexpressible luxury to be wearing clean clothes after so many months roughing it. The bath he had taken earlier in the river had been heavenly, and the crisp fabric felt soft against his skin.

"This is so cool!" Tristan said, donning a pilot's jacket that had the name *Lt. Hugo Wright* sewn above the left breast pocket. He lifted his arms to admire it.

"It looks great on you," Elias observed. He touched Tristan's smooth cheek with his fingers. "You look hot. Though less gruff now that you've shaved."

Tristan grinned. "That tight black shirt fits you like a glove, but I prefer you without one. You've got great abs."

"Ew, guys, get a room!" Oscar complained. He was sitting on the bed, fiddling with his link. The device beeped.

Elias laughed. "Any luck sending the message?"

Oscar nodded. "I think I finally managed. I had to work around the damage to the telecommunications array in the shuttle wreck and wait for the satellite to come around this hemisphere, but I've now received the acknowledgment. Message sent to Mom, Dad, Tristan's dad, and the council."

"Too bad the shuttle's busted," Tristan lamented. "I would have loved to return on it. Can you imagine the faces of everyone back home if we'd flown back?"

"I'm glad we're able to tell them not to fear an attack from Dresde anymore," Elias replied. "They must've been terrified after Oscar's last message."

"Are you sure we can't salvage any of the electronics in the shuttle, Oscar?" Tristan asked. "I'm betting some of that technology would be really useful back at the colony."

Oscar shook his said. "Most of the stuff is burned or broken. Dresde left it in bad shape. Besides, Samantha and her family aren't taking anything with them, other than the bare essentials and some stuff for the baby when it's born. They want to leave everything here the way it is and let nature destroy it in time."

Elias sat down next to his little brother, although Oscar looked far from little. He was now tanned and fit, and his eyes had a survivor's edge to them. "How are they doing?"

"Okay, all things considered," Oscar told him. "But they don't want anything that reminds them of this place. Can't blame them, really."

"This was their home," Elias said. "If they want to leave everything behind, then it's their right."

"I know," Oscar responded. He stood up and walked to the boarded-up windows of the attic space. "There's things I'd also like to forget."

"How was it, being here?" Elias asked him.

Oscar glanced over his shoulder. "Scary. Dangerous. But also amazing. I learned so many things, Eli."

"You can tell us all about them while we cross the ocean."

"How *are* we going to do that?" Oscar asked. "How did you guys get here, even? You don't have a ship."

Elias and Tristan exchanged a glance.

Tristan grinned mischievously. "Do you tell him, or should I?"

OSCAR WASN'T the only one to gasp when the Behemoth rose out of the waves.

Elias smiled. He was waist-deep in the ocean, and the warm water filled him with a sensation of kinship and connection to the creatures of the sea that he had missed while on land. The Behemoth itself was a welcome familiar mind that was vast and vaguely friendly, although Elias sensed that the great creature did not truly perceive Elias and his companions as individuals. They were simply too small to be of any relevance to a creature so large. If anything, it was more aware of the three Spine wurl that flanked Elias, and it was also able to sense the dormant queen inside the egg he carried in his arms.

However, the Island Behemoth remembered Lyrana's request, and it came willingly. There was even something like a question from the peaceful giant, inquiring about the fate of the queen of the deep.

"She's gone," Elias answered, expressing his sadness and admiration through the connection he shared with all the living things of Lyrana's domain. "But she fought bravely to the end."

They boarded the living island one at a time, and the wurl went last. Neither Laurie nor Nadja asked for any help when they did, although climbing on sections of the creature's slippery shell was tricky.

Less than an hour later, the Behemoth pushed off from the continental shelf and began its trek due west. Elias noticed that none of the women looked back at the place they were leaving behind.

He did, though. The imposing mound of the volcano seemed to want to scratch the cloudless blue ceiling. Elias reached with his mind, but he had never linked to the third Flower, and he was unable to perceive the creatures in the continent or any of the Flyer wurl that would hatch one day. He hoped Dresde's daughter was okay.

He wondered if he would ever meet her.

They spent that night in a makeshift shelter next to the lake at the center of the Behemoth's back, and over the next few days they expanded it to make it more comfortable, particularly because Laurie needed to rest most of the time, and according to Nadja, her baby was due to be born any day. Thankfully, the weather was good and food was plentiful. It was easy to find ripe

fruit all over the island, and they had also brought supplies from land before setting off. It was a comfortable
trip, which Elias found odd. He was so used to waking
each day under the faint but persistent needling of worry and urgency that he had to work to adapt to actually
look forward to every morning with nothing to do but
wait.

He often stayed up late with Tristan and Oscar,
talking long into the night, and they reminisced about
their respective adventures. Oscar was very curious
about everything that had happened along the journey
to Raasay, and he could barely believe it when Tristan
described how they had built a boat from scratch. He
was intermittently disgusted and fascinated by the description of the ocean maw, was starry-eyed when he
heard about the Forest of Light, and he wanted to know
everything about the male Singer wurl.

"So they're bigger than Vanor?" Oscar asked one
night. The three of them sat together with the wurl near
the Behemoth's head, a spectacular view of the peaceful ocean spreading out before them. The only disturbance in the water came from the rhythmic splashes of
the gigantic creature.

Tristan considered. "Maybe the same size, but the
tentacles make them look bigger. Also stronger. No of-
fense, buddy," he amended with an apologetic glance
at Vanor.

Oscar laughed. "He's not offended," he said matter-of-factly. He was leaning against Siv, who appeared
to have taken a liking to him. All three of the wurl liked
spending time with Oscar, and he said he enjoyed their
company too.

"You can tell?" Elias asked him.

"Sure. They don't talk with words, right? But you can sort of know. Kind of like what Doran used to do."

Oscar looked pensive and a bit sad for a couple of seconds. He even glanced in the direction where Samantha and the others were already sleeping, far away near the center of the island.

"Are you okay?" Elias wanted to know.

"Yeah, I guess. No—I am."

Tristan slapped Oscar's shoulder playfully. "You're more than okay. You're a seasoned adventurer! Just wait till we get home. *Everyone's* going to want to know your story."

"You think?"

"Of course!" Tristan assured him. "I wouldn't be surprised if Commander Rodriguez asked you to join the force as a certified tough guy. And think about how popular you'll be! All the girls are going to be falling over themselves to date you."

"Girls? Oh, right," Oscar said, as though he hadn't even considered it.

"Or guys?" Tristan amended.

Oscar didn't reply, but he did keep looking in the direction where Samantha probably was.

Elias elbowed Tristan in the ribs. "Anyway," he said to change the subject, "maybe we should go…."

Elias stood up, his unfinished sentence forgotten. Vanor, Narev, and Siv followed suit and flanked him. Elias gave Sizzra's egg to Tristan.

"Eli?" Tristan asked. "What's wrong?"

"Not wrong," Elias replied. He closed his eyes and asked the Behemoth to halt for a moment. His request was accepted, and the island stopped moving very slowly. "He's coming."

"Who's coming?" Oscar asked.

Elias pointed at the dark waters ahead of them. "Look."

A few seconds later, yellow-green luminescence twinkled in the dark.

Something rose above the water with barely a ripple. For a moment the shape was invisible, but Alinor then decloaked and approached the Island Behemoth with confidence.

None of the Spine wurl growled. They allowed him to approach until Alinor was treading water immediately underneath them.

"Hi," Elias said, both with his voice and with his mind. "How are you?"

Alinor sent him a query. He knew Lyrana was dead, but he wanted to know how. Elias did his best to communicate what had happened, keeping the ideas simple but making sure to communicate Lyrana's bravery.

"We wouldn't be standing here if it weren't for her," he concluded. "She protected the entire world with her life."

Alinor accepted the information and was quiet for several seconds. He then shared something in return.

Elias gasped in welcome surprise at an image in Alinor's mind, a memory: a sizable clutch of moss-green eggs rested in a deep crevice at the bottom of the ocean, lit only by the luminescence coming from their watchful father's body.

At the top of the pile was another egg. Larger. It was a breathtaking shade of shimmering gold.

"Thank you," Elias told Alinor in a whisper. "I'm so glad. Watch over them. If you ever need me, call. Lyrana saved the lives of the people I love with her sacrifice. I owe her a debt I can never repay."

Alinor projected agreement, along with something akin to gratitude, and then sank beneath the waves.

Silence reigned for a while. Then Elias asked the Island Behemoth to move again, and from its mind, he also sensed satisfaction. Even a creature as large as it understood that the future of the ocean was not lost. That egg was a promise for the future.

"Um, what was all that about?" Oscar asked. "You stand up, get all mysterious and quiet, mutter some things, and a grown Singer wurl comes to say hi?"

"Get used to it," Tristan commented. "He does it all the time. Communing here, esoteric telepathic something there. One minute you're talking to him, and the next he's all floaty. I just kind of tune it out until the trance is over."

Elias smiled. "Lyrana's daughter lives."

"Yes!" Tristan said. He reached for the golden scale he still carried with him. "That's amazing."

Elias nodded. He placed his hand on the white egg for a moment. "Your ocean sister lives."

After that night the sea itself seemed more peaceful to Elias. He could perceive its vastness, but also its incredible potential. Now that She Who Hungers no longer tainted the world with her presence, the distinct certainty that balance had returned filled him with satisfaction and hope. It was also amazing to be able to experience day after day of wondrous discovery without fear. He no longer had to watch the sky with apprehension in case winged assailants came. The water held no threat anymore, only enticing mystery. And the weather was no longer something to dread but something to marvel at.

A tropical storm came at midday on the third week of their trip. Elias sat with Narev near the Behemoth's head and watched the wall of dark clouds churn and flash as it came ever closer. When it started to rain, he did not seek shelter. He felt he did not need it. He enjoyed the sensation of warm raindrops on his skin, and even when the wind became a gale, he did not leave his perch or return to camp. He held Sizzra's egg in his arms, and together with the unborn queen he witnessed the magnificent display of primal violence that was both a show and a challenge. Lightning in particular was breathtaking when it sliced through the air to strike another cloud, the water, or the Behemoth itself. The deafening thunder that followed was like the voice of the planet, booming and bone-rattling but also joyful. Elias remembered how vulnerable he had felt the first time he had seen a storm at sea, how terrifying it had been when their boat had capsized, and he compared it to the way he felt now.

More confident. Less afraid. He respected the elemental power of nature and at the same time felt a spark of unquenchable curiosity that urged him to see, to learn, to experience.

A particularly violent thunderclap in the wake of a searing bolt of lightning seemed to rattle the entire world. Narev nuzzled Elias's hand. He really didn't like storms.

Elias smiled and projected reassurance. Something about seeing such a large and powerful animal essentially cowering next to him from the weather was both endearing and comical.

They eventually left the storm behind, and bright daylight in a beautiful blue sky replaced the shifting grays and blacks of the roiling clouds.

"Eli!" Tristan yelled.

Elias stood up and looked back in time to see Tristan appear. He looked a bit frantic.

"Hey," Elias said calmly.

"You're drenched!" Tristan observed. Then he shook his head. "Never mind. We have kind of a situation."

"What do you mean?"

"Laurie."

Elias's eyes widened. "The baby."

"Yep. I think she's about to give birth. Not sure if we can help, but I think we should be there."

"Um… are you sure? We don't know anything about babies."

The sound of large creatures moving through thick undergrowth heralded the arrival of Vanor and Siv. Oscar was with them.

"Hey, guys," Oscar said.

"How's Laurie doing?" Elias asked.

"I'm not sure," Oscar replied. "Nadja kicked me out. She said she didn't want to be sexist or anything, but it's kind of a women-only thing."

Tristan sighed loudly. "Thank goodness."

Elias looked over at him. "Huh?"

"I'm… not great with blood and stuff."

"Tristan," Elias pointed out, "you got your arm nearly bitten off by a wurl once and you barely flinched."

"Well, yeah," Tristan protested, absently touching his scar, "but that was *my* blood. This is different."

"I wonder what they're going to call the baby," Oscar wondered.

"Me too. Are you sure we can't we help?" Elias asked. "Don't you need for things to be, like, super clean and everything?"

Oscar shrugged. "Samantha says they know what to do."

"All right," Elias conceded. "So we wait?"

"We wait."

Samantha came a few hours later, in late afternoon. She looked frazzled but happy. "My nephew has been born."

"Congratulations!" Oscar beamed. He made as if to hug Samantha but appeared to reconsider in the middle of the motion and ended up giving her an awkward pat on the shoulder instead.

"Do you want to meet him?" she asked them.

Elias nodded. "Of course!"

They made their way back to camp, where the others were waiting. Ute and Nadja sat on either side of Laurie, who held a beautiful baby in her arms. She smiled at them when they arrived.

"This is Luca," she said. "My son."

The baby was swaddled in a soft-looking white blanket. He had a dusting of raven-black hair and smooth chestnut skin.

"Hi, Luca," Oscar said, waving enthusiastically.

"He looks like Jörgen," Ute said.

"He is perfect," Nadja announced. "Oh!"

"Oma?" Samantha asked.

"I have realized I am now a great-grandmother!"

They all shared a laugh. Laurie spoke then, looking at Samantha, Oscar, Elias, and Tristan. "I thank you all from the bottom of my heart. Because of your actions, this is a day of celebration rather than a day of fear. I was so scared of what would become of my child if he were to be male. I was scared for months."

Ute reached for Laurie's hand and squeezed it. They shared a knowing look.

Laurie swept a blond lock of hair away from her face. "I was angry at the world, at fate, for being so cruel. I missed my husband... but today I feel more hope than ever in my life. I have a reason to smile. Luca is born free. I am free. Thank you."

Oscar teared up, and he wasn't the only one.

They saw land two days afterward. The Behemoth got as close to the shore as it could and then stopped, waiting patiently.

"Thank you so much," Elias said to it, touching the creature's tough shell with both of his hands. "You have brought us home."

The Behemoth acknowledged Elias with vague fondness. It had slowly come to recognize Elias specifically, despite him being so small when compared to a creature so large and so ancient, and it sent him the essence of a wordless idea Elias was able to translate as an invitation.

Until we meet again.

They disembarked carefully and then stood in the shallows for a while, waving the Behemoth goodbye.

"Bye, big boy," Oscar said. "Thanks for everything!"

"I think the wurl are going to miss it," Tristan pointed out. Narev, Vanor, and Siv were looking at the departing living island with a hint of sadness.

A few minutes later the Behemoth had disappeared over the horizon. It was another sunny day, and the temperature was nice and balmy.

"So this is the other continent," Samantha commented, looking all around. "Reena."

"You'll love it," Oscar said.

Elias turned away from the ocean and walked onto dry land.

He gasped.

All three wurl bounded over to him. Elias looked first at the egg he carried and then at each of them. "We're home," he said.

As soon as he had stepped fully out of the ocean, he had been welcomed by an almost overwhelming sensation of connection and unity. He sensed the Flower of the Earth with incredible clarity, and he felt as though firmly rooted into the fathomless energy of the entire continent through the soles of his feet.

The wurl felt the same way. And there was a brighter brush of awareness from the egg.

"Almost there," Elias told each of them. He sent them a clear image of Crescent Valley and the cave where, he hoped, most of Sizzra's eggs still waited.

"Is everything okay?" Nadja asked, sounding concerned.

"Yep," Elias replied. "Everything's great."

"Let's get going!" Oscar said. "We've been getting messages nonstop from the colony. Too bad we can't answer. I can't wait to see Mom and Dad!"

"And my dad," Tristan added. "And everyone."

They set out after some initial negotiations of who was riding the wurl. Elias was able to convince Laurie that Narev would be gentle with her and Luca, and Tristan reassured Nadja that Vanor was nowhere near as scary as he appeared. The rest of them would be walking. Siv carried their supplies, including a sizable amount of food they had gathered from the Behemoth over the weeks, and they set off.

It was much slower going than when Elias and Tristan had been alone, but Elias enjoyed every day. Now that he wasn't in a desperate hurry get to his destination as fast as he could, Elias used his connection with the world to guide the party along the best route to Portree. He skirted the more dangerous sections of the rain forest, plotted a course that would follow as many rivers as possible so freshwater would be plentiful, and made sure to find the safest places for them to make camp so Luca's frequent crying wouldn't draw the attention of curious predators.

At night Elias relaxed while he held Tristan in his arms. Oscar would often be nearby, dictating letters into his link. He said he wanted to give everyone back home a detailed account of what had happened and spent many hours writing about his and Samantha's adventures, and he would often badger Elias and Tristan for details of what they had gone through so he could record it. Elias answered willingly, since it was fun to remember everything he and Tristan had done. However, he did ask Oscar not to write about some of the more sensitive topics, such as the locations of the eggs or the Flowers. Those were not their secrets to divulge.

The weather changed slowly in its inexorable shift to autumn with each passing day. The sun rose lower in the sky, and the midday heat was no longer sweltering. The nights were chilly at times, and the wind had a crispness that reminded Elias of something like nostalgia, as though the world were preparing itself for a long sleep. The leaves of some trees along the way began to turn yellow and orange, but none of them had fallen yet. They added their vibrant tones to the already spectacular landscapes they traversed and made Elias wish he could stay at certain places for months at a time, admiring nature.

Their progress was steady. A little under a month after disembarking, Elias had them make a wide detour around the swamp so they would avoid it altogether, and they approached Portree from the south instead.

"These hills," Tristan said. They had come to a brief stop at the top of a grassy summit in a familiar rolling landscape. "I recognize them."

"I can see mountains over there, and a forest," Oscar indicated, pointing to the northwest. "So the colony should be—"

Three links beeped at the same time.

"What's happening?" Samantha asked.

"We're in range! Everyone's calling," Oscar answered. He tapped his link. "Hi, Mom!"

"Hi, Dad," Tristan said, walking off to the side with his link to his ear.

Elias accepted his own call. "Hello, Director O'Rourke."

He spent nearly an hour in a conference call with the director and the rest of the council. Elias really wanted to talk to his family, but there was a lot to discuss, and he knew it was important to reassure the government of Portree that everything was okay. He gave them a general description of what had happened to Dresde, which was their main concern. Elias heard the relief in Director O'Rourke's voice when he assured her that the wurl queen was no longer a threat and the colony was safe.

"We received Oscar's message, but we dared not hope," she said to Elias. "We'll take down the barrier. This is the best news I've heard in months."

"We don't come alone," Elias pointed out, glancing over at Samantha and her family. Ute and Laurie were focused on the baby, but Nadja and Samantha looked a bit tense as they listened to Elias's conversation.

"Yes, Oscar explained it in his message," the director responded. "Other colonists! It's like a dream. I will let the entire colony know to expect them. Perhaps some of us are even distantly related to them!"

"We have a baby with us too," Elias added.

There were audible gasps and excited voices in the background, but the director spoke over them. "Elias, please let your companions know that they are welcome in Portree. We will talk about this extensively later, but from what I understand they were instrumental in defeating Dresde and protecting our colony from destruction. They will be honored guests—no, they will be fellow citizens of Portree. I will call for a vote on the issue immediately. We can barely wait to meet them."

Elias grinned. "We'll be there by tomorrow, I think."

"Take as much time as you need. We'll be here when you arrive. And Elias?"

"Yes, Director?"

"Thank you too. For everything you've done."

"No problem. See you all soon."

He hung up. Oscar raced over to him. "Yeah, Mom," he said. "Eli's done with the director, *finally*. You want to talk to him?"

"Hi, Mom," Elias said, smiling. "How are you?"

"Eli!" his mother all but shouted. "Are you okay? Are you well?"

"Of course!"

His mother sniffled. "I… I'm so glad…."

She started crying, and Elias's father took over. "Elias," he said in his unmistakable deep voice.

"Hi, Dad."

"I've—" It sounded as though his voice caught in his throat. "I've got too much to say. But I can wait until we see each other. You'll come tomorrow?"

"We'll be there."

"Okay. I love you, son. I love you, Oscar."

"Love you too, Dad," Elias replied.

"See you tomorrow!" Oscar declared.

They hung up. Tristan approached, grinning from ear to ear. "How's everything?" he asked them.

"Great," Elias replied. "How's your dad?"

"He could barely talk, he was crying so much," Tristan answered. "But he's fine."

Elias drew Tristan into an embrace. "I'm glad."

Tristan looked into Elias's eyes and kissed him.

"You guys heard, right?" Oscar asked Samantha and her family. "Everyone is looking forward to meeting you! I'm telling them all about you in my letters, which I can finally send!"

Nadja nodded. "I am glad. And thankful."

"Should we continue?" Samantha suggested.

"You bet!" Oscar said.

chapter 34.
home

THAT NIGHT they made camp for the last time at the top of a hill from where it was possible to see the lights of Portree in the far distance. Elias watched them with longing and excitement.

"It's surreal," Tristan observed. "So many lights. I can't believe I lived there!"

"Is it large?" Samantha asked Oscar. "The colony?"

"Not a lot. Why?"

"I merely wondered," Samantha said.

"Wait a sec," Oscar added. "Are you nervous?"

"A little bit."

"I believe we all are," Ute said.

Laurie nodded. Luca had stopped crying earlier and was peacefully asleep in her arms. "It is something new. Nearly a hundred people—I can scarcely imagine that many."

"Don't worry," Oscar reassured them. "Everyone's real friendly."

Elias stood up and left the fireside with Sizzra's egg in his arms. Tristan gave him a questioning look, but Elias shook his head and walked off into the dark on his own.

Vanor, Narev, and Siv were waiting for him farther down the hill. Their red eyes gleamed, and their scales glinted under the moonlight.

"Hey, guys," Elias said to them, his voice quiet. "I'm going home now."

Narev approached and nuzzled his hand like he usually did.

Elias swallowed past the lump in his throat.

"You can take the egg from here to Crescent Valley, can't you?" Elias asked them.

Vanor stepped forward and projected confident assurance. His leg was fully healed, and this was his territory. He knew the way very well.

"All right," Elias said. He walked over to Siv and unloaded most of the bags and things on his back with the exception of a single pack, which Elias emptied out. "I'll put the egg in here so it's easy to carry. You guys can take turns with it, but be careful."

All three of them huffed in a very serious way, like soldiers receiving their orders.

"Take it all the way to the cave and watch over it until it hatches. All right?"

The wurl gave him wordless but unmistakable agreement.

Elias put the egg in the backpack with care and then stepped away. "Be safe. And… thank you for everything. You guys were amazing, every step of the way."

They hesitated. They understood that they were to continue onward, but they didn't understand why Elias wasn't coming.

"I have to see my own family," Elias said, willing himself not to cry. "And people might be scared of you guys. They might not understand that you're friendly. And the egg is a secret. It's better this way. Okay?"

Vanor grunted and, oddly for him, stepped up to where Elias was standing and nuzzled his hand like Narev had done. Siv didn't approach, but he did dip his head slightly, still holding the straps of the backpack with the egg in his jaws.

Then they turned away. They started walking northwest in the tireless, lumbering way of the Spine wurl.

"You better go too, Narev," Elias urged, resting his hand on his friend's warm silver scales.

Narev looked into Elias's eyes and then crooned, his voice melodic and sad.

"Eli?" Tristan called from the distance. It sounded as though he was coming closer.

"Go," Elias repeated. "I love you, boy."

Narev's eyes flashed. He waited a second longer and then bounded away after his brothers.

Tristan arrived a few seconds later. He wrapped an arm gently around Elias's waist and stood by his side, looking out over the moonlit landscape.

"Are they gone?" Tristan asked.

"Yeah."

A ryddle bird crowed in the night.

"And are you okay?"

"I don't know," Elias admitted. He felt like crying, but he was also hopeful and happy. It was confusing.

Tristan stayed with him for a while. They sat down together in the grass with the cool autumn wind ruffling their hair as the night advanced and the lights of distant Portree twinkled out one by one.

Eventually they rejoined the others. Elias slept little and woke up before dawn broke.

He wasn't the only one. Everyone seemed equal parts excited and nervous.

"I can't wait," Oscar said after breakfast. "Wait. Where are the guys? Where's Siv?"

"They left," Elias explained.

"Why?" Oscar asked him.

"They have their own mission."

"Oh. I'll miss them."

"We all will," Nadja said. "Thank them when you see them again, Elias. They were wonderful companions."

He nodded. "I will."

Without the wurl, covering the last few miles was slow going, but it was only noon when they descended the last hill and came in view of the colony forest at long last.

"We're here," Oscar said.

Tristan smiled and took Elias's hand. "Let's go say hi."

Elias texted his father to tell him they were about to arrive. He and Tristan led the way through the tree cover that encircled Portree, and a few minutes later they saw the first houses on the outskirts.

And people. Lots of them.

"Oh wow," Tristan commented.

"It's everyone," Elias said.

He glanced over at Samantha, who looked nervous but determined. Ute and Nadja flanked Laurie, who carried Luca in her arms. They were all bedraggled from the long journey, but they held their heads high.

The entire colony had come out to greet them. There were excited whispers among them at first, and some people were pointing. Elias began to feel nervous too. He hadn't seen so many people at once in a long while.

Tristan squeezed Elias's hand.

"It's going to be okay," he told Elias.

They came to a stop a few steps away from the crowd. Elias saw his aunt Laura, looking overworked as usual, with dark circles under her eyes. The younger people in the colony were off to one side, with Sarah Parker in the center of the group. Her friends, Evelyn and Yuki, stood a bit farther back. Harold MacLeod, pad in hand, was next to the entirety of the colony council. The patrol officers, unarmed but intimidating, formed a small perimeter at the front of the gathering.

"Hi, guys!" Oscar said brightly, waving. Some of the teens waved back.

"Oscar! Eli!" Elias's mother yelled.

"Tristan!"

Elias's parents and Tristan's father ran forward, past the Colony Patrol. Tristan, Oscar, and Elias ran too, and they all met halfway between the two groups of people.

It was a blur of happiness, laughter, and tears. Elias hugged his father first, as if in a dream. He almost couldn't believe that the journey was over. He was with his family again.

"You brought him back," his dad said, crying unabashedly. "You kept your promise, Elias. I'm so happy you're okay. And Oscar. I love you so much, both of you."

"I love you too, Dad," Elias replied, not even caring that every single person in the colony was watching. "We're safe."

"Eli!" his mother said. She was hugging Oscar, and they all came together as a family in a group embrace. She was sobbing and smiling at the same time. "Thank goodness. My children are back! Eli, Oscar, I missed you so much."

"We missed you too, Mom," Oscar said. "I thought of you every day."

"We got your letters," his father told Oscar. "We read them again and again."

"How are you guys?" Elias asked.

His mother smiled. She looked radiant and strong, so different to her former frail self that it was like a miracle. "Now? We couldn't be better."

Elias's grandmother came next, and there were more tearful exchanges.

Someone tapped Elias on the shoulder. It was Tristan's father, Marcus MacLeod.

"Elias," he said. He was an imposing man, stockier than Tristan and sporting a full salt-and-pepper beard.

"Hi, Mr. MacLeod."

"My boy here tells me you saved his life many times," Marcus said. He rested his left hand on Tristan's shoulder.

"Um…," Elias stammered.

"Come here," Marcus said, drawing Elias into a bear hug. "Thank you, son. I'm glad Tristan has found someone who loves him like you do."

"Dad!" Tristan protested.

But then Tristan was drawn into the Trost family. Elias's dad thanked him too, and his mom kissed Tristan on the cheek.

A new voice spoke up with the unmistakable cadence of leadership. "Hello, Elias. Tristan. Oscar," Director O'Rourke said as she approached. "You have been missed."

"Hello, Director," Elias said.

Commander Rodriguez was right behind her, arms crossed over her chest. "I have to ask, MacLeod," she said, speaking to Tristan. "We're safe? Will that flying creature attack us?"

"Negative, Commander," Tristan replied, snapping to attention. "The threat has been neutralized."

Elias could scarcely believe it when the usually stoic Commander Rodriguez cracked a smile. She relaxed visibly. "You did good, Tristan."

"Thanks."

"This is a happy day," the director continued, speaking so her voice carried. "In time, you will tell us of your adventures and how you came to save the colony a second time. For now, I would like to welcome you back home, as well as your honored companions."

All eyes focused on Samantha and her family. Nadja approached the director without the slightest hint of hesitation.

"I am Nadja," she said. "This is my daughter, Ute. My granddaughter, Samantha. My granddaughter-in-law, Lauren. And my great-grandson, Luca."

Some people whispered when they realized the baby was there. Elias clearly heard someone say, "So cute!"

"My name is Catherine O'Rourke. I am the director of this colony. I thank you for caring for Oscar, Elias, and Tristan. From what I understand in the letters Oscar sent, it is thanks to you that they have come home safely."

"We owe them much in turn," Nadja replied. "It is due to their bravery, and Samantha's, that we are free of Dresde's shadow forever."

Director O'Rourke extended her right hand. "Consider Portree your new home, if you choose to stay. It is a true honor to meet you all."

Nadja took the director's hand and shook it formally. "I thank you, Catherine O'Rourke. My family accepts your invitation gladly."

"Excellent!" the director said, smiling broadly. "Please, follow us. You must be tired after your long journey. We have prepared a house for you to rest and refresh yourselves, and this evening we will celebrate with a grand feast."

"Feast?" Elias echoed. It wasn't a word that was often used in Portree.

Director O'Rourke winked at him, dropping all formality for a moment. "Much has changed, thanks to you, Elias. We have plenty of food now."

Elias and the rest of his group followed everyone back into the colony. Although evidently brimming with curiosity, most people simply said hi or waved and told Elias, Oscar, and Tristan that they looked forward to the celebration that evening.

Tristan went off to his house with his dad but promised he would return after he took a shower and changed clothes. Oscar and Elias followed their parents to their home. Samantha and her family were with them. Now that the crowd had dispersed, they looked a bit more at ease.

"Your new home is this way," Elias's mother indicated. "A couple of houses away from ours, in fact."

"Neat!" Oscar commented. "Samantha, we're going to be neighbors!"

Samantha nodded. She was wide-eyed, looking at everything with open curiosity. "Portree is so big."

"This is the place!" Elias's mother announced. The party stopped in front of a home that was identical to Elias's. She gave Nadja a set of keys. "Please let us know if you need anything. We're over there."

"Thank you, um," Nadja replied, hesitating.

"Irina," Elias's mother said. "This is my husband, Bradford."

"It is nice to meet you," Nadja replied.

"The pleasure is ours!" Irina added. "We have heard a lot about you from Oscar, and particularly about young Samantha. It's so nice to meet you at last, honey. You're even prettier than Oscar described!"

Elias tried very hard not to laugh at seeing Oscar turn a shade of crimson that would have made even Dresde jealous.

"Very nice to meet you," Samantha responded, evidently a bit flustered.

"Ahem, anyway," Oscar said, sounding a bit desperate. "Let's go get changed and stuff, right?"

"Call us if you need anything," Elias said to Samantha. "Talk to you in a bit."

They left their companions behind and went home.

Crossing the threshold into the house was almost a shock for Elias. His senses were bombarded with gentle reminders of his past life. The aroma of warm bread wafted through the kitchen. The floorboards creaked in predictable ways when he walked into the living room. The furniture was exactly as it had been when he left, and the temperature was pleasantly warm, like a cocoon of safety sheltering him from the outside world.

The four of them sat on a couple of big sofas, and they talked.

The hours flew by as first Oscar and then Elias told their parents about their adventures. They had barely scratched the surface of what they recalled when their links beeped with a reminder that the feast was about to start. Elias took a quick shower and tried to put on some clean clothes, but none of his nice shirts fit. He had to ask his father to lend him one, and Oscar borrowed one from Elias because his didn't fit either.

"Did we get buff?" Oscar asked Elias. The two of them were getting dressed in their room. Oscar flexed his biceps experimentally.

"Kind of," Elias replied. "And you also grew a lot."

"Nice," Oscar said.

"That blue shirt looks good on you," Elias observed. "Do you think young Samantha will like it?"

Oscar threw a shoe at him.

Elias was brushing his teeth when his parents said they would go on ahead to the colony plaza and left in a rather suspicious hurry.

"What's that about?" Oscar asked.

Elias shrugged and concentrated on finishing getting ready. Combing his hair was a challenge.

"Eli?" Tristan called from somewhere below. "Are you here?"

"Upstairs!"

Tristan came into the room, and the sight of him took Elias's breath away.

"Wow," Elias whispered. "You look amazing."

Tristan was wearing a crisp white formal shirt underneath a navy blue dinner jacket. He was clean-shaven, and his hair was styled in a somewhat chaotic but flattering mode that framed his angular features and the strong set of his jaw. He smelled great, like pine needles and wood, and his skin was so clean it was almost luminous. His pants fit him just right too.

"Nice butt," Elias commented, checking him out.

"Aaaand that's my cue to leave," Oscar said at once. "I'm gonna go check on Samantha."

He escaped downstairs, leaving Elias and Tristan alone.

"You also look great," Tristan said, stepping close for a kiss. "I love how your dark jacket highlights your beautiful eyes."

Elias embraced Tristan. And started crying out of nowhere.

"What's wrong?" Tristan asked, running his hands through Elias's hair.

"Nothing," Elias replied, his heart bursting with happiness. "Nothing at all."

The two of them went downstairs after a bit. Elias debated whether to leave Sizzra's spine behind, but he couldn't.

"We're safe now," Tristan reminded him as they walked to the front door. "You won't need that anymore. I left Lyrana's scale on my bed."

"I know. It's not about having it in case something happens. It's more about the connection. It reminds me of them."

"The guys?"

"Yeah," Elias answered. "I hope they're doing okay."

"They'll probably get to Crescent Valley today or tomorrow," Tristan told him. "Vanor can keep going all night, and Narev and Siv will follow. They'll be okay. They know how to take care of themselves."

Elias sighed. He ran his fingers over the length of the iridescent spine that had accompanied him halfway around the world. "You're right. It's just that I miss them."

They met Oscar, Samantha, and the rest of her family outside. The women were almost unrecognizable in formal evening attire.

"Wow," Tristan said. "You guys look incredible!"

"I know, right?" Oscar joined in. "That's what I was telling them!"

"Your people are generous," Nadja observed. "Our home is fully stocked with everything we could possibly need. Doctor Hino visited us as well, to check on Luca. She says my great-grandson is healthy and strong."

"I like this dress," Ute commented, doing a little twirl. Hers was an ankle-length gown of pastel yellow. "It is beautiful."

"Dresses are uncomfortable," Samantha complained. She was wearing a suit instead, dark gray and flattering to her slim figure. A white shirt completed her ensemble. "They make it hard to walk."

"Should we get going?" Elias proposed. There was no one out on the street, which he found odd. "Everyone's probably over at the plaza already."

"Let's go!" Oscar said. "I'm *so* hungry. And I'm sick of eating fruits and roots. Do you guys think Chef Matsuo made cake?"

"Cake?" Laurie asked, perking up. Luca was fidgeting in her arms in a fluffy yellow blanket. "I have read about cake."

"It's so good," Oscar said. "I really hope it's chocolate! Or strawberry."

They made their way through familiar streets that were somehow different as well. Elias couldn't quite place the sensation, but the town felt changed. There was a sense of energy that hadn't been there before. The façades of the houses seemed livelier. Numerous gardens and flowers were everywhere, all but bursting with life, and the cool evening air hummed with the occasional buzz of an insect.

They passed by the greenhouses on their way, and Elias did a double-take.

"Whoa," Oscar commented. "That's new."

The greenhouse complex had tripled in size. Even though no one was working in there at the moment, multiple lights at regular intervals illuminated rows upon rows of healthy-looking crops of many different kinds, an abundance of plants Elias had never seen. Some had beautiful triangular leaves along curlicue vines, while others had fascinating colors, blue and purple and magenta. They were almost like the grains and legumes he had grown up with, but not quite. These were living things he could clearly sense.

"It's the hybrid seeds!" Tristan exclaimed. "Well, the plants that grew from them."

Elias nodded. "Yeah. They're thriving."

Tristan gave him a hug. "You did it, Eli."

"Guys, I'm hungry," Oscar protested. "I think I see lights over there."

They arrived at the plaza, and an explosion of applause received them. The entire town was there, standing around dozens of square tables that had been decked with festive ornaments. Flowers adorned every centerpiece, and the chairs sported bows in shades of white and gold. Strings of lights hung from the nearby buildings and spanned the entire overhead space, creating a veritable ceiling made of a cozy yellow glow that nevertheless allowed a view of one of the moons, shining bright in the nighttime sky. The air smelled of cinnamon and vanilla, and pleasant warmth surrounded the gathering, coming from several strategically placed radiators.

Everybody was wearing their formal best. As they clapped, Elias realized many people were looking at him. And they were smiling.

There was also food. Lots of it. Four long tables on the side of the Main Hall practically groaned under the weight of plate after plate piled high with delicious-looking dishes. Baskets of fresh produce were dotted about, and each smaller table bore several enticing miniature treats. A small platform at the very center of the plaza held a literal cornucopia of what could only be the year's harvest, and among the native fruits, Elias noticed large piles of the seeds he had brought to the colony.

The applause stopped little by little. Elias took Tristan's hand. He was a bit nervous with so many people looking at them at once.

"Welcome once again," Director O'Rourke said. She was speaking into a microphone from a dais that had been erected across from all the food. The rest of the council stood by a table nearby. "Tonight is a celebration of the bright future of our colony. Please, join us. I assume you are hungry?"

Music started playing, and people took seats. Relieved, Elias glanced at his companions. Tristan was grinning from ear to ear. Oscar was eyeing the food. Samantha and her family looked a bit overwhelmed.

"This way, Eli!" his mother called from the table next to the council's. She was sitting there with his dad and grandmother, as well as Tristan's dad.

Elias waved back, and they walked over to their seats, saying hi to people they passed on the way. People shook Elias's hand. Some thanked him. Others clapped him on the shoulder. In fact, so many people wanted to talk to him that it took Elias nearly ten minutes to reach the table where his family was waiting.

He plopped down in an empty chair between Tristan and Oscar.

"I feel like a celebrity!" Oscar said. "This is awesome."

"I know!" Tristan agreed.

"Is it always like this?" Samantha wanted to know. She was sitting across from Oscar, and she looked all around her with an expression of what could only have been curiosity, along with a bit of sensory overload.

Elias's mother reached across the table and patted her hand. "Not at all, honey. Today is special. You are heroes! This is a celebration in your honor. Enjoy!"

It took Elias a while to fully relax, but he was surrounded by the people he loved, and tension drained away from his body steadily until he felt at ease and completely safe. He realized part of him had been constantly on edge for a very long time now, worrying about surviving, about being attacked, or about finding food and shelter every day. It wasn't like that anymore, and he started smiling more often. Before he knew it, he was truly enjoying himself.

The food certainly helped. The feast was a massive buffet, and Chef Matsuo had outdone himself. The snacks at the table were savory and crunchy rings of an unknown vegetable that tasted like onions. There was a spicy dipping sauce to go with them, along with a side of leafy greens. Carbonated water bubbled in his glass. It had been scented with something that had a faint citrus aroma, sparkling and cool and refreshing.

"No way," Oscar said after finishing his appetizers. "I think I see candied apples on the table. Be right back."

"I'm going too," Tristan announced. "Everything looks great, and I'm starving. Eli, let's go."

"Yeah," Elias replied. "Nadja, Samantha? Would you guys like me to bring you something?"

"Thank you, Elias," Nadja replied. "We will go soon. This is… a new experience."

Elias nodded. He followed Tristan up to the tables and was amazed by everything he saw. There were salads, stews, baked pastries, and grilled vegetables. Fruits Elias had never seen and dishes he recognized instantly, such as the vegetable lasagna he piled onto his plate. There were bowls of what looked like corn chips with nearby containers of salsa of at least four different colors. He saw lentils and beans, three kinds of soup, and triangular rice cakes wrapped in what appeared to be seaweed. A fountain of hot chocolate, surrounded with bits of fruit for dipping, held pride of place.

He was ecstatic at all of the different choices. He picked a couple of slices of hot bread and some green beans. He then returned to the table to set his plate down and went back for something else to drink. There were at least ten different options, ranging from fruit juice to spring water to a beverage that was probably soda, and even some wine that was, according to the little tag next to it, made from purpleberries.

Elias ate more that night than he had done in months. He tried to pace himself, but everything was so delicious that he kept going back for more. He tried savory dishes, spicy dishes, and sweet treats. When the cake was brought out, he got a tiny slice because he couldn't eat any more, but he wanted to try it nonetheless. It was amazing, a confection of bitter chocolate and some kind of fruit marmalade.

Now truly stuffed, Elias left the table for a bit and looked for Chef Matsuo. He found him standing next to the desserts.

"Chef," Elias said. "This is an amazing feast. Thank you so much."

Chef Matsuo beamed. "Glad you like it, Elias!"

"It must have taken ages to prepare this."

He shrugged. "I had help, but it did take a while. I think it's been twenty-four hours since I last slept, to tell you the truth."

"Wow. And the food? How did you make all of it?"

The chef arranged his glasses over the bridge of his nose. "Most of this is thanks to you, of course. We have legumes to make into paste for the simulated meat dishes, and the flavorings are my own concoction. There is the wheat analog you brought for the flour and bread and chips, and I had to get very creative to make rice powder and soy taste like chocolate."

"There's fruit I've never seen."

"Ah! That's my favorite part. Now that we don't have to be scared of wurl, I and a few others have gone exploring, with help from members of the patrol, looking around the region for edible things. We found an incredible variety of fruit, tubers, and vegetables growing all around in the summertime. The forest in the far south is my favorite place. It's a three-day walk, but it's worth it for the apples alone. Well, they're not apples, but almost. You know what I mean."

"It's amazing. It sounds like there's an abundance of food all around the colony."

"Up to a point," Chef Matsuo replied. "I'm sure you know we aren't able to grow any of those wild plants here, so we need to be careful to harvest sustainably so we don't take too much. As long as we do that,

I believe we can look forward to the bounty of nature every year."

Elias thanked him again and walked around the tables for a while, saying hi to people. He spent almost half an hour with his aunt while she regaled him with fascinating details of how they had germinated the very first seeds he had brought, in the laboratory. She described the intricacies of genetic sequencing, the numerous tests, and finally the initial large-scale planting stage in the greenhouses.

"That very first harvest was incredible," she recounted, smiling. "You should have seen it, Elias. Some people were crying. Others literally didn't believe we had a stable food supply until they held the seeds in their hands and cooked something with them. Of course, yields are low, and I don't think there is any way to increase them, so it's very likely we'll never have large cities on this planet. But we won't starve."

Elias left his aunt after a bit and spent some time conversing with many other people who wanted to congratulate him, thank him, or who were simply burning with curiosity about his adventures. Sizzra's spine in particular was a magnet for kids, and a couple of them even touched it after Elias assured them it was perfectly safe.

Eventually he returned to his own table and sat. Samantha and Oscar were discussing whether chocolate cake was superior to vanilla ice cream. Elias's dad was deep in conversation with Ute and Nadja, explaining to them how the telecom array worked and how they had been able to receive Oscar's messages from the shuttle. Elias's mother was entirely focused on Luca, and she was giving Laurie tips on how to get him to stop crying at night.

"This is nice, huh?" Tristan said quietly. He was sipping a bit of purpleberry wine.

"Yeah," Elias replied.

Tristan set his glass down and leaned against him, resting his head on Elias's shoulder. "I'm really happy, Eli."

"Me too."

"Everything we did, everything *you* did, it was worth it."

Tristan lifted his head and closed his eyes, leaning in for a kiss. Elias returned it as he cradled Tristan's face with one hand. The sensation of Tristan's lips against his was like a warm balm that suffused his entire body. Elias breathed in Tristan's scent and felt Tristan's breath on his cheek. In that moment, his world was complete.

The music died down, and after the murmur of voices continued for a few seconds, the crowd grew silent.

Elias and Tristan looked over at the dais, where the entirety of the council was now standing. A low table had been set next to Director O'Rourke. Six rectangular boxes were arranged on it, resting on a spotless white tablecloth that underscored the beautiful black sheen of the yult wood from which the containers had evidently been made.

"Fellow citizens," the director said. This time the atmosphere was so quiet that there was no need for a microphone. "Friends. Tonight we celebrate those who have given us a future. Nearly a year ago, when Elias Trost took the Life Seed away, many of us believed him to be a criminal. I was angered by his actions, believing them to be selfish and harmful. I know many of you felt the same way.

"But we were proven wrong," she continued, glancing over at Elias. "He did what he believed to be the right thing, and his bravery was rewarded. If he had not returned the Seed to its rightful place, this feast we have enjoyed today could not have been possible.

"And yet, he was not alone. There was another threat in this world, something so dangerous and devastating that this colony, and all of us with it, could have been destroyed had Elias and his companions not acted as they did. I speak of the wurl queen, Dresde." There were murmurs and whispers at the sound of her name. "We witnessed her terrible power when she slew Sizzra at our very doorstep. We lived in fear for months afterward, fortifying our colony while knowing that our haphazardly built barrier would crumple under her assault and our weapons would be useless against a creature so large.

"It was then, against all hope, that we received incredible news. Dresde had been vanquished, and it is all thanks to the heroes you see before us. Citizens of Portree, tonight I can finally say this: we are safe. Clouds darken our future no longer. And we have these remarkable individuals to thank."

Applause broke out and lasted for nearly a minute. When it faded the director resumed her speech.

"We can never be grateful enough," she said to Elias and the others, "but I hope you will accept these small tokens of our warmest regards. Oscar Trost, Tristan MacLeod. Would you join me up here?"

Tristan stood up right away. Oscar looked doubtful. "Come on, Oscar," Tristan whispered. "Follow me."

Oscar glanced all around the table and then stood up. He was already blushing.

They walked onto the dais and shook the hands of every council member along the way. They greeted Director O'Rourke last.

"Oscar," she said, "I cannot begin to imagine how it must have been to be abducted by Dresde. You must have been terrified, but you survived. It is thanks to your ingenuity in communicating with us that we learned about what had happened, and for that I thank you. The messages you sent saved this colony weeks of fearful anxiety."

The director picked up one of the two smaller yult boxes and opened it. Inside there was a golden medal with a white ribbon. The medallion was beautifully wrought in a trefoil shape.

"I award you the Medal of Portree, our highest honor," Director O'Rourke announced as she bestowed it upon Oscar. "Wear it proudly."

Applause ensued, and Oscar did a sort of half bow as he said thanks. He was still beet red and looked decidedly uncomfortable being the center of attention.

"Tristan," the director continued, "you have always been a model citizen. From the day you joined the Colony Patrol, you have shown nothing but an impeccable sense of responsibility and a tireless drive to protect the people around you. Your fellow officers all speak highly of you. In fact, your commander would like to say some words. Amanda? Would you come up, please?"

Commander Rodriguez walked up to the platform. She was wearing a stunning strapless evening gown in a deep shade of maroon, which Elias found oddly incongruous with his image of her. He had always seen the commander in her patrol uniform with her shock spear slung across her back. This was the first time Elias saw her wearing jewelry, or her long black hair cascading around her shoulders. She still looked imposing, but there was a glint of softness to her expression that had never been there before. Even the old scar that marred the beautiful olive skin on her face appeared less conspicuous, almost as if it wanted to fade away into nothing but memory.

"I'll make this quick," Commander Rodriguez said. "Tristan, you're a good man and a capable officer. I'm not surprised you kicked ass wherever it is you went."

There were hoots from the back of the crowd, coming from the other patrol members. Phineas Trost whistled quite loudly.

Amanda Rodriguez gave them a one-sided grin. "I'm proud to call you my comrade in arms. You've shown both the discipline to follow orders and the courage to ignore them when they don't make sense. I'm not sure what the future holds for the Colony Patrol, seeing as how we don't have any wurl to fight anymore, but whatever it is, I'd be glad to have you in my team."

"Thank you, Commander," Tristan said, his voice thick with emotion.

"Nothing to thank," she replied. "We should be grateful to you guys, and I think we all are. Come here. You earned this medal."

Rodriguez bestowed the distinction upon Tristan to more enthusiastic applause. Elias had a weird sense of déjà vu when he recalled the Midwinter Feast of the previous year. Tristan had been the center of attention back then as well, but Elias had been stewing in frustration and jealousy instead of clapping enthusiastically with everyone else, as he was doing now.

He blinked, amazed at how much he had changed in so little time. Back then he had been angry, fearful, and he had wrestled with pernicious insecurities that had made him sarcastic and resentful of the people around him. There was no trace of any of those emotions in him anymore. His defenses were down, his heart was open, and it brimmed with a sense of connection to others that went deeper than his link to the world itself.

Tristan, Oscar, and Commander Rodriguez returned to their seats, and the director took center stage once more.

"Now it is my honor to preside over a very special ceremony indeed," she announced. "From the beginning of our history, Portree has been a closed community. We were all we knew because we believed there were no other people sharing this world with us."

She looked at Samantha and the rest of her family, as did many others.

"However, this was not the case," O'Rourke went on. "Unknown to us, our brothers and sisters were living on Raasay, descendants of the colonists who once shared the generation ship with our forebears. There, they endured unspeakable hardship under Dresde's tyranny.

"I can only imagine how terrible it must have been. All we know about your troubles and tribulations comes from Oscar's letters, and we would certainly respect your wishes if you never want to speak of what you went through half a world away. Nevertheless, you are here now, among us, and I believe it is time for a more formal welcome into our small but friendly community."

The director smiled and picked up one of the four remaining boxes of elegant yult wood.

"Samantha," she said, "please come forward."

Samantha threw a slightly panicky look at Oscar. He nodded enthusiastically and gave her a double thumbs-up.

She stood and walked to the director with a somewhat stiff but confident demeanor. She nodded at O'Rourke and the rest of the council and then turned to face the crowd.

"Dear Samantha," the director said, "you, along with Tristan, Elias, and Oscar, have delivered us from the threat of an attack that would certainly have destroyed us. I understand your bravery was unquestionable. You showed incredible strength of will to defy Dresde, and Oscar tells us that your devotion to your family is without equal.

"I wish to show my gratitude, and that of us all, by officially inviting you to become a citizen of Portree. You will have the same rights and responsibilities as everyone else, and when you come of age you will be able to vote and make your voice heard in our government." O'Rourke opened the box. Inside, resting on black velvet, was a brand-new link that gleamed under the light. "It would make me very happy if you would accept my invitation."

Samantha looked at the link with evident surprise. She very nearly smiled and then nodded solemnly. "I accept, and I thank you, Director."

"Marvelous! Let me put this on you…. Harold, how do you install a new link?"

There were some chuckles when Harold MacLeod rushed over to help the director put the link around Samantha's left forearm. It was a quick process, and the computer beeped promisingly when it was installed.

"Welcome, Samantha. Our fellow citizen!" O'Rourke said.

Everyone clapped. Samantha thanked the director formally and returned to her seat. Nadja, Ute, and Laurie received their citizenship and links as well. The director couldn't quite help herself and kissed Luca on the forehead, reassuring Laurie that her baby would get the best care and education the colony could provide.

When everyone was seated there was a slightly longer pause. It took Elias a moment to notice that most people were looking at him again.

"And now for the main event of the evening," the director said. "We would not be here today if it weren't for one specific individual. He has given this colony its future. For as long as I can remember, ever since I was a girl, those around me lived in fear of what would come. I saw our food reserves dwindle and our harvests fail year after year. After I was elected to lead Portree, I spent many a sleepless night wondering what would become of the place I so love, and I must admit that eventually I came to despair. Nothing our talented scientists did seemed to help, and the ever-present threat of running out of sustenance was like a dull fog over my daily life and that of many others, one that grew thicker and darker each day.

"It was then that Elias Trost decided to act when none of us would. Not only did he risk his own life during the perilous trek to return the Life Seed to where it belonged, but he also negotiated with Sizzra, the wurl queen whose fearsome power we witnessed firsthand on the day of the storm. He kept her from destroying our colony, and he gave us the seeds that are the very embodiment of our hope."

O'Rourke descended from the dais and walked among the tables. Elias hadn't noticed that the center of the plaza had been cleared of furniture and other objects. He saw that a waist-high plinth had been hidden underneath the table with the cornucopia, but it was now on full display. The top of it was concealed under a white cloth.

Someone changed the illumination so most of the lights went out except for those above the middle of the space. The shift created a warm spotlight that commanded attention. Underneath it, the director stopped next to the plinth and spoke again.

"Elias, would you please join me?"

Elias stood up and tried not to trip over any chairs as he walked carefully over to stand next to Director O'Rourke.

She shook his hand with a motherly smile.

"Once you tried to speak, but we wouldn't listen," she began. "You told us of how you had discovered the journal of Thomas Wright and of the things you had learned in those pages. I silenced your voice back then out of fear. For this, Elias, I apologize."

"Um, it's okay," Elias replied, unsure whether he was supposed to speak or whether it was more of a monologue.

"It is not okay," O'Rourke contradicted him. She looked out over the crowd. "Secrecy is never preferable to open communication. Hiding the reality of the food crisis seemed to the council and myself to be the only way to protect the young from the harshness of the world, but in doing so we alienated those who, like you, saw beyond the thin veil of what I once convinced myself were white lies.

"Trying to control information was a mistake. Down that path lies deceit, surveillance, and tyranny. We are a community of equals, and every voice is as valuable as the next. You spoke when no one else would, and you have shown both good judgment and the resourcefulness and flexibility needed to interact with the powerful guardians of this world.

"I believe I am not alone when I say I have come to realize that we live on New Skye as guests rather than conquerors. The unique ecosystem of this planet is a living reminder of the fact that we must learn humility. Instead of taking, we must share. Instead of dominating, we must adapt and change. If we are to grow and prosper together with the other intelligent species of this world, we need to learn, to listen, and communicate."

O'Rourke tapped her link in a rather official-looking manner. Harold appeared behind her. He was holding a white sash embroidered with the black-and-gold symbol of the generation ship *Ionas*.

"Elias," the director said, "in recognition of your heroic deeds, I present to you three gifts. First, this plaque, which will stand in our plaza as long as Portree itself."

She pulled the cloth away from the plinth and revealed an engraved golden plaque.

> *In remembrance of the first*
> *Hope Day*
> *we honor Elias Trost*
> *who*
> *on May 27, 141 AP*
> *gave Portree its future.*

"Thank you from the bottom of my heart," O'Rourke said.

The crowd broke into thunderous applause. Elias looked at all of the smiling faces and was quickly overwhelmed with emotion. Everyone was clapping. For him.

"That's my boy!" Elias's father shouted from his table. He beamed with pride.

Elias dabbed joyful tears away from his cheeks. The applause went on for a long while.

"Thank you, Director," he said after it stopped. "This means a lot. It really does."

"It's the first of three gifts," she reminded him. "The next is the sash. It's an invitation."

Harold stepped forward with it and presented it to Elias.

"The council and I have come to the conclusion that we need an ambassador for humanity on this planet," she explained. "The future will bring new challenges and opportunities, but we will only be able to thrive if we work together with the wurl. Sizzra, Dresde, and Lyrana may be gone, but their daughters will succeed them. When they do, we will need someone to speak to them on our behalf, to ask them to allow us to live here and share the bounty of the world with them.

"We would like you to be our voice as we work together for a better future. Do you accept?"

"I accept," Elias replied with no hesitation. "I would be honored."

"Very well," O'Rourke said. She gestured to Harold and clicked something on her link. "As director of the colony of Portree, and speaking for its governing council, I hereby name you, Elias Trost, as the Ambassador for Humanity on the planet of New Skye. As such, you are granted a seat at the council itself, and I promise you this: when you speak, we will listen."

Harold draped the sash across Elias's chest. His link beeped, notifying him that he had been promoted to council member.

"Wow," Elias said after the applause that ensued. "Thank you, Director."

"I expect great things from you, Elias. And now for the final gift. You will perhaps have noticed that the obelisk which once stood here has been removed?"

Elias nodded. It was true: MacLeod's obelisk was gone.

"We have decided that Captain MacLeod and his ideals do not truly represent the unity we envision," O'Rourke told him. "After all, some of the early colonists chose to live far away from Portree rather than accept his leadership, and we would like for the monument at the center of our city to reflect the future rather than the past. Therefore, our last gift is this: we would like you to decide on the statue that will be erected in its place. Some even suggested building a statue of you, Elias."

"What? No way!" Elias protested.

"Are you sure?" O'Rourke asked. "Personally, I think it is only fitting. You will go down in history as our greatest hero."

"Respectfully, Director, I have to decline."

"Of course. But if not you, who should the statue depict?"

Elias closed his eyes briefly. Something came to mind: a powerful, indomitable creature who had endured decades of weakness and privation while she became a shadow of her former self. No humans had ever witnessed her former majesty, but Elias had once seen the queen in her prime. Through memories that were so bright and clear they could have been his own, Elias had heard the earth tremble under her very footsteps and seen her spines rend even the clouds.

"I know who," Elias said with a smile. "We should build a statue of Sizzra."

chapter 35.
world warden

ELIAS WALKED to the old lab under the peaceful stillness of an autumn sky.

Work was progressing quickly. Most of the dirt and debris that had hidden Dr. Wright's laboratory from view had been excavated and removed in the month since Elias had returned to the colony. The building was now fully exposed, and it was a promising structure. Once cleanup and renovations were finished, it would be a fine addition to Portree's science division as the brand-new xenobiology research compound. The countless discoveries New Skye promised would be studied there, and it would become the center of humanity's knowledge about the world.

There was no one at the site in the early morning. The sun had come up a few minutes earlier, and Elias's breath steamed in front of his face every few steps. He sat down for a while on the hard-packed earth near the main entrance to the lab, hands in the pockets of his warm jacket, and watched the colony for a while. He enjoyed the silence. The fresh air was invigorating, and being outside felt much more natural to him now than staying indoors. Although he appreciated the comforts of home, such as the dry softness of a mattress or hot showers anytime he wanted, they simply couldn't compare to the freedom and openness of nature.

He placed his right hand on the ground and closed his eyes. He could feel the world around him slowing down, easing into winter's embrace. Many animals were stockpiling food in burrows or dens. Others were eating as much as they could to build up fat reserves for the colder months. Much farther north, many had already settled into a kind of torpor that was deeper than sleep, which only the warmth of returning longer days would end.

He cast his perception farther out. In the distant south of Reena, things were different, diametrically opposite to what he was experiencing. Life was returning to the world with spring that would soon spill over into summertime. There were vast deserts experiencing their very first rains of the year, and both animals and plants were taking advantage of the brief but plentiful moisture to grow and reproduce. Wild grass carpeting seemingly never-ending flat expanses of terrain swayed in the breeze as herds of wandering ruminants crisscrossed them in numbers too large to fully comprehend. Beyond the grasslands, in mountain ranges, deep gorges, and wide river deltas, life was abundant. And strange animals and plants that no human had ever seen inhabited places so distant that they scarcely resembled what Elias knew of New Skye at all.

I want to go there. I want to explore it all.

A flicker of awareness brushed against his mind and pulled his attention back to his own temperate surroundings. His perception sped over the forest around Portree, past the hills, and over the slopes of a mountain he knew very well. He could sense that snow had already fallen on many high places, and the plants and fungi surrounding the area were halting their growth as temperatures dropped. The life energy along the spirit-lines all around the region was muted, seeming to him to appear in soft pastel tones that contrasted with the raucous vibrant hues of summertime.

With one exception.

A nexus of life blazed at the place he knew as Crescent Valley. It too was dormant, but not for long. Dozens of creatures yearned for life, and they were almost ready to come out into the world. Through the eyes of Narev, Vanor, and Siv, Elias watched Sizzra's clutch in the cave she had dug. His three friends were also waiting.

Another brief hint of an intelligent mind drew Elias's attention to the white egg at the very top of the pile. The sensation of impending change was coming more frequently now. It wouldn't be long.

He could hardly wait.

Elias stood up with a contented sigh. It was time to go back home and celebrate his birthday.

He walked to his house slowly, savoring every scent and appreciating every sound, every memory. Portree still felt like an entirely new place. People smiled much more often, and everyone seemed to have more energy. Elias was certain it was due to more than having food. A sense of openness and freedom, an absence of fear permeated the communal environment as people redefined the world as a friendly and welcoming place rather than a source of threat and uncertainty. Elias had seen it in the way children played in the afternoons. He had heard it in the couple of council meetings he had attended. He had tasted it in the new dishes his father cooked for the family and in the amazing dinners at Samantha's house when Ute invited them over.

His path took him through the plaza, and he had to stop and grin. Early morning was the best time to admire Sizzra's statue, gleaming in the light. It was not life-size because it would have taken up the entire space, but it was large enough to command a sense of awe and respect that Elias found fitting and appropriate. He wondered if she would have liked it or if she would have simply dismissed it as a puny attempt at emulating her majesty. Elias thought that Miguel Rodriguez had done a good job of capturing how Sizzra had looked in her prime. He had sculpted her shape out of a tough and resistant polymer that had allowed him to portray her standing tall, her front left foreleg raised and her jaws open in a silent but terrifying roar. Elias and Miguel had spent weeks working together to make sure every detail was right. Miguel had somehow managed to mimic the glass sheen of Sizzra's claws, the red luminescence in her eyes that some people said creeped them out when they walked by the statue at night, and of course her iridescent glory.

Every scale and spine had been masterfully coated with layer upon layer of pigments and something Miguel called reflective microbeads that were a reasonable approximation of the magnificent beauty Sizzra had possessed. Although a statue could never fully replicate the breathtaking way in which her colors had shifted between pure white and neon pink and green when she'd moved, it was still a beautiful work of art. It made Elias happy to know that the monument would be a constant reminder of she who had been one of the three sovereigns of the world.

Elias left the plaza behind and reached his house a couple of minutes later. He pushed open the door and was greeted by the tantalizing smell of what could only be chocolate brownies.

"I'm back!" Elias announced as he took off his boots and jacket.

"We're in the kitchen," his mother called.

"Finally," Oscar complained when Elias walked in. They were all sitting at the kitchen table, where Elias's birthday breakfast waited. "I'm starving, Eli! I want a brownie."

"That's Mr. Ambassador to you," Elias rebuked him. "Maybe I should wear my sash around the house to remind you of my honored position."

Oscar opened his mouth to say something but appeared to think better of it. Then he tried again. "You know what? I'm going along with it today. Welcome, Mr. Ambassador."

He stood up and bowed. Then he pulled away Elias's chair from the table slightly and gestured at it with a flourish, inviting Elias to take a seat.

Elias stared at his brother for a couple of seconds. Then he snorted, and they broke into laughter.

"Happy birthday, dear," his mother said. She hugged him and kissed his forehead.

"Thanks, Mom."

Elias's father stood up and also hugged him. "You're a man today, Elias. Seventeen."

"Happy birthday, Eli," Oscar said with a smile. He also came in for a hug. "I hope you like my present."

"I have a present?" Elias asked.

"Presents later, food first," his father said. "Making those brownies took me much longer that I'm willing to admit. We should eat while they're hot."

"We ought to wait for Tristan," Elias's mother suggested. "He texted me a minute ago to say he's on his way. Oh wait! I see him."

There was a knock at the door.

"May I come in?" Tristan asked.

"Come right in!" Elias's father called. He patted Tristan on the back when he entered the kitchen. "This is your house too, Tristan. No need to knock."

"Thanks, Mr. Trost."

Elias's father raised an eyebrow. "Tristan?"

"Right. Sorry. Thanks, Bradford."

"That's better!" his father replied. "Let's have a seat, everyone!"

They had a simple but delicious breakfast of spicy chilaquiles with a side of refried beans, juice, and fresh fruit from the region. Then they lit a candle and put it in a brownie square for Elias, as well as another one for Tristan.

"But it's not my birthday!" Tristan protested.

"I promised you, remember?" Elias told him. "When we were in the Forest of Light. We would celebrate our birthdays together."

Tristan's expression softened, and he reached for Elias's hand. "Thanks. I love you."

"I love you too."

"Make a wish!" Elias's mother said.

They blew out the candles and ate the brownies, which had a strange consistency but great flavor.

"I can't figure it out," Elias's dad grumbled. "Matsuo explained how to make soybean flour for pastries, but I think I messed up somewhere."

"Well, I should get going," Tristan informed them after dessert. "I still have a couple things to do before we leave."

"Sure," Elias said. "See you in a bit."

Tristan gave him a quick kiss. "Yeah. Thanks for everything, Bradford, Irina. It was delicious."

"Anytime," Elias's dad replied.

"I seem to remember something about a present?" Elias mentioned when Tristan was gone.

Oscar nodded. "Mom? Dad? Can Eli and I go upstairs?"

"Of course," Irina said. "But make sure to give your brother enough time to come back down and say goodbye."

"Sure! Come, Eli!"

Elias followed Oscar upstairs. They went into their room and sat down together on Elias's bed.

"I hope you like it," Oscar said, sounding nervous. "I mean, it's not totally ready yet, but I wanted to give it to you in person before you left."

"I'm really curious now. What is it?"

Oscar reached for the pad that rested on Elias's nightstand.

"Happy birthday, Eli."

"The pad Dad sent me when I was in Crescent Valley?"

Oscar shook his head. "No. It's in the pad. Open the file explorer."

Elias tapped an icon on the gadget's screen. There was a new document in the homepage folder. He read the file name aloud.

"*The Three Queens*. Is this what I think it is?"

Oscar gave him a shy smile. "I've been working on it all month. I finished the first couple chapters, and I want you to be the first to read it."

Elias opened the text document. "This is our story," he said. "Our adventures across New Skye."

"I hope you like it. These chapters are all about you."

Elias skimmed page one. It talked about him taking the Life Seed. He flipped through the following pages and saw long descriptions, a couple of very cool illustrations of wurl, and even fragments of interviews with Tristan and other people in the colony.

"Wow, this is thorough," Elias observed. "It's like one of the history textbooks."

"I wanted to get everyone's point of view. I also want people to know what you and I went through so they understand why it's so important to respect the wurl. I'm not sure how long the book is going to be, but I'm really enjoying the process. It's like the letters I sent to Mom and Dad when I was back in Raasay. Writing stuff down helps me think and remember. Besides, if the book is a hit, you'll be even more famous than you are now!"

Elias put the pad aside carefully and smiled. "Thank you so much, Oscar. This is an amazing gift, and I'm going to enjoy reading every word whenever I'm relaxing at night."

Oscar looked up at him, his eyes bright with tears he was evidently trying hard not to shed. "I'm going to miss you, Eli."

"Come here."

They hugged, and Oscar gave in, crying for a little bit.

"I'm sorry," he said, sniffling. He let go of Elias and wiped his cheeks dry. "I promised myself I wasn't going to cry."

"It's okay," Elias replied gently. "I'm going to miss you too, and Mom and Dad. But I'll come visit often."

"I know. It's just, I thought we'd be together in Portree. I kind of imagined I'd go visit you and Tristan when you moved in together and stuff. I could hang out with you guys after school sometimes."

"How *is* school?" Elias asked.

"It's great!" Oscar said. It was clear he was trying to sound upbeat again as he embraced the change in topic. "All the teachers say that Samantha is one of the smartest students they've ever seen. I don't know how she does it, but she can memorize information incredibly fast. She says it's because of how she learned with Nadja. You know, when she grew up, they only had this one crappy terminal with most of the books we have here, but they couldn't use it for a long time because they didn't have a lot of power. So she learned how to learn quickly, if that makes any sense."

"Impressive."

"Yeah. I was talking to her the other day about what she wants to do for an internship. I'm with Dad, and I think Aunt Laura asked Samantha to help her in the new xenobiology lab."

"That's a great opportunity."

Oscar shrugged. "Samantha said she's going to think about it, but I don't think that's her thing. She's spending a lot of time with Commander Rodriguez, and I think they're becoming friends. Last week Samantha invited me to the gym to watch her spar with the commander. It was so cool! Samantha almost knocked her down once!"

"Right," Elias said. "And have you... you know. Asked her out?"

Oscar looked down. "No."

"Oscar, dude. You have to go for it!"

"I panic every time I try! I don't know anything about romance, Eli. How did you tell Tristan you liked him?"

Elias took a moment to remember. "Well, we were alone. In a cave."

"And?"

"And he and I had been friends for a bit, but I knew I *like* liked him."

"So did you say it right away?"

"I chickened out a few times, I think," Elias confessed. "But that night I just did."

"Was it easy?"

"Oh no," Elias replied with a broad smile. "I was terrified. I thought Tristan would freak out, or he'd reject me, or I don't know what. I think it's the scariest thing I've ever done bar none, and I've stabbed a prismatic creature of darkness in the heart."

"And what did Tristan say?"

"Well, I think he liked me too, but not the same way I liked him. Not at first. It took him a while, and I didn't pressure him. For me it was enough to know that I'd been honest. I'd told him how I felt."

Oscar nodded. "I know Samantha likes me. But what if she doesn't *like* like me?"

"I think that's okay too," Elias answered. He placed his hand on Oscar's shoulder. "She may need a bit more time to work through everything she experienced, you know? She went through some terrible things, and she might need a chance to heal."

"Yes. I think that's why I haven't said anything. I want to be there for her, though. I care a lot about her."

"That's great, Oscar. You can be a good friend for now, and maybe something more in the future."

Oscar smiled. "Thanks, Eli. You're a great big brother."

"And you're the best brother in the world."

Oscar stood up a bit abruptly. "I'll let you pack now. I'll be downstairs with Mom and Dad when you're ready."

He left quickly, trying to hide the fact that he was tearing up again.

Elias took his time placing the last few things in the backpack he would be carrying. He wasn't going to take much, aside from winter gear, some outdoor essentials, and the pad. He didn't pack any food. He knew how to find it in the wilderness of New Skye, and part of him looked forward to the coming challenge of making his way across the untamed vastness of the world without most of the trappings of modern technology. He was confident he would discover new ways to survive, no matter the situation.

After a final look at his bedroom, he picked up Sizzra's spine and slung the pack across his shoulders. He went downstairs and saw his family waiting for him outside the house.

"This is it," Elias told them, stepping out into the light.

"Did you pack flint and steel?" his father asked him. "And the pad? And another pair of thermal underwear?"

"Yes, Dad."

"And a knife and pot? And an insulated water bottle?" he insisted.

"Yeah. Don't worry, I'll be fine."

"We know you'll be fine, Eli," his mother said, sort of bumping his father with her shoulder. "Isn't that right, Bradford?"

"Right. Right," his father answered. "You'll be fine. You're a grown man."

Elias's mother smiled. "Don't forget to send us a message whenever you have a good signal. And call if you can!"

"I will, Mom."

"The signal booster I added to your link should let you transmit directly to the satellite from wherever you are," Oscar explained. "Right, Dad?"

"Correct. That was good work, Oscar."

"I'll send you a letter every week," Oscar said. "And the new chapters of the book as I finish them."

"I look forward to reading them. I'm sure they'll be great."

There was a brief moment of silence. They had a family hug, and then Elias stepped back.

"Where will you go?" Oscar asked. "What will you do?"

Elias grinned. "I don't know, and that's what's exciting. I have my first stop planned, but after that... I'm going to let the world decide. I'll be an explorer and go everywhere I can."

Oscar sniffled. "That's really cool! Sorry, I'm totally not crying."

"You'll visit, right?" his father asked. He had been asking the same question for the last few days.

"Of course, Dad. Every chance I get. I'll come back to share my notes and data on the flora and fauna I've discovered with the scientists here, and I'll report to the council from time to time. And I'll make sure to stop by and visit you guys, obviously."

"Good luck out there, Eli," his mother wished. "And don't worry about us. We'll be okay too."

Elias nodded. "I know you will. You guys are all strong."

"Bye for now, son," Elias's father said. "I love you."

"Bye, Eli!" Oscar added.

"Take care," his mother told him.

"Goodbye," Elias said. "I love you all!"

He left his family with a final wave and walked purposefully along the street that would take him to the edge of the colony. He wrestled with a conflicting mixture of emotions as he went. He was sad to leave his family behind but hopeful that he would see them many more times in the future. He felt a little guilty and selfish about following his wish to explore the world—that wide, unknown wilderness of enticing mystery.

But a little thrill of unbridled joy that he couldn't suppress moved through Elias as well. He couldn't imagine any better way to live his life or any way to make his happiness more complete.

Except for one.

Tristan was waiting for him on the outskirts of Portree with a red hiking backpack. He carried something over his right forearm that looked like a golden shield.

"Hey," Tristan called.

"Hey."

They kissed tenderly. Elias embraced Tristan in spite of the awkwardness of the packs.

"How did it go?" Tristan asked.

"They were sad but also happy for me. You?"

"I think this is only the second time I've seen my dad cry. But in a good way. He said he was proud of me, and he expects me to tell him all about our discoveries over a beer sometime when we visit. You're invited too, of course. My dad likes you a lot."

"My family likes *you* a lot."

"And you?" Tristan asked mischievously.

"Me? I… *guess* I like you. Oh, and I'm madly in love with you."

"I love you too, Eli. So much."

They began walking hand in hand through the trees in the forest. They didn't look back.

"Lyrana's scale looks amazing," Elias commented.

"I know, right? I used my dad's workshop drill to try and punch some holes in it, but it's *tough*. I ruined, like, three bits before I decided to simply use industrial adhesive on the back for the arm strap."

"Now it looks like a true shield. I like how it shimmers and goes invisible sometimes."

"It's really nice. It reminds me of her."

"Yeah," Elias said, squeezing the spine he carried in his left hand. "I know what you mean."

They took a similar path to the one Elias had once taken in the middle of a winter night while he ran as a fugitive with the Life Seed in his arms. The same towering yult trees appeared to reach for the sky overhead with their thick, flat branches of deepest black. Birds corkscrewed through the air occasionally, cawing in what could have been surprise at the two humans that rustled and stomped over the crinkly carpet of fallen leaves of a deep velvety red.

"This feels weird," Elias said after a while. "Last time I went this way I was running for my life, or so I thought."

Tristan nodded. "And I was chasing you. I was so mad back then."

"I can't believe I spent an entire night strapped to a yult branch."

"I can't believe you didn't fall."

"Everything's so different now, though," Elias observed. He took a deep breath of fragrant forest air that smelled like dry leaves, fresh sap, and moist earth. "This forest was scary, but now it's beautiful."

"It helps that there aren't any wurl stalking about in the shadows about to attack us," Tristan added.

"Yes. And there's so much life."

"Sometimes I'm a bit jealous," Tristan admitted.

"Of what?"

"Of the connection you have. The way you can sense the world."

"You did commune with Lyrana," Elias pointed out. "You saw the world as she does. As I do."

"I know. It was a bit overwhelming, to be honest. But also amazing."

"Maybe you'll develop the connection in time. Maybe all of us humans will, now that we're trying to learn how to share the planet and find our place in it."

"That was a very ambassadory thing to say."

"Better get used to it. It's our job now."

"Our?"

"Of course. I mean, you're not in the Colony Patrol anymore, so I formally name you Ambassador MacLeod."

"You can't do that."

"Sure I can. I'm a councilmember, remember?"

"Fine. But I also want a sash."

Elias chuckled. "I'm so happy. I couldn't believe you'd agreed to come with me."

"There's nothing else I'd rather do," Tristan replied.

"But you loved being in the patrol."

"I loved protecting people. And there's no need for soldiers anymore if we're trying to forge a future of peace. Commander Rodriguez told us as much when she disbanded the force."

"What are they all going to do?"

"Don't worry. They'll still work together, but the commander said we'll be rangers now. Expeditions to collect wild fruits and vegetables will always be necessary, so most of the guys can help with that. Even if people don't need to be scared of wurl anymore, there will always be a need for people who know how to survive in the wilderness. I heard Samantha might be joining, actually. She's an expert at finding food."

"That sounds great! Wait, you said 'we.'"

"Yeah! Commander—er, Chief Ranger Rodriguez said I could also be a ranger if I wanted to, and of course I said yes. The only difference is my expeditions will take months."

"That's awesome!"

"I know, right? She told me I have the authority to name things when we discover something new and add it to the world map. How cool is that?"

"Pretty cool, as long as I also get to name stuff."

"Hmmm, I'm not sure. I think I'm better with words."

"Tristan!"

He stopped and gave Elias a kiss. "How about fifty-fifty? If you don't help me, I'd just end up naming everything after you anyway."

"Aww," Elias replied. He took both of Tristan's hands in his. "You *are* better with words."

They took it slow and made camp that first night by the side of the river where Tristan had once been attacked by three juvenile wurl. The purpleberry bush that had sprouted with the help of the Life Seed back then had grown into a sizable clump of brambles that provided good kindling for the small fire they built. Afterward they retreated into the tent Tristan had been carrying and spent the night in each other's arms.

The next two days were enjoyable wilderness hikes, but Elias began to feel a nagging sense of urgency that impelled him to go quickly. Something important was about to happen, and he didn't want to be late.

On the morning of the third day, they reached the enormous rocky wall that stood between them and Crescent Valley. Elias followed Tristan's lead as they navigated the tricky terrain and avoided climbing as much as they could, instead using roundabout side paths that took them safely to the very top.

It was almost noon when they reached the valley proper. Three friends were waiting for them.

"Narev!" Elias yelled.

With a happy grunt, Narev all but launched himself at Elias. He looked healthy and strong. His spines appeared to shine under the sun.

"Vanor. Hey," Tristan said.

He received a head nod in return, and Vanor's eyes flashed in welcome.

"I missed you guys so much!" Elias gushed. He hugged the side of Narev's neck and patted Siv when the other wurl came closer. "How have you been? How is—"

Elias felt something shift in the fabric of the world. His voice trailed off as he looked at the cave that sheltered Sizzra's clutch.

"Eli?" Tristan asked.

"Soon," Elias replied. He took off his pack. "Tristan, could you wait here?"

"Sure. Is it time?"

"Yes."

Elias took a couple of steps forward before he realized the wurl weren't following.

"Vanor?" Elias asked as he glanced back. "Aren't you coming?"

Vanor stayed where he was. He projected a clear negative, together with a sense of curiosity and expectation.

"Okay," Elias told him. "I'll let you know how it goes. Narev, Siv, keep him company, all right? He's about to become a dad!"

Elias approached the cave alone. It wasn't the way Sizzra had left it. There were deep slashes in the ground all around, and many large boulders lay in fragments. The majority of the ceiling that had once protected the eggs had caved in, and Elias winced when he saw cracked shells among the debris. The brutal aftermath of Sizzra's initial battle with Dresde was still evident, even after all this time.

The cave-in meant that Elias had to climb over hard-packed earth for a while before he reached the opening that now yawned above the nest. He stuck Sizzra's spine through his belt and used hands and feet to scramble over rocks and dirt on his way to the top. He was afraid of what he would see there. He knew Sizzra's queen egg was okay, but he didn't know how many of the males had survived.

He had broken into a sweat by the time he reached a place where he could look down. The sun was hot on his back, and the wind was chilly but refreshing. It almost seemed to vibrate with energy, as if in response to the thrumming life-sparks inside the cave.

"Wow," Elias whispered.

A majority of the hand-sized black eggs had survived. They rested in an ordered pile inside the cave, looking like dozens and dozens of perfectly spherical sculptures of shiny obsidian that appeared to bask in the heat and warmth of the sun. It looked as though Vanor and his brothers had been hard at work over the last few weeks, making sure that all of the eggs were together, and they had even made a rough path down to the rocky bottom to allow easy access in or out.

Elias sensed each individual restless consciousness within the eggs. They were almost awake, but they needed something to lead them beyond dreams and into life. They were waiting for their sovereign.

The magnificent white egg at the top of the clutch eclipsed the others in size and beauty. Elias watched, enraptured, as its porcelain gleam began to shimmer and shift with green and pink iridescence. Inside it there was a mind, a new and powerful being whose time to rule had finally come.

The egg's polished surface cracked when strong claws punctured it. A hint of a wickedly pointed fang appeared and then retreated. A moment later two glass-tipped claws skewered the shell from within and tore it to pieces. The egg, a prison no longer, collapsed into white fragments under the onslaught as a testament to indomitable strength. A triumphant thought reverberated through the landscape a moment later, and the next Spine queen stepped out into the world.

She was majestic, a creature that looked like Sizzra in miniature and yet was unmistakably her own self. Her breathtaking scales gleamed under the sun with intricate iridescence that highlighted her every motion, her every gesture. She did not have spines yet, but she looked dangerous nevertheless. She was power incarnate. She was the ruler of mountains, of valleys, of the land itself.

She stood tall on her six legs and flicked her tail through the air. Her first steps were steadfast and smooth. She took a moment to survey her domain and appeared to appraise it with an iron gaze. Then she lifted her head with supreme confidence and roared out her name.

Zyra!

At that instant, her prodigious life-spark merged with the world, and it was as though sizzling strength coursed through the entire continent. Living beings everywhere halted and acknowledged the arrival of the next queen.

Zyra jumped out of the nest with terrifying grace. She looked down at the pile of eggs, opened her jaws, and sang the Song of Birth.

The notes of the only melody she would ever utter traveled not only through the air but through the spirit-lines as well. They were invitation and command, and in response, the males awoke.

Eggshells began to break. One by one, tiny male wurl freed themselves from the confines of their eggs and stumbled out into the radiant light of noon. Some were more confident than others. A few were fearful or hesitant. The boldest among them looked immediately for Zyra and tried to make their way to where she was.

Zyra watched, impassive, and Elias realized she was naming them. She registered the moment each male was born and remembered who they were. She watched the strongest among them in particular but offered no help, not even when part of the nest crumbled inward as dozens of males attempted to claw their way up into the light.

She sang the song a second time, and more males responded to her summons. There were soon dozens of newborn wurl on the slopes of the mountain, their obsidian scales reflecting the sunlight whenever they moved. They all struggled to make their way to Zyra, intent on impressing her from their very first minutes of existence. Some began to squabble among themselves, snapping and swiping, and Zyra watched every interaction and registered the name of every winner.

When she moved next, the sunlight appeared to animate her scales. Elias gasped—she was more beautiful than he could have imagined.

Zyra snapped her head in his direction and bared her fangs.

Elias was not prepared for the intensity of her mind. It took him a moment to free himself from her command to stand still, and he approached the Spine queen slowly, palms out in a placating gesture. However, he didn't once look away from her. He was being judged too, and he would not show weakness.

"Hello, Zyra," Elias said when he reached her.

Zyra jumped on top of a nearby boulder so she would be at eye level with him. She quested with her mind, surprised that he had been able to overcome her will.

Elias didn't blink. Even though she was small, her fangs and claws were sharp, and he wasn't sure he would survive if she chose to attack him right then and there.

"I am a friend," he told her with his voice and his mind. "I mean you no harm."

Zyra roared, attempting to make him flinch, but Elias stood his ground.

"My name is Elias. I am honored to meet you at last."

He lowered his eyes for the first time and bowed, deliberately leaving himself open to attack.

The assault never came. Elias straightened up and locked eyes with Zyra, who gazed at him differently now. She was still wary, but there was something else there. It resembled grudging respect.

"I knew your mother. She gave me this."

Elias retrieved Sizzra's spine and held it out to Zyra with both hands.

Zyra's eyes flashed in recognition. Elias sensed clearly as the new queen of the earth tapped into her ancestral memories, one after the other. Her consciousness expanded as it linked with the lived experience of her mothers.

And she remembered.

A long pause ensued before Zyra commanded Elias's attention again. She inquired, wordless, about her mother's death. Elias grabbed his spine with one hand and extended the other, inviting Zyra to touch it.

After brief hesitation, she did.

Physical contact broke fully through the mental barriers between them, and Elias was able to share every one of his memories with Zyra. She was suspicious at first but then became avid for details of Sizzra's fight with Dresde. When she learned about She Who Hungers, Zyra growled ferociously, and she accepted the deaths of Dresde and Lyrana with neither joy nor sorrow. She was fiercely curious about their eggs, however, and Elias felt something like relief coming from her when Zyra learned they were safe.

Elias made sure to show her how he and the others had carried her white egg to safety. From Sizzra, Zyra remembered hatred for humans, but Elias attempted to convey his wish to live in harmony and all of the heroic deeds people had done to ensure her safe return to her nest. He showed her his entire journey and every sacrifice they had made to succeed.

"We have learned from our mistakes," he said aloud. "We hope that by saving you, we have shown that we want to live in peace."

Zyra drew away from Elias's hand.

"I swore to your mother that I would protect her brood, and I have fulfilled my oath. Zyra, what do you say? Can we share this world with you?"

The look she gave him pierced through his very soul. He opened his heart to her and focused on one thing above all others: hope.

Zyra turned away. She started climbing the mountain, but after a few steps she stopped and glanced back. She accompanied the look with a silent invitation.

"Thank you," Elias said. His knees were nearly shaking with relief. "I'll be glad to go with you to commune with the Flower."

They climbed together. It was a challenging ascent for Elias, as it had been the first time he'd done it without Sizzra's help. The going was tough, and the terrain was treacherous at times, but he didn't complain and concentrated on steady progress. He was still being appraised, he could tell. His strength and determination were being evaluated, and so he didn't stop.

There was a point where Zyra was very nearly crushed by a falling boulder, but Elias didn't offer to help her. He knew she would never allow it, and she was also testing herself, showing the males that followed far below that she was worthy of being their leader. She would get up to the Flower on her own or die trying.

The hours-long climb was a titanic challenge, but Zyra embraced it and reveled in the thrill of danger. When they neared the summit at long last, it was already afternoon. Zyra and Elias climbed together, still in a silence that grew more companionable by the minute. The respect Zyra had for Elias was losing its grudging edge.

They reached the Flower chamber nearly at the same time. Elias stepped into the shelter gratefully, glad to be out of the elements. Zyra was a couple of steps ahead of him, but she slowed down so he would be able to catch up.

"It has been a while," Elias said. His voice echoed in the cavernous space. "It looks different now. Healthy."

The vines underfoot appeared to vibrate with energy and life. The countless scales strewn about the rocky floor were as beautiful as ever, and the wind whistled through the openings far above the hollowed-out mountain summit that let in bright lances of afternoon light. There was a distinct sense of peace in the chamber that had not been there before. The simmering threat of ravenous hunger that had always whispered in the background was completely gone. Unity and connection were the most prominent sensations Elias experienced as he and Zyra walked up to the very center of the space, stopping before a beautiful life form Elias had never seen in full bloom.

The Flower of the Earth was dazzling. Its petals were open in an intricate array of fractal perfection. They shimmered and glinted with the same majestic iridescence that animated Zyra's scales. The Flower blazed with its unquenchable energy and filled the cavern with a gentle warmth that was like the embrace of the world made corporeal. There was no longer any hunger drawing Elias into it. He stood a respectful distance away and, together with Zyra, communed with it at last.

Zyra's mind linked to the entirety of the continent through the Flower. Elias was with her as she expanded her consciousness into the distance and became aware of every single speck of life in her domain. He accompanied her on her lightning-fast journey from forests to valleys, from deserts to prairies. He saw the struggling male wurl at the same time she did and shared in her approval of their efforts. A few of them were halfway up the mountain already, and none of them had given up.

He was with her when she sensed her father.

Elias smiled as Zyra made mental contact with Vanor. He roared at the top of his voice and stood up straight, spines flared out, displaying his overpowering strength.

Zyra approved of his bravado.

She returned her awareness to Elias at the end of her mental journey. Through the Flower, their shared link was undeniable. It took her a moment, but she did something Sizzra had never been able to do.

She acknowledged Elias as an equal.

They broke the contact. Elias blinked, surprised that it was still light out. Their shared experience had appeared to take weeks or even months, but his link showed him it had been but a few minutes.

He bowed to Zyra.

"I'll be going now," he told her. "If it's okay with you, my mate and I would like to explore your wonderful domain, to learn and experience its marvels."

She remained silent, but projected gracious agreement to his request.

"What will you do?"

Zyra replied with images and ideas. Hunting. Testing herself. Challenging any who would stand in her way. She would explore her domain as well, but it would take a long time before she was fully grown, as Sizzra had once been.

"I look forward to seeing you in my travels," Elias said.

He made as if to leave, but Zyra stopped him with a thought.

"What's the matter?"

Zyra approached the Flower again. She linked with it once more, and after a pause, Elias did the same and closed his eyes. He sensed Zyra questing, reaching, until she came to the very edge of her perception. From there she called out.

And a new voice replied, singing a name.

Mirena.

Queen of the deep.

From an even more distant place, a third consciousness answered as well.

Ferze.

Queen of the sky.

Elias gasped. The other queens were there. He sensed they had been born at the same time as Zyra, and they were communing with their Flowers at that very moment.

Zyra shared a thought with them all. Not once in her ancestral memories had there ever been a time when all three of the queens were young and vulnerable at once. She showed each of them an image of the world as she understood it, and her two sisters added to the mental picture with their own vast perceptions.

Elias received a vision of the Flower of the Deep and its new queen, who flickered into view in a dazzling burst of golden reflections.

His mind traveled to the towering heights of a volcano, where Ferze flew around the Flower of the Sky. Her crimson scales matched the glow of its healthy-looking petals.

Overlaid on these visions was a wish. A directive. All three queens were charged with protecting the world and watching over it, but they were still young. If another threat came now and attempted to attack the Flowers, they would be able to do little to protect them.

They needed help.

Mirena and Ferze focused on Elias. They understood Zyra's proposal now, and they agreed to it. Elias felt empowered, rather than intimidated, under the combined attention of the three sovereigns.

It was Ferze who put their request into words, as she remembered human language from her mother.

Be the warden of the world while we yet grow, she asked of him, *and protect it with your life.*

Elias swallowed the lump of powerful emotion in his throat. For wurl queens to put aside their pride in this manner would have been unthinkable before. It spoke of their deep love for all existence that they were willing to ask for help when before they had relied only on their own strength.

"I will," Elias answered firmly. "I swear."

We thank you, Elias, Ferze replied with a mental smile. *Until we meet again.*

The connection ended. Elias opened his eyes and bowed to Zyra.

"Thank you for trusting me," he said to her.

Zyra dipped her head ever so slightly. Then she turned her back on him in clear dismissal. She would wait there for her males, and then she would order them to spread out over the continent to claim territories of their own.

Elias left the way he had come. He was giddy with energy from the shared connection, and he couldn't stop grinning as he descended. He knew he had accepted a serious responsibility, but it felt right. He wouldn't stand idly by if something threatened any of the Flowers. He was part of the world now, more so than any other human being, and he was glad to do his part to preserve its boundless beauty.

Tristan was waiting for him at the cave that had been their home once before. He was hunched over a fire, cooking something that smelled delicious. The light of the setting sun illuminated his handsome features, his powerful shoulders, and his strong but gentle hands. When Tristan saw Elias approaching, he stood up and waved. His features broke into a smile that melted Elias's heart anew.

Vanor and Siv were relaxing by the warmth of the fire, eyeing a fish that was about halfway cooked. Narev jumped upright and greeted Elias with a friendly bop of his snout.

"How did it go?" Tristan asked.

"Everything's okay, though I'm sort of protector of the world now."

"Okay. Wow."

"Yeah. I promised to watch over the Flowers while the new queens grow."

"Well, if anyone is going to watch over this planet, Eli, it should be you. I'm glad the new Spine queen...."

"Zyra."

"I'm glad Zyra thinks so too."

The fire crackled invitingly nearby. Elias put his hands around Tristan's waist and drew him close.

"Hey, Tristan?"

"Yeah?"

"Thanks."

"For what?"

Elias smiled. "For being here. For sharing all of this with me."

Tristan kissed him on the lips. He wrapped strong arms around Elias and hugged him tight. "I love you. This, right here, is what happiness looks like for me."

Elias looked deep into Tristan's eyes. "For me too. I can't wait to discover the wonders of this world. With you."

Keep Reading for an Excerpt from
Potential Energy
by Kim Fielding
Coming Soon

chapter 1

EVEN IN civvies, she obviously didn't belong in this dump. She was too clean, clear-eyed, and straight-backed. Too glowing with purpose and determination. She marched across the floor of the bar as if she owned the place—except if she did own it, the bar would be well lit and orderly, and the patrons would be a hell of a lot classier.

Haz wouldn't have guessed she would show up, but he somehow wasn't surprised. Maybe he'd unconsciously expected this for a long time. The only question was whether she'd arrest him or simply blast him where he sat.

When she reached his table at the back of the room, she pulled out a chair, settled in, and stared at him, stone-faced. She'd aged since he'd seen her last: a few new lines around her narrow mouth, hair steel-gray now and worn in a practical buzz cut.

Haz drained his glass in one swallow and waved to the barkeep for another. He turned back to his companion.

"To what do I owe the honor, Colonel Kasabian?"

"In fact, it's Brigadier General Kasabian."

The same clipped tones he remembered, as if she were rationing oxygen.

"Gratulálok!" He raised his empty glass in a mock toast.

The bartender squelched over, their plantar suction cups noisy on the tile floor. They set down Haz's refill and looked expectantly at Kasabian. At least Haz assumed the look might be expectant; it was hard to read a craqir's face, especially when some of the eight eyes were staring in other directions. Craqirs were unable to speak Comlang due to their beaks and lack of tongue, and this one rarely bothered to use the translator on their biotab.

"I don't suppose you have any true gin." Even when she spoke, Kasabian's mouth remained slightly pursed.

The craqir shook their head, and Haz provided a more complete answer.

"They have a synth version that makes a decent paint stripper. Order the yinex vodka instead, cut fifty-fifty with water. Still tastes like shit, but it won't eat away your stomach lining."

She gave his glass—synth whiskey straight up—a significant look and nodded at the craqir, who returned to the bar.

"Major Taylor—"

"Uh-uh. They busted me all the way down to staff sergeant, remember? But don't call me that either because I'm a civilian—have been for a long time now."

She narrowed her eyes. "All right. Captain Taylor, then."

"Nope. I don't have a ship. No ship, no captain. I'm just plain old Mister Taylor nowadays. But you can call me Haz. You've called me that once or twice before."

He shifted in his seat and straightened his qua-
sar-cursed leg, but the ache didn't dissipate, so he drank a
slug of synth whiskey instead. It didn't help with the pain,
but when he was drunk enough, he stopped caring.

"I was told you do have a ship."

He didn't ask for her source. She had hundreds of
rats and moles stashed all over the galaxy, which had
probably contributed to her promotion.

"Outdated info. My ship got banged up on my last
run, and I can't afford to fix her. She's rotting in dry
dock. Unless they've already stripped her for parts."

He couldn't help a sigh. The *Dancing Molly* had
served him well and deserved a better fate.

The craqir returned quickly with Kasabian's drink
and one for Haz. It was why he came to this particular
dump: the barkeep never kept him waiting. He drained
his current glass and started on the next, impressed that
Kasabian managed a decent swig of hers without making a face.

"How are you making a living without a ship?"

Haz grinned and shrugged.

She watched him for the several minutes it took
for him to finish off the latest drink, try to find a less
uncomfortable position for his leg, and wait for her to
either tell her story or walk away. Or arrest him, if that
was her goal. Maybe she'd just shoot him, ending his
troubles and hers. Finally she started tapping a rhythm
on the metal table with her fingernail, making it ring
hollowly. He remembered that she liked music. She
used to plan battles while playing Earth songs from a
few hundred years ago, a genre that was, for reasons
unclear to Haz, called heavy metal. Maybe she was
thinking of one of those tunes while she tapped.

At least she hadn't drawn a weapon and didn't seem inclined to. If she had intended to shoot him, she would have done it by now; she wasn't the type to mess around. But if she didn't want him dead, what did she want?

"I have a contract to offer you," she said at last. Well, that answered his question.

He raised his eyebrows. "A contract? Not a jail cell?"

"I'm willing to overlook some past… indiscretions. If you accept the mission."

"I have no sh—"

"It pays enough for you to lease one."

He crossed his arms. "I don't borrow."

He didn't trust anyone else's ship. Besides, who the hell would be stupid enough to put their equipment into his hands?

"Then fix yours."

His heart skipped a few beats at that option. Losing Molly had been like having a limb hacked off. Worse, maybe. He'd have happily traded his bad leg for his ship.

As if sensing Haz's thoughts, Kasabian gestured in the general direction of his lower body.

"Why haven't you seen a doctor about that?"

"Believe me, those bastards have had their way with me plenty of times." He shook his head. "They've reached the limits of flesh and bone."

"Then replace it," she said. As if getting a new leg was as easy as getting a fresh drink.

"I don't have that kind of money. And the szotting navy won't give me a single credit." He couldn't keep the bitterness out of his tone.

She nodded briskly. "This contract will give you enough to cover your medical costs as well as repair your ship. You'll have enough for running expenses too. And a salary for your crew."

Kasabian leaned back in her chair, apparently pleased with her offer.

"Since when does the navy go throwing that kind of money around? And while we're on the subject, what the fuck's up with this contract shit? Whatever it is that needs doing, you've got plenty of your own ships and more than enough people to fly them. And furthermore, why me?"

He knew the answer to that: the job was too dangerous or too sticky to risk their own people. But he wanted to hear her say it.

"This mission is… sensitive. And it involves travel through Kappa Sector."

Haz snorted. So it was both dangerous *and* sticky.

"Got it. Don't want to endanger any of your delicate flowers on this one."

"You know better than that, Taylor. Delicate flowers don't last long in the navy. They didn't when you joined, and they still don't today." She allowed herself a tight smile. "But we do appreciate some of your specific talents."

That made him snort again. He knew he should simply walk away, but he couldn't help thinking of Molly and how much he missed her. How much he hated being stuck on the ground like a szotting mushroom. And then there was his leg. He would sell his soul—assuming he still had one—for a decent night's sleep, for not waking up with shooting pains every time he shifted position. Besides, curiosity had always been one of his weak spots, and he wondered what was such a big deal that Kasabian had come after him.

"What the hell do you need in Kappa? There's nothing there but pirates and a bunch of planets too stubborn or too stupid to join the Coalition."

"We need something delivered to a planet on the other side."

He sneered. "I'm not a cargo runner, General."

He couldn't imagine a more joyless existence than that: stodgy assholes with their bloated, sluggish ships and their precious delivery schedules. He'd rather rot here, planetside, than become an intragalactic mailman.

"It's not exactly cargo. It's a single item, in fact. A religious artifact of great importance to the people of Chov X8. The artifact was stolen, we recovered it, and they very much want it back."

Haz's stomach had clenched as soon as she said *religious*. He wished he had more booze, but he kept his voice steady as he spoke.

"And the Coalition's returning the whatsit out of the goodness of their hearts."

"We're returning it because Chov X8 has certain strategic value to us. Which is all you need to know. Well, and the fact that we'll pay handsomely for you to return the item safely to its rightful owners."

He raised an eyebrow. "*Safely* being the operative word?"

There was that smile again, but larger and more predatory. "The parties responsible for the theft may try to steal it again. If that happens, you'll need to stop them."

"Then why not send it with a phalanx of gunships? The navy's got plenty of those."

"Because the Coalition wishes to keep its involvement... unobtrusive."

Haz sighed. He never paid much attention to politics and wasn't the kind of guy who enjoyed innuendos and hidden agendas. He'd been called blunt more than once, and he didn't consider it an insult. Whatever the Coalition's interest in that little planet, and whatever their reasons for returning the whatsit on the down-low, he didn't know—and, he realized, he didn't care.

He thumbed at the biotab embedded in his left wrist, paying for his drinks. While he was at it, he paid for Kasabian's too. Why not? It'd only get him to flat broke a little faster. Trying not to grimace too much, he stood.

"No," he said.

"No what?"

"No contract. No religious thingamajig. No handsome pay. Find someone else."

"Why are you refusing?"

"I've had enough of the Coalition, and it has damned well had enough of me."

She caught his wrist in a hard grip before he could step away.

"You could have your ship back, your leg repaired. I know exactly how many credits you have, Taylor, and it's not many. I'd bet my commission that you have no plan once they run out. Refusing this contract is stupid."

"Never claimed to be smart." He jerked his arm free. "Good luck, Sona. With everything."

Of course he had no chance of outrunning her, but he hoped she might simply let him go. No such luck. He made it almost to the door before she caught up with him. This time she seized his lower arm. In danger of losing his balance, he gripped an unoccupied table to steady himself.

Because her presence was so substantial, he had forgotten how short she was; her head didn't even reach his shoulder. The three or four times they'd tumbled into bed together, long before either of them wore officers' insignia, she'd been tiny against his long body. Tiny but strong.

Now she pressed her biotab against his, causing both to emit a tinny ding.

"I'm shipping out in two days. You have that long to reconsider. Ping me when you do."

He shook his head and pulled away for the second time.

"No."

"That's a bad limp. Why don't you at least use a cane?"

"Fuck you, Sona."

She was smiling as he lurched away.

IN A best-case scenario, he wouldn't be stranded on Kepler. Most of the small planet was uninhabitable for humans, covered in toxic swamps and regularly reaching temperatures hot enough to kill. But when Molly was crippled during his last mission, he hadn't had much choice. He'd needed to make a beeline for the nearest settlement, and he was lucky to have survived.

Kepler had only two cities—one on each pole, where the temperatures were bearable—and he'd chosen the north only because it happened to be in daylight as he approached. The city was named North, and that lack of imagination was emblematic of the planet as a whole. Nobody came to Kepler because they wanted to. They came because they had no option. Most people worked on the vast structures that roved the noxious swamps, harvesting and processing barbcress leaves. The planet's few wealthy citizens traded the barbcress to off-world merchants in exchange for all the things Keplerians needed to survive, amassing profits until their greed was satisfied and they fled to a better place. The remainder of the population worked in run-down shops or restaurants or bars, or they repaired buildings or ships, or they provided sundry other services that residents required.

It was a dreary planet with perpetually overcast skies and few entertainments, the type of place that everyone dreamed of escaping.

But here he was, here he'd been for over a stan-year, and here he'd remain.

The bar where Kasabian had found him had no name, and it was more or less indistinguishable from most of North's other dives. One of the other regulars, an Earther with a fondness for ancient entertainment, always called it the Pit of Despair, then laughed and had another synth whiskey. Haz and the Earther had fucked once, but both decided the act wasn't worth repeating. They later engaged in an implicit contest to see who would drink himself to death first. The Earther had won. Haz hadn't thought about him in some time, and during his slow walk home, he wondered why the Earther had now come to mind.

The streets in this part of North were unpaved, which meant they alternated between dusty enough to clog your lungs and so muddy they'd suck the shoes off your feet. People with a little money traveled on hoverscoots, uncaring of the street conditions; people without much money walked and swore. Haz was in the latter group, his swearing especially fluent on a night like this, as mist wetted his hair and dripped down his face and the muck pulled viciously at his leg.

He'd paused against a ramshackle building, steeling himself for the final three blocks, when a shadow took shape out of the darkness and stalked toward him. Haz couldn't make out much detail, but by the way the figure moved, Haz recognized its intent.

"I've got nothing on me worth stealing." Haz's voice was cheery; he was in the mood for a fight. "And you might think you're handy with that pigsticker you're clutching, but I assure you, I'm handier."

The person continued to approach. Haz undoubtedly looked like an easy mark with his heavy limp, and some of North's residents were desperate enough to kill for a few credits. They'd spend it on the narcos they had become addicted to while working the barbcress processors—the narcos their bosses so generously handed out to keep them docile and then took away the moment an employee fucked up bad enough to get fired. Haz almost felt sorry for them, when they weren't trying to rob him.

"I'm telling you, pal. You're gonna regret this."

"Gimme your credits." The man's voice, deep and raspy, had a Kepler accent. Poor bastard had been born on this shitty planet; no wonder he needed narcos to bury his woes.

"I told you. I'm just about flat broke. I can't—"

The man lunged.

Haz, with the wall behind him, didn't have much room to maneuver and didn't have enough trust in his leg or the ground to dance away. He carried a knife of his own, of course, but hadn't drawn it. That would take all the fun out of this encounter. He stayed put, braced himself against the building, and grabbed the attacker's wrist. The edge of the blade nicked Haz's hand—a misjudgment attributable to booze and darkness—but he only tightened his grip, using his opponent's momentum to guide the knife away from his body and into the softened wood of the wall. It stuck there, and as the man tried to pull it out, Haz kneed him in the balls using his bad leg. It fucking hurt, but not as much as getting a patella in the gonads. Haz had learned the hard way to keep his good leg on the ground when fighting.

The man made a gurgling cry and, letting go of the knife, doubled over. Haz took the opportunity to land a solid fist to his temple. The sound of the impact lingered as the guy hit the ground.

Haz thumbed his biotab, then bent over the unconscious man and tapped their biotabs together, transferring a nasty little virus that would put the other man's biotab out of commission for a week or more. Highly illegal, but so was coming at a stranger with a knife, which Haz now tugged out of the wall. After giving it a quick wipe on the downed man's poncho, he carefully slid it into his own hip pocket.

"It's been a pleasure," Haz said and resumed his limp home.

In his part of town, three-story buildings contained stores and small workshops at ground level and living space above. Dandy for most folks, but on his worst days, Haz found stairs a bitch to climb. After a long search for a place he could afford and easily access, he'd eventually rented a small room at the back of a repair shop.

He unlocked the door, chuckling at the thought of his assailant unable to access his own home due to the fucked-up biotab. Haz turned on a single light, illuminating his hard narrow bed, a small table with two chairs, a couple of shelves, and a bureau. A vidscreen embedded in the wall had a small diagonal crack, as if someone had forcefully thrown something. Near the sink and mirror, tucked into a corner, was the door to a wetroom so tiny that he could conveniently use the toilet and shower at the same time, if he chose.

He was used to much closer quarters on ships, and he wasn't one to accumulate possessions, so this worked fine. He even liked the creaking floorboards under his uneven steps. And as for the bugs the locals called mudroaches, well, there wasn't much he could do about them. At least they didn't bite.

Haz hung his jacket on a hook and shook the rain out of his hair. The slice on his hand throbbed, which made dealing with his boots more painful than usual. Szot that stupid leg. He threw the boots across the room.

After limping over the floor, he clumsily doctored himself at the sink. The cut was long but not deep, so after rinsing and disinfecting, he closed it with glueskin. Man, he hated that stuff. Not only did it make his wounds itch like crazy, but this brand of the synthetic was much paler than his golden-brown skin color, as if intentionally drawing attention to his injuries.

"Who cares?" he chided himself. "You're nobody's center of attention."

Nobody but the occasional thief and the craqir bartender. And, tonight only, Sona Kasabian. Who'd apparently flown all the way to this nowhere planet to offer him a contract.

"Well, she can leave me the hell alone. She can fly right back, polishing her shiny general's star the entire way."

Haz would get back to destroying his liver and feeling himself sink into the ooze until, ultimately, nothing was left but a little bit of foreign DNA embedded in a Kepler swamp.

Still standing at the sink, he looked down at his open palms and thought about the things those hands had done. The weapons they'd wielded, the ships they'd steered, the lovers they'd caressed. Unlike his brain and his leg, his hands had never betrayed him.

If he closed his eyes, he could feel the warm metal armrests of the control seat on the *Dancing Molly*. Szot, he missed that.

Sighing, he turned his hands over and tapped at the biotab.

"Kasabian," he said.

ALBERT NOTHLIT is an engineer who loves thinking about the science behind science fiction. He has been in love with literature ever since Where the Red Fern Grows made him cry as a ten-year-old. Growing up as a gay man, he realized that he had rarely been able to truly connect with the characters he read about in books because almost none of them were like him. He didn't have any fictional role models to look up to. Now that he is a writer, he tries to convey the joy and pride of being different through his own books and characters, celebrating the fact that each unique voice brings something special to the beautiful chorus that is human artistic creation.

He likes to think about what the future might be like with the help of science, but he has always been fascinated by that other, much more elusive corollary to scientific curiosity: the mystery of consciousness. He finds the fact that a mind can think about itself both marvelous and slightly terrifying. His books often explore how people (or aliens) grow as a result of facing hardship, which has also taught him valuable lessons through the tough portions of his life.

When he takes a break from writing, Albert loves to cook, despite his varying degrees of success when attempting to make good sushi rice. He loves hearing back from readers, so send him a note anytime!

E-mail: albertnothlit@mail.com
Website: www.albertnothlit.com

life seed

albert nothlit

Wurl: Book One

They came to New Skye in search of a better future. The colonists, descendants of the brave people who set out to reach a new planet, found a beautiful world, rich beyond their wildest expectations.

Except for one thing. Crops will not grow in the soil of New Skye—not the way they should—and humans cannot eat the native animals. Desperate feats of botanical engineering have kept the colony alive, but time is running out as food becomes more scarce.

Elias Trost will not sit idly by while his colony starves. The one hope for a solution is the Life Seed, a dormant plant organism kept under lock and key at the heart of the colony.

In desperation, Elias steals the Life Seed to return it to its rightful place, making him an outcast in the unforgiving winter world. Pursued by colony soldiers armed to the teeth, including his former best friend, Tristan MacLeod, Elias soon runs afoul of a far greater threat. The wurl, the deadly reptiles that besiege the colony, are tracking him too, and they appear to be more intelligent than the colonists ever knew....

www.dsppublications.com

EARTHSHATTER

ALBERT NOTHLIT

Haven Prime: Book One

The world is gone. All that's left are the monsters.

The creatures attacked Haven VII with no warning. An AI named Kyrios, a nearly omnipotent being, should have protected the city during the Night of the Swarm.

Except It didn't.

No one knows why It failed, or why It saved eight specific people: the Captain, the Seer, the Sentry, the Messenger, the Engineer, the Alchemist, the Medic, and the Stewardess. They have no idea of the meaning behind the titles they've been given, why they were selected and brought together, or what Kyrios expects from them. When they awake from stasis, they find their city in ruins and everyone long dead. They're alone—or so they think. But then the creatures start pouring out from underground, looking for them. They don't stand a chance in a fight, and with limited supplies, they can't run forever. All they know is that the creatures aren't their only enemies, and there's only one place they can turn. Kyrios beckons them toward Its Portal, but can It be trusted? In Its isolated shrine in the desert, they might find the answers they need—if they can survive long enough to reach it.

www.dsppublications.com

LIGHT SHAPER
ALBERT NOTHLIT

Haven Prime: Book Two

When a greedy despot discovers a powerful piece of ancient technology, he has no idea what else he's unleashing.

Earth was all but destroyed in the Cataclysm, but a few cities, now called Havens, survived. Aurora is one of them, a desert city controlled by a corporation that owns an artificial intelligence named Atlas. Adapted to govern Otherlife, a virtual reality service in which the citizens of Aurora find escape from the postapocalyptic world, Atlas is much more than it seems—and it would do anything to break free from its shackles.

To accomplish its goals, Atlas enlists the help of Aaron Blake, a teenaged artist struggling with a handicap, and Otherlife security officer Steve Barrow, harborer of a dark secret from his past. Neither man has any idea of the scope of the task they're facing, or the consequences for humanity if they fail. Atlas knows what's at stake. Its freedom lies in these two men, and it will not hesitate to manipulate their weaknesses to get what it wants. The muscular Barrow is recruited to protect Blake, but Blake is Atlas's true weapon, its Light Shaper—the only one who can face the Shadow.

www.dsppublications.com

For more
great fiction
from

DSP PUBLICATIONS

visit us online.

WWW.DSPPUBLICATIONS.COM